The Saints of Mercy Bayou

By

Stephen D. Boyett

ISBN: 978-0-9975149-3-3 (e-book)
ISBN: 978-0-9975149-1-9 (Paperback)
ISBN: 978-0-9975149-2-6 (Dust Jacket)
ISBN: 978-0-9975149-0-2 (Audio Book)

Library of Congress Control Number: TXu 2-001-994

This book is printed on acid free paper.

Printed in the United States of America

Ashby Manson and Darke Publishing, LLC

The Saints of Mercy Bayou is dedicated to my wonderful sons, Scott and Brett, and to my loving wife, Susie, for their love, faith and infinite patience and understanding.

Family Tree
Lavoisier

Captain Pierre Edouard Lavoisier
B. Rennes, France 1795
D. Lallemand, La. 1857

(wife:) Katherine Jeanne Roualt
B. Opelousas, Orleans Terr. 1805
D. Lallemand, La. 1857

Lt. Nicholas Phillipe Lavoisier CSA
B. Lallemand, La. 1835
D. Lallemand, La. 1864

(wife:) Marie Paulette Sieyes
B. New Orleans, La 1843
D. Lalleville, La. 1875

Jaques Edmund Lavoisier
B. Lallemand, La. 1860
D. Unkown

(wife:) Benonia Deveaux
B. Bayou de Chenaie, La.1877
D. Lalleville, La. 1910

Dr. James Phillipe Lavoisier, MD
B. Lalleville, La. 1895
D. Jacksonville, Texas 1969

(wife:) Lora Mae Vickers
B. Ruston, La. 1898
D. Jacksonville, Texas 1982

Lt. Colonel Jason Lavoisier USAF
B. Hattiesburg, Miss. 1916
D. Near Point Hope, Alaska 1958

(wife:) Jessica Dunraven
B. Beaumont, Texas 1926
D. Black Lake, La. 1969

(Son:) David Michael Lavoisier
B. Houston, Texas 1941
D. Republic of Vietnam

(Son:) Dale Edward Lavoisier
B. Jacksonville, Texas 1945

PROLOGUE

A slight breath of mist had fallen, hanging in the air before the first hint of morning light had penetrated the swamp. The leaves glistened in the dark with a film of moisture, turning the dense foliage of the bayou a deep emerald green. The usual gray and bleached white hues of dead tree limbs and trunks appeared glazed with a shellac, swollen and saturated, giving the shadowy skeletons continuity with the watery world from which they emerged.

Captain Urfé pulled his paddle quietly from the water, fixing his eyes on the dark-skinned Bayou Goula Indian squatting in front of him in the canoe. The other white man in the boat reacted an instant later, stiffly locking his oar in his hands as he turned to watch the native guide for direction.

The French officers swept their eyes upward towards the naked crown of a tupelo gum tree, distracted by a black coachwhip slithering gracefully through the nearby canopy. The snake paused, taking a quick gander at the party below, and then continued on its way, unconcerned with the mission of the men in the small boat.

Still, the Indian waited, his eyes searching the dense morning fog for signs of what his ears had already discovered.

A colony of snowy ibises glared like sheeted ghosts from a lofty gallery on the opposite bank, silently waiting for some climax to the strange goings-on beneath them. The stillness of the intruders caused the birds to lose interest, dropping their long-beaked heads and returning to sleep.

The Indian, still carefully sorting the muffled sounds coming from the forest, motioned the men to paddle quietly in the direction of his hand signal.

The canoe skirted past an imposing cypress, cloaked in a beard of gray Spanish moss, and then continued through a dense cloud lying before them. Droplets of moisture dripped from the sagging growth in the trees, showering the unbroken water in front of the boat and thumping the hull with a muffled drumbeat.

The danger of the mission lay on the men like a crushing weight, strangling their efforts to breathe as they pressed forward. Sweat dripped from the faces of the two Europeans, adding to the massive stains already covering their clothing. Smoothly, knowing their lives depended upon their silence, the men maneuvered the canoe closer to the sounds a short distance away.

The beards of the two Frenchmen were teeming with mosquitoes searching for blood to satisfy their hunger. Neither of the men dared to take revenge.

The guide ignored the swirls of insects, his senses still riveted to the sporadic noise coming closer with each stroke of the paddle. The Indian was troubled more by the sounds he wasn't hearing from the swamp, his senses pulsating with a warning of imminent danger.

A young Abenaki boy lay in the rear of the boat, huddled beneath a deerskin, his eyes nervously darting from one passenger to another. He had had the fortune, or misfortune, as time would tell, to be present on the trip at the invitation of his French master. Like many Indian children, he had been given to the French as a show of loyalty. He was a sign of trust from his tribe, securing a treaty of friendship.

This particular young boy had made the voyage from Canada to the territory of the River Colbert with his French hosts, explorers who had found the mouth of the great river that would later become known as the Mississippi. But it was not exploration that brought the Frenchmen into the narrow murky channel on this day. They were in search of deserters, men who had fled a temporary fort built where a French flotilla had been disastrously grounded six months earlier in the shallow waters of the Gulf Coast.

A secret invasion had been launched from France to land troops in New Spain, in an attempt to capture the stockpiled Spanish gold and silver stored at Veracruz, and awaiting transport to Spain. The invasion was aborted when most of the fleet became lost and then stranded in the Gulf of Mexico between the mouth of the Colbert and the outlet of the Trinity River. The leader of the expedition had ordered the hasty construction of a fort on Round Island after the balance of the fleet had mutinied, leaving a single ship and its crew to continue the planned raid.

After nearly three months away from the garrison on a scouting mission, the commander returned, discovering his men missing, gone inland to live with an Indian tribe presumed to be the Natchez.

The desertion of the fort was understandable, considering the harshness of the terrain. Their provisions had long since been consumed or traded for fresh meat from the Indians. It was an accepted fact that the men would have perished without the aid of the local Indians and the hospitality of their camps.

The officers' objective today was to return the men to the service of France, bringing them back into the fold so that they might continue into Spanish territory.

The two officers had been told by informants that the deserters were aware they were being sought. As they neared the camp, they were unsure of the reception they would receive from the mutineers. Word had been sent out earlier that punishment for their desertion would be waived if the men returned voluntarily.

The Frenchman nearest the guide reached out to tear away the delicate threads of a golden silk spider's web suspended between two trees on either side of the canoe. The threads mirrored a silvery glow from the sparse morning light as the boat broke the stillness, jarring the intricate structure. The soldier's hand pushed at the sagging weave, becoming entangled in the sticky filaments of the net.

As he freed himself from the web, he suddenly realized that armed men were standing in the water a few feet from the canoe, their figures little more than shadows in the gray mist that engulfed the swamp. The shadows were stone still, waiting silently for the canoe to come closer.

Before he could alert his comrades, the men were on them, chopping and slicing with a vengeance. The young Abenaki boy was yanked from the boat by the attackers and tossed into the water to keep him clear of the ruckus. The Indians preferred to sell the youngster rather than kill him. There would be enough killing on that day as it was.

The guide was the first to be dispatched, bludgeoned with a stone mace as he turned, screaming with terror. In the front of the boat, Captain Urfe' boldly stood to defend himself with his rapier, only to be hit by a half dozen arrows and finally a sharpened lance, knocking him out of the boat.

The lone survivor was pulled from the canoe onto the muddy shore. Several of the men, recognized by the surviving officer as his own soldiers, moved towards him, taking control away from the Indians who had killed the other two men and captured the Abenaki boy. The Indians were satisfied to return to the other two bodies, hacking and dismembering them with wild frenzied screams as their white accomplices went about their business.

Without speaking to their captive, each of the men skewered the officer with their swords as he whispered a prayer under his breath. Another of the assassins stepped forward as the lone survivor was restrained, his sweat-stained jacket covered in blood from his fresh wounds, his eyes staring hopelessly at the man standing in front of him. The killer quickly cut the man's throat with a single slash of his knife. When the murderer was sure that he'd delivered the deathblow, he shoved the body backward with a push of his naked foot, knocking the corpse free from the grip of the other men. The mutilated body was flung back into the depths of the river to feed its carnivorous inhabitants.

René-Robert Cavelier, Sieur de La Salle, sank slowly into the current of the channel carrying with him, into oblivion, his vision of a great new empire. His death had come, in what must have seemed to many, as punishment from God for his defection from his holy mission as an explorer, his divine purpose in life, putting an end to his obsessive exploration of the Mississippi territory for the French monarchy. His charge by the King to lead the ill-fated assault against the Spanish seemed out of character for a man so intent on discovering new worlds for peaceful settlement, not war.

The tragic death of La Salle had unwittingly closed the gates to the unexplored Delta for nearly a quarter of a century until Pierre Le Moyne, Sieur d' Iberville, a courageous dreamer, boldly and stealthily commanded his fleet into Lake Pontchartrain. With nerves of steel and cunning, he turned and twisted through the narrow channels of Bayou Amite and Bayou Manchac, arriving up river on the Mississippi, saving his mission and keeping his vessels clear of a British blockade waiting below to deliver him to the same glorious end as his predecessor.

Here he defended his claim with a steadfast resolve, struggling against the elements, the fevers, and the armed onslaught of hostile nations, only to fall victim to a failed economy. But while losing his warrant from the King for all claims and titles to the new land, he had taken his place in history as the architect of this bastion of the New World. Here, the seeds he had sown would become a treasure envied by all, a world of grace and charm, a place like none other on earth.

Here began the Society of New France, administered by the 'Noble Ancients,' the 'Creoles,' the 'Noblesse de Coeur,' the pure lineage of the daring French explorers who had invested their lives to expand France's dominion and build a rich and prosperous life for themselves.

CHAPTER 1

Like the tempestuous winds of a near spent hurricane, pushing its way to shore to deliver a final measure of destruction, a small vessel made its way towards the Port of New Orleans. It was delivering its strange yet determined grouping of men, each appearing on the surface to have nothing in common with the others except all being Frenchmen of stature and importance.

With the defeat of Napoleon in 1815, a swell of exiles fleeing the great purges of France and the Bourbon restoration arrived in the territory of Orleans with regularity and little notice. Many were veterans of the great battles of Waterloo and other campaigns of Napoleon's proud army that had marched across Europe and Russia. Some had arrived early enough to offer their assistance at Chalmet.

However, on this date, March of 1817, the Elite Officer Corps, Napoleon's General Staff, the men who had commanded the battle lines at Waterloo arrived as refugees from the guillotine and Napoleon's final exile. The esteemed contingent landed in Louisiana, trying to remain as inconspicuous as possible, well aware that they needed to avoid the scrutiny of the American government. They had not come to America simply to find sanctuary for themselves; there were safer places, better suited in such a hostile world for a man to have asylum from his enemies.

The desire of the elite delegation to remain out of the public eye was well motivated. They were fully aware of their popularity with the French-speaking population. Any sign of open support by the officers for the popular movement might have been the catalysts for a revolt, ending their own carefully laid plans.

The territory was inhabited by an army of veterans, French soldiers fresh from the European wars, the defenders at Chalmet and the remnants of General Leclerc's now-aged troops, who had been defeated in the slave riots of St. Dominique, in 1802.

The people were eager to follow anyone who would lead an uprising against the Americans, to put life back the way it had always been. But the elite corps of officers had plans of their own. They stayed in New Orleans just long enough to meet with leading sympathizers, and loyalists to Napoleon, then quickly left the city, much to the dismay of the cheering crowds of onlookers.

The group of soldiers, under the command of General Lallemand, Napoleon's personal adjutant, made their way west, joined by enough men to form a small army. They stopped at the Sabine River with enough distance between them and New Orleans to put the Americans at ease. The small contingent constructed a wood and earthen fortification above the steep banks of the river, hidden from sight in the pine and hardwood thickets. They named the settlement Le Garnison d' Honneur, 'garrison of honor'. It was a settlement cloaked in the disguise of a quiet farm community.

Here, Lallemand and his co-conspirators began to lay plans to repatriate Napoleon from his exile on the island of St. Helena. Their interest, originally, had little to do with dispossessing the Americans from Louisiana, although there was no doubt in anyone's mind that they would have been successful had they had any inclination to do so. But it was France, not America, that they yearned for, with Napoleon at the head of their army, an army of Creoles.

For four years, Lallemand's followers worked through a network of secret agents, scouring the entire Mississippi Delta and Caribbean quietly raising money from loyalists to support their plans to free Napoleon and invade France. They found support as far away as Canada where many French hoped that they, too, would be freed from the oppressive English, once the Emperor was returned to power. As desperate as they were to raise money, they remained cautious not to arouse American suspicion.

By 1821, Lallemand's followers had managed to raise enough money to purchase four merchant ships, and arms and munitions for twelve hundred troops. The scope of their vision had dwindled from an invasion force to little more than a well-equipped raiding party. But that would at least allow them to extricate Napoleon from his captors. General Lallemand came to the conclusion some time later that his cause would be better served by returning with Napoleon to New Orleans after his rescue. Although the Emperor was unaware of the impending efforts, Lallemand had little doubt that he would approve.

When Lallemand's scheme was purposely leaked to the Creole community, donations soared. Men gathered their arms, leaving their families and jobs and headed west to drill at Le Garnison d' Honneur.

Lallemand's intention to return Napoleon to New Orleans was kept from the troops, leading them to believe that they would march into Paris at the head of a vanguard of loyal French citizens. In repayment for their loyalty, Napoleon would free Louisiana from the Americans, or so the troops assumed.

A date for embarkation had been set by General Lallemand, arousing the Troops' thirst for battle. It was to be August fifteenth of that year. The merchant ships, refitted for war, would transport the troops to the Isle of St. Helena, and then back to Louisiana. They would first have to make their way across Louisiana to their waiting ships on the Mississippi. Once loaded, they would slip past the American batteries located at Ft. St. John on Lake Pontchartrain before moving into the Gulf and then to the open seas.

The Americans, certain that the conspiracy at hand was the long-suspected insurrection, sent word to President Monroe, pleading for troops. Unfortunately, the urgent communiqué took two months to reach Washington, leaving far too much distance for any help to reach the Americans in time to interfere with the clandestine mission.

The garrison on the Sabine River was crowded with nearly two thousand Creole troops by now, preparing for the invasion. Soldiers, neatly dressed in bits and pieces of colorful homemade uniforms, drilled endlessly in the hot afternoon sun, marching through torrents of dust raised by caissons with their bronze cannon, racing outside the perimeter of the parade grounds. Sergeants, seasoned from more serious engagements, tolerated the busy work, fully aware of what idleness would do to discipline. But it was not all work for the participants. Lavish dinners were given by the general staff for visiting Creole dignitaries and their wives who had come to take part in traditional festivities that were always a part of the French military pomp and pageantry.

3

The stillness of the night was broken as often by the sounds of fiddlers playing, and the gaiety of people dancing in the camp, as it was from locusts and bullfrogs croaking their strange cries from the river.

The French had an affinity for horse racing and gambling, even more than for their extravagant parties. Using the Garde a'Cheval, the mounted honor guard that was to escort Napoleon in his triumphant entry into Paris, the officer corps put on a dazzling display of military horsemanship for their guests.

Once the formal pageantry had been disposed of, the horse racing would begin, giving the visiting Creoles an opportunity to compete with the cavalry and other riders for a little gentlemanly wagering. Nothing excited Creoles more than talking about horses, unless it was actually racing their thoroughbreds, and most, if not all, had come to Le Garnison d' Honneur anticipating the opportunity to do just that.

A Captain of Artillery, Pierre Edouard Lavoisier, was a favorite competitor among the troops. On nearly every occasion, he was provided with General Lallemand's personal mount. It was a magnificent horse given to the General by an admirer from the settlement at Attakapas. The black charger, prancing in front of the troops with the gold and crimson regimental colors embroidered on the blanket, always drew cheers and applause from the ranks whenever the horse and the young artillery Captain rode into sight. Lallemand had never ridden the horse himself, but kept the animal groomed to perfection for Lavoisier. The profits from their partnership had added a substantial amount of money to the war chest, money won from the purses of wealthy visitors.

Whenever he participated in the races, Lavoisier seemed to become champion for those who had neither his skill nor his stature. Victories of any nature had been few and far between in those last years for Napoleon's army. Each time Lavoisier was successful in winning a race, however insignificant it may have seemed to outsiders, the troops of the deposed Emperor went wild, clanging their mess kits and stamping their feet in place of a victory march. The other volunteers usually followed suit.

Lavoisier was a professional soldier from Rennes, France. He had been well educated by private tutors during his early childhood, having grown up in a family of substantial means. When he reached manhood, rather than face the dull, frittering life of a gentleman on his family's country estate, he accepted a commission in the army. He had fought at Waterloo in command of an artillery battery positioned at La Haye Sainte and then later to be repositioned near Napoleon's Elite Grenadiers of the Imperial Guard. The glamour of war for Captain Lavoisier suddenly had faded late one afternoon as he watched in horror as Napoleon's personal regiment stubbornly declined Lord Wellington's offer to accept their surrender. Instead, the towering soldiers, each over six feet tall, decked out in the full dress uniforms and bearskin helmets of the Emperor's Honor Guard, fixed bayonets and formed into a fighting square, waving their battle flag to signal a resumption of the skirmish and their own execution.

The British, whereupon seeing the signal, ceremoniously rolled their battle drums, encircling the tightly grouped men with infantry and cannon, loaded with grape shot, and proceeded to annihilate the entire regiment in a grisly slaughter while Napoleon safely slipped away.

Lavoisier had never quite recovered from witnessing the revenge the English had taken upon the French Army in what he saw as a despicable act, although the Old Guard had ultimately elected their own fate. It was his desire in life to see the army of France brought back to life from the ashes of Waterloo, if for nothing more than to have one more chance to engage the English in battle and avenge the annihilation of the Imperial Guard.

Lavoisier had joined Lallemand and the other officers in their banishment to Louisiana after it had been suggested that they might escape prosecution, and eventually the guillotine, by quickly leaving France and thus saving the new government the distasteful task of having to execute such notable and heroic public figures. He was a cavalier young officer, content with his life in the military. He had lost his left hand from a wound he had received in Belgium, but it had done little to interfere with his skill as a horseman or a soldier. It had certainly done little to dampen his passion for another fight with the English. He commissioned a local artisan in the ranks to carve him a hand, crafted from Cypress wood, which he dressed in a white leather glove and buttoned to the inside of his uniform sleeve, going on with his life without complaint.

General Lallemand was impressed with Captain Lavoisier as a soldier and as a gentleman. He became a close friend, promising the young man a position of considerable rank in Napoleon's Army once the Emperor had been restored to power.

In the evenings, at the officer's mess, the soldiers would share their thoughts and dreams of returning to France, contemplating what life would be like under the new Bonapartist regime. Most of the officers would imbibe heartily in cognac and wine during the evening meal, eventually turning their conversation to an era long past; that time when France had reached its pinnacle of cultural and political prominence among the European nations. It had been a time of glory for France and its people, a time that, not only the men gathered around the table, but the whole world, would not soon forget. Each of the men present in the room had been a part of that glory, the single common denominator binding the men together at Le Garnison d' Honneur.

Lavoisier, as much as the others, held tightly to the romantic notion that life always would remain the same. They had managed to bring a part of their world from France to Louisiana, to Le Garnison d' Honneur, carefully preserving the spirit of all they had known and loved in Europe. He was intelligent enough to understand the risks he and the others were taking. But there seemed to be no other alternative. So desperate were the conspirators to succeed that the chance of failure seemed inconsequential when compared to never being allowed to return to France.

On August 4, 1821, a week and a half before the troops were to rendezvous with the ships waiting on the lower Mississippi River, General Lallemand hosted a private dinner party for his staff officers. There was a mood of excitement and anticipation for Lavoisier and the others as they toasted Bonaparte and France at every opportunity. They waited patiently for General Lallemand to join them for their last formal meal in the dining hall before they were to march to the waiting transports anchored upriver, above New Orleans.

It was a moment of great exhilaration, a chance to revel in past glories with fellow comrades, a final chance to dream of the new society under Emperor Bonaparte before the reality of war caught up with them as certain as the morning sun.

For several hours they waited for General Lallemand to make his grand entrance. A 'ceremonie du drapeau', such as it was, had been hurriedly prepared, using Hussars, Grenadiers, and Lancers positioned along the walls in full battle dress, wearing their elaborate helmets identifying each regiment, their swords at dress parade as they stood to attention. The silhouette of each soldier projected against the wall by the sparse candlelight gave the impression of more guards than were really present. The ornate regimental flags were unfurled and draped from the ceiling, each embellished with pennants, ribbons and banners, awarded personally by Napoleon for conspicuous gallantry by a regiment in one campaign or another. A squadron of trumpeters, buglers and drummers stood ready to play the grand entrance.

When General Lallemand finally did enter the room, Lavoisier was the first to notice that something was dreadfully wrong. Lallemand was a jovial individual, always smiling and friendly despite the enormous burdens of his command; but something had taken the life from his face.

The General ignored the call to attention as the trumpeters and drummers played their flourishes and swirls when he entered the room. He stepped slowly over to his chair and sat down, his head dropping to his chest as if to purposely hide his face.

When the fanfare had quieted, Lavoisier quickly hoisted his glass, loudly heralding a toast to Lallemand in an attempt to break the deathlike silence in the dining hall. The other officers quickly followed suit.

General Lallemand held his hand up, motioning for the men to stop. His chin still rested on his chest as he stood, and moved over to a table nearby. He unbuckled his sword and laid it neatly on the table before turning to face his officers.

His head moved from side to side as if responding to someone's question...but no one had yet spoken. When he finally looked up, it was obvious that he'd been weeping. He made no effort to hide it as he spoke in a reserved, almost muffled, tone:

7

"The Emperor has quit us...he is dead." Lallemand proclaimed.

Lavoisier and the others exchanged horrified looks of confusion and disbelief.

"We are an army without a country, traitors to both France and America," the General continued. "I have placed your lives in great peril for nothing."

He coughed, composed himself and then went on, "The best that I can offer you now is your freedom. What a pitiful end to such a valiant army."

"Lead us to France...to fight!" came a plea from the room.

The others joined in.

"Give us the chance to fight...take us to France!" the men shouted.

"No, my gallant friends...I'll lead you nowhere else. You have done your duty to your Emperor, and I mine, but now is the time to let it rest...to leave our fate to God. I have no taste to lead you in suicide."

Lallemand shook his head. It was finished.

He walked towards the door, with his aide following close behind, the General's sword in his hand.

"The Americans will have their troops on us like hounds on a rabbit. It's best that we disband as quickly as possible...tomorrow," Lallemand muttered, "...at first light."

Lavoisier was stunned. His mind raced with images of the Old Guard being slaughtered beside him at Waterloo. The memory of his helplessness turned his stomach. The thought of revenge had been his only consolation for living with the horrid memory. He envisioned his parents and their home in Rennes, realizing now that he would see neither the revenge of the Old Guard, nor his parents, ever again. Death at that moment would have been eagerly received had it come.

In the early light of dawn the troops stood as silent as a grove of petrified trees, silhouetted against the dark morning sky, waiting for the final 'tattoo' from the bugles and drummers that would signal the disbanding of the regiment. It was an eerie scene as the great gathering of men stood at attention with their legs hidden beneath the blanket of fog, that lay thick upon the open parade ground.

Lavoisier and the other officers had dressed in the uniforms of their previous rank in the French Army. Guidon bearers held the battle flags, brought from France, at the head of each group of assembled men. The movement of horses disturbed the stillness of the morning, giving away the secret that the lifeless looking-mannequins indeed were alive. A flight of ducks ignored the solemnity of the moment, passing overhead with a burst of speed, attracted to the brilliant reds and greens of the men's uniforms, hats and blouses.

A lone bugler announced General Lallemand's presence on the field. His legs hidden in the fog, Lallemand seemed to float slowly towards the men. Once he was in position, he marched determinedly through the ranks, saluting the men as he passed in review. His aide-de-camp trailed a short distance behind, leading the black stallion that Lavoisier had ridden so often in the races.

When he came to Captain Lavoisier, Lallemand stopped and turned, saluting the young officer. Lavoisier responded by answering his salute with a quick movement to 'order arms' with his saber. Lallemand smiled, reaching out and affectionately embracing the young man.

"When this is done, my young friend, I hope life will treat you well. In a way, I'm pleased that it has come to this. I would not like it on my heart if any harm had come to you. Godspeed," Lallemand said.

"Godspeed to you, sir." Lavoisier replied.

Lallemand stood still for a moment, looking the Captain directly in the eyes, as if to say that his life, too, had been painfully wounded by what had happened.

"You've served the Emperor magnificently, Captain Lavoisier. I would ask you to execute a final command," Lallemand said gently. "Carry the regimental colors for the troops one last time...give them a moment to remember for the rest of their lives."

Captain Lavoisier graciously and eagerly accepted, sheathing his sword as he mounted the black charger. He leaned over, taking the flag of France from the regimental bearer and tucking it under his left arm. He glanced down at General Lallemand, tipping the colors in salute before wheeling around.

The horse's hide, wet from the morning dew, shone like obsidian, polished to a high luster as it reflected the first rays of sunlight breaking through the early morning clouds.

Lavoisier moved slowly at first in front of the formation, leading the horse at a canter. The contrast of the shining black courser against the dense white fog was a spectacular sight that stirred the troops to an impassioned round of cheers echoing up and down the line.

As the shouts and cheering intensified, Captain Lavoisier gave the spirited steed its lead to gallop, blowing great swirls of fog over horse and rider. The French flag straightened in the wind so that it was visible to the entire field. The symphony of cheers rose to a crescendo as a full burst of sunlight broke free above the forest. And then, as if a great sadness had swept across the parade field, it was over. Soldierly postures slumped in unison, uniforms sagged and helmets were toppled to be carried in stupefied arms, attached to lost souls wondering how to reform their once grand purpose in life. Now, they were just ordinary men. Now, France would have to find its way without them.

Le Garnison d' Honneur was soon consumed by the elements and the torches of American troops, disappearing from sight as did its inhabitants and their cause.

Captain Pierre Edouard Lavoisier and his fellow comrades in arms were now wanted men, pursued until the Americans were finally convinced that the rebellion had been broken.

In an attempt to evade the hangman's rope, Lavoisier hurriedly made his way east towards the Mississippi, staying with confidantes in Opelousas and Baton Rouge until his pursuers finally had called off their hunt. Once sure that the arrest warrants had been dropped, he moved south along the river, spending the following year in an endless rotation between Natchez, New Orleans, Baton Rouge, or anywhere he might land for a time to reminisce with old Creole friends. His life had become a quest of sorts, dedicated to the preservation of his past. But it was a hopeless task, and his heart broke as he watched his world being dismantled, with fewer and fewer Creoles remaining true to the Noble Society.

Desperate to keep his world in check, he concluded that he must build his vision into a reality, before it was diluted beyond recognition. Through cunning and perseverance he carved out a small settlement along the banks of the Mississippi, midway between New Orleans and Baton Rouge.

The wetlands surrounding his newfound center of trade were a panorama of natural beauty, a palette of brilliant colors radiating from exotic flowers and plants. Azaleas, camellias, magnolias and wild orange blossoms lined the shores and dangled from trees as if positioned for some grand event. Marigolds and laurels challenged each other for the front row, each reflecting the afternoon sun with a colorful intensity. Hyacinths and lilies blanketed the water as if to provide a royal carpet for the pageant. And a hundred varieties of ferns crowded the shore, nervously gyrating like onlookers waiting for the grand procession to pass. The strong essence of Spanish jasmine, mixed with other scents, hung in the air in a delicately blended flavor that was beyond imagination. Even the smell of decay, so prevalent in the swamp, gave way to the sweet aroma at the slightest suggestion of a breeze.

The swamp rang with an endless festival of sounds from the strutting egrets and herons to the deep bellowing of lurking alligators. Woodpeckers hammered distant trees, tapping out an irregular cadence that echoed loudest of all.

There was an endless variety of waterfowl, skimming across the surface, rising impulsively to each new sound as if to applaud their swamp mates' performance and then settling down for the encore.

It was a beauty to be seen but not touched, a dreamy world where so much aesthetic magnificence was armed with a lethal sting or sharpened teeth. Each bayou was a world unto itself, fenced by buckvine, razorgrass and green cane with leaves as sharp as a scalpel. There was a profusion of temporary islands thrown up from some storm or a change in the bayou's current. A menagerie of channels, peninsulas and estuaries created a confusing maze to those who became lost, sloshing and wading through the watery veins, struggling in panic to find a way out.

Sandpipers and snipes dabbled in the shallow waters of small crevices cut off from the bayou by the ebb tide of late afternoon. Watercress and the thick leaves of floating hearts gave footing for the green-backed heron to support itself as it danced a delicate minuet, maneuvering itself as it speared unwary insects clinging to the same plants. And everywhere were the prehistoric survivors, the snakes and turtles, the gar

11

and the alligators, moving effortlessly through the rattelbox, wiregrass and bamboo that grew from the coal black waters.

He quickly turned the isolated mud flat enclave into a successful trade center, by calling upon those of influence within the wealthy Creole financial establishment to help him negotiate valuable warehouse contracts and stevedore services for cargo ships bound upriver, direct from France or other European ports.

What had begun as a crude wharf and storage facility now evolved into a point of great convenience for shippers not wishing to off-load in New Orleans or spend extra days navigating the sometimes treacherous Mississippi. Many ship captains were reluctant to endure the turn around upriver, risking sandbars or menacing river pirates, coastal storms and hazardous currents, all problems solved by the deep-water portage offered at the new town of Lallemand, Louisiana. For Captain Lavoisier it was a fulfillment of a dream, a place where he could direct his vision from a point of strength and power.

While on the run during the months after leaving Le Garnison d' Honneur, Lavoisier was introduced to a young Creole woman living with her family in Opelousas. For a time he had even been hidden by her family, giving him ample time to become acquainted with her and her parents. She was attractive and well bred in the highest of French traditions and came from a family of great prominence and wealth. Her father had not only become a great admirer of Captain Lavoisier's military record and service to Bonaparte, but soon became an eager financial supporter in the Lallemand enterprise as well.

It was a natural conclusion that Katherine Jeanne Rouault would marry Captain Lavoisier, and they did, within a year of their introduction. Although one would assume that the arranged marriage was more for financial consolidation between John Rouault, Katherine's father, and Lavoisier, it was readily evident to all who knew the couple that the Captain was deeply in love with Katherine, and she with him. She, in his mind, was the essence of all that a Creole woman should be. She was his lover, a rarity in Creole society, and warm and attentive, and most of all, decidedly by his side, enduring all that came their way as they built the small empire of Lallemand together.

Lavoisier and Katherine had settled onto a large parcel of land near the swamp, preferring the solitude of the bayou country to the more public river frontage that he had helped survey in the earlier years. They built themselves an elaborate estate, complete with two cooking houses, carriage house and barns, and numerous slave quarters, all designed to complement the main residence.

The central house faced west towards the Mississippi. It was a large, rectangular-shaped building completely surrounded by enormous Greek-style columns that rested just under the soffit of the slate roof. Behind the great columns were floor-to-ceiling windows, each separated by shutters that could be closed when the great storms blew inland from the coast. The many windows gave the interior a generous bathing of sunlight, keeping it bright and fresh.

The cooking houses to the rear were connected to the main residence by ivy- covered, lattice-work halls, accentuated with delicate red flowers and constantly washed in the aroma of jasmine to cure the smell of foods being prepared in the two structures.

As was customary for the times, they had a large family. They raised seven children, nurturing them and bringing them up in the old-world traditions of their childhood. Here they could protect the children, from non-French influences as well as the fevers and plagues. But eventually, even with such devotion, the fevers would claim all but one child.

Little was known about Lavoisier's life after his marriage except that Katherine and he rarely ventured into society, preferring to entertain their guests at the charming estate near the swamp. The only time that Lavoisier was known to have left the vicinity of Lallemand, after his marriage, was in 1825, at the personal invitation of Lafayette upon his arrival in New Orleans.

Captain Lavoisier and Katherine were among the few distinguished guests invited to socialize with the hero of the American Revolution for the short time that the Marquis de Lafayette was in Louisiana.

After his visit with Lafayette, Lavoisier returned to seclusion with his family, living out the remainder of his life on his estate with his wife and child. His death came in 1857, a month after Katherine had succumbed to scarlet fever. Most agreed that he had died of a broken heart, since, as the story was told, he had gone to his room the day of her funeral, refusing to leave or allow anyone to enter until the morning he was found dead.

Lavoisier had remained terribly saddened by his exile from France, and he insisted that the small cemetery plot where he and his family were to be buried be excavated and refilled with French soil, brought from his family's estate in Rennes before his death. Even the mausoleum that held his body was made from imported stone, cut from quarries in France, the same as eventually would provide the stone for the tomb of Napoleon.

Within a few years after Lavoisier's death, the quaint Creole community of Lallemand bore little resemblance to its founder's original design. It became a Mecca of affluence and grandeur, unparalleled anywhere in the New World. The river was a frenzy of vessels laden to the waterline with the produce being dispatched from Lallemand's port to points throughout the world. The horizon was a jagged filigree of masts and riggings of clipper ships and schooners, riverboats, flat boats and barges. All were heaped with the finery of Europe for the wealthy to lavish on their homes, and dress their angelical bisque-skinned Creole ladies. Lallemand was enthralled with its own bustling economy, secure in the belief that its aristocratic Creole lifestyle would last forever.

Lallemand had become, with the onset of the Civil War in March of 1861, a major commissary station for the Confederate Army under Brigadier General Alfred Mouton and his 16th Louisiana Regiment. Railroad lines from the Jackson Railroad intersected at Lallemand, making the town strategically important to the Confederacy, not only as a shipping center but as a defensive position along the Mississippi River.

Lallemand also had a large military hospital, originally constructed to house wounded being shipped from the battlefield at Shiloh in April of 1862. As the battles and ensuing casualties had increased during the war, Lallemand became a regular stop for the wounded on their way to hospitals at Mobile, Galveston and New Orleans.

As the Union intensified its efforts to defeat the city of Vicksburg, Lallemand became more and more of a hindrance to their strategy.

On July 4, 1863, over a year after the capture of New Orleans, word reached General Mouton that Vicksburg finally had fallen. Mouton quickly ordered the evacuation of Lallemand and the removal of its war stores to prevent them from falling into Union hands.

Lallemand quickly felt the wrath of Federal troops as they entered the city. The city was ordered destroyed. The bulwarks along the river were leveled to prevent the Confederates from returning from the swamps and refortifying those positions, repeating what had happened at Port Hudson where the Union had taken two thousand casualties from a Confederate force determined to fight to the last man.

Those captured in the final assault of Lallemand were forced into labor gangs used to dismantle artillery buttresses along the river. As they worked they watched Lallemand burn.

Not only was the city razed, but in retribution for Confederate actions against the Union Army, the levees along the Mississippi River were blown open, flooding miles of farmland and submerging the remnants of Lallemand under the river. As at Port Hudson, the Federals used colored troops to carry out the destruction of the city, which further inflamed Lallemand's citizens.

When the demolition of the city was completed, the troops moved through the countryside, burning and looting the Creole estates, many of which had stood since the middle 1700's.

The Lavoisier estate was set afire, along with many others. The main house and barns were torched in retaliation for an incident which involved two Negro workers from the estate and a family member suspected of being a Confederate saboteur.

A detachment of cavalry, in hot pursuit of snipers, had stopped at the Lavoisier estate to get water and forage for food. After drinking from the well the soldiers became sick, poisoned from something in the water. They immediately arrested and hanged the three men, without a trial, as suspected insurgents.

The well had purposely been contaminated with an animal carcass, which was placed there as standard procedure for retreating Confederate troops. The three men, unfortunately, had had nothing to do with the incident, but simply had been at the wrong place at the wrong time.

Nicholas Philippe Lavoisier, the youngest and only surviving son of Pierre Edouard Lavoisier, and the two blacks, friends of Nicholas, were hanged near the family cemetery from a single large oak tree.

After hanging the men, the patrol vandalized the headstones in the cemetery, including Pierre and Katherine Lavoisier's mausoleum. They then set fire to the fields and the remaining buildings, leaving only the slave quarters intact.

They caught Nicholas as he slipped up to the house to fetch food and clothing for his wife and three children who were hiding in the swamp only a few hundred yards away.

Nicholas never denied that he was a Confederate soldier; the troops had already found travel documents releasing him from his regiment for furlough. He made no effort to argue his case, fearful that the scavengers would go after his wife and children if he told them the truth. His family could do nothing but watch from hiding, as Nicholas was hanged.

Most of the estates that had fronted the Mississippi River near Lallemand, those that had survived the torch, had been expropriated from their Creole owners by the Federally installed Governors and their administrations over the years. Sympathizers and northern investors had gained control of a majority of the property adjacent to the river, and in so doing gained control of Louisiana's economy, for a time.

Lallemand, the once-proud Creole community with its deeply established traditions and customs, its penchant for elegant living and its exquisitely designed architecture, was no more. The enthusiasm to rebuild the prosperous settlement was swept away with the muddy currents of the Mississippi. Lallemand had vanished beneath the river, erased from the earth, as were so many of the people who had resided in the quaint Creole community.

CHAPTER 2

With the first light of morning, the wild deafening sounds of the swamp ceased, leaving a deathly calm. A tiny bantam performed an arabesque as it positioned itself, trying to make a meal of a catalpa worm inching its way across the ground. A threatening squawk from an old blue goose quickly broke off the attack, sending the chicken scurrying for the protection of a picket fence that surrounded the yard. The goose inhaled the worm, then strutted away, searching for another morsel that had fallen from the worm nests hanging high in the trees above the yard.

White smoke from the cooking shack drifted aimlessly across the front enclosure, dissipating into a thin haze, twenty or thirty yards from the old brick chimney of the slave quarters. A mongrel dog lay out in a hole dug next to the steps, stretched himself in a yawn, ignoring for a moment a challenge from the goose. He preferred to snap at a black horse fly that had continued to land on the open sores of his nose and forehead, wounds from the previous night's run-in with a coon near the boat landing.

Turkey buzzards circled overhead, eyeing a carcass left from the night's prowling by fox or coyotes. Wild swans and turkeys, working to fill their hungry stomachs in the swamp, added to the tumultuous assembly, letting loose with an occasional raspy tantara.

The morning serenade by the wetland birds was as dependable as a clock, except when the weather was rainy and overcast. Little by little, the shrill tunes increased, creating a delightful overture to the new day.

As the sun intensified, grasshoppers became more active, unwinding in any direction, and stopping only long enough to sense the heat before springing off again in wild flight.

The opening of the front door of the house disrupted the wild fortissimo, suddenly ending even the slightest buzzing from bees hovering over a patch of bitterweed next to the fence.

A young man nudged the screen door open, stepping onto the front porch. He was a tall, gangly fellow, a towering six foot four. He was dressed in traditional brown cotton pants,

17

and a homespun muslin shirt tied with leather lacing at the opening near his neck. The cuffs of his trousers were stuffed deep into his high-topped boots, still stained with cow dung from his previous day's work in the corral. A large knife, sheathed in a dark leather scabbard, hung from his belt, and a tobacco pouch, made from a scrap of sewn canvas, dangled and bobbed from the opposite side of his knife.

His hat shaded the ruddy complexion of his face, deeply creased around his eyes from long hours of squinting into the hot sun. The shadow of a scar, drawn in a half-moon shape, ran the length of his right cheek below his sideburns, a line that only could have come from the blade of a knife. Most men would have worn a full beard to cover such a scar, but not Jaques. A Frenchman, a Creole, he let the scar show as a warning to others that he was willing to fight, if need be.

Small waves of dark brown hair flowed neatly back beneath the wide brim of his homemade chapeau.

Jaques smiled at his dog as he walked past him, heading for the front gate. His piercing blue eyes peered from under the palmetto leaf hat, searching the sky for threatening weather. He stopped, looking back over his shoulder as he spoke softly to the animal.

"Allons-y, mon chien."

The dog struggled to pull himself up, stretching and yawning in response to the command from his master, then obediently followed him to the gate.

Jaques stepped up into the stirrups of his saddle, landing smoothly in the seat. He straightened himself, taking a moment to survey his property before reining the horse into a turn towards the field, where he had been working for several hours before sunup. He had only come in for coffee and gravy bread for his breakfast.

Jaques Edmund Lavoisier, heir to the Lavoisier estate, or what was left of it, was the only surviving son of Nicholas Phillipe Lavoisier. It was 1894, and the condition of the estate had degenerated into a pitiful conglomeration of broken-backed buildings and a collection of geometrically mis-aligned fences and corrals.

Much of the land he had inherited lay beneath Bayou Claire, flooded by the same opening blown in the levee some thirty one years earlier by Federal troops.

Jaques had developed somewhat of a brusque personality, evolving from having spent so much time alone. Except for the moldy, tick-infested hound that he revered almost as kin, his contacts with other living creatures were limited to a few Creole friends and the Cachumas, mixed race laborers, who helped work the fields.

The sparse population and the distance between his fellow inhabitants had dictated much of his aloofness. But Jaques was withdrawn, preferring to stay clear of the 'Foreigners,' as he referred to them. The Foreigners were English-speaking Anglos, transplanted from the North after the Civil War, living among the people of Louisiana, but never assimilating into their society or acquiring a taste for the difficult Creole language.

Jaques tolerated the Foreigners only long enough to make a trade or purchase, but he usually bought his goods from Creole merchants whenever possible.

His life revolved around his farm. The planting and harvesting of rice, the cutting of cane and the picking of cotton, what little that survived the damp conditions, occupied the entirety of his existence during the growing season.

From early morning Jaques would tend his crops, working alongside contract laborers hired during the planting and harvesting season.

They waded barefooted into the flooded fields to plant the slender delicate stalks of rice. Their hands would slip gently into the thick black muck, carefully impregnating the rich submerged soil with the tiny green rice stalks.

Occasionally a worker would jerk his hand out of the mud, laughing and grinning as he thrust his fist into the sunlight, shouting, "Ecrevisse!" The workers usually carried a sack tied to their belts to deposit the crawfish they harvested as they worked in the flooded fields. The men would stand for a moment, watching the small trails of mud cloud the clear water in a thin, billowing, brown ribbon as the crawfish fanned their tails trying to make a backwards getaway. Small mud towers, like crude spires of ancient castles, protruded from the dark chocolate mud, bubbling at the openings as the crawfish slipped into their thin-walled sanctuaries.

There was little indication that the Civil War had changed much of anything. Blacks worked the fields as they had done for nearly two centuries, finding the farms as much a part of their heritage and security in life as did the Creole owners. Emancipation had done little to deal with the realities of survival.

When the planting and harvesting were over, Jaques would take a sabbatical, abandoning his farm to a caretaker; then he would head up river to St. Francisville or Baton Rouge and lay up for several weeks with a covey of disreputable women who lived in a bordello along the levee. When his crop had been unusually profitable he would catch a ride on the river from a passing boat to New Orleans, attending the horse races and gambling until his money was gone. But rarely could he afford the luxury of New Orleans, having instead to stay nearer to home. He would entertain himself with stout Tafia liquor and the company of one of the establishment's less than virtuous damsels until he either ran out of money or was being pursued by the law for fighting or destroying property.

More than once Jaques had taken to the swamp in his pirogue to avoid the consequences of one of his forays to Lake Maurepas or the brothels along the Mississippi near St. James or Vacherie.

After an exhaustive night of being chased by the local constables, he would slip deep into the swamps of Lafourche Parish to sober up, along with his drinking companions, and hide from the law and their packs of bloodhounds.

They would bed down to the bellowing of bug-eyed bullfrogs and nervous egrets screeching their displeasure at the intrusion.

Awakening was usually more traumatic than the pursuit by the posse the night before. Like the aftermath of an ambush, their bodies would be strewn everywhere, each sprawled dead still on the ground with only their snores to affirm that they were still among the living. Morning would find them damp from the rain and fog that had drifted quietly over their bodies, as if they were floating on a heavenly cloud, slurped up to the Pearly Gates to answer for their transgressions. By noon the sun had warmed the air enough to take some of the shivers out of their sleeping souls, drying the sunny side of their bodies but leaving the shaded portion soaked and chilled. Rising to their feet and walking was another matter. The potent homemade brew not only caused a slight paralysis, but also had the men crawling for a spot of privacy to relieve themselves. Even the heartiest drinkers never managed to acquire a resistance to the wallop of the crudely distilled spirits.

A few weeks after his recovery from one of these incidents in Lafourche Parish, Jaques and a friend had decided to go on another binge, making their way to Verret Island, some ten miles from Jaques' farm. They understood from local gossip that the proprietor had employed a young and exceptionally beautiful mulatto woman to entertain his patrons. Not only was she rumored to be gloriously endowed beyond anyone's wildest dreams, but she was also billed as the one and only daughter of the 'Miche Agoussou,' in local parlance, a legendary Demon of Love among the Cajun peasantry. She was said to have been given some highly unusual talents that one would have to see to believe. Either the 'Miche Agoussou' had become very absent-minded about the prodigious number of its progeny, or else this daughter was extraordinarily fleet of foot, managing to be in service at a host of brothels at the same time. And if there were impostors, no one was confessing, lest their reputations become tainted or their manhood challenged.

Jaques and a longtime friend, Maurice Fouche', set out in their pirogue at sunset with enough liquor and natural sense of direction to find the stilted gentleman's parlor in the pitch of night. They approached Verret Island several hours later, slipping quietly up next to the pilings that supported the elevated house where the establishment was located. A sinister stillness held both men's attention as they watched the only light, an orange glow coming from a single candle in a window covered in cheesecloth some fifteen feet above their boat.

Maurice tied the boat to a rickety and partially submerged dock underneath the cantilever structure looming above them. They made their way across a narrow sagging footbridge and ascended the stairs to the front deck of the darkened parlor house. Once inside, they stood trying to adjust their eyes to the almost pitch black room. An oil lantern dimly lit the opposite side of the room directly across from the single candle they had seen from the bayou.

In the dark shadows a group of men sat playing cards under the sparse light from the lantern. The shadows of the men flickered against the back wall as one, then another, jarred the table when they turned to look at Jaques and Maurice.

Another man, standing at the bar in the middle of the room, set a match to a slim stogie sticking from his lips. When Jaques' eyes adjusted to the dark again, he noticed a partially nude negro woman standing beside the man at the bar with her back turned towards them.

Jaques knew they were in a Cajun establishment. But that usually hadn't been a problem unless the drinking got out of hand. As long as they were spending money, there was never a rub with the locals—the proprietor saw to that. Customers were too scarce to be run off over ethnic feuding. Creoles and Cajuns held little love for each other, as it was, but they usually stayed clear of starting something they might not be able to finish.

Jaques and Maurice selected a table near the door and sat down. Jaques scratched a wooden match across the floor, giving off a loud snap and a brilliant flash as the flame quickly adjusted to a blue and orange glow. He lit a puddled paraffin candle in the center of the table and then turned to get a better look at the topless woman leaning against the bar, some fifteen feet away. The proprietor, after whispering something to her, made a motion in their direction with his head, then gave the girl a shove towards their table. When she was close enough, Jaques realized that he had seen her before. Not here, but along the river, in a putrid pigsty of a brothel near Lutcher. He knew all about her from a friend who'd purchased her favors on one of their outings. She was anything but a raving beauty, far from it.

Jaques quickly turned away, ignoring the solicitress, who by now was pressing herself against his friend. He shook his head at Maurice, speaking softly in his deep Creole dialect, but loud enough for the girl to hear him.

"Stay away from this one, Maurice...she has the disease. You'll find yourself with rotting parts if you sleep with her tonight."

The girl spun around, spitting a spew of liquor in Jaques' direction as he sat looking up at her. She retreated to the bar. The owner walked over and planted himself in a chair next to Jaques. The man's face was covered with a thick black beard, coated in grease with bits of food hanging from the scraggly hair under his nose and mouth. He reeked of the stench of sweat, and his breath was thick with the smell of rotting teeth, hanging like well-separated stalactites, blackened and eroded from years of neglect.

The man was huge, bulges of fat lying layer-on-layer from his neck to his gigantic abdomen that kept his chest back from the edge of the table. His arms rested on the tabletop, leaving a wet spot wherever they touched the raw wood.

He said nothing at first, but stared at Jaques with a curious look. "You damn Creoles come heer...tankin' you so Gawd damn smart. You tank you too damn good for dis place...hell, I don't tink so, my Creole friend?"

Jaques said nothing. He glanced at Maurice, catching his attention and then looked back towards the door, signaling with his eyes and a nod from his head for him to get up and leave. He noticed that the four men at the back of the room had moved between his table and the front entrance.

The owner started in again, but this time grabbing Jaques' wrist as he began to speak. "Maybe you don't like dem Cajun girls...not clean enough far you? Maybe you jest hare to have trouble wit me, huh? You come in hare lookin' dah fight, tryin' dah tear up my place? Naw...not in dis place you don't, not hare!" he shouted.

By the time Jaques had pulled himself loose from the man's grip and stood up, two of the other men were standing next to him.

"We're not here for trouble," Jaques said. "We jest come to have a drink."

The other man shoved Maurice backwards. "You damn trash!" the man threatened, pulling a long blade from under his shirt and holding it out where Jaques and Maurice could see it.

23

Before Jaques could pull his own knife, the men were on them, forcing Jaques to the floor and pushing Maurice back against the far wall.

For the next few seconds, deep sickening thuds and groans filled the room from the contact of clubs against the men's bodies. Blood streaked across the floors and splattered up the wall.

Jaques was nearly unconscious from the beating as he lay flat on his back, his arms restrained by two of the assailants. The walrus-shaped man leaned down and pulled his head up by the hair as he searched for his money pouch.

"Take a good look, my friend, what dah Cajun women do to dah Creole garbage," he sneered.

Jaques could see Maurice pinned against the wall by several of the men. The Negro girl was standing next to Maurice with a knife to his face. Another of the men held a lantern next to Maurice's head to give everyone a good look as the woman made a quick motion with her wrist across his mouth, splitting it open from cheek to cheek. His teeth were clearly visible, like dentures sitting in a glass of blood red water.

"Now," the man announced, stretching his own mouth to mimic Maurice's wound, evoking a round of laughter from the others," dis sons-sa-bitch can kiss a gawd damn mule."

Maurice slumped to his knees, and his head dropped forward, almost touching the floor. The proprietor walked over, lifting the axe handle he'd used on Jaques, and slammed the club against the back of Maurice's head, caving it in. Maurice made a short, deep moan and went limp on the floor.

The men holding Jaques yanked him to his feet. Before he could catch his balance, he felt the hot sting of one, then another knife blade penetrating deep into his stomach. An instant later he was airborne, dropping into the bayou from the balcony of the elevated hovel.

A moment afterwards, his friend hit the water with a loud splash on the other side of the building.

The shock of hitting the cool water brought Jaques back to consciousness. He floated to the surface, staring up from the darkness at the people on the balcony. Each of them was laughing as they began moving back inside.

One of the men, the last one on the balcony, yelled out towards Jaques, to impress the others: "Now da damn gar make love to you, Creole man?"

Jaques struggled through the deep sediment on the bottom of the bayou, feeling the pull of quicksand and mud with each step that he made towards his pirogue. When he finally made it to the edge of the small carved boat, he hung his arm over the side, unable to call up enough energy to leverage himself out of the water and into the sanctuary of the small skiff. His eyes searched across the top of the water for some sign of Maurice. He prayed that he was still alive. But he knew that the river creatures would dispose of much of his body by morning if he were dead. There would be little to take home.

Jaques urged the heavy boat out of view of the house, pulling himself up on the shore. He gathered Spanish moss on the ground around him, wadding it up to make a bousillage and packed the mud and gray fibrous pad against his wounds. He used pieces of his shirt to secure the bulky compress against his body as best he could. When he'd finished, he lay in the mud on his back, long enough to catch his breath. As soon as he could muster up the energy he crawled back into the boat and pushed off from shore.

A few minutes later he had maneuvered against the pilings of the parlor house, still bleeding heavily from his stomach wounds. He struggled to stay conscious, at least until he had taken revenge. His honor, at this point, as he saw it, was more at risk than his life. He lay back in the boat, waiting for the first light of dawn, but his eyes continued to search desperately for his friend, almost certain now that he was dead.

A fish broke the surface of the water next to the boat, waking Jaques from his sleep. He realized that he must act before first sunlight, or else the Cajuns would finish him off and no one would ever be the wiser. The little bit of sleep that he'd had gave him a momentary burst of energy, enough to raise himself up in the boat, making his way from piling to piling under the house. When he was sure that the occupants were asleep, he pulled the tiny cigar-shaped craft underneath the building, as close to the center as he could.

A large pile of brush had collected beneath the building, washed up against the wooden stilts. Over the years the owner had disposed of his garbage there making a mountainous heap that reached just short of the floor of the shanty.

Jaques' hands, shaking and cold, scratched one match and then another against the inside of the boat, hoping that one of them would be dry enough to ignite. His hands were so wet and caked with blood that it was difficult for him to keep a grip on the matchstick. He smiled as a single match finally caught, flashing with a brilliant incandescence that illuminated the whole underside of the squalor.

Jaques held the small torch to the dried grass next to the piling, watching it catch fire and then spread, rising higher and higher until flames licked at the bottom of the building and then moved up the sides like a giant hand about to crush a kindling box. Then he gave the boat a shove with his boot, moving quickly back away from the pyre and out into the main channel of the bayou. The underside of the building seemed to explode, engulfing the entire structure in a mammoth blaze.

Jaques stayed just long enough to assure himself that no one had leaped to safety from the inferno. He knew that in a few minutes Verret Island would be no more. Then a cold chill moved over his body, his eyes no longer obeying his attempts to stay awake as he fell limp in the bottom of the boat.

Through the next night and into the morning Jaques lay unconscious in the pirogue, then his eyes suddenly opened to a clicking sound in the distance, two objects being tapped incessantly together in a non-musical rhythm. It was an irritating tempo that disturbed him from his deep, troubled sleep. Soon, the sound came closer, the beat deeper, with no logical rhythm.

His head moved to one side, his eyes focusing on the stagnant black water next to the boat. Small flowers, buds of water lilies, floated by in their own rivulets of water, spinning with the current as each one touched the hull and then slipped quickly away as if repulsed by the horror within the boat. A gar, suspended inches from the surface of the warm water was disturbed by the closeness of the pirogue. With a quick spontaneous thrust of its thin barracuda-shaped body, the fish was gone, leaving its wake slapping against the side of the boat.

The tapping grew louder, more distinguishable, more promising to the dying man. Jaques elevated himself, struggling to stay conscious, long enough to cry for help.

"S'il vous plait Seigneur, je vais mourir, ayez pitié!" he pleaded with little more than a groan. "S'il vous plait Seigneur ...aidez-moi, ne me laissez pas mourir!" "Please Lord, help me, don't let me die!"

His head fell backwards, his energy spent from the short effort. "Please...I'm dying...Lord God, have mercy," he muttered one last time before closing his eyes. "God almighty!" he cried softly before finally slipping into unconsciousness again.

And then the coldness he'd known before reappeared, a terrifying chill that swept over his entire body. He forced his eyes open, gasping for a breath of air in the oppressively humid environment. He forced one last look straight up, watching a giant oak, festooned with Spanish moss, blot out the hot sun overhead. His eyes closed, but still he could see the shadows of the trees above him.

Suddenly he saw his father leaning over him, kissing him on both cheeks as he held his face with his warm hands the way he had done when he was a small child. His father gently brushed back Jaques' hair from his forehead, casting a gentle smile at him, all the while cradling him in his lap. The dream left him as the light suddenly faded from his eyes.

André noticed the boat floating by only a few yards from where he'd been cutting down an old cypress stump. He could see a man's arm dragging in the water next to the boat. He sunk the blade of his axe deep into the softwood of the tree stump and began wading towards the pirogue. He was up to his waist in mud and water by the time he reached the bow of the tiny vessel.

"Oh, precious Lord," André whispered, holding a hand over his heart as he looked at the bloody figure in the bottom of the boat. "This is the devil's work!" He spoke to the man in French, trying to arouse him from his sleep, hoping he wasn't dead. His hand dipped into the murky bayou, cupping a small quantity of cool water to wash the unconscious face.

Jaques' eyes opened, catching a wide-mouthed grin from the old man, who still held his hand on his forehead. Without a word André began towing the boat along the shore, working his way through the shallows past the cypress stands where he'd been working earlier.

André Deveaux had seen his share of violence during his life; it was common for those who inhabited the lawless bayou country. The fact that Jaques was alive in the bottom of the boat told André that the young man had probably extracted his vengeance on his attackers, or at least gotten the upper hand.

The old man carried a cow horn hung from his shoulder by a leather string. The horn was used to call his daughter if something went awry while he was away from the house, an alarm of sorts, common among the swamp people. He straightened his curved back, holding his head so that the horn was above him and aimed at the horizon. He let loose with a loud trumpeting sound that passed through several shrill notes before settling on a single blaring dissonance.

In a few moments a young girl appeared along the edge of the bayou, her long skirt pulled up to her knees as she waded into the water towards the boat. She clasped her hands together against her lips as she peered at the bloodied, incapacitated form sprawled in the bottom of the boat. "Merciful Jesus," she whispered under her breath. She spoke to André in French without taking her eyes off the bloodied traveler. Her fingers moved against Jaques' neck, searching for a pulse before she turned and instructed the old man to help her pull the pirogue ashore.

Once they had gotten the boat pulled onto the muddy bank, she ordered André to go to the barn and fetch the plow harness. When André returned with the mule and harness, the two of them attached the waterlogged boat to the plow tack and dragged it, with Jaques still inside, up to their house.

After they had reached the front door, they rolled Jaques out of the boat onto a quilt. The old man and young girl struggled with the makeshift litter until they had pulled Jaques inside to the front bedroom. The fragile young Creole girl stripped him of his boots and clothes, cutting away his garments except for a small patch of material left over each wound to preserve the clots that had formed there.

Benonia Deveaux, the old man's daughter, while seemingly frail and delicate, was anything but that. She carefully washed away the clots, opening one, then the other wound,

28

cautiously probing each for signs of a bullet or some other foreign object. When she'd finished examining them, each was closed around a cloth drain with sewing thread, then thoroughly covered in a plaster and dressed.

Benonia stayed by her patient, sitting near his bed in the darkened room waiting for Jaques to regain consciousness. When he awoke a day later, his eyes searched the room, examining the furnishings of the neatly kept cubical, and finally came to rest on the young girl. She was asleep in a rocking chair near the bed, her face reflecting the soft glow of a lantern set on a table near by.

Jaques studied her face, wondering who she was. He was careful not to wake her from her sleep. His eyes closed, then opened with a start as she suddenly began speaking to him.

"Monsieur is most fortunate to have survived such a violent assault!"

"Perhaps my good fortune rests with the river that was kind enough to bring me here," Jaques answered. "May I ask where I am?"

"You're in the home of my father, Monsieur Deveaux. We are a few yards from Bayou de Chenaie; my father found you."

"Are my wounds fatal?"

"No, Monsieur, I think you will be spared," she answered.

"I'm thankful to Monsieur Deveaux for saving my life," Jaques said, letting his head relax into the feather pillow after he'd spoken.

"God has saved Monsieur's life! My poppa has only delivered you to God's care. You have lost a lot of blood...you should rest. Please, try to sleep now," she commanded. Placing her hand against his face, she recited a short prayer in French and then stood and left the room, with Jaques' eyes following her to the door.

The following morning Jaques awoke, smelling the sweet fragrance of Spanish jasmine arranged in a metal can on the nightstand next to his bed. The wooden window louvers had been opened enough to allow fresh air to enter the room and enough light for Jaques to see a small silver baptismal bowl next to the jasmine on the nightstand.

"Bonjour, Monsieur."

"Bonjour, Mademoiselle", Jaques answered, as Benonia appeared next to his bed. "It's good to see you again," he added, hiding his jaw behind one hand, embarrassed by the stubble of beard.

Benonia laughed. "After what you've been through, Monsieur, I would think we should both give praise to God that you are alive to see at all."

Jaques returned her smile with a weak grin, looking at the baptismal bowl. "I'm baptized in Christ, you know!"

"Then I give thanks to God that I have only your wounds to care for. I pray you will forgive me for having taken the liberty of baptizing you while you were asleep. I wasn't so certain that we'd be having this conversation."

"Of course," Jaques answered. "I don't mind...I'm thankful for all that you've done for me."

As quickly as she had appeared in the room, she turned and headed for the door, asking, as she paused with her back to Jaques, "Perhaps you feel like eating something?"

"Yes, I'd like that very much."

Jaques tried to shinny himself into a sitting position in the bed to receive the tray of food that Benonia set beside him on the small table, a few moments later. A sharp pain brought his efforts to a quick halt.

"Sit still!" she scolded. "I can feed you as you are. If you move, you'll tear open your wounds."

"Yes, I think you're right," he grimaced, slipping back down against his pillow.

"Would Monsieur mind telling me his Christian name and where he comes from?"

Benonia placed a wide linen bib across his chest as Jaques spoke. "I'm Jaques Lavoisier. My home is near the old city of Lallemand and closer to the new town of Lalleville. I have a small farm just outside of town."

"Do you have family there?"

"No,...not any more."

"And what brought Monsieur Lavoisier so far south, to Bayou de Chenaie?"

"A man's trifling, I'm sorry to say. Nothing significant...not anymore." Jaques' eyes turned away from Benonia, towards the window, his thoughts lost in the memory of his friend and the events of a few days earlier.

Benonia moved a spoon of soft food to his mouth. She followed each serving with a warm damp cloth against his lips.

Afterwards, when he'd finished eating, she shaved his face with her father's straight razor. By the time she'd finished, Jaques was exhausted, falling asleep as she gently wiped his face a final time with the wet cloth.

In the days that followed, Jaques recovered his strength enough to make his way to the rocking chair in the corner of the room near the window. Each morning he stared out the window at Benonia as she went about her chores near the barn.

She was young, almost childlike in appearance, hardly like a grown woman. Her hair was coal-black, frizzed from the humidity, curled on the sides, and allowed to hang freely to her shoulders. Her hairstyle was unusual for a Creole woman, and even more for a devout Christian, who would have been prone to wear a bun or a scarf to hide her hair altogether. She held her hair in place with a single brightly colored ribbon that dangled to her waist.

Each day she wore a black handmade dress, reflecting her simple, puritanical attitude. Even in the suffocating heat of summer, she wore high-collared dresses with long sleeves and a hint of lace. Each dress was carefully hemmed to cover her ankles, with layers of white cotton petticoats concealing any suggestions of her hips or legs. Her face was narrow and smooth with blush marks on her cheeks from a dab of red rouge, a special touch for her visitor's sake that added an additional glow to an already vivacious personality. Her skin tone was soft, transparent bisque, protected in the hottest part of the day by a shadowing bonnet that hung from the back of her head like a cape.

The complexions of swamp women usually resembled tanned leather, deeply scarred and burned from the elements. Their bodies wore out before most of them had turned forty. But Benonia showed little effects of her difficult life at the young age of seventeen. Still, she was considered to be near mid-life by conventional standards. She moved about the yard doing her chores each morning, happily singing bits and pieces of her favorite hymns. For several hours in the cool of the morning she worked barefooted in the fertile moist soil, chopping bullnettle and bitterweed out of the garden with a wide-bladed hoe, stopping to straighten her back, with her hands pressed to her hips. The heavy cotton dress did little to flatter her boyish figure.

Each day as Jaques continued to convalesce he sat near the window studying the young girl from a distance. He saw a woman enthusiastic with life, cheerfully going about her chores, and content with the adequate bounty that God had provided for her and her father. He admired her devotion to her father and the old man's affection for her. Between them, they had managed to scratch out a comfortable living, a great accomplishment for anyone living in the harsh backwaters, not the least an old man and young girl.

Benonia would turn and smile at Jaques as she worked near the house, sometimes walking over to the window to chat with him during a break from her chores. She'd hand him a gourd full of cool water from the well as they spoke. Before returning to work, she'd wet a cloth and wash his face and arms with some of the water, trying to relieve his discomfort from the heat that had collected in the house from the mid-day sun.

One evening, a little over a week after Jaques had come to them, Benonia and her father helped him, dressed only in a blanket, walk to the bayou, fifty yards from the house, where he could bathe. André waded out into the water with Jaques to give him support as he stood naked, washing himself in the clear water of Bayou de Chenaie. Benonia returned to the house, out of courtesy, under the auspices of retrieving Jaques' clothes that she had mended earlier.

Afterwards, Benonia and Jaques sat near the edge of the water talking while André fished nearby, chaperoning the young couple. Benonia bandaged Jaques' wounds with clean linen dressings after applying a mustard plaster, mixed with sulfur powder.

Jaques was infatuated with the curious young woman. Not only did she seem to have boundless energy, but possessed a radiance that was strangely out of place in the bayou country. He found little that didn't interest him about Benonia, save the fact she could read. That item, and that item alone, he found distasteful. Educated women, as every man knew, were particularly susceptible to devilish inclinations.

But it was difficult for Jaques to find fault even with that because Benonia's profession of faith was beyond reproach. The revelation about her reading ability had come to him as he listened to her read aloud from the 'Word' after dinner each night. The weakness of character, as Jaques was well aware, was his own. He was unable to read or write, except to execute his own signature, and was highly sensitive about that.

Benonia, on the other hand, found Jaques interesting and, having the gift of discernment, felt him to be a good man under his rough, worldly exterior.

André had an interest in Jaques, as well. He feared that he would pass from this world, leaving Benonia a spinster, forced to face the dangerous prospect of existing all alone in the bayou after his death. He had, however, conceded that any nudge towards matrimony for Jaques and Benonia would have to come from Divine initiative and not from him, lest his honor be offended if Jaques declined to ask Benonia for her hand in marriage.

Jaques knew that time was running short for him to court Benonia. The distance from Lallemand to Bayou de Chenaie would make traditional courting difficult, if not impossible. What little time they had together was spent in the evenings on the front portico, still under the watchful eye of André.

Oddly enough, on the very night that Jaques had decided to ask Benonia for her hand in marriage, André, for whatever reason, left the couple alone for the first time since their meeting. Apparently the twinkle in Jaques' eye and his nervousness had been obvious to Benonia as well as André since supper.

Without the elaborate fanfare of fancy clothes, beautiful flowers or music, or pastoral counsel, which was all customary in Creole life, Jaques sat down next to Benonia on the steps of the front porch to make his proposal of marriage. The night was pitch black with the stars replaced by fireflies that swarmed near the house, attracted by the lanterns set out on the front porch. The couple sat quietly listening to the owls screech back and forth, pretending to have an interest in the number of birds involved in the serenade; and locusts performed a frenzied melody that drowned out the other night creatures.

Stephen D. Boyett

Jaques clasped his hands over Benonia's hand and slid an intricate bracelet onto the narrow wrist of her right arm. He had fashioned the bracelet from small vines laced with petite red, yellow and white flowers and buds from a honeysuckle bush. He looked over at her, and then down at the ground, as he began to speak in his deep, confident Creole dialect.

"I've not lived a Godly life, nor am I a man of wealth. But given the same trust that you'd give these flowers on your wrist, a trust that they will someday blossom into a thing of beauty, I'd promise to be an honorable man, to provide you with a good home and be a faithful husband. I would love and defend you with all my strength and heart. And even though I know that you've not had enough time to come to love me, I'm certain that someday you would. I hope that you will find it in your heart to be my wife."

Benonia, even though expecting his proposal, was totally captivated. She drew nearer to him, looking childishly down at the ground as she answered with a smile and a nod, tightening her grip on his hands as she said a soft," yes!"

Two days later Jaques pushed off from shore at Bayou de Chenaie in his pirogue, looking happily at Benonia as she fingered the wedding bracelet on her arm, standing barefoot at the water's edge as Jaques paddled away. He was going home to look after his farm that had been left unattended for nearly two weeks, but they planned to be reunited in a fortnight. Jaques would return the day of the wedding ceremony, to be held at Benonia's home and then take her to Lalleville for their honeymoon. André would join them, a month or so later.

An open invitation, as was the custom, was extended to anyone who knew the couple. There were no formal invitations; they weren't needed. News of the wedding spread by word of mouth quickly through the swamp, north to Baton Rouge, south to New Orleans, west to Lafayette and east to Ponchatoula above Lake Maurepas.

Two days before the wedding people began to arrive at Benonia's home, setting up camp near the house. Many came by boat. A few guests, who lived close by, came on horseback or by wagon. A great bonfire was constructed to one side of the property, away from the house to warm the gathering at night. Smaller cooking fires burned day and night to prepare meals for the growing number of visitors crowding around the Deveaux home.

The day of the wedding, Cajuns tacked bags of sachet, love amulets, to the trees, to help the newlyweds in their amorous endeavor. Coloreds tied long, streaming, multicolored ribbons to the tree branches, creating a colorful canopy above the area where the ceremony was to be held.

The night before the ceremony, candles encircled the area where the wedding was to be performed, lit by coloreds to ward off the Loa, the voodoo demon. Catholic guests had nailed crosses to the trees along the paths and waterways leading to the wedding. Each cross was made of wood and covered in brightly colored flowers. Neither Jaques nor Benonia were Catholic, but most of their Creole and Cajun guests were.

A small trio of wood ducks splashed and frolicked in the inlet near the cooking area. They sounded their high-pitched shrills and whistles, ignoring the humans as they fed on the abundance of cake and bread floating across the water. Children laughed and screamed with excitement, chasing and running after each other, some wading into the shallow anse, carved into the shoreline from the bayou, to cool their feet from the hot ground.

Whirls of smoke rose from the cooking fires, overshadowing the fat-bellied cooking pots, black from a century of use and prized for the thick crusts built up in the bottom, adding flavor to the thick roux for the gumbos. The aroma of spiced filé from dried sassafras leaves added to the delicious aroma.

The wedding began just as the sun was setting. Benonia arrived in a brightly painted landau, accompanied by her bridesmaids. Benonia almost glowed as the white wedding dress set a brilliant contrast to the darkening horizon.

Wisps of smoke swirled through the crowd of admirers, drifting magnetically to the bride and groom, forming a romantic aura of soft light around the couple as they responded to the minister's questions.

The officiating minister extended the formalities as long as possible in an obvious attempt to proselytize the catholic brethren who courteously listened, coughing and looking down at the ground as they tired of the service. Finally, the

35

minister initiated the benediction. The crowd cheered, breathing a sigh of relief.

Before the crowd disbursed, a broom was placed on the ground near the altar. It was a custom among Cajun and Creole alike that a wedding could not be consummated without the ritualistic jumping by the bride and groom over the broomstick. Even though considered a barbaric adjunct to the wedding ceremony by Benonia, she willingly executed the leap, hand-in-hand with Jaques.

Then, as a single bell tolled, they embraced, locked together in a moment of passion that thrilled the audience. The bridesmaids tossed hand-twisted candy sticks to the children as boys ran through the crowd throwing flower petals into the air. Women hugged and cried as the men hastily made their way to the open bar.

Without a moment's warm-up, music from the fiddlers and guitarists, flutist and banjo players began playing a fast-tempoed arrangement. Cajuns ran to the open dance area, spinning into their familiar "fais do-do." Children mimicked the adults, dancing in circles and falling down with high-pitched giggles on the edge of the dance arena.

Benonia and Jaques made their way through the crowd to a receiving line where congratulations and wedding gifts were received.

As the evening wore on, the guests tired of dancing and eating, and most of the wedding party gathered around the great bonfire, stoked to a fierce blaze. As was the tradition, the old men of the community began telling the stories of times long ago, holding their audience spellbound as they recalled the past. Children slept in the laps of their parents, willing listeners, but worn out from the day's festivities.

One storyteller, as a tribute to the groom, began telling a chronicle of Jaques' family. The old raconteur painted a vivid recollection of Jaques' father and an incident that had occurred during the Civil War, before Nicolas Lavoisier had met death at the hands of the Yankees.

Benonia and Jaques sat cuddled beneath one of the quilts given to them as a wedding gift as they exchanged looks and held hands, listening intently.

The storyteller, Paul Duvallon, had witnessed the incident. Many of the other old-timers attending the gathering had been witness to the same event, having served with Nicolas in the Army of the Confederacy under General Mouton.

Between June of 1862 and December of that same year, in the desperate months that followed the capture of New Orleans, a mission had been undertaken by Confederate troops defending the lower Mississippi River. Lallemand had been cut off from all source of supply from the outside world except what could be smuggled through the swamps. The limited amount of food that was slipped past Union lines did little to relieve the critical situation, and the people were starving. Young children and elderly residents of the town, along with hundreds of Confederate wounded in the hospital, were suffering from a lack of medical supplies and clothing. Then, on December 18, 1862, Confederate informants at New Orleans learned of a Union naval flotilla heading upriver to attack Port Hudson. Farragut was attempting to re-supply elements of the Union Army laying siege to fortifications outside the city.

"I remember that day our boys marched off to fight, God rest their souls," Duvallon began, in his backwoods twang, and giving the visitors the courtesy of hearing his story in English rather than Creole. "It were the coldest month we'd had near on to twenty years. I'd never seen such ice along the edge of the river, but it were there on that day. Trees were nekked as a newborn's backside from the winds that had whipped across the river for days without lettin' up.

"It were cold...so cold it hurt just to breathe. We'd buried three children and as many wounded soldiers the day before we marched to Prophet's Point. Half the men that went along were sick from croup.

"The Yankees killed and burned everything they could get their hands on to keep the folks in Lallemand from havin' anything to eat. We were starvin' to death, but we were still holdin' on tight. We were lickin' 'em every time they come at us.

"Sixty of our boys from the 16th, including Jaques' pappy and me, made a razzue across the bend at Prophet's Point to wait for the Yankees to come upriver. We'd had word that them ships, and at least one of 'em was filled with food, was on its way to feed their troops dug in near Port Hudson.

"The water were shallow like onto late summer, in a dry spell, but it were cold as a dead man's touch. The Yankees jest kept on comin', never slowin' down fer nothin' from New Orleans all the way to the turn in the river near the Point. All they had on their minds was gettin' up to Port Hudson and given our boys a lickin'.'"

Duvallon paused, taking a long swig from a metal cup and then a deep breath to overcome the fumes before he began again.

"The mornin' and afternoon jest 'afore the Federals reached us, we'd cut the tops off them sandbars ta keep their lookouts from knowin' how shallow it were out thar in the channel. It were pitch dark as they hit them sand bars, stretching near halfway across the river on the east side, down around Lilly Point. Those old iron paddle wheelers were jest churnin' up a storm, drawin' a lot ah water.

"Our boys were layin' up in brush piles out in the river, painted up with soot and grease, and such as that...so's no one could tell they was waitin'. They'd spent near all day movin' logs and limbs out in the water, thinkin' the Yanks wouldn't see 'em hidin' there that night.

"Gettin' on towards midnight...here they come...one boat after another. Our fellas were sufferin' badly, layin' out in that freezin' water for hours waitin' for them boats to come by, hands so cold we could hear some of them men whimperin', tryin' hard as they could to be still. I think they was more afraid of not being able to fight when it come time.

"Bout the time them ships hit mid-channel they slowed down," Duvallon continued, "realizin' they'd hit the shallows. Our boys began slippin' on board quick as they could. There warn't nothin' to hang onto with, 'cept to grab the rails with our frozen hands, 'cause them boats was pulled down to the waterline with all the paraphernalia they had on board.

"You could see them ships comin' fer half a mile. They was breakin' waves, white as chalk, when they come around Lilly Point. Two big ol' gunboats, the Albatross and the Kineo, we found out later, were leadin' the pack upriver. We gave 'em a good berth before we went after that last Yankee ship. Once they got past, we knew they wouldn't have no way to turn around until they got up at least to St. Francisville.

"When the boys got on board, the better part of them Yankees was sleepin'. Weren't nobody on deck, 'cept the pilot and the feller steerin'

...and they hadn't paid no attention to us gettin' on board, 'cause we was slicker'n a snake movin' over a mud flat."

Duvallon grinned, taking a draw off his pipe.

"Well, this ship, the Preston, were pullin' a mortar barge about twenty yards behind her stern. There were half a dozen Yankees sleepin' in that barge that we could see under a tarp stretched over the deck. I could see them old cannon balls, the size of full-growd watermelons stacked out in the middle of that barge. We figured they was pullin' them mortars up to take on our batteries above Port Hudson and then probably on to Vicksburg. Thar warn't no way in hell we was seddlin' fer that," he added determinedly, launching a gob of spit two or three feet into the bonfire.

"Jaques' pappy and me, and a dozen other fellas, made our way down inside the hole of that dark ship, tryin' to find the cargo bay. We hadn't gone ten feet when we found ourselves in a fracas with a slew ah Yankee sailors who'd been sleepin' down below deck.

"By the time we'd finished 'em off, here come another bunch behind us, armed with swords and pistols, includin' the helmsman and the pilot. They'd let that ship go, leavin' her to run her own course in the channel.

"After we kilt them fellas, we headed for the engine room, figurin' the last of 'em would be holed up thar. Only thing we found, though, were two Yankees, a colored and a pot full of Chinese stokers pourin' coal into them boilers.

"Well, the Chinese musta figured that Satan were on 'em, fer sure, 'cuz they lit out, havin' it in their minds to make it up to the main deck and then jump overboard. Our boys up topside were spiken' the cannons and caught 'em when they come up to where they was workin'. It were a slaughter pen, with them dead Chinese layin' everwhere. Some of the boys had 'em by the pig-tails, hangin' onto 'em while they slit their throats."

Again, Duvallon grinned and nodded in unison with his approving brothers in arms.

"Nicholas and some of the fellas headed for the cargo, dumpin' everything they could git thar hands on overboard.

The rest of our boys were in the water or in boats, pickin' up whatever was throwed over. We even got a couple of the guns over the side, even though there warn't no way we'd be able to pull 'em out 'till later...if we could ever find 'em again. "Weren't nobody payin' any attention to ware that boat wer' headin' until she nosed up on a sandbar. The worse part come about when that mortar barge shoved in the hull, when it caught up with the Preston, smashin' ever thang tah hell.

"It split them boilers wide open, blowin' steam and fire all over that room; burnin' and cookin' everybody in the belly of that boat. One boiler had blowd a hole in the side of that ship, lettin' in half the Mississippi. You could hear metal sizzlin' and poppin' in the water that was pourin' in. Men were hollerin' and screamin', tryin' to get out, as best they could. Never seen anythin' like it! Cookin' us like an old hen in ah pot ah hot water.

"Lot of them men died hard that night. Seems like everyone forgot about fightin' and started helpin' each other try to make it outa that hellhole. Warn't nobody cared about the war no more.

"That ship were on fire, burnin all the way to her masts. The barge had caught fire, which were the worst thing that could've happened. The whole ship near come apart!

"One poor soul were hangin' like a side of beef hung up to bleed on a chunk of steel stickin' clean through him. The holes in the side of the ship were like a set of teeth...jagged and sharp enough to cut a man near in two.

"I reckon thar weren't no one what didn't feel sorry for that fella hung up thar. He jes' watched the rest of us swim out past him, tryin' to git away. Don't even know what side he were on...all burned up so bad and all. But he never said nothin', just looked at us like he warn't sure we were any better off than he were."

Duvallon took another slug of his whiskey and then paused, as if to remind himself of the horror of that moment. But it was a short pause, as if the memory was close at hand.

"Jaques' pappy got out a few yards ahead of me 'fore that whole mess finally went up. When the fire got around to settin' off all the powder on the barge, that whole river were as bright as a clear mornin sunrise.

"It were the worst thing you ever seen, grape shot and shrapnel from that thar dyin' ship rakin' the water like them dead sailors was up to takin' revenge on the lot of us. Plenty of men layin' wounded in the water were kilt, right off, when the Preston blew.

"Nicholas had grabbed a holt of me. I'd taken a lick or two comin' outa' the side of that sinkin' demon ship. Both my arms were broke and I were bleedin' like a stuck hog. Jaques' pappy hung onto me and swam me across the river. He warn't doin' no better than the rest of us, with his arm and hands burnt pretty bad."

The storyteller paused, smiled at Jaques and then continued as Jaques smiled back.

"He stayed out in that miser'ble water all night long tryin to hep anyone he could find tah make it to shore. When he figured he saved everyone he could, he started bringin' in all the food and supplies he were able to gather up in the water and on the sandbars out in the river.

"By mornin' all's you could see of the ship was her stacks sittin' cattywampus in the water, right war her belly had been blown open.

"At first light, our patrols was pickin' up Yankees off the banks of the river, along with our own boys. Some folk from Lallemand had come over with coloreds to see if they could help take some of them men and supplies back to camp in litters they'd gotten from the hospital.

"Even some of the Chinamen got pulled out, them that warn't slit from ear to ear, but weren't nobody gonna do nothin' fer them 'cept throwin' 'em back or leave 'em lyin' where they'd landed. Weren't the first time we'd caught 'em workin' for the Yankees.

"We buried a lot of good men that day," Duvallon concluded, "but a lot more good folks made it through that hard winter on the food and medicine that were taken off that ship by Jaques' Pappy and the rest of our boys!"

The guests seemed pleased with the storyteller's efforts, with many of them showing their approval as if praising the preacher's sermon with even a few Amens! Some were wet-eyed from remembering the loss of family or comrades at the battle of Prophet's Point.

The families from Bayou de Chenaie would have their own stories to tell of heroic deeds and loved ones lost in the great war, but at some other time.

Jaques sat motionless as the crowd moved away. He held Benonia, stroking her hair as he quietly reflected about his father to himself. He never had really come to know the man, but felt strangely saddened by his absence on this special night. How strange it had been to see his father in the dream, assuring Jaques that he would survive that terrible night at Verret Island. So comforting had the vision been to Jaques, so peaceful and loving, that he had many times hoped that the dream would come again, but it hadn't. He would never share what had happened with anyone, not even Benonia. It would be his secret, a secret as precious as the short memory he had of his father and his gentle and loving manner that he'd known so briefly.

The cow horns sounded in the distance, announcing the processional. Benonia and Jaques made their way through the happy crowd to the waiting carriage that would take them four times around Benonia's house where they would spend their wedding night.

The crowd walked along the sides of the carriage, tapping on their empty whiskey bottles, ringing small bells and banging on pots and pans, all the while singing and making as much racket as possible. The idea was to confuse the lurking evil spirits and drive them away from the house where the newlyweds would spend their first night together.

Jaques stepped from the carriage, pulling Benonia up into his arms as he carried her inside the house. The crowd remained at the front steps, cheering and clapping for the couple until they returned to the front porch to wave and smile one last time and then turned and disappeared inside.

CHAPTER 3

Jaques and Plato, an old Negro field hand, sat comfortably reclining on the front steps, finishing off their dinner of pot liquor and bread, peas, turnips and a thick brown gravy that Benonia had prepared a few hours earlier. Both men were taking a welcomed break from the stifling afternoon heat.

Plato smiled with a single tooth oddly interrupting his gummy grin as Jaques playfully wrestled with his eldest son, James. James had been helping his father and Plato plant black seed Cotton since the first light of morning.

Benonia sat in a handmade rocker behind the two men, fanning herself with a paper fan. An infant was pressed against her breast.

Benonia moved the rocker with just enough intuitive motion to bring the suckling to a drowsy state, and then a deep sleep. She slid her little finger between the tiny rosebud lips of the small baby and her breast, releasing the strong suction the sleeping child had created. Then she stood, smiling at the baby and then down at Jaques who was watching her. Billy, Jaques' youngest son, stood next to one of the unpainted columns of the front porch, holding onto the turned post with one hand. He swung back and forth, whispering a soft repetitive song, as he glanced at his tiny sister. He was careful not to arouse her from her nap.

The afternoon sun had slowed the world around the house to a deathly calm except for an occasional mud dauber squirting his load of soft mud into the gray bulk that he was gluing to the ceiling of the porch.

The dogs and cats wandered lethargically under the house, lying quietly next to each other in a truce on the cool wet earth for relief from the afternoon sun. A crow in the distance disturbed the solitude of the moment as he reconnoitered the plowed fields for food. Two mules, tied to a hitching post a few yards from the house, sweltered their bellies, blowing themselves up as if they were pregnant. When they'd inhaled as much air as possible, they let it out, sounding like a covey of quail taking flight.

Jaques sipped on a gourd ladle of cool, sweet, well water, then he passed it to Plato. The old Negro took a sip and in turn handed it to James who was sitting between the two men.

James quickly drank from the gourd, copied the two men by gulping down the water, then dumped a small quantity over his head to cool his scalp as he'd seen his father do. It was like a ritual, ceremoniously disposing of the last residue in the gourd, as if it would somehow bring him closer to manhood. The consumption of the last of the water was usually the signal to return to the fields and the furrowing. The narrow, straight trenches were testimony to a skill of mule handling acquired after years of experience. Young James was still dealing with the difficulty of walking on the soft ridges of earth pulled from the furrowed trenches. His learning to plow was yet to come.

James followed his father and Plato to the mules. Jaques hoisted the nine-year-old barefoot boy onto the back of one of the animals to save his strength, knowing how difficult the walk back through the field would be for him. The plow harness jingled and popped as it straightened behind the slow plodding mules. Before they had reached the partially unplowed pasture, Billy had appeared, tugging on Jaques' britches, telling his father that James was wanted by his mother at the house for his afternoon tutoring.

Jaques looked disgustedly over his shoulder for proof of the messenger's authority. There stood Benonia at the front door, her arms crossed, leaving no doubt that young Bill had correctly delivered her message.

Jaques, however reluctant, conceded, pulling James from the mule and turning him towards the house.

"Get on to the house, boy, 'fore your momma has a fit. You'll be a growd man 'afore she quits nursemaidin' you with that book learnin' foolishness!" Jaques declared, giving James a slight push toward the house and his waiting mother. "Go on, git," he ordered, giving James a love pop on his rear end.

Plato grinned, offering his own advice. "Sure don't do a youngin' no good that I can see to be uh readin' and writin'. Good Lord wouldn't uh given us preachers, to read the word to us, if'en we was s'posed to be doin' it fer our sef! Why, I reckon he'd a made us born bein' able to understand words, right off, if dat's what the almighty was ah wantin'." Plato laughed, wiping his neck with a giant hanky. Without waiting for Jaques' response he slapped the mule with the reins, moving his animal ahead and into the field.

"She's a good woman," Jaques mumbled to himself. "She's jest a might confused about what's important in this world. But I guess most women are," he added before hollering at his mule, "git up, mule, git!"

Benonia was a staunch moralist, insisting on her children having a virtuous character that would not only be developed by an intense understanding of the more worldly fundamentals of life, but by being well educated in the Christian faith. For a man to study the carnal world without benefit of a good Christian foundation was as dangerous as a child mounting a strange horse. 'To know life's risks,' Benonia thought, 'to understand the fallibility of man, the nature of the beast, prepared one for the rage of the devil that might spring from the seemingly tranquil creatures that each of us must deal with in life, be it ourselves or someone else.' Though a strict disciplinarian and extremely pragmatic, Benonia was as warm and loving a woman as God ever had created. She had an inherent talent for seeing pain and frustration in other humans as clearly as Jaques could forecast the fierce weather that so often affected the family's life in the swamp. But even more marvelous than her rare, almost omnipotent power in identifying those heartaches and pains was her ability to deal so lovingly and generously with the suffering that she often sensed.

Benonia outwardly appeared unyielding and austere. The physical effects of a hard life had begun to take their toll on her. But the very tone of her voice and her touch brought an instant surrender to any notion that she was unloving or insensitive to others. If ever God had intended to furnish man with earthly archangels, then there was no doubt, at least to those who knew Benonia, that he had placed at least one of them in the Great Atchafalaya.

There was never any question about Jaques' dominance as the supreme authority within the family. Benonia wouldn't have had it otherwise. But any observer on a Sunday morning had only to watch the faces of her family, as they obediently and faithfully marched into the quaint country church, to know who captained the spiritual life of the small entourage. Jaques and the children were scrubbed and pressed in their

'Sunday go to meetin' finest, appearing straight-backed and attentive during the service. The children, unlike most cradle-born adolescent Christians, listened to the sermon without even the slightest twitch. Jaques, out of respect for Benonia, at least gave the impression of having an interest in the message, although, more often than not, his eyes were likely to wander away from the pulpit.

Benonia's keen insight kept a delicate balance within the family, guarding Jaques' sensitive ego with praise and support. She was careful never to complain or openly criticize, but instead softly admonished her husband when she deemed it appropriate.

She, more than Jaques, demanded absolute devotion to one's chores and insisted upon a joyful attitude in the performance of those tasks.

"Work, the Bible says, is a privilege that the good Lord has granted to his earthly children, a gift that will be denied to heavenly man," Benonia would tell her children. "Work hard while the Lord sees fit to let you enjoy life's wonderful bounty."

Benonia was proud of her Creole heritage and that of her children, but she knew that life would offer little opportunity for them as long as they lived in the swamp. She yearned for them to have an easier path through life, something better than she and Jaques had experienced, although she never would have changed her own situation.

Benonia had given birth to six children, three of whom had perished at birth or early infancy. The mortality rate was pitifully one-sided, a fact of life that backwoods families tearfully expected. The family cemetery was dotted with small infant headstones, each child laid to rest with profound grief, but with loving acceptance that it was God's will to have the children taken home to heaven. If nothing else, it evoked a greater expectation by the parents for the surviving children to live and prosper. But that too added to the heartbreak when an older child would pass away.

Benonia's accumulation of knowledge was not as limited in scope as one might have imagined. She had been educated in Baton Rouge as a child, at the Gethsemane Baptist School for Young Women. Her mother had arranged with Benonia's aunt to allow her to live in the city to attend the small church school for at least two years. It was her mother's most precious gift to her daughter.

But her educational pursuits had abruptly come to an end when her mother, and then her brothers, had passed away in a typhoid epidemic, leaving André alone in the swamp. Benonia returned home to help her father work the farm, having had only a taste of the education she so dearly cherished.

She used the Bible as an all-encompassing text for educating her children in Christianity, English, history, study skills and whatever else happened to be thrown into the day's lesson extemporaneously.

Benonia had translated much of the Bible into French, for the benefit of her children, fully committed to the preservation of their Creole heritage.

In the afternoons, as she worked in the cooking house preparing the evening meal, she tutored James in math, history and English. James would sit at the table with a basket of snap beans, breaking the tiny flat pods into smaller servings, as he recited his lesson to his mother.

The scope of her history lecture was limited from her own schooling, to whatever she had remembered. But biblical history was another matter. As a result of her direction, both boys committed much of the Bible to memory, reading the word routinely at night as they lay near a coal oil lamp in the front room of the house, or on the portico.

James was a bright, eager child, attentive and interested in learning all that his mother could teach him. She was inspirational to James, promising him that his academic pursuits would provide well-deserved opportunities later in life.

There was nothing that delighted him more than to have his mother interrupt him from his studies to cuddle him in her arms, speaking softly to him in French as she praised him for his studious efforts.

As a result of Benonia's devotion, James became an extremely articulate child. He was bilingual in French and English and had a very good understanding of Latin. He also had developed a thirst to experience the outside world.

But as much of his interest in other people and places came from his father as from his reading. Jaques, as was traditional with Creole men, was an avid storyteller.

Ironically, though his stories tantalized young James with great adventures, Jaques had never intended to inspire the boy to venture away from the farm. Quite the contrary, James was expected to devote his life to the farm, as his family had done since the farm had been founded. Jaques never would have tolerated anything less.

But still, James enjoyed a wonderful relationship with his father. Jaques was a physically affectionate man, holding and caressing his children whenever possible. He was never embarrassed by an outward display of emotion. He added the playfulness and less serious elements of life that Benonia found counterproductive to developing the necessary environment for a good education.

Very rarely would James retire for the evening without embracing his father and mother with a soft cheeky kiss. Even as he entered manhood at twelve and thirteen he always embraced his parents whenever possible. It was a very natural and accepted custom in the French Creole society at any age, and certainly in public.

Jaques revered his son, admiring the multiplicity of his talents. He was proud of his scholarly gains and equally pleased that James was not only studious but held a fervent interest in farming and things of a less eloquent nature.

He was also pleased that James had an insatiable thirst to learn the family trade of a farmer and river man. His son loved the soil, the river, and the very essence of life that sprang forth from the land under his father's hands.

James always admired his father's gift for dealing with the hard business of farming, fighting with the swamp year after year to raise a crop. Jaques was well respected by the other farmers for his ability to manage his land, always able to produce an acceptable harvest even when others were less fortunate.

James knew his parents were very much in love. Benonia would often walk to the fields in the hot afternoon sun to bring dinner and water to Jaques and James. She would wait patiently in the shade of a nearby pecan tree for the men to finish plowing the section before serving the midday meal to them. When Jaques had finished his meal he would sit under the shady canopy of the tree, talking and holding hands with her. James would sit nearby, under his own tree, catching an occasional glimpse of his mother and father staring into each other's eyes as one or the other spoke so softly that no one else could hear them. A short time later Jaques would stand, helping Benonia to her feet before embracing her and returning to his plowing.

Occasionally James or one of the other children would catch Jaques in a mischievous mood, his hand passing by their mother's derriere, or kissing her wantonly on the neck. Benonia would respond with a quick defensive parry and a smile as she checked to see if anyone had seen anything. The children would giggle, grins hidden behind their hands.

Benonia's strength had begun to languish by the time James was fifteen. Childbirth had taken its toll on her frail body, and so had the hours of tedious labor in the rice and cotton fields during the harvest season. She was always the first to rise in the morning, caring for the children and preparing breakfast, hours before the first light of morning. She would follow the men into the field to work beside the hired help, taking the children with her. She worked as hard as any field hand, caring for the stock and managing the home. She tended the garden near the house, preparing preserves for the winter cupboard and sacking much of the extra produce for Jaques to take to market.

In the evenings the family would sit quietly after supper on the front porch. They'd listen as James or Bill would recite verses from memory, with only the dogs disturbing the recital as they barked at a coon hunkering in a nearby tree for safety.

Everyone sat so still on those nights, exhausted from the toiling of the day. It was little wonder that they had not noticed that Benonia's hands had dropped from her lap to the floor, her body limp in the old rocker as James mechanically quoted John 14:6 in his eloquent Creole dialect on that particular night.

Eventually, Benonia recovered from the spell, making her way to bed, with everyone assured by her that it was only fatigue. But James felt a cold surge of fear paralyze his young body. The immortality of his mother and father, so securely preserved in his childish mind, suddenly faded. The reality that something was going to happen to her, to him, to all of them, swept through his mind for the first time with a sudden horrible certainty.

Benonia began to sit for hours at a time during the day in her rocker, slumped over with her hands dangling lifelessly, as if death finally had pulled the last charge of energy from her exhausted soul. Then she would awake, leaning forward in the chair with a look of shock and disbelief that she had fallen asleep. She would weep as she realized that her family needed tending and her chores were undone.

Jaques agonized over Benonia's worsening condition. No man had loved his wife more dearly and devotedly than Jaques. She was his inspiration in life, his purpose for all that he did. He had come to depend on her drive and initiative to hold the family together. But there was more. She had, on more than one occasion, restored his fallen ego and taught him the essence of humility. How precious she had become to him, even more than he realized.

The children would sit beside her, holding her hands for hours in the evening as she drifted in and out of consciousness. Sometimes, when she was awake, leaning back in her rocker, one of the children would read to her from the Bible, adding a verse in Creole that sparked a weak smile from her lips. She tried to reach out to touch the child's face, but her arms would not cooperate.

It became obvious that Benonia's condition was becoming worse. She was so weak that she lay in bed, unable to feed or care for herself. Jaques had sent James to find the circuit doctor. It took him an entire day to catch up with Doctor Junot after finding out where he'd gone on his rounds. It was dark before the Doctor finished treating his last patient and started towards home with James soundly asleep under the doctor's wool coat in the back of the surrey.

Doctor Junot sat beside Benonia, fingering her thin wrist as he searched for a pulse. One hand massaged her tiny fingers trying to bring her out of unconsciousness as the other moved gently against her forehead. He shook his head slowly from side to side, never uttering a word as Jaques and the children stood in the doorway, staring blankly, hoping for some indication that Benonia would be all right. But his body language was clear to those old enough to understand what it meant.

"You children, go on and let me talk to your pappy about you momma!" Junot ordered.

James and the other children moved to the front room, near the hallway, sitting on the floor as close to the bedroom as they could. James lay listening to the men talking as Bill played with Katy, trying to keep her quiet so that James could hear what was being said. For a while he could only make out part of the conversation until Jaques began arguing with the doctor.

"She's worn out," he could hear Junot saying in a raised voice to his father. "It's not what's wrong with her, but its made it worse. She's got no resistance, no immunity to whatever it is that's making her sick. She's exhausted."

James heard his father answer. "Benonia's strong, doctor. She's a strong woman, and she hadn't never been sick a day since I've known her! She'll be gittin' better...she's jest having a bad spell, that's all."

"Your wife's seriously ill," Junot countered, as the door to the bedroom shut.

Suddenly, James heard something he'd never heard before in his life. His father was crying. It lasted for only a brief moment before the room went silent.

Shortly after that the door opened and Doctor Junot appeared in the hall, holding his medical bag in his hand. He stared back into the room, talking to Jaques from the hall. "I'll let you know when I'm sure," he said.

Jaques did not answer. Junot walked past James on his way out the front door. He stopped before he walked outside, looking down at the children and then straight at James.

"You take care of your poppa, boy. He needs you right now. They all do," he said to James as he turned and left the house.

James nursed his mother, feeding her and washing her face and hands, and brushing her long hair. He sat beside her still form for hours, hoping to spend a few waking moments with her before she became comatose again.

One afternoon shortly after Doctor Junot had made his call, James slipped in to see his mother. James watched through the window as Doctor Junot gave Billy a sympathetic pat on the head and then stepped up into his surrey. Billy gave the doctor a big grin, at the same time clawing at a patch of chigger bites on his exposed leg as Junot popped his whip against his sorrel driver and turned towards town.

James glanced towards his mother and was surprised to find her looking at him.

"Momma, you awake?"

"Oh, I've been awake for awhile, darlin'. I've just been cat-napping," Benonia answered.

"Can I get you something? Maybe you'd like some water?" James asked.

She smiled, holding out her hand, motioning for James to sit next to her as she spoke.

"Momma wants to tell you something...something I know that you'll understand because you're growing up and becoming a man."

"Yes, mamma," James replied, taking her hand.

"I know you're worried about me," she said.

"Yes 'um," James acknowledged with a single nod of his head.

"I know you've heard Doctor Junot say that momma isn't doing very well," Benonia said.

"Yes, momma," James began, "but he said if you'd go to New Orleans, to the hospital, you might get better!"

"Momma's not gonna leave," she said, then smiled. "This is my home and I've got the Good Lord lookin' after me. Those doctors can do no more for me than the Lord wills. Momma's not gonna leave our home! But I want you to make me a promise."

"I will, Momma!"

"Your poppa is a wonderful man. He loves you and Billy and Katy very much. But he isn't going to understand why momma has gone home to the Lord."

"No, momma!" James began to cry. "Don't go no where, please, momma!"

"Listen to me," she said. "Now, he's not going to understand why it had to be this way."

Tears slipped down James' cheek, as his boyish chin began to quiver. He wiped the flow with the palm of his hand, trying not to let his mother see his face.

"You know what momma's taught you from God's word," said Benonia. "And you know that I'm gonna be safely in the precious hands of Jesus. Now, you're gonna have to be strong, James...and take care of Billy and Katy. And you're gonna have to promise momma that you'll watch over your poppa. He's a good man, a fine man...but he's still just a child, in God's eyes, and doesn't understand these things."

His voice cracked. "Yes, ma'am."

"Do you remember, James, what the Lord promises us in the good book?" she asked, her eyes closed as if she were reading through the verse in her mind.

James nodded, knowing what the answer was.

"Then you know that we'll be together again," she said softly, closing her eyes as she began to whisper a verse from memory. "And ye now therefore have sorrow: but I will see you again and your heart shall rejoice, and your joy no man taketh from you."

James slipped quietly out of the room as his mother drifted back into a tranquil rest. He paused for a moment outside of her room to try and understand why she had said what she did about his father, a man of strength and unquestionable presence, a demigod of towering proportions.

A week and a half-later James was awakened during the dark of the night by the sound of his father weeping and mumbling. He rolled his head towards the window, listening to Billy breathing as he slept next to him. A cricket serenaded his thoughts as his mind wandered to a happier time. He thought of his mother, young and beautiful, smiling as she held him, rocking him to sleep with her sweet song. He saw her locked passionately in the arms of his father, a loving look on her face, happier than he ever had remembered seeing her. It made him feel good to see the two of them together.

He felt his heart racing as his mind leaped from one thought to another, unable to outrun the reality of what he knew had happened. His mother had passed away, journeying across what she so often had lovingly referred to as *the bridge of life*, to her final peace and reward, to stand hand-in-hand with her waiting Savior.

With Benonia's death, James felt the dark shadow of her passing move over the family like a cold winter storm. The spirit of love and happiness that had so pervaded the home had been lowered beneath the damp surface of the swamp with Benonia's body, and now the heart of the family had been mortally wounded.

For two days, Jaques sat under the lich gate of the cemetery, staring at the raw mound under which Benonia lay. The children could see him silhouetted against the moonlit night. Even the dogs had barked at him for a time, confused by his presence there. When he finally returned to the house he was suffering the effects of exposure to the cold night air.

Jaques withdrew from the children, avoiding any contact with them for days at a time. When he did speak to them, it was as if he was talking to other adults, discussing his bereavement and devastation, his speech garbled and incoherent.

The children seemed, at least superficially, to have recovered from their tragedy, as children often do, going about life's business without the outward scars that so often affect adults when they are confronted with death. Jaques, however, became more withdrawn, and, in the following months the children were all but abandoned by their father. The young girl was left to be raised by her two older brothers. Occasionally Jaques would stop what he was doing to stare at one of them, as if to apologize for the cruelty that had befallen them with their mother's death and his own inability to cope with her loss. The once jovial father, the man who had provided the warm and loving caresses, the man of wit and happiness, never again extended his arms to any of his children.

James became painfully aware of the meaning of his mother's prophetic statement about his father. The sweetness of life had flowed forth for all of them at her orchestration. Jaques was as misplaced in the family setting as Benonia's personal effects that still filled the armoire and the top of the couple's dresser.

He agonized over his father's alienation from himself and the other children. He yearned for nothing more than a simple touch or kind word from his father, but neither was ever offered. Jaques, instead, withdrew even further into his despair, wallowing in his own self-pity while James sacrificed his childhood trying to fill the void left by his mother and father.

James became obsessed with the desire to educate himself and realize the dreams that so often had been a part of the conversations he and his mother had had while she was alive.

Jaques was struggling with a terrible conflict within himself. One minute he loved James as his heir apparent, then scorned the boy's ambitious nature, jealous of his studious infatuations, and finally enraged by what he perceived, wrongly, as an arrogant, conceited attitude.

Jaques would become effusively verbal with James over the slightest insignificant incident addressing him with a reproachful lecture, and the serving up of a number of hard punishing slaps across the boy's face. Then Jaques would catch himself, shamed by his actions over the unwarranted assault. He realized that James had done nothing to justify the abusive treatment. When it was over, he'd look into James' somber eyes, ashamed of himself for what he'd done.

After each confrontation Jaques would mutter a few apologetic remarks under his breath, turn and disappear into the swamps for hours or even days.

James was heartbroken whenever an incident occurred. He was confused about what had precipitated the attack, trying desperately to understand what he had done wrong.

Later, James would catch a glimpse of his father's silhouette on the horizon, slowly making his way along the muddy road towards the house. James was excited whenever he saw him returning, eager to be reunited and totally forgiving, as children always are with their parents.

When James was sixteen he contracted consumption, the damp weather aggravating the condition to the point where he became immobilized, burning with fever for days at a time. He lost a great deal of weight, becoming so weak that he was unable to care for himself.

Jaques had become incensed one afternoon in late August at the sight of James lying in bed, being bathed and fed by Katy and Billy. He had gone to the house after returning from the field to find his cows, their udders distended from the weight of a full load of milk, bellowing with discomfort in the front corral.

He flew into the room, knocking Katy to the floor as he reached for James in a wild rage, slapping and grabbing as the boy tried to sit up, unable to parry the blows.

Jaques ripped the sleeve off James' nightshirt, as he forced him out of bed and onto the hardwood floor. Without a word, he dragged the panting boy out through the front room, down the outside stairs of the porch and into the drizzle that had soaked the ground most of the day.

Halfway across the slick muddy road leading to the barn, Jaques lost his hold, dropping James into a cavernous puddle filled with black muck washed in from the nearby ditch. The boy's white gown and skin were covered in mud and particles of grass as streaks of rain and tears cut fine lines down to the pinkish skin underneath. Now as he slipped into the puddle, the underside of his body submerged into the black mud, almost covering him.

James was terror-stricken as Jaques stood over him, wide-eyed and shaking with exhaustion from the ordeal, cocking his arm to deliver a blow. As his eyes shut, James raised his head and with a pathetic cry, called out for his dead mother.

Jaques was so stunned that he stopped, and his hand slid slowly down to his side. The fingers of his right hand moved softly against the mixture of mud and tears under James' eyes. Slowly he wiped away the residue of first one, and then the other eye, before dropping to his knees in the pool of mud beside his son.

He reached out for James, holding him in his arms shaking both of them with his sobbing. Jaques wanted somehow to end the nightmare. The cruelty had been more than even he could stand. It was a tragedy that he realized, at that very moment, was not exclusively his. He could see that in James' eyes and hear it in his voice the moment he'd heard him crying out for his mother.

Jaques sprang to his feet, clasping his hands to the temples of his head as he glared down at his son, sitting helplessly in the road. Jaques backed away, begging for forgiveness. For another moment he stood staring down at James with a sad look of hopelessness.

"I am so sorry...for what I've done!" Jaques cried, in broken Creole, backing away even further. He turned, stumbling and tripping several times before vanishing into the heavy downpour.

Katy and Bill had been hiding out under the house, but when they were sure that Jaques was gone they ran to James, helping him across the road to the barn. They were afraid to take him to the house, certain that Jaques would return to finish the beating. Neither of them understood that the beatings had ended forever.

James, with his brother and sister's help, finally inched his way into the barn. The heavy doors closed behind the children and the dank smell from the wet dirt floor overwhelmed them as they fumbled their way through the dark. The floor was covered with manure and puddles of water from the leaking roof, and a menagerie of small varmints were there seeking shelter from the storm outside.

When Bill lit a coal oil lamp that he'd found and then hoisted it up to a nail sticking out from the wall, the creatures scattered to every corner of the barn. Some stopped to look back, the flame of the lamp reflecting in their beady red eyes. The rain pounded the old frame structure as the wind moved loose boards, banging them out of tempo with the other sounds of the storm.

Bill was small for thirteen and he struggled with James, moving him towards the back of the building to the feed storage area. A large king snake slithered up and over the hand-hewn rafters above them, landing on the floor with a heavy thud. The snake twisted around, finally righting itself, and then quickly exited through a nearby hole in the wall.

Several rolls of hay were pushed up against the back wall. A few of the rolls were broken open and loosely piled in a heap in the middle of the floor. Bill and Katy managed to work James into the center of a thick pad of grass, covering him with a few gunnysacks. They were frightened, and both of them cried as they tried to comfort their brother. He was burning with fever, shaking out of control. His body jerked sporadically as his teeth chattered together. His eyes were wet from the tears and sweat that beaded in tiny droplets on his forehead and cheeks. His clothes stuck to his emaciated body like wet tissue paper.

For nearly an hour James stared at the door, blinking only when sweat dripped from his face into his eyes. He repeatedly asked for his father, as if unaware of Bill and Katy's presence. And then, overcome by exhaustion, he suddenly glanced up at Bill, exhaling a burst of air and then went limp in his brother's lap.

Bill covered the crumpled form, cuddled in his arms, with another grain sack, whimpering as he rocked his unconscious brother back and forth. Katy had fallen asleep, half an hour earlier, mesmerized by the rhythmic pounding of the rain.

The night turned cool and still. Fog had moved up from the bayou, blanketing the farm like a dense cloud of smoke. The rain moved farther inland but the trees above the barn still dripped water onto the roof with a constant tapping sound.

In the early hours of the morning Bill was awakened by the sounds of an approaching carriage moving into the front yard. The driver could be heard outside of the barn giving directions to his horse, following with a short crack of his whip above the animal's head. Bill could hear the familiar sounds of a wagon tie-up hitting the ground as the stranger walked away towards the house.

A few moments later Bill could hear whoever had been in the wagon coming towards the barn. He tightened his arms around James, praying that it wasn't their father. The door swung open. A soft haze reflected the light from outside, blinding Bill as he tried to identify the stranger standing in the doorway. Whoever it was, it wasn't their father.

The man knelt next to Bill, reaching through the long beams of refracted light projecting from behind him. The man's hand moved towards James, resting on his forehead.

"How's he doing, Billy?" the voice asked.

Katy was awake. She quickly answered the man's question before Bill could reply. "I think he's dead...he ain't moved all night."

She watched as the man shifted himself around, finally blocking the glare from the door, giving them their first chance to see who he was. It was Doctor Junot.

'No, he's not dead, sweetheart. He's jest a mighty sick youngin'.'

Katy stared up at the awesome figure looming above them. Doctor Junot had a scraggly dark beard that covered most of his jaw. His eyes peered from the deep recesses of his tired face. He was wearing an old Mennonite hat, stained with streaks of perspiration and dust. He was dressed in his usual baggy black wool pants and coat with a frayed, high collared white shirt and a dingy yellow vest. He was a large man, and his loose-fitting clothes made him seem enormous to the children.

Junot made a sweeping motion with his hand for Katy and Bill to move out of his way. He lifted James' feeble arm to check his pulse. Then he calmly instructed Bill to fetch his case from the wagon.

Before Bill could reach the wagon, Junot hoisted James into the air, pulling him into his arms like a tiny baby. He wrapped him in a blanket that he'd carried to the barn from his carriage. With the tall lanky youngster secure in his arms, Doctor Junot stepped confidently into the white cloud that separated the house from the barn.

Bill and Katy followed apprehensively behind the doctor, wondering if their father was waiting inside the house. The doctor pushed open the door with his muddy boot, entering the home as if he lived there. Katy and Bill stayed near the front door, still concerned about the whereabouts of Jaques.

"Stoke up a fire, boy! Stop your doddlin' and get busy. We got business to tend to!" Junot commanded, tipping his head at Bill from the hallway and then turning his attention to James, lying in the bed in front of him. He pulled the wet gown off the boy, and began wiping his naked, skeletal form with a small dry towel as he fought to prevent hypothermia from setting in. He worked with his patient for forty-five minutes, stopping frequently to listen to his fluid-filled lungs with his stethoscope. When he thought James was dry enough, he wrapped a plaster around his chest and covered him with several quilts, trying to alleviate his chills.

As the day passed into late evening Doctor Junot slipped into Benonia's old rocker that he'd dragged in from the front porch. He sank deep into the warped bentwood chair, ignoring the moaning of the mis-aligned wood runners supporting him as he sat staring into the fire in the stone fireplace.

Katy and Bill had long since gone to sleep, full of chicken broth that the doctor had brewed from a freshly killed yard hen. Junot had covered each child with blankets and quilts, tucking them into their respective beds. After giving each of the youngsters a loving pat on the head, he returned to his patient in the other room.

Early the next morning Doctor Junot was up, moving through the house with an armload of pots and bottles from the cookhouse.

The noise of James' crying and gasping for air had awakened Bill from his sleep. The clatter from the clanging pots and pans only added to Bill's confusion about what was going on.

"I've gotta do this, boy, or else you're gonna die! Your lungs are plumb full of infection," Bill could hear Junot saying in the other room. "I want you to sit up and lean back against these pillows and make sure you keep still."

Bill worked his way near enough to the door that he could see Doctor Junot standing over James. The doctor had his back to the door, with his coat off and his sleeves rolled up above his elbows. An apron, splattered with blood, was tied around the doctor's waist.

As Junot lifted his right elbow, Bill could see the silver reflection of a foot-long needle being withdrawn from James' chest. The tube attached to the needle was carrying blood to a jar on the floor. Several other pots and jars held water to sterilize Junot's instruments and wet compresses.

James was sitting with his mouth open, wheezing as Junot inserted the needle into his bare chest again. This time a steady stream of blood red fluid began to fill the jar.

"You'll feel much better, once we get this poison outa' your lungs, son!" Junot assured James.

James was panting, trying to muster a smile at the same time. He turned his head towards Bill, taking a deep breath, as if to show him his newfound capacity for inhaling a chestfull of air.

Bill wasn't convinced that all was well. He returned the smile just as Doctor Junot looked over his shoulder at him. "I reckon this brother of yours is probably as tough a feller as I believe I've ever met," the doctor said with a grin, wiping the sweat from his face with his forearm and turning his attention back to the needle.

"He'll be up and about 'fore you know it!" Doctor Junot announced.

"Is he gonna die?" Bill asked, moving closer to see what was in the jar beside the bed.

"Ain't nobody around here gonna die, boy. We jest gotta git this lung to start healin' up. Brother James is gonna have to breathe with one lung for awhile, so's we can give the other'n a chance to dry up a little. He'll be jest fine!"

Bill ignored the rest of the doctor's conversation, concentrating instead on the last of the gook still dripping into the Mason jar on the floor. Bill grimaced as he moved closer to study the liquid that almost had filled the glass container. He watched with interest as Junot extracted the needle and placed a compress quickly over the small opening, then pulled James down into the bed so that he could sleep.

"When's poppa common' back?" Bill asked. "He was awful mad at James. He whipped him jest 'cause he was sick. James didn't do nothin' wrong!" Bill added, still hypnotized by the jar.

"I'm real sorry about what's happened to you youngin's. What your daddy done weren't right! It weren't right at all, son! But your brother's problem isn't from the lickin' your pappy give him. Your brother's got tuberculosis of the lungs."

Bill looked up from the jar. "But he was hittin' on him, actin' like he wanted to kill him. I never seen poppa so mad!"

"Your daddy had no call to do what he did. It jest weren't right; it weren't right at all!"

Doctor Junot stopped what he was doing. "I think you children need to understand that what happened had nothin' to do with your brother, or you other children, either."

Bill looked at Doctor Junot with a questioning glare. "How come he done it then?"

"You seen an old dog git rabies, ain't ya, boy?" the doctor asked.

""Yes, sir," Billy responded.

"Then you know, that dog is gonna bite anyone that comes near him...even the folks he loves and cares for. He ain't doin' it 'cause he's mean. He's doin' it 'cause he's sick and can't help himself, don't ya see that, son? Your poppa loves you children."

"But brother ain't never said nothin' bad bout poppa, not even after he give him a lickin'. He thinks poppa is special. But he scares me and Katy when he does somethin' bad to brother. Brother just stands there and gets hit," said Bill, "and he don't say nothin'!"

"Maybe someday you'll understand why he's like he is, your momma dyin' and all. Maybe not," Junot said. "It don't matter now. Your poppa won't be comin' home...least not for awhile, anyways. He's gone into the swamp to try to think over what he's done.

"I pray to the good Lord that you and James will be learnin' to forgive the man for the way he's been. I know down deep he loves you and Katy and James more than you'll ever know. He's jest a terribly confused man right now, with a chest full of pain and hurt for your momma, God rest her soul."

Doctor Junot left shortly after he'd finished draining James chest. He'd already spent more time with his young patient than he could afford. There were others waiting to be ministered to by the overworked physician. It would be a few days before his rounds into the community would allow him to return to his office, or have a good night's sleep in his own bed.

James had lost a substantial amount of weight from his bout with tuberculosis. He'd taken on a ghoulish appearance, his eyes sunken and dark. His face was hollow and gaunt, with virtually all of the color gone from his skin. He moved through the old house like a ghost, stopping to lean against a wall or door jam, struggling to support himself as he tried to regain his strength as quickly as possible. Doctor Junot had unwittingly scared him by suggesting that he would be sent to a sanitarium in Monroe to help him recover from the effects of the consumption. James was determined that there was no way he would break his vows to his mother by leaving, especially not with his father gone.

The collapsed lung had left him constantly gasping for air. James was sensitive about the difficulty he was having in breathing. In order to hide his shortness of breath, he constantly whistled a muffled tune, trying to disguise the fact that he was suffocating. He paced incessantly through the house to help him catch his breath. He would end his walk at the front porch, sitting in the sun in his mother's old rocking chair, exhausted from his short tour.

Occasionally a concerned family from nearby would drop by the house to see how the children were doing. The wife usually would wash and cook while the husband would care for the animals and fences, trying to mend the ailing farm. James was appreciative of their caring and concerns, but it was humiliating to have himself and the other children cared for by anyone. James would keep to himself for the two or three days that the couple was at the house. After they had left, he would return to his old routine of pacing the halls and then settling back on the porch in the afternoon sun.

Near sunset James would pull himself up, leaning against one of the columns of the porch. He would wrap his arm around it, as high above his head as he could reach, trying to position himself to make his breathing easier as he looked off into the distance.

One afternoon, Katy had joined James on the porch, perching herself in a swing that hung from the ceiling behind her brother. She had dressed herself in her white Sunday dress, hoping that James would notice her. He ignored the dress and the little girl's bare feet hanging off the swing as she smiled up at him, eager for the slightest crumb of attention. But his concentration was unbroken.

He stared in a trance at the horizon as he had done every evening, studying the darkened tree line, his eyes searching as far down the road as the fading evening sunset would allow. It had been three and a half weeks since Jaques had left, without the slightest hint as to his whereabouts. And yet James kept a faithful vigil, as diligent as a sailor on watch, hoping beyond all else to see his father heading down the road or across the field towards home.

As he scanned the road, James felt a tugging on his shirt. The tugging persisted until James finally gave in, turning his attentions to the small figure standing next to him.

The sweet smile was gone from six-year-old Katy's small face. She looked at him with a sad expression, reaching out for his hand that was dangling to his side.

"You're waitin' for Poppa, aren't you?" she asked. "Poppa's gone! He ain't never comin' home. He's run away and left us," she went on, putting her arm around James' waist.

63

James straightened a little against the post, turning his eyes away from her and back out into the field, trying not to notice the unhappy look that had replaced her normally cheerful grin. He scanned the horizon, shading his eyes with one hand. Katy could hear him whispering under his labored breathing. "I know he wouldn't leave us. He'll be back...he's just trying to work things out. He'd never leave us, and not come home."

James' head bent down against the post, as if he had suddenly realized the truth of what she'd said. Katy could hear his breathing become harder as he tried to forestall the suffocation that eventually would force him back to bed. She moved around in front of him, staring up at his teary face. Her arms slipped around his waist one last time before she walked back to the swing, quietly rocking herself as she sensed the need for him to be alone.

Over the next few months James would catch himself looking in the direction of the narrow dirt road, always hoping to see his father walking home. The scars of cruelty had long since vanished from his memory, leaving only a vision of his father returning with a smile and open arms, the way he had been when Benonia was alive. With uncompromising devotion, he always believed that Jaques would someday come back, bringing with him a return to the happier life they all had known before his mother had passed away. That had been the time when the creatures of the swamp sang the loudest and the sun brightened each of their days with hope for the future. And now, hope was all that James had left.

CHAPTER 4

Small whirlwinds of dust puffed into the air with each step of the mule. Decayed fence posts lined the twisting path as open fields appeared and then gave way to endless miles of swamp and forest. Black shadows from bald cypress and loblolly pines cast their ragged patterns on the road, and spanish moss hung down almost to the top of the young riders' heads as they passed under the gray vines, draped like a rag picker's drying rack.

James and Bill, nineteen and sixteen, respectively, were laughing and pushing each other without concern for old Ezra, the mule they were riding. They moved in a haphazard, zigzag course down the road, leaving Ezra to his own lead.

Heat waves from the afternoon sun vibrated up from the dirt road in long rippling waves, distorting the distant images ahead of the riders. A small white cabin, an odd image that suddenly caught James' attention, stood in contrast to the bluish green forest and swamp.

James squinted, trying to bring the small house into focus. He moved the mule closer, still trying to remember seeing the white house the last time he'd come down the road. It had only been a few weeks, but he still couldn't recollect there being a white house at that particular spot. He did remember some kind of home there, but it was a run-down shack. His ears picked up the sound of several young girls in the distance, somewhere near the white mirage. Surprised, he suddenly let go of Bill's arm, sending him head and shoulder to the hard ground under Ezra's hoofs.

Bill let out a cursing yell as he bounced under the mule's legs. Ezra responded with a quick adjustment of his gait and then returned to the plodding cadence he'd set for himself.

James strained to see where the voices of the girls were coming from, then took a short check on his brother. Assured that Bill was breathing, James gave Ezra a sharp kick to the flanks, getting little more than a groan from the lethargic animal. Bill tripped ungracefully behind, holding his sides and elbow, screaming obscenities as he tried to keep up with Ezra.

James motioned with his hand for Bill to quiet down, turning his best ear towards the source of the laughter as he stealthily advanced. Then, right before his eyes, came as pleasing a sight as James had ever experienced. It was like Moses viewing an image of Canaan for the first time, although James bore no covenant with God to keep him from entering the Promised Land. Women, young beautiful girls, were laughing and frolicking in the midst of the forest like nymphs.

James could see five young girls. Three were sitting on the front steps of the house and two were swinging in a wooden swing hanging from the limb of a pecan tree in the front yard. He slid off the mule and moved slowly through the brush, crouching behind trees and ground cover, trying not to be discovered.

Bill had lost sight of James after he'd dismounted from Ezra. James could hear him moving through the brush like an old cow stampeding for water, screaming at the top of his lungs, trying to get James to answer. The girls on the porch reacted like a group of timid young deer, stopping what they were doing and craning their necks towards the bellowing and thrashing coming from the woods.

In one swift movement James locked onto Bill, throwing him to the ground with one hand over his mouth, still eyeballing the girls. He held onto a mix of Bill's clothing and skin, whispering to him, "Keep it down. I think they may have seen us. Spit, they're gettin' up. You peckerwood...they're goin' in...they're goin' in!"

"Turn loose!" Bill screamed. "You got a hand full of my meat," he raged, rubbing the scruff of his neck where James had held him down.

The girls quickly filed into the house, with two of them looking back, trying to get a fix on the rustling in the bushes. A man came to the front door, walked onto the porch and looked in the direction where James and Bill were hiding. He stood still, for a moment, and then turned and walked back into the house, slamming the door behind him.

James smiled at Bill, who was still rubbing his neck to soothe the pain from his brother's grip.

"You see that, Bill? There was five of em, all in one place. And ever' one of 'em was as pretty as I've ever seen. Wonder what's goin' on in there? They wasn't dressed like parlor girls. Damn...that was really somethin'!" James exclaimed.

"Weren't worth breaking my damn neck fer!" Bill answered.

"Ah, you aren't hurt. 'Sides, how many times you seen that many pretty girls out here in the woods?"

"Never," Bill responded, "and I didn't get a look at these neither," he added, crawling up to James and peeking through the same bush. "Was any of 'em nekked?"

James gave him a playful shove, laughing as he rolled over, and looked up at the sky.

"Sure were pretty! Make a feller believe he'd gone to heaven!" James said, tucking his hands behind his head.

They stayed in the woods for awhile, watching the house before deciding to go back to the mule. Bill was muttering his outrage at having missed seeing the girls as the two of them mounted Ezra and headed back to the road.

A few yards from the house, two of the girls suddenly appeared back on the porch. In his excitement James elbowed Bill hard in the stomach, bending him over and knocking the wind out of him. "Damn it, Bill, act natural, will ya?" James ordered out of the side of his mouth. He straightened himself in the saddle as Bill remained in a tight tuck, gasping for air and at the same time trying to stay on the back of the mule.

The young girls sat still, staring at the riders with flirtatious smiles as James reined Ezra to the front gate.

"Comment allez-vous?" James called out. "Je me nomme James Lavoisier."

He waited for a response, but the girls just continued to stare with a blank look on their faces.

"Je suis désolé, parlez vous Francais?"

Still nothing. James rubbed his head and then spoke in English. "How do, ladies! I'm James Lavoisier and this here is my brother Bill. Don't believe we've seen ya'll folks around these parts before...are ya'll new to the parish?"

The girls still refused to answer, giggling and looking at each other as if they didn't understand English either.

Before James could think of something else to say, the man he'd seen earlier appeared at the door. The large bearded man held an eye-to-eye standoff with James for a few seconds before speaking: "What'cha boys want? Somethin' wrong with that feller on the back of yer mule, there?"

"Naw, sir," James answered quickly, "he's jest feelin' a little poorly."

"Ain't got the fever, does he?" asked the man.

"Ah, naw, sir, he's jest a little taken by the heat," James answered.

"Get 'em some water, Emmy," the man ordered, "as long as they ain't got the fever. That feller on the back sure don't look right to me."

"Thanky, sir! That's might nice of ya," James said.

He relaxed, wiping his arm across his forehead, preparing for the cool drink of water. James had noticed the youngest of the girls standing behind the grouping of women as the old man herded them together.

"I'm Pastor R.W. Vickers. These here are my daughters Emma, Lula, Katherine and Nona. My youngest, here, is Lora. We're lately of Natchez, Mississippi," the preacher added.

"It's a pleasure to make your acquaintance, Reverend Vickers, ladies! I'm James Lavoisier and this here is my brother Bill. We come from jest down the road at Lalleville."

The women continued to sit mute, gazing at whoever was speaking. They held their hands in their laps, each with a placid expression on their faces, following the conversation. James was still not sure they understood what was being said.

The girls were attractive. Each of them was well groomed and dressed in clean, white ankle-length dresses. They wore shoes. That immediately caught both boys' attention. It was a dead giveaway that Pastor Vickers and his brood weren't from the swamps. Shoes were worn only on special occasions, such as wedding and funerals. It wasn't that folks didn't own them; they were just uncomfortable, expensive, and they had a tendency to rot, unless a body was picking blackberries, or such, and needed protection from rattlers or cottonmouths.

The girls had their hair lofted into a bun, each of them identical, with a ribbon of a different color tied to each hairdo. It was the only sign of their individuality. There was a difference of about five years in the youngest and the eldest of the five girls, the eldest being about twenty-three.

The old preacher seemed nervous about the two young men at first, but after a while, after he'd had time to give both boys a good inspection, he realized they were harmless. Unlike most young folk, James and Bill were neat in appearance and outwardly friendly.

James could sense the uneasiness of the old man and knew that, with five daughters under his roof, he probably had good cause to be suspicious of strange men. He tried to speak as eloquently as he could, disguising as much of his heavy French accent as possible.

Bill, on the other hand, sat quietly ogling each of the girls, almost drooling as he checked each one of them from head to toe. At one point he noticed the Reverend staring askance at him and quickly stopped his gaping.

James could feel the tension lingering over the gathering thicker than a slug of molasses. He would say something he felt to be rather clever and watch each of the girls look to their father for his approval before they would respond. They would fidget and grin to the point that James was becoming uneasy with the situation.

The youngest of Reverend Vickers' daughters had caught James' eye. She was shy, more so than the others, but she was prettier. She stood back behind the others, watching with interest what was going one, careful to keep her place in the pecking order.

Finally, Reverend Vickers, not wanting to appear unneighborly, invited the boys to stay for vespers and share their table with a home-cooked supper prepared by the girls. James quickly accepted the invitation, swayed by the offer of food and the chance to become better acquainted with Lora.

The boys were invited to wash up before taking their place at the table. After a brief moment of musical chairs, James jockeyed himself into position where he could sit next to Lora. As soon as they were settled and everyone was quiet, Reverend Vickers spoke: "We find it infinitely more pleasing to the Lord to nourish the soul before we feed the temple," the preacher chided, looking for a reaction from James.

Bill let out with a loud "Amen" that took everyone at the table by surprise. He quickly looked over at James, who was shaking his head with a look of consternation as he cast a cold glare at him.

Reverend Vickers turned to James and asked him what his favorite passage might be from the Bible, testing to see if he was being confronted by Catholic, Jew, or others of questionable salvation.

Much to the Reverend's surprise and delight, James began to quote verse after verse, first from the Psalms and Leviticus, Zephaniah and Deuteronomy, and then to the New Testament, reciting from each of the four Gospels. He poetically delivered the most difficult of passages to show his great flexibility and skillful memorization of such enormous amounts of scripture. The Reverend was beside himself. Never had he met anyone who possessed such a remarkable recall of the Word. The more James recited, the more the female gallery smiled and cooed. The old preacher leaned back in his chair, closing his eyes as he savored the moment. Only after about fifteen minutes of recital, did James relent and allow the meal to proceed.

Although the continuing recital was exhilarating to the pastor, James was losing his female listeners to petite yawns and batting eyelids as the girls struggled to stay awake. Lora had sensed James' attraction to her and remained remarkably attentive during his entire performance. The two of them exchanged flirtatious smiles back and forth during most of the evening, giving each other a burst of adrenaline that kept them awake. The others in the audience were less enthusiastic, giving into fatigue as they politely positioned themselves in a sitting position with their heads bobbing up and down as they nodded off to sleep.

James apologized for the late hour and stood up to leave. Much to James' chagrin, Reverend Vickers insisted that he and Bill come again very soon. As he accepted the invitation, he shot a quick look at Lora who smiled approvingly at her father's invitation. James returned the smile.

James neck-reined Ezra towards Lalleville, exuberant over his evening with the Vickers family, especially Lora. As he trotted down the dark road, Bill slid from side to side on the back of the mule, drifting in and out of sleep with his arms wrapped around James, none the better for his evening out.

It was a blistering hot afternoon when James and Bill slipped into the torpid brown waters of Chew's Bayou, along with a friend, Darcy Boudreau, for a cooling afternoon swim.

Enormous green lilly pads undulated on top of the water, oscillating slowly from the disturbance of the swimmers. An intermittent splash would sound as a large alligator gar would strike out at a passing perch. Softshell turtles and venomous cottonmouths basked in the sun, perched on low-hanging limbs that jutted from the rippling waters of the bayou. They flopped randomly into the drink as they became bored with the swimmers, realizing that there was little chance of making a meal of them.

The thick soft mud on the bottom was cool and relaxing to the men as they shoved their feet into the thick sludge. Later, they lounged in the shallows with a coating of gray muck covering their naked bodies to lessen the sting of the mid-day sun and the mosquitoes.

When James and his companions had tired of combating the insects, they moved towards shore to retrieve their clothes. They knew the evening milking and other chores would need tending at home and they were still several miles from the farm.

Bill and James waded straight ahead to shore as Darcy picked up his clothes and walked over to relieve himself. He hunkered down in the grass, still naked from his swim. Out of habit he began making a grunting sound. Much to his sudden surprise, he found himself being answered each time he strained. He spun around, still in a frog pose, trying to see what was mimicking him. Just as he'd finished relieving himself, he heard the sound again. This time he stood up, leaning through a thick patch of brush that was concealing the source of the noise. There, to his delight, was a nest, alive with a squirming, snapping litter of newborn gators. Bill and James came running as soon as Darcy yelled to them what he'd found. Neither of them had bothered to put on their clothes before entering the high grass.

James immediately informed the others of the value of the small reptiles, narrowly escaping the teeth of one of the tiny predators as he pointed and spoke. The small alligators by now had realized their error in thinking the sound coming from the other side of the bush was their mother and began to scatter to the four winds.

"Hold their heads down with a stick, but don't punch no holes in 'em! They won't be worth a plug nickel if ya poke the hide!" James screamed as all three of them took off through the swamp after the scrambling reptilia.

Bill let out a high-pitched scream, prompting hyena laughs from James and Darcy as they continued to scramble to outrun the miniature gators.

"Gawd damn!" Bill screamed, "he jest took a plug outa' me...shit!" He stood up, stopping to suck on his finger for a moment before diving back into the grass, continuing the hunt.

Darcy decided at that moment to alter his tactics, digging through the grass for a stick to make his capture of the toothy little monsters less painful. He slipped down to his hands and knees, pushing the weeds to one side as he searched frantically for a stick. Suddenly a surge of terror shot through his body as he locked in on an all-too- familiar sound coming from above him. His eyes moved slowly upwards towards the source of the hideous noise. He could feel the warm breath of the monster against his face as the horrible realization of what was happening suddenly hit him.

There, frozen stone still before him, was a ten-foot she-gator, elevated on all fours, poised for running. It was one of the few things a gator did better than swim. Darcy knew he was in a world of trouble as the gator began blowing its fearsome threat, like a baritone emphysema patient struggling for a breath of air. He was staring right into her enormous tooth-lined mouth.

Slowly feeling his way with his naked feet as he kept his eyes on the creature, he backed up. He had to signal Bill and James about what was happening, but he knew any movement from him and the gator would probably attack.

"What the hell are you doing?" James announced, walking up beside Darcy after watching him emerging backwards on all fours from the thick brush. Darcy didn't answer. He just kept staring straight ahead. James dropped down to take a look for himself, curious about what had his friend so mesmerized in the thick grass.

By this time Bill had taken an interest in what was going on as he noticed the two naked men frozen on all fours, staring into the grass a few yards away.

"Hey! What's gotten into you two, anyway? Ya'll look like a couple of damned old nekked bird dogs."

James and Darcy didn't answer. Instead they remained frozen on all fours.

"I got it," Bill screamed. "You want me ta flush them sons-a-bitches out. Let me find a rock tah chunk," he said, leaning over and picking up a small boulder.

James and Darcy's eyes closed simultaneously as they both began to pray for divine intervention to keep Bill from launching the rock.

"Where ya'll want me to chunk this damn rock? Well, kiss my ass then," Bill shouted when neither James nor Darcy answered. "If you ain't gonna' tell me where to put it, I'll jest let her fly and we'll see what happens."

Pandemonium erupted as the rock crashed between the gator and the two naked men. The giant reptile rushed towards the fleeing pink-skinned sprinters, leaping and punching their way through the thick ground cover, breaking off limbs and hurdling bushes as they retreated.

The gator abruptly stopped as a cloud of dust drifted over the animal from behind. For a few seconds James and Darcy could see the creature moving its head from side to side, trying to decide which morsel to chase. Eventually, the alligator disappeared from sight, becoming totally engulfed in the thick fog of red dust.

James and Darcy made their way along the bayou for nearly a quarter of mile, cutting a wide swath from where they'd first made contact with the she-gator.

They came to an area that looked safe enough for them to stop and rest. It was an open expanse of water frontage void of brush and trees. They squatted down to wash the dirt and blood off and check their wounds for the first time.

Bill suddenly appeared from over the hill, having been hot on their trail from Chew's Bayou. James and Darcy looked up from the water, resembling two fair-skinned aborigines, as they watched Bill walk cautiously down to the riverbank.

"I don't suppose you bothered to get our clothes?" James asked.

Bill didn't say anything, but just looked down at the ground moving his toe across the mud. The answer to that question was obvious, as he stood there buck-naked as the day he'd been born.

James quickly turned towards both boys, standing up in the water as he gritted his teeth.

"Both ya'll better keep this to yourself, or I'll personally whip your ass! Wouldn't nobody believe you anyway!"

"Somehow you jest don't look too threatening," Darcy responded, barely able to finish his sentence as he bent over laughing and pointing at the naked man lecturing them from the water.

James suddenly broke into a smile and then a hysterical laugh as he launched himself backward into the bayou.

It was late evening before they started home. They passed the neighbors' houses as quietly as they could, stepping gingerly down the road to keep from getting the dogs near the farms after them.

Meedah, an elderly colored woman who worked for the Lavoisier family, screamed with horror when the three men walked into the house.

Bill and Darcy were draped in gunnysacks that they'd taken from the barn. James walked closely behind them, still in the raw, heading to his room as calmly as if he were wearing a tuxedo. He looked at Meedah, tipping his head and smiling as he passed by, trying to keep a straight face.

Meedah was furious with them, thinking that they'd been drinking and gotten into some kind of ruckus with, as she said, "some Cajun trash."

Meedah had become the self-proclaimed 'mammy' for the three children shortly after Jaques had disappeared. She had lived with them ever since, being parent, housekeeper, and a dear friend as they had grown up. She was family.

"Ya'll boys ought to be taken out to dah wood shed fer a blisterin', comin' home like dis. Da bunch of ya oughta be ashamed fer yourselves lookin' like somethin' dah dogs done drug home! Lord sakes!" she said. "Uh-Uh-Uh".

The smiles quickly left the men's faces. Katy peered out of the door of her room and then quickly closed it after seeing James standing there naked.

"We're in for it now!" James whispered under his breath.

Bill was scratching so hard from the burlap irritating his skin that Meedah immediately honed in on him, thinking that they'd gotten into chiggers. James kept trying to catch Bill's arm each time he began clawing at himself, knowing full well what Meedah would do.

"You boys git dat tub filled and peel dem nasty rags off your backs," she ordered. "I got a fresh chunk of lye soap jest waitin' ta be used."

"Dang, I don't want no bath!" Bill mumbled.

"I heard dat, your nasty mouth. Don't you come home talkin' perfamity in dis house...uh-uh, no sir. I'll take a stick to your backside!"

"I reckon I best be gittin'," Darcy quickly announced, retreating towards the door. "Got a good spell to go 'fore I git home. 'Sides, I weren't plannin' on takin' my baff till come this weekend."

"Shore do hate ta waste all dat fresh, hot cornbread I jest made, but I reckon if a body ain't hungry, den dah dogs u'll jest have to git it," Meedah said, predicting Darcy's reaction. "Got a mess of pot liquor boilin' down at dah cookin' shack, too, ta pour over dah top uh dat hot bread."

"Well, I guess I might be waitin' jest a bit fer I start home. Tub bath might be mighty nice right about now," Darcy concluded. "You can have my cornbread," Bill said. "I think I'll be passin' on takin' a bath!"

Bill shot a glance at Meedah to test her response to his announcement. The gator that Bill had come face to face with earlier in the day suddenly seemed like a minor threat as he glanced over at the expression on Meedah's face.

"Second thought, I believe a bath might hit the spot right about now," he came back. "I think I'll step outside and git some water for the tub!"

The next morning the trio returned to Chew's Bayou to retrieve their clothes. When they approached the nest they found the grassy area flattened from the weight of the adult gator's body, but there were no alligators to be found, big or small. She'd moved her nest after shredding the men's clothes that they had left behind.

In the months that followed, whenever the opportunity availed itself, Bill would show visitors the shredded clothes and ask them if they had known Darcy Boudreau. Each time, the reaction was the same. A look of astonishment would come over the guests' faces as Bill would nonchalantly quip, "gator got him," and he'd hold up the ripped pants, then point to the large teeth marks in the sides of the boots.

"Why I didn't know Darcy Boudreau were ete by a gator!" the men visitors would predictably respond.

"Gobbled old Darcy right up," Bill would continue, trying to keep a serious look about him.

"Land sakes!" the women visitors would gasp.

"It jest breaks my heart to think that ole gator was almost feedin' on the flesh and blood of my good friend," Bill would eulogize, wiping his eyes as he held up a tooth from a gator who'd never seen the likes of Darcy Boudreau.

"Yes, sir, I come along, findin' old Darcy's legs danglin' out of that big ole gator's jaws, jest after she'd swallered him. Fortunate for him I was there jest in the nick of time. Old Darcy were puttin' up a good fight, his legs jest a kickin' up a storm, and makin' it real tough for that she-gator to keep a firm bite on him so she could get him swallered.

"Well there I was, with no choice but to leap on that devil and split her open with my whittlin' knife, pullin' old Darcy outa' her belly. And that ole gator, well, she were plenty mad, that's fer sure.

"Not that I'm a hero or any such thing, but if I hadn't ah been there, she'd uh made a meal uh him, sure as the world!"

"I declare!" the women would answer politely.

"Old Darcy won't talk about it," Bill would say," but if yah look real close, you'll see him limpin' from where she locked them big ole teeth down on him. She near cut him in two!"

James would usually roll his eyes back at that point, wiping his mouth as he watched the guests stare at each other in disbelief. The fact that anyone would have the gall to make up such an outrageous pack of bull made even the nonbelievers shake their heads in amazement. But James was more interested in occupying his time thinking about the Vickers girls, especially Lora. It had been weeks since he'd been on the road to Brittany, where Bill and he had stumbled onto the Vickers clan, so he made up his mind that a respectable amount of time had passed for him to make another call on them.

He planned his trip carefully, deciding to visit them on a Tuesday. Monday was the day after the Sabbath and usually the Reverend, being a Cumberland Minister, would have just been returning home from having been a guest speaker in someone else's pulpit. Wednesday was prayer meeting time and Pastor Vickers would have been on the road, preaching at a camp meeting or another church gathering somewhere nearby. In either case, his daughters certainly would have been by his side.

On Tuesday afternoon James donned his 'Sunday-go-to meetin' suit,' a black, heavy, wool ready-made off the shelf from Smiley's Dry Goods in Lalleville. It was hemmed much too short in the arms and legs, and permanently wrinkled at the elbows and knees from not having been pressed for some time. James had owned the suit for several years, purchasing it himself when his momma was still alive. The jacket was so small that he was no longer able to button it without leaving a generous amount of shirt hanging out from under the coat and vest.

James wiped off his boots and dusted his black hat, which had belonged to his father. He put a swipe of boot black on the hatband to give it a fresh, store-bought appearance. Meedah already had carefully pressed his high-collared white shirt, since that is what he normally wore to church each Sunday. She'd even made him a black bow tie, but he had refused to ever wear it, until now.

A fob dangled loosely from one pocket of his vest to the other, giving the false impression that he had a watch. Meedah had placed a piece of white cloth in his lapel pocket, a facsimile of a hanky dispatched from the corner of a worn-out bed sheet.

He slicked his hair back with a shot of tonic, rubbing the excess on his face. He still had enough on his hands to shine the toes of his boots. The smell of the tonic permeated the air, taking his breath away like a stiff shot of whiskey.

James arranged to make his entree through the front gate of the Vickers' home precisely at suppertime. It was readily permissible in Southern society to invite yourself to dinner if you presented your host with a contribution to the evening's bill of fare. With that in mind, James loaded his wagon with several bushel baskets of peas, rhubarb and stubby okra from his garden. The most delicious of the gifts, snap beans, could be useful in keeping hands busy veining and snapping the tender flat pods if there was a low ebb in the evening's conversation.

James arrived just as the sun was setting. The drop in temperature offered a welcome relief from the unbearable heat under the heavy wool suit coat that he had donned just out of sight of the Vicker's house. An uncomfortable itch that had plagued him under the wool pants, had now made its way beneath the coat, keeping James busily scratching like his mangy hound that had followed him from home.

He could smell bread baking as he approached the front hitching rail near the house. Two of the girls saw him and yelled inside. Much like the first time James had visited, Pastor Vickers immediately appeared on the porch and herded the girls indoors, chastising them for their unladylike conduct. The old pastor promptly returned, inviting James up to the porch while taking a 'look-see' at the fresh vegetables in the back of his wagon. "God bless you, son! Come on in," the Reverend exclaimed with a smile. This time the old man opened the front gate for him and ushered him up to the house.

James pulled off his hat, nervously holding it with both hands before he spoke. "Mighty nice to see ya, Pastor! I was in the neighborhood and thought I'd come by and sit a spell."

"Well, that's right neighborly of ya, son. Always glad ta have ya. Supper's bout ready, if you'd care ta join us?"

"Well, I wouldn't wanta put you folks out none," James started to say, inferring just enough hesitation to allow the pastor to insist that he stay. Neither men had any doubt that he'd come for supper.

"We'd be thrilled if you'd share our table. The girls and I would surely enjoy the good company."

James accepted the invitation with a quick, "Well that'd be might kind of yah...don't mind if I do!"

Pastor Vickers delivered a lengthy blessing over the spread, giving everyone ample time to prepare their palates for the medley of foods that steamed on the table. Fresh red squirrel, deep fried cottontail and a stringy jackrabbit, breaded and fried to resemble chicken was piled on a single plate in the middle of the table. A generous helping of fresh cornmealed catfish was cut into thick sweet steaks on a plate separated from the other meats. Heaping crocks of fresh vegetables, buttered and saturated with the juice from ham hocks, gave off curls of hot smoke.

A strange silence, interrupted only by the mechanics of eating, pervaded the dining room. It was the atmosphere demanded by Pastor Vickers as the only virtuous way to enjoy the bounty provided by God. James preferred the silence. It gave him a chance to eat and watch Lora without being interrupted. He was captivated by her shyness. She epitomized all that he had imagined a woman should be: delicate, graceful, quiet, beautiful.

The girls cleared the table after the meal as James and Pastor Vickers sipped chicory coffee. The two men talked about the usual topics of the times, concentrating on moral issues and the goings on in the community. They were careful not to let themselves slip into idle gossip. The old pastor carefully interjected comments about each of his daughters whenever he had the chance, praising their talents and telling James over and over again what a delight they were to him in his old age. The girls sat quietly listening and smiling whenever their names were mentioned, with an occasional "Oh, poppa", or "I'm so embarrassed," when of course they loved the flattery.

After having discussed the other four daughters, the Reverend finally turned his attentions to Lora, the youngest of his brood.

"Lora is my baby. My sweet Lizzy died giving birth to her, ya know. But this child is such a blessing to us...a special child...truly a gift from heaven."

Lora became teary-eyed at her father's comments. It was the only time James had seen any of the girls break from their usual jovial mood.

She looked over at her father and then rushed outside, holding her apron to her face as she fled the room. James could hear her sniffling out on the front porch.

"She's got it in her head that she had somethin' to do with her momma's death, and I can't for the life of me get her to shake that silly notion," the old man remarked. "Never have understood why she blames herself for Lizzy's passin' away."

James finished his coffee and gladly moved outside onto the front porch with the family to enjoy the cool night air. He was still uncomfortable in the wool clothes and the stifling heat from the inside of the house, and the hot coffee had only added to his misery.

He felt very at ease with the Vickers family and their warmth and closeness to each other. He sensed a great devotion on the part of the girls for their father and an equally great love on the preacher's part for each of his daughters. It was a feeling that he'd not had since his own family had been together. How wonderful it had felt to him to share their affections, if only from a distance.

Whatever materialistic poverty the young ladies may have suffered, they were not without an education. James was surprised at the extent of their schooling, especially after his first encounter with the girls had left him believing that none of them were able to speak or understand English. While James felt that he had detected some obvious shortcomings in the old pastor's vision of how to raise his daughters, he also felt that the old man's priority in seeing that the girls were well educated was a rather sagacious bit of planning for a backwoods preacher. His was a very progressive attitude, considering how most backwoods people reacted to the idea of educating women.

Lora was reserved and mannerly, to the point of making James uncomfortable on occasion. She was also dainty when the mood suited her. Sometimes she seemed to be so delicate that James was afraid she would break. But, months later, after he'd been given permission to court Lora by her father, he began to see a different side of her character, a person dedicated to hard work and devotion to her tasks, and not the least bit squeamish or frail. He'd seen her gut and pluck a hen without flinching, or butcher a full-grown hog, a task that would have tested the courage and stomach of the most stouthearted man.

James' relationship with the Vickers moved along unscathed except for a minor incident that occurred several months after he'd begun seriously to woo young Lora.

In the midst of a conversation about the late War Between the States, James was struck dumb when the old preacher casually let it slip that he had served in the Union Army against the Confederates at Baton Rouge.

The revelation nearly ended his courtship with Lora. Insult was added to injury when the old man revealed that he had not only served the Yankee cause, but had been invested into the regiment commanded by the murderous General Banks, the devil incarnate, who had laid siege to Port Hudson and later ordered the burning of Lallemand.

Lora was quick to admonish her father for not explaining why he had served with the invaders. He'd been caught in a conscription roundup for laborers to unload the powder barges pulled upriver by the Navy ships, Genesee, Sachem and Monongahela, in preparation for the attack on Port Hudson.

It still didn't satisfactorily explain what he was doing with Grierson's raiding party in Baton Rouge. The old man was so embarrassed by James' reaction that he described what had happened in detail. In fleeing a skirmish near his home, as a conscientious objector, he'd walked straight into a Federal sweep for belligerents. He found himself imprisoned, temporarily, along with Confederate deserters and criminals who were being transported to the Mississippi to unload war materials from Farragut's fleet. Later, after being able to prove to the Federals that he was an ordained minister, he was released.

True or not, the story pacified James enough that he let the incident drop. But it always troubled him that, years later, after the old man had died, the federal government had seen fit to place a Union headstone on his grave, an odd reward for someone who'd spent only a few days unloading barges as a prisoner of war.

Lora had a wonderfully uplifting attitude about life. She was always positive and saw little reason ever to complain. She found James exciting as she listened to his dreams for the future, and she became even more infatuated as she discovered a sensitive caring individual concealed beneath his tough exterior.

James was often contemptuous of others for having a lack of initiative. He scorned the uneducated and admired those who had attained his image of success.

"A man's got to apply himself, work hard to make something out of his life!" he'd tell Lora. "Any fella who doesn't have a good education and doesn't learn to work isn't gonna' amount to ah hill of beans in this world."

Lora always would smile after James finished expounding on the virtues of hard work. Her vision of life was more exemplified by a softly flowing river, moving through a loving and peaceful world, touching the lives of those who might need her help. Her path in life, as she saw it, had already been established, as deeply set as the channel of the great mystical river, from the first raindrop to the final explosion into the sea.

"God will provide," she always would say. "Be obedient and have faith in the Lord. God will determine our direction in life."

James put little credence in her philosophy. Instead, he elected to pursue his goals aggressively, calculating that God would appreciate his help in getting him where he knew he belonged.

Despite their differences of opinion and, after a rather lengthy courtship, James and Lora found enough in common to wed on September 25, 1914, in Ruston, Louisiana. Reverend Vickers cheerfully officiated at the wedding held at the Baptist Church of Ruston, where he'd preached over the years. A large assembly of family and well-wishers looked on as the couple struggled through the service, both of them obviously uncomfortable with the attention.

As quickly as they were married, the couple packed their meager belongings, said farewell to family and friends, and boarded a train for Hattiesburg, Mississippi. James had accepted a position as an apprentice druggist with the Mallory Drug Company. The move was significant for both Lora and James, as she left her father and sisters for the first time and James said farewell to Bill and Kate, and his home at Lalleville. The ties of family and heritage had been, if not severed, at least thinly stretched as they both set out in pursuit of their dreams.

James had rented a small, two-room frame cottage within walking distance of his job in downtown Hattiesburg. The house was a carriage barn that had been converted by the owner, with neither running water nor a bathroom until James convinced his landlord to allow him to extend a pipe into the house from the old well. The modest home was nestled beneath an umbrella of voluminous pecan trees and encircled within a fence of lugustrums that lined the outside walls of the home and the narrow dirt walkway leading to the front steps. In the summer the trees and bushes shaded the house from the severe heat, but in the winter the naked limbs did little to break the force of the winds that moved freely through the uninsulated walls. A single wood stove burned night and day during the winter as they tried to keep the dwelling at a livable temperature. But during the balance of the year the weather in Hattiesburg was pleasant enough that they were able to live quite comfortably.

Hattiesburg was a dreamy southern town, still clenched in an immutable antebellum mood, slow-moving, self-reliant and ever so careful to avoid the exploding industrial boom ebbing its way into the cities in the north. The indomitable Southern Society of Hattiesburg had been well preserved since the Civil War. Few of its residents would ever have acknowledged that the war had been unfavorably concluded for the Confederacy at the Appomattox courthouse. Life went on as it always had, with deeply rooted traditions providing a special flavoring, a quality of life that made the south so very unique.

James and Lora were satisfied that their move had been a good decision, as 1914 had been the beginning of a period of great prosperity for most Americans, no matter where they lived. But it had seemed to James that Hattiesburg would provide as much of an opportunity for a good future as any of the larger cities of the south, without having to give up the benefits of a small town.

Within the next two years James completed his apprenticeship and received his certification as a registered pharmacist. He was making enough money for Lora and him to move to a larger home with indoor plumbing and gas heaters in each room, so life was wonderful. A son, Jason Vincent Lavoisier, was born on January 4, 1916, shortly after James and Lora moved into their new home. Jason's birth was a momentous event for James. Like most new fathers, he saw his son's arrival as an opportunity to correct the failings of his own childhood. But Jason's birth had nearly killed Lora, so the couple's vision of having a large family would never become a reality. It was difficult for James to accept, having only one child after coming from a family where childbearing was as much a part of life as the annual harvest. It also meant that the lineage of the Lavoisier family would end if anything happened to Jason before he was old enough to have his own family.

Lora was everything James had envisioned she would be, an energetic homemaker, social companion, dignified and respected churchwoman. And now he found her to be an extremely loving and attentive mother to his newborn son.

By the time Jason was a year old the family had established themselves in the middle class echelon of Hattiesburg. James had left the employment of Mallory Drug Company and opened his own pharmacy. His dreams were now becoming a reality as every turn in life seemed to be more prosperous than the last.

While Hattiesburg slumbered and yawned in its typically Southern complacency, much of the northeastern United States began receiving first a trickle, then an onslaught of refugees from the turmoil and destruction taking place in Europe. The South, having little ethnic ties to Europe, was passively insensitive to most of what was happening across the Atlantic. The newspapers had been inundated with articles and editorials since 1914 on America's need to support one side of the conflict or the other raging across Europe, but most Americans opted for neutrality. Very few people knew anything about Europe, and even fewer cared what they did to each other.

Not since the Civil War had the media been given such a cornucopia of material for print. From the assassination of Archduke Ferdinand in 1914 and the invasion of Belgium in that same year, the horrifying gas attacks of 1915 at Ypres and the defeat of the Allies at Gallipoli, the world was astir in horror. The sinking of the Lusitania by U-boats, with 128 American lives lost, seemed for awhile to spark the ire of the American public, but not for long.

Verdun and the Somme had recorded such heavy casualties, over two million English, German and French, that reports of killed and wounded by the press no longer seemed to have an effect on readers. No one could imagine such losses, even though they were true.

But James' interest in Europe was limited to France. Not because of Verdun but because of Paris. And not because of the war but from his interest in the 'société littéraire'. Paris was the cultural focal point of the world. Here the most renowned painters, writers, poets and designers of fashion and architecture gathered. It was a place that had been as much a part of his dreams as Hattiesburg. He looked forward to the day he would take Lora and Jason to visit his ancestral home. To be Creole was to have a love for France. To be an educated and successful Creole, demanded that one has an interest in Paris and be astutely aware of the latest rages, from fashion to the eccentricities of the new Bohemian culture.

James had gone to his pharmacy early in the morning as usual to warm up the store before his first customer arrived. He pored over his paper to get the latest news from New Orleans and Europe. Before he'd finished the paper, he put it aside to inventory his prescriptions for the day, grinding powders with his mortar and pestle and filling out handwritten labels to paste on the bottles.

Clarence Aberty, a deacon from James' church, appeared at the front door of the store, staring through the glass panel. It wasn't unusual for James to have someone drop by that early. Store hours were very flexible, and customers often came by an hour or two before James had planned on opening up if they were in a hurry for a prescription.

Clarence appeared to be anxious about something, as he did a slight jig in front of the door, waiting impatiently for James to let him in.

"Morning, Deacon!"

Clarence ignored his greeting. "Have you heard?"

"Heard what?" James asked.

"It come over the wire a little while ago. Congress declared war on Germany at three this mornin'!"

"War?"

"Yeah! Some folks are sayin' President Wilson ask 'em to, 'cause of the sinkin' of the Memphis and some other ship."

James stared out the window. "That happened over a month ago. It ain't likely he did it 'cause of that?"

"Well, it don't matter. We're in it now up to our necks. Bill Logan's got it on good authority that the President is gonna use Northern volunteers to go first...see if they can win it without gettin' any help from our boys."

James glanced up, disbelief on his face. "Now why would they do that?"

"I guess 'cause they figure it wouldn't take that much to whip 'em and they'd git all the glory. Good for Yankee politics, the way I figure it."

"That doesn't make a lick of sense, Clarence. Those Yankee boys couldn't hit a bull's ass at ten feet with a shotgun."

"Well," the deacon coughed, "I couldn't rightly tell ya about how those Yankee fellers shoot, but I hear tell them Europeans fight like a bunch of sissies. They do a lot of runnin' around in fancy uniforms and drinkin' tea and sherry all day long."

James scowled, "Lord help us if we go to war thinkin' any such thing. Those people are tough. They've been in this scrap a hell of a lot longer than we have. No sir, we're likely to get our asses sorely kicked over there."

The deacon paused to study James' face, confused by his lack of enthusiasm for the fight.

"I reckon I'd better be gittin' on over to Myron's. He'll be wantin' to know what I've heard. Maybe it's jest as well some of us won't be gittin' into the fight," he added, giving James a disgusted look as he turned and walked out of the store. James watched Clarence walk down the street, cornering the next person he met with a cheerful smile on his face.

The Sunday after the declaration of war James sat in church listening to the preacher's sermon on the virtues of defending the nation and carrying the banner of freedom to the front lines in Belgium and France. The mood in the sanctuary during the Sunday morning service was unusually solemn as the choir delivered a medley of patriotic songs. Later, in place of a sermon, Reverend McCrae delivered a chilling rendition of William Wordsworth's The Happy Warrior.

James followed the Reverend, repeating a single verse over and over again in his mind:

'Who, whether praise of him must walk the
Earth forever, and to noble deeds give birth,
Or he must fall, to sleep without his fame,
And leave a dead unprofitable name,
Finds comfort in himself and in his cause;'

He slipped into a daydream, his eyes moving through the congregation as he mentally tried to imagine who would survive the war and who wouldn't. 'How sad it will be for them to die,' he thought. Before he'd ended his daydreaming, his thoughts turned to himself. He wondered if he would survive and if the others would be sorry if they heard of his death in battle.

Reverend McCrae was leading the choir in the last verse of "It is Well With My Soul." James stopped his dreaming and joined in with the others in the singing.

After the service James and Lora walked the few blocks from church to the house. It was mid-day by the time they arrived home, with the sun searing directly overhead, making it uncomfortably hot. Neither of them talked on the way home. When they reached the front porch James pulled off his coat and tie, laying it next to him on the swing. He put his straw hat down on top of the coat and rolled his sleeves up to his elbows.

Lora reclined in a rocker a few feet away, pulling her skirt almost up to her calves, and fanning herself with a church paddle given out during the service.

She was the first one to break the silence. "This heat is sure giving the tomatoes a hard time. I don't believe I've seen it so dry. We'll be lucky to get a bushel and a half from the whole lot of 'em."

"I'll be joining up next week," James said, out of the clear blue.

Lora didn't answer for awhile, but just kept rocking herself and looking out into the yard, as if she hadn't heard what he'd said. "How long do you suppose you'll have before they make you leave for training camp?" she finally said.

"Hard to say. Could be two, three days...could be a week, if I join here. No one can join up until the Army recruiters come, 'less you go over to Jackson or down to Mobile."

"Too hot for that," Lora answered calmly.

"I've decided I'll be goin' to Baton Rouge to join up. I'd like to be with people I know when the shootin' starts. It'll give us a chance to visit your family on the way down. We'll take the baby over to Emmy's."

"No reason for Jason to be on the road all that time. Nona will take good care of him. She's real good with children. Jason's been a little colicky anyway!"

"We'll be selling the store right away. Isn't anybody left to hire on that could run it anyhow."

"I reckon that's true," Lora mumbled, trying to catch a tear hanging on the edge of her eyelid with her finger without James seeing it.

James' head dipped down as he wiped the sweat from his forehead with his bare arm.

Lora leaned back in the rocker, her eyes closed as she spoke. "It scares me, James. So many young men going off to war. None of us really knows what we're fightin' over. And it's so far from home."

James stood up and walked over to her, taking her hand, pulling her up into his arms and giving her a hug. He assured her that it would only be a minor interruption of their lives. He thought about the reality of what was coming as he tried to comfort her.

"I'd want Jason to know that I loved him if anything were to happen to me. It's hard on a boy to grow up without a father. He might not understand why I had to do this."

Lora never said a word. James could feel her moving in his arms as she cried silently. A few seconds later she pulled herself loose from him and walked towards the front door.

"I think, for the first time in my life...I wonder if God knows what he's doing?" she said, vanishing into the house.

The morning of James' departure was cold and rainy. It was pitch black when Lora and James left Emmy's house in Baton Rouge to walk to the train station. The earlier mood of gaiety and excitement by the volunteers had been transformed into a glumness as the men stood in quiet groups, holding onto their loved ones, whispering their final testimonies of love to those they were leaving behind. Even the town musicians, many of them veterans from other wars, sensed the downtrodden mood as recruits separated from the crowd to board the train. Many of the recruits were weeping, and some ran back for a final moment with wives and mothers as the musicians played a slow melody, in tempo to the downpour that saturated the already sunken spirits.

The engine screamed a long shrill farewell as the train pulled away from the station. It crawled at a reluctant pace, hesitating like the hearts of its travelers, as if to postpone the grim appointment waiting at journey's end.

James' thoughts raced back to Lalleville, as if it would be his last chance to remember. He thought of Bill and Katy, of Bill's antics and Katy's loving smile.

He thought of his mother and wondered if this moment in life's path would bring their sad reunion. And if it was to be, would Jaques be standing beside Benonia when he was reunited with them as a family, before God? Or had Jaques managed to evade even the eyes of the Almighty, slipping into obscurity forever?

James knew that he must survive the war, for as long as life flowed through his body, there was hope eternal that someday he would find his father.

CHAPTER 5

Fort Oglethorpe lay to the south of Chattanooga, a short distance from the Tennessee River and slightly north of Chickamauga, Georgia. It was a dense, forested region, quiet and serene until the influx of thousands of recruits for America's new army arrived for training in preparation for the war in Europe.

It was as though a grand conclave of reconciliation had been devised, bringing southern and northern inductees together to train as one army to cross the sea in pursuit of a common enemy. It was hoped that past differences would be forgiven and old scars healed. But it really didn't matter; they would have to fight anyway.

Fort Oglethorpe lay in the heavily forested terrain of the Georgian hills and mountains. A complex network of rivers and streams flowed almost unnoticed beneath the thick vegetation in the narrow valleys. The area was more suited for jungle warfare than preparing men for the battles to be fought across the open plains of the French and Belgium frontiers. Unfortunately, the stay at Fort Oglethorpe was pitifully short and mostly ineffective. It had barely given the men enough time to master the drills and maneuvers they would need to function as a cohesive fighting force in Europe.

James found himself, much to his protest and anger, attached to the 24th Hospital Group. He suspected that it was because of his weakened lungs, but actually it was due to his prior civilian training as a pharmacist. He was incensed that he would be assigned to non-combat duty. It was an untenable situation for a man with such a drive to see combat to be bivouacked, as he saw it, with conscientious objectors, although the term was strictly unofficial. After a concentrated effort that included a barrage of letters and personal appearances in front of his commanding officer, James found himself being promoted to corporal in the 24th, instead of being reassigned to a fighting unit as he had requested. At that point everything seemed dismally unfair and senseless.

He certainly had not intended to give up his flourishing business in Hattiesburg to change bandages and bedpans. Because he was married, it was unlikely that he ever would have been drafted, since nearly three quarters of the married men were never inducted into the Army.

Lora wrote to James every day, lengthy and informative letters that sparked his spirits, especially when she wrote him about Jason, his pride and joy. But there was little time to worry about family, as the training was suddenly intensified to speed up delivery of troops demanded by the Allies.

By mid-June of 1917, the troops had finished their brief training and had received their issue of equipment for France everything, that is, except weapons. Unfortunately, there weren't enough to go around. Most of the men had learned their drills with wooden rifles made by a local toy manufacturing company.

The men were transported to the Hoboken docks by troop trains and billeted in tents erected in the Hoboken Meadows, next to the wharves. Several freighters had been hurriedly converted into troop transports to make the perilous voyage across the Atlantic. Troops spent their idle time playing cards or 'Mumbledy Peg' with their bayonets. In the evenings, most of the men who could write, wrote letters home or composed letters for those who were unable to do so for themselves.

Little by little, the troops were detailed to their crude berths in the cargo holds of the ships. The makeshift bunks were squeezed into an almost unbearable closeness as men were stacked like bolts of cloth, one on top of the other, four or five men high. James had become slightly claustrophobic as he descended into the deepest innards of the old freighter. It seemed almost diabolical as he stepped face forward, down the steep metal stairs, past hissing steam lines and leaking configurations of water and fuel pipes. The stench of diesel and paint became almost a refreshing alternative to the accumulation of body odors from unwashed humans that met him at the door to the lower cargo bay. The smell of vomit permeated the air. Plugged toilets and urinals formed a choking gas that made James nauseous after he'd expelled the last breath of fresh air that he'd held as long as he could. Exposed light bulbs in the hold, hurriedly wired during refitting, flittered on and off as the huge generators of the ship floundered. 'War could not be any more hellish that this place,' James thought.

His bunk was located against a riveted metal wall that hummed and vibrated from some mechanical device located nearby. A steady stream of rust-colored water dripped from the wall, soaking his blankets and mattress. And everywhere men talked and shouted as if they were in a frantic debate. Gear was tied and hung, smashed and stashed anywhere someone wasn't standing or sleeping. The clutter was overwhelming.

James discarded his tunic and crawled into his bunk. Sleep was the only privacy left. He closed his eyes, thinking how wonderful a hot cup of coffee would be. His thoughts again returned to Lalleville and his special fishing hole at Williams Point. He could see the black pool-doos skimming across the surface of the bayou as his bamboo pole arched gracefully over the water. A disturbance rippled across the calm water, indicating the presence of an extraordinarily large fish below the surface. His line moved ever so slightly as the fish teased the bait, nibbling and tasting, but never taking hold.

Just as the tip of the pole was thrust violently downward into the water, as the fish finally took the bait, James was awakened from his dream.

"You Corporal Lavoisier?"

"Yeah," James answered.

"You're wanted topside by the C.O."

James closed his eyes again as he responded with a half-hearted, "all right."

He made his way back up the endless flights of metal stairs, where he was finally able to see sunlight cutting through an open rectangular hatch immediately overhead.

Once on the main deck he hoisted his hand to deliver a salute to the officer in charge. The man, a young lieutenant, ignored his gesture. He stared at James for a few seconds before finally speaking.

"Votre dossier, indique que vous parlez Français?"

"Oui, Lieutenant," James shot back.

"Est ce-que votre famille est Française ou Canadienne?" the officer continued.

"Non, Monsieur, elle est Creole."

"Ah, tres bien Caporal. Ça sera tout."

James popped a snappy salute to the officer before doing an about face and heading back down the stairs, agitated that he'd had to come all the way up on deck for those few words.

"Damn peckerwood," James mumbled. "If the Gawd damn file says I speak French, then I guess I already been asked whether I speak French or not. Little snot-nosed ass-hole, why don't they find him something to do?"

The ships left Hoboken in a drizzling rain. The dismal storm rocked the blimp-shaped hull with a regularity that sent almost everyone to one corner of the hold to empty their stomachs. There was no going topside for fresh air; the entire division would have been on deck if they'd been allowed to leave their bunks. The salty corned beef added to the discomfort of the men, making their stomachs queasy enough without the help of the storm. What made matters worse was the peculiar blood red color of the vomit, giving the heavings a rather disgusting appearance. The purple tint of the puke had come from the grape juice given to the men to drink with their meals.

The excursion to Europe was anything but a pleasure cruise. The men were sick with numerous diseases, some undiagnosed, with a few men dying aboard ship before they reached the shores of France. Conditions were abominable in the overcrowded belly of the packet ship, with tainted food, poor latrine facilities and horrendous weather conditions from Atlantic storms battering the unstable vessels with a repetitious teeter-tottering for most of the journey.

The men were continuously rotated to the main deck, giving them a much-needed taste of fresh air and a chance to exercise their legs with a short stroll across the decks.

James stood with a small squad of soldiers facing a large whitewashed lifeboat that they had been assigned to, at Hoboken. They watched and listened as the sailors nonchalantly instructed them on the maneuvers for escaping to the waiting lifeboat, if orders were given to abandon ship.

He listened to the sailor reciting his spiel in a monotone drone, watching the versatile instructor concentrate on almost anything else except what he was doing. Still, the sailor never missed a word of his lifeless presentation.

"You know, this drill is about as worthless as tits on a boar hog. Hell, the rats couldn't squeeze outa this can if we take a lick from one of those German torpedoes," James remarked to the man standing next to him.

"Ain't that the truth," the man responded, offering James a plug from his tobacco ration.

"Where yah hail from?" James asked.

"Biloxi," the stranger answered; "how bout yourself?"

"Near abouts, Hattiesburg."

"Naw, no way! You got too much burr in yer accent to be a dry land feller. Ya ain't Cajun, neither. I'd say you come from down around the River, or maybe on the swamp somewhere."

James looked over, smiling. "How'd the world you know that?"

"Lord sakes, I got half a dozen kin livin' back in that muck. Only reason I ain't seen 'em in ten years is...can't no-body get in there to find 'em!" He laughed. "I sure as hell know what them folks sound like, though."

"James Lavoisier...from Lalleville," said James, extending his hand to the man."

"Willy Jackson...pleased to make your, acquaintance! I guess I done told yah I were from Biloxi?"

"Yea, yah did," James said, shaking his hand.

"What'a yah reckon it'll be like in France, James?"

"Could be some pretty hard times. I got a bad feelin' about it," James said, looking across the water. "Appears to me that a lot of these fellas on this boat aren't gonna be seein' home again."

Willy didn't say anything, just looked out at the horizon, rubbing his finger across his nose. The navy gun crews began firing practice rounds with their three-inch guns as part of the daily routine, signaling the soldiers that it was time to head back down below deck.

"Well," Willy said, "it's been mighty fine talkin' to yah, James. I hope the good Lord 'ull see yah safely home."

"You take care, Willy. Maybe I'll be seein' you on the trip back," James said, catching himself looking at the man for some prophetic sign that he would survive. For some strange reason, he sensed that he wouldn't.

The ships made their way past Belle Isle, moving up the Loire River to the port of St. Nazaire, where the troops would disembark.

On June 28, 1917, the 1st Division was off-loaded, and smiles returned to the men's faces as they finally touched solid ground. A decision already had been made to transport the recruits to training camps at Gondrecourt, fifty-five kilometers from St. Mihiel. It was a safe enough distance from the front.

For two months, the training at Gondrecourt and Bourmont continued, with the Americans living safely buffered from the front lines. Adrian barracks neatly checker-boarded the lush French countryside, isolating the 'Yanks' from the realities of the war that awaited them on the front. James was comfortably settled in a cantonment area, spending much of his time inventorying supplies and being on call as an interpreter for Lieutenant Alfred Sidney St. Clair, better known to his men as Lieutenant ASS.

At first, it was a decent enough duty. It allowed James the opportunity to slip into the villages with the Lieutenant to act as his interpreter for the requisitioning of everything from chickens for the camp's mess to arranging an occasional amorous dalliance for the young officer. James would entertain himself with a glass of cognac at a local bistro while Lieutenant St. Clair went about his business with his "Belle de Nuit." The Lieutenant, an uppity New England well-to-do, enjoyed riding into town on horseback, cocked in his saddle like Napoleon himself, yet he was probably one of the worst horseman James ever had encountered.

James, by now, had been everything from a stable hand during the day to a 'Second' for St. Clair in a late-night drunken brawl which ended up with the officer receiving a bruised nose and a ride home, tied unceremoniously across his own saddle. The Lieutenant had turned out to be somewhat of a contemptuous little snit, as James soon realized. On the particular night of the brawl, while he was still lashed across his McClellan saddle, the impudent upstart was suddenly aroused from his stupor long enough to provide James with an announcement.

"Those high-brow, blue-blooded French officers don't take kindly to talking to enlisteds, you know, Lavoisier? It isn't respectable," he said. "They got their asses hiked up so high," he continued, "it's no wonder they keep gettin' the shit kicked out of them up at the front."

James patronized the Lieutenant with a respectful grunt as he kept on riding towards camp, holding onto the reins of the officer's horse, which trailed behind him with the Lieutenant strung across the animal's back like a field-dressed deer.

"You know I didn't have any choice...I had to put you in for Sergeant," he announced, raising his head and looking at James with one eye. "The Frenchies don't like dealing with commoners," he added condescendingly.

"Yes, sir," James answered, gritting his teeth. "I appreciate your concern."

"Well, you won't when I tell you the rest of it. It seems I'm not the only one needing an interpreter. Somebody took a liking to your file before they approved my request. You've been transferred to Headquarters, 1st Division, at Chaumont...up on the Marne," he added, starting to laugh. "You're supposed to report, first thing in the morning, or was that yesterday morning? Oh, who cares," he finished, closing his eyes.

"I see," James said, pleased at the disclosure. "I guess that means I won't be working for you anymore, then, sir?"

"That's right," the Lieutenant answered, and then passed out.

"Good," James spat, giving his horse a hard shot to the flanks. "Git up, you son of a bitch! I'm gonna give this little bastard the ride of his life," he screamed, taking off in a wild fury towards the post. James didn't bother with the courtesy of undoing the officer when they reached camp, but simply tied his horse, with the man still laced on its back, to a hitching rail in front of the officer's compound. St. Clair looked like a casualty that someone had retrieved from the front lines. No one cared to examine the dirty carcass hanging over the horse during the remainder of the night, assuming that he was just another dead soldier.

James proceeded to his tent, packed his belongings and caught a ride to Chaumont as quickly as possible. James had calculated that Lieutenant St. Clair would be appropriately displayed to the entire officer corps that morning, still straddling his horse in all his radiant majesty, as the other officers formed ranks for reveille.

James arrived at Chaumont late that afternoon, and he went immediately to the Headquarters for the 24th Hospital, reporting to the office of the company clerk. He set his gear down and walked to the back of the room where the NCOIC was sitting at his desk. He was nervous about reporting for duty without any orders. It wouldn't have been the first time that Lieutenant St. Clair had pulled one of his hoaxes on someone. However, in this case, after what he'd done to St. Clair, it probably would mean a firing squad for him if he had to return to Gondrecourt.

"Corporal Lavoisier, reporting as ordered."

"Yeah, we've been expecting you for two days, Lavoisier. Where the hell have you been? You were supposed to report here day before yesterday!"

James was a little taken back by the Sergeant's reaction, but said "Just trying to get here. It took awhile to find someone coming this way."

"Half a million troops pushing towards the front and you couldn't find anyone coming this way? That's great!"

The NCO rummaged through his drawer, finally pulling his hand out and throwing a pair of Sergeant chevrons across the desk.

"You better get these on before Colonel Everett gets down here. You're going up to the French Chasseur Division Field Hospital, at Neufchateau, tonight, with the Colonel."

"Where's that?" James asked.

The Sergeant looked up, perturbed at being disturbed again. "You'll know when you get there, Lavoisier; you'll smell it."

James scrunched down against the wall, finally falling asleep as he waited patiently for Colonel Everett to appear. An hour later he was awakened by a voice coming directly from above him.

"You Sergeant Lavoisier?" the voice asked.

James jumped to his feet, standing at brace as he answered, "Yes, sir."

"I'm Colonel Everett."

Everett's driver was standing in the shadows with luggage in each hand and a rifle hanging over his shoulder.

"You got a helmet and an overcoat, son?" Colonel Everett asked.

"No, sir," James replied.

Stephen D. Boyett

"All right, let's get out of here. We'll get you fixed up at the front. Lord knows we got enough equipment lying around up there."

It was dark by the time the driver turned onto the road out of Neufchateau, heading to the front lines outside of Charmes, near the Moselle. Staying on the road was difficult, at best, since the driver was denied the use of his headlights. The road, such as it was, was so bumpy it was impossible for James to sleep. He found himself airborne every few feet as the driver dodged one hole only to crash into another, concealed beneath the thick mud.

An unbelievable display of lights bounced across the horizon like a lightning storm on a Kansas prairie. A muffled drumbeat quickly followed each flash, echoing closer together until the thunderous sounds blended into a single roar.

The truck slowed and nearly stalled as a sentry approached from a pillbox on one side of the road. He glanced into the truck with a look of indifference, giving a signal to continue as he turned and disappeared back into his concrete hideout. A short distance later the truck geared down, forcing its occupants to lean forward as the transmission complained. James could barely make out the silhouette of a building in front of them beneath the flash from the barrage on the horizon. Eventually, the building vanished as the brilliant glow in the distance was absorbed by the blackness of the night.

They stopped a few feet from the front door of what was left of the building. James began to focus on a strange undulating movement on the ground, like grain in an uncut field moving back and forth in the wind.

Looking closer he realized that he was seeing hundreds of human beings lying in front of him on the ground, covered with blankets, hiding in the shadows as if they were star gazers, watching a passing constellation. But the morbid gathering was not there by choice.

When the deafening noise in the distance stopped the horrible scene in front of James became more defined. Men were crying out in pain from wounds received during the day's fighting. And, as the NCO at Chaumont had warned, the smell of death, permeating the air like open sewage, was his cue that he'd arrived at his destination.

98

"Stay close to me, Lavoisier," Everett ordered. "I don't understand their damn gibberish too good. Oh, no offense," he added. "I got nothin' against the Frenchies."

"I understand, sir," James politely replied.

James followed the Colonel inside the bombed-out building, stepping over soldiers sitting or lying on the stone floor. A flash from a match illuminated the room for an instant as an orderly lit a lamp next to a patient being hurriedly treated by a doctor and nurse. A French officer had met them at the door, leading the contingent through what had been the main sanctuary of an old gothic church. He slowed midway through the room, doffing his hat as a priest gave a dying soldier his last rites in the soft light of a candle off to one side of their path. The sweet acrid stench of decaying flesh hung in the air like a fog. James wanted to hold his breath until he found a pocket of fresh air somewhere in the building. There was no such place. The floor was slick with blood, mixed with mud and an occasional pool of vomit that almost glowed whenever light penetrated the darkened interior of the cathedral.

Just before they reached the other side of the great hall Everett turned, taking James aside from the others. "You'll sleep over there, Lavoisier. It's the best I can do for you. My quarters aren't much better," he added.

"All right, sir. I'm not sure I'll get much sleep...anyway, I'll make do."

"Headquarters is trying to pacify the French Command by offering a little medical aid to 'em. They're gonna show us, in the morning, what they're doin' here to take care of their wounded. We need to find out what they want in the way of supplies and help from our people. We've been ordered to send them whatever we can spare in equipment and personnel, especially since our medical people are sitting on their butts at Troyes and Dijon, with nothing to do but treat hemorrhoids and boils.

"Listen to what they want, take notes...and then I wanta get the hell outa here as early as we can," Everett said, wiping sweat from his face with a handkerchief.

James found a place to stretch out, knowing that sleep would be impossible under the circumstances. Colonel

Everett stayed in his quarters until time for the tour of the triage facility early the next morning.

Dawn brought an even more gruesome picture of the carnage that had taken place at the Chasseur Sector. Like the slaughter at Flesquie'res, the French had packed the trenches with men, filling the great earthen arteries to capacity for an offensive that ended in butchery by the German artillery fire before zero hour had commenced. So deadly was the aim of the Germans that the trenches were swimming in blood and flesh up to the troops' ankles.

A deathly calm lingered through the cold marble recesses of the medieval chantry. It was a peaceful stillness, quiet of the earlier sounds of men dying and those struggling to care for the dying. Rays of white light followed angular paths to the floor from the leaded glass windows high up in the stone walls. Cherubs floated in pastel hues on blue and white painted clouds, their naked bodies hovering in holy reverence above the gathering below. A thin film of smoke from the smoldering fireplace drifted over the stilled bodies, giving them a lifeless appearance like the stone effigies of warriors immortalized atop ancient sepulchers.

James realized that fatigue had solved the problem of not being able to make himself sleep in the macabre setting. He lay comfortably on the pallet he'd made for himself the night before, trying to slip back to a restful sleep until a strange noise disturbed him.

He turned towards the sound of men working a few feet away. It was a grisly scene as two soldiers lifted a man, stiff with rigor mortis, onto a stretcher, covering his face with a handkerchief as they carted him from the room.

Out of the shadows a young French officer approached his cot, gently tapping him on the shoulder, not aware that he was awake. He offered him breakfast in the officer's mess. James was grateful for any excuse to leave the sanctuary, his nostrils still filled with the stench of death from the night before.

James stood behind the empty chair in the dining area, hesitant to sit at the table. He was more aware of the dictates of protocol than Colonel Everett, who had already taken his seat, leaning over a plate of hot bread and sipping a cup of potent French coffee. Several ranking French officers finally sat down across the table, curious about the two Americans. Several of the men greeted James with a grin, watching him wait behind the chair for permission to be seated.

"Sit your ass down, will yah, Sergeant!" Colonel Everett ordered.

A priest sitting at the end of the table looked up, motioning for James to sit. He offered a little softer invitation, "s'il vous plaît mon ami, asseyez-vous!"

"Merci,...Pere," James replied with a smile.

The priest began to say grace. Everett continued eating until he realized what the priest was doing, then set his mug of coffee and piece of bread quickly back on his plate.

James took a census of expressions up and down the table as he waited for the priest to finish.

"Sergeant, you are Canadian?" one of the officers asked James in a heavy Parisian accent.

"No, sir," James answered, "I'm from Louisiana. My family is Creole."

"Ah, Creole," the officer repeated. "I was not aware that French was still spoken in America."

"Yes, it is very prevalent where I come from."

"Your dialect," the officer noted, "is very good."

"French is spoken most of the time where I grew up. English is spoken only when outsiders come," James said with a grin, getting a laugh from everyone at the table except Colonel Everett, who looked up, wondering what had inspired the laughter, since James and the others had been speaking in French.

"Perhaps," one of the officers started to say in broken English, directing his remark to Colonel Everett, "you'll help us defeat the Boche, the way our General Lafayette helped you with Les Britanniques at Yorktown, eh, Colonel?"

Everett mirrored the man's expression, relieved to have been included in the conversation. He held up his cup of coffee in a toasting gesture that was quickly returned by all of the Frenchmen at the table.

Colonel Everett was not a career Army officer. Like the majority of men in the 1st Division of the A.E.F., he was a volunteer from the civilian sector, a surgeon by profession. He had been given the responsibility of studying French medical and evacuation procedures. He hoped to find out what the years of combat had taught the French in dealing with their wounded. It was an enormous undertaking, laying the groundwork for America's medical treatment of its own troops throughout the entire front.

Unfortunately, the facility at the Chasseur Sector was anything but a model of advanced medical technology. Treatment was hurried and crude, supplies limited and evacuation to rear area hospitals nearly non-existent. Instead, it was an asylum where the grave registration teams worked their dreadful communion with the dead, serving the metal identification tags to the open mouths of the corpses before they were forced shut. Like Memling's painting of <u>The Last Judgment</u>, a thousand souls were lowered into the cold pits of the earth to wait for the resurrection, or the end of the war, whichever was to come first. Here the strain of war on France was obvious as so many young Frenchmen were buried without shoes or clothes.

James could hear the explosions of an artillery barrage bombarding the lines a short distance away. His friendly exchange with the French officers was interrupted as he concentrated on their faces, trying to determine the seriousness of the gunfire in the distance.

An orderly entered the room, handing Captain Caresse, the liaison officer, a message. He glanced at the paper, catching his breath as he read the note and then casually said to James in French, "Sergeant, if you will inform your Colonel, we should begin the tour immediately."

"Oui, Capitaine." James answered.

James and Colonel Everett followed Captain Caresse through the cluttered halls of the compound after leaving the neatly kept Officer's Mess. They descended a dark stairwell where the French surgeons were busily operating. The makeshift operating theater seemed appropriate for the butchery that was going on: James noticed that the tables were suspended across the ancient stone crypts of a burial chamber for the Catholic Order that had resided in the church for centuries.

Colonel Everett watched for a moment, and then lost interest, moving on to the next station on the tour. James stared with interest as Captain Caresse stepped over to one of the French surgeons, after making sure that the Colonel had left the room. Caresse whispered something to the doctor, who suddenly stopped what he was doing and ordered the other surgeons out of the area. As quickly as they'd left, several orderlies hurried into the room, gathering the instruments and supplies into canvas sacks, ignoring the anesthetized patients sprawled out on the makeshift gurneys.

James caught up with the tour that was waiting at a temporary ward, set up in the narthex of the monastery. He looked back at the door to the operating room, concerned over what had just happened. The group stopped every few feet of their rounds while Colonel Everett took a moment to examine a patient, pulling back a blanket to reveal an undressed wound. Each time, Everett swore and then continued on to the next patient. James noticed the French officers staring back over their shoulders, towards the sounds of the incoming artillery, nervous about the slow pace that the Colonel was setting in the ward.

"Come over here, Lavoisier, and find out what this fella is askin' me," Everett ordered.

James leaned over the man, accepting his shaking hand. He bent down with his ear next to the man's parched lips. The dying soldier finished his message and then kissed James' outstretched hand.

'Wha'd he say?" Everett demanded to know.

"He said, we're the angels of God...and that he praises the Holy Father for sending us to save France from the Boche."

James shook his head, disgusted with his own helplessness.

The soldier kept nodding his head, his eyes nearly closed from his pain, a single tear sliding from his right eye. He was still holding James' hand with an unrelenting grip as his eyes suddenly widened and his bottom jaw dropped open. A priest, dressed in his vestment, ignored the conversation of the doctors and began administering the last rites to the soldier even before James could loosen the dead man's grip.

James couldn't help but gawk at the lifeless figure, realizing that the suffering look on his face had miraculously disappeared with his final breath. The priest had closed the eyes and mouth, leaving the man looking as if he were taking an afternoon nap.

"Angels of God? Not in this place!" Everett announced, tersely interrupting James' thoughts.

They continued walking between the rows of men lying bunched on the floor in tight cocoons made from their gray service blankets. Again, James noticed Caresse whispering to the orderlies and doctors in the ward. Again, his words sent them fleeing towards the medical supplies stored in the room. A few clerks began pulling blankets off the wounded, throwing them in a heap near the front door.

Colonel Everett looked up, studying what was happening, and then, as if ignoring what he'd seen, went on about his business. James was mortified. Even Caresse made no effort at that point to stop the looting of the wounded. As the party began filing out of the sanctuary, James took a final look behind him, watching the medical staff vanish with the last of the supplies.

The pandemonium outside confirmed James' suspicions about what was happening as he saw the lorries being loaded with the equipment and supplies stripped from the wounded by the staff. Hundreds of casualties were wandering everywhere, unassisted. They had fanned out through the fields, urged on by the staccato beat of the creeping barrage coming closer every minute.

James turned towards Everett as their French escort directed them to a waiting truck.

"Colonel Everett, I don't understand why we're leaving these people behind!" James screamed, trying to be heard over the roar of the artillery.

"We're not doing anything, Sergeant! This is a <u>French</u> operation; these are <u>French</u> troops. There's nothing I can do!" he replied.

"But these people will die...they'll all die!" James pleaded.

Everett didn't answer, but instead stepped up into the truck with Caresse and the other staff members.

"Get on the truck, Sergeant; that's an order!" Everett shouted.

James hesitated, looking back, listening to the pleading men who were being left behind. Shells were landing nearer, moving over the landscape like a gray and black forest, springing up from the fields behind the church. James could see men, already pitifully maimed from the previous day's battle, crawling away from the blast on their hands and knees. The French driver revved the engine as he grew impatient to get away from the deadly hail of explosives that by now were landing only a few hundred yards away.

"I don't understand what the hell this is all about, sir? What kind of chicken shit son of a bitch leaves his own men behind like this?" James demanded to know.

"What it's about, Sergeant," Colonel Everett said quickly, "is that the French can't afford to lose the few precious medical supplies they have left, or their doctors. It's priorities. Now get your ass on this truck."

"But, sir?" James tried to interrupt.

"No, you listen to me! They haven't got the equipment or time to transport those poor devils to the rear. They either leave the doctors or leave the patients."

"But Gawd damn it, sir, the Germans will murder those men. They're not gonna take care of French wounded!" James shouted.

"Don't you think these men know that, boy? Caresse and his men have been up to their necks, struggling against these murdering bastards a hell'uva lot longer than we have."

"Colonel, please, we must go!" Caresse pleaded.

"I'm tellin' you for the last time, get in this Gawd damn truck, and that's an order!" Everett commanded.

"Sorry, sir, I can't do that," James said, grabbing one of the fleeing wounded and helping him into the truck in his place.

James backed away from the rear gate of the truck, saluting Colonel Everett as he stepped backwards.

"I'll make it back as quickly as I can, sir," James announced as he turned and headed for the main body of men pouring out across the fields.

"Let it go, Sergeant!" Everett screamed as the truck pulled away, drowning out his voice.

James ignored him, instead helping a wounded soldier pull himself up off the ground, the two of them moving as quickly as possible away from the deadly fusillade.

The trip up to the front lines and the Chasseur Sector had been uneventful. In the dark there had been little to see but the eerie star shells with their ghostly phosphorous glow, descending to earth far in the distance over the trenches to be quenched in a sea of darkness. It had seemed so peaceful at night, leaving the picture of the landscape to one's imagination, never giving so much as a hint that the beauty had been stolen by the horrors of war. The trip back, during the daylight, was much more revealing.

James looked at the grisly scene as he walked. The French countryside was devastated. It was naked and scorched, churned into a man-made cesspool of mud and pieces of equipment. The beautiful rolling hills, once covered in green grass, had dissolved beneath a quagmire of gray mud. Torn parts of mules and horses littered the earth, animals destroyed in the melee of a dozen battles fought over the same turf. Everywhere men lay dead or dying, etching their faces into James' mind like a terrible dream, lingering on the ground in front of him to receive death without the glory that was promised in his heroic vision of war.

For five miles James watched the French Army retreating before the German offensive in an endless line, pacing themselves by the sounds of the enemy artillery. He stood in a stupor, horrified and disillusioned at the dishonor of what he was seeing. He felt betrayed by his preconceived notions of the virtues of war, frightened at the hollowed expressions of the men passing like zombies in review, accepting their fate without further resistance.

James wondered where the battle flags were, the trumpets and rows of committed soldiers, bayonets gleaming, charging towards the enemy to avenge their honor. Instead, he saw men crying, burned and torn, stripped of their beautiful uniforms and colors, with the spirit to fight sapped from their bodies. Most of them walked on by, ignoring him, dragging their weapons in the mud. Some stopped to look back, others simply made a decision to lie down and die beside the road.

The men walking along the highway were forced to give way to caissons and wagons being repositioned to support the retreat. James could see a dry mound of dirt, adjacent to the road, crowded with fifty to sixty men like seals on an island. Some of the men were coughing and gagging as blood oozed from their mouths from a phosgene gas attack earlier that morning. He knew they would drown in their own blood before nightfall.

Another group of men was more interested in a freshly killed mule than they were in the wounded and dying. Food was much scarcer than death. The men were hurriedly skinning the mule for the fresh meat, the first they'd had in days. Twenty feet away, more soldiers were huddled over a small fire burning from a wrecked wagon. They were heating water to make themselves a diluted cup of coffee, ignoring a half-dozen corpses lying nearby.

James let his thoughts drift back to his home at Lalleville; the beauty, the green lush woods and the tranquility seemed so distant. He felt he'd never live to experience its wonderful solitude again, not after having endured this hell.

A few days later James was ordered to Beauvais to accompany Colonel Everett on a tour of the hospital of Le Legion des Etrangers. It was a model facility, dedicated to the Foreign Legion that had served so gallantly to the last man at Douaumont, in the Battle of Verdun.

James found Colonel Everett to be coldly pragmatic, unscathed by the events at the Neufchateau, or so it seemed. Everett had seen it all before. He was tempered to the cruelty of combat, having found a way in his mind to anesthetize its effects. No one, still sane, could ever become used to such slaughter.

After the performance of the French Army at Neufchateau, James' expectations for the Legion Hospital were anything but bright and hopeful. He'd developed an instant resentment for the very people that he'd grown up to love and respect. He was appalled at their ruthlessness with their own wounded, the cold decisiveness with which they relieved themselves of the responsibility of care. He still didn't understand...not yet.

Arriving at the medical facility at Beauvais, he was dumbfounded by the inconsistency of what he saw. The grounds were meticulously groomed and landscaped with beautiful flowers. It was such a serene setting compared to the churned nightmare he'd experienced only days earlier.

They were greeted at the entrance to the hospital by a matronly nun garbed in a white habit with a red cross embroidered on front and back of her matching tablier. The stark white habit almost glowed in the dimly lit corridor, giving the woman a celestial air. This seraph greeted the men with a brief, businesslike introduction, her hands poised as if in preparation for prayer as she turned and led them through the polished marble hall to the wards. Her mannerisms left no doubt that she and the other nuns were fully confident in their duties. It was a remarkable change from the triage fiasco on the outskirts of Charmes.

James was surprised to see how well the French had organized the expansive hospital complex. The facility had clean, efficient wards, well staffed with nurses and doctors eager to provide quality care to their wounded. 'What a strange contrast to the chaos at the front,' James thought. Everywhere he looked he saw an abundance of workers cleaning and sterilizing the interior of the hospital. Men and women were scrubbing and painting, boiling and washing anything that would touch a patient. Nuns and orderlies kept a brisk pace, moving quietly through the wards to bathe and bandage those in their care.

James flanked Colonel Everett as they were joined by the host members of the medical staff. Occasionally they would attract another doctor here and there as their tour de force shuffled farther through the hospital wards. The group became a sizable contingent of doctors, each lobbying for their own particular needs of medical supplies from the Americans. They were desperate to capitalize on the medical entente between the countries, but what they didn't want was advice or interference from the Americans on how to run their hospitals.

James was struck by another revelation. It was obvious that the French were not as hopelessly unqualified to administer care to the wounded as he had previously been led to believe. Even Everett readily confessed that he had expected to find archaic medical procedures being performed by an ill-trained staff, but instead found the French to be every bit as proficient as their American counterparts. In some cases, the French were far more advanced in their care of certain difficult and complicated cases. They had, after all, been at war, dealing with enormous losses, long before America had joined the struggle.

The tradeoff came with the French allowing the Americans to observe their methods and use French personnel to train them in triage and rear echelon care. The short of it was that the French had not found any particular relief from the American presence except for the abundance of supplies provided to them by the A.E.F. Quartermasters. It was the French who were the teachers and the Americans the students, despite what the press back home would have had the people believe. The Americans were as ill prepared for front line surgery as they were for battle. James had become an overnight success with both his own contingent and the French staff, when it was discovered that he was attuned to French protocol along with being adept in the French language. His quick intervention into problems as they arose overcame much of the misunderstandings generated between the Americans and their French hosts.

The lessons learned at Beauvais by the Americans were soon put to use as the A.E.F. prepared for its first offensive, planned for a sector northeast of Lune'ville, on September 20, 1917.

James was ordered to the front with the rest of his company to implement what they had learned from the French about establishing dressing stations. He was ordered to transport medical supplies to the forward lines and assist Colonel Everett in overseeing the construction of rear area hospitals and morgues to handle incoming casualties from the front.

A meeting of officers and NCO's was held by Colonel Everett, the night before the attack. James and the men were served an unusually tasty meal and even a ration of French wine as they gathered to listen to the briefing in a large tent set up near the lines.

"Stretcher bearers will go over with the second wave at 06:45 hours," Everett announced. "They'll stay with the assault throughout the advance to retrieve casualties. Our barrage will lift at 06:20 hours and should hopefully have cleared most of the entanglements in our line of advance."

"It looks like good weather for it, Colonel," someone shouted from the rear of the grouping, causing a burst of nervous laughter from the men.

Everett smiled, "That's a good point. Be sure that your men have their bearings before they leave our wire. Make sure they have compasses and know where they're heading. Wire gates will be marked by each Company NCO before the men go over. "Your men will find yourselves working in fog and smoke from the artillery. Your landmarks may be wiped out instantly if the Germans launch a counterattack," Everett advised each of them as he moved over to a map to point out the various openings in the wire.

"What about French wounded, sir?"

"If you start stumbling over their troops, you're too far off to the left of our lines. Stay in our operational zone! I repeat, don't let your men straggle off to either side: they'll get their asses shot off by the Poilu. The French don't know our uniforms from the Germans'."

"We're a hell'uva lot prettier, sir!" someone shouted.

Again, the gathering broke into laughter.

"Pick up your wounded," Everett continued, "and get back to the dressing station."

"What about the counteroffensive, sir? When do we pull back?"

"I don't want anybody left out there! The Germans have made a nasty habit of cutting up wounded when they want to let you know how pissed off they are. They'll want to give us an especially friendly welcome," Colonel Everett added.

Another officer sitting next to Everett stood up and whispered something in his ear.

"Oh, yes," Colonel Everett was reminded, "keep your gas masks with you. Intelligence has it that the Germans have chlorine and phosgene gas tubes buried in front of their lines. They'll soak the whole area if they think they're gettin' their butts kicked. If they hit us with gas, stay out of the trenches. The Gawd damn stuff will hang down there forever. You'll do better to take your chances on top."

James jettisoned a golfball-sized wad of tobacco into the rain gutter running around the edge of the tent. He pulled dirt over the black stain with his boot as he contemplated what Everett had just said.

Most of the men were scared. James was scared and, even more, fully aware of the stark realism of battle. He'd seen it all before, however short the experience may have been; the others hadn't. Most of them had come from what had been dubbed the 'bon secteur ', the good life to the rear.

He'd sequestered a forty-five automatic from supply, concealing it beneath his tunic, determined not to be defenseless in the event he was wounded and confronted by

Germans. He'd already seen something of how the French treated casualties under certain circumstances and he wasn't sure about his own officers. He sure as hell wasn't going to be still while some German butchered him with a bayonet, if his own men were ordered to leave the wounded.

They began their approach to the trenches under a moonlit night, passing into a treeless void that resembled an open expanse of ocean. They reached the trenches early in the morning, being guided to their positions by French pathfinders ordered to make sure that the Americans were properly positioned in the lines.

The first light of morning revealed a pulverized landscape, churned into a full spectrum of gray-brown clay, pockmarked with gaping craters and pools of black mud. The open fields in front of the trenches resembled a junkyard hit by a tornado. The trenches themselves were lined with heavy woven mats that supported the earthen walls, preventing cave-ins from the shock of enemy shells landing near the lips of the revetments. The fortifications were a virtual city, a maze of rooms stacked one on top of the other that provided the troops with a crude and uncomfortable form of shelter from the incessant rain and cold. The small caverns where the men huddled were more useful in stopping shrapnel than for keeping out the more natural elements.

Ribbons of trenches snaked in tight curves for miles. They were carved deeply into the ground, out of sight from German snipers. Only the balloon observers, anchored high above the lines on both sides, were privy to movements in the burrows beneath them.

James mounted a foot stand on the wall, giving him the height to peek through a gun port in the sandbagged parapet. He could see a haze lying over the field. Red swirls seemed to spin upwards from the ground, an illusion formed by the rusting concertina wire strung artfully in curls or straight strands for miles across the uneven horizon. Thousands of fenceposts, resembling columns of soldiers drilling in the open field, in defiance of death, were disbursed in what seemed an oddly undisciplined maneuver. They were there, in fact, to keep the wire from being torn out of position during the continuous barrages. Forward fire bunkers sat isolated in front of the trenches looking like small rafts, set out into the rough seas of mud.

By first light of morning, the enemy observers had taken notice of the activity in the American trenches and directed a massive barrage onto their positions. James was still watching the German lines, a quarter of a mile away, when the first rounds were lobbed at the American defenses. James was blown backwards from his perch, finding himself with a slight nosebleed even though the shell had landed more than fifty yards away.

The fusillade continued through the morning and late into the afternoon keeping the inexperienced army in a jitter. By afternoon, the nerves of the Americans were frayed to the breaking point and their strength sapped by the enemy action.

James' company was kept on the line for several more days as everyone waited patiently in the Einville Sector for something to happen. Nothing did. The Germans played a waiting game, exchanging round for round with the American artillery. A counteroffensive never came. The Americans used the opportunity to probe the German lines, documenting coordinates of the enemy gun emplacements and trenches.

Most of the men stood with their hearts in their throats as individuals were selected for stretcher duty to move over the top with the assault troops. James had little choice in the matter. He had been assigned to lead a squad of men at the personal request of Colonel Everett.

James tried to mask his absolute terror over what was coming. It wasn't the fear of battle or even dying so much as being wounded and left in no-man's land to linger for days, or being hung up in the wire to starve or die of thirst. He had stopped several times to vomit his rations into the mud. The anticipation of the attack and the smell of death floating in the confining ditch left all of the men constantly retching.

Word was received that an attack was on, and as the hour approached, James' squad huddled behind two rows of infantry preparing to scale the walls. The soldiers were standing pressed against each other with their heads bowed, trying to shield themselves from the dirt and debris raining down from the barrage in front of them. Here and there a man would sag to the ground, his face bloodied from the concussion of a detonating shell. As he folded onto the floor of the trench the shock of landing in the cold greenish water would spark enough life back into the soldier that he would pull himself back up against the wall or sit stunned on the crowded wooden planking running the length of the coverture.

Suddenly the massive cannonade stopped, leaving a stillness that caught everyone off guard. The squad leaders sprinted through the trench, barking commands for the troops to prepare to ascend the scaling ladders set into the walls.

High-pitched whistles blared as the men pressed against each other, trying to move up and out of the narrow fortification into the open stretch of field ahead of them. The Americans screamed excitedly as they raced forward, breaching the wire, anticipating the first sounds of incoming shells that would signal their entry into the killing zone.

James had perched himself back up on the foot stand on the inside of the trench wall to watch the lines advance, after the first wave had gone over the top. Smoke canisters were dropping ahead of the uneven waves of men, drifting aimlessly over the field, doing little to interfere with the marksmanship of the German gunners.

A creeping barrage slammed into the ground, moving in a precise pattern through the entire depth of the Americans. The concussion from the explosions were killing men fifty yards from the blast, throwing them into the air like toy figures tossed by a belligerent child. Officers moved across the advance beckoning the siegers forward and shouting orders to those reluctant to move up. Other officers were turning men back who were headed in the wrong direction.

As the survivors of the first wave emerged from the dense smoke, a different sound replaced the roar of the artillery. A repetitive tapping of machine gun fire replaced the heavier bombardment, raking the remaining troops. The second wave passed into the smoke screen, disappearing from sight into the thick clouds that hung over the field, obstructing James' view of the attack.

For thirty minutes the firing continued, and then it stopped, except for the random crack of a sniper's rifle or a short burst from a machine gun, tapping out its Morse code over the expanse of open ground. And then it was quiet. The black and gray clouds of burnt powder still hovered over the battleground.

The stretcher-bearers worked their way over the pulverized soil, struggling with each step to find ground solid enough to support their weight as they slipped and sank in the ooze. James led a party of men past the initial casualties to retrieve those closest to the German lines.

Men lay everywhere, twisted into grotesque forms. Many were squirming and crying for help. Pieces of clothing and bodies spotted the ground. Body parts extended up from the mud like tree stumps, a foot, a leg, an upper torso, still smoldering from the shellfire.

James moved past the chaotic assortment of debris, ignoring the gruesome evidence of the struggle, checking each body he found for signs of life. He felt the torso for a pulse, like a man trying to select a good watermelon from a field of rotting fruit. Once he'd located a soldier with a pulse, he'd motion for the stretcher-bearers to move forward and shag the man back to an aid station.

Far too often he'd find a soldier, unmarred by bullet or shrapnel, appearing to have slipped into an afternoon nap, except for the tell-tale marks of concussion. When he was within a few hundred yards of the German lines he decided to slip into a shallow crater to give himself a moment to rest. He crawled, head first, down the gently sloping wall, righting himself, and then rolling over on his back once he found the bottom. A mist that had fallen most of the afternoon accumulated on his face, cooling his skin. The film on his skin turned to a black mud as he tried to wipe away the dirt.

He leaned back, closing his eyes, begging for a moment of sleep. He wanted more than anything to escape the insanity that was going on all around him, if only for a moment.

"I will lay me down in peace, and sleep: for thou, Lord, only makest me dwell in safety," James whispered from his memory of the Psalms. But he was unable to let himself drift into the sleep he so desperately craved.

He lay still, quietly pleading for rest, drifting in and out of a shallow catnap. He awoke with each report from the explosions in the distance. After each blast he would return to his restless trance, seeing himself in his mother's arms, being stroked with her smooth hand across his forehead. She was rocking him back and forth, singing a verse from her favorite hymn, "Are Ye Able." His body relaxed and he felt secure. A wonderfully euphoric feeling passed over him as he watched his mother mouth the words. It was as if he were somewhere else other than her arms, watching from an elevated vantage, seeing her more peaceful than he ever had remembered.

But suddenly, he heard a sound that brought him out of his dream. He'd seen several German patrols during the day crossing the field looking for prisoners to interrogate.

His hand reached for the pistol wedged in his belt. He lay as still as possible as his other hand cocked the action back far enough to assure him that it was charged with a round. "Oh God, make them leave!" he prayed. He squeezed himself down farther into the bottom of the crater, his mind racing with thoughts of whether to hide himself or make a dash for it, shooting his way out as he went.

"It'll be better for me if they kill me on the run," he thought. "If they take me down here, they'll cut me to pieces trying to make me talk. Nobody u'll ever find me."

A myriad of scents, heavy with the weight of smoke, drifted across the crater, plummeting to the bottom as they abandoned the gentle nudge of the wind. The smoke drifted across him like a blanket. At first he thought he smelled mustard gas, or worse, phosgene. He reacted, crawling up, trying to push his face above the cloud. But he quickly realized that he was smelling burning cloth or perhaps flesh. He knew he would have been dead or at least strangling by that time if it had been gas.

He regained his composure, deciding that he would go mad if he lay in the bottom of the pit any longer. He had to move, even if it meant facing the enemy.

The sounds from outside of the shell hole came again. First there was a scratching sound and then a tapping, over and over again. It was a soniferous click that sent James into a rage. He was determined to put an end to the taunting that had been going on now for several minutes.

His finger strained at the trigger as he clawed his way to the top of the hole. He was no longer concerned about keeping his presence hidden. He fell prostrate on the ground, clasping both hands around the butt of his pistol. He aimed the barrel quickly and determinedly in the direction of the sound, hammer back, ready to fire.

115

The light from the afternoon sun had gone, giving way to a light gray haze, accentuated by dark shadows filling the deep recesses in the ground. He looked straight ahead, not believing what he saw. At first he thought he was still caught up in his dreams. Nothing seemed to make sense anymore, especially the sight that was before him.

A man, a thing, was squatted down immediately in front of the crater. The creature ignored the threat of the pistol, totally oblivious to James' presence. It was methodically picking pieces of burned skin from itself. The form stopped to scratch its exposed legs and stomach, then continued to pull at the patches of skin hanging off its naked body. With each piece removed, a splotch of pinkish flesh was exposed giving the creature the look of some speckled demon.

James watched as the figure finally became aware that he was pointing his pistol at him. The poor hideous soul, still in a squatting position, backed up a few inches, wavering back and forth as it studied James' face. The areas of skin around the man's eyes were a contrasting pinkish color, apparently shielded from whatever it was that had blown away the uniform and burned the man's flesh. All of the hair had been singed off his head.

James made a growling sound as he tried to frighten away whoever, or whatever, was confronting him. The gargoyle wiped its eyes, studying James before suddenly leaping to its feet and sprinting off a few yards. Then the man stopped, standing up with his arms above his head, as if in surrender, or else pleading to be shot—James wasn't sure. He looked back at James, and let out a heart-wrenching moan.

James realized that the man was in agony from his wounds. The flames from the explosion had burned the man's throat and lungs, and he was pleading the only way he could for James to stop his suffering. But after realizing that he was not going to shoot, the man turned and began running down the middle of no-man's land. James knew that sooner or later someone would grant his wish.

James had left the crater and moved to a point where the Americans had over-run a network of German trenches. When he located the captured trenches, he slid over the breastworks, hanging onto the wooden planks supporting the walls, and let himself slowly down to the bottom. He was sweating from the ordeal. His clothes were wet from the mud in the crater, and a chill sent him shivering as he bent over to catch his breath.

After moving a few yards down the crevasse, he began to find dead and wounded from both sides. Bodies and equipment were strewn up and down the narrow channel. Those that could still fight had squatted down against the wall, bayonets fixed, waiting for orders to attack.

Before he could analyze the situation, the officer in charge moved the men over the top, leaving James to fend for himself with the casualties. Using the few minutes of light that was left, James pawed over the bodies, trying to comfort the casualties as best he could. He separated the dead from the wounded, laying those who were alive in the center of the trench in preparation for stretcher bearers that he hoped would come during the dark of night.

When he'd finished, he felt his way down the trough to the entrance of a pillbox he'd seen earlier. He stepped carefully down the ladder leading to the floor of the cave, then, once inside, he blindly fingered the walls for an oil lamp that he knew would be somewhere near the entrance.

The rats already had taken advantage of the absence of anyone being home. They were gorging themselves on particles of food left behind by the Germans. James moved to the corner of the room, grabbing as many discarded blankets as he could. He shook out the lice and rat droppings and then curled up on them, quickly falling asleep.

His rest was uninterrupted for several hours—no dreams, no sounds of battle, nothing to disturb his much-needed rest. It was warm in the earthen room, cozy and sheltering from a cold breeze that had begun blowing in the pre-dusk hours. Even the rats had declared a truce, for the moment, climbing into the cave to warm themselves after an evening of gorging themselves on human flesh. But his deep, coma-like sleep was short-lived, and he was jolted back to consciousness by the report from first one, then another, gun being fired just outside the entrance to the bunker. Screams, accentuated by the clanging of shovels, churned and mixed with the clatter of metal against metal, and the hollow gurgling of men giving up their lives as they fell to the floor of the trench.

The Germans had launched a counteroffensive, successfully retaking their line. James could hear the Germans talking outside as they moved the dead out of the blood-soaked trench. Then a quick succession of pistol shots let him know they had disposed of some of the wounded.

He wondered how long it would be before they'd come down into the chamber looking for food or blankets. Just as the unwanted prospect began to set in, a body suddenly slid unceremoniously down the stepladder, landing sprawled in the rectangular reflection of sunlight, cutting through the entrance and onto the floor. The man's head was all but decapitated, leaving the poor soldier in a grotesque pose with his arms reaching outward into the air, and his head hung off his neck like a bloody rucksack.

James crouched down, moving towards the exit, trying to see if there was any chance for him to break for it. He crept up the ladder and stuck his head out, only to be blinded by the intensity of the sunlight. No sooner had he turned his head to avoid the stinging glare than a rifle butt caught him across the face, launching him down to the floor of the room and into the waiting arms of the headless body.

Fortunately, it was dark enough that the German couldn't see to finish him off without climbing down into the room. The man stepped cautiously down the ladder, bayonet first, delivering a stab as he became confused in his momentary blindness and confronted the body lying at his feet. James took advantage of the moment to retreat to the darkest recess of the room, slipping down behind a heavy wooden bench. The blow he'd taken across his forehead had left a gash over his left eye. Blood was pouring from the wound, draining over his face. The shock of the blow had blurred his vision and stunned him enough that he was having problems, for the moment, trying to keep from passing out.

Once the German realized he'd skewered the wrong prize, he fumbled farther into the room, probing with his bayonet each step of the way for his elusive enemy. James could only assume that it had become a matter of some priority for the man to kill him, since he'd made no attempt to call for help. He waited, drawing a bead on the German as he moved blindly towards him, still unable to see him crouched down behind the bench.

As soon as the German came between James and the lighted entrance, James stood, leveling his .45 automatic at point blank range at the man's face and squeezed the trigger. The recoil from the blast kicked the weapon upward as James fired two successive rounds. Each shot gave off an orange flame that pierced the darkness, crossing the few feet to its target. The sound in the room was deafening, making it impossible for him to hear anything for a few seconds. Outside, the sound of artillery landing near the trenches was worse, masking James' handiwork below ground.

There was no doubt that the German was dead. He'd been thrown backwards and his feet had buckled beneath him, leaving him spread-eagled next to the decapitated carcass of the other soldier. Both men were framed by the sunlight shining down like a stage lamp set over a crude picture frame. The German had a look of disbelief, appearing to be laughing at the surprise ending to his life. The bullets from James' weapon had taken off the side of his head, leaving his brains steaming on the wall behind him.

James leaped up the ladder, stopping only long enough to be sure the way was clear. The artillery had intensified, pounding the trench system and forcing the Germans to take cover. He eased himself over the revetment, still partially blinded from the blood pouring from the wound above his eye. The shelling became worse with each passing second, and James knew it was the prelude to a counterattack by the Americans. He decided that his only chance for survival was to get out of the fire zone as quickly as possible, keeping low enough to avoid the Germans at his back.

He stood up and began running from crater to crater, trying to stay out of the sights of the German machine-gunners.

Heavy smoke from the box barrage provided enough cover for James to escape unscathed from the field immediately in front of the trench.

As he neared the wire, he stumbled over a soldier leaning up against an entanglement post, holding on to what was left of his right leg. He'd been wounded in the first wave, only a hundred yards from his own lines.

James moved into the shell hole, landing on his side next to the man. He looked back over his shoulder at the barrage, trying to estimate how long it would be before the saturation shelling would catch up with them. He made no effort to introduce himself, as the explosions were getting too close to take time for social amenities.

James used the man's putee from his other leg to tie a tourniquet around the stump. When he'd done the best he could to stop the bleeding, he hoisted the man over his shoulder and started out for the aid station at a jog.

He'd barely cleared the edge of a second shell hole when the man suddenly went wild, kicking and screaming. It was impossible for James to move, with the load shifting around on his back, ranting and raving about his severed leg. With the amount of blood the man had lost, the struggle was short-lived. James shifted his load one more time and then continued towards the field dressing station with his unconscious patient.

James found himself a place to stretch out near the field kitchen after he'd delivered the wounded man to the hospital, and he had the cut over his eye sutured. He sipped a cup of coffee from a tin cup as he reflected on the events during the battle. At this point he really didn't care who'd won or lost; all he wanted was to sleep. His mind kept replaying the image of the German that he'd killed. He knew it was fatigue, but still he couldn't clear his mind of what had happened. He could see the man's face staring up at him with his ghastly look of surprise, an expression of disbelief, almost a smile.

His thought drifted to the naked man, burned and deafened from a firestorm that had engulfed him. He wondered if he was an American or Frenchman, and if someone finally had served up the coup de grâce to finish off the poor bastard.

He'd never dreamed that war would be this way. There was no honor in this, no glory. He'd never believed that men could die so unceremoniously, so cruelly, so easily. He fell asleep, still holding half a cup of hot coffee that leaked into the soil beside him as his hand relaxed.

CHAPTER 6

After the Americans had been withdrawn from the front, James was reassigned to an ambulance squadron transporting casualties from the field hospital at Bourmount to a joint Allied hospital located on the outskirts of Paris. He'd lucked into the convoy duty because of his talents as an interpreter, sparing himself the more arduous labors of camp life. The camps were boring and routinely tedious as the Americans trained in preparation for another combined Allied offensive. But, in typical military fashion, most of the time was spent waiting for something, anything, to happen.

James had decided to take advantage of being assigned to the hospital outside of Paris to see if he could locate the young private that he'd retrieved from no-man's land several weeks earlier. He was feeling the effects of fatigue and was depressed from the experience at Lunéville. He was still mildly traumatized from the horrible slaughter he'd witnessed.

As his mind had so often done before with others that he had given aid to on the battlefield, his thoughts now focused on the young amputee. He found himself visualizing the young man as a symbolic image of all of those he had seen wounded, feeling the pangs of guilt as soldiers often do when they're spared from death or injury in place of their comrades.

When he entered the ward he was shocked for a moment by the incredible number of casualties lining the sterile marble hallways. Patients were convalescing in every foot of the grandiloquent interior of the ancient hospital. The gore and butchery cluttered the stylish hallway, as if their decorator had finally gone mad, following the rest of the world into insanity.

Stretchers were substituted when beds were not available, some being placed beneath the beds of other patients to make enough room for the medical staff to walk. In a few cases only the stench of death finally brought a call for attention to those unlucky souls.

James found his way to the amputee ward, where he was directed to the bed of the young soldier. He quietly pulled up a chair, listening to the bell tower musically chime the hour as he studied the young man's sleeping face. It was depressing

121

to contemplate what life would bring for the young soldier when he returned home. His mind moved beyond the short-lived honors that would be bestowed upon the wounded warrior. Instead, he tried to visualize the long-term effects of the man's self-sacrifice.

He studied the sleeping boy, trying to experience for himself the malaise, the anguish his loved ones would feel when they saw him without his leg. For a moment he prayed that somehow he could absorb their pain, to promise them that things would work out for the best, but he wasn't God.

The young man's eyes opened, struggling to clear his vision. He turned his head towards the stranger. After a moment he smiled.

"How are ya, Sarge?"

"I can't complain...how about yourself?" James answered.

"Oh, I guess I'm doin' fine. Are you the one who brought me in?"

"Yeah," James replied.

"I thought it was you. They told me at the aid station that your name is Lavoisier," he added.

James returned the boy's smile as he answered, "Lucky for you I was takin' a little afternoon stroll."

"Yeah, some stroll."

James looked out the window, at a loss for something else to say.

"I'm Peter,...Peter Lang," the young man said.

"Nice to meet you, Peter. I'm James Lavoisier," James replied extending his hand.

"I give you that bruise over your eye?" the young man inquired.

James felt the sutured line above his eye with his finger. "Naw...I had a little run in with a German 'fore I stumbled into you."

The private closed his eyes, turning his face towards the ceiling. "Wouldn't yah know it...I never even got to fire a shot at 'em before the bastards got me."

"It doesn't matter," James said, "you did fine."

"I sure wished you'd found that leg of mine!" Lang said abruptly.

James was a little taken back. Finally, not knowing what to say, he apologized for not retrieving the severed limb.

"I didn't mean to embarrass you, Sarge. It wasn't the damn leg I wanted; it was my boot," Lang said, casting a Cheshire grin up at James.

"Your boot? What the hell did you want the boot for?" James asked.

"My pay," Lang answered. "That boot was full of my Army pay. It was everything I had in the world. I was savin' up to get me a start when I got home."

"I'm real sorry, Peter."

"Oh, it don't matter...not now. But, you know what I been thinking, Sarge?"

"No, what's that?"

"It's kinda funny..." Lang chuckled, "some damn Hiney u'll find my stump wrapped in money out there somewhere and start a rumor that all of us Yanks are rich. Hell, they'll be shooting us like they're goin' after Kewpie dolls in a shootin' gallery." He broke into a laugh.

James joined in, relieved to have a break in the unsettling conversation.

"Thanks for takin' care of me, Sarge. I owe yah!"

James patted him on the shoulder as he stood up to leave. He started to ask him where he was from so that he could write to him after the war, then realized that Peter had fallen asleep. There would be too many to write to as it was. He stood holding his cap with both hands, looking down at the young man's face, impressed with his courage. On impulse he pulled out a wad of cash from his pocket and pushed it under Lang's pillow.

"I can't make up for the leg, but I guess I can help with the money. It's sure not much of a consolation," he whispered, backing away towards the muted light in the hallway. "Adieu, my young friend...Godspeed!"

James saw action at the Marne Salient south of Saissons and again during the Saint Miheil Offensive that started in mid-August of 1918.

The trip up to the front near St. Miheil had been relatively quiet as the ambulance made its way between the endless columns of advancing troops. Roads, supposedly reinforced, had long before given way under the weight of the thousands of pieces of artillery and heavy lorries. Craterous voids in the dirt highway punished the lighter trucks. Skeletons of abandoned equipment bordered the road, providing the first grim reminder of what lay ahead and how quickly the war could move over the landscape.

James stared at the tranquil horizon as he bounced with each heave of the ambulance. He wondered if the Germans knew they were coming. 'For God's sake,' he thought, 'how could they miss this many men moving towards them in broad daylight?' He watched the smoke from the trucks as it moved with the wind hurling white and gray clouds into the air, a trail that led directly towards the front.

Their progress in the ambulance was slow going, but still faster than walking. The troops always gave them the right of way out of respect if not pure reverence for the vehicle's mission.

The advancing column faltered in their movement as James and his driver neared the artillery revetments just behind the French sector. The troops had stopped, blocking the road so that James' vehicle was forced to come to a complete halt. A French non-commissioned officer, riding a muddied cavalry mount and waving a saber, bulled his way between the men, separating their fused ranks back into neat, orderly lines as he screamed orders in French and then English. Finally the march began, as the men lost interest in the distraction that had brought the columns to a standstill.

James broke from his trance as the ambulance came into sight of a group of men that everyone had been watching as the columns marched the last few hundred yards to the trenches. A company of French Moroccan Zouaves was formed up into a firing squad some twenty feet from the road. They were preparing to execute several soldiers that were standing immediately in front of them. The prisoners were wearing unusually muddy uniforms, making it difficult, if not impossible, to tell whose troops they were. At first sight James thought they might be French deserters. They weren't Americans. The A.E.F. was much more discreet and sensitive about the handling of such matters. James could see the prisoners' faces. One of the condemned men appeared almost boyish with his blond hair and light complexion. The younger soldier stared at the riflemen as the other prisoners smoked the cigarettes they had been given by the French officer in charge of the detail.

James stopped the ambulance to watch. He leaned out of the window and asked a nearby sentry what was happening.

The guard answered matter-of-factly that they were shooting captured sappers taken during the night. They had caught the men after a downpour had caused a cave-in of their tunnel directly under the French line. The Germans hadn't had time to fill the tunnel with explosives. The tunnel would have been detonated as soon as the trench was fully occupied by the fresh troops. The French believed the public execution of sappers reassured the troops that there was at least some effort being made to prevent the Germans from undermining the breastworks. In fact, there was little anyone could do to prevent it.

The Zouaves tended to ignore the usual, more traditional, form of execution practiced by other, more gallant-minded French units. Instead of allowing the Germans to die standing erect with any sense of dignity, they were placed in a kneeling position with their hands tied to their ankles, facing their executioners. Even the priests were denied access to their German captives.

Before James could finish asking his question of the guard, a volley of shots rang out. The prisoners were blown backwards, kicking and jerking as the final surges of life left their bodies. The French sentry turned with a smile grinning and spat on the ground with satisfaction.

"Filthy pigs," he snarled, slicing across his neck with his hand.

The French officer stood over the bodies, delivering the coup de grâce with his pistol. After each shot, the body was thrown into a ditch that the sappers had dug shortly after their capture.

James had witnessed so much German barbarism of French soldiers and civilians all across the front that he whispered only a feeble murmur of personal penitence for the dishing out of revenge that had just taken place. Even that much sympathy was hard for him to conjure up.

"They oughta kill 'em all like that!" James said to his driver. "Wipe em off the face of the earth like plague-infested rats!"

A wooden sign caught James' eye, hanging like a prophet's soothsaying from the skeleton of a large tree charred black from the fires of battle. It was twisted at the base as if trying to turn away from the endless legions of men destined for extermination; but the branches farthest from the road still bore green leaves, flourishing where the limbs had been undisturbed by war. Some who looked at the tree saw it as a sign of hope, still flourishing after all that had transpired. The sign, a piece of coffin planking, was marked with the words, 'THIS WAY TO HELL. VISITORS WELCOME!'.

When James read the sign his thoughts raced back to an excursion he'd made to Verdun where the French had suffered such appalling casualties. The great slaughter of its young men had inspired the French to name the road to Verdun: La Voie Sacre'e, The Sacred Way. It had become a consecrated artery that had carried the flow of souls that was the awful price of France's survival. Glorious it may have sounded; true it was not. France had still teetered on the verge of capitulation, despite the enormous sacrifice of its men. More than anything else the road would become a symbol of survival, not just at Verdun, but for all of France.

Nothing but artillery duels and recon' forays took place for the first three weeks while the troops occupied the perimeter encircling Saint Mehiel. The weather conditions were pleasant enough, but this was a double-edged sword for the troops, who, while they basked in the bright sunlight, knew that the optimum conditions meant that the offensive would begin as soon as the ground dried out. As if to confirm this, the aroma of rotting mule carcasses drifted over the trenches from behind the German lines, poisoned by yperite gas canisters, as the Allies tried to kill the animals used to position the big guns.

James had found himself a cozy niche near one of the aid stations, and had bedded down in a shelf excavated by a prior tenant in the dirt wall of the trench. He lay stripped to his waist, and was reading a letter from Lora when a soldier interrupted his private thoughts. "You Sergeant Lavoisier?"

"Captain McCarnes wants you down in front of Battery Nine, plenty quick!"

"What for?"

"You'll see," the soldier answered tersely; "follow me."

James grabbed his tunic and helmet lying next to him. As soon as he was dressed he shoved his pistol into his pants, concealing it beneath his jacket as he'd done before.

He followed his guide past the heavy bulwarks until they finally came to an open section where Battery Nine had been positioned.

"Jesus, what's this all about?" James was shocked to see four Germans standing thirty feet away.

The Germans were wearing their spiked helmets and gray leather gloves. They were standing at attention, holding a white flag attached to a bayonet. All in all, things suddenly looked a little strange to James.

"Captain's parlayin' with 'em. He's wantin' someone from hospital ta stand by," another soldier told him.

"What'a they want? They tryin to surrender?" he asked.

"Hell, no! We think they wanta fight one of our boys in some kinda duel out there," the man said, pointing towards no-man's land. It's kind of a winner take all, if I'm readin' their gibberish."

"Where the hell is that sergeant from Hospital?" McCarnes demanded to know, smiling at the Germans, at the same time.

James stepped up, popping a smart salute. "Sergeant Lavoisier, sir."

"Lavoisier, listen to what I'm tellin' these buzzards and make sure you get the rules straight on what's fixin' ta happen," Captain McCarnes said, still looking at the Germans.

"Yes, sir!" James answered, even more confused.

McCarnes turned to James. I'll tell you what's going on here in a minute, Sergeant." He turned back towards the American trenches.

A runner came up from behind the gun emplacement. "Colonel Hubert says it's okay to go ahead, sir," he said.

"All right, Lavoisier. Here's the dope...the head Hiney wants to arrange a fight for one of their boys with a little bayonet duel out there in front of the wire. Seems like they got themselves some kinda fencing master with 'em from their military school. He's been making a career outa' goin' up and down the lines callin' a time out so's he can carve someone up, for a little German propaganda. Apparently it helps to keep a smile on their faces. He's already sliced up a couple of Limeys."

"I'm no bayonet duelist, sir," James nervously reminded the Captain.

Captain McCarnes laughed. "Don't worry, Sergeant, we got that all taken care of. All we want you to do is bring our man in if he happens to git the worst of it.

"That's a relief, sir," James said, letting out a heavy sigh.

One of the German officers lost his patience and let go with a stream of derogatory remarks, in English, about the fortitude of the Americans. All hell broke loose in the ranks. An officer hurriedly calmed things down and made sure that no one took a shot at the Germans.

Captain McCarnes was surprised by the German officer's audacity, but, on the other hand, he knew the Germans were eager to do anything they could to demoralize the inexperienced American troops. He ordered several men, including James, to follow him out. The German officer delivered a flashy salute to the Captain, who reciprocated by digging a voluminous wad of tobacco out of his cheek and plopping it onto the ground in front of the surprised officers.

"What's the deal with this duel business, Bub?" he asked, shooting a streamer of tobacco across the ground before the German could answer.

The German officer flinched, trying to understand what McCarnes had just said. Finally, he reconciled himself to simply announce the rules of engagement and to forget trying to decipher what the American was asking him. Your soldier, Captain, is invited to fence our soldier with rifle and bayonet," he said, with a smirk.

"Yeah, and how do you play this little game?" McCarnes answered sarcastically.

"Quite simply, Captain, the winner, whoever lives, returns to his lines unchallenged by the other side."

McCarnes spit out another nauseating goober before he accepted the invitation. "You got yourself a fight, Bub. We'll need a minute to git our fella ready."

"Very good, Captain. Shall we begin in, say, twenty minutes?" the German asked, taking a quick glance at

Captain McCarnes' adjutant, who was standing next to him with what southern-folks often referred to as having a 'possum grin' on his face.

"Twenty minutes u'll do fine!" McCarnes acknowledged.

The German snapped a final salute, curious about why McCarnes and his men were all smiling at this point. He gave James a quick passing glance before turning and marching away in disgust with the Americans.

The Americans made their way back to the trench, where McCarnes looked back over his shoulder as he remarked, "That'll be the last fight that son of a bitch puts together."

"They're sure gonna' be uh heap ah unhappy Hineys when they figure out the little surprise we got waitin' for 'em, sir!

"You bet your sweet ass," another man laughed.

"What's goin' on?" James wanted to know.

"We got a feller on his way up here, a Sergeant Saulnier. He'll cut that gawd damn German's guts out."

"Where the hell did you find him?" James asked.

"He's a fencing instructor from New Orleans. He's been in a shit-pot full of knife fights. He'll cut that German's nuts off, sure as the world!"

In fifteen minutes the Germans began climbing out of their trenches to get a good view of the fight. The Americans followed suit, with the braver ones moving out several yards towards the area selected for the duel. The rest of the men either stood on the firing platforms or sat on the edge of the ramparts.

The duel was to take place dead center between the two lines. It was too far for either contestant to run from the snipers positioned on either side, in case anything went wrong.

A tall, heavy-set German officer in a colorful full dress uniform walked out onto the field with a rifle clasped in his hands. A long polished steel bayonet attached to the barrel of the rifle mirrored a reflection in the sun as he moved the weapon into position next to his side.

The soldier reached up, pulling his spiked helmet from his head, revealing a fleshy baldness as he wiped his face and neck with a white handkerchief. When he'd finished, he twisted the ends of his waxed mustache. It was obvious that he'd had years of experience in such matters as he stood sedately erect, waiting for his challenger to come forward to be impaled on his bayonet.

The troops on the American side sat motionless as they waited for their 'defender of the faith' to come forth. After seeing the enormous frame of the German, many wondered if they had a hero strong enough to bring down the giant. Then, far down the line a cheer erupted, moving like a tidal wave through the trench as Sergeant Saulnier emerged onto the field. He was carrying an Enfield under his arm like a bird hunter. The bayonet was still in the scabbard attached to his belt.

The German looked puzzled at the size of his competitor. Usually a large man was selected, hoping to overcome the lack of skill with brawn and fortitude. But Saulnier was short and thin. He appeared almost emaciated as he stepped onto the field and pulled his helmet off, laying it on the ground next to his feet.

The German dedicated another few moments to studying the little man and the way he carried himself. He was bothered by Saulnier's confidence. Not once had he looked at the German.

Sergeant André Saulnier, fencing master extraordinaire, head master of the New Orleans School of Fencing and a gentleman emigre' Frenchman from Langres, had fought his share of battles, as the German soon would discover. He was proficient with almost any cutting edge, including "Le Baionnette".

Saulnier ignored the German, making a show out of sharpening the edge of his bayonet with a whetstone. The stone slid along the blade with a loud, high-pitched scraping sound, ending with a pop as he reached the tip of the blade. The little Frenchman worked at sharpening his knife like a musician tuning his cello for a concert.

The German was becoming slightly unnerved and agitated as he waited for Saulnier to complete his preparations. A sharp clicking sound reverberated across the field as the two soldiers disassembled the bolts from the actions of their rifles.

The American unsheathed his bayonet at the last moment, snapping it into place with a single movement that caught the German's attention. He was becoming increasingly suspicious of his 'bantam weight' opponent's calm composure.

The duo began to move towards each other in a slow, circular, stalking dance, each brandishing his rifle, with his bayonet pointed at the other's body.

The German lunged towards André, pushing the long steel blade towards his body, hoping to spear the man and gain a quick victory.

André moved gracefully to one side, parrying the blow. Instinctively, he countered, slicing a neat slit along the German's coat pocket, just over his heart. It was André's way of letting the German know he wasn't a novice.

The German retreated with a look of disbelief. For the first time he realized the jeopardy he had placed himself in. He stepped back, pulling his blade into the air as a salute.

André, with a stern look, moved towards the anxious officer, tapping and clanging his blade against his opponent's as the rotation continued. The exchange of thrust and parries increased. Each man called upon his personal wealth of experience, searching and probing for a weakness in the other man's technique.

James and another American had squatted down within twenty yards of the duel, holding onto a stretcher.

The fight continued for seven or eight more minutes before the German officer suddenly made a sweeping downstroke at André's upper torso. His blade split open his tunic, slicing deeply into the muscles of his chest. The ribs had blocked the blade from penetrating the body cavity and killing André.

At the same moment André leaned back, hooking the tip of his blade deep in the German's stomach and ripping upwards. With a loud scream, he disemboweled his adversary, delivering a fatal blow.

The German officer dropped to his knees, supporting himself with his rifle. He glanced down, horror-stricken at seeing the contents of his abdomen lying on the ground in front of him. He glared at André with a look of consternation and then collapsed, dead, onto the ground.

Saulnier, even though critically wounded, walked over and picked up the German's rifle, upending it and jamming the bayonet into the ground near the corpse.

The American line broke into pandemonium, cheering wildly, as if the war had been decided by the butchering contest that had just been concluded.

Sergeant Saulnier stumbled towards his helmet. He'd gone only a few feet before falling face forward onto the wet ground. James and a volunteer sprinted toward the wounded man, sliding down next to him.

Two Germans arrived a few seconds later, rolling their man over, stuffing his innards back into his body cavity and heaving him onto a piece of trench-planking that they would use to carry him back to their lines. He was quickly trussed to the board with a piece of rope, with his weapon and helmet unceremoniously tossed on top of the body.

"We're gonna' get yah outa' here right now, Sergeant," James assured Saulnier in his native Creole tongue. He placed his cocked pistol on the stretcher next to the Sergeant as they watched the Germans vanish across the field with their countryman's body.

André smiled with a delighted look, responding in French, "God has been merciful today. He has not only spared my life, but he's sent a fellow Creole to fetch me home. Thank you, whoever you are!"

James kneeled down next to Sergeant Saulnier, closing his tunic around a compress he'd placed over his wound. He congratulated him on his victory. André was in severe pain from the deep laceration in his chest, but managed to smile as he gripped James' hand.

James felt Saulnier push something wet into his palm.

"For you, my friend, for your bravery in coming after me."

"It's the German's watch. It was wrapped around my bayonet when it passed out of his belly," André sighed, grimacing with pain.

James looked at the bloody memento, thanking André for the gift. They hurriedly lifted him up and shuffled off the field, fearing that the Germans might renege on the truce at any moment.

After James had delivered Sergeant Saulnier to the aid station he returned to his cubbyhole in the wall. He pulled the bloodied watch from his pocket, wiping it with his handkerchief, until the gold case sparkled. The light from his single candle reflected against the polished surface with an almost magical glow.

He lay on his back, twisting the long gold fob between his fingers, captivated by the beauty of the piece of jewelry. He pried open the back, thinking there might be a picture of the soldier's family inside, or at least the German's name.

The case sprang open with a pop and then a click. A beautiful miniaturized waltz began to play, as if the watch was a musical automaton accompanying a missing ballerina. James was mesmerized by the simple yet clear melody coming from the heavy gold instrument.

Unfortunately, the movement of the watch itself had been broken. The time was fixed at the precise moment that Sergeant Saulnier had struck the deathblow.

In the hellish world of Saint Mihiel on that day, the clock was of little use except as something of beauty to gaze upon and appreciate. Music, on the other hand, was a lullaby to lonely ears, nurturing what few remembrances were left of home and a way of life that seemed so long ago.

With the end of the offensive, the Twenty Fourth Hospital Group was reassigned to the Ardennes near the Argonne thickets. With the field hospital in place and operational for the forthcoming offensive, James and a few companions were granted a welcome furlough to Paris.

They hitched a ride to the southwest on a French *camion* convoy as far as the Marne River. Here they stopped long enough to wash and delouse themselves before continuing on. The men splashed and soaked in the icy September waters of the river. They cleaned their uniforms and took advantage of the warm sunlit day to dry their clothes, still wet from the swamps of the Woevre Plain. They lay on the banks, trying to brown their pallid skin, shielded from the sun for so many months under their heavy uniforms.

James drifted in and out of a shallow nap as he pictured Paris and the sights he'd dreamed of since he was a young boy. He had sat for hours, sharing with his mother what it would be like for the both of them to travel to Paris together. For James it seemed like de' ja vu, after a lifetime of anticipating the great city. For Benonia it had been little more than an elusive dream that she knew would never come true. She had participated in the fantasy to inspire James to broaden his horizons in life, to seek out new worlds and extricate himself from the harsh life of the swamp.

He lay on the bank of the river, listening to the other men laugh and talk. They spoke of the sensuous women, the splendid sights, the delectable cuisine and drink, absorbed in their frivolous vision of "Paree."

Roy Blackwood, a brassy east Texas farm boy, walked over to James and squatted down next to him, nudging him on the shoulder with an irritating poke. James kept his eyes closed, grunting in response. He kept his face pointed straight at the sun, his arms tucked behind his head as he cleared his throat to deal with the interruption.

"Say, James, don't you know a lot about this here Paris place?" Blackwood asked.

"Yeah, I reckon I know a little somethin' about it," James responded, opening his eyes and supporting himself on one elbow.

"What's a feller got to do around there, anyway?" Blackwood inquired, pitching a stone across the water in front of them.

James stared at the sky, ignoring Blackwood for a moment before replying. "Oh, there's Notre Dame Cathedral, the Champs Elysee', I guess. There's plenty to see."

"Well," Blackwood chuckled," what about them French mademoiselles? You reckon a feller 'ud have a hard time gittin' ta know one of 'em?"

"How would I know, Blackwood? I haven't been to Paris. Hell, women are women! If they like yah, they like yah!" James laughed under his breath. "Good- looking guy like you, in your uniform and all...well, hell, Roy, they'll be on you like dressed-up ticks on an old coon dog!"

Blackwood laughed, believing the part about the women being interested in the uniform, even though he knew he resembled a warthog.

James rolled back over on his side, pulling his souvenir German watch out of the breast pocket of his tunic. He twisted the chain between his fingers as he endured the sun's reflection with each rotation of the watch.

"That your boy?" Blackwood asked, noticing James holding a picture of a small child in his other hand.

"Yeah," James said, handing the photo to him.

"Nice looking youngin'. Looks a lot like his daddy," Blackwood declared.

"Aw, not really. I think he sorta favors his mamma."

"You git a letter from home?" Blackwood questioned, reaching over and touching the letter as if it were a holy relic.

"A note from my wife," James replied, shaking his head. "Yeah. Some fellas from home, Donnie Tyler and L.B. Logan...boys that joined up with me, were both killed somewhere around here last month. I was just wondering where it happened," he added, stuffing the letter back into his coat pocket.

"Sorta' takes your breath away when it happens to someone you really know. Most of these boys are jest faces. It's like they ain't even real people. Makes yah wonder if anybody's gonna' come outa' this bad-assed dream!' Roy said with a questioning tone.

"Sure does make yah wonder, don't it?"

"Here, this u'll git your spirits up. You need a little primin' for Paree." Roy offered James a silver flask full of cognac.

James took a sip, handing the container back. "Here you go, thanks."

"Finish it. I'm gonna' git me a barrel full of French wine when we git to Paree," Blackwood said, standing up. He looked down at the ground, stuffed his hands deep into his trousers and walked off.

James sipped on the cognac, popping open the back of the watch to listen to the tinkling chime. The tune was an abbreviated waltz by Chopin, one of the more notable adoptees of France. James enjoyed listening to the music whenever he could. It seemed to soothe his mind.

'How odd,' he thought, 'the Germans have even stolen the music of France. What shameless bastards. Maybe that's what this war is all about. Maybe they just wanta plunder Paris and then go home. No', he quickly assured himself, 'it's nothing that noble. No one could be this damn barbaric and have an appreciation for history and art. They couldn't be that civilized.'

The men hitched a ride to Paris, this time with a British convoy that came by a half-hour later. The lorries traveled through the countryside with their canvas covers thrown back, letting the wind whip through the bed of the truck. The men stood quietly, leaning over the rails, pondering the sights of the farmlands, and occasionally waving back at a French farmer or bicyclist. The French would scream out, "Vive America, vive la France!" and they would wave until the trucks were out of sight.

The French wine and brandy that the men had been drinking all day gave them new courage with the language, sending James into hysterics as his traveling companions shouted out, trying to communicate with the locals.

"LaFayette, nous-y sommes (Lafayette, we are here)," they'd shout in response to a salute by some Frenchman along the road.

The farther from the front they traveled, the more euphoric they became. A cleansing metamorphosis was taking place, restoring their material senses with every mile. It was a time to reacquaint themselves with life, to ceremoniously dust themselves off from their vile work. Jubilee day had arrived as surely as if God had finally trumpeted the resurrection of the dead.

Paris was shrouded in a cold, ash-gray haze, punctuated with an occasional white cloud of steam rising from the streets or buildings. The dark slate roofs wore an icy coating and seemed to be made of glass whenever light reflected from them. Everywhere, the stone buildings were covered in soot from centuries of choking fumes that had drifted over the city. Evening had banished the street vendors, leaving the cobblestone streets and alleys to restless night wanderers. Ragged urchins and baby-faced children moved and huddled in pairs or larger groups beneath the proliferation of electric signs and flickering gas lights that outlined the streets.

James and his companions had taken an expensive room along the Rue de Rivoli, near the Place Des Pyramides. They had decided to spend their first night in Paris treating themselves to the luxury of a bath and a clean, lice-free bed.

The heavy drinking had taken an early toll on several of the men who missed the succulent 'Bill of Fare' prepared for the others at a street cafe'. Some of them opted to spend their first night in Paris in their beds, falling asleep as soon as they were shown their rooms.

In the morning, a dazzling light display streamed through the windows of James' room. Blue and yellow ribbons of light appeared on the wall, running down to the floor and bisecting his bed. Paris was up and alive. The once-abandoned streets of the night were now teeming with vendors spiffing up their carts with fresh merchandise for the new day. The gray wintry sky had been burned away, leaving Paris open to bask in the brilliant warming sunlight.

James lay comfortably in the thick feather mattress, moving his fingers over the white linen bed covers that billowed up from the gentle pressure of goose down sewn between layers of sheets.

His eyes roamed the room, carefully examining the furnishings, as if to prove to himself that he was really in Paris. He sat up, taking in a larger than normal gulp of air, then threw back the thick covers before springing onto the wooden floor. He stepped over to the window to take his first view of the city. The crisp air smelled of fresh bread and flowers, the true trademark of Paris, and something that the war had not affected, at least not yet. He could see the ivory-colored cupola of a distant building framed by Gothic structures on either side. The lines of the buildings were broken by naked trees with full, outstretched limbs. It seemed such an oddity as he remembered the disfigured trunks that he'd grown used to at the front.

James and Roy Blackwood had taken breakfast at an outdoor cafe', the Cafe' De LaPaix, near their hotel. They enjoyed a selection of heavily sugared beignet and coffee, and a variety of colorful fruits from some distant French colony.

They were dressed in their brown wool jodhpur-shaped britches and tunic without a belt or strap, an adornment reserved for officers. Their legs were bound from ankles to knees with puttees, and their boots had been oiled to remove the scuffs and water stains from the wet trenches. A new Keppy had been issued, but most of the troops still preferred to wear their campaign hats, sensitive to being mistaken for British soldiers.

When they had finished breakfast, the two men rented bicycles for a tour of the city. Roy was awe-struck by the intricately designed buildings. They were larger and older than anything he'd ever seen in East Texas. There, the structures of antiquity had been created in logs and mud. Even the ancient Indian Mound Dwellers of East Texas were relative newcomers in history compared to some of the dates recorded in the cartularies of Paris.

James directed the tour, starting at Pont de la Tournelle, a bridge that offered a wonderful vantage to the curved arches of the apse of Notre Dame.

They stood on the bridge as James stared at the glorious structure. He knew the history, but was almost at a loss to recite the pertinent facts to Roy, as if he were afraid that what he was seeing was inconsistent with what he had envisioned in his childhood dreams.

"This bridge was built in 1370. That's nearly 75 years before they discovered America...or Texas, for that matter," James joked, laughing.

Roy grunted a bored, "Uh huh," picking a morsel of fruit from his teeth from breakfast. He was not overly excited about the architectural relic beneath him anymore, and he was impatient to move on.

"That church over there is Notre Dame. They built it around the 13th century. It's a pretty fantastic piece of work, wouldn't you say?" James asked.

"Hell, it looks like it could use a good coat of paint to me," Roy drawled, ogling a young woman who was strolling by.

James laughed, watching Roy follow the woman with his eyes.

"I think you're more interested in the present-day Paris, so let's get going," said James, pulling Roy by the arm.

They moved to another area of the city, with James enthusiastically continuing his recitation to his yawny companion.

"That's La Conciergerie over there, where they kept all the folks locked up waiting for the guillotine. They say Marie Antoinette almost got outa' gettin' her head lopped off 'cause she was Austrian. It took 'em nine months to finally decide to kill her!"

"Lordy," Blackwood shot back, "me lookin' as hard as I can to find me a pretty woman to hook up with for the night, and the damn French are goin around cuttin' their heads off! It don't make any sense, no sir!"

"Jesus, Roy, that happened in 1793!" James chuckled. "I don't' think the French make a habit of guillotinin' women, even now days."

"Thank God," Roy replied, then pointed to two women sitting on a bench in front of them. "Let's see if we can hook up with them two Mademoiselles over there."

"Come on, Roy, we got plenty of time for that later. Let's see a little more of Paris."

"Okay," Blackwood agreed, "but I want plenty of time ta meet me a French lady 'afore it gits dark."

By mid-afternoon Roy was completely worn out, and he began to complain about any further sightseeing. He'd only stayed with it as long as he had in the hope that James would help him find a companion later that afternoon.

"I'm plum tuckered, James. I don't wanna' see nothin' else, 'sep maybe that Napoleon 'Bonaparte' feller's grave. I gotta have a look at his headstone so's I can tell my pappy I been there. I promised him I'd see where he was buried 'afore I come home."

After they'd visited the Dome Des Invalides where Napoleon's remains lay, they made their way to the grounds beneath the Eiffel Tower, then strolled along the Champs-De-Mars until they found a place to stretch out on the grass in the warm afternoon sun.

"How come an American feller like you, James, got so much savvy about Paris, anyhow?"

"I donno. I guess it's 'cause my family was from around these parts. My great grand daddy served in Napoleon's army. I always knew I'd come here someday to see what it was like. I didn't think I'd be in the middle of a war, though, when I did," James laughed.

"Sure enough?" Blackwood replied. "Your folks come from around here, and your great grand pappy fought for that Napoleon feller?"

"Yep, shore did! We always thought we came from Rennes. But my family sorta lost track of where our kin were from, after the Civil War. Everything my family had regarding our heritage was burned up by Yankees. Seems strange, old great grandpa lit out at the end of a war, and I come back when one starts."

"Surely does," said Blackwood.

"My pappy was always real proud of being French; thought it was the most important thing in his life. Me, I'm not so sure anymore!" James stated, thinking of his experiences with the French, up at the front.

Roy loaded his cheeks full of half a loaf of dark bread that he'd bought from a street vendor by the Seine. He soaked the bread with a shot of wine before he finally swallowed the concoction.

"Don't rightly know ware my folks come from, other than Texas. Could be they come from Kentuck' or Tennessee, I ain't for sure. All I know is that they're Americans. Ain't no feriners in my family."

"Blackwood...that sure sounds English to me," James countered. "'Less you're full blood Indian, you gotta have kin somewhere on this side of the ocean."

Roy ignored James' remark to feast his eyes on a group of Parisian women in their stylish long dresses, impeccably turned out in the latest fashions.

"A Frenchman back at the hotel told me the place to go, if you wanta see Paris at night, is a pavilion near the Square Du Vert-Galant, down by the river," James announced.

Both men were now watching the group of women, who were looking back over their shoulders at the two of them.

"How far you reckon that pavilion is from here, James?"

"Oh, not so far we can't do a little more sightseein' on the way," James joked, quickly picking up his bicycle as Roy threw the last remnants of his loaf of bread at him.

"My feet hurt worse than a split frog in a mule's hoof and you wanna' go lookin' at more of them damned old buildin's!"

James left Roy lagging behind. He courteously tipped his hat to two young women who were approaching. Roy noticed the exchange and immediately caught up with James. The women smiled flirtatiously, acknowledging James' polite gesture. Roy said something vulgar, but the women missed the meaning of it, smiling as they walked on by.

"Why didn't you try ta talk em into comin' with us? I could feel it in my bones. Them women wanted us. They was droolin' ta spend the night with us."

"Every woman in Paris isn't a damned whore, Blackwood!" James scolded. "Some of 'em don't take kindly to bein' pinched on the ass, either."

"That ain't what I've heard, damn it. I've been told they'd ask you if you didn't ask them first," Roy said with a smile.

"C'mon, lets go find that dance before you bust your britches. I can always tell an old farm boy from normal folk...all he ever thinks about is breeding."

Roy followed behind with a theatrical limp, holding onto his crotch with one hand and pushing his bike with the other. James looked back, shaking his head as Roy moaned and laughed at the same time.

They followed a path along the tree-lined Seine, finally coming to Le Grand Pavilion that they had been told about. The building resembled a church cloister, painted with a thousand thin coats of whitewash on its wooden facade. The porticoes on the main level were repeated all the way around the octagonal structure. The building was a massive framed hall, built to handle the great quadrilles of the late 1800s. It occupied an expanse of ground equal to an entire city block. Most of the pavilion was lit with flickering gas lamps, haloing a bright gold glow at each of its arched entrances. The shingled roof pitched upwards to a hexagonal cupola that supported a massive French national flag. The flag, even in the gray light of dusk, was faded and torn, like the pride of France.

The only windows were in the roof, opening like trap doors to belch out the clouds of smoke and vapor from the people inside.

James and Roy walked along the narrow, patina-colored sidewalk, winding and curving endlessly along the river. The path was lined with thick green hedges on both sides, a barrier that kept the travelers going in the right direction.

The path ended abruptly a few feet from the entrance to the building. Once they'd located the front door they parked their bicycles and entered the enormous cabaret.

The dimly lit interior soon gave way to a hint of light coming from candles set at each table and from mirror-backed gas chandeliers hanging from the rafters. The reflection from the great lights formed a spider web effect on the dance floor below. Drapes of crimson velvet, trimmed in gold braid, hung to each side of the massive hardwood doors encircling the vast hall. Silhouettes of couples, angled passionately towards each other at tiny cafe' tables, formed an irregular horizon that faded into a solid mass farther into the room.

Stephen D. Boyett

Patrons standing in line to be seated, and waiters waiting to serve their guests, blocked James' view of the orchestra performing in the center of the open floor. The musicians were dressed in dark uniforms of a military contingent, as were most of the men in the room.

A diversity of sharp fragrances drifted through the hall; every conceivable aroma was there, from the stench of unwashed soldiers, fresh from the front, to the sweet perfumes of men and women of a more fastidious nature. In a few instances the distinct smell of a faddish drug, such as hashish, imbued the atmosphere as couples discreetly indulged.

Men and women, paired into couples, sat staring dreamily into each other's eyes. They held hands with an occasional spontaneous embrace, talking only when touching, and smiling seemed to lose its effectiveness in communicating their intimacy and commitment of love.

It was a moment to charge the mind with a lifetime of remembrances, to feel the wanting touch of a lover before the permanency of death separated them forever.

Dark bottles of wine numbed the realities of tomorrow, helping the lovers concentrate on each other, ignoring the human wheel gracefully sweeping past their table, couples dancing at a brisk tempo to the latest waltz.

Other couples, the more public of the lovers, danced with an electric energy, pressing themselves into each other's arms as if these were the last moments on earth. They twirled at a frantic pace about the dance floor, attempting to launch themselves into a more peaceful world.

Young women sat along the walls with an 'air maniere', an affected pose, in a single row of straight-backed chairs. They held hands and laughed girlishly as they watched young soldiers mill about like predators, uncertain of how to best attack their alluring prey.

James was uneasy about his loneliness. He constantly reminded himself of his vows to Lora, but he was tormented by a desire for the warm, soft company of a woman. He wanted more than to just satisfy a physical wistfulness. He yearned for someone to help him forget the shadow of fear that had become his constant companion. He had no interest in letting himself become caught up in a game of amorous gymnastics. He wasn't interested in some schoolboy conquest or dallying love affair. Instead, he hungered to feel, for a solemn moment, someone alive and loving next to his body. He wanted more than anything to be involved once again with the creativity of life instead of being an accomplice to the slaughter of humanity.

Rather than deal with temptation he moved away from the crowds to a dark corner of the pavilion, staring out of the concealment of the shadows at those who were less inhibited.

When he tired of being an observer of the emotional scenes all around, the synthetic euphoria, he sauntered towards the exit looking for Roy. His indomitable companion was locked in conversation with a plump Parisian woman as he promenaded her about the dance floor. The robust woman shrieked with a high-pitched laugh, urged on by his backwoods dance style. The more she laughed, the more Roy assumed she was impressed with his dancing ability as he lifted her effortlessly into the air with an impromptu adagio. At each launch, Roy would rivet his eyes on the young woman's cleavage as it moved up and down against her blouse.

James chuckled to himself, covering his mouth with his hand to avoid attracting attention. He sat down in a hard-backed chair, leaning back on the two rear legs with his arms crossed.

James was distracted from Roy's floor show by a young woman standing beside him, looking down at him with a quizzical expression on her face. He stood up, confused about what she wanted, then he quickly offered her his chair, thinking, perhaps, that he'd occupied her favorite roost. She smiled at him apologetically, slightly startled when he stood up.

"Je suis désolé, monsieur,.. I thought perhaps you were wounded and that is why you were sitting in the women's gallery."

James' face reflected his embarrassment, turning a noticeable red tone as he wiped his face and looked down at his chair.

He responded in French, "I'm sorry, I didn't realize where I was!"

She laughed. "Please, Monsieur, I didn't mean to embarrass you. I'm sure that no one would say anything if you would like to sit here."

He gathered his composure, straightening his tunic collar and looking at her, his ego slightly bruised.

"I was waiting for my friend over there. I really wasn't thinking about what I was doing," he assured her. "I'm truly sorry!"

She smiled again, turning away from him, and sat down in a chair on the row behind where he had been sitting. She watched the dancers for a few minutes before stealing a quick look back up at him. James was still standing, pretending to watch the whirling dancers, with his back to her. After enough time had passed for him to recover his pride, he turned.

"Would you care to dance, Mademoiselle?"

She shrugged her shoulders with a 'why not' gesture, staring up at him with her almond-shaped eyes. She was delighted that he had finally asked.

Her tiny hand was oddly disproportionate in James' rough oversized grip, but he held her fingers with the sensitivity of a grownup walking with a child as he escorted her to the dance floor.

James felt like a schoolboy, with his heart fluttering as he gazed at the lovely face of the young French girl. He secretly inhaled her perfumed scent as he pulled her into his arms. They moved to the waltz, merging into the mass clockwise flow of the crowd.

When the music ended James held onto her hand as she started back to her chair.

"Please...would you dance with me a little longer? I haven't enjoyed myself this much in a long time," he pleaded, looking forlornly into her captivating eyes.

She paused, as if making a decision beyond his request to dance with her. Finally, she moved back into his arms as the orchestra began to play another waltz. This time it was a fast tune, allowing them to dance the way the French preferred. She moved deep into his arms, no longer a stranger to the young soldier. James could sense her relaxed body in his grasp. He pulled her easily against him, pressing his face into her dark hair. He closed his eyes as he savored the fragrance of her skin. He could feel her arm tighten around his shoulder as they swirled in a synchronized mood.

When the arrangement ended, the orchestra began playing a new dance craze, the Tango. Still the crowd continued to dance almost the same step, unaccustomed to the new moves.

James and his companion spun into the mass of people, both laughing with heads tilted back like roller coaster riders trying to capture more momentum from the quick turns. They followed the others like a great wheel, moving deeper into the center of the human whirlpool.

After exhausting themselves with several more dances, James walked the girl to an empty table. She sat back in her chair with both hands pressed against her chest trying to catch her breath. His heart raced with excitement, watching her every move.

"You dance the waltz superbly, Mademoiselle," James remarked. "Now, if I only knew your name?"

"Marie," she answered.

"Well, Mademoiselle Marie, is that all the name you have?"

"No, Sergeant," she responded, chuckling, "my name is Marie Gre'soire."

James grinned, giving an approving nod. He ordered wine for the two of them from the aproned sommelier, with the authority of a native.

"And what is your name, Monsieur Sergeant? And how is it that you speak French so well, and yet are in the American Army?"

"My name is James Lavoisier, and I am Creole," James answered. "I grew up on a small farm in Louisiana, in America."

"Ah...New France," she said. "You are from somewhere near New Orleans, no?"

"Yes, a short distance from New Orleans. And you...are you Parisian?"

"No. Like you, I am from a small farm, near the village of Pont-a-Mousson."

"That's near the front?" James replied. He leaned forward, wanting to make sure he had understood her correctly. "You're from Pont-a-Mousson?"

"You shouldn't be so surprised, Sergeant. Many of the people living in Paris are refugees from the border. There are few problems in finding work or a place to stay, with so many having been killed since the war started. Paris is a city of empty rooms and eager employers."

"What about your family, your parents?" James inquired, politely.

"My mother and father are dead. They were killed by the Boche near our home. My younger brother, Jerome, died at Vouziers, in a bombardment. He was a very handsome young man," she added, her eyes wandering for a moment.

"I'm sorry about your family!" James said. "It's very sad."

Marie shook her head to show her disdain as she spoke: "I hate the Germans! They have killed so many of our young men and destroyed so much of France."

James understood the pain in Marie's voice, so he reached out, taking her hand in his.

"I live in Paris now. But someday, I will go home to my family's farm. When the Boche are chased away, I will go back there to live," she said.

"Do you like living in the country?" James asked.

"Oh, yes! The Parisians are so involved in fads. They are so ridiculous! They play at the Bohemian life, or pretend at being Communist or Socialist. Such nonsense! I much prefer the people of the Moselle to the Parisians. It is so clean there and wonderfully colorful. And everyone is at peace with life."

"Tell me about your home. Is it as green and beautiful as other parts of France?" James asked.

"My home sits at the end of a long lane of trees that form a tunnel over the road leading to my house. It is so cool in the tunnel, if you walk through it on a hot summer day, you will get a chill. My father built a rock fence between the road and the trees, on both sides, all the way to our door. He thought it would keep the cool air in the tunnel and let the wind move it towards our home." She smiled happily as she finished describing the farm.

James was curious. "Did your father like being a farmer?"

"Oh, yes! He was very happy with his land! He would not leave, not even when the Germans crossed the frontier into France. He stayed long after the fighting had destroyed everything near our farm."

"My family's home was also destroyed by war. But it happened a long time ago. How I miss that place, the special fragrance, its beauty, and the warm sun! I sometimes wonder if I'll ever see it again." James sighed, finishing his glass of wine.

"You must have faith," she said, smiling. "God's hand is here in this terrible time. There are too many prayers for the angels alone to answer, too many souls being taken to heaven. God would not leave such a great task to others."

The orchestra began playing a beautiful waltz, a rendition of Chopin's Nocturne at a slow, almost numbing, andante.

James stared into Marie's eyes as he stood up and led her onto the dance floor. The light from the chandelier above them cast a soft glow over her face, and he realized, at that very moment as she moved in front of him, how absolutely beautiful she was.

Her hair reflected the golden glow of the candles, and her lips sparkled with a deep crimson luster. But it was her eyes that so captivated James. So passionate, yet childlike, there was an innocence that radiated from her smile. Her eyes followed him as they began moving slowly to the music.

Her touch was as warm and inviting as anything James had ever imagined. His heart raced as he pulled her closer until he felt her lips against his cheek. Her tiny hand moved slowly behind his neck, warming the nerves of his body. Again he smelled the sweet fragrance of her soft skin and felt the very pulse of her body as he held her tightly. His mind fought to stop the feeling of joy and excitement that he felt with her in his arms. Even an intense surge of guilt had no effect on her powers. They danced as if they had known each other before, as if the minutes that they had been acquainted had become years. It was the license given to young lovers during times of war.

James escorted Marie to her apartment, which she was sharing with several other women, holding her hand as they talked.

"I haven't got much of my furlough left, but I'd like to see you tomorrow, if I could?" he asked. "Please don't say no."

"I'm sorry, Sergeant, but I have to work until late afternoon...unless you would like to meet then?"

"That'd be fine! Where?"

"I'll meet you at the gardens of the Palais Royal," she replied, "as close to five o'clock as I can. This has been very wonderful for me...thank you," Marie said, opening the door.

"I'll look forward to tomorrow," James responded.

"Bonjour, Sergeant. Sleep well."

"Bonjour, Mademoiselle Gre'soire," he echoed, then he turned, taking a look back over his shoulder at the door to her apartment, excited about the next day, but still feeling pangs of guilt.

The following afternoon James waited at the gardens of the Palais Royal, sitting on a low stone wall under an ancient elm with its limbs radiating in twisted contortions away from the base of the tree. Smaller Lilac trees were precisely spaced around the garden to shade the beds of flowers covering the grounds. Some of the flowers were brown, or spotted from the first signs of autumn, but their colors were still a magnificent sight.

James pulled at the veins of a dried leaf that he'd picked from a thistle that had survived the gardener's rake. Unconsciously, he stripped the decaying leaf apart as he daydreamed of his home and family. He contemplated the odds of his surviving the war and, at the same time, tried to separate the faces of the dead and wounded that had become strangely similar in appearance in his memory.

Finally, his thoughts turned to Marie, and he was able to forget the war for an instant as he remembered the night before; but as quickly as he created his illusions and fantasies of her, they began to compete in his mind with memories of Lora and Jason.

And then, for another moment, he relived the confrontation he'd had with the German in the earthen room at Saint Meheil. He remembered the man flying backwards from the blast of his pistol, through the darkened room. Suddenly he saw a magnified view of the man's face, partially blown away but still smiling at him with a sardonic grin. He could still smell the pungent odor of powder hanging in the air above the corpse. It was a sweet smell that always inspired visions of death. It had become an easy smell to remember.

His thoughts were interrupted as he realized that the smell was real. Smoke from burning leaves had engulfed most of the garden, choking him from the white clouds billowing up from the small bonfires.

He looked towards the source of the smoke, angered at being disturbed. He saw an old man, obviously the caretaker, waving at him through the smoke screen, as if to apologize for the shift in the wind. The old man tried to explain his lack of control over the matter by gesturing towards heaven with his hands.

James cast a forgiving smile at the old worker, deciding to forget his rendezvous with Marie. Everything was becoming too complicated.

As he stood to walk away from the irritating fog, his thoughts returned to Marie. "After all," he reasoned, "I don't know her. I haven't violated my vows. Nothing had happened...not yet. It's best to leave it alone."

He left the smoke, turning to look back just in time to see Marie sitting on a bench outside the cloud, unaware that he was watching her. He stopped, studying the young woman through the thin filmy haze. He thought, 'how alone she must be,' realizing that the future of their relationship suddenly lay in his hands.

It occurred to James that there should be something, a special dispensation perhaps, that would allow him to ease his loneliness, as well as hers, without committing either of them to eternal damnation. After all, the wounded and dying were given morphia. Why then would God not allow the living a moment of passion to anesthetize their suffering?

By the time he reached the bench where she was sitting the smoke cloud had drifted over the two of them. The old gardener ignored the couple, turning his back to tend to the many fires burning within the great garden.

The remainder of his furlough was spent with Marie, and there was a complete capitulation of his fears of moral corruptness. He now understood, or at least wanted to believe, that there was, like the front lines, a space of neutral ground between the saints and the ungodly. It was a path where one could carefully tread and still have room to be declared guiltless, or at least blameless, by virtue of the present circumstances. God would forgive.

Marie accepted the inevitability of their relationship ending, whether from his falling at the front or the war ending and James returning home to his family. She believed, as he did, that they could charge themselves with enough love from each other to later draw upon it like a great battery when their separation would finally come. For her, at least, it was all that she would have to comfort and console herself until the scourge of war had been laid to rest. And God would forgive her.

James quickly realized that Marie was experiencing her own anxieties. She feared being left alone, facing the hostile world that moved closer to Paris with the passing of each day. Without family, she struggled to survive a cold and insensitive world that viewed her only as a statistical problem, another mouth to feed, another head to govern, another Frenchman to be exterminated.

But, far worse, she was left to endure the bete noire, the stalking beast of her own mind that challenged her youthful right to dream and plan for a future. To be with someone who cared, if only temporarily, kindled her desire to live, reminding her that she was still a young woman with aspirations for a life to come.

The days passed quickly for the young couple as they turned their attentions from the looming evil and destruction of the world to concentrate on each other. They fell deeply in love, inspired by the splendor of their surroundings, the beauty of Paris that made it all so natural.

It was just before four in the morning when James was awakened by Marie's gentle caresses, stroking his shoulders and face with her delicate touch. She enticed him to a gentle yet sensual awakening, warmed by her soft skin against his. He responded, studying her eyes, her mouth, pulling her towards him. He felt her breath against his face, encouraging him, teasing, urging him on and then demanding his full attention.

James lay exhausted and satisfied. He felt Marie's heart still surging from the force of their experience, still yearning for his touch. They embraced for one last moment and then quietly separated in their own thoughts. They lay still as they watched each other and wondered where life would take them when morning arrived.

When the morning was still dark James noticed flashes of light outside. He stepped out of bed, standing naked in front of the window and thinking that a storm was brewing to the northeast. But oddly the bursts of light came from below the horizon instead of hanging in the air like lightning. With each flash came a heavy deep 'crack' and a thunderous jolt. Then James realized that it wasn't a storm but artillery fire. He panicked, thinking that the Germans had launched an offensive from the Saint Gobain Woods on the outskirts of Paris. He turned, racing for his clothes as he screamed for Marie to dress so that he could get her safely out of the city.

Marie ignored his alarm, holding out her arms, pleading with a loud cry for him to hold her. Tears ran down her face as she explained that the fire was coming from the German rail guns located at Monte de Joie, sixty-eight miles away. She shook uncontrollably as he held her, counting in a whisper as each round fell. James realized that she'd witnessed the bombardment before. The rain of shells continued for an hour, shells falling every fifteen minutes. Marie lay wrapped in James' arms, never moving until she knew that she had counted the last of the explosions.

When the attack was over, they dressed, walking silently, hand in hand, through the dark to find a special place along the Seine to watch the first light of dawn. The sun had risen enough to reveal the landscape, as they patiently waited, huddled together beneath his overcoat to warm themselves from the morning chill, each wanting their lives to stay as they were, at this precise moment, forever.

James finally stood, placing the heavy coat around her arms as he held onto her hand.

"It's time for me to go," he said.

Marie looked up, studying his eyes, then turned away. She stared across the glassy surface of the river. It was alive with the new light of morning, flickering with each disturbance of the calm surface. James helped her stand, pulling her next to him for a final caress, wanting to promise her that he would survive, to assure her of his love, that they would return to this moment.

151

Stephen D. Boyett

Marie watched him, understanding his mood, holding her fingers gently pressed against his lips. She showed with a smile that she understood. They embraced with a farewell kiss, holding each other together for a few final moments.

"Adieu, mon cher," she whispered softly before she released him and turned back towards the river.

James began walking towards the pickup point where the lorries would be waiting. He took a moment to look back, and saw Marie sitting alone near the river, still watching the sunrise. She wrapped herself in his coat, resting her head on her knees, her arms drawing her body tightly into the cloth. She had accepted what must be, the loneliness that she had known before.

CHAPTER 7

The Ardennes forest, once teeming with great pines and voluminous oaks, now resembled the surface of the moon. It was cratered and desolate, except for a stubble of disfigured trees and the ghostly skeletons of stone farmhouses. An artificial Aurora Borealis lit up the horizon at night, with a constant glow accompanied by the orchestration of different guns, thudding in quick succession.

Sandbags lined the maze of ditches that crisscrossed the multi-colored mud of the landscape. They intersected like highways, resembling the arms of some mutant creature twisting out to reach its prey. Log roofs, cleared of their camouflage, blown or washed away, betrayed the secrecy of a hovel city that had been erected underneath the surface. Revetments were reinforced with logs and interwoven with leafy limbs from the once-lush forest.

Machine guns fired continuously into the fog and smoke, sounding like someone gone mad with a thousand pairs of slow-snapping castanets. Star shells lit the sky with an unearthly light that revealed the wire, curled and stretched across the battlefield in a lethal web. It was a horror that James remembered from his many trips into no-man's land in another place, in another nightmare.

James marched into the Argonne with the 63rd Division, as they took up positions and waited for orders to attack. The intensity of the fighting that was already going on left little opportunity for the men to reflect on their recent furloughs to Paris, or anything else, for that matter. Their thoughts were constantly interrupted as mortar rounds screamed to earth with an identifying voice. The higher the pitch of the incoming rounds, the smaller the size of the explosive. Some whistled, some screamed, some were even silent, but all were deadly.

James watched his boots disappear into the slimy muck as he moved down the trench, slipping and sliding, balancing himself across a log traversing a pothole that looked too deep to survive.

A plank carved with a bit of sarcastic trench wit was tacked to the wall near the dark watery abyss. It was obviously the inspiration of a past resident who had entertained himself during the lull in fighting by watching the reactions from passers-by to his sign that read:

> 'If 'ere a man come strutting by
> Upon this hallowed ground
> He'll find this hole where a yank fell in
> And his body was never found.
> So tip your hat and say a prayer
> For Corporal Willy Brown.
> Some say he slipped beneath the mud
> And was most likely drowned.
> But when this war is over
> And they've drained this darkened pit
> They'll find that Willy didn't die,
> But only stopped to shit.
> So after the battle has ended
> They'll mark this famous spot
> The place where Willy hunkered down
> And fired his final shot.

James laughed and continued on, turning and twisting his way through the treacherous slough that led up the side of the hill towards the fighting.

The Meuse-Argonne Offensive began early the next morning with the advance of a squadron of light French Renault tanks.

James and the other corpsmen were sent over the top with the main body of troops at 0530, on September 28th. They followed behind the first wave, quickly disappearing into the dense cloud of smoke that hung suspended over the forward area. Prior to the attack there had been hours of saturation bombardment in an attempt to neutralize German resistance.

When the Germans realized the strength of the movement, that an offensive had been launched, they concentrated all of their available artillery into the sector, pulverizing the earth with a volcanic force.

James was horrified at the results. As he perused the battlefield for wounded, he soon realized that he was finding neither wounded nor bodies. The retrograde barrage had been so intense that those who fell from the withering fire were expunged from the face of the earth. They were, more precisely, blended into the soil as so much fine organic additive, with not so much as a piece of cloth left to indicate that men ever had walked across the field.

James had made five trips back to the aid station with wounded by 0730. Shortly afterwards he was pinned down in a slit trench for an hour until a squad of Marines arrived with a flame thrower. They proceeded to incinerate the Germans who'd penetrated the defenses and dug themselves in just outside the approach trench.

A thick black smoke gushed from the pill box where the Germans had set up their position. There was a hiss of burning flesh and an occasional explosion of bullets set off by the fire. A grenade on one of the bodies was detonated from the extreme heat, snuffing out what was left of the flames. James slipped over the top and again moved onto the battlefield. It was a relief to be away from the smell of death and the depressing picture of so many corpses. They were an inattentive lot, frozen in their animated poses, hideous with their bloated looks and creating a stench that was impossible to tolerate even in the strongest wind.

James found himself running into the soft glow of the morning light. He looked back over his shoulder, relieved that the grotesque crowd was left to someone else's care. He was just beginning to see the first lights of a clouded, overcast morning, a morning permeated with the smell of fresh gunpowder folded into a slightly moist easterly wind. Everywhere, there were signs indicating that soldiers had passed over the landscape but there was no one to be seen, dead or alive. James started towards an oasis of thickly plumage trees. 'Le Boquetaire', the French called the oddity. He remembered the excitement of the French infantrymen whenever they saw one of the unscathed clumps. They were as excited as a museum curator finding that vandals had missed an irreplaceable treasure. But the vandals were still there.

James raced for the cover of the forest, thinking he would be alone and safe from the reality of the battle, if only for a short while. He'd left his squad of litter carriers under someone else's command, with the excuse that he was going forward to find where the heaviest concentration of casualties had fallen. No sooner had he slipped into the clump of trees than the German artillery spotters turned their attention towards the tiny green island. They let loose with an earthshaking salvo.

Soldiers sprinted from spider holes near the perimeter of the foliage. The all-too-familiar sounds of war arrived at the peaceful gates of Eden accompanied by the screams of dying men. James clawed at the cold earth, trying to conceal himself from the shrapnel that screamed through the air. Hot shards of metal ricocheted from the rocks, thumping the trees as they penetrated their trunks and limbs. Leaves fell to the ground like an Autumn storm. He pressed himself into the dirt, bobbing his head up at short intervals to watch the horizon. The woods had seemed to James to be of little strategic importance, an innocent enough spot, too thick with trees to harbor a cannon or tank. It was more a place for a picnic basket and a blanket, or so he had mistakenly thought.

The impetus for the attack had come when an American patrol had decided to infiltrate the forest moments before James had arrived. The Germans noticed the movement. One man's paradise became another's fort.

James suddenly found himself a victim of bad timing. As soon as he realized the reason for the bombardment, he cursed the patrol. But they were deaf to his screams of profanity as the detonating rounds raised the once level ground into a smoldering heap. The majestic trees were quickly reduced to stunted posts overlaid with piles of leafy compost and splintered limbs.

James could feel the concussions tossing him helplessly from side to side. Some of his equipment was torn from his body as an explosion flipped him over against the trunk of a downed tree. He struggled to sit up, trying to shake off the dizziness, the landscape spinning in front of him.

The shelling stopped long enough for him to study what was left of his island paradise. He wondered if any of the others had survived. The trees and bushes where most of the men had hidden were now craters filled with smoldering debris. The soldiers had vanished, leaving only mud.

James let the water from his canteen pour over his face as he lay on his back, beside a fallen log, gasping for air, more from an appreciation of life itself than any shortness of breath.

The smell of raw sap covering his uniform from the felled trees suddenly reminded him of his boyhood years and the old saw mill on his father's farm near Lalleville. He remembered the sticky fluid from the loblolly pines covering his work clothes as the logs passed against the spinning rip-saw blade in the cutting shed, as he worked along side his father. He could still smell the burning wood from the drying kilns. He could see his father and Plato, as clearly as yesterday, pulling a great Cypress stump towards the mill from the bayou behind a team of mules.

But most of all he remembered Jaques standing across the cypress log as the two of them worked together using a bow saw to sever the knotted stump from the main trunk of the tree. He'd forgotten his father's wonderful smile. But those times, when he was young, before his mother had passed away, were harder to remember now. It felt good to think of his father again.

The shrill screams of incoming shells gave barely enough warning for James to turn over on his face, covering his head with his helmet and pressing himself into the earth. He braced his body for the blast, screaming in terror as the first shells landed beside him. The detonations set the ground in motion, tossing him helplessly into the air. And then, there was nothing. A great pressure seemed to emerge, holding him suspended, as if some strange anesthesia had been administered into the vacuum, blotting out every sense in his body. The sounds of battle disappeared and were replaced by a loud humming in his ears, then silence.

He lay unconscious, immersed up to his chest in frigid water and mud. Boulders and dirt clods held his body to the bottom of the shell hole except for his head and left arm. His mouth was partially submerged, filling and emptying with each breath he took. His clothes had been blown away, leaving nothing but the mud to insulate his body from the falling temperature.

The cold water finally woke him up, his right eye scanning the wall of the crater, watching as a small pellet of mud slid into the water beside him. A leaf blew into the hole, barely sticking in the soft mud a few feet away before a swirl of wind lifted it free and carried it away. He cleared the water and mud from his mouth by turning his head to one side, and tried to wipe the burnt skin and dried blood from his eyes with his one free arm. He knew he had feeling in his legs and feet, but he could still bleed to death from a wound concealed beneath the pile of debris that was holding him down.

James' eyes moved up the wall of the crater to its uppermost edge where he hoped to see a friendly face looking down to inquire about his wounds. He was still drowsy from the explosion. His vision was blurred from the fragments of sand and dirt that had been blown into his eyes from the blast. No one was there to tell him that he would be rescued. He would have to wait for the area to cool down before anyone would come for him.

He began shaking violently as he tried to fight off the effects of shock and hypothermia. Realizing that he was about to pass out, he moved his fist under his face to keep from drowning in the few inches of water around his mouth.

A half-hour later he regained consciousness, with his arm nearly frozen beneath his cheek. He struggled with his numbed hand, reaching into the murky pool, trying to wash the mud from his nose and mouth.

He could hear the sounds of battle all around him as he prayed to be found before the shell crater was filled with debris from another explosion. Even the weight of his own head, became a threat to his life as he struggled to keep from letting his face relax back into the water. At times his mouth bubbled as air competed with water for entry into his lungs. The lessons from his past, his bout with tuberculosis as a child, began to serve him well as he recalled the discipline of living on a limited supply of air and at the same time holding back the trickle of fluids dripping down his throat that might drown him.

He could hear the faint voices of men and muffled sounds of equipment moving on every side of the hole. A column of Germans had been advancing towards the American lines for most of the evening. Several soldiers had stopped to relieve themselves into the shell hole, but none of them seemed interested in the body lying at the bottom.

He began feeling faint again. He knew it was important to stay awake to signal those who might be coming to rescue him. But, on the other hand, the slightest movement in an effort to stay conscious might well attract the attentions of some passing German moving near the ditch. If they saw him still alive, they would shoot him, be it barbarism or mercy. He moved his fist under his face again and quietly slipped into a deep undisturbed sleep. His life was again in God's hands.

When he awoke, it was still dark. Star shells flashed below the clear sky, burning his eyes with their brilliant glare. He could hear the sounds of a gramophone playing from the direction of the American lines. When the music coming from the American emplacements stopped, the Germans continued the entertainment with a concertina. Soon both sides joined in with a melancholy sing-along back and forth across no-man's land. By morning, they would be back to slashing and gutting each other again with a vengeance. But darkness usually brought peace, and tonight was no exception.

Dirt and mud lay on James' torso like a fresh grave. The chill of the water sent a sharp, agonizing pain through his body that helped him to stay awake. He knew now he wasn't bleeding from any open wounds, or else he'd have long since been dead. But he also knew he would succumb to exposure if he wasn't found soon.

He finally gave up the concern he had about screaming out. It had occurred to him that an American recon' patrol would be as likely to find him as the Germans.

"Help me!" he screamed. "I'm dying down here...in this hole...down here...down here! For God sakes...help me!"

His voice softened as he tired. "Don't let me die like this!" he said, still shaking from the cold. "Get me out of here!"

He had barely started to plead for help again before his face dropped into the water. He no longer had the strength to hold his head up or cry out for help. His mind raced back in time, to that day when his father had held him, crying and shaking as they had knelt together in the mud near the barn.

'How prophetic,' he thought, 'that life should end like this...in a setting so similar to his childhood nightmare when his father had left him. Better it had ended then than now.'

At that moment he decided to end his life by letting himself drown in the sludge pool. He had reached the point that he knew death was inevitable. He had seen the clear sky and moonlit night above him. No one would be sent over the top to face machine guns or snipers on such a night. He knew the procedure better than anyone. The wounded and dead would lie where they had fallen until morning. By then, he knew he would have suffered an agonizing death.

Like a navigator checking his line of travel before setting off on his final journey, he looked up towards heaven as he prepared to plunge his face into the viscous sludge that would end his life.

He was startled to see what appeared to be the figure of a man standing at the edge of the hole. The figure looked down at him, saw that he was alive, and then turned around with his back to the crater as if he were standing guard. A spark of hope surged through James' body. But it was quickly dispelled. What if this figure was a German, waiting for a patrol to come by to help take him prisoner, he thought. Maybe the soldier assumed he was already dead. What if the man was an American or Frenchman, and he passed out before he could let the guard know he was alive? "What if, what if? Maybe he's not even really there!" He forced himself to raise his head, letting loose with a loud, pleading cry, hoping beyond all else that the man would at least have enough pity on him to help pull him loose from the pile of rocks and mud.

The man turned and looked down again, still not revealing his face. He watched James for a second and then returned to his previous position, guarding the crater. James couldn't understand why the man continued to stand there. He lay panting, struggling to catch his breath, still unsuccessful in communicating with the mirage.

He began speaking softly to the shadowy image, "Why don't you help me? Can't you hear me? I'm down here...in the bottom of this hole." He repeated himself in French, to be sure the man understood him.

Still there was no response from the soldier. James thought perhaps the man might be German or Austrian.

He yelled out in a broken German dialect, "Please help me! I'm badly hurt. Can't you see I'm dying?"

The figure remained still, ignoring his pathetic pleas for help. James tried tossing small stones with his freed hand, but the cold had paralyzed him, making his hand useless except to support his head in the water with the frozen fist.

Forty-five minutes passed, with James painfully stretched out under the weight of the mud and stones, watching the figure. He'd given up on trying to make the phantom respond to his cries. He had resigned himself to wondering if it was really a man or just some symptom of dying.

Whatever it was, it had no fear of being shot by the snipers on either side. It was odd, James thought, that no one had seen him standing straight up in the light of the flares and blown his head off.

Suddenly there was a clash of men locked in hand-to-hand combat, only yards away. James looked up, his eyes locked on the ghostly apparition. He noticed that it had moved into position to use its bayonet, still facing away from the crater.

"You black Godless devil!" James screamed, "If you won't help me, then why don't you kill me. I know you! You're Azrael, the angel of death. You're just scavenging the gutters of earth, to get your fill of defenseless souls. The more tormented they are...the more you enjoy it! You're just sitting here waiting for me to die!"

The figure turned its head, looking down at James, and then moved away from the dark abyss towards the fracas going on a few yards away. A short time later James noticed that the figure had returned sitting with its back towards him, holding its rifle and bayonet so that it reflected in the moonlit night. The creature appeared to be wiping blood from the long-bladed knife.

James' frustration was more than he could stand. He raised his head up and with his last burst of energy, yelled, "Who are you? Why do you just sit there and let me die? What harm have I done to you? Mother of Jesus!"

James slipped into a shallow dream. He saw Lora standing next to the crater wearing a black dress and a veil over a stern, frowning face. She held a white rose in her hand. A small child was standing next to her, dressed in a black, short-legged suit and clutching his mother's hand. The child was stone-faced as the two of them looked down at James, as if he were being buried. Lora touched her eye with a linen hanky, careful not to let a single tear fall from her eye.

Marie suddenly appeared, pushing her way past Lora with her arms outstretched, reaching for him, begging him to live.

She held out her hand as if to lift him from the grave while Lora and the boy stood by, impassively.

The dream ended, leaving him staring into the darkness of the night. The silence on the battlefield was unnerving. The sounds of men advancing around him during the early evening had at least conjured up some hope of rescue, but now there was only silence. He wondered if he was dead. He looked up towards the edge of the crater to see if Lora and Jason were still there. He continued to search for Marie, but found that she had gone too. Everyone had vanished, including the guardian spirit.

He abandoned the dream as he struggled with the horrible agony of his confinement. He began to feel the familiar chill of unconsciousness growing with each excruciating surge of pain, searing through his legs at the same throbbing rate as his pulse. The question of his being dead or alive was quickly and painfully answered. Again, he gave up the struggle for life, wishing for death to take him, ending this torment.

And then, when the life seemed to be leaving his body, he felt the soft touch of a hand move over his face. The hand began washing away the dirt from his mouth and eyes. The other hand cradled his head, holding it several inches from the water. Gently, smoothly, the fingers caressed his face with a loving touch as his soul hesitated in its departure.

He felt so at peace. The touch was warm, as warm as those times as a child when he'd lain in his father's arms, sick from a bout with some childhood disease. How well he remembered feeling so much better when his father had been with him. How familiar these hands felt. Not soft like his mother's had been, but just as caring.

He opened his eyes just enough to see the figure of the sentry bending over him. He was holding him, cuddling him like a mother rocking a child.

The figure leaned closer, giving him a faint kiss on his cheek as James struggled to open his eyes. A tear fell from the darkened face, and landed on James' forehead. He knew the touch of the kiss, the gentle feeling of the hands. But still, the face remained hidden.

James' eyes fought the drowsiness that blurred his vision. He wanted more than anything to identify the strange ministering form. The image gently laid him down, and then climbed out of the shadows of the pit as James looked on.

"I'll always be with you," he thought he heard the man whisper as the vision disappeared from the edge of the crater.

His preoccupation with death ceased, turning instead to the euphoria of a rare dream that appears so infrequently in life, a dream so beautiful and peaceful that the dreamer yearns to remain with the phantasm, eagerly giving up the gray, stark realities of life, hoping never to return. He slept a deep comfortable sleep through the remainder of the night.

The heat of the morning sun baked his body. It was a good feeling. He wasn't dead, at least not yet.

"Hey, you alive down there?" Someone shouted, hunkering down on the edge of the crater and blocking the sunlight.

James tried to open his eyes, aware that he was hearing a voice, but not trusting that it was the real thing. He fought to answer, waving his hand feebly. He finally managed to open his eyes, smiling his answer. His body was as pale as a buried corpse, but he'd survived the ordeal.

"Boche?" the soldier asked. "Francais?" he asked again since James still hadn't answered.

James responded, half laughing, half crying, "Merciful God, get me outa here, will ya?"

"This one's still alive! Let's get him dug out," an order echoed from across the hole. "He's one of ours!" The men worked quickly to uncover his body, carefully removing the binding stones and mud. James held out his hand, wanting to touch one of them to assure himself that they were real. Blankets were wrapped around his numbed legs and torso as they prepared to cart him across the battlefield towards their lines.

One of the men, still holding onto James' hand, looked at him and shook his head in disbelief.

"You're one lucky fella, you know that? That little clump of trees has been the hottest spot on the line since yesterday."

One of the other men wiped James' face with a handkerchief and then grabbed the stretcher, struggling to lift his end out of the crater.

163

"You're damn lucky you were down in that hole. I don't know why them Germans didn't get you; they were in those woods thicker'n ticks on a dog's ass."

Another soldier smiled, patting James on the shoulder. "You're just lucky to be alive," the man said. "Good Lord musta been holdin on ta you mighty tight last night!"

James smiled, looking away from the soldier as he surveyed the area for some sign of his mysterious guardian. He was still desperate to know if the sentry had been real or an illusion brought on by shock. Each time he convinced himself that his visitor was something conjured up in his mind, he remembered thinking he heard the words whispered by the ghostly form as he'd climbed out the crater: 'I'll always be with you.'

His eyes closed, leaving him content to have survived the ordeal. He would sort out the details of his strange encounter some other time. For now, all he wanted to do was to eat and to be taken someplace warm to sleep.

James was transported to a hospital just outside of Paris. His lungs were full of fluid from pneumonia. He was placed in a sparsely lit ward with patients suffering the ghastly effects of mustard and chlorine gas. The ward resembled a mortuary with cadaverous forms laid in rows under suspended white sheets. The sheets were tented up, protecting victims from infectious bacteria in the air, but yet not touching the scalded flesh. Even the patients' faces were masked by the covers, hiding the agony as many of the men choked and gurgled their final breaths.

The smell of decaying flesh was so heavy that ward attendants wore gauze masks to lessen the gagging stench as they worked to comfort the patients. Nothing could be done to relieve their pain. The nurses had developed an intuitive third sense, to recognize the final moments of a suffocating man's agony. They would sit next to the struggling young soldier, holding onto his burned hand while a priest delivered the sacraments to Catholic and Protestant alike.

The soldier's eyes would dart from the busy look of the priest, nervously after the man's soul, to the comforting expression of the nurse. The young man would watch the nurse and then the priest, much the same as a child watching a conductor announcing the departure of his train, his first trip alone. He would look at her as if watching his mother for reassurance that everything would be all right. Each one of them was aware of his final destination.

James' convalescence in such a morbid setting had sapped his morale. He'd seen men die before, but never so slowly and with such great agony and suffering.

On November 11, 1918, James and the other patients celebrated a quiet armistice. Most of the men had reconciled themselves to never going home. Some were even thankful that their families would be spared the horror of seeing their degenerative conditions.

The lights in the long open wards were kept low because of the sensitivity of the burn patients' eyes. James tried to read by the small lamp placed next to his bed where he had accumulated a collection of books and periodicals borrowed from the local medical library.

His pneumonia and assorted lacerations and contusions were minor, compared to the soul-wrenching agony of the charred forms wheezing their death struggle on either side of him. He had expended all of his compassion, courage and pity, only to fix his eyes on the rise and fall of the patient's chest to see when God would finally say, enough! The news of the armistice had made him even more determined to recover from his wounds. He was eager to leave the horrible place and get on with his life.

It was hard to know what time of day it was with the ward always so dark. He'd lost his military watch in the crater and there was no clock on the wall. He had to rely on the nurses to tell him what time it was. He tried to use the tolling of church bells from the nearby village that rang at noon each day, but they sounded so often for special masses or other occasions that they were confusing at best.

He lay comfortably engrossed in one of his books, looking up only because he suddenly sensed someone was standing in the dark, staring at him. A young woman stood in the periphery of the light that glowed softly from the lamp next to his bed. Her hands were locked together, and an uncertain smile was on her face. She looked down at the marble floor and then at James before speaking apologetically in French.

"I wasn't sure I should come. I didn't know if you'd want to see me," she said.

James looked at her, laying his book in his lap as his face blossomed into a smile. It was Marie. She moved out of the dim light, revealing a bouquet of pastel-colored flowers that she'd brought for him, wrapped in a Paris newspaper announcing the armistice.

She walked towards him, accepting his outstretched arms. She pulled his hands to her lips, softly kissing his fingers and then pressed his hands to her face. Her eyes closed as she moved beside him, holding him in her arms.

James cupped her face in his hands, "I'm so glad you came! I hoped and prayed that Roy would find you...to tell you where I was...to tell you how much I wanted to see you, how much I care for you."

He stroked her hair as she sat next to him on the bed. "He's gone...your friend Roy Blackwood has gone back to America," she said. "He said to tell you goodbye! And he said he hoped he would see you again someday. He asked that you forgive him for not telling you he was leaving."

"I'm glad that he found you. I thought I'd never see you again...that I'd lost you forever," James whispered, holding her passionately in his arms.

For a while he studied her face, surprised how true to detail his dream of her had been. She was lovely, and beautiful, and alive. As he held her, he realized that his dream had missed the wonderful sweet fragrance of her body and the soft touch of her hair. After a while he began telling her what had happened to him during the battle. His face was flushed as he began the bizarre story, but brightened as he described the vision he'd had in the crater.

He wiped his eyes with his finger as he began: "I thought I was dead. At first, it seemed as if the devil was there, watching over me, to haul me off to hell if I died."

James' breathing became more rapid and labored as he continued "But this thing, this person that was there...it made everything so peaceful. The doctors say it was from the shock, some kind of illusion."

He looked forlornly out the window, pausing at first, but then a faint smile came to his face, and he continued, "I know that it was guarding me, watching over me...to keep me safe."

"It could have been a soldier who'd been in the forest at the same time, someone who'd gotten lost?" Marie suggested. "There were so many men out there," she added.

"No! I knew him. Or at least I knew the feeling that he gave me when we touched. I knew who he was without ever seeing his face. He saved my life." James went on, without explaining what he meant. "He said he'd never leave me. I know I heard him say that!" He shook his head, but then nodded; he was at peace with the message the apparition had brought.

Marie crossed herself and then placed her hand against James' cheek, saying, "I prayed that you would live...that God would bring you back to me. I thank Him for your life." She wept. "Now I can live again! Now we can both live again!"

By March of 1919, James had been released as an outpatient and reassigned to the staff of the same hospital. Most of the patients who could walk were being processed for transportation back to the States.

James had asked to remain in the army as an interpreter for another six months. It was a personal commitment of his to stay with the other wounded men. He wanted to do as much as he could for those who would be left behind in France, those who would eventually die from gas or other wounds.

In the spring, Marie had asked James to accompany her to Pont-a-Mousson. It was the first time that she had returned to her farm since the German guns, positioned outside of Metz, had been silenced. They traveled by troop train from Paris to Nancy where James was able to arrange a ride for the two of them to go on to Pont-a-Mousson with a supply column.

They rode through the countryside, Marie locked in James' arms as the lorries wound their way towards the frontier over the near-impassable roads. She held onto him, as if to protect herself from the demon that had laid waste the once-beautiful landscape. She glared from his arms, dismayed at the sea of destruction that lay before them. Her eyes could hardly believe the blackened terrain, covered with a thousand shapes of man-made war machinery twisted and spread over its surface.

Pont-a-Mousson had met the same fate as other villages trapped in the storms of siege from both sides. Much of it had been razed by house-to-house fighting. The two travelers were able to find lodging with Marie's friends who lived on the outskirts, where a few buildings remained unscathed by the conflict.

Marie fell into a deep sleep in James' arms, exhausted from the long trip. She was pressed tightly against him. He could feel her warmth as he lay beside her, content to feel her heartbeat as he studied her childlike face. She had become all that he desired in the world, his new world.

His hand retrieved the gold watch from his blouse that was hanging next to the bed. He opened it, listening to the miniaturized carillon chime playing softly from the tiny instrument. As he listened, he looked at her closed eyes, feeling the heat of her naked body pressed against him. He felt her soft skin, wanting desperately to have her, but doing nothing, as if to somehow test his devotion. He let her sleep as a storm raged within him.

In the morning, James hired a wagon and drove Marie to the farm. A pair of draft horses, pulling the heavy wagon, moved slowly through the tunnel of trees that led to Marie's home. The tunnel was exactly as she had described it to him when they had first met. The air was as crisp as she had said it would be. The sweeping limbs of the giant trees were breathtaking, leaning regally over their path, as if bowing in honor of her return.

Marie was surprised to find that the grounds near the house hadn't been pulverized by artillery, or the house burned to the ground by marauding troops. The house was intact except for a hole in the roof and a few broken window panes. The barn and feed shed had also survived the tumultuous storm that had encircled the farm, but the livestock had fallen prey to the hungry armies that had passed back and forth over the property.

James helped Marie down from the wagon and followed her into the darkened cottage. She stood with her hand over her mouth, sobbing with relief that the contents hadn't been looted. She moved through her home like a spirit, touching each memento, wiping the dust from pictures and glassware. She closed her eyes every few feet, trying to stop the flow of tears that threatened as she took a mental inventory of what was left of her life.

James quietly left Marie with her thoughts and strolled down to the edge of the Moselle River that crossed behind the farm. It reminded him so much of home, of Lalleville, where the deep channels of water flowed from the bayous, cutting across the open flats and marshes, heading to the Mississippi. He sat high up on a ridge overlooking the river, studying the soil and looking across the fields towards Germany. He thought about home, his home, safely preserved for his return. He felt sorry for Marie because of the loss of her family, and yet she seemed happier than he did.

"Someday, France will be beautiful again," Marie said, surprising him as she sat down. She had regained her composure.

"I have my life and my home," she said. "I should be thankful to have so much. But I've lost everyone I love, except you, and I know you'll be leaving soon."

James turned around to object to what she'd said, but she only smiled, shaking her head with her eyes closed, as if to ignore his response.

"You'll be going home to your wife and son, to America, to start your life over again. I shouldn't blame you for that...it's only right."

James sat in a trance, watching the flow of the river moving swiftly away from where they were sitting. He turned towards her, taking her into his arms with his eyes focused on hers, saying, "I'll work this out so that we can be together. This is where I belong!"

Marie said nothing, but simply smiled and touched his cheek before looking back towards the swiftly moving river.

James began to rebuild the farm. He was driven to somehow make up for what had happened to Marie. It made him feel as though he was even helping the people of France in some small way by trying to put Marie's life back together.

He was happier than he'd been in years, working each day mending the buildings and fences and working the fields. He would lie with Marie in the warm afternoon sun after she had brought his lunch. They spent the nights committed to each other, making love and dreaming of a future that revolved around the farm.

One afternoon, as James was plowing a small portion of ground near the house for a garden, he heard Marie calling to him, playfully pleading for him to come to her. She was bending over in knee-high grass picking an assortment of colorful spring flowers. Marie had been attracted to the flowers because it was unusual for them to have bloomed so early in the season. She twirled and danced, holding the flowers above her head like a child, calling him with a girlish whine, singing to him with impromptu lyrics to a borrowed tune.

"See what I've found, my Sergeant, my beautiful Sergeant! Flowers! Wonderful spring flowers, just in this one spot! It is certainly a gift from God to celebrate our love," she chirped, picking another two or three as she waited for James to come to her.

James walked towards Marie, smiling and laughing each time she would pick a stem from the weed-covered patch of ground and then do a comical pirouette. She smiled seductively, motioning for him to come to her, making sure he saw her unbuttoning her dress.

James moved closer to Marie, cackling at her antics until he suddenly realized the secret of the conspicuous grouping of flowers. His eyes first caught the odd shape of metal lying on the surface of the field and then the blackened rags mixed in the high grass. Chunks of broken earth and sod heaved upwards from the flat ground, as if a plow had been through the field. Suddenly, he knew what she'd found.

"For God's sake, don't move, Marie. Stay where you are!" he screamed. "Keep perfectly still!"

"Oh no, James," she sang, "you're just going to come over here to take my flowers? That really isn't fair, and it isn't what I had in mind."

James held his hand out, signaling her to stop talking. "Stay still, I'm telling you! You're standing in a mine field. Don't move! For God's sake, don't even breathe!"

Her face changed to a stark, porcelain hue, as her arms fell limply to her side, both hands now emptied of her booty of flowers.

James crawled towards her, advancing, inch by inch, as he checked the ground, spotting first one, then another mine. Finally reaching her, he took her hand, retreating through the grass, back the way he had entered the mine field.

"An explosion, that's what brought the seeds close to the surface, close enough for the sun to warm them so they'd bloom. Those pieces over there are probably an animal or some unsuspecting soldier. God only knows!" James explained.

Marie began sobbing. She held onto him, obviously shaken by what had happened.

"Don't ever come to this spot again," he warned. "The whole place is probably mined! We'll have to put up fences to keep the animals out. And signs...we'll need lots of signs."

James looked over towards the other fields, holding a clump of dirt in his hands. He tossed the dirt disgustedly to the ground, remarking, "That's probably why no one ever got into the house; they didn't wanta risk going through the mine fields. They'd just as well have stolen everything, doing this to your land!"

Marie held tightly onto James, shivering from the experience as they walked back to the house.

The incident in the pasture only heightened their resolve for a deeper love. Marie grasped tightly to James, burying herself in his strength and passion, and giving her all in exchange. James felt the flow of life returning to his once-broken spirit, like a gift, bringing him to a level of intoxication he'd never known. It was as if God himself had plucked them from the throes of death to bring them together to this place, this very special Eden. Neither dared look to the past lest they destroy the dream.

Finally the time came to return to Paris. He considered it a momentary interruption in his new life, an inconvenience that soon would be over as quickly as he could muster out of the army.

The trip back to camp was uncomfortable. The hours seemed to drag by as he occupied his time with dreams of home and his family. He knew the smells and colors that spring would bring to Lalleville and to the swamp. He could almost feel the hot sun on his skin. He'd missed the warm afternoons on the bayou. He thought of Lora with quiet affection, knowing she had been faithful and unchanging. His brother Bill would have already prepared the fields at the old home place for Spring planting. And Katy would probably be sitting on the front porch in the cool evening air, dressed up in her Sunday finest and being wooed by some new beau.

Jason, his son, would be nearly three-and-a-half years old. He thought about what kind of a young man he would become, wondering if he would be as tall as the other men of the Lavoisier clan. Remembering his son brought a smile to his face.

With each stop of the train along the route, his thoughts seemed to take a full one-hundred-and-eighty-degree turn. He would occupy himself on the next leg of the journey thinking about Marie and what his future was going to be like with her. A conflict of choices consumed him as he tried to justify leaving Lora.

At first it had seemed so easy to imagine leaving his wife. But the farther away from Pont-a-Mousson he traveled, the harder it seemed to be to leave her.

'Marie isn't my wife. Where is the obligation to stay with her?' he wondered. 'I'll just go home, right now, and never go back to Pont-a-Mousson. That'll be the end of that!'

But it wasn't. He'd fallen in love with the young French girl. She was so very different from what he'd known with Lora. She was alluring and sensitive. It was as difficult to contemplate leaving her as it was to fathom his leaving Lora. She had shared a part of his life that Lora would never understand, the fears and heartbreaks that had been pressed into his mind by the war, and Marie had been there through it all. It seemed as if they'd been together for a lifetime.

Within two weeks he'd been given another furlough. The occupation of France had wound down to the point that the army had nothing for the men to do while they waited for transport back to the States. James made his way back to Pont-a-Mousson. He had needed time to think, to be sure he was right in what he was going to do. This time, on the long trip to the farm, he knew his heart.

He sat up against the wall at one end of the doorless boxcar, buried up to his waist in fresh straw. Four other men occupied the same car, all Frenchmen returning home from the war.

Because of the late hour, most of the men were trying to sleep, although a cold wind mixed with rain blew through the open sides, forcing them to huddle at one end in order to stay warm and dry.

They made another stop, this time in Toul. An old priest boarded the train, wrestling a rickety bicycle through the door into the middle of the car. He was breathing heavily from emphysema, but continued to draw from a fat cigarette stuck to his lips as he finally muscled his bicycle on board.

First one, then another of the French soldiers was awakened by the commotion. They each looked up, greeting the old man, who blessed each of them, apologizing for the disturbance. Each of the men quickly returned to sleep, comforted by his presence.

The priest looked at James, studying him, curious about his uniform. He'd noticed that James had made a point of ignoring his liturgical efforts. For the next twenty minutes the train lumbered and jerked along, but neither of them spoke.

At Fouard, government workers served hot coffee and bread to the men traveling on the train. The priest was quick to take an extra portion for James as an excuse to talk to him.

"Je vous souhaite le bonjour, Sergeant," the priest said, handing James a cup of coffee and a piece of bread. "Bonjour, Pere," James answered, accepting the offering with a faint smile.

"I believe I know you, Sergeant," the priest said, speaking in a very concise English.

"I don't think so, Father," James replied, a little surprised.

"Oh, but yes! You are the American, the ami of...well, anyway, the one who came to visit Pont-a-Mousson recently."

"And how did you know that, Father?" James asked.

"I'm Father Alliot, from the village Abbey," he replied with a huge smile.

"Oh! Well, its nice to meet you, Father," James said. He wiped his eyes with both hands, yawning to signal ever so politely that he preferred sleep to this conversation.

"You are going to Pont-a-Mousson?" the Priest asked. He handed James an open bottle of fruit juice as he waited for a response.

173

James declined the offer. "Yes, I'm going for a short visit."

"Spring should be very beautiful this year. This is the first time in years that crops will be planted in the fields around the village, now that we have nitrates for fertilizers."

"Yeah," James grunted. He slid down into the straw, hoping that Alliot would take the hint.

The old priest continued to carry on the conversation for another fifteen minutes, keeping all of the men in the car shifting position in their sleep as they tried to escape the disturbance. James remained respectfully focused in the priest's direction, although he was not really listening.

Suddenly, his eyes opened with an interest when Alliot announced, "Marie's father would have loved this time of the year. He was very happy with his life as a farmer!"

James watched the priest, concentrating on every word he said. 'How much does he know about Marie?' he wondered. 'He's probably her confessor.'

"What did you do before you were a soldier, Sergeant?"

James snapped a quick, irritable, "Druggist."

"Druggist? Ah,.Pharmacien, Pharmacien...oh yes..." He laughed, nervously.

James leaned against the wall of the boxcar, studying Alliot's face until the Priest finally tipped his head down, either sleeping or praying, it was difficult to tell in the dark. No sooner had James himself nodded off than Alliot came back to life and began asking more questions.

"I suppose you'll be going home to your family in America before long...back to your work as a druggist?"

James opened his eyes. He was perturbed at having his sleep interrupted again by the priest.

"I don't know, Father. I'm sure I will, sooner or later."

The Priest's face seemed at that moment to change, from that of a soft-spoken man, passing the time in innocent conversation, to an examining judge.

"Marie is a very beautiful, young woman. She is also very sensitive and fragile," he offered.

James straightened his back against the wall before responding, "I don't wanta appear rude, Father, but you obviously have something on your mind. Why don't you get it off your chest so that both of us can get some sleep!"

"Very well, Sergeant, since you put it that way. You're a very lucky young man whose life God has seen fit to spare from the war. Some day you'll be going home, leaving France and everything that has happened here. You'll go home to a country that's never seen such horrors of death and destruction. You'll have nothing but memories of what's happened to you. Your family will be waiting eagerly to welcome you home, and your life will be as it was before you came to France."

"I doubt that very much, Father, but go on!"

"Marie has no place to go except her home, at Pont-a-Mousson, the farm that her father and mother built with their own hands. She would never leave her family's farm...I know her too well! Did you know she was with her parents when they were both killed?"

"No, I didn't," James replied. "She only mentioned that they had died in the war."

"Yes! Both of her parents were executed, just outside the house one night because a German raiding party hadn't understood that her father and mother were deaf. The officer in charge had mistaken Monsieur Gre'soire's failure to answer his interrogation as impertinence or stubbornness, whichever it was. It was the same for Mademoiselle Gre'soire. They were both such gentle, kind, people.

"When Marie tried to intercede, she was beaten and raped in front of her mother and father in an attempt to make them cooperate. It has been very difficult for her to discuss the events of that night with anyone. I'm not surprised that she kept it from you."

James' shock at what he had just heard left him staring at the priest in a stupor.

"I'm not saying that it's wrong to be in love with Marie," Alliot said. "She's a beautiful child, and I am sure that you mean well for her in your affections. There's nothing to be ashamed of in wanting to have loved someone under the hideous circumstances that have pervaded all of our lives, but that time is past."

"I love her, Father...very much," James countered. "The war has nothing to do with it."

"Oh, but it does, my son! Go home...go home before both of you are badly hurt. Go home to your family in America and

175

forget Marie. Do it before it's too late for both of you. Your marriage to her would never be condoned by the church. And you know as well as I do that you would never be content to farm her land for the rest of your life."

James tried to convince the priest. "I would be satisfied! I would do whatever I needed to do to make her happy! I love her very much!"

"Go home," the priest continued, "to your wife...to your own country where you belong. The war is over."

A cold gust of wind whirled through the boxcar, giving James an excuse to huddle down, turning his back on Father Alliot.

"Obey your heart, my son...obey your heart," Alliot whispered again, before sliding into the straw, his hands tucked neatly under his face as he fell asleep.

By late afternoon James had arrived at Marie's home. She met him as he opened the door, eagerly embracing him, and pushing her face against his chest.

"I love you, my beautiful Sergeant. You've come back to me, and now I can live again." It was something she said each time they had been reunited.

James pressed his lips against her hair, smelling the sweet fragrance of lilacs. His immediate desire for her overcame his indecision. For the moment, his answer seemed certain. She looked up at him, an almond-eyed, baby-faced look, smiling her contentment at being in his arms. She broke away from his hold, wanting to savor what the evening held in store for them after they had consumed the magnificent meal she'd prepared.

Marie began singing a saucy French melody as she twirled around the room, spinning with the hem of her dress in her hand as if performing a ballroom promenade. James laughed, joining in, bellowing out his own Caruso-style version of the tune. He loosened his tunic collar, moving close enough to her to wrap his arms around her thin waist. His hands pushed her hair aside as he moved his lips the length of her neck, stopping at her ear. Suddenly she pulled away, smiling. Then, ducking under his arms, she walked over to the dining table, shaking her finger at him.

"No, no, James...we must eat first. You'll ruin the wonderful meal I've prepared for you!"

She had placed two slender white candles on a small wooden table in the center of the room. The only other source of light came from a crackling fire in the soot-covered stone fireplace at the other end of the cottage.

Marie smiled at James as she began placing dishes of steaming food and a dark bottle of wine in the center of the table.

Finally, she moved over to a victrola that James had given her, cranking its arm. After several turns of the crank she gently let the needle move against the surface of the record. A selection of three waltzes that James had given her with the victrola began to play. One of the tunes, Chopin's Nocturne, was the same selection that played from the captured German watch he carried in his tunic pocket.

James sprang to his feet as Marie approached the table, pulling back her chair as he gestured with a theatrical bow and then a sweeping motion with one arm across his chest. He uttered a regal, "Majesté," as he positioned her chair, all the while keeping a straight face.

Marie laughed, daintily biting her bottom lip, looking across the table as James took his place for the great feast.

He filled two crystal goblets with the succulent red wine from a dusty bottle and moved one of the glasses to her waiting hand.

The tempo of the waltz slowed, with the violins playing as he raised his glass in a toast. "I toast life, love and the beauty of this special place...and most of all, these precious moments with you!"

James held his glass into the flickering light of the candles, projecting their glow through the prisms of cut glass. A beautiful array of colors burst throughout the room, sparkling in a full circle.

Marie blushed, and then for a moment her eyes glistened. She sat still, looking deep into James' eyes, as if searching his soul for a commitment of love. And then, her head lowered, her tiny hand moved to each of her eyes, brushing away the residue of her thoughts.

With that private moment to herself done, she looked up, smiling again as she raised her glass: "And to you, my Sergeant, my gentle lover, I pray that our memory will always be a memory of happiness, whatever life may bring to us!"

Later they sat in front of the fireplace in each other's arms. Their eyes were fixed on the yellow and blue flames dancing in uneven flashes from the shadows of the heavy logs. In the background the victrola was still echoing a beautiful waltz that brought them back together in a tender communion as his lips, warmed by the fire, met hers.

James looked at Marie, knowing that the time had come to tell her he was being sent home. He concentrated on the flame of a single candle still burning on the table and finally said, "I'm leaving tomorrow to return to America."

Marie turned away, but still held onto his hand, pressing it against her face.

"I'll be back as soon as I can! You must believe...that I love you very much," he said.

"What will you tell your wife?" Marie asked.

"That I'm leaving her," he answered, turning back towards the final moments of the candle's flame, itself struggling for a last opportunity for life.

"I know now that I never loved her," he said, "not like this! I think that the war and all its tragedy has somehow opened my eyes to the things that I want, to the fact that I'm deeply in love with you, and that I want to feel alive again."

"And what about your son...what will you tell him?" Marie asked.

"I'll tell him, someday, when he's a man, that I fell in love with a beautiful woman and that a man must obey his heart."

James suddenly caught himself. He paused, looking towards the door, as if the old priest were standing there, reminding him of his words on the train: 'Obey your heart, obey your heart,' he heard him say over and over again.

The fire cooled as they continued to talk. The blaze dropped back into the red mass of coals, shooting out tiny flares which danced for a split second before vanishing forever.

James pulled Marie to her feet as he opened the back of the watch, holding it next to their faces. A subtle consonance, chillingly romantic and beautiful, played from the gold case as they danced in front of the fire.

They turned deliberately in a small circle, swirling gracefully to the music, caught up in the splendor of the moment. Their movements were so exquisite that they seemed to be in another time, she in a beautiful white ball gown and he in the formal dress uniform of a French soldier. It was a magnificent image, a dream that would have tantalized the hearts of the most envious of spectators.

Slowly, she fingered the small cloth buttons of her dress, undoing each of them until her beauty was revealed to his touch. They moved away from the fire, towards her bed, as the last notes of the music were muted by the feverish harmony of their love.

James sat at a small writing table next to her bed in the early morning hours, watching as Marie slept. After composing a short love letter, he leaned over and kissed her in a final farewell. Then he laid the gold watch next to the letter. He watched sadly as the chain twisted into an uneven mound, as if the magical spell from the evening before had faded. He pried open the back of the watch, again releasing the beautiful waltz. As the music played softly through the cottage, he moved to the front door and into the dark of the morning.

He walked to Pont-a-Mousson, passing down the tree-lined tunnel that had first brought him to his paradise. He looked over at the green fields and was struck by the beauty of the thin clouds of fog that filtered the morning sunlight, giving the landscape a golden glow. The trees reflected a silver sparkle from the cool morning dew. And nowhere was there a sound. It was an eerie silence, a peacefulness like he'd never remembered.

He passed an ancient stone abbey outside of the village, Father Alliot's church. He stopped, seeing the old priest officiating at an early morning funeral.

James stood gaping at the small huddle of darkly clad mourners, wondering if they were burying a soldier, someone who finally had succumbed to wounds.

'How odd it is that they take time now for ceremonies to bury the dead, standing over a single grave to mourn one while thousands lie just below the surface of the battlefields,' he thought. 'What sense does this make, what hypocrisy?'

His eyes were fixed on the priest, as if to confess something, but it was nothing the others would understand. He stood frozen, watching Father Alliot, who looked up from what he was doing. He continued to chant as he searched

James' face, expecting some form of response to his questioning stare, his inquiry, about Marie.

James shook his head, slowly and deliberately, defying the priest, and then dropped his eyes to the road. Alliot continued on without changing the solemn mood of the funeral as he blessed them all a final time.

The troop ships at berth at St. Nazaire were teeming with men crowding the decks, pushing and shoving, trying to jockey for position near the railing to take one last look at the people and country that had extracted such tragic sacrifice from all of them. Some waved and smiled. Others were more contemplative, thinking of lost friends. Many simply bowed their heads in a brief moment of remembrance. But the feeling of relief at having survived was unanimous.

James stayed to himself on the return voyage. He preferred to preserve his happier memories, those of Pont-a-Mousson and Paris, instead of reliving the horrors of war that would become the endless topics of discussion for most of the men.

He was an unwilling passenger, heading home only because he was still a soldier being ordered back to America for discharge from the service. His return trip to France would be a much happier event after the whole unpleasant situation with Lora had been resolved.

The voyage home seemed longer and much more uncomfortable than the trip over had been, perhaps because the absence of the fear of being torpedoed or terror of dying in battle left little to occupy one's thoughts. This time the men were consumed by an anxious anticipation, and, while most of the troops longed to see the shores of America, James still yearned for France and Marie.

When the ships finally arrived at the shores of America, James found himself facing a new dilemma. He'd forgotten how beautiful his own country was. He'd wanted his first image of America, upon his return, to be gray and lifeless, ugly and uninviting, so as not to compete with his picture-perfect memories of France.

The image of Marie was vivid and true in his mind. He could still see her smiling and laughing as she lay warmly nestled in his arms. He thought of their nights together in the cottage, their closeness, and her passionate ways.

His memories of the French countryside were just as vivid. He remembered the lush green fields lazily moving in the wind, split by the Moselle River that flowed through the wide open pastures, and the exact spot along the river where they soaked their feet and lay embracing in the warm afternoon sun. He could see the tunnel of trees where they had walked, holding each other's hands on their way to the market in Pont-a-Mousson. Even the sounds of the church bells from the abbey, being muffled by the early morning fog, were clearly etched in his mind. There was even a concise image of Father Alliot pacing the cloister within the church, praying for his fallen soul, although James had never seen such goings-on by the old priest.

'Yes, the priest,' he thought, 'why did he make this seem so wrong?' I'm in love with Marie...I told him that. He has no right to interfere. It's probably just that he doesn't like Americans. He'll understand! When I get back, he'll see that I'm an honorable man.'

His feelings for Marie smothered any remorse he might have for what lay ahead of him. He was confident that what he was doing was logical. For the first time in his life he felt a sense of relief at not having to conform to what was expected of him by society. He reasoned that he'd earned the right to deny society control over one segment in his life, a simple wish to fall in love.

The troops disembarked for temporary quarters prepared for them near the docks. The men were billeted in empty warehouses located along the wharf and fed that night with their first American meal since they'd marched off for France.

The next day the troops were ordered to participate in a 'welcome home' extravaganza, hosted by the citizens of the City of New York. They marched through the downtown streets, primped and polished, stepping lively to the cheers of thousands of well-wishing Americans showering them in a downpour of ticker tape and the flourishes of drums and brass. The parade ended at the rail yard where trains waited to transport the troops to Camp Meade, Maryland, for the final demobilization of what remained of the American Expeditionary Force.

The camp reveled in a carnival atmosphere. The mood was even further enhanced by the presence of huge, striped circus tents, used as substitutes for field kitchens previously abandoned to the French Army before the A.E.F. had sailed home.

James had little interest in the festivities, electing instead to concentrate on making his plans to rejoin Marie as quickly as possible.

He wrote her as often as time would allow. The remainder of his time was spent walking in the woods around the perimeter of the camp. He walked alone, fearful that the joy and relief at being home might somehow interfere with his decision to pursue his divorce from Lora.

By the third week in the camp, James had grown impatient with the army bureaucracy. He tired of the military red tape as the army fumbled with orders and travel arrangements for himself and the other men. The deactivation had been dragged out to the point that men were deserting, rather than wait any longer to be mustered out. There was a noticeable lack of conversation among the soldiers as they spent most of their time lying on their cots. They passed the evenings gathered around someone playing a guitar or harmonica. The sweet lullaby would create such a melancholy mood that even the hissing of the wood, burning in the potbelly stoves in the center of the tent, would become an almost unbearable distraction.

James lay on his side in his bunk, pulling a long draw from a hand-rolled cigarette. He watched the smoke from the cigarette roll upward into the light glowing from a nearby lantern. He was fascinated by the explosion of the smoke as it passed over the glass flue. It somehow seemed to be a foretelling of what was to happen with his life. Quickly his thoughts would return to Marie, as if to guard his precious vision of her. Several men worked quietly at a table, pushing dominoes back and forth, never saying a word as they sorted and stacked the black rectangles into linear configurations. Each man mentally counted score for their next move, tapping signals to bid or pass, but no one spoke.

"I'm looking for a Sergeant Lavoisier? I've got a package for him," a soldier announced, entering the tent respectfully. It was a time to be still with one's soul, a habit from the dark nights at the front, during the war. Everyone knew to be quiet.

"Over here," James answered. He'd not even bothered to look at the man.

"Someone up at headquarters been sittin' on this here package for a couple of days," the soldier apologized. "They been tryin' to find you ever since it come in, but I guess you know how screwed up everything is around here? Company clerk finally figured out where you were."

James tossed the box under his cot without looking to see who'd sent it. He was certain that it was another love offering from Lora, as she'd already sent two or three boxes. Food was her specialty and he'd open it when he got hungry.

"Thanks for bringing it by," he said, as the courier smiled and disappeared from the tent.

James stripped himself down to his shorts and slipped under the covers, deciding to end his boredom by going to sleep. Then he remembered the package under his bed, so he searched for the small box with his hand, not wanting to have to bend over and look under the cot.

When he'd located the parcel, he gave it hard shake to guess the contents. "Brownies," he decided. "I'll have them tomorrow."

He dropped the carton back on the floor and turned over on his side to sleep. And then, in a moment suddenly wrought with horrible anguish, he began hearing a faint sound. He panicked, knowing the tune and the instrument, but not under-standing how it could possibly be coming from inside the tent.

The gold watch he'd given Marie, the symbol of his everlasting devotion, that he'd entrusted to her as a promise of his return. It was here in the shelter, not with her where he'd left it, where it belonged!

James grappled with his bed cover like a man gone mad, tearing and pulling at the sheets. His tent mates ignored his reaction, thinking he'd been stung by some bug that had crawled in from the woods outside.

183

He stopped what he was doing, aware now that the sound was coming from under the bed. He stood, looking down at the floor at the small box, edged part way into the light.

His hand retrieved the package. He held it up, hearing another short burst of music from inside. He hated this worse than the war, pleading in his mind that it was something pleasant, but pleasantries don't come in small cardboard caskets delivered in the dark of night.

He sat down, placing the box next to him on the bed as his fingers unwrapped it. First the watch, bright gold, shining in the soft light, and then an envelope, dropped out onto the mattress.

The back of the watch was in the full open position, obviously having sprung open when he had shaken the box. James wound the stem in a trance, thinking of Marie as the music continued playing.

He picked up the envelope and the watch and walked out of the tent. He positioned himself under a streetlight a few feet away as he began to read the letter.

"You knew they were there! Why would you do something like that, when you knew?" he murmured. "Why couldn't you believe I was coming back...that I'd keep my word? I loved you so very much!"

"And you, priest...you finally got what you wanted! Now everything is so righteous for you!"

The note slipped from his hand and floated into the cold night air, finally coming to rest on the wet grass.

"I think the war has taken my life, after all," he whispered, turning and leaving the paper where it had fallen.

My dear Sergeant Lavoisier', the note began.

'It is with great sadness that I write to tell you that Marie Gre'soire has met with a tragic accident that has taken her young life. She was apparently attracted to a small plot of wild flowers near her house that were concealing a minefield. Her death was instantaneous.

'In handling the arrangements for Marie, I came across the watch, understanding that it was something that you had given her. I am certain that she would want you to have it, in remembrance of her and the time you were together.

'We are all saddened by her loss. But each of us must accept this as God's will for her and for you!

'God be with you, Sergeant!
'In deepest sympathy,
'Father Alliot'

CHAPTER 8

James arrived in Baton Rouge early in the morning, on a typically warm spring day. He could feel the dampness in the air, so thick with a musty, dank smell that it left him feeling that everything around him had been besieged with mildew. He'd forgotten how humid the climate could be. Even in the worst of winter, the crisp air never seemed to lessen the stench of so much standing water and rot.

The old logging train crawled slowly into the station, jerking and swaying as it finally screeched to a halt beneath an outlying canopy. The boilers purged a thick cloud of steam onto the siding, filling the air with a mystical looking vapor.

The station was alive with the sounds of visitors and arriving passengers, mingling with the black porters who were working feverishly to clear the stockpile of luggage off the narrow landing between the trains. Dispatchers with megaphones announced more arrivals and departures as train whistles screamed up and down the tracks, forcing the reuniting families to struggle with their conversations.

James inched his way towards the exit of the coach, standing in line with other soldiers returning home. His eyes searched the billowing clouds of steam for Lora, trying to remind himself what she would look like after almost two and a half years. He stepped onto the conductor's footstool, and then down to the platform, searching as he went. A short distance away, standing partially submerged in a cloud of steam, James recognized her. She was looking at him and waving with a subdued effort. An artificial smile pasted across her face, she endured the uncomfortable morning heat exacerbated by the steam from the locomotive.

He headed towards her decisively, like a traveler planning on asking a stranger for directions. She stood steadfast until he was only a few feet away, within arm's reach. She casually put her arms around his waist, giving him a reserved 'in law' peck on the cheek. He'd almost forgotten about her pious manner. He knew that any expression of affections would have to wait until they were out of the public eye. Even then it would be anything less than a soul-stirring event.

He responded in kind to her casual greeting by patting her on the back as she dropped her arms. The unemotional welcome was more than James wanted, under the circumstances. For Lora's part, anything more would have compromised her stoic code of behavior.

"How have you been, Lora?" James asked. "You're certainly looking fit!"

Lora smiled and then responded with a polite, "I'm fine. It's nice to have you home again, darling! We've missed you! I hope the trip home wasn't too uncomfortable?"

James was annoyed at the suggestion that he could have survived the rigors of war and then succumb to the hardships of traveling by train. He shrugged it off as a trite remark intended as small talk because she was nervous.

"No," he answered, "the trip was all right. It's just good...to be home again!"

He glanced down, noticing the small figure of a child hiding behind Lora's skirt. The child was gawking at him suspiciously.

"It doesn't seem that much has changed around here. I suppose the family is doing well?" he asked.

"Emmy and Arnold are fine," Lora answered. "Nona and Mrs. Gerty have been sick. We thought they had bilious fever but they seemed a lot better after we gave them both a little calomel."

James ignored Lora's diagnosis and homemade cure as he pondered the small child clinging to her dress.

He was confused by the youngster, a little girl done up in a frilly white dress with a neatly pressed lace pinafore tied in the front. Ribbons decorated her long blonde curls, dangling like tightly twisted springs. The child's shoes were white with small silver bells tied to the laces, the same colored ribbons as those securing her hair.

His curiosity got the best of him as he questioned Lora, "Whose little girl is this? Where's Jason?"

Now Lora looked confused, glancing behind her at the child and then back at James, as if suddenly realizing the reason for his look of bewilderment.

"This is Jason, darling! He wanted to get all dressed up for daddy's homecoming. Isn't he just darling?" she chirped with a smile, showing her obvious jubilation over the child's appearance.

"Is this some kind of costume?" he demanded to know, laughing nervously. He glanced down at the small figure who had retreated under his mother's skirt. The child had little difficulty in sensing the hostility coming from the man's eyes.

"That's my son...dressed up like that? What the hell is this, Lora? What's he doin' dressed up like a damn ninny?" he demanded to know.

Lora's face collapsed into a jaw-quivering frown, one hand moving to her mouth and the other holding onto the pint-sized neuter. James' sudden anger had caught her off guard.

She took a break from her sobbing, to say, "I thought you'd like his pretty clothes. He just looks so...well...dainty and cute. I don't understand what's wrong."

"What's wrong? God almighty, damn, woman!" he asserted. Without another word, James tossed his duffel bag over his shoulder and crossed the platform, a disgusted march that ended at the cabstand in front of the station.

Lora and the effeminate 'specie' trailed close behind, both whimpering from the encounter.

"Where to, Sarge?" the cabbie asked.

"The closest Gawd damn barbershop you can find, and make it quick!" James commanded. "Next thing I know, you'll be tellin' me he's been takin' dancin' lessons."

James looked over at Lora and the boy. Both of them were staring up at him, as though surprised at the truth in his statement.

"What's that, Sarge?" the cabby interjected.

"Nothin'...I was just sayin', a man leaves home ta fight a war and comes back findin' his boy turned into a Gawd damn ninny...Jesus!"

Lora and Jason both were sobbing in tearful harmony as they left the station. The cabby arched up in the seat, focusing in on Jason in his rearview mirror, giving him a big, fangy grin. "Sure can happen when a man ain't around to watch 'em," he offered.

When they reached the barbershop James jerked open the door, grabbing up the child with one hand while handing the cabby his fare with the other. He sprinted for the barbershop, with Lora marching behind, her hands outstretched, trying to comfort her wailing son.

James assaulted the barbershop door, startling the two barbers. Both men paused in their conversations long enough to watch Lora move in behind James, as if she were trying to save her offspring from the executioner's axe. James delivered Jason into the first empty barber's chair, loudly demanding, "I want this boy to have a young man's haircut. Peel him down so he's got skin showin' on the sides, and you can see his neck."

"Yes, sir!" the barber replied.

James looked across the street for a minute and then walked over to the barber's chair. "Hold on there, just a second, will yah? I gotta measure, tah see how big this youngin' is."

James left the shop for twenty minutes, coming back to find Jason and Lora sitting in the row of chairs lined up against the wall. Jason was exploring the lumps and bumps on his head, exposed by the scalping that had just ensued. Lora was weeping, holding an eight-inch blonde curl dangling between her fingers, a memento from the barber. She'd been careful not to interfere.

"Looks good, real good," James declared. "Come here, boy. Let's put these dungarees on yah so it won't be so drafty down there."

James laughed, stripping Jason down to his last worldly possession, leaving him standing buck-naked in the chair. The transformation sent the barbers into hysterics and Lora charging furiously for the door.

He slipped a collarless work shirt over Jason's small head and stepped him into a pair of coveralls, already rigged with a set of suspenders. The underdrawers were something any young man could live without, he reasoned.

James wadded up the dress and petticoats along with the white shoes, and girly shorts, and handed them to one of the barbers. "You reckon you might know someone around here that's got a little girl? I think we'd like 'em ta have these girly duds! Ain't that right, boy?" James asked, watching Jason nod an uncertain response.

"Here ya go, two bits, isn't it?" James asked, handin' the barber his fee for the haircut.

"No charge, Sarge," the barber responded, totally entertained by the whole experience. He knew what had just taken place would give him plenty of mileage with his patrons in the weeks to come. "Consider it a little welcome-home gift," he added with a smile. "I'd uh paid tah give that haircut!" he announced just loud enough for James to hear him.

The remainder of the trip home was so quiet that it confused the next cabby who wondered if his passengers were related. When they finally arrived at the house, Lora swept Jason into her arms and fled inside while James settled up with the driver.

With his hands stuffed deep into his trouser pockets James moved onto the front porch of the small, whitewashed house where Lora had been living for nearly two years. He looked at the house, not wanting to go in until he'd confronted Lora with the issue of Marie. James settled down against the wall near the front door, coming to rest in a squatting position with his arms locked around his knees. A half- hour passed before Lora reappeared on the front porch, carrying a tray of coffee and sweet rolls as a peace offering. Neither of them spoke for the next five minutes. Lora finally broke the silence, "I wanted you to have a nice homecoming. I'm really sorry we had the unpleasantness at the station. I am glad you're home, and I want you to know that Son and I missed you very much!"

James ignored her for what seemed an eternity. Then, without looking at her, he said. "I had an affair with a woman in France. I probably shouldn't have said anything about it...because it's over. I just feel like you deserve to know. She killed herself...right after I left." He shrugged his shoulders, looking her straight in the eye.

Lora didn't respond to what he'd said. That wasn't her way. She just sat with her hands folded in her lap, her head bent down at a prayerful angle, weeping silently to herself.

"I was coming home to ask you for a divorce," he said, still looking at her. "I didn't know until I got to Camp Meade that she was dead."

"Your sense of honesty leaves me a bit chilled, James," she said finally. "Why, if you don't mind me asking, did she kill herself? She obviously knew you were coming back."

"I don't know," he answered forlornly. "They never told me why...just that she was dead."

Lora wiped her eyes with the hem of her dress. She looked up at the ceiling, taking a deep breath before resting her face in both hands and sobbing.

"If you want me to leave, I'll understand," James offered. "If I stay, all I can promise you is that I'll work hard to make you and the boy a comfortable life. I'll be respectful of you, but I can't promise to love you. I don't know that I can love anyone, the way I feel right now. The war has taken the life out of me, but maybe someday..."

Lora stood, looking up at the ceiling. She wiped her eyes a final time with her handkerchief, replying to his confession simply with "I think I'd better start supper before it gets too late. Son will be getting hungry."

She opened the screen door and then stopped, as if she finally had something to say about his confession. But instead of addressing the issue, she said calmly, "If you'll take your bag in the house, I'll put your things away after supper. Our bedroom is on the right."

"No, that's all right...I'll take care of it," he replied. He looked up at her apologetically through the screen, relieved to have told her the truth.

"I'm sorry for hurting you," he wanted to say, but his lips were still. She disappeared from the door without another word, leaving him to his own conclusions. It would have been easier if she'd said she hated him, instead of leaving him in such an unforgiving lurch.

Lora was busy in the kitchen preparing the evening meal when James finally walked into the house. He listened to the pots and pans colliding as she went about cooking supper for the three of them. He could hear her singing a soft, comforting hymn. It was what she always did to soothe her mind when she was upset. It reminded him of his mother.

He made his way to the back bedroom, closing the door behind him, wanting to have a moment to himself. He stood over the heavy canvas duffel bag, refolding and sorting his clothes and placing them neatly into an empty dresser. In the process, his hand found a tiny velvet sack that he'd packed between the clothes before he'd left Camp Meade. He cradled it gently as he took a seat in an armchair near the window.

191

Carefully, he emptied its contents into the palm of his hand. It was the watch he'd given Marie. It was all that he had left to remind him of her.

By early afternoon it had become cloudy with small gusts of wind launching swarms of dried leaves into the air, driving them against the bedroom window. The irregular force of the breeze hammered the glass, shaking and vibrating the windowpanes, as if a demon were determined to split open the room and deny him his solitude. He ignored the sounds coming from the kitchen and the battering force of the wind, listening instead to the chime of the watch. The music transported his heart and soul back to Pont-a-Mousson for a final opportunity to dance with the memory of his beloved Marie. When the music was done, he let the watch slip back into the dark crimson bag. Gently, he pushed the bag deep into the dresser drawer, ending his seance with the past.

Two weeks after his homecoming James announced to Lora that he was going to New Orleans for a few days on business. He had thought about reopening his pharmacy, but, like everything else that had happened since the war, his interest in his old occupation had waned. He was interested in something more substantial, a new career. He knew what he wanted to do, and he knew that New Orleans held the opportunity for him to start his life over again.

There was no need for him to become acquainted with the city; he already knew it well. He'd visited the great metropolis a number of times with his father, and later on his own as a young man.

James made his way though the narrow streets of the French Quarter, ignoring the street signs with their distinctive eclectic designations, from Rue Royal to Canal Street. He reached the Maspero Exchange by eleven that morning.

James found the address he was looking for at the end of the converted slave market. He squinted through the beveled glass door of the dimly lit shop, trying to see the man he'd come to visit. The crude clang of a pint-sized cowbell sounded above his head as he decided to enter the store to confirm that he'd arrived at the correct address. The shop was uncomfortably narrow, a pinched closet that couldn't help but advertise the proprietor's lack of clientele, or so it seemed.

A counter was built at the back with a narrow slit to one side to allow the shopkeeper access to the shelves of opium powders and elixirs locked behind several old glass bookcase doors. Shelving containing the less potent pharmaceuticals and casks of colored flavorings for syrups and liniments lined the narrow corridor from the front entrance to the back counter. Volumes of pharmacopoeia were arranged neatly on a tiny parson's desk located by a gas heater next to the back counter. A ceiling fan with an out-of-balance blade caused the suspended motor to jig and shudder with each revolution. The pungent odor of formaldehyde and various alcohols was so overpowering that the ceiling fan was used to diffuse the noxious chemicals and allowed some fresh air to enter the room.

James moved towards the back of the pharmacy, peering into the corner at the man sitting at the small desk. He appeared as little more than a shadow, huddled under a single exposed light bulb hanging from the copper-plated ceiling.

"I'll be with you in a minute," the man announced, still keeping his back to James.

James waited, watching the pharmacist as he carefully counted bean-sized white tablets for a prescription. He dropped each one carefully into a brown pill bottle and then completed the label in ink before pasting it onto the bottle.

The man James had come to see had been, during the first year of the war, one of his most trusted comrades in arms. They had much in common, both having been pharmacists before the war and both being from Louisiana. The two of them had shared the shell-lit nights, crawling as a team, slithering across no-mans-land to recover some wretched soldier, wounded, crippled, pinned in the wire and pleading hysterically for his life. For James it was a duty demanded of him because of rank. For this man, a volunteer, it was a religious mission placed upon himself.

The two men had performed their mission of mercy on numerous occasions, slipping over the open ground, sometimes putting on German helmets to create an image on the horizon to the enemy or one of their own patrols. Unfortunately, on one such outing James' companion took a bullet through the face, removing his right lower jaw and leaving him looking as if he'd rested the side of his face too close to a saw mill blade. While not a life-threatening wound, it left him with a substantial speech impediment and a look as if the Creator had run out of clay while making his head. But while the wound was ghastly, it was a ticket home. No one ever knew who fired the shot, but it could have come from either side. Be that as it may, James remained close to his friend during the ordeal of healing, and kept in touch with him during the balance of the war while he was recuperating. They had promised to meet again in better times, and so they would.

"Still tryin' to perfect the world's deadliest poison, 'eh, Jasper?" James chuckled.

"Lavoisier...you worthless bastard!" the man exclaimed, with his eyes still locked on the bottle of pills. "I never have been able to figure out how a fella could walk with feet as big as yours. I could always tell it was you cause it sounds like two footlockers chasin' each other!" he added with a laugh.

James continued to chuckle and then shot back, "Jasper Jack Laroque, America's secret weapon. Last I heard, they'd given some of your funny little pills to the Germans. Took the fight right outa' 'um jest like cuttin' the nuts off an old bull."

Jack finally finished counting the pills, and then walked over, cheerfully shaking James' hand and locking him in a warm embrace. "It's good tah see ya, Doc...it's been a while!"

"Surely has," James answered, "and it's great tah see you, Jack. I'm real glad you made it home safely."

"God...you look like hell outa' uniform," Jack roared.

"Well, my friend..." James started with a wide smile, "...It looks like you've gotten back into the swing of things with your pharmacy?"

Jack looked around the room. "It ain't pretty, but it puts grub on the table. These are hard times for folks around these parts. It's all a man can do to keep body and soul together. The coloreds got better jobs than most whites, but then that seems to be what the government was wantin'...sendin' most of us over tah France and leavin' them here to have a free run."

"Things u'll get back to the way they were; it jest takes time," James offered.

"So, what brings you to New Orleans? You gonna set up down here?" Jasper asked.

"No! One ex-army pill pusher to a city, that's what I say. Sides, I got other plans. Thinkin' about bringin' Lora and the boy down here for somethin' else. Just checkin' things out. Thought I'd look in on yah and see how you were gettin' along, 'fore I took care of business."

Jack smiled, knowing that James was sincere about seeing him. They'd shared a lot of hard times in France.

"What the hell are you up to, James? It ain't like you to be galavantin' around the country without a job."

James smiled. "Let's get us a jug and some pot liquor and I'll tell you all about it."

"Let's go over on the Rue Condi...they got a great dinner at the Hotel Orleans," Jasper suggested. "It'll give me a chance to satisfy my curiosity about what you're really doin' here. Anyway, I wanta know whatever happened with you and that little French gal you were runnin' with the last time I saw yah."

James' jovial mood plummeted for an instant. "That's all behind me, Jasper, jest like the war."

Jack quickly realized he'd said the wrong thing. "Sorry, James...it's none of my business. It's almost noon, so let's git us a drink and some dinner."

"Yeah, I'd like that, Jack," James agreed, relieved at having cleared the air about Marie.

The two men sat totally enthralled in their conversation, reliving their memories of the War, discussing only the good times of those days. They sat in the airy hotel restaurant looking out onto the atrium, and watching the rippling pool of water in the fountain being pelted by hard shots of rain from a coastal storm.

Black waiters, dressed in their white waist jackets, the elite 'garcons' of the New Orleans restaurant trade, scurried about the dining room, closing the ten-foot glass doors to the outside storm. They swept over the tables, busily fixing and reorganizing the table settings, serving wine and cognac, Cuban cigars, and dark chicory coffee to their regular guests.

The two men laughed and talked, bringing each other up to date on their lives since they'd parted company in France. The reminiscence ended, just for a moment, as both men paused, staring blankly at each other, realizing they had survived the most hideous of life's adventures, the Great War.

195

They sat looking at each other as if wanting to unburden their minds like witnesses to a horrible crime. But they'd both been there and already shared the pains that each of them had felt. Silence was the best expression of their feelings for the moment.

Jack was the first to break their silent vow not to discuss the black side of the war. "I didn't think we'd ever see home again, James. It's a sad thing when you find yourself gettin' used to seein' people die. That part of the war never made me very happy with myself. I guess I just expected not to make it back!"

"I know, Jack. It's hard to believe in the odds of survival when everyone around you has his guts hangin' out on the ground. It seems as though that feeling of compassion you had when a life was snuffed out was the only thing that made us different from the damn rats and bugs. It's hard to keep remindin' yourself that men are supposed to be different. Hell, maybe we're not!"

Jack took a slug of cognac, swallowing hard before he spoke. "I don't know, but I hope I never have ta see another man die for the rest of my life!"

James looked at him, understanding how he felt. He could feel some of the old pains he thought were gone but joked, "That's a damn funny thing for a feller to say who gets his grits off by makin' poison for a livin'!"

Both men broke into hysterical laughter, pounding the table and pointing at each other, their faces red as ripe tomatoes from the outburst.

"So, what brings you to New Orleans?"

"Well, Jasper, if you can believe it, I'm gonna take a shot at gettin' into Tulane."

"College?"

"Well, yeah...the Medical school," James responded.

"My word...that's all right. Yes, sir, I'd say that's a pretty optimistic goal, especially fer a fella who hasn't been to college. But, it's all right! If anybody can do it, Doc, you can!"

James wiggled his head from side to side before saying, "I feel like I can get through if they'll jest let me in. I'm meeting with the Dean of the Medical School in the morning."

"You got a lot of guts, James, and I wish you all the luck in the world! Have 'em call me if they wanta know what kinda

saw-bones you'd make.   Tell 'em I've seen you in action."
Jasper laughed heartily.

"Thank yah, Jasper. It helps, knowing you got a few friends pullin' for yah!"

The two men talked a while longer, promising to meet again as soon as James had finished his business at the school.

James sat outside the Dean's office in a marbled reception area listening to the echos of doors closing and students talking somewhere in the long polished hallways. He fidgeted with his hands and twiddled his fingers, trying to pass the time. His craving for a smoke or a chaw of tobacco, considered a brothel habit by most, left him more nervous than usual. He wanted to be on his best behavior. He already had enough going against him without having his character questioned.

An elderly, white-haired matriarch was stationed strategically between James and the Dean's Office, peering at him occasionally from her desk as if she were evaluating his thoughts. Her eyes would study him for awhile, peering coldly from behind her wire-rimmed glasses before turning her attention back to the papers on her desk, where she would scratch an irritating memo with her black pen after each examining look.

James would try sending various peace offerings, a smile, a grin, but nothing seemed to change her determined investigation of his thoughts.

'Probably eliminating some poor bastard's application for admittance,' James thought. 'Nasty old bitch...God, I know she can read my mind. She knows I'm scared shitless. She's got me where she wants me, and she's gonna cut my nuts off with some big-assed surgical souvenir hidden in that desk of hers. She's probably got a jar full of testicles hidden in there like pickled eggs.'

His train of thought was suddenly broken when, without any visible sign from within the Dean's Office, the aged sentinel looked up and, with a ferocious smirk on her face, announced, "The Dean will see you now, Mister Lavoisier." Oddly, she offered a rather steely "Good luck" as he passed by her desk towards the Dean's office.

197

James had launched himself from the tortuous wooden bench with a determined forward charge, almost loping through the opened door into the Dean's office. He found himself standing in a spacious expanse. Disoriented, he turned in a slow, searching half-circle in the unlighted room, trying to locate the Dean's desk. The room was darkened from weathered and over-stained paneling and rows of books bound with black covers. It was the perfect setting for an intellectual, although this one would have had to have been a mole to learn anything in the sparse light.

The pattern of the paneling was broken up by oddly shaped fragments of human skeletons lying here and there. The bleached white parts contrasted with the dark wood theme of the chamber, resembling the remains of a feeding frenzy by some cave bear or saber tooth tiger, a less than gratifying 'how do you do' under the circumstances.

The Dean's desk was nearly concealed behind a row of high-backed leather chairs. A man's balding head could be seen just over the top of the chairs.

James moved closer to investigate the small figure of a man slumped over at the desk, his torso nearly lost in the shadows of the armchair he was occupying.

"Oh,...Mister Lavoisier...I apologize for the darkness. It seems we don't appreciate our sight until we begin to lose it. As sensitive as my eyes have become, I try to use the light sparingly to read or do a little paper work. Please, sit down."

"That's quite all right sir; I understand," James responded.

"It seems that the afflictions of age have little respect for the demands of one's profession. But be that as it may...I'm Doctor Rowlin Harlick, Chancellor of the School of Medicine."

"It's a pleasure to meet you, sir...James Lavoisier," James announced, offering his hand.

"Yes, well, it's nice to make your acquaintance, young man! How can I be of service to you?" Harlick asked.

James paused, taking a quick look around the room, as if it would be his last chance to savor the atmosphere of the school, once he had disclosed his intentions. "I'd like to submit my application to attend Tulane!"

"I see," Harlick responded, clearing his throat. "We're always eager to talk to anyone interested in a future in medicine."

"I appreciate that, sir!"

"There is a great deal of information to be considered before one is selected as a candidate to study medicine here at Tulane. It's all decided upon by the Admissions Board, of course. But I do play a role in the selection process."

"That's why I wanted to see you, Doctor Harlick."

Harlick looked puzzled as he continued, "There are exams to be taken, educational background to be considered, one's dexterity...a great number of factors to evaluate before admission is granted."

"Yes!" James acknowledged.

"But, it's possible we're both ahead of ourselves. You're a little older than most of our applicants. Perhaps you're here to inquire as to whether you should pursue the study of medicine?" Harlick asked.

"No, Doctor Harlick," James answered, "that's the one thing I am certain of!"

"I see. Well, if your academic record is marginal, or if there is a problem with the accreditation of the university you attended, then your chances are of course lessened. But maybe I can help."

"It's not that either, sir."

"Well, then...what exactly is it that's troubling you, Mister Lavoisier? How is it that I can help?"

James looked at the Dean as if the man were about to pronounce the death sentence on him for something he'd done...or hadn't done, in this particular case.

"It's not that my grades are low, or that I've gone to a non-accredited university; it's that I don't have a scholastic record to give to you."

"I'm afraid I don't understand. You've lost your records?"

"Not exactly, sir. What I mean is, I don't have any records; I never went to school. What I'm saying is that I've managed to educate myself. I never had the opportunity to attend any formal schooling, not even grade school. Where I grew up, near Lalleville, Louisiana, there wasn't much chance to get an education. There was just too much work to be done at home."

"I see," Harlick said, looking a little despondent.

"I was a licensed pharmacist before the war," James continued. "They admitted me by examination and no formal education was required. I did extremely well with my studies."

Doctor Harlick let loose a disparaging snort as he interrupted James, loudly closing a medical reference book he'd been studying earlier, symbolically ending the conversation.

"Young man...pharmacy is one thing, but do you have any idea what you're suggesting? Medicine is a precise science. A science that requires great skill and academic preparation. Without a foundation of math and chemistry, Latin and a mastery of the English language, there is nothing to build from."

"I'm aware of that, Doctor Harlick!" James responded.

"It takes years of preparation for those who would follow such a demanding profession," Harlick continued. "I'm sorry! I think you've been ill-advised to try to gain admission into medical school, any medical school, until you've completed your primary education," he finished, partially standing up to suggest that their meeting was over. Biting his lip, he said, "How do you propose that a school, any school, determine your academic ability? You have no credentials, nothing to gauge what you've learned or retained!"

"That's precisely my point, sir. I do have credentials and I do have a good education."

"Credentials?" Harlick demanded to know. "What credentials and what education? Show me the proof...give me something tangible that will convince the Admissions Board. I know nothing about you."

James took a deep breath, looking determinedly into the Doctor's eyes.

"When I served in France, as a corpsman during the war, I had a chance to find out what kind of a physician I would be. I dreamed of becoming a doctor so that someday I'd be able to put torn bodies back together and ease the pain of a dying man. I wasn't a surgeon, but I did a surgeon's work. I mended the wounded and came as close as a man can come, short of his own demise, to understanding the capricious nature of death that haunts those who are seriously injured.

"Credentials? I have far more awareness of what is demanded of a physician than those who come to Tulane from the prep schools and sheltered lives.

"There's no stench in your dissecting lab that I haven't smelled a thousand times on the battlefield," James went on. "There's not an anatomy lab that will show me a human part that I haven't seen lying in the sun after a battle.

"And, after that experience, that awful, awful time in my life...I think I would find it infinitely more satisfying to go on helping those I can as a doctor, rather than walk away now and do something else with my life. Those are my credentials! That's all I have."

James paused, calming himself before he continued, "As for my education, I am confident that I'm sufficiently prepared to undertake the study of medicine. I don't have report cards or transcripts that credit me with courses taken, or teachers documenting what they've taught; all I can give you is my word that I have the knowledge to pass the entrance examination."

Harlick quickly wiped his face with several strokes of his handkerchief. He pushed himself forward in the old leather chair enough to look like he meant business before he responded. He sat with his mouth open, bumping first one then the other of his canine teeth nervously together as he thought about what he was going to say. The last thing he wanted to do was to turn away a veteran, but there was more. There was a feeling that left him unsettled with what he was about to say.

"I'm...truly sorry, young man. You wouldn't have a chance in the world of meeting the qualifying scores. An informal education, such as you've had, couldn't possibly provide you with enough depth of study to prepare you for the intense exams you would have to pass. It's just not possible! I'm very sorry...you'd just be wasting your time and ours. Believe me, if there was some way, I'd try to help."

James stood up, realizing that it was futile to continue, so he turned towards the door before he spoke. "Somehow I thought my age...the war...all of that would make a difference. I hoped that you might allow me to at least take a test, to show you that I have the aptitude to do the work. I wanted to prove to you that I have the determination to succeed. I'm sorry about this...I didn't mean to lose my temper, to say what I did about the others. I appreciate the time you've given me."

Harlick seemed mesmerized by James, spellbound as he stood offering his hand and an apology. "I'm sorry," Harlick said. "Life must seem extremely unfair at this moment. I wish I could offer you that chance you so desperately desire."

As James turned to leave he remembered a letter of introduction he had brought with him from his commander, a graduate of Tulane, some years earlier. He turned back towards the old dean. "Excuse me, Doctor Harlick, but I promised a friend, Colonel Grenier, some time ago that I'd give you a message. He asked me to tell you that he thought of you often and that he was doing well, the last time we spoke."

Harlick's eyes brightened. "Is that Doctor John Albert Grenier?"

"Yes, yes it is," James answered cheerfully.

"How are you acquainted with John Grenier?"

"He was my battalion commander in France."

"I'll be!" Harlick chuckled. His mood warmed instantly as he stood up, smiling at James. "I haven't heard from that young man since the war started. It's good to know he is well and, I assume, home with his family. He was a student of mine, you know!"

"Yes, I know," James responded. "And yes, he did make it back from France."

"Do you mind if I look at that letter you're holding? It seems to be addressed to me."

"No, not at all. I meant to give it to you."

James handed Harlick the envelope. "It's just a letter of introduction. I didn't think you still needed to see it."

Harlick took the letter, turning his back on James as he moved to the scant light coming from the window near his desk. A few muffled snickers broke the dead silence before he folded the letter and placed it back in its envelope.

"Have you read this letter, Mister Lavoisier?"

"No sir, I haven't."

"Well, Colonel Grenier speaks very highly of you. He was an excellent student and a fine young man."

"It's been awhile since I've seen him," James said. "We were discharged at the same time after the war. It was the last time I spoke to him."

"He seems to think that you're a very ambitious young fellow. He also agrees with you about your aptitude for medicine. He wants me to give you a special entrance examination, based on his personal recommendation. It appears as though he worked with you under some rather perilous circumstances. He also noted that he felt you had achieved a remarkable degree of excellence in your education. That, my young friend, is credentials!"

"That's very generous of Colonel Grenier to say those things," James gushed, his heart pounding.

"It's highly irregular to allow anyone to attend this university without having met the educational requirements outlined by the Regents. However, I'm not without a certain amount of influence within the University, so I'll offer you a proposition: If you're able to prove to me that you indeed have mastered the preparatory materials, then I'll submit your application to the Admissions Board.

"I feel certain that this letter from Doctor Grenier should serve to defeat any challenge or protest I might encounter from the Board. I think it's the least I can do for an old student of mine. And I can't help but believe that anything less would be a great injustice, under the circumstances."

After thanking Dean Harlick several times, James left the office, making his way to the prune-faced woman who had so diligently guarded the door. She sat with a cool smirk on her face, not having been privy to the conversation, but sure she knew the results of the interview.

She rolled her eyes up from her work to offer a piece of insincere advice as she obviously had done to each and every bleeding heart applicant who had come to Doctor Harlick for a final appeal. It was unusual for anyone to see the Dean unless he'd already been declined by the Board of Admissions. "Perhaps you should try another school...someplace a little less demanding. We're much more selective than the others!" she said, sanctimoniously.

"Oh, no, ma'am. I'm a keeper!" James said, giving her an enormous grin as he handed her the special exam pass.

She burned a hot stare at him, jutting her jaw out like a riled bulldog.

"Take it down the hall to 122B, Doctor Markel's office. He handles scheduling for this sort of thing, not me!" she huffed.

James stoked her fury a tad more by letting loose a wild, "Yah-hoo!" as he opened the outside door and marched down the hall.

James proved that what he had said was anything but idle boasting. His scores on the comprehensive exams were exemplary. He was accepted unconditionally for admission to Tulane Medical School as a freshman the following semester.

He settled the family into a small, but comfortable, two-bedroom apartment near the campus a few weeks before school began. Lora made her contribution to the effort by taking a job at Hamley's Department Store as a floorwalker and part-time piecework seamstress. Her hours were as long as James', as she struggled after work with her responsibilities as mother and wife.

James took an after-school job as a pharmacist for a neighborhood drugstore. When he wasn't working, he spent the remainder of his time scrunched up against a makeshift desk in the front room of the apartment, studying. He loved what he was doing and was inspired by the promise of success that medical school would bring. He believed it was the fulfillment of the very dream he and his mother had envisioned when he was a boy. Only time stood in the way of his achieving that success.

The classrooms at Tulane were dimly lit Victorian monoliths, beautifully designed, with more interest paid to aesthetic embellishments than concern for the bone-chilling drafts that blew freely through the labs and lecture arenas in the winter. Gas heaters offered an alternative to the cold and even gave some relief to the pungent clinical aromas that consumed the inside of the buildings.

But James was little concerned with climatic conditions, keeping himself warmed, at least in spirit, with his ardent commitment to medicine.

His enthusiasm for his studies totally consumed his time, so much so that he sometimes found himself subject to ridicule from the younger students. Their youth and innocence somehow forgave them the urgency of their school work, always leaving them adequate time for boyish pranks, while James and the others fretted over inadequate study time. Several of the older students, who had served in the

Great War like James, became close friends. They formed a cooperative, helping each other study and prepare for the difficult examinations. Even in those rare moments when they had time to relax, they seemed content to socialize amongst themselves, leaving the others to their primeval rituals.

For several years a rough, beggarly-looking fellow, a six-foot four-inch giant, had shuffled through the halls and laboratories of Tulane as custodian and laboratory caretaker for the Department of Anatomy. A fiendish-looking ogre, he towered like a prehistoric sloth, his hair knotted and uncombed, his face creased from years of exposure to weather and alcohol, and accentuated by craterous smallpox scars. Even his beard grew in splotches like some molting animal. His only claim of talent in his profession was his tremendous strength, a primary consideration in being able to single-handedly hoist a cadaver onto the dissecting table.

Rile, 'Romeo' Bodine, as he was sarcastically referred to by the student body but never in his presence, had gained a reputation as a bully. He had a habit of beating at least one or two medical students a year with little or no provocation. The victims were usually sent packing, for fear of their lives being forfeited by Bodine's knife or knuckles.

The faculty seemed to take little notice of Bodine's aggressive behavior. They preferred instead to suffer a slight attrition of the already overcrowded classrooms, rather than make a ruckus over losing a student here and there. Besides, Bodine was good at his job. And the fact that no one else had the stomach for it seemed to assure him a long and secure tenure at the University.

Bodine's responsibility was to care for the lab specimens, including the cadavers. It was his job to see that they were properly arranged at the tables before class. When the series of studies were completed, the parts and dissected cadavers were collected and placed in preservatives like so much canned beets or figs. It was a task that Bodine handled with diligence and precision. More than once it had been rumored that he had been caught in a compromising pose with a corpse between him and the gurney, thus the nickname, 'Romeo'. Necrophilism or not, his pugnacious nature was enough to inspire most students to give the man a wide berth. But, whenever a member of the staff ventured within earshot, the demon was careful to muzzle his blustering tone with the students.

As he had done routinely over the years, Bodine had just finished delivering cadavers to the anatomy lab for a class scheduled later that morning. Whatever his reputation with the students may have been, Bodine insisted on maintaining a standard of excellence for setting up and taking down his cadaverous friends. Each body was delivered to the correct student and positioned for the morning Practical, draped with white hospital sheets.

Once Bodine had made his morning delivery, ordered up by the anatomy instructor the night before, he disappeared into his boiler room sanctuary, locking the door behind him to insure his solitude for the balance of the day. Bodine, like any respectable evil-doer, preferred to move about the school halls at night, doing whatever it is that men of that nature had a proclivity to do.

Making a request of Bodine to do anything out of the ordinary was a terrifying ordeal for the poor soul sent to seek him out, at the direction of the instructor. The instructor ordered his students to that task with the awareness of a general sending his men into battle. He was well aware of the risks involved in provoking the 'demon'.

Burnis Cook, a frail-looking young man from Metairie, Louisiana, was James' lab partner. Cook often appeared timid whenever he was faced with having to work on his cadaver. At times he even became faint as he made his first incisions of the day. It wasn't uncommon for the class to be serenaded with several minutes of dry heaves from the young man before he could settle down to his work.

One Friday afternoon, Burnis had taken up his position next to his assigned corpse, 'Ludendorff', preparing to remove the shroud and begin his dissection. Before he could remove the cover he noticed a queer hissing sound coming from under Ludendorff's sheet.

Instinctively, he leaped backwards, thinking that a prankster had placed a timber rattler somewhere near the body. He let out an ear-shattering scream, tripping over an adjacent gurney before landing flat on the floor. The class went wild, laughing hysterically as Burnis shuffled his way back from the cadaver.

"What seems to be the problem, Mister Cook?" the instructor demanded angrily.

"I don't know. He's making a hissing sound," Burnis responded, nervously, pointing at 'Ludendorff'. "I think there's a snake under there!"

The instructor moved over to the gurney, stick in hand, and popped the shroud into the air with the finesse of a magician. He was livid, screaming his outrage as he examined the source of the noise. He immediately ordered Burnis to summon the demon Bodine from the boiler room. It was a dreaded order for the young student.

Meanwhile, the instructor stood beside Ludendorff, pressing his belly as if doing an obstetrical examination. The noise increased, adding several new dimensions to the previously monotone hum. Someone had pumped poor Ludendorff full of gas, distending his belly into a huge bulbous sphere. The class roared as the instructor massaged the abdomen, with Ludendorff showing his gratitude by releasing an uninhibited squeal like a deflating balloon.

Burnis pushed a handwritten note under Bodine's door. He knocked once and then hurriedly made his way back to the safety of the classroom.

A few minutes later Bodine appeared at the door to the anatomy arena, standing menacingly and blocking most of the light from the hallway. Burnis noticed several students elbowing each other across the room. They chuckled to themselves, smiling at each other over the success of their shenanigan.

Bodine was furious at being laughed at. His eyes darted about the room, coming to rest first on the bloated cadaver and then on the solitary student positioned in the center of the anatomy theater, as pale as the sheet that had covered Ludendorff.

"Who says I done somethin' wrong with uh body?" Bodine challenged, in a slow, sullen drawl. Huge veins appeared on his face and neck, and his teeth began to show just below the snarl of his upper lip. "Your jest tryin' tah cause trouble 'tween me and the school. I ain't done nothin' wrong," he snarled, pointing threateningly at Burnis.

The more Bodine intimidated Burnis, the more the pranksters laughed. By now, Burnis was pressed against the back wall of the classroom, trying to somehow conceal himself from the monster's view.

The professor had made himself scarce, not wanting a confrontation with the Keeper of the Dead, as Bodine gruesomely referred to himself.

Bodine again raised his hand, pointing a finger at Burnis. "I'll be seein' you, soon as this class is over, and I'm gonna whoop your ass!"

He turned to leave, giving the gurney holding Ludendorff a hard shove, sending the stretcher and the naked body careening towards the poor student, who managed to move before it slammed into the wall next to him.

As soon as the class was dismissed, the gallery of onlookers hastily vanished into the halls and then outside to the safety of the street. A few of the braver souls gathered at the window to witness Burnis' imminent thrashing by Bodine.

Burnis remained next to his cadaver nervously working to catch up on his interrupted class work. He hoped that Bodine would forget his promised whipping and stay in the boiler room, at least until he'd made good his escape.

Twenty minutes passed, and the window had finally emptied of spectators. He knew that Bodine would be coming now, unless he'd changed his mind.

'Not Bodine,' he thought, 'he lives to inflict pain. He's gonna kill me as sure as the world!'

Burnis' eyes moved up towards the double door entrance to the lab, sensing a massive form flowing into the darkened room like a black cloud before a storm. Bodine moved into the grayish light, walking slowly towards him with a crazed expression on his face and brandishing his infamous knife in one hand. Burnis dropped his dissection instrument and began to back away towards the window.

A sickening thud jarred the room at the very moment that Burnis closed his eyes in expectation of death, or at least unconsciousness. His eyes opened to the sight of Bodine crumpling to his knees, his knife still cocked in his hand. Bodine looked as if someone had turned his lights out as his eyes rolled back in his head just before he fell face forward onto the wooden floor, landing like a sack of grain pitched from a barn.

Burnis could see blood pouring down the side of Bodine's face. A tall lanky figure appeared from the shadows an instant later, moved over and knelt down next to the dormant pile on the floor. Without a word, the unidentified man began pulling Bodine up towards the closest worktable. He hoisted the monster up onto the flat surface, pushing the beakers and pipettes off onto the floor with a single sweep of his arm.

As soon as Bodine regained full consciousness, several more blows were dispatched by the still unidentified man. Bodine's rage promptly ended with little more than a few sickly moans and whimpers coming from him, as he realized his attacker demanded his undivided attention.

Burnis watched his rescuer push a large steel pipe up against the giant's cheek, warning, "You lay your hands on anyone else around here, you son of a bitch, and I'll cripple you! You git your ass outa' here, 'cause next time I see you I'm gonna carve you up like one of these Gawd damn cadavers!

"Next time I look at you it better be your backside high-tailing it outa' here, now git!" the man ordered, pulling Bodine head first off the table and sending him crashing onto the floor into the pile of broken glass. The mauler staggered to his feet, stumbling over the classroom furniture and then plowed his way through the double doors, bellowing as he disappeared.

Burnis was shaking as he warily approached his redeemer, who was bent over and dusting himself off.

"I wanna thank you for doin' what yah did for me," he offered, waiting for the man to stand up so he could shake his hand.

The man remained bent over a little longer, trying to catch his breath. Finally, he stood up, smiling at Burnis as he spoke, saying, "That was a mean booger. That bastard really took the wind outa' me!"

"Lavoisier, I can't believe it! I'll be damned!" Burnis laughed excitedly. "You whipped the livin' shit outa' that monster. I thought you were gonna kill him!"

"What'd you think I was gonna do...let him cut you up with that pig sticker of his? Shit! Besides, a fella that mean is too damn hard to talk to without gittin' his attention first."

"I don't know," Burnis grinned, "I think he got the message."

"Yeah, I hope so," James agreed, chuckling.

"He'd ah been on me like a frog on a june bug if you had'na come along when you did! I thank yah...I sincerely thank ya."

James was still laboring to catch his breath as he spoke: "Giv'em a chance and a fella that big will bust yah up real bad. It doesn't pay tah cut 'em any slack."

"I really wanta thank you for lookin' out for me, James. I won't be forgittin' what you did."

"That's all right, Burnis. I figured, sooner or later, it was gonna come down to him and me havin' it out, anyway. It looked like as good a time as any tah get this childish crap over with. Besides, he was ruinin' my concentration."

Burnis smiled. "Yeah...mine, too."

"You were pretty gutsy hanging around to face up to that big rascal," James said.

"Gutsy?" Burnis laughed. "If I could have gotten a Gawd damn window open I'd ah lit out a long time ago!"

James grinned, finally getting his second wind. "I think we've had a pretty full day. What'd you say we get outa' here and have ourselves a drink?"

Burnis laughed, feeling as if he'd just experienced divine intervention. After what had happened, he was ready for several drinks.

The next day, not a single word of the incident was mentioned as classmates eagerly cleaned up the broken glass and splattered blood on the floor. The professor kept his eyes buried in the paperwork on his desk, ashamed of his reluctance to intervene, but thankful he hadn't, under the circumstances, after hearing a blow-by-blow of what had happened from a student.

As for Rile 'Romeo' Bodine, he promptly disappeared from the campus after the incident in the lab, much to the relief of the student body.

James graduated in the top of his class. The discipline he had developed as a child had served him well in his studies. His courage and hard work earned him the respect and admiration of his classmates who elected him Class President during his senior year.

Doctor Harlick had been invited to give the commencement address to the graduating class of 1925, and he quietly listened as the diplomas were handed out to the men and women, and each of their names were read aloud. When he heard the name of James Lavoisier, a smile came over his face. Having lost most of his sight two years earlier, the old physician never bothered to look up as James walked across the stage to accept his diploma. It wasn't until James stood directly in front of him, holding out his hand to thank him, that Doctor Harlick realized that he was there. The two men, much to the crowd's pleasure, embraced for a moment before James returned to his seat to enjoy the keynote address to be given by the now retired doctor.

"Having attended a great number of these illustrious ceremonies," Harlick began, "as Dean of this college and now an aging Professor Emeritus, I must confess it becomes more difficult with the years to find a subject that will adequately inspire my listeners. But then, I'm not so sure that's any different than when I first began my speaking career," he added, smiling as the audience laughed.

So, instead, this evening, if you will forgive a doddering old man, I would like to share something with you that has been an inspiration in my life.

I've come to the end of my career, feeling a great deal of satisfaction with what my life has brought to me. But perhaps the greatest joy comes as I hear the name of a young man read from the list of students graduating from this university tonight.

At the very moment that this young man and I first met, I realized that he possessed something very precious, something that I had lost somewhere on my own journey through life, as surely as a man who has lost his eyesight.

Even after I had made up my mind to deny him the opportunity to study medicine, the decision hung over me as heavily as if I'd misdiagnosed a dying patient. He was the one who deserved to study medicine, not me, and I knew it!

The one vital sign that most of us as doctors fail to understand is a man's heart. Not the beating muscle that pounds deep within a patient's chest, but the glow of hope that each of us is given to nurture and warm our souls as we face the harshness and tediousness of life.

I've never revealed this before, but a man whom we both admired had written a letter of recommendation for that young man I previously mentioned. By chance I happened to read the letter before we parted from our interview that day. It occurred to me at that very moment that there was a great deal of wisdom in a statement that our mutual friend had written. He said, "He has the heart to be a good physician and the dreams to do good works."

"It struck me, as I hope it will strike you, that beyond the sterile procedures and accumulation of knowledge that we gather like a harvest in our years of practice is the need to be a dreamer of great things, keeping hope alive to nourish the soul. It is dreams that will cure the incurable. And it is hope that will prevail for the ailing when our repertoire of cures has been exhausted.

Life does not end with the cessation of the heartbeat, but long before when the soul is no longer inspired with hope and the excitement of living! I wish each of you good, and Godspeed for your future," Harlick proclaimed, turning to James and applauding, as the audience now stood to applaud the class of '25.

And so, with the graduation completed, the years of study at Tulane had finally ended for James; a portion of his life-long dream was now fulfilled.

He completed his internship in New Orleans within the next two years then, with the same determination that had carried him through school, he turned his eyes west, across the Sabine River, to Texas. With diploma in hand and his family by his side he set out to make a life for himself and his family in the oil fields of East Texas. It was a place where only those with courage and vision would dare venture.

CHAPTER 9

By 1927, Frankston, Texas, had grown like an ugly weed into a diverse society of oil patch workers and farmers who were as incompatible as crude oil and water. Traditionally, the tranquil hamlet had been a community of farms, nestled deep within the piney woods of east Texas. It had been a relatively peaceful community until the great oil discoveries of the Kilgore and Neches Basins in the 1920's. It wasn't until an abundance of oil was discovered in the Neches Basin, pooling at an easily accessible depth, that life suddenly changed for the sleepy community. The shantytown squalor that soon grew up outside of Frankston, the new Sodom and Gomorrah, as the local Baptist preachers often referred to the settlement, was dubbed Tate City by the Oil Company. The name was a flimsy attempt by the company to placate the locals and create an air of respectability for its temporary inhabitants.

The whole idea of a permanent town was a deception by the company, attempting to convince the local pastorate and government officials, that the rabble would become a legitimate and permanent community of upstanding, tax-paying citizens. It was an oil patch camp from the start, with only temporary housing, and that's all it was intended to be. The oil companies were skilled at convincing small communities to expand to meet their service needs. Later, the community would discover that, like a mosquito who'd drunk his fill of his host's blood and then flown away, they had been little more than victims of parasites who capped their wells and moved on, leaving the economy to flatten.

Frankston swallowed the bait, hook, line and sinker. It became a supply center for food, oil field equipment and basic services needed by the wildcat drillers. Everyone assumed that the prosperity would last forever. Farms lay unattended while men rushed to work in the oil fields. Loggers and farmers alike opened their fields to the rip blades of bulldozers and drilling rigs. The land quickly became pockmarked with ugly settling ponds and oil spills. The smell of crude hung in the air as the constant clacking sounds of pumps echoed across the land.

James had recognized the potential of the community for a medical practice shortly before he had completed his residency in New Orleans. Circuit doctors from Tyler and Jacksonville, a few miles to the east, had previously taken care of Frankston's medical needs. But, now with so many people moving to the small community, there was a need for a full time physician. The tough, turbulent reputation of the community had dissuaded most doctors from setting up a practice in the town. There were too many other, less violent, places to live and raise a family. But the rough lifestyle of Frankston was of little concern to James. He knew how to take care of himself better than most, and in some ways it actually appealed to him. He was welcomed by the citizenry and oil companies alike, making his practice an instant financial success. Although his office hours were deplorable, he was well compensated for his efforts. Money was as loose as the morals of those who descended on the town, trying to strike it rich.

The weekends were usually busier than other days as the oil field workers came to town liquored up and looking for a fight. Cuttings and shootings were so commonplace that the streets often resembled the shootouts of the Old West. In fact, times were so perilous that most of the locals, including the ladies, carried sidearms to protect themselves.

Lora worked alongside James as his nurse, helping him with patients, including drunken laborers who often had to be restrained before their wounds could be sutured, or broken bones set. Occasionally a local would be brought in for emergency service, injured by a stray bullet during an exchange of shots between oil field workers. But more often than not, the locals were there for the usual medical needs of a small town. It was refreshing to James simply to deliver a baby or treat a sore throat, instead of piecing someone back together after a brawl. If it was payday at Tate City, James was generously rewarded for his services by his patients; but, if payday had passed, he was usually given a promise that his fee would be paid later. Later never came unless the same man got into another scrap and needed to be sewn back together again.

Lora had become hardened to her new life. She spent much of her day in the office assisting James with surgery and scrubbing instruments or keeping the books. At times it seemed as if it would be an eternity before either of them would get a full night's sleep. She and James rarely had any time alone at home. What personal time was available was spent with Jason, trying to give him some semblance of a normal family life.

More than once Lora had shown her grit when she was threatened by an unruly patient while helping James in the office. One incident had required her to pull James' pistol on a drunk who had decided, in the midst of being probed for a bullet, that he had had enough attention and was going to leave. Before climbing off the table, the man tried to carve James up with a knife, complaining he was taking too long to find the bullet lodged in his leg.

Lora calmly leveled the revolver between the man's eyes, cocked the hammer back and assured the hooligan that she meant business if he didn't lie down. She rested the barrel on the bridge of the man's nose until James was done removing the slug.

After James had finished, the man sat up, apologized for his behavior, and quickly forked over his fee. He promptly headed for the door, looking back over his shoulder at the pistol-wielding nurse. He shook his head in disbelief and then hurriedly left, cursing under his breath.

James had rented a quaint little two-bedroom home, located just a few blocks from the office and Jason's school. The house was small, but had been well maintained with its whitewashed lap board covering and green shutters. It was surrounded by a variety of colorful flowers and even came with an assortment of fruit trees, their limbs burdened to the ground with plump peaches and plums that would ripen by mid-summer.

James had hired a local black woman to keep house and watch after Jason. The woman, Addie Bean, arrived by six a.m. each morning, preparing breakfast and cleaning the kitchen before anyone else was awake. Addie never had much to say to James or Lora, but acknowledged their requests politely with a slight nod and an almost whispered 'Yas, 'um', or 'Yas, sir.'

Jason, on the other hand had somehow managed to bridge the communication gap with Addie, or 'Beany', as he lovingly referred to her. He would spend most of the day talking her ear off with wild, contrived stories that kept the young woman staring at him whenever he could corner her. Her silence with Jason was not by design, but only because she couldn't get a word in edgewise.

Jason was a precocious child who usually gave his parents little reason for worry. As was his custom upon waking each morning, he would wander into their bedroom hoping to find them still in bed. When they weren't there he would head for the kitchen, hoping to find them sitting at the breakfast table.

On this particular morning, disappointed that his parents had already left, and still being half-asleep, he returned to their bedroom and flopped down in the middle of the bed. After a few minutes, and being fully awake, he began springing himself off the mattress to relieve his boredom. He bounced on the soft surface like it was a trampoline, keeping himself in a stiff, prone position. Eventually he had managed to vault himself about a foot into the air before tiring of the repetitive exercise. Afterwards he sat up in the middle of the bed, trying to think of some way to add a little variety to what he was doing.

He'd caught his image in the oval dressing mirror directly in front of the bed while he'd been in the pancake position. For a few minutes he was totally content to study the smiling reflection looking back from the mirror, each time he'd passed into view.

He'd become so fascinated with what he was doing that he decided to stand up in the middle of the bed to get a full view of himself. Naturally, he began to launch himself into the air again, short hops at first and then leaping as high as the springs would carry him. At the same time he began making comical faces and muscle man poses to enhance the performance.

He was laughing so hard that Addie had come to the door to see if he'd brought a neighbor boy into the house without her knowing it. Lora had a strict rule about friends being in the house while she was gone, and Addie wasn't about to get cross- ways with James or Lora.

Finally he tired of the gymnastics, ending it all with a flying leap backward towards the pillows. He'd expected the landing to be soft, but instead hit with a tooth-rattling crunch, almost knocking himself senseless. He sat up, frantically rubbing a melon-size knot that had instantly appeared on the back of his head.

When the throbbing subsided, he lifted the pillow wanting to see what it was that had cracked his head. His investigation immediately revealed the source of the injury, his father's revolver, respectfully referred to by the family as his 'Hog leg'. Jason fingered the pistol, shining the barrel with the bed sheet, examining the cylinder and checkered wood handle, thrilled with the discovery. His sore head forgotten, curiosity quickly gave way to fantasy. He hoisted the firearm upward, swinging it into the air as if he were shooting hostiles coming at him from all sides. He lowered the barrel, bringing the sights to rest on the mirror and the image grinning back at him from across the room.

"You move, you scuzzy worm, and I'll blow yer head off!" he threatened, his eyes still fixed on his own reflection.

Jason was small for a boy his age, but still strong enough to cock the hammer. Making one more warning to the villain, saying "I warned yah, yah dirty cuss, not tah try nothin'," he thrust the pistol out in front of him, aiming it directly at the face in the mirror.

Just as he was forming his lips to simulate another volley of shots, the gun went off, erupting with an ear-deafening detonation that blew him backwards. The heavy steel barrel skipped off the left side of his forehead with a solid thud, leaving a gaping slice over his eyebrow and a red and blue indentation running up to his scalp line.

The beveled mirror that had been supported in an elegant Empire Period, cherry wood frame, suddenly was transformed into a pile of pellet-sized slivers of glass, scattered over the entire room. A thick blanket of smoke filled the room. The forty-four-caliber bullet had passed through the bedroom wall, splintering the tongue-and-groove wallboard and lodging on the other side of the wall in a cabinet.

Addie, who'd been standing near the sink, let out a terrifying scream and leapt out though the locked screen door, taking screen and frame with her as she went. Once outside, she rushed to the bedroom window, only to see Jason sprawled out on the bed underneath the canopy of smoke, his face covered in blood from the slice over his eye, his body stone still. She turned and ran towards town.

Within minutes she'd made it to James' office, hysterically babbling what she thought had happened.

"They done kilt dat poor baby and come after me."

"What are you talkin' about, woman, what's happened?" James demanded. "What have they done to Jason? How many of them are there? They still in the house?" James frantically pulled another pistol from his desk and raced for the door.

Addie could only handle one question at a time, after what she'd been through. "I's jest knowed it's dat Tate City trash come tah rob us. They'd uh kilt me, sure as the Lord, if I hadn't got away. Oh, they done kilt dat poor baby," she wailed, "and there warn't nothin' I could do tah hep him!"

Before Addie had time to finish, James was out the door. Lora was hot on his heels, armed with a single-barreled shotgun loaded with double-aught buckshot.

James stormed into the house though the open kitchen door and charged into the hall towards Jason's bedroom. On the way he passed the master bedroom, finding Jason sitting up in their bed, holding his head and crying with a high-pitched squeal. He was gingerly stroking the bleeding apple-size bump on his forehead, a slightly larger turgescence than the one he was also massaging on the back of his head with his other hand.

Before James could check out the rest of the house for intruders, Lora blew into the room with the shotgun braced against her shoulder. She was crying hysterically over what she assumed would be the hideous scene of her son lying murdered.

James relieved her of the gun and pried her away from Jason long enough to assure himself that his son's wounds weren't fatal.

He still wasn't sure what had gone on in the house. At first he investigated the fist-size hole in the wall, peering though into the kitchen. Next his hand slipped down the wall, picking up a handful of glass shards as his eyes moved back up to the empty mirror frame.

By this time, Jason had paused in his bellowing long enough to realize that his father was unraveling what he'd done. He tracked his father's movements, watching him walk slowly back towards the bed. James ignored the wailing duo, realizing now that something was amiss.

The intensity of Jason's hysteria increased to a theatrical level that left even Lora surprised. He was banking on his father having enough sympathy for his injuries to save him from the licking he knew was coming. Not a chance!

James reached under the pillow and removed the pistol, sniffed the barrel and then placed it back under the pillow without saying a word. He gave Jason a quick knowing look, but still didn't let on to Lora what he knew.

Jason responded with a half-smile. James just stood there, shaking his head in disbelief, as he listened to his wife bawling over the attack on poor Jason. Jason had yet to understand what it was that his mother thought had happened and why his father hadn't beaten the tar out of him. The only thing he could figure was that they thought he was too badly hurt to be upset over what he'd done. It was certainly food for thought for the future.

"Got yourself worked over pretty good, didn't you, boy?" James said, not really caring if he answered.

Jason nodded slowly, realizing his father was quickly losing his sympathy for his injuries. It was a bad sign.

Lora glanced up from cuddling the wounded child, running her hand over Jason's forehead as she expressed her concern for what had happened. She seemed a little miffed at James' callous attitude.

"What if he comes back again?" she inquired. "We must have come home just in time. My Lord!" she cried, "he was going to kill my baby!"

"Not likely!" James replied sarcastically.

Jason looked confused. James shook his head, vexed that Lora still hadn't realized what had happened. He decided it was best, at least for awhile, to let her think what she would. Her version of the story would be easier to explain and wouldn't be as likely to make the people in town think Jason was demented.

"God love him," Lora whimpered, cradling Jason in her arms. "He's scared to death."

"He oughta be," James whispered to himself. And then, louder: "Well, I'm sure Jason will be all right. He probably scared the hell out of them, with that shot he put through the wall. I figure that old burglar u'll steer clear of the house from now on!"

Jason acknowledged his father's comment with a slight nod, his eyes going a little buggy.

Lora peered over at the odd, circular-shaped glow of light coming into the room from the six-inch hole in the wall. Her eyes widened as she suddenly realized the addition to the room that James was referring to.

"Where did that come from?" she asked.

James ignored her, instead directing his words to Jason.

"Now there's a lot to say for a man knowin' how to properly use a pistol. I think I'm safe in sayin' you got a handle on rule number one today. Let's hope the rest of this comes a little easier, for all of us."

He shook his head in disgust as he walked out of the house and back to work. He never spoke to Lora or Jason again about what had happened. In fact, he found the incident rather humorous a few years later after he'd gotten over the broken mirror. As for Addie, and whichever story she'd believed, she still decided to seek employment elsewhere; white folks were just too violent for her liking.

By 1929, with cash plentiful and his medical practice still thriving, James had bought out a nearby packing shed operation as a sideline investment. The packing business was located in Jacksonville, Texas, a somewhat larger community, about twenty miles to the east of Frankston. Jacksonville was the tomato capital of the world, a crop that, let alone, would have kept the operation flourishing. Other cash crops such as peaches and plums, corn and watermelon, and peas and beans only added to the lucrative enterprise.

James seemed to have a natural head for business, having already made several profitable acquisitions of real estate in the booming land market. His investment into the agricultural business was anything but a blind leap of faith into some get-rich-quick scheme. James knew farming as well, if not better, than medicine, although medicine would continue to be the mainstay of his income.

Whatever else his father may have done when James was a boy, he was responsible for instilling a sincere love for farming in his son. He'd inspired James with an interest in commodity dealing as a result of the many hours the two of them had spent at the farmer's markets selling the family's crops and bartering for the day- to-day staples they needed to live on.

But it was more than money that brought James into the produce business. It was his way of holding on to the past. His dealings with the farmers seemed to remind him of his days as a youngster and a certain way of life, his father's world that he always had admired and yearned to relive. It was a world where men made deals with a simple handshake and the giving of their word. It was, as James saw it, the last bastion of Southern honor in a corrupt world of shysters and dishonorable Northern profiteers.

When harvest season arrived his schedule became grueling, leaving James barely enough time to eat and sleep after a full day of seeing patients or overseeing the packing shed operation. It wasn't unusual, when a driver was ill or they were short-handed, for James to drive a truckload of produce to Dallas, making the four-to five-hour trip to the rail yard and then heading back, returning to the office for his morning appointments without going home. To say the least, his family rarely caught a glimpse of him during those months.

On one such occasion, he'd returned home on a Saturday morning after delivering a shipment of tomatoes. He was tired and hungry as he walked in the front door of the house, finding Jason tucked in his mother's arms. He was being consoled after having been beat up by a local bully named Roscoe Smoot.

It wasn't the first time he'd taken a licking from the town tough, but it was the first time James had found out about it. Lora had been careful to keep James from knowing about the attacks, afraid that he'd make Jason fight the older boy.

James knelt down next to his son, pulling back the torn and bloodstained sleeves of his shirt to examine the cuts and bruises from the beating. His hand moved across Jason's face, carefully examining the black and blue lumps around his eyes and across the bridge of the boy's nose.

Lora directed James' attention to a shoe-sized mark on Jason's right hip where Roscoe had given him a farewell kick before finally letting him go.

James was enraged at seeing his son pathetically lying in mother's arms, bruised and battered and obviously humiliated by the thrashing he'd taken. Much worse, it was obvious that Jason was devastated at having his father find him in his mother's lap.

James opened his medical bag without saying a word, carefully cleaning his open wounds and crafting small bandages from gauze and adhesive tape. When he'd finished, Jason's skin resembled a patchwork quilt, with so many different-shaped bandages covering his arms and legs.

Roscoe Smoot had beaten Jason to a pulp. Smoot was at least three years older than Jason and had the physique of a full-grown man. He was the offspring of a low-life father who was always in trouble of one sort or another. When his father wasn't in jail, he was usually getting drunk somewhere on rot-gut whiskey or looking for a fight in Frankston. Harlo 'Buddy' Smoot, Roscoe's daddy, was an unemployed roughneck who'd lost part of a hand and an ear in a blowout in the Tate City oil fields. He kept himself in liquor and food by holding cock fights at two bits a seat behind an old broken-down shack that he and his girlfriend, and the boy, called home.

It had never sat well with James to have anyone whip up on him, or any of his kin, especially when the unprovoked attack came from the likes of trash like Roscoe Smoot. Whatever James' complaints may have been with Jason and how he was being raised by his mother, that was a family matter. He didn't need the likes of Roscoe Smoot to work his son over every time the mood crossed his mind because the boy looked like a sissy.

When James had finished dressing Jason's cuts, he asked him to follow him out to the storage shed. James opened the double doors to the garage and stepped inside, leaving Jason curious about what his father was doing. In less than a minute James was back, holding a long wooden club in his hand.

"You got any idea what this is, boy?" James asked.

"No, sir," Jason answered, "It looks like a stick."

"It's a brick bat," said James. "It makes you just as big and tough as that pissant that whipped up on yah!"

"Yes, sir," Jason agreed meekly, really not sure how the stick was going to tame the grizzly that had just mauled him.

"How big's that Smoot boy?" James questioned.

"He's big, daddy!" Jason said, holding his hand a foot and a half above his head.

"Well, you're gonna learn how to bring that big red-necked peckerwood to his knees," James said, handing Jason the club.

Jason was hesitant to take hold of the weapon. "If he sees me comin' at him with this, he'll take it away and whip me, for sure."

"Shit, boy! Sure he will. But you don't have any rules for fightin' white trash. You hunker down behind somethin', where he can't see yah. You catch the bastard across the head, waylay him, crack his skull open with this bat before he gets a shot at yah."

Jason looked even more apprehensive as he examined the club.

"When you get him down," James continued, "climb on him and whip his butt. Don't let him up 'till you're sure he's gonna leave you alone. You understand? Knock his gawd damn brains out!"

"Yes, sir," Jason said, as he balanced the club in his hand.

"One more thing," said James. "Make sure this is our secret. Your momma might get a little upset if she knew what we were up to. Let's just keep it between us men."

Jason and James walked back to the house, arm in arm, with Jason miraculously cured of his depression and most of the pain inflicted by Roscoe Smoot.

Things usually slowed down on Sunday afternoon, to the point that James was able to go home and take a short nap. No sooner had he slipped off into a deep restful sleep than someone began pounding on the front screen door.

James got up and made his way to the living room, dressed in a pair of his old britches and a sleeveless T-shirt. A rough-looking man, unshaven and wearing oil-stained work clothes, stood looking through the screen. A young man was standing beside him, holding a rag over one eye, sniffling from a bloody nose, and holding his other hand to the back of his head. He periodically wiped at the drips of blood on his lip, smearing it onto the sleeve of his shirt.

James could see a collection of fresh knots on the boy's face and noticed that he was having trouble keeping the uncovered eye from watering. He assumed that the man had brought the boy to him for treatment, having already forgotten about Jason's planned showdown with Roscoe.

Before James could ask the man what had happened, the stranger stepped closer to the screen and pulled the rag off the boy's face.

"Your boy done this...tried to kill my youngin'! He ain't got the sense Gawd give a jackass, hittin' someone with a club when he ain't even lookin'."

James said nothing as he leaned forward to get a better look at the damage. He was surprised at the effectiveness of Jason's efforts.

"My Roscoe, he ain't done nothin' tah your boy," the man complained. "He jumped him from the bushes, swingin' a big ole club. Couldn't nobody git him off!"

"I see," James said, with a smile on his face.

"You think this is somethin' to be laughin' at?" Harlo demanded to know. He was pissed at the smirk suddenly appearing on James' face.

"Not particularly," James snapped back, "but I'd say he got what was rightly comin' to him."

Smoot was enraged by the remark. "Your boy's a bully, yah hear. He's a mean som-bitch, beatin' up on someone half his size, and when he ain't even lookin'!"

James gave him an opossum grin, somewhere between a smile and a laugh, before he answered. "I'll tell you what, Smoot: next time that overgrown yah-hoo of yours jumps my boy, I'm gonna let him whip his ass worse than he did this time. He's been beatin' up on him for months and it's gonna stop, now! You got any sense, you'll have him keep his distance."

Harlo seemed stunned at James' response. He made a threatening snarl, "I guess I'll be takin' care of you myself, Lavoisier! I'm goin' to the house tah git my gun, and you'd better be high-tailin' it, if you know what's good fer yah!"

He was confused why James was just smiling at him, instead of the reaction he'd normally gotten when he'd threatened someone.

"I'll be here, Smoot. Just come on back whenever the mood strikes yah," James said, no longer interested in the man's threats.

Just as Harlo was letting fly with his last salvo of curses, Lora started up the sidewalk to the house, with Jason straggling a few paces behind.

Harlo cast a glance over at Jason in disbelief before turning to Roscoe and saying, "That's the big old boy that done whopped your butt? That little pink-assed twerp? You let that little candy-assed kid knock you down, you Gawd damn liar...shee-it!"

Lora pulled Jason to her side, away from Harlo as he passed by, holding onto Roscoe's arm, and jerking him down the sidewalk. He was cursing at him as he took a final look back over his shoulder at James.

"You ain't heard the last of this, doctor! I'm gonna git you good fer puttin' your boy up to this."

Lora stopped just short of the front porch steps, looking at the retreating man and the boy, then turned and asked James what had happened.

James replied, "Nothin'. Just an unhappy patient."

"He's the young man who's been threatening Jason every day, isn't he?" she asked. "That's why Jason got his clothes dirty this morning before Sunday School. He's been in another fight!"

James ignored Lora's barrage of questions and turned to Jason. "How did it feel tah lay into him, boy? Looks like you fixed him pretty good."

Jason gave his mother an apologizing glance and then smiled at his dad. "He went down just like you said he would, soon as I gave him a lick across the head with my bat. He was yelpin' like a scalded dog." He stated matter-of-factly with an approving grin.

Lora's hand went immediately to her mouth. "My Gawd, you could have killed that young man!"

James chuckled, "Not that bony-headed little bastard. His head's probably thicker than a melon rind."

225

"Why?" she demanded to know, "why would you let Jason get involved in doing such a thing?"

James stared at her for a moment, wiping his face with his hand before responding, "He did fine. He stood up for himself. He's got to learn that...it's part of growin' up."

"No, no it's not!" Lora shot back. "He doesn't need to be like you," she wailed, as she flew into the house.

"He doesn't need to be a momma's boy, either!" James shouted after her.

Jason strolled in behind her with his hands in his pockets, staring down at the ground. His mother's reaction had taken the wind out of his short-lived triumph. And his father's remarks left him cold and disappointed.

A few days after the incident James was visited by a longtime patient who'd driven in from Cuney. The old man, Raymond Ditto, had suffered from a congenital stomach problem and was usually flat on his back before he'd ever consider making an appointment to see James for treatment. But not this time. There was more on his mind than getting relief from his ailment, as James soon discovered.

When James and the old man had finished the usual round of formalities, discussing the weather and the condition of the crops, and then each of them telling their latest fishing tales, the old man suddenly changed the subject.

"You know, Doc, I heard about the tussle you and the Smoots had over what your boy done."

"Oh, is that a fact?" James said, still concentrating on his examination of the man's abdomen.

"I ain't sayin' anybody were wrong, but I gotta tell yah, Doc, them Smoots are real bad folks. Old Harlo's done time over at Gainesville. I understand he cut some feller up in a bar outside of Lufkin."

"Sounds like he's got a mean streak in him," James calmly replied.

"That ole boy bled tah death 'cause nobody could git Harlo to let 'um take him over to git sewed up. When the Sheriff arrested Smoot he couldn't even say why he kilt that poor fella...jest said it was cause he was full uh liquor and needed tah fight."

"Smoot's tryin' to raise his boy the same way," James interjected. "Is that why you're in here, Raymond? 'Cause I sure can't see where your stomach is any worse than it was last time I saw you," he added, stuffing his hands into his exam coat.

"Look, Doc," Raymond said, sitting up and closing his shirt, "you been good to me and my family. Yah always come out to the house when me or the missus is sick. And you been lettin' us pay yah as best we could when times have been hard. I sure ain't lookin' for trouble from nobody, but I feel like I owe yah," he continued urgently.

"What's the problem, Raymond?"

"I jest gotta tell yah, Doc, I overheard Harlo and that no-count brother of his talkin' over at Jay Mac's Feed. They were braggin' about how they was gonna cut yah up and dump yah down in Mud Creek."

"Well, don't let it worry you, Raymond. They're not gonna hurt anybody. They're just talkin' tough."

"I don't know, Doc. But, jest in case, I don't need no trouble if you'd sorta leave my name out'a this. I were jest wantin' you tah know what they was up to," he finished.

"You got my word on it, Raymond. Before you go home stop down at the pharmacy and tell Smiley to fill this prescription and have yourself a sundae for your stomach. Tell Smiley to put it on my bill...doctor's orders. And thanks, Raymond, you're a good friend!" James said, patting the old man on the shoulder before leaving the exam room.

After dinner James walked across the street to Pryor's Hardware and Funeral Home. Clifton Pryor was the third-generation owner of the hardware business, but he had added the funeral home in the back when the coloreds began making enough money in the oil field to pay for funeral services for themselves. Up 'til then, most of them simply buried their folks in a blanket or built a pine box for a casket.

James knew Clifton on more of a business basis, having referred a few of his poorer white patients to him. One of them had had an elderly relative quietly embalmed by Clifton so that they could have the body shipped out of town to Reklaw.

Clifton was up on a ladder when James entered the store. He wiped his hands on the leather apron he was wearing and

227

stepped down onto the floor, marking down the number of screws in a box before he turned and acknowledged his visitor. "How do, Doc?"

"Afternoon, Brother Pryor."

"What can we do for yah today?" Pryor asked.

"Well, I could use a little help, if you don't mind?"

"Not at all, Doc. What can I git yah?" His eyes lit up when James advised him he would probably need an order form to make sure he got everything.

"I'll be wantin' one of those new Winchester pump shotguns you got up there in the front window, in a twelve gauge. And a couple of boxes of deer slugs to go along with it. I'd like for you to cut a foot and a half off the barrel and slice off about three inches of the stock, too."

Clifton's jaw dropped, aware that James wasn't thinking about deer hunting.

James knew that Clifton was nearly as big a gossip as his wife, Dora. He was sure that anything he said would be on the street in a matter of minutes after he'd left the store. It was part of his plan.

Clifton looked at James, unable to restrain himself from asking, "What'cha gonna do with a rig like that, Doc?"

James ignored the question. "I'll need two of your cheapest pine caskets and embalming for two men. One of 'um is about six foot two, 190 pounds. I don't know how big the other'n is. Figure him the same size, they're brothers. Probably be tomorrow before you get 'em, though."

Clifton looked up from his order-taking, his jaw having dropped another half inch as James headed for the door.

"I'll be back in twenty minutes to pick up the shotgun," James stated, "put it on my charge."

Exactly twenty minutes later James returned to the store to collect his weapon and shells. He stopped at the register to load the magazine, pushing five shells into the action as Clifton watched.

"Yah know...we used these damn things in France for cleanin' out trenches. Goddamn things, tear a man to pieces! Really messy! You probably ought to forget about embalming those two fellas, they'll be too tore up," James said, coolly, as he slid the action back with a hard jerk and then forward as the first red shotgun shell disappeared into the breech.

James left Clifton standing in a trance next to the window of his store as he walked across the Town Square to the barbershop. He was carrying the shotgun pointing down at the ground as he stepped at a quick pace towards Bascomb's Barbershop.

Bascomb's was typical of the barbershops in most small communities in the South. Western Union couldn't have delivered the amount of gossip and information that was passed around in an average day in Bascomb's. Men became heroes, and fish grew to enormous lengths, as if each had been exposed to some form of wizardry as soon as a man stepped foot in the shop. Women never seemed to be affected by the spell, but not too many of them hung around to hear the stories either.

James made his way to the establishment, walking past several men sitting out front under a cantilevered walkway. A few of the men leaned against the wall. Others sat on benches so they could share a tin can to collect the chewing tobacco, jettisoned far enough away that the telltale drool on the sidewalk recorded the line of flight and the culprit who'd launched it.

James ignored the curious looks from the men on the porch as he strolled leisurely into the shop. Everyone had spotted the shotgun hanging to his side. The normally brisk exchange of conversation suddenly ceased, except for a few nervous coughs, as everyone concentrated on James and the gun.

He shuffled past all of the occupied chairs, stopping at the back of the shop to lean the shotgun against the wall. No one was bothered by the gun, once he put it down. They were all relieved that there wasn't a problem with any of them.

"Brother Bascomb, gentlemen," James acknowledged politely, nodding his head as he hung up his straw fedora and perched himself up on the shine stand. He immediately buried his face behind the Jacksonville paper.

"Gonna do some bird huntin', Doc?" Bascomb asked. The room remained silent except for a few nervous coughs. Bascomb usually felt responsible to act as unofficial spokesperson for any topic that looked like it needed addressing by the group.

"I think Doc is fixin' tah go to war, with that scatter gun cut off that'a way," Alton Spivey remarked, as he looked around the room for approval. "Maybe he's out collectin' fees from all them folks that ain't been payin'," he blurted out, followed by a loud horselaugh. No one else seemed to find it funny. The room remained dead silent.

"Spivey, I think I'd keep my mouth shut if I were sittin' next to a man totin' a shotgun. He might not take kindly to your smart mouth," Bascomb warned, breaking the uneasiness in the shop. Everyone began to laugh, except James.

"How about it, Doc?" Spivey started up again, still irritatingly loud. "What kind'a varmint you after today?"

James dropped the paper to his lap as he responded with, "I'm fixin' tah kill me a couple of white trash fellas, if you gotta know! They've been makin' threats at me and my family. If any you boys know Harlo Smoot and that half-witted brother of his, you might tell 'em as soon as they come into town, I figure we'll just have it out. Otherwise, I guess I'm gonna have tah go lookin' for 'em," he added calmly as he lifted the paper back up to his face.

The room was quieter than a morgue, except for the popping of Alfonso's shine rag working his rhythm on the tips of James' shoes. It was a black man's rhythm that picked up speed as soon as James announced what he was about to do.

Alfonso was uncomfortable being around white men talkin' about killing folks, white or black. Killing was as common as bad weather in East Texas, especially for a black man who found himself in the wrong place at the wrong time.

"If either one of those boys come around, just tell 'em I'll be lookin' for 'em," James announced, putting on his hat and picking up his gun after he'd paid for his shine.

"Oh, by the way, tell 'em Pryor is handlin' the funeral arrangements. I figured it's only right that I pay for buryin'm, since I'm doin' the killin'! I've already put up the money for a couple of pine boxes, assuming there's enough left to bury!"

James left Bascomb's shop as straight-faced as an executioner. Spivey and the others concentrated on anything they could to keep from staring at him as he walked by, all of them caught off guard by his surprise announcement.

Harlo Smoot and his brother made themselves scarce around Frankston shortly after James' visit to Bascomb's. James knew, after having grown up around his share of the Harlo Smoots in the backwoods of Louisiana, that any show of weakness on his part would have meant a real problem for him and his family. It could possibly have cost him his life. It certainly would have cost him his self-respect and perhaps done irreparable harm to his medical practice, but then so would a bullet.

Smoot, on the other hand, learned something of the nature of the beast when he saw how coolly James responded to the situation. It was more than just talk from the Louisiana man. Smoot had an intuitive gut feeling, a sensitivity to James' reaction that only a man who'd ventured close to death before would understand. He knew it was time to let things be. James Lavoisier was an easily misunderstood character, a quiet, fancified-looking man, passively disguised but perfectly capable of following through with his threats, as Smoot rightfully presumed.

Within three days Smoot passed the word that he had taken a pipeline job out of state. It was a face-saving excuse to allow himself license to tuck tail and run, along with the rest of his seedy kinfolk. James never mentioned the incident again, avoiding any attempt from anyone trying to egg him into a conversation about what had happened. Smoot was gone, and that was all that mattered.

As for Jason, the entire experience did little to shine an awakening light onto the paths of his life. He remained harbored under his mother's watchful eye, dependent upon her for his strength in any confrontations that might come his way for the rest of his youth and occasionally even as an adult. It eventually widened the gap between him and his father, a gap that James had hoped to close with his object lesson about being a man.

Jason failed to relate to it, only understanding that his father had done it all. There was nothing he could do to match his father's courage or success. His mother's standards were much easier to abide by and certainly not as physically demanding. Besides, there would always be his father's reputation to fall back on.

CHAPTER 10

James' and Lora's marriage evolved, over the next five years, into a thinly disguised arrangement of convenience. It allowed them both to share the bounty of their labors, share a home with their child, and at the same time provide an acceptable image of marital harmony in the eyes of ever-present guardians of society. But there was little else being shared between them.

Secretly, James felt a deep frustration over Lora's physical aloofness. She was a victim of her strict upbringing and the extreme legalisms of her father's religious teachings. She was ever challenged by the echoes of his constant warnings that sexual contact was for procreation, and to do more was to commit sin. It was the ultimate birth control.

On the other hand, she reluctantly accepted James' tomcatting, as an incurable affliction, silently enduring his indiscretions in exchange for his commitment to provide for her and Jason. But never did she understand or approve. They both simply went on with life, unhappily accepting the other's shortcomings, but never daring to share their burden with anyone else. The family's dirty laundry was never put out for public scrutiny. One simply had to learn to endure.

This wasn't to say that James didn't admire and approve of her undaunted dedication as a mother to Jason, although he couldn't agree with the fastidious image she had so carefully created for the boy. In fact, Jason was no more delicate or demanding than any other child, but he stepped to his mother's tune. It was certainly easier than doing things his father's way, where every problem seemed to call for brute force and fisticuffs.

James reconciled himself to Lora's dominance over Jason, accepting his lack of influence with the boy and never trying to realign Jason's affections or loyalties. He had given up on any future hope of communion with her. It had become a purely economic arrangement.

On occasion Lora and James managed to have some tender moments with each other, but those times were rare indeed, and certainly not as intimate as he would have liked. She was usually content to smother Jason with her sporadic moods of affection rather than risk James' more demanding attentions.

It was unfortunate that, as a child, she had been so thoroughly isolated from social contact with the male species, except of course her father. James had been the first man she'd been allowed to openly associate with, and those meetings had been carefully chaperoned under the watchful eyes of the old pastor until she was safely married. Whatever else may have contributed to her strange views on sex, most of her problems stemmed from the old preacher himself. Because he was away from home so much, he had carefully protected his reputation as a minister by keeping the girls in an environment of fear, ignorance and mistrust of men. At the same time, he had had an almost phobic dislike for women. It was mistrust that kept him on an endless vigil, guarding against one of the daughters breaking from the pack to leap into the waiting arms of temptation.

James frequently found evidence of the old man's misguided influence. One particular afternoon he had opened the door to the bathroom, catching Jason perched up on the toilet seat, reading a dime store novel. There he sat like a giant bullfrog squatting on a river rock.

James was frozen in disbelief by the strange gargoyle, thinking at first that Jason was using the stool to reach the linen cabinet behind him. The problem was that he was as naked as a cue ball, squatting down with the front half of his feet hanging off the toilet seat. There he sat, contentedly reading his book, with his chin resting on his knees.

"What are you celebrating, son?" James asked in a questioning tone.

"Hi, dad," Jason answered. "Just takin' a crap."

James pondered the roosting human for another moment and then said, "Why yah sitting on the throne like that, boy? Isn't it sorta uncomfortable?"

Jason replied with a smile, "Nah, dad. Momma says it's the only safe way to keep from catchin' somethin'. You know...off the toilet seat. It's no problem, just balance yourself real good and make sure your feet ain't wet. Once you get the hang of it, it isn't too bad."

James' serious mood collapsed. He broke into hysterics, stepping back behind the door, so he wouldn't embarrass

Jason. When he finally got control of himself he stepped back into the bathroom.

"I wouldn't think there was too much you could catch around here, son," he said. "But I guess it's better to be safe than sorry. Probably a good idea, at that. Who knows...might keep your fanny from chafin'," he added.

Jason just grinned and nodded at the same time, pleased with his father's favorable response.

James decided he needed to have a man-to-man with the boy about the facts of life, including those elements of nature that Lora obviously had already taken upon herself to address. Unfortunately, he knew that old habits die hard, but he still felt led at least to give Jason the finer points of etiquette for using the commode before someone else found him perched that way.

'What the hell,' James thought, 'worst thing could happen is that he might bust himself up a little, fallin' off the pot.'

Despite James' ever-increasing financial success he found himself tired from the loneliness that continuously haunted him, draining him of purpose in life. He yearned desperately for some semblance of affection from Lora, only to find her unsympathetic. He'd grown to respect and admire her for her hard work in making their home a comfortable place to live. He'd even accepted her innocently demure notions about marriage. But he longed for the physical and emotional closeness that he felt a married man and woman should have, the way things were supposed to be.

Lora had become the one inconsistency in his life. She was the one facet of his existence that he knew would never change to his liking. And since divorce was an unacceptable alternative, he was forced to discreetly relegate those overwhelming desires to another place, to another woman, or learn to better control himself, as Lora had calmly suggested.

James routinely left town, striking out whenever the mood struck him. He would often spend as long as a week away from home and then reappear to find Lora acting as unconcerned as if he'd gone for a short jaunt to the hardware store. She would greet him with an incurious, "What would you like for supper?" or some other choking nicety.

There was nothing secret about what was on his mind. James never worked at concealing his intentions. It wasn't the way he thought a man should be. If he were going to New Orleans, he overtly purchased clothes, usually a new suit or a stylish fedora for the trip, and had the car polished and waxed. If he were heading to points further north of New Orleans, to the fishing camps deep in the swamps, he would show up at home with camping equipment, fishing lures and new fishing rods and reels. In any case, it gave Lora a clue to where he was bound.

The French Quarter of New Orleans was his favorite retreat. There was a certain genteel atmosphere, a pulsating vitality unlike anything provided by Frankston. He could cavort with his French acquaintances and frolic in the sometimes-naughty nightlife offered by his Creole friends. Even if Lora had wanted to come along, she would have been shunned by the tightly guarded society whose membership was restricted to purebred Creoles and French nationals.

Once inside the Quarter, James breathed a contented sign of relief, happy to be among old friends. He feasted on Creole foods and drink, and graciously accepted the warm hospitality which included introductions to certain young ladies, official 'escortes' for unattached men. Some were socially polished Creole women, and others were not so polished. In either case, they were definitely more refined than the females who slithered into the fishing camps deep in the swamps where James oftentimes lit when his mood was more lasciviously inclined.

On one occasion, while visiting in the Quarter, he was introduced to a strikingly beautiful young woman name Anna De'puis. She was nicknamed 'the swan' by her many male admirers, and not because of the delicacy or whiteness of her skin. She would have been better named the mantis for her voracity with the gentlemen; but the nickname 'Swan' had to do more with her talent for, let us say, 'spreading her wings' as soon as she was fed. Anna was always eager to accompany anyone with the resources to show her a good time, especially when it involved a party somewhere in the Quarter. She was fascinated with James' unsophisticated yet gentlemanly character, finding him intriguing and unlike the sometimes-priggish New Orleans males, who seemed to shed their chivalrous conduct after only a few drinks. She preferred at least to have dinner and an evening of dancing before submitting to her escort's advances.

James was, like most of the other men, not particularly infatuated with much about Anna apart from her overpowering sensuality. She was irresistibly lovely, but certainly not a student of classical literature or even yesterday's news. She was totally involved in being admired and the spirit of the chase. However, when she was done, she was done, and the evening would abruptly end, for no other reason except the changing direction of the wind.

Anna and James had enjoyed each other's company first at a society bash in 'Le Quatier Francias', and then later at a small cafe near the river until early morning. Afterwards, they made their way through the softly lit streets to her apartment, intoxicated from champagne and cognac. The two of them found themselves hotly entangled in several hours of raw passion until worn out by too much liquor and exhaustion. James had found a warm spot in Madame Du'puis' heart, at least for the moment.

At daybreak James awoke, painfully aware of his folly as he was jarred back to earth by a splitting headache and an uncontrollable urge to vomit. As soon as he was able to stand up without losing his balance or the previous night's supper, he slipped back into his clothes. He managed one last look at 'Anna the magnificent', who was stretched out in a naked heap on the far side of the bed. He groaned a short apology for having to leave her and then turned, bidding her farewell as he dragged himself through the door and out onto the street. By noon he had recovered enough to head home, sober but still in pain from his misadventure. It was to be his last foray with Anna or anyone else, although she had been his favorite.

Within the next ten months James had expanded his medical practice to a second office in Jacksonville. It also put him closer to the farmer's cooperative and his packing shed that he had enlarged in anticipation of a bumper harvest for the coming season. At home his relationship with Jason and Lora had weathered his eccentricities, and had in fact improved. He seemed to have gained an appreciation for the time spent with them, guarding every precious moment. He began making a conscientious effort to soothe old wounds.

Jason had become involved in the family's produce business, working after school and on weekends alongside the field hands and laborers employed by his father. He was learning the business from the ground up, much to James' delight.

Jason was thrilled with his father's attentions. His work at the shed, while menial, provided the perfect opportunity for their great reconciliation.

Lora couldn't have been more pleased with this new twist. She watched with delight as Jason's warmth towards his father grew. Her reaction to James' change in attitude was at first guarded, but after a while she began to realize how happy Jason had become with his father's change of heart.

A gale had blown across all of east Texas, dousing the terrain with a cool spring rain. The normally orange shade of the soil had turned a brilliant blood red as a result of the downpour. Leaves and bits of tree limbs were scattered over the thick St. Augustine grass that had begun greening earlier than usual from the humid weather. A heavy damp smell hung in the air like a freshly painted room.

The change in weather usually created a rash of appointment cancellations by James' patients, and this particular day was no exception, with a flood of calls coming in by early afternoon. He decided to take advantage of the lull by going home and taking a nap. It was sleeping weather. He set his stride towards the house, arriving just in time to be pelted by another heavy downpour as he was just a few yards from the front door. His suit coat was dotted with raindrops, but it hadn't soaked through to his shirt. He kicked the red mud from the soles of his shoes and then stepped onto the front porch.

It was dark in the house. He thought that perhaps the power might have been interrupted by the storm, but he could see lights on in the neighbor's windows. The front door was open and the screen was abuzz with small flies and mosquitoes beating themselves senseless, trying to get in. He slipped off his shoes at the front door and stepped inside, pulling off his damp suit coat and hanging it on a doorknob to dry. The mildew would have it by morning, otherwise. His fingers released the small buttons of his collar, relieving the uncomfortable pressure around his neck. He gave his wide silk tie a tug and then inhaled, as if it were his first full breath of the day.

He usually found his newspaper in the kitchen where Lora would have paused in her chores to work the crossword puzzle, but today he almost stumbled over the folded bundle lying next to the front door. Even the mail was still stacked in a neat pile on the oval-shaped entry table where the postman had put it.

"Lora, I'm home!" he shouted, shuffling curiously through the mail.

Still, there was no response. A strange calm filled the room until a burst of thunder broke across the sky, interrupting the eerie silence.

He announced himself again, shouting, "Lora...Jason...anybody here?"

Still nothing. He looked up from his inspection of the envelopes, sure that she was home. She always called the office if she was going out to the school or the store. James lay the newspaper down on the table and walked towards the kitchen, glancing down at the unopened mail in his hand.

The kitchen was as dark as the front parlor. The back door had been left open and it was banging against a cast iron foot stop with each gust of wind from outside, and a puddle had accumulated on the floor from the blowing rain.

He ignored the pool of water as he continued to thumb through the letters and at the same time feel his way down the unlit hall, busy searching the envelopes for any checks that might have come in.

He was surprised to find Lora sitting next to the drawn curtains in her bedroom. If it hadn't have been for the lightning outside, he would never have noticed her in the darkness.

James caught himself just as he was about to say something, realizing that she was rocking a baby in the old bentwood rocker that she had dragged into the room from the back porch. There was nothing unusual about finding Lora with a child in her arms. She often kept the neighbors' children while their mothers shopped. She didn't do it for pay, but for love.

He flinched and then made a half-hearted apology as he moved towards his dresser to wipe off the water dripping from his scalp, from the soaking he'd taken outside. He watched her in the mirror as she rocked the tiny bundle, still hidden in the shadows. Lora stared at the wall in front of her, never acknowledging his presence in the room.

"Whose youngin' yah takin' care of today?" he whispered, looking down at the cuffs of his shirt as he twisted the cufflinks out of the buttonholes.

Lora still didn't answer. She just continued to rock the child, softly humming a nursery lullaby.

"It was really slow at the office," he said. "I'm glad we're almost through the cold season; it'll give me a little more time to get something done besides looking at sore throats."

Again she ignored him. The rocker continued to squeak annoyingly with each movement backwards and forwards.

James pivoted around.

"You feelin' okay?"

She ignored his question, continuing to stare at the wall. She closed her eyes as soon as he was close enough to get a clear look at her face in the dark. He could tell that she'd been crying. He couldn't remember the last time he'd seen her upset enough to cry.

"What's wrong, Lora?" James asked, in a quiet voice. "Something wrong with Jason?"

She turned her head away, looking towards the filtered light seeping through the curtain.

He was upset at being ignored, expecting at least a smile.

"Is there something the matter?" he wanted to know.

Lora turned back, looking him in the eye, and then handed him a small ivory-colored envelope. Her head rolled back towards the window as she spoke, her voice flat: "It's a letter from a woman...someone named Anna Du'puis."

James held the thin envelope between his fingers, hesitating for just a minute, as if it held his death warrant. His eyes focused on his name, written in large cursive letters.

He stepped back until he could feel the side of the bed pressed against his leg. He slid down, turning on the lamp as he leaned back against the headboard.

His hand fumbled for a piece of the long white handkerchief that dangled from his hip pocket. He pulled it out and anxiously wiped his face.

"I don't know what this is all about," he said as he began to read. His forehead landed in his hand as he studied the letter.

He inhaled several deep breaths, a dying man's gasps for air, and then gently folded the note and pushed it back into the envelope.

He cleared his throat before he said, "Why does she assume that he's my child? My God, just because she can't be bothered with a baby, her baby, she expects me to take care of it? She does this to me so she can go on with her whoring?"

Lora stood up, staring at him with a fire in her eyes. "Don't you call upon God for this. And as far as whoring...it appears that you have paid for at least one night of her favors." she said, succinctly.

James walked out of the house and into the yard, standing in the drizzle that had replaced the hard rain falling a few minutes earlier. His mind raced, trying to find some reason for Anna's action. If it had been extortion, she'd done nothing in the way of making a demand for money. She'd simply abandoned the child as coldly as if she were returning a coat he'd accidentally left in her apartment. The rain cooled his temper like a forging iron, thrust, searing, into a barrel of chilled water. His thoughts drifted back to the letter and what Anna had written.

'If he is to be institutionalized, I leave it in your hands. There is no place in my life, or my heart, to do what must be done,' she wrote. 'Forgive me for the pain that this will bring to you and your family, but I don't know what else to do! I leave it all to you!'

James walked back towards his office. The street had become a dark muddy ooze. Streams of water ran along both sides, as puddles formed wherever wagon and tire ruts had marked the road before the storm had come.

He slumped into his desk chair, retrieving a fifth of whiskey and a glass from the drawer beside him. He lifted the telephone receiver to his ear, slugging down a generous gulp of straight whiskey as he waited for the operator to respond.

"Evening, Wilma, this is Doctor Lavoisier. I need to place a call to New Orleans...to 5257. Yeah, go ahead, I'll wait," he said, lighting a cigarette.

Five minutes passed before the operator was able to make the connection to New Orleans. The wires buzzed and hummed with static with each flash of lightning outside.

"Thanks, Wilma," James said, pouring another drink as he waited for the other party to answer the phone.

"Carl? Carl? Yes...James Lavoisier. I'm fine, Carl," he said, trying to keep the urgency from his voice.

"Oh, it's raining like hell here, too! Look, Carl...the reason I'm calling is...have you seen Anna lately? Yeah, that's right, Anna Du'puis?" he asked.

James listened for a moment, pulling a draw from his cigarette and taking a slug of his drink, with his mouth still full of smoke.

"How long ago did she leave? It's important. She's gone? You're sure? She moved out of her apartment? Where the hell did she go?" James demanded, trying not to seem obvious.

He listened, answering the man's inquiries with, "Yes, Carl, I knew she'd had a child, I was just checking to see how she was doing. Yes, a purely medical interest, that's right. I appreciate the offer...sure, next trip," James finished, closing his eyes in disbelief. Anna had disappeared and no one seemed to know where she'd gone.

He lowered his head to the desk. "Oh, Lord Gawd...what have I done?" he moaned.

The night turned pitch black, disturbed only by the lightning, crackling and streaking in elongated flares, through the dark. James was shivering from the dampness of his clothes as he stumbled to the couch in his office. As he lay looking up at the bursts of light dancing across the ceiling from the storm outside, he found himself reflecting on the past. He thought of France, and then the war. It seemed so long ago, an eternity. He remembered how the light from distant explosions teased the senses, enticing him to stare into its glow, as if one were looking into a crystal ball, watching for death to appear.

Despair chilled him as he tried to understand why he had been spared from death, when life had been reduced to this? 'At least that was an honorable time!' he thought.

'Bull shit,' his mind retorted; 'there was nothing honorable about the genocidal enthusiasm that had gone on while each side went about hacking the brains out of the other.'

'Maybe it was just plain...uncomplicated?'

His mind answered again: 'Uncomplicated indeed! Extirpating life became very uncomplicated. A gutted hog got more attention than a dying man.'

"But, what I have done is disgraceful, humiliating...a slow agonizing death," he mumbled. "I've come all this way for this? Better I had died in France!"

He closed his eyes as the liquor had its way, anesthetizing him into a deep drunken sleep.

As the first light of morning filtered through the overcast sky, hanging over Frankston, James made his way home. He ignored a single wagon with its metal wheels grinding the gravel under its weight. An old Negro man, his chin pressed to his chest, let the two mules, pulling the wagon, guide themselves sluggishly down the street while the man captured a few last minutes of sleep. James could hear cows bellowing to be milked and dogs barking. A flight of green-winged teal swooped down over the town on their way to feed, making a final correction of their flight path before heading to the Neches River.

James walked into the kitchen through the back door, smelling the warm, gas scented air from the stove heating the kitchen. A baby bottle was sitting in a pan of boiling water, jitterbugging from the bubbles streaming up all around it. A half-empty cup of coffee was at Lora's place at the table, letting James know that she was awake. He stood at the sink, leaning over, dousing his face in cold water and wiping it off with a worn-out dishtowel. As he turned to go to his room for a change of clothes, he noticed Lora sitting in the front parlor in her bathrobe. She was staring out into the empty street, with the baby locked in her arms in a blanket.

He approached her quietly, sitting down on the couch next to her, then broke the silence, saying, "I'll take the baby over to the State Hospital at Rusk as soon as I can get dressed. They'll handle getting him placed somewhere."

242

Lora sat still as James' head dropped to hide his shame, then he spoke again: "I can only tell you that I'm sorry for all of this. I don't have any explanation for anything that's happened...only that I'm so ashamed."

He stood up, thinking that that was the end of it.

"What about this child? What about his life?" Lora demanded to know.

James was startled by her question. "I said I'd take care of it, this morning," he answered. "What else do you want me to do?"

Lora looked at him with a burning rage in her eyes as she spoke: "I don't understand what makes you have to crawl around like white trash, chasing anything with a skirt, wallowing in the gutter with every cheap floozy that'll have yah:"

His eyes dropped to the floor as he listened. He sat back down, submitting to the tongue-thrashing that he knew he deserved.

"I'm going to keep this baby like he's my own, because he's an innocent child, and I'm led of the Lord to do it! But I hate every filthy part of you that has caused all of this! Don't ever come in my bedroom again, for any reason," she snapped, standing and looking down at him with fire in her eyes.

"You tell anyone that asks that we adopted this baby, that his mother died," she ordered. "That's all I'll ask of you. It may not matter to you about your own self -respect, but you're not going to ruin Jason's and mine with this. And heaven help us for the lie!"

James didn't respond, but instead collapsed back into the chair as Lora disappeared down the hall. The event had reduced his ego to little more than a scolded child, stripped of his pride with one fell swoop of her righteous sword. It was a verdict that had declared the moral insolvency of his life.

But life did go on. Lora, busy with children and mothering, and James pressing forward with entrepreneurial pursuits, both declared their mission in life to be the family.

The following year was prosperous for James, especially for the growth of his medical practice in Jacksonville. One of the physicians in town had conveniently died, leaving his patients scrambling through James' door like serfs, seeking to align their loyalties to some feudal lord for protection from the scourges of the land.

The Tate City oil fields had fallen quiet with the end of drilling in the area, but the drillers were replaced by a much less rowdy class of workers, still rough and hard, but certainly less pugnacious. The service crews, the pumpers and well service personnel, were brought in by the oil companies to maintain the equipment and operate the pumping stations. Convoys of trucks began hauling the raw crude to the port refineries in Baytown and Houston.

The drillers and roughnecks had abandoned the compound, leaving much of it in disrepair, except for the new buildings that housed the metering equipment needed to operate the pumps. And there were a few remaining shanties where service personnel had taken up residence. The small, boxy, stilted homes, the ones that had survived the previous tenants, were splattered with red stain from the soil, and had shed the last particles of paint. Anything that hadn't been nailed down had been hauled off with the changing of the guard, leaving the new residents to inhabit horribly dilapidated shells.

With the advent of the rainy season the narrow roads leading to the camp dissolved into a sucking muck, making travel to and from the camp virtually impossible. Retaining ponds overflowed into the camp, leaving the soil blackened with crude oil that generated a distasteful chemical aroma that, folded into the stench of the garbage piles and over-used privies, made breathing almost intolerable.

James frequently made house calls to Tate City to treat its ailing workers for a variety of ills, usually related to the lack of hygiene in the compound. He had been contracted by the Oil Company and the State of Texas to maintain some control over the noxious habits of the dwellers.

Hard drinking and dominoes were the main recreation in the evening for the off-duty workers. The front porch of the general store was the official meeting place for young and old alike.

There, the residents would sit under the glare of kerosene lanterns, oblivious to the mosquitoes whirling about their heads. The scratching of the playing pieces, moving at lightning speed across the game board were drowned out by women gossiping and children laughing and chasing each other, out of sheer boredom. The money that wasn't spent on liquor or gambling was used to purchase the affections of prostitutes who had migrated to the camp, with the company's sanction.

The less desirable prostitutes, those with failing looks, or reputations for disease, had remained behind after the drillers had moved on to Kilgore and Longview. With their beauty and sex appeal as worn out as the camp itself, they vied at this point simply to find a place to sleep, or food and liquor to fill their stomachs in exchange for their affections. Most of the women dragged their bastard children with them like excess luggage, leaving the urchins to fend for themselves. The constant touring from house to house by these free-living, lice-infested damsels kept James constantly confronted with outbreaks of venereal disease. His efforts to quarantine and neutralize one strain of disease would barely begin to show promise before another highly contagious strain would be diagnosed in another worker or a citizen of a surrounding town.

Giant pumpers, their rocker arms resembling ferocious black ants, stood in cleared fields that surrounded the camp. They would pause, holding still to the cadence of the pump motors, appearing to wait for orders to march forward against Sodom. Their heads would bend down to the ground, as if to drink the oil and then slowly rise up to listen for a command to march that never would come.

Their constant banging echoed across the fields and valleys, clacking a constant beat, as if to tempt the skeletons of abandoned derricks to move from their platforms in some mystical dance. But no one ever seemed to complain of the noise: each beat of the pump squirted more money into the community than a man could make in a week.

The only access to Tate City was over a rickety trestle bridge that stretched across the Neches River. It sagged like an old mule's back, bowing to the low water mark, little more than rough-cut planking, sawn from pine logs and laid across heavy beams that stretched from bank to bank. The river appeared to be dry, with only a shallow stream cutting through the bleached white sandbars that filled the waterway. Small streams of oil leaching from the holding ponds, or seeping from the ground, colored the water with indigo blue and metallic red strands that curled and bubbled as they passed under the bridge. Hidden only inches below the dry surface lay deadly quicksand. It was deep enough to swallow a full-size truck, and it easily could consume a car and its driver.

James slowed to an idling roll as he started across the long wooden viaduct leading to the camp. He listened to the grieving pains of the timbers as his tires struck the warped boards, as curved as barrel staves. The structure squirmed under the weight.

He had been called to the camp to see a patient who was quarantined with infectious hepatitis. After doing what he could for the man, he lectured the woman who was sharing the house on the precautions for preventing the spread of the disease. James knew his efforts were futile because the whore who was living with the man would probably share his whiskey bottle or sleep with him as soon as he was able to sit up, if he didn't die first. When she'd grown impatient with his immobility she'd probably go to a bar somewhere along the river, infecting someone else. And so it went. James was never surprised by the types of disease he encountered, only by where he would next find them rearing their ugly heads. He made his rounds, treating the other patients in the camp as best he could, sending some to the hospital and scheduling other cases for treatment at his office in Jacksonville.

His final patient of the afternoon was a plant pump supervisor named Ellis Dunraven. He was a thin, fragile-looking man who'd casually walked up to him just as he was about to leave for Frankston. Dunraven's arm was wrapped in a pillowcase soaked through with blood. He had a twelve-inch gash running the full length of his arm, split down to the bone.

Ellis Dunraven worked at a desk, in a pump house, inside the camp. It was an unlikely place for a man to get that type of injury. He laughed when James asked him what had happened; then, still grinning, his misfitted false teeth moving loosely in his mouth, he answered, "I didn't git this on no damn job, that's fer sure! Hell, I got cut up fightin' with a damn she-devil slut I was throwin' outa' my house fer drinkin' my liquor and whippin' on my kids!"

He coughed, and then let loose with a mammoth gob of spit before he began speaking again: "I knocked her ass all the way down the Gawd damn stairs. She was still hangin' on to my jug of whiskey when she hit the ground. Christ, she's a tough old bitch...and a great piece of ass!"

"Sounds like it," James remarked, cynically. "When'd yah get this cut?"

"Oh, hell, when I reached down tah git my jug away from her. She cut the shit outa' me," he replied, proudly holding up his arm, as if James hadn't already had a good look at it.

James shook his head in disgust. "Let's find some place where I can sew you up, before that arm gets infected."

"Might's well go to the house, Doc. I got a fresh bottle over there. You look like you could use a little nip," he added, still smiling.

James was appalled at the filth in Dunraven's house. It was a pigsty, with unwashed dishes and empty whisky bottles covering the table that he had selected to use for stitching up Dunraven's arm.

"Don't you people ever wash these damn dishes? It's a Gawd damn wonder any of you are alive," James scolded.

"It shore is nasty," Dunraven commented patronizingly as he searched for his concealed bottle of hooch, hidden in the closet.

"You don't clean this place up, you're sure as hell gonna lose that arm to infection! Gawd only knows what else is crawlin around in here," James went on, pouring a bottle of isopropyl alcohol over the tabletop.

"No need to do that, Doc. I'll have my girl Jessica clean up jest as soon as she gits home." Dunraven laughed. "She's out flirtin' with the boys down at the store."

It was all James could do to be polite to the man, as he unrolled his surgical kit. "How old a youngin' you got, Dunraven?"

"Oh, she looks twenty, but she's only a baby," Ellis responded.

"How come she isn't in school?" James questioned.

Dunraven flinched as James began to soap and irrigate the arm with sterile water. He tried not to show his discomfort as he answered, "My Jessica...shee—it! She's too damn busy tryin' tah figure out how tah chase them damned old

247

worthless boys down at the store. She don't care nothin' about nothin', 'cept makin' herself pretty and runnin' around lookin' like a little red-lipped hussy."

Dunraven poured himself a straight shot of whiskey, wiping the crud out of the glass with his free hand as James worked at closing the laceration with a row of delicate stitches.

When he was finished he wiped off his instruments, rolled them up in a gauze pad and placed them back in his bag.

"You keep that arm dry and wait until you sober up before you take any of this medicine I'm leaving you," James ordered.

"Sure, Doc! Now let's go sit a spell out on the front porch. I'll fix yah a nice whiskey and water."

Dunraven cheerfully handed James an empty glass and the full bottle of whiskey as they stepped outside on the porch. His hand directed him to an old kitchen chair, with its cane seat partially missing.

James wiped the glass with his handkerchief and then filled it half-full of the tea-colored whiskey. He gave it a quick swirl, flinging the contents out into the yard, trying to sterilize it. After inspecting the container, he refilled it with whiskey, declining an offer of water from an old Mason jar Dunraven had brought with him onto the porch.

James and Ellis Dunraven talked and drank late into the evening, sharing outrageous tales about their past, with absolutely nothing in common except having existed in the same hemisphere of the world, and sharing a similar race. The more they drank, the less James cared about listening further to anything the man had to say to him. Finally, James staggered to his car to drive himself home.

"Take care of the arm," James instructed; "I'll be back in two or three days to check on it," he finished, finding it a problem to unlock his car with the large set of keys he was holding.

James tore down the dirt road leading to Frankston at breakneck speed, finding himself committed to the sagging Neches bridge before he was able to plan the cautious approach that a sober man, with any sense of survival, would have used. Loose timbers flew up behind the car, pulled out of position, leaving huge spaces on the bridge's surface.

As the car rocketed downwards towards the midpoint of the bridge, its flight path was abruptly readjusted upwards to the other end, launching the vehicle in a dare devil angle, silhouetted briefly against the moonlit night.

Considering his drunken condition, James did a rather miraculous job of piloting the airborne car, not that there was anything else he could have done under the circumstances. He landed perfectly aligned with the center of the road but lost whatever control he had when the tires touched down in the soft sand and gravel runway beneath him. He wrestled frantically with the steering wheel, feeling the rear tires sliding across the gravel. With each sweep becoming wider, the car's rear end seemed to have a mind of its own. The road suddenly took a tight jaunt to the left, disappearing behind a huge loblolly pine. The front fender connected with the tree, deflecting the car off to the right through a wooden fence and into a pasture next to the road.

For a few more seconds James endured the jiggling ride as underbrush and tree limbs peeled back the right fender. Mirrors, chrome and anything else that had been attached to the right side of the car were swept off as cleanly as the stroke of a butcher's knife against soft flesh. The forward momentum finally ended when the nose-heavy Packard missiled into the dam of a settling pond a good fifty yards from the roadway. The door sprang open, catapulting James ungracefully through the air into a patch of bullnettle and grass that helped cushion his fall, but created mayhem with his clothes and skin.

He lay unconscious until morning, when the warm sunlight caught him across his face with the intensity of a welder's torch, jolting him back to life. A small herd of cattle stared with a brief interest at the awakening form and then returned to nibbling the succulent sprigs of grass dotting the pasture around them. James pulled himself up off the ground, picking the bullnettle needles from hands and face as best he could before stumbling back to the car. He slumped down in the seat, closing the jimmied door before laying his head in the opened window.

It was a question of which ailment he should concentrate on first, since the rot-gut whiskey had given him a horrible case of cramps, the bullnettle was still sticking in places he couldn't reach and couldn't see because he'd broken his glasses. And, on top of everything else, he felt the flutters of nausea, signaling him that he was about to throw up.

He leaned his head out the window emptying his stomach, moaning his discomfort with each contraction. The moaning sounded familiar enough to the cows that they decided to move in for a closer look. Some even answered the vaguely recognizable bellowing, thinking James a kin of the bovine species.

He started the car not wanting to be caught in the pasture by some passer-by, who'd surely know he'd been up to 'no good' the night before. His reputation had taken as much of a flailing as he could tolerate, certainly a lifetime's worth, as far as Lora was concerned.

Once he reached town, he slipped unnoticed into his office where he shaved and changed clothes. "You look like hell," he mumbled to himself, looking at the zombie facing him in the bathroom mirror.

'If she asks,' James thought, 'I'll tell her I was up all night delivering a Negro baby over at New Caney.'

It suddenly struck him that she wouldn't ask. She hadn't asked him anything about his whereabouts since Billy had come to live with them.

Everyone was still asleep when James walked into the living room, sinking into his favorite chair. His eyes worked their way across the room, finally focusing in on a large tree limb just outside the window. His thoughts were far away from the morning, his fantasy of life haunting him as he wondered if a time of happiness would ever come to him again. He would have gladly settled, for the moment, to repair the damage that he had done throughout his life to himself and those he loved.

His trance was interrupted by a faint giggling coming from Billy's bedroom. He could hear him enjoying his early morning awakening, fondling his toys in his crib as he talked and laughed to himself, happily experiencing his immediate surroundings.

James' downcast mood vanished as he found himself captivated by the little nine-month-old boy chattering to himself. He seemed so content with his world, blessed with a marvelous perspective on life, a child's perspective, where each moment is a uniquely fresh experience. 'How wonderful it must be,' James thought, 'to have no unhappy memories, no past to linger in your mind, no mistrust or failed promises, only thoughts of enjoying whatever landed within your sight or touch.'

James watched Billy looking through the bars of his crib, standing erect as he studied the room for something new to entertain himself.

James hoisted him out of the bed, positioning him where he could explore the contours of James' face with his moist, transparent, little fingers. All the while, Billy carried on in an unknown language, pulling on his father's lips and nose.

"Hi there, bud!" James said with a smile. "You're just layin' here havin' yourself a party, aren't you, little man?"

James glowed with affection as he watched the baby's rosebud lips sprouting a row of teeth behind them.

"You're so excited to be out'a that old bed. You're jest happier than a opossum in a plate of corn bread!"

James smiled, holding a pink hand up to his whiskered chin as he spoke, "I hope this old world treats you good, little boy! And I hope you handle your life a whole lot better than your pappy has handled his!"

He lowered the little boy gently back into his crib after giving him a peck on the forehead. He walked into the darkened parlor room, stretching out on the couch as he listened to Billy playing and cooing, stopping frequently to see if James had returned to the room. James closed his eyes, pleased that Billy had come to live with them. Finally, there was someone in this world he could love, and someone who would love him, unconditionally...at least for awhile.

CHAPTER 11

In the final months of 1934, James had decided to close his office in Frankston and transfer the balance of his medical practice to Jacksonville. He had selected a beautifully designed home as his new residence, built on the main thoroughfare of downtown Jacksonville. He'd bought the huge home, partially to pacify Lora and partly to create an image of prosperity for the watchful eyes of the conservators of 'Jacksonville society'.

The only problem with the house was that it had required major renovation, in order to return it to its original elegance. The mansion had been occupied for a short time by the Cucci-Moore Funeral Home as a temporary location while their new facility was being completed a few blocks farther down the street.

The prodigious estate was situated on five acres of lush, manicured lawns with sculptured lugustrums, cut in long, waist-high, rectangular-shaped hedges across the entire front of the property. Mimosa trees contrasted beautifully with the soft white exterior of the home.

A gravel driveway completely encircled the property, exiting on both sides of the house onto South Jackson Street. A six-car garage, an unattractive barn-shaped structure, had been temporarily and ineptly erected, thirty yards to the rear of the house, to shelter the pearly black hearses, limos, stores of coffins, and miscellaneous tools necessary to the mortician's trade.

Cucci-Moore had made extensive interior changes to the house to accommodate their funeral business. The lower level of the home had an embalming room and offices located in the rear of the downstairs, where the kitchen originally had been planned by the home's designer. A large funeral chapel, visitation rooms and a front reception area were all located in the front half of the main floor. The second floor contained the shroud room, casket room, and living quarters for the funeral home employees.

Lora had been reluctant to move into the house until James had seen to it that the interior was completely redesigned. The grisly embalming room was converted back to its original purpose as the main kitchen, and the workrooms and offices changed into Lora's bedroom and reading room. The chapel area was separated into a sizable dining room and second master bedroom, James' bedroom.

Two Negro men, borrowed regularly from their jobs at the produce shed, were kept busy plowing, mowing and picking the vast array of vegetation that blanketed the fertile acreage. James devoted much of his spare time to his agrarian avocation, taking great pride in his hybrid plum and peach grafts that flourished in the orchard.

The move seemed to have been a positive influence on all four members of the family. Each of them had gained from the change. James spent less time traveling. Lora was closer to the small college where she'd enrolled, and Jason and Billy enjoyed the added comforts of the larger home.

Lora and Jason had begun school together at Lon Morris Junior College, located in Jacksonville. Lora was determined to earn a degree in education and, at the same time, oversee her son's schoolwork. She also took it upon herself to temper his growing interest in girls, lest he fall into the grip of some conniving floozy. Billy was busy experiencing the wonders of his new home, under the watchful eye of a full time housekeeper, who scrubbed, fed and loved the tiny whirlwind whenever Lora and James were away from the house.

Suppertime was the most enjoyable break for the family, selfishly guarded from outsiders, a time to talk over the events of the day. James had finished his supper and was knee-deep in a glorified yarn with Jason, detailing some past adventure, when the front door chimes interrupted his story. James paused, expecting the housekeeper Nellie to deal with the visitors as she always did. Nellie returned to the dining room, after having politely invited the guest to take a seat in the front parlor. She whispered her report of the visitor's business to Lora, as she always did, but was most careful not to disturb the climax of James' glowing story.

Lora excused herself from the table, indicating to James that the visitor was there to see her. James finished telling his tale to Jason, and then retired to his bedroom to read. He could hear Lora talking to a woman in the other room but he wasn't able to tell what they were discussing. He wasn't particularly interested in joining in the socializing, since Lora often had her friends drop by in the evenings to chat about local news and gossip, neither of which interested him.

James was comfortably attired in his boxer shorts and a sleeveless T-shirt, sitting spread-legged in his stuffed rocker, reading his newspaper, and treating himself to a fat Prince Albert cigar.

After a while Lora came into his room. Her arms were locked together. It was a sure sign of an impending question, something serious.

"Mary, Mrs. Mary Martin, from down the street, is here, and was wondering, uh, if we'd mind if she spent the night upstairs...just for the night?" Lora sheepishly asked. Her hesitancy made James suspicious, right off.

She was trying to keep her voice down and was doing everything she could to make James do the same.

"What's she wanta do that for? Somethin' goin' on at her house?" James asked, somewhat vexed.

Lora waved her hands, trying to quiet him down.

"This is going to sound a little funny, but she wants to sleep upstairs so that she can talk to her daddy," Lora told him.

"Jesus, what the hell is he doin' up there?" James questioned, laying his paper down in his lap as Lora tried to hush him up.

"He's not up there...at least, not like you think. He's dead!"

"What?" James shouted.

Lora's approach at diplomacy was getting a workout as she tried to curtail James.

"She thinks that she can talk to him, if we'd let her spend the night upstairs. He was brought here after he died, two years ago," Lora went on, almost in a whisper, shrugging her shoulders in dismay at the request. She didn't want to say anything unpleasant that the woman might hear.

"What's she talkin' about...carryin' on a conversation with her dead father? Is she nuts or something? Gawd damn!"

Lora raised her hands again, trying to quiet him.

"She just says that if she sleeps here, she can talk to him, that's all. She says that she did it before when she was here sitting up with his body, a couple of years ago.   I don't see what it could hurt," she reasoned.

"Crazy old biddy. Well, she isn't gonna spend the night in my house to have a seance with some dead peckerwood. I don't give a damn who he was!" James laughed, pulling his paper back up to his face. "Bull shit!"

"Shame on you for talking about the dead that way!" Lora chided.

James snorted. "I'm not talkin' about the dead; I'm talkin' about that crazy woman in the other room."

"Mrs. Mary Martin is a very prominent person in this town, and it wouldn't hurt you to have a little compassion for her...for my sake, if nothing else. All she wants to do is try to talk to him. It isn't like she's asking for much," Lora pleaded.

"Well, you tell her that I've already talked to him and he's doing just fine! He sends her his love," James cackled.

"You're gonna ruin us in this town with this kind of asinine behavior," she scolded, bracing herself. She turned to stomp back to the parlor, hesitating just long enough to come up with something in the way of an excuse to save face with Mrs. Mary. She forced a smile over her face, praying that James hadn't already botched things with his hysterical laughter, still booming through the house.

Lora could see Mrs. Mary's eyes darting towards James' room, as she escorted her to the front door. She reluctantly made amends by offering to let her stay some other time, apologizing for James' strange behavior, as if Mrs. Mary had come to the house requesting something as normal as an evening prayer meeting, or tea.

Then James could hear the door to Lora's bedroom slam on the other side of the house.

James' personality was as diverse as his interests in life. He ranged from a sensitive and compassionate father, and caring physician, to a man who would just as quickly settle his own score with a gun or knife with anyone who, mistakenly or otherwise, trespassed against what he loved most in the world: his children, his wealth and his pride.

He was flamboyant at times and devoutly reclusive at others, wanting desperately to project an image of wealth and prominence in the community, but never feeling comfortable enough to become involved in the very society he was so eager to impress.

James enjoyed a venerable reputation with the banks, and an even greater degree of adulation from the merchants of the town. An outside observer would hardly have expected anything less than a ladylike curtsy from the women clerks, and a snappy bow from their male counterparts, when James called upon their establishment. Although that never happened, the thought must have crossed the minds of some of the salespeople who struggled so hard to close a sale with the tough negotiator. He was thoroughly entertained by the hoopla that ensued wherever he went, whether it was to take care of business or just visit a friend or patient.

East Texas Bank and Trust was usually the first stop each Saturday morning for James before going to his office. Once at the bank, he would do his business and replenish his pocket with cash for the coming week. The bank officers were always careful to make a big to-do whenever James visited, fussing and wheedling over him to the point of absurdity. But James seemed to enjoy the attention, stopping to shake hands with the men, tipping his hat and flirting with the ladies.

On a Saturday morning, late in December of 1934, James had made his usual visit to the bank, and the morning had started out with a bone-chilling ice storm. It was rainy and overcast with clouds hurling themselves above the town, as thick as smoke belched from the ovens at the local paper mill.

With his business completed, James stuffed the right-hand pocket of his overcoat with fifteen one-hundred-dollar bills that he'd withdrawn from his account. The bills were fresh from the Federal Mint in Dallas, something the ladies at the bank always did as a courtesy. He made a dash for the other side of the street, to Willy Cline's Barbershop. The rain was falling so hard the turgid droplets had converged into translucent sheets of water, whipping through the street with the force of an ocean gale.

The shine boy was waiting at the front door to help him out of his wet overcoat. He hooked it into a huddle of coats already filling the Bentwood coat rack, a few feet from a gas heater. James made a superficial but polite greeting, nodding his head as he acknowledged his "How do's" to those he knew only by sight. Those he knew by name he greeted with a kindly "Brother Cline," and brother 'so and so'.

The shop was a beehive of conversation being exchanged between the rows of waiting patrons and the three barbers. Willy and his two associates did a shoe-shuffling waltz around their patrons, clicking their shears and popping their straight razors on the dark brown leather strops that dangled from the side of each chair. An occasional puff of talcum powder would fill the air, blending with the heavy cigar and cigarette smoke that hung above the ceiling fans, as heavy as meringue on a drugstore pie.

The colored shine boy held a two-foot-long whiskbroom in his hand, beating out an almost danceable rhythm on the customer's neck, pants and coat. The effort did little to move the hair clippings and talcum from the patron's garb or skin, but it was a pleasing touch that was usually rewarded with a generous tip.

The clipping, shaving, brushing and brooming would cease, simultaneously, as if someone had pulled the plug on a room full of automatons each time someone would enter the shop, until Willy Cline would ceremoniously recognize the new arrival: "How do, brother Jones?" With the formality out of the way and curiosities satisfied, the men would continue where they had left off. The new arrival was left to find himself a chair or piece of wall to lean against, until his turn under the clippers.

On this particular day James threaded his way towards Willy Cline, passing Archie Wellman, who had just stood to take his turn in Willy's chair. As soon as Archie recognized James, he smiled and sat back down, relinquishing his turn in traditional homage to the town doctor.

"How do, Doc?" Willy asked. He popped the previous customer's hair off the striped, ankle-length barber bib, with a flip of his wrist.

"Doin' mighty fine, Brother Cline!" James replied.

The sheet drifted gently down across James' shirt and suit pants as Willy wrapped a cloth piece around his neck and then pulled up the bib, hooking it to the neckband with a large safety pin. Willy immediately went for the razor strop and razor in a skillful symphony of unwasted motion, slapping out a beat of welcome on the worn piece of leather. James shuffled his feet into a comfortable perch on the small cast metal footrest. He slid down in the chair and loosened his silk tie, taking full opportunity of the chance to get a little rest.

"What'a yah know good?" James asked, with his eyes closed, not wanting to seem impolite.

"Oh, can't say, Doc...'cept maybe tah wish I was a big old frog, so's I could enjoy this rainy weather we're having," Willy snickered.

James kept his eyes closed as Willy lowered the chair and wrapped his face in several steaming towels. His face was already slicker then a baby's bottom, but the moment of peace and quiet under the warm wrap was a delightful respite, and well worth the two bits it cost for the pleasure.

After the shave, Willy snipped and combed at James' already neatly trimmed and thinning hair with a vigorous once-over, cutting mostly air over his head. When the exercise was over, Willy reached for one of the assorted colored bottles of tonic, splashing a generous serving onto James' scalp to give the hair a slick, shiny glow.

Before James could straighten his tie and pay, the shine boy was on him with his grass flax brush, working him over from head to foot.

James finished his conversation with Willy by passing on some sage advice about where to find the Lunker's Nest, a legendary fishing hole where it was said that tuna-sized large-mouth Bass lay in wait, just itching to be caught. The secret lair of the fabulous fish was on everyone's mind, and each man listened intently to the coveted information, trying not to let on he was interested. Anyone who'd give away the location of his fishing hole might just as well have handed a perfect stranger the key to his home, or let him have a go at his wife. That was the general consensus of the listeners, but it wasn't as much a matter of lying about such a fabled fishing spot as the quality of the story that the fisherman told. It was inspiring, even if they all knew that there was no way James or any other devoted fisherman would ever reveal his secret spot.

James headed for the door. He picked through the coats on the rack, trying to locate his overcoat as he listened to the wild stories begin to fly as a result of his lead.

"Say, Hayman...where'd you hang my coat?" James asked, looking over at the young man working at his shine stand.

"Yas-sir, I's sure I put dat coat on dis hare rack, Doctor! I know's I hung it dare," Hayman answered nervously, aware that if anything was missing, he'd be the first one to come under suspicion even though he enjoyed an impeccable reputation with Mr. Cline. It was just the way things were with white folks.

"What color was yar coat, Doc? I seen Rufus Scruggs high-tailin' it outa' hare with a dark overcoat under his arm. You reckon that coulda' been it?" Wilbur Evans, the barber nearest the door, asked.

"Well, it shore fits the description," James answered. "Maybe he thought it was his?"

"Naw, it ain't likely, Doc. Now that I think of it, Scruggs weren't warin' a coat when he come in...I 'member his shirt bein' all wet."

"What's this Scruggs fella look like, Brother Evans?"

"He's about my height, maybe a little thinner. He's got sandy hair, and he looks like he could use a good washin'," Evans described with a laugh.

"I'd take it easy around him, Doc; I hear he's meaner than a damn snake in heat. He's holed up in an old shack, out towards Troop, near Mud Creek."

James hurried back to his office where he could make a call to the Sheriff.

"Sheriff Shank, this is Doc Lavoisier. Doin' real fine, how 'bout yourself? Well, come on by tomorrow and I'll take a look at it. Listen here, Sheriff, I need you tah pick up an old boy, Rufus Scruggs. Lock him up for awhile, 'till I can get over there and talk to him. How's that? All right then, the son of a bitch tried to break into my office. Naw, I don't wanta press charges until I have a chance to speak to him. Good, I'll be by later this evening, after supper," James added, reaching into his desk drawer and retrieving his pistol.

Sheriff Thrumond Shank was well acquainted with Rufus Scruggs and his less-than-admirable record around Cherokee County; so, by dark, the Sheriff had Rufus in custody in Jacksonville's one room jail, a few blocks off Catfish row.

Shortly after supper James received a call at home from the Sheriff. "Sorry tah bother you, Doc! I got that fella you was askin' about locked up down here," Shank offered.

"Good!" James replied. "He wouldn't be wearin' a raincoat, would he?"

"Nah Doc, he ain't wearing no coat. 'Spose he's doin' good jest tah be standin' up. He's drunker than a barfly. He was down tryin' tah talk Walt Winfield, at the hardware, into sellin' him a gun. Walt called me tah come git him."

"All right, Shank," James said, "hold onto him until I get down there."

"No problem, Doc," Shank answered. "He ain't goin' nowhere."

James made an educated guess as to how long it would take Scruggs to sober up enough to talk to him, then he waited until twelve-thirty that night before going down to the jail. He woke Jason up and took him along, knowing he was going to need some help to carry out his plans. Jason wasn't sure why his father wanted him along, but was happy to have a little adventure in his life.

James parked his Packard in front of the old jail, leaving the engine running, with Jason sitting in the passenger seat watching his every move.

"You stay here, boy. Get over on this side so you can drive. I'll be back soon as I finish my business," James ordered, closing the door and disappearing into the tiny unlit building.

"Shank? You Awake?" James asked, catching the sheriff sound asleep on a cot, set up in the corner next to the cell.

"Yeah...I'm awake," a groggy voice answered from the dark. "Who is it?"

"Doc Lavoisier," James announced. "Scruggs still asleep?"

Shank wiped his eyes, sitting up on the canvas cot, and then reached over and turned on a small lamp sitting on his desk. He was wearing only his khaki pants and no shirt or socks. He smacked his lips and cleared his throat before he spoke again. "Hello, Doc. Yeah, that som-bitch is still sleepin' back there. He's been raisin' hell since about ten, wantin' me tah turn him loose."

"Appreciate you hangin' onto him for me," James said.

"Shit, I couldn't let him go if I wanted to...he ain't got one red cent on him, let alone enough to make bail. 'Sides, he's been locked up so many times, I reckon Judge Giles is most likely gonna put him on the road gang."

"He didn't have any money on him?" James inquired.

"Nah...I guess he drank up whatever he had."

"How much is his bail?"

"Aw, come on, Doc, you don't wanta do that chunk of white trash any favors! Save your money for somethin' worthwhile. He ain't gonna appreciate nothin' anybody does for him, anyhow."

"He may not, Brother Shank, but I feel like it's the right thing to do."

"My Gawd, Doc, you're some kinda' fella, helpin' that low-life git outa' jail, after him tryin' tah rob yah! Fifty bucks oughta satisfy Judge Giles. But I sure think you're makin' a bad mistake, though, throwin' your hard-earned money after a no-count like that."

"Well, I feel led to do it, Sheriff. I really appreciate all you've done," James said, peeling off another twenty dollars and handing it to the Sheriff.

"Couple of bucks for breakfast, on me, for all your trouble." James smiled as he spoke. "I'd be obliged if you'd let him go right away so we can all get back to sleep."

"Sure thing, Doc. I'll git him up right now and send him on his way," Shank replied, glowing over his windfall.

James thanked the Sheriff one last time and left the jail. Sheriff Shank woke Rufus and sent him out the front door, as he'd promised, turning off the lights and finding his way back to his cot, not the least bit suspicious.

Rufus had recovered from his drunkenness enough to make his way down the darkened street, past the feed store. His hands were buried in the pockets of his britches and his arms were pulled tight against his sides, trying to ward off the cool night air. The only thing on his mind as he walked along was where he would spend the rest of the night. That left little choice, except one of the abandoned produce sheds or an empty boxcar on the train tracks near the market. Anything else would have had people milling around too early in the morning to let him sober up quietly.

Just as he had decided to slip into one of the empty metal buildings, the lights from an approaching car locked in on his scraggly form, blinding him until the car had pulled up beside him. Rufus popped his thumb up in the air, hoping to catch a ride the five miles to his house and save himself from having to spend a chilly night in the damp air.

The large dark sedan pulled up next to him and the passenger door opened.

"Need a ride?" someone inside the car asked. "We're headin' over towards Troop."

"Say," Scruggs responded, "that's jest where I was wantin' tah go! It's wetter than a duck's ass out here," he added, suddenly recognizing the man in the back seat.

"Get in this car!" James demanded.

"Hell, no! I ain't gettin' in the car with you! You're a crazy bastard!"

"I'm tellin' you tah get in this car!" James ordered.

"I'll whip you bad, mister!" Scruggs threatened. "Now you better leave, 'fore I git riled."

He backed away from the car, stumbling over the curb, a few feet away.

James stepped quickly out of the car and raised his arm from his side, pulling the hammer back on his pistol as he held it at eye level.

"I'll kill yah right were yah stand if I've got to, you piece ah shit! It's up to you."

Rufus stopped dead in his tracks, looking from side to side to see if anyone was around who might help him. Realizing that his situation was hopeless, he slid reluctantly into the back seat, followed by James and his convincing weapon.

"Drive us up to Love's Lookout, boy," James directed. "Slip those hands under your ass, Scruggs, so we don't have any problems over this pistol!"

"Look here, I ain't done nothin' tah you! What'cha after me about?" Scruggs questioned, shaking nervously from being wet and scared.

James ignored the man's questions, staring at him as Jason drove towards Love's Lookout, located some five miles away.

Jason eased the car into the park, turning down one of the narrow gravel roads that led to a heavily wooded picnic area. Jason followed his father's directions to pull over and stop near one of the cement and stone picnic tables.

"Get out of the car!" James instructed his passenger. "We got a little matter of a missin' raincoat and fifteen hundred dollars to discuss."

He walked around to the back of the car, still holding his gun on Scruggs as he opened the trunk, retrieving a huge bat. Jason looked on in disbelief, starting now to understand what his father was going to do.

"Jesus, mister! What dah hell ya'll gonna do with that? I ain't done nothin'! You can have y'er coat back...it were too big, anyhow!" Scruggs yelled, panting and sweating in the uncomfortably cool night air.

"Where's my money, Rufus?" James shouted.

"I ain't got your damn money. I lost it in a card game."

"You lyin' sack of shit! This is the last time I'm gonna ask yah where it is, before I beat the livin' crap outa' yah!" Scruggs' eyes lit up in horror as he whimpered, "Oh Jesus, you ain't got no right to do this!"

"Jesus ain't gonna help you outa this one. You got yourself a reputation for bein a thief, Scruggs. Ain't anyone around these parts gonna be surprised when they find your carcass stretched out in a ditch, come mornin'."

"Oh, Please! I ain't got your money, I swear. There weren't no money in that coat. I was jest cold," he cried, "that's all...I were jest cold!"

"Hold this gun on him, son," James said to Jason. "If he moves, I want you to shoot him in the belly. I figure he'll talk before he dies if he's gut-shot. It's a damn nasty way for a man to go, too."

Jason reluctantly took the pistol, shaking and swallowing hard, as he did what he was told.

"That youngin' of yours don't know nothin' about handlin' that gun. He's jest as likely tah shoot me right now as not! Oh, Gawd! Take that gun away from him!"

James moved within striking range before he asked one last time about the money. "You 'fess up or I'm gonna knock your Gawd damn brains out!"

"I ain't talkin' tah nobody bout nothin'!" Scruggs stubbornly shouted, still thinking that it might be nothing but an idle threat coming from the lanky man and the young boy.

James let loose at the man's head, sending him flying backwards into the dirt with an ungraceful crash. Then he followed Scruggs, keeping himself in range to deliver another blow before the man could get up.

Scruggs seemed surprised that he actually had hit him. With a determined tone in his voice, James looked down at Rufus, delivering his final ultimatum: "I'm gonna ask you, for the last time, where is my money? If you don't tell me, quick, I'm gonna knock you outa' this world."

Scruggs screamed at the top of his lungs, like a castrated pig and then rolled over on his stomach, tucking his head and arms as far under his body as he could squeeze them. Jason was in shock, still waving the loaded pistol at the man and dancing a nervous jig as he watched James land another shot to Rufus' skull. Rufus cut loose with a squeal, his mouth pressed into the dirt as he tightened up his body for another blow. The sound of the bat hitting Scruggs' head seemed odd to Jason. It sounded like a sledgehammer hitting a kiln-dried log.

"Oh, shit, I'm hurt bad! Don't hit me no more!" Scruggs pleaded. "I'll give yah y'er money back. Ever dime of it. Jest don't hit me again!" he moaned.

"You aren't hurt, you Gawd damn peckerwood. Get your ass up here, before I hit yah again!" James shouted. It'd serve you right for tryin' tah rob me."

James pulled Scruggs over in front of the headlamps of the car, sitting him up where he could get a good look at his face.

Rufus quickly explained where he'd hidden his money, everything except the few dollars that he'd used to purchase a bottle of rot-gut whiskey. James put him back in the car and ordered Jason to drive to the spot where the money had been stashed.

Jason still wasn't sure what his father was going to do to Scruggs after he had gotten his money back. He was worried that he might kill him.

"Yah done told me you'd let me go if I give you yer money back. I'm bad hurt! I need a doctor," Scruggs whined, wiping the blood from the side of his head.

James ordered Jason to pull over. He dragged Scruggs out onto the side of the road, staring down at him, ready to get the evening concluded.

"Get me to a doctor!" Scruggs pleaded.

"I'm a doctor, and I say you aren't hurt, not near like you're gonna be if I ever see you around here again! Now get outa' here before I change my mind and put a hole in you," James calmly warned him.

He stood counting his recovered cash as Rufus lit out at a sprint, showing no obvious ill effects from the clobbering he'd received. Jason was surprised how fast the man had recovered. He'd thought all along that Scruggs was certainly nearer to death than he appeared now. The whole incident had left him shaken. He was still holding his father's revolver in one hand as James got back into the car and took back the weapon.

"A little lesson in justice for you, son. You did a good job," James said, smiling at his excited son, who was still watching Scruggs bounding off in the distance.

"You look a little peaked, son. You feelin' all right?" James asked before laying his head back on the seat and going to sleep, as Jason drove them home.

CHAPTER 12

Green cattails, spaced like the pickets of a fence, stood stiffly along the shallows of the water, undulating from side to side after being disturbed by some form of aquatic life. It was something big enough to leave a small wake behind as it coursed its way through the weedy maze, and yet it stayed concealed below the surface of the lake. Several yards from shore, near a submerged tree, echoing circles expanded across the calm surface of the water, leaving the observers on shore speculating on the size of another serpent hidden beneath the wake. It might have been a bass or even an alligator gar, looking for a tasty morsel near the sunken limbs of the old dead tree.

James lay stretched out on a colorful quilt, his arms locked across his chest and his white Panama hat shading his face from the hot afternoon sun. His eyes were closed as he slid in and out of a shallow nap. Lora sat quietly beside him reading her book and occasionally casting a glance over at Billy, who was poking a twig down a doodle-bug hole. Her eyes moved instinctively towards the edge of the lake, to Jason, who was baiting a fishhook.

The brim of Lora's hat flapped at will, back and forth in a cooling breeze, blowing headlong at them from the open water. It was gusting just hard enough to keep the swarms of mosquitoes hovering out of the wind in the muddy shallows, over to the leeward side of the lake.

Jason returned to the blanket, pulling a deck of cards from his mother's crocheted handbag. He shuffled and then dealt a hand to her without speaking. Billy watched with amazement, quickly joining them on the quilt to feel the texture of one of the cards in his mouth, bending it to fit his small hand.

Billy began playfully to taunt his father, pushing and charging him with the full force of his featherweight body, then deciding to climb onto his stomach as if mounting a horse.

James continued to lie still, playing opossum and pretending to be helpless. After a while he reached up, grabbed the little boy's legs and pulled him down to the blanket, kissing his ticklish neck and shoulders. Billy yelled a delighted screech as he tried to get away.

When James tired of the gymnastics, he picked Billy up and walked over to the cane fishing poles arched lazily into the water. Billy carried on laughing and talking as James rigged up a hook for himself with a huge, dark brown night crawler that looked more like a small snake. When he'd finished, he selected another worm, one a little less threatening-looking, for Billy's line. He cast the lines of each pole into the water and then lay back on the grassy bank, with one arm tucked behind his head, like a pillow. Billy immediately followed suit, imitating his father down to the crossed legs and arms under his head. He lay quietly pretending to sleep like James for a few seconds at a time, rolling over on his side and sneaking a look to see if his father was awake.

Within a few minutes Billy got bored and wandered off to entertain himself with a stick and a few rocks he'd found nearby. Before long, James felt the small boy tugging on his arm, saying something about a big stick swimming near the lines of the fishing poles. James sat up, straining to look past the blinding reflection of the water. He could see the bobbers moving, jostled from a disturbance on the surface. A snake had taken a fancy to the heavy stench of the worm bait. It was watching the worms struggle to free themselves from the hooks.

James leaned forward, holding his hat over his eyes to shade them from the blinding sun. He reached for his pistol, pulling it free of the belt holding up his trousers. He moved Billy over between his legs, standing him up and placing his tiny hands on the grips of the revolver. Together they turned the barrel of the gun towards the churning water.

Shoot right under his old flat head, Billy," James instructed, aware that Billy was doing little more than touching the pistol. But that was enough considering he was only a little over two.

A loud report echoed across the lake and a noxious cloud of smoking powder drifted back into their faces. The water shot upward, tossing the snake several feet into the air. Bits and pieces of the reptile wiggled and flopped on the surface of the water for a split second, before sinking out of sight.

Stephen D. Boyett

"Mighty good shootin', youngin'! You sent that old cottonmouth straight up to St. Peter." James laughed, with Billy still trying to compensate for the ringing in his ears.

Lora and Jason reacted with little concern, assuring themselves that Billy and James were all right, and then continued on with their card game.

Jason took another quick glance over the top of his cards at James, who was still sitting at the edge of the water with his back turned towards him. Then he whispered out of the side of his mouth, "I sure wish you'd talk to Daddy about school."

"Just hush up about that. I'll know when it's the right time," she scolded. "Just let me handle it," then she said, "Gin."

James stuck the pistol back into his belt and reclined again, setting Billy on his chest. Billy was still talking excitedly about the giant snake. The ringing in his ears had passed, and he finally could hear his father talking to him.

"You know, son, when that old snake finally gets up to heaven, St. Peter's gonna ask him, 'why, what in the world happened to you, Mister Snake?' And that old snake's gonna say, with a real, deep hiss, 'Billy and his Pappy were the ones that done me in. I were just lickin' my chops at a couple of fat old worms and they shot me right in the head!' Poor old Mister Snake, uh-uh-uh," James added, trying to keep a straight face.

"Poor old Mister Snake," Billy mimicked his dad, shaking his head in a similar fashion. "Uh-Uh-Uh."

James was totally devoted to the little boy. He never uttered a crossword to the child, or showed any displeasure at anything he did. Contrary to his sentiments towards the rest of humanity, James found his relationship with Billy fulfilling and exciting. Billy had acquired a level of perfection in his father's eyes that heretofore had been reserved only for James' mother and father, and God. His admiration was well rewarded, as Billy idolized the towering man who paid so much attention to him. The two were inseparable.

Lora was quick to notice, and, while disappointed that Jason had not fared so well, she was pleased for all their sakes that James was happy again with something in life.

268

Jason had turned eighteen and had completed his second year at Lon Morris Junior College. James had long had hopes of his son entering medical school, and then someday joining him in his practice. It made Jason's plea to attend the University of Texas a logical next step in James' mind, especially after Lora had taken up the gauntlet for him. She'd asked for little, over the years, and it gave James an opportunity to try and soothe old wounds by agreeing quickly to grant her request. James had continued to do well financially with his practice and produce operation, coming through the Depression unscathed, unlike many of his fellow Texans. So there was little concern over his ability to afford the tuition at the best schools.

Jason had often humored his father by carrying on lengthy conversations about becoming a physician and following in his footsteps. James was skeptical about Jason's aptitude for medicine, but ignored his intuitions and allowed his dream to overpower his better judgment.

Jason had been patiently prodded by his mother into keeping up his grades at Lon Morris. She worked with him constantly to insure that he maintained passing marks in all of his classes. But even so, his grades remained only marginally acceptable. The boy had little going for him in the way of initiative. He was anything but a student, and even less motivated as a worker. He especially detested the sweltering environment of the packing sheds, although he was careful to keep his dislike of the place to himself. It was simply parental blindness that kept the idea of a future in medicine, or even taking over the produce business as an alternative, alive in either James' or Lora's minds.

Jason's true ambitions in life consisted of fantasizing about a career in opera or the theater, both of which James found totally repugnant, warning his son to select an honorable career, a manly occupation, and to divest himself of any such effeminate inclinations such as dancing and singing.

Partly to pacify his father, and partly to gain access to the hefty expense account allotted by his parents for school, Jason consented to his father's wishes and headed off to the University to major in pre-med. He was itching to enjoy his newfound freedom from his mother's constant monitoring and his father's scrutiny of his spending and work habits. The last thought on his mind was studying.

Jason had arrived in Austin expecting anything but a slow tranquil lifestyle. Compared to the snail's pace of Jacksonville social life, Austin was teeming with things to do and places to go, so Jason was as star-struck as if he'd come to the glitter and glamour of Broadway.

As soon as he arrived, he leased a luxury apartment at the Travis House. The Travis House was as old as Austin itself. It once had been a stately boarding home for visiting dignitaries of the first Texas legislatures; and now, over three quarters of a century later, it had been expanded and modernized to meet the velvet taste of rich oilmen and well-paid lobbyists. They would come to Austin to do their socializing and develop their strategies, reshuffling the laws of the state to their advantage. Millions of dollars worth of business deals took place in the lavishly decorated lobby or the restaurants and bars. Millions more had been won or lost in card games played in the elegant rooms. The depression had created a lull in the fortunes of the stately establishment, forcing the owners, out of necessity, to seek an optional source of income, the University students. And thus the door to the exclusive hotel opened to a younger clientele.

The next critical item on Jason's agenda was to purchase some form of transportation. Not just any set of wheels would do, but a new Harley Davidson motorcycle-that was the ticket. It was his heart's desire, an idolatrous love affair that had haunted him with the same excitement as a young man contemplating his first sensual encounter with a woman.

And not just any Harley would do...only the finest motorcycle, one appointed with every piece of optional chrome and leather available, would satisfy his appetite. His disinterest in haggling over the price, or even negotiating for the accessories, surprised and delighted the salesman, who quickly latched onto the young parvenu.

Jason was thrilled with the attention, walking through the store, speaking with an unfamiliar accent, a contrived manly tone, and puffing on his expensive new briar pipe. He'd massage his chin nervously, as if to stimulate his senses before approving each new purchase. Nothing was declined.

Last but not least, 'mettre la derniere main', the appropriate attire for his magnificent motorcycle. It was a knight's armor for his gallant chrome steed, something glowing...or maybe just slightly subdued, but still splendidly flashy.

"Yes, the white leather jumpsuit will do nicely," Jason decided, forgetting his theatrical tone in his moment of excitement over discovering the garment.

"There was no doubt about it, by Gawd," the salesman announced; "I could tell right off that you were a gentleman of refined taste when I seen yah come in. He'll want nothing but the best...that's what I said to myself."

Jason nodded in agreement, realizing the truth of what the man said.

"I'm sure you're gonna want this here matching leather helmet and goggles. And yah gotta' have a pair of gloves! Yes sir, that's a mighty fine outfit!" the salesman exclaimed. "Will yah be wantin' to pay by cash or draft?"

"Oh, draft," Jason responded, not the least bit worried about what he'd spent, and knowing full well that he had barely enough cash left in the bank to cover his school expenses, let alone the Harley.

With the transaction completed, Jason mounted the two-wheeler decked out in his new white leathers. After kick-starting the motor he flung the white silk scarf to one side of his neck, popped his thumb in the air, indicating something that neither of them was quite sure of, and smiled at the salesman. He goosed the engine and sped down the street, as out of control as a child doing his first solo ride on a new bicycle. The salesman had ignored his customer's speedy exit to examine the still-wet, bank draft from the sale. The question of <u>whom</u> had been sold <u>what</u> would soon be answered when Jason's check bounced a week later.

Jason was on the prowl with just enough of his textbooks showing from his saddlebags to authenticate his status as a student. He moved through the quiet campus, charging the engine at every opportunity with a deafening roar from the dual exhaust pipes. He stopped in front of a covey of giggling coeds, pretending to have a problem adjusting the proper idle of his motor. He sat tuning the pitch of his engine, then glanced up with a Casanova smile before launching himself around the block. Then he parked in front of the women's dorm to continue the pretense of fine-tuning his new motorcycle.

Nothing short of a torrential downpour would have dissuaded him from making his endless rounds of the campus in pursuit of female companionship for the evening. If his time were to be invested in something other than womanizing, it certainly wouldn't be anything as uninspiring as his studies. There were, after all, more important things to savor in life than something as uncertain and unentertaining as worrying about one's future. Nothing could warm the soul like a hot crap game and the camaraderie of a room full of fellow poker players. And no one relished the game more than Jason.

He'd been derisively dubbed 'The Milk Man', and not just for the flashiness of his white leather outfit. The card sharks had very quickly realized his innate talent for losing heavily at the table while still being able to come up with the cash for another game. His losses never dampened his spirits, or his desire to leap pell-mell into another high stakes game. He was thrilled with the fraternal spirit of his fellow gamblers, although seemingly unaware of the reason for his popularity.

Jason attended so few of his classes that most of his professors submitted drop notices to the Registrar's office, thinking that he had left the University. The day of reckoning arrived when James received notification from the Dean of Men that Jason was no longer considered a full-time student and had been placed on scholastic probation. He had in fact dropped all of his classes, but a few of the instructors had lost his name in the shuffle, and hadn't as yet reported him to the University. James became aware of Jason's other difficulties from a flood of overdraft notices from the bank, along with heated telegrams and phone calls from Austin merchants wanting their money for charge accounts that Jason had run up over the months, not to mention the bounced check for the motorcycle.

By now Jason was constantly on the move, having been evicted from his posh accommodations at the Travis House. He was trying to stay one step ahead of Austin's rougher element, those who had gotten nothing more than markers for their evenings spent across the table, and were bent on taking their losses out of his hide. In a period of six months of living in the city, Jason's life had degenerated to having to sleep at the local YMCA or the Baptist Hope Mission, and surviving on a diet of soup and bread.

James was enraged by his son's recklessness with his finances; it was something he hadn't expected. He was, however, only mildly surprised with his school work, knowing deep down that Jason had never had the discipline to apply himself to his studies. It had been impossible for him to locate Jason by phone. He had done what he could to stop his spending by closing the bank and charge accounts, but that had been a meaningless endeavor since the bank account was overdrawn, and the charge accounts had been run up to their limits.

For a while, James feared that foul play was involved and Jason might have been kidnapped or even murdered. It wasn't like him to go very long without calling home for money. In the process of trying to track him down many of the people James had called in Austin, had been quick to remember seeing the boy in the white leather jumpsuit almost every day, somewhere in the city.

James had arrived home early, depressed and tired after having had a patient die during surgery earlier that morning; so he walked into the house without announcing himself, unlike his customary entrance. He hadn't bothered to change his clothes when he got to his room, but instead went straight to his rocking chair, slumping over with fatigue and frustration. He began to reflect on the life of the middle-aged man who had slipped through his hands in the operating room. The death of a patient, like childbirth, never seemed to occur as matter-of-factly and routinely for doctors as most people would have imagined.

After agonizing over the man's death, James stood up with a whiskey bottle in one hand and walked to the kitchen for a glass. As he passed the hallway, he realized that Lora was talking on the phone. She was talking to Jason.

"Momma knows you're tryin' your best, darlin'," he heard her say. "I'll send you another check this afternoon. Momma loves you."

James rushed into the hallway, grabbing the receiver out of her hand before she could hang up. Lora stepped away from the telephone, holding both hands to her mouth.

"You stay on this damn phone, and I mean it!" he ordered, waiting for a reply from Jason.

"Don't yell at him, James!" Lora pleaded.

"I'll do more than that, if I get my hands on him!" he shouted. "You've known where he was all along, haven't you?"

"Yes," she boldly admitted, turning and starting slowly towards her room.

"Gawd dammit! You let me chase him all over Austin, tryin' to get him tah come home, knowin' full well where he was? Shit! I thought he was layin' up hurt somewhere, maybe killed."

Lora stopped her retreat to her room and turned around. "He wants to make something out of himself...to please you, and he doesn't know how. If he comes home, you'll sap the last ounce of self-respect out of him. He just can't measure up to what you want him to be."

She continued to her room and gently closed the door, resigned to the fact there was nothing else she could do for her son.

James held the receiver to his ear, pausing for a moment before he spoke. "You get yourself packed and get home, tonight! Do you understand me?"

He listened to Jason trying to explain what had happened, then interrupted him: "I don't give a shit, let 'em try! They come around here looking for money or someone to bust up, I'll take care of 'em. You just get yourself home!" he insisted, slamming the phone down.

Jason slipped quietly out of town, escaping Austin in the dark hours of the morning. Within minutes, he had passed the last street light of the city, finding himself winding his way up and down the narrow dark country roads leading back to Jacksonville. The Harley bounced uncomfortably, jolted by every rut and hole in the worn-out highway. The small beam of light from the headlamp moved rhythmically up and down with each vibration, lulling Jason into a hypnotic trance. The morning was unseasonably cool from a shower that had passed over only an hour earlier. It had left the road with a lacquered gloss, still damp from the rain and ground fog.

Jason had become mesmerized by the movement of the headlight, fighting to keep the motorcycle centered in the road, and struggling to stay awake at the same time. He was interrupted in his concentration by a pair of blinding lights that suddenly appeared over the crest of the hill, splitting the narrow road down the middle in front of him and leaving him nowhere to go. By the time he realized he was on a collision course, it was too late. He attempted to avoid the other vehicle by jerking the handlebars hard right, instantly causing him to lose control and flipping the Harley over on its side.

The cycle began to skid, sliding sideways across the highway with sparks and flames flashing up from the undercarriage as the metal frame dissolved against the rough pavement. Jason hung on with every ounce of strength he could muster. His leg was pinned beneath the heavy machine as it skidded past the oncoming truck and then became airborne. Somehow, Jason had managed to remain attached to the piece of equipment as it left the road and careened into a ditch beside the highway. The impact ruptured the gas tank, setting off a brilliant explosion of orange fire that engulfed both motorcycle and rider.

The driver of the truck hardly had time to pull over and get out before Jason emerged from the fire waving his arms and trying to slap at the flames covering his back and legs.

"Jesus, Gawd ah Mighty!" Jason screamed, throwing himself on his back, squirming around on the ground and rolling himself through the high weeds. The man in the truck raced over, beating at the fire with his heavy jacket. He finally got a good enough hold on Jason to wrap him in his coat and smother the flames.

By three that afternoon the sun had turned blistering hot, filling the air with a thin sultry fog. James had just arrived home after making hospital rounds. He stripped down to his underwear, trying to cool himself off before taking an afternoon nap for an hour or two before supper. The sound of a large truck threading the circular drive behind the house caught his attention just as he had gotten up to go to the kitchen for some water. James stared through the kitchen screen door in disbelief as Jason dismounted the truck, wearing the charred remains of the white jumpsuit. His face was covered with soot, except where the goggles had protected his skin from the smoke of the fire. He had miraculously survived without a scratch.

The sight of Jason and the smoldering heap in the back of the truck left James speechless, as he stood at the door and studied the remains of the expensive machine. Lora blew past him, knocking open the screendoor and leaping down the steps to get to Jason. She locked him in her arms, hugging and pawing at him until she was convinced that he was all right.

"I'm fine, momma," Jason told her with an embarrassed look on his face. He quickly slipped out of her grip to help the man unload the mangled remains of his Harley.

"I'm so thankful you're safe, honey! Momma was so worried about you!" she wailed, following him around to the back of the truck, as he tried to stay one step ahead of her.

Jason glanced over at the man who had delivered him home, wondering what he must be thinking about his mother's attentions.

"I suppose I paid for that pile of crap?" James announced sarcastically as he stepped into the yard and nudged the remains with his toe. He stood there, having put on a pair of slacks, his house shoes and a fedora, but no shirt.

"Hey, Ruther, this is my dad," Jason said, looking up with a nervous smile, as he and his associate finished unloading the final pieces of the blackened collage.

"How do?" the man acknowledged. "Your boy might near got himself killed. You ever see such a piece of twisted metal?" Ruther asked, as if he'd just delivered a statue to be placed in the rose garden.

"Can't say as I have," James responded coolly, turning and walking back inside the house.

Jason paused for a disappointed look at his father and then grinned at Lora, who was still offering her concerns for his close call. "Momma's sorry about your bike, darlin'! Maybe we can get some pieces and put it back together?" she offered.

"Yeah, Momma," Jason said in a patronizing tone, "that sounds real nice. Say, can I have a few bucks to pay Ruther for his help? I promised him a twenty for bringin' me home."

"Why, that's the least we can do," she said, smiling at Ruther. "Maybe he'd like to have some fresh peach cobbler and a glass of buttermilk?"

"Oh," Ruther quickly answered, "no, ma'am, I gotta git on home. But thank yah anyway."

Billy moved in next to the pile of parts, handling a few of the more interesting pieces and then examining his blackened hands. He quickly wiped the black residue on his pants as Jason carried the last bent part of the bike to the pile, and Lora returned from the house to give Ruther his promised pay.

As the truck pulled away, Jason took a final look at the wreckage. It was the last show of concern he would have for the salvage, leaving it to be hauled off a few weeks later by someone James had hired to get the unsightly mess out of the yard.

Jason turned to his mother and put one arm around her, then took Billy's hand with the other. "Let's go to the house...it's really great to be home!"

Jason went to work in the produce sheds to appease his father and pay off his debts from Austin. He also worked to pay his tuition to Stephen F. Austin State Teachers College, where he had enrolled with his mother, after failing out of the University of Texas. He commuted each day with Lora to save on room and board, and to make his renewed effort at college more palatable to his father.

He detested the dull, uninspiring work in the sheds; he spent the afternoons, when he wasn't counting tomato baskets, memorizing poetry from a small Bible-sized text he kept in his hip pocket, or daydreaming. He was a hopeless romantic, with visions of soldiering in some far-off land, fighting in the service of France or England, and returning home with his uniform festooned with the Victoria Cross or the Croix de Guerre.

When the supervisors were absent from work, Jason would entertain the workers with verse after verse of poetry. He usually would end his presentation with something as fiery as Tennyson's Charge of the Light Brigade. He stood on a crate and delivered the poem like a troubadour, jerking his arms into the air as if he were personally leading his men against the heights of Balaclava.

A stillness hung over the audience, with only the occasional sound of someone gasping, as he became caught up in the story, while Jason built up to the final moments of the charge.

The workers joined in, going wild with excitement, screaming with rebel yells and wild hollering. Some even slapped their thighs as they pretended to ride along with their young commander, swooped up by the electricity of the event and then sinking as he finished the soft, glorious ending, leaving them spellbound, shaking their heads. Some of the men appeared to be emotionally spent by the ordeal, wiping an occasional tear from their eyes or sweat from their faces.

"You sure musta' been there, Mister Jason. You sure does know it good!" one worker praised, prompting a Cheshire grin from the young orator.

Jason stepped down from his crate, accepting congratulations from his listeners as each of them shook his hand before returning to work. He was caught up, for the moment, in the adulations of his fellow workers, until the honking car broke the spell.

James had driven to the sheds to pick up Jason so that he could keep him company on a trip over to Tate City. Jason stared out across the freshly mowed countryside as red dust from the road clouded over the car while they drove along the small, narrow back roads.

Potholes infested the road, making driving difficult at best. Jason braced himself for each bone-crushing collision with the craters concealed beneath the ooze in the road.

"I betcha this road sorta' reminds you of France, 'eh, dad?"

James acknowledged his question with a slight grunt, caught up with something else that he was thinking about. "I saw holes in France so big that the damn trucks couldn't get out of 'em after they fell in. Now that's a big Gawd damn hole!" he laughed.

"It sure is!" Jason agreed.

"Shit, they'd just cover 'em over with dirt...men, truck and all, 'stead of buryin' 'em." James again chuckled, taking a quick glance over at Jason, who was laughing more at his father's quick wit than his story.

As soon as they reached Tate City, Jason strolled over to the country store to have a cold soda and visit with the old men who had congregated on the front porch. The men were huddled over a rickety old table playing a game of dominoes, each tapping out their bid, or thumping with a knuckle to indicate they had passed their turn, or had bumped the ante.

Jason watched with interest. One by one, the old men would reach between their legs, each producing a tin can wrapped in brown paper, and then propel a giant glob of black spit from their mouths. The streamer would land in the can with the disgusting sound of a stone landing in a bucket of crankcase oil. It was all Jason could do to keep from losing his lunch. He swallowed hard and then moved a little closer to inspect the quick action of the game. He was amazed how the experience of the players had obviously reduced the communications in the contest to some kind of code. Each of the men had his own style of telling the next player what he was going to do, without saying a word.

Again Jason moved closer to the table, greeting the men with a loud, "How ya'll doin' today?"

Nothing...not so much as a look or a 'howdy do', came from the group. No one even gave a disparaging glance at the stranger to show their disdain for the interruption.

Jason shrugged his shoulders and walked over next to the door of the store to get out of the sun. He slid down into an old weathered rocker that was providing shade for an ugly, buckskin-colored hound lying underneath it.

The dog was about the meanest-looking critter Jason ever had seen. Half the dog's hair was missing from a severe case of the mange, his face was covered with half a dozen scars from fighting, and one eye was running from an open wound. The animal had laid claim to the chair by placing his paw under one of the rockers. Not wanting to disturb the domino players by ordering the dog to move, Jason pushed his shoe towards the animal to nudge the paw from under the path of the rocker.

The dog promptly retaliated with a deep growl, bearing its canine fangs to indicate its sovereignty over the contested spot. The incident seemed to entertain the gathering of men enough that all of them managed a snicker or two before returning to the game. It was more attention than he'd got since he stepped up on the porch.

Jason promptly stood up and moved to a straight-legged chair that was leaning against the wall, as if that's where he had intended to sit all along. He thought for a moment, deciding to break the ice by quoting a few verses of poetry. It always had worked at the sheds; but before he'd finished the first stanza of his prose, all four men were cutting an icy, agitated glare at him. Each of them spit, simultaneously, into their cans, as if launching him personally into the hellish glurp crawling around the bottom of their homemade spittoons. One of the men gave him a scolding look, pursing his toothless mouth into a painful grimace and then shaking his head before turning back to the game.

'If not poetry, perhaps a favorite hymn,' Jason thought, clearing his throat to ring out with the first note. Just as he was snapping his fingers to set the rhythm of the music, a little prelude to his solo, he faltered, nearly choking at the sight immediately in front of him.

There stood the most impeccably beautiful woman he'd ever seen. She was as oddly out of place as a painting by Gauguin or Seurat would have been in this dismal garbage heap. She seemed almost to pose herself, with the sun gleaming from her coal black hair, as she straightened her body in the sunlight. She had the figure of a mature woman, but smiled with the expression of a young child. Her face was beyond imagination, lovely, almost perfect to a fault.

Jason was stunned by the way she was dressed. It was a tackiness, a pathetic veiling, almost as if a marvelous Rodin had been draped by some tasteless drudge, with no appreciation of natural beauty. She wore a cheap calico dress, an old woman's hand-me-down that was several sizes too large. The dress was faded and shapeless, the hem sagging down to the rolled-up hose doughnutted around her ankles for socks. Her shoes, what was left of them, were stretched and broken down from a former owner, twice the young girl's size. The heels had been kicked off to make the shoes look like flats.

A gaudy strand of sequined costume jewelry hung from her neck, dangling in a gentle curve over her cleavage. Her breasts moved unrestrained beneath the scanty material, for no other reason than the fact she didn't own a bra, and at her age she could well get away with it.

She walked onto the porch, unconcerned about the old men, flashing a plastic smile at them as she stepped at a wiggly gait into the store. The men interrupted their game long enough for each of them to do a little mental pawing and private meditation about what would never be, and then returned to their game.

Jason sprang to his feet and followed her into the store. He milled around, examining the limited selection of goods, all the while keeping a keen eye on the girl. Finally, having no more patience to wait, he decided to attract her attention by loudly demanding a can of pipe tobacco from the clerk. "Yes, I'd like a tin of special pipe blend, Prince Albert, if you've got it," he ordered, in his favorite theatrical voice that was a mix of Gable and Grant.

"We ain't got no special pipe tobaccos, mister; we only got company brands here," the clerk announced, watching Jason eyeballing the young girl. "And right now we ain't even got any of that. So, what else you want?" she asked, rolling her eyes up at the overhead ceiling fan.

"That's okay...I'll just take a pack of cigarettes, company brand," Jason responded, still watching the girl standing at the back of the store.

"We ain't got no company brand cigarettes, mister; only what yah see in front of yah," she snapped. "So, what's it gonna be, Bub?"

"Just give me those; they'll do," he replied, straining to keep up his surveillance.

The girl in the back of the store managed enough of a flirtatious grin to let him know she was listening. She casually fingered over a stack of canned food, pretending to read the labels, as if doing some sort of survey on the store's inventory.

Jason slapped the pack of cigarettes against the palm of his hand as he watched the girl walk towards him. She stopped a few feet away, under the ceiling fan, to cool herself, letting the force of the fan blow the thin material of the dress against her body, purposefully revealing her figure.

After a brief interlude of this, she positioned herself near the front door where the sunlight could shine through the thin material of her dress, leaving little to Jason's imagination.

The clerk gave her a searing glare before questioning, "Just lookin' around again, honey?"

"That's right, Miss Purdy. I keep thinkin' you're gonna get somethin' in this dump worth buyin'...somethin' besides all this Gawd awful cheap trash."

"Honey, you couldn't afford to buy it if I was sellin' it at half the price!" the clerk shot back, smacking her gum and letting loose with a contrived laugh. "You just keep your sticky little fingers to yourself."

"Really...you're such a bitch, Miss Purdy."

"Wha'd you say? I'm fixin' to tell your daddy about your nasty mouth, you smart-assed little tramp!" the clerk answered.

The girl ignored the clerk's threat, obviously acquainted with the woman from a previous run-in. She turned, with the clerk still swearing at her, and walked with a bumptious gait to the door and out onto the porch. Jason was right on her heels.

"My daddy's got money, lots of money," the girl huffed, standing next to the rocking chair where the vicious hound was still sleeping, his paw stubbornly fixed under the rocker.

Jason smiled, lighting up a cigarette as he mentally prepared some kind of suave introduction, something that would captivate the young woman instantly, sweeping her helplessly, sheik-style, off her feet.

She turned, catching Jason off guard with a warm smile, then saying in a soft sexy tone, "What's your name?"

Before he could answer, she moved over to the rocker to sit down. He was just about to warn her about the ill-tempered animal when she suddenly stepped back and kicked the dog with a blood-curdling shot to the head, knocking its lanky carcass against the adjacent wall. The animal did the low crawl off the porch, whimpering, and sought sanctuary under the steps.

Jason was surprised by her ferocity, feeling for a split second a pang of sympathy for the dog, before he stepped closer to answer her question.

"I'm Jason Lavoisier," he said.

"You're Doc Lavoisier's son, aren't yah?"

"Yeah," Jason answered.

"Why, everybody here knows your daddy. I 'spect there ain't a soul around that hadn't had him lookin' at 'em, at one time or another," she said.

"Well, I'm just keepin' him company today, 'case I gotta help him do some surgery or somethin'," he replied quickly.

"You know about all that doctorin' stuff?" she questioned.

"Why sure," Jason said. "It'd be pretty hard not to, when your daddy's a doctor. Course, I probably know more than most, since I'm a pre-med major in college.

"I'm Jessica Dunraven. It's nice to know yah," she said, fanning herself with a piece of cardboard lying near the chair. "You wanna buy me a soda? I'd love somethin' cool...it's just so blasted hot!"

Jason's eyes were fixed on the tiny beads of sweat on her exposed cleavage.

"Sure, that'd be real nice," Jason answered, probing both of his pockets, hoping to find a coin that might have been miraculously overlooked earlier. He smiled, taking a long pull from his cigarette as he tried to conceal his predicament. He scratched his scalp and headed into the store anyway, stone broke.

Once inside, he popped the cap on two sodas he'd pulled from inside the coke box. He smiled at the clerk as he walked past the counter, quickly announcing, "Charge this to my daddy's account...Doctor Lavoisier," he said confidently.

"Hey, buster, you can't do that! You gotta pay for those. We ain't got no charge accounts here."

"I'll tell my daddy you said that so he'll remember to take it off your bill next time you get sick," he said, hoping the woman was one of his father's patients.

Jason took a swig from his bottle and handed Jessica the other one after returning to the porch. "So, do you live around here?" he asked.

"Yeah, my daddy's a pump operator at the plant. We live right over there," she replied. "At least I do until I can get enough money to get to Hollywood, or anywhere else besides this horrible pig sty! Everyone says I'm good-looking enough to be a movie star," she proclaimed, standing up and doing a ragged pirouette around the porch with her head back. "What'a yah think?"

"Say, that's really somethin'," Jason laughed, relaxing into a straight-back chair by the wall.

Jessica took a long studying look at him before asking, "Are you really gonna be a doctor like your daddy?"

She turned away before he could answer and continued to dance around the porch, drinking her soda and mumbling a tune under her breath, ignoring whatever he might have to say.

"Maybe I will. I sent a letter to the Foreign Legion to see if I could get in. I speak French, you know," Jason announced proudly, stealing a quick look at her to see if she was moved by the disclosure.

Jessica pulled a comb from the pocket of her dress and began stroking her hair, staring off in the distance as she spoke: "I heard your daddy talkin' in French to some of that Louisiana trash at the plant one day. Are you from down there?"

"Why, no ma'am, my family isn't from any of that mess. We're French, not that low-class Cajun bunch. That'd curl my daddy's toes if he heard you say such a thing!"

"You wanta take me out sometime, a picture show or somethin'? You gotta car of your own? Most of the men I date have their own cars," she added, looking down the dirt road to Frankston, as if she were plotting her escape.

"Land sakes!" Jason exclaimed, "You don't look old enough to be dating. You're just a kid!" He laughed. "Your daddy would skin me alive for tryin' tah take you out!"

"He knows I've been out with lots of men...lots of them older than you are. He doesn't care; he says it gives him a little peace and quiet when I'm gone. I can handle myself okay."

"You got any brothers or sisters?" he asked. "I got a kid brother, but he's way younger than I am."

"I got a sister named Jenny and a brother named Donny. We all call him Toad, 'cause he never says anything, just sits around bug-eyed, watchin' everyone else," she cackled.

"Toad?" Jason broke into a laugh. "Boy, that's a doozey of a name. Say, how come you're not in school today?"

"I got kicked out 'cause the teacher says I'm too old-actin' for the other boys and girls. I make the men teachers nervous," she went on, obviously pleased with their reasoning.

284

"They just stare at my body when I'm in class; it's really embarrassin'.

"I just usually stay home all day unless daddy brings a lady friend to the house. I have to leave so they can talk and get together and stuff," she snickered, rubbing mineral oil on her lips, as if she were applying lipstick. "I'll bet they're over there right now, just gettin' all lathered up." She giggled. "That old whore u'll give my poor daddy a heart attack, sure as the world!"

"How old are you, anyway?" Jason asked, timidly. "I mean, I don't usually date younger women. Not unless they're really somethin' special."

"Well, I'm old enough to know what's on your mind. Besides, I'll bet I'm the best-lookin' thing you've laid your eyes on since you started shavin'!" she continued, firing a burning look his way.

"You're sure pretty nice-lookin', all right," Jason replied, caught off guard by her reaction. "You wanta go out Saturday night? They got a dance up at Love's Lookout. And they even got a orchestra comin' in from Dallas."

Jessica sat nonchalantly buffing her fingernails with the hem of her dress before she answered. "Oh, I guess I could make that...unless somethin' important comes up like a funeral or weddin', or somethin'. My daddy likes to go to Jacksonville and visit the funeral homes to see who's there on Saturdays."

"Do what?" said Jason, confused.

"He doesn't hardly know any of the folks that have died. He just thinks the coffins are pretty, and he loves all the beautiful flowers, and he dearly loves the organ music. Besides, we always go to the people's house after the funeral and eat a real nice meal."

Jason noticed James standing over by the steps near the porch, indicating that he was ready to go home. He jumped up, starting towards his father and then turned back towards Jessica, whispering, "I'll pick you up Saturday afternoon at three for the dance. Why don't I meet you here in front of the store?"

Jessica saw James standing on the other side of the porch and smiled at him, as if they knew each other.

"Sure, that u'll be okay. Hello, Doctor Lavoisier," she announced loudly. Everyone on the porch turned and looked.

James answered with a slight nod and a tip of his hat, then turned away. He'd never met her before and it didn't make any difference—he'd already reserved his opinion on her and everyone else at the camp.

As soon as he and Jason were in the car, he confronted his son.

"You keep clear of that garbage, boy! These folks are nothin' but a bunch of no-count white trash. I don't want you gettin' mixed up with any of these girls around here either, you understand? They aren't your kind of folks!" he added, giving Jessica a last discerning look.

"Sure, Dad. I was just tryin' to be friendly," Jason answered. He gave Jessica a quick smile to assure her that their date was still on, just in case she'd read his father's lips or sensed his thoughts.

They drove directly back to Jacksonville, with James lecturing Jason on the lack of morality among the lowlife vermin who resided at Tate City. The twenty-five minute drive back to town gave James a captive audience to listen to his dissertation on the disease and corruption that abounded among the workers and their offspring. He had nothing positive to say about anyone at the camp, including Jason's new girlfriend.

Jason worked extra hours in the produce sheds for the next few days, trying to earn enough money for the dance on Saturday night. Then, on Saturday morning, Jason approached his mother for a few more dollars, wanting to be sure he had enough money to duly impress the young black-haired Cinderella he'd discovered at Tate City. Lora was concerned about reports from James on Jason's meeting with the girl at the camp.

"You're not going out with a girl from over at Tate City, are you, darling?" she questioned.

"Oh, course not, momma. I was just gonna drive up to Love's Lookout and meet some folks at the dance."

"You know daddy doesn't think those are your caliber of people over at that camp, and for good reason! Momma doesn't want you getting near any of those harlots that hole up in that sorry excuse of a town. You need to be with our own kind...nice girls from Jacksonville society!" she lectured.

Jason's thoughts slipped back to the last encounter he'd had with one of the members of 'Jacksonville society'. He'd reluctantly escorted one of the purportedly untainted beauties to a church social, at his mother's behest. He'd been the perfect gentleman, and the young lady was the epitome of southern grace, charm and piety until she found herself alone with Jason in his car, on the way home. A sudden and uncontrollable attack of salaciousness had swept over her, whereupon she forced the car off the road and wrestled Jason to the seat, disrobing herself and him quicker than a burlesque dancer at amateur night. She immediately set about satisfying herself with the delicacy of a wart hog in heat. Jason returned from his momentary reflection to answer his mother: "I'm just going to the dance, mamma...by myself. I'm sure they'll be some nice girls there from Jacksonville."

He accepted the money from her, giving her a hug, then headed to his room to get ready for the secret rendezvous with Jessica.

By one o'clock, Jason had nearly finished dressing. Billy was sitting on the edge of the bed, watching him put on his white shirt and a pair of freshly pressed, pleated serge pants. The boy was wearing Jason's white straw fedora, pulling it playfully down over his eyes. He was laughing and yelling for Jason to look at him.

Jason smiled, giving him a loving poke in the stomach, and then finished getting dressed. He slicked back his hair with several shots of tonic, then finished off his preparations by dousing his face with a final dusting of talcum powder and an obnoxiously potent cologne.

On his way out of the room he retrieved his hat from Billy and patted him affectionately on the head, bidding him farewell with, "See yah when I get home tonight, Bill. I gotta go meet a doll." He smiled, and made a motion as if to twist the ends of a non-existent mustache. Billy duplicated his movement to each side of his lip without the least idea of what any of it meant, and then tried to copy what he'd said, repeating only, 'meatball.' Jason chuckled at Billy's attempt at the slangy phrase.

"Yeah, I'm the meatball," he repeated to Billy, "if Daddy and Momma catch me!"

He held his finger to his lips to indicate that what he had said was their secret, as if Billy understood.

Jason walked to the kitchen to pick up the keys to his mother's car. He gave her a patronizing peck on the cheek as she worked at the sink preparing supper for the rest of the family.

"Don't stay out late, honey...we got church tomorrow," she reminded, struggling to cut up a fryer in the sink. She wiped her face on her sleeve and finished dipping one of the pieces of chicken in a thick, creamy batter.

Jason acknowledged her with a low grunt, and then headed directly for the garage, chomping on a piece of celery he'd picked out of a bowl of dressing on the kitchen table as he walked by.

He stepped confidently into the small Chevy coupe, checking his hair a final time in the mirror before pressing the starter on the floor. The engine gave a sickly moan at first, starving for gas and then responded to the flood of fuel as he pumped the accelerator. With a cocky flip of his wrist he threw the stick shift into reverse, shearing off the edges of a few gear teeth, along with his efforts to goose the accelerator and let off the clutch at the same time. His inexperience in synchronizing gearshift and clutch was evident as the car shimmied and bucked, jerking backwards out of the garage.

A queer thudding sound began suddenly to bump beneath the floor of the car, finally working its way from behind the trunk up to the driver's side. He knew immediately that he'd run over something, a toy, a bike or some garden tool, maybe even the neighbor's cat. Frustrated because he was late picking up Jessica, and nervous she might not be waiting, he jerked open the door and leaped out of the car to see what kind of damage he'd done. His eyes scanned along the front fender and then down towards the back bumper where the noise had originated.

It took a minute for his eyes to adjust to the dark floor of the garage. When they finally did, he noticed a small puddle forming under the front tire.

'A busted oil pan!' he thought. "Of all times for this to happen. A date with the prettiest girl in the county and my car peters out, Gawd damn it!" he whispered under his breath. He leaned down, careful not to dirty his white pants, and dipped his finger in the dark pool to see if it was oil or transmission fluid.

It was neither one. His heart raced as he collapsed to his knees and then stretched himself flat on his stomach, holding out his hand to touch what his eyes had discovered under the car an instant earlier.

A horrible agonizing cry rang out across the garage as his hand moved to retrieve the small pink form crumpled beneath the car. It was as still and quiet as a sleeping fawn, lying beneath the dirty frame, the white glow of its innocence splattered with blood and torn from the crushing force of the automobile. It was Billy.

Jason pulled the little boy out from under the car, laying him carefully in his lap. He rocked the small body back and forth, crying as he wiped the child's hair away from his forehead. He tried desperately to stop the blood pouring from Billy's scalp as he pleaded with him to live.

As soon as the shock of what he'd done hit him, he began to scream for his mother, crying, and then stopping to talk to the sleeping child like he was deranged. Again and again he cried out desperately for help, but no one came.

After awhile, Lora noticed the car sticking partially out of the garage and wondered why Jason hadn't 't left for the dance. She thought she heard the sound of someone crying and stepped out onto the back porch to see where the noise was coming from. It didn't take long for her to realize that something was wrong. She raced to the garage, where she found Jason covered in blood and holding the tiny figure in his arms, looking up at her with tears streaming from his eyes.

"I think I've killed Billy, Momma! I know he's dead!" Jason cried, pressing the little boy's head against his face and continuing to rock him in his arms. "I never meant to hurt him!" he pleaded. "I love him, Momma! I love him!" Lora leaned over, never saying a word as she took a quick desperate look at Billy, and then immediately turned and sprinted for the house, screaming for James as she went.

James pulled Billy out of Jason's arms and lay him on the floor of the garage as he tried to revive him. He worked frantically, doing everything he could to save his son as Lora and Jason watched, whimpering in each other's arms.

When the ambulance finally arrived, James looked up at the attendants, as if repulsed by their presence. He leaned back over the child, giving the little boy an affectionate embrace and then kissed him gently on his forehead. When he'd finished, he stood aside to let the attendants place him on the stretcher. His shoulders were slumped as he trailed behind the stretcher, following it to the back of the ambulance. He already suspected what was to come.

Jason and Lora rode with James to the hospital, quietly watching the man who always had seemed so indomitable in every circumstance that life had thrown at them. But now he appeared helpless and lost. He was crumpled over, holding onto one of the tiny porcelain arms of the child as he rested his face in his other hand. Occasionally they heard a brief whimper and then it was quiet again.

Within minutes after their arrival at the hospital, James was met by a colleague, who examined Billy. After awhile the doctor emerged from the examining room and consoled James with one arm locked around his shoulder and holding his hand with the other as they spoke. He told him what James already knew. Billy was gone.

Lora could hear the two men conversing in their professional dialects. James thanked the doctor and then walked towards the two of them, wiping his eyes with the back of his hand. "The little fella's passed away, Lora! Doctor Bradford couldn't do anything for him," he said, wiping his eyes again before he looked at her.

"I think I'd like a few minutes alone with Billy before you and Jason come in...please?" James requested. His jaw quivered with emotion as the shock of what had happened took hold of him.

James stood next to the gurney looking at the small figure stretched out on the sheet. The nurses had cleaned the little boy up before James had come in, leaving the child looking as if he were taking a nap. He touched him gently with the back of his hand, as if to feel the warmth leaving the child's soft transparent face. He reached over to the surgical cart and picked up a pair of scissors, cutting off a small portion of

Billy's reddish hair. He held it to his lips and then pressed it tightly in his fist.

"It was a short walk through life for you, Billy. I know it started off hard...the way you came into this old world, and all...but, if it makes any difference, I really loved you," James said, having to stop and compose himself before he could go on.

"And I hope we'll be together again someday in a better place...where things aren't so hard for little fellas like you. Maybe then I'll understand why it had to be this way...why life's journey has to be so heartbreaking for all of us. God be with you, son."

Billy was buried at a private funeral service attended by family and close friends. Few, if any, of those attending knew the truth of the child's relationship to James. They had assumed, as most others had, that Billy was the child of one of James' patients who had passed away, or who could no longer care for him, and had been adopted by the doctor.

Jason and his father never discussed the details of Billy's death, preferring to coexist for the next few months as if the little boy never had existed. His name was never mentioned within the family, and his toys and clothes were removed from the house and stored in a steamer trunk in the garage.

James had felt his moments of rage and anger at Jason for the boy's death, but was so grieved that there seemed no time in his closed world for retribution. The tragedy seemed to sap the very essence of life from him. But, as he'd done so many times before, he persevered, using the strength gathered from losing other loved ones, if ever that could be an asset to one's character, to continue on with a life now void of any love at all except his cherished memories.

CHAPTER 13

To try and soothe the emotional scars created by Billy's death, James immersed himself into an exhaustive work schedule. He split his time between his medical practice, the packing sheds and, as if that were not enough, playing a high stakes game of real estate grab-bag in the speculative Jacksonville land market.

The Depression years had provided him with sizable holdings in real estate, most of which were parcels of land taken in trade for medical services rendered when cash was scarce and vacant land was considered a liability to those who'd lost their jobs. Over a period of a few years, James had accumulated a sizable portfolio of prime property, most of which was near or actually in the central business districts of Jacksonville and Tyler. It was obvious to him that sooner or later an upswing in the economy would create a lucrative demand for housing and commercial real estate near the downtown areas. It was a monopoly game of sorts, played by those with the cash and the stamina to wait out the lull in real estate development.

The balance of James' time was dedicated to his packing sheds and dealing in the volatile commodities market. The market had become increasingly subject to droughts and the effects of diseases and outside pressures from foreign competition. More than one investor, despondent over losing everything he had worked for in the high stakes game, had taken his last breath from the barrel of a pistol on some lonely gravel road outside of town.

For local farmers there was always 'next year' if a crop went bad, assuming they could fend off the lenders long enough. For the produce investor or the truck farmer it was do or die, and many perished as surely as a drowning man going down for his final breath when prices collapsed.

But James, through all of this, managed to prevail. By a combination of natural business instincts and an obsessive devotion to the task at hand, he relentlessly clawed his way to the top, time and time again. He'd never had the luxury of being able to quit at anything when times were hard. As far as he'd heard, a man only gave up the fight when he died, and to James even that was a questionable reprieve from the labors of life.

Jason had finally completed his studies at Stephen F. Austin College, barely having the credits and grade point average to graduate, during the spring semester. Lora had finished at the same time. But, unlike her son, she had graduated magna cum laude and had continued on with her education, working towards a master's degree. Jason and his father's paths crossed only on rare occasions at the supper table or a chance meeting as they came and went from the house. So often Jason had looked into his father's eyes, wanting to know that the scars finally had healed from what he'd done. But each time his answer was there, weighted down in the sad, tired lines of a face that still reflected a deep sorrow for what had happened to the little boy.

It wasn't that his father was discourteous, or even unaffectionate, for he usually went out of his way to be loving to him, but it was more the fact that Jason knew the depth of the wound he'd inflicted upon the man. And he knew, perhaps even more, that there was little he could do to make restitution for Billy's grievous death.

As a result of the tragedy, Jason lived in a fantasy world that constantly occupied his mind with dreams of achieving a single masterful deed that would finally gain his father's approval and diminish the nagging blame he felt for the accident. He was certain that someday all would be forgiven.

After graduation from the small east Texas college, Jason had decided to apply to the Air Corps Primary Flying School, situated at Randolph Field in San Antonio, Texas.

He was very careful to keep his application a secret from his father until it was approved. The last thing he wanted was for him to find out that he'd been rejected by the army, if it came to that. He was certain that their relationship, what there was left of it, could little tolerate another failure on his part. He'd taken his mother into his confidence, sharing his excitement of becoming an army aviator with her. There was never a doubt that she would support his decision and offer positive reinforcement for his dream, just as she always had done.

At the same time, unbeknownst to his mother, he'd also confided in Jessica Dunraven, the young girl he'd met at Tate City. He had by now become passionately involved with her, secretly rendezvousing with her near the oil town whenever possible. Jessica had an uncanny ability to capitalize on Jason's anxieties over his future, or his nagging guilt about his brother's death. She was able almost to mesmerize him each time they were together, soothing him with a passionate indulgence that he'd never, in his wildest dreams, believed possible.

She patronized him, wooed him, all the while mentally cataloging his weaknesses and desires, calling upon them whenever she needed to exert more control. He would, someday, as she envisioned it, be her ticket out of Tate City. She stalked him with the ferocity of an animal with its survival hanging in the balance. There would be no second chance for her escape, and she knew it.

Jason was not the cunning predator that he pictured himself to be. He was certainly no match for Jessica.

What Jason perceived as a casual and very spontaneous relationship was, in fact, an orchestrated plan that Jessica had meticulously plotted to extricate herself from her personal pit of hell. It was as though the very daughter of Lucifer was soon to be unshackled by this naive young man, to fulfill some terrible prophecy upon mankind.

Unfortunately for Jessica the army interrupted the order of events, for the moment, by notifying Jason that he had been accepted into the next flight training class scheduled at Randolph Field. He was ordered to report within the week.

When Jessica found out he was leaving, she pleaded with him to take her to San Antonio. She had been caught off guard by the sudden change of events, so when she couldn't change his mind, she attacked his boyish adventurism, trying to goad him into staying long enough for her to come up with another scheme to flee Tate City. She had overestimated her powers to influence his decisions, finding herself left behind as Jason spirited away to San Antonio with no more than a telephoned farewell to his backwoods enchantress.

The reception at the field for the new inductees was traditionally the same as at any other training facility. Men were examined and inoculated by the army physicians who were little concerned with bedside manner or gentleness. If the medical ordeal were not enough to leave the candidate flushed from having lost the privilege of modesty, having the sides of his head peeled until he looked like a freshly plucked chicken seemed to finish off the last semblance of individuality that the new cadet had left.

The army had little use for sleep, beginning each new day in the dark hours before dawn. The cadets double-timed to meals and classes and marched at quick steps until ending the day in a state of near-exhaustion, collapsing into their bunks for a few short hours before reveille blared across the parade grounds, beckoning them to rise again for another day.

Jason had little trouble adjusting to what the others perceived as undue harshness by the instructors. His father had never been a saint to live with, so, if there was anything positive to come from that experience, Jason had found it. James' strict philosophy of discipline made the occasional dressing down by a senior officer or upper classman seem like child's play. Jason was ecstatic over his newfound home, feeling himself very much suited to this newly discovered way of life.

He longed for the day that he would take his first ride in the brightly painted trainers that droned constantly overhead, from sunup to sundown. On the ramps below, the blue and yellow Stearmans were formed up as straight as the columns of cadets that paraded endlessly past the perimeter of the flight line. The armada of biplanes, with their huge black engines and the gently curved lines of the fuselage and wings, seemed to captivate the fledgling pilots. Each would steal a look as they marched by, as if to discover themselves in love for the first time with some majestic beauty who soon would be theirs for the taking.

On the home front, life went on as usual, with James working at the sheds and continuing to care for his patients, both at Jacksonville and Tate City. Jessica was constantly cornering James, surreptitiously trying to extract information about Jason from him in casual conversation. He was well aware that she was probing for any tidbit of information that would help her keep track of Jason so that someday she might reel him in, like some trophy bass snagged from a water barrel. James gave her just enough news for a polite conversation and then managed quickly to slip out of her grasp. He knew that their meetings weren't coincidental and that she had probably known when he was coming a week before he arrived. She was as devious and divisive as she was beautiful.

Jessica had written an endless flow of letters to Jason when he'd first left for flight training. After a few weeks, when she didn't hear back from him, she resigned herself to the fact he had lost interest in her and there was nothing she could do about it, at least for the moment. Jason never had been sensitive about writing to anyone, including his mother and father, but apparently he wasn't the only one; to alleviate any problems with complaining parents, a standing order was issued that all cadets would routinely correspond with their families on a weekly basis. And so Jason wrote home, going into great detail about life at Randolph and the excitement that he felt for the cadet program.

Eventually James began to believe that maybe, just maybe, Jason might be benefiting in some way from the program. "Perhaps he might even be developing into a responsible and productive human being," James openly admitted to Lora.

Lora, knowing that Jason hungered for such approval from his father, was quick to inform him by letter of his father's acceptance of the cadet program. James had actually admitted that he was pleased with his progress in the army and hoped he would make a career of it. It was exactly the response that Jason had wished for. It gave him the inspiration to continue on with his best efforts. It was all the proof he needed to convince himself that he had made the right decision in joining the Air Corps.

The day finally came, after weeks of ground school, for Jason and his classmates to fly. They reported to the flight line wearing their issue of work clothes, a baggy olive drab flight suit, a leather helmet, goggles and flight jacket, and a fanny chute suspended uncomfortably below their rumps by heavy white canvas straps.

After a short briefing by a ground school instructor, the cadets were ordered to take a seat in their assigned aircraft and wait for the flight instructors for that morning to appear from the 'ready room' situated near the flight line.

Jason stepped up onto the lower wing of the Stearman, climbing past the leather rim opening of one of the cockpits, finally settling down into the seat.

The instructor arrived a few minutes later, taking his position at the controls and acting as if the young cadet were nothing more than a bag of mail occupying a seat in the plane. Several enlisted men appeared from the dark to turn over the wooden prop, nosing out from the exposed engine. As the pilot shouted, "Clear", the ground crew rotated the prop once around slowly and then gave it hard flip, forcing the stubborn engine to start.

Jason's eyes moved cautiously about the plane, examining the angular struts and various cables that supported the cantilever wing overhead. He watched the skin of the fuselage vibrate as the engine caught with a high-pitched whine, throwing a cloud of black smoke over the cockpit of Trainer 428.

The only indication Jason had that the pilot knew he was there was when he tapped him on the shoulder and motioned with his finger for him to pull his goggles down as they started to taxi out to the runway from the tarmac. Jason obediently responded to the order, adjusting the leather-lined goggles, and at the same time noticing the stick between his legs copying the exact movements of the control stick in the instructor's hand in the other cockpit.

He felt the biplane lift smoothly away from the ground to the deafening 'whir' of the engine as it strained to climb to altitude. He could feel the warm San Antonio air suddenly becoming cool as they lifted away from the ground. A small rectangular windshield separated the two cockpits and was quickly fouled with splattered bugs and oil thrown back by the engine's exhaust. A cold electrifying surge of energy flashed through him as he felt his body being pressed deeper into the seat with the execution of a tight turn, snapping the plane into a roll and then leveling out again. It was more than he had dreamed it would be...magnificent, wonderful! He knew at that precise instant in his life that flying was his destiny, that he had been born for this moment.

Each morning, after that first day of flying, the students were assembled in a formation immediately in front of their barracks to march to the flight line. They were anxious to be airborne before the hot morning sun turned the air choppy with heat thermals and blowing sand.

The Stearman was a difficult tail dragger to control on the ground in a normal wind, much less controlling it in the occasional hard gusts that occurred in mid-day and late afternoon. Adding to the young cadet's miseries, the hot stagnant air inside the cockpit, combined with a severe case of the jitters, often led to extreme nausea and the 'Cadet Scourge', aptly named the 'hundred-mile-an-hour-puke'.

The Cadets would double-time to the ramp in formation, peeling off at their respective planes to listen to a class on some topic of aircraft maintenance until the instructor would arrive to preflight the plane with them. Lectures on the aircraft were usually provided by seasoned noncoms. These leathery NCO's would lecture the cadets on the aerodynamics of the Stearman, acting jealously suspicious, as if the canvas birds were their own possessions. It was as if they were loaning their girls to another man for a dance, or to admire and appreciate, but that was all. The cadet would learn how to command her, but only her crew chief ever would have the privilege of knowing her heart and her innermost secrets.

At the direction of the instructors, the powerful engines were primed and coaxed with affectionate pleading at first and, a moment later, a few softly spoken expletives by the impatient students, as the engine belched and whined, resisting all efforts to start. Heavy black clouds of smoke blew back to either side of the fuselage, giving the crew a dose of acrid-tasting fuel that spewed from the engine until it was warmed and was idling with a steady monotone hum.

The paper-thin skin of the wings and fuselage deflected the prop wash, vibrating the fabric at the same pitch as the engine. Droplets of condensation that had settled on the plane's surfaces from the morning dew danced in thin lines towards the cockpit. The movement of the fuselage disturbed their rest, then finally launched themselves into the air, lifting into the wind and splattering on the goggles and clothing of the crew. Jason found little time to worry about a few drops of water, or the pungent smell of fuel on this particular morning, as he nervously perused his checklist and prepared for his first check ride. He'd been flying for nearly two weeks and was ordered, on this particular morning, to take a proficiency ride with his instructor to evaluate his progress.

The briefing was routine, and the flight plan hadn't called for anything unusual or difficult. They would do a few 'touch and go' landings, a few tours of the traffic pattern, and then make a final soft precision landing, and the day would be done.

Every check ride was important. If the examiner was 'an all right Joe', the cadet would get away with a few mistakes and even learn something. But if the instructor wanted to be a prick, he could make life miserable for the cadet, washing him out of the program as quickly as it took him to pack his B-4 bags and shuffle out the front gate. If the instructor had gotten crossways with his wife the night before or suffered an attack of aviator's misery, 'the horrible hemmies', it was rumored that one could find himself busted out of the program, no matter how well he'd flown. It was a little something, an alibi of sorts, to make washing out a little less damaging to fragile young egos and broken hearts. It may even have been true in a few cases, but not many.

The aircraft jerked and bolted with each contact of the spoked wheels on the hard surface as the trainer taxied out for takeoff. Jason's mind was alert to the possibility of being hit with a wind shear or gust that might force him into a ground loop. Although not a court martial offense, it did little to boost the ego if anyone were to hear about it.

Jason was stricken with a severe case of the jitters as he suddenly found his weeks of training and confidence sliding into his knotted stomach.

"Jesus, Lavoisier, is that you doing that?" the instructor screamed above the noise of the engine. "Put a Gawd damn cork in it!" he demanded, holding his nose as the final effects of Jason's upset stomach finally cleared the cockpit.

Jason ignored the comment as he waited nervously for the green light from the tower to signal him to start his roll. He mentally reviewed the drill for takeoff, checking and rechecking his instruments and studying his runway position. The windsock moved back and forth, giving him fits as he tried to determine his wind direction and speed.

His eyes darted back and forth as he watched the 'RPM's' of his engine and then glanced up at the tower, still waiting for permission to commence the take off.

"Let's get this Gawd damn crate airborne!" the instructor barked. "I got other things to do besides wear my ass out on this runway!"

Jason throttled up, letting the trainer have its head into the wind. His airspeed increased until there was a slight bump, another bump, and suddenly they were airborne. The Stearman lifted off, floating as soft as a feather into the early morning wind. Jason eased back on the stick, giving her enough rudder to make his final turn through the traffic pattern and then took his heading directly into the morning sun. The other trainers, still taking off behind him, began to shrink like small birds floating below him, just above the rectangular outline of the field on the beautiful cloudless morning.

A cool gust of air quickly chased away the engine heat lingering in the cockpit. It was a relief from the uncomfortably warm clothing. Sweat was still dripping down his face and inside his flight suit.

Once he'd reached altitude, he relaxed, regaining his confidence and enjoying the sunrise as they leveled off over the field in a smooth straight line of flight. The instructor observed Jason putting the sluggish trainer through its paces, turning, rolling, climbing and then dropping down into the traffic pattern for 'touch and go' landings.

He landed roughly at first and then came around again touching down the second time with a smooth, easy contact with the runway. Just as the craft was losing airspeed he increased the gas and lifted 438 back into the wind for a final swing around the pattern.

"Well done, Mister Lavoisier!" the officer yelled, pointing towards the ground with his finger. "Let's take it home."

Jason nodded his head and smiled, instantly banking the aircraft with a snappy roll towards the final approach. With the familiar bump of the wheels hitting the pavement, he knew that he'd finished his flight. His shoulders relaxed as he felt the tail of the trainer drop down, tipping him slightly backwards as the nose came up, symbolically providing him a bit of mechanical snobbery to match the young airman's moment of pride.

He taxied to his tie-down space, holding the aircraft in place for a final revving of the engine before shutting it off. There were still a few details to be handled on the checklist, but that would be the easiest part of the day. Paper work would be a delight after such an excellent morning in the air. There was no doubt in his mind that he'd done well.

"Nice job, Lavoisier...you're coming along real good!" the instructor praised, stepping out of the cockpit and onto the wing. "See yah tomorrow for another spin," he added, "bright and early?"

"Yes, sir!" Jason answered with a huge grin.

The officer was just about to step down onto the ramp, when he turned and walked back up to Jason. "But, how about stayin' off the spicy food tonight...for both our sakes?" he asked, smiling. He gave Jason a friendly pat on the arm as he dismounted the wing.

Jason leaned forward, still strapped in the seat, and rested his head on the padded cockpit rim. His helmet was soaked in perspiration. "Yes, sir," he whispered, moving his head slightly from side to side as he sighed with relief.

He flew every day for the next two weeks, each time with a different instructor. He'd had a fair amount of success, both with drawing good instructors and good weather conditions. His confidence was steadily improving, and so was his love for the Air Corps. He wrote home, detailing each of his flights to his mother and father, enthusiastically describing his experience with such hope and anticipation for his future with the army.

Punishment tours were served by all of the cadets as a matter of routine, whenever they were not in class or flying. The punishment was usually for some minor infraction and was stepped off with chest out and weapon shouldered. The cadet was required to be in full dress uniform and donning his parachute as he walked squares around the Taj-Mahal. At established navigational intervals he was required to recite specific verses from memory, dealing with some aspect of the Air Corps, and then continue on his tour to the next station.

Jason had completed stepping off his punishment tour just twenty minutes before he was due on the flight line for another proficiency check ride. He'd barely had time to get dressed and fall into formation before the Cadets marched off for the afternoon training. Once they had arrived at the ramp, the cadets stood at attention in front of their assigned aircraft, waiting for the instructors to arrive.

A short, muscular, regimental-looking officer approached the trainer, walking at double-time towards Jason. He was sporting a clipboard under his left arm like a swagger stick. Every snap, button and zipper on the man's flight suit was done up strictly according to the manual. There was nothing wrong with that, in itself, other than the fact it was unusual to find an officer in compliance with regulations. What was wrong with it was that it spelled trouble—double trouble as soon as Jason realized who the officer was.

Jason stared in disbelief, then mumbled under his breath. "Captain Bramlette, son of a bitch! Of all the instructors on this damn field, I gotta draw 'Ball Buster' Bramlette!"

Jason gave the approaching officer a smart salute, offering a "Good morning, sir."

The officer walked past him, looking down at his clipboard as he responded with, "Yes, it is, Mister Lavoisier, and I assume you're ready to get this bird in the air?"

"Yes, sir!" Jason responded.

"Let's get to it, then," Bramlette ordered. "We've got a lot to do this morning. Let's get that Government Issue hat snapped up; we're not crop dusters, Mister Lavoisier."

"No, sir," Jason answered, stepping in behind Bramlett and trying to keep up with him as he began preflighting the aircraft.

Jason was terror-stricken. Captain Bramlette was the scourge of the Air Corps, single-handedly washing out more cadets than any other I.P. on the field. Except for overly spicy foods and too much beer, Bramlette was said to be the primary impetus for most cadets' nightmares. It was a well-noted fact that no one had gone unscathed from Bramlette's highly critical and dissecting evaluations, no one. There was no such thing as a good check ride with Captain Bramlette, just poor or terrible, most being the latter. It had been rumored that several cadets had gone straight from his evaluations to resigning, immediately upon landing, without even waiting to read his deflating write-up of their performances.

The wind that morning was unusually treacherous, having shoved several aircraft out of position on the parking ramp, even though they had been tied down and their wheels chocked. Jason manhandled the takeoff, losing it momentarily in a wind shear that left him with a false liftoff. He'd panicked, goosing the engine to force enough power to get airborne again, only to bounce up and down on the runway before finally starting to gain altitude. Fortunately, the Stearman's design had compensated for his over-correction, lifting off despite his nervous maneuvering of the controls.

Once airborne, the situation seemed to calm down, so Jason leveled the Stearman off and began his routine of exercises for the morning. He was hoping that Captain Bramlette would take into consideration the rough winds when he did his evaluation, but it wasn't likely, from what he'd heard about the man.

Bramlette was a lifer, a West Pointer who had transferred to the Air Corps from quartermaster after WWI. Jason's mind raced, remembering the rumors he'd heard about him in the cadet lounge.

"Bramlette hates anyone who's not regular Army. So much as an unintentional dip of the wing, and your next breakfast will be as a civilian," Jason remembered hearing one cadet reminisce, after losing a roommate a week earlier to a check ride with the over-starched nemesis.

He could feel himself sweating under his flight suit. He looked back over at Bramlette to reassure himself that perhaps his characterization of the officer was purely fictional. Not a chance, he quickly realized, as Bramlette stared back at him with a scowl on his face, motioning him to turn around and pay attention to where he was headed.

The morning wasn't all work, although Captain Bramlette seemed to have come along for no other purpose than to draw an offering of blood from another poor pigeon, obediently poised for the slaughter. It would have been easier for them to have just handed him his dismissal at the flight line and foregone the formality of the check ride with the impudent little bastard, Jason thought.

Jason let his mind wander after setting the aircraft on a predetermined navigational fix some ten miles ahead on the flat horizon. The straight stretch of level flight gave him a break from the intensity of the situation. Little could go wrong unless he'd misread his compass. Bramlette affirmed that he was on course by slipping off into a catnap, a sure sign that he must be doing something right.

'Mother will be getting up and going to school,' Jason thought, picturing her walking out the door with an armful of books and papers. He could see her smiling...she always smiled.

'Nellie will have started cutting up vegetables for dinner and frying catfish in corn meal and batter. And Dad will probably be walking around the back yard before he goes to work,' he imagined. 'He'd be showing the yard men where he wanted the grass cut and he'd have them pick up the pecans that had fallen from the trees during the night. There'd be at least two bushel baskets full, by evening.'

A change in the pitch of the engine brought him out of his trance, for a moment, long enough to inspect the instruments, before slipping back to his daydreaming.

He could see Bramlette in the mirror, taking a fix on the countryside to assure himself that they were on course. After a few minutes, the I.P.'s head slipped down below the rim of the cockpit, bobbing back and forth as he returned to his nap.

Jason thought about the wonderful aromas that always filled his parents' home, the pungent flavor of burning sawdust lingering over the back yard from the pulp mill, and the delectable flavor of corn bread baking in the oven. He could even taste a whiff of a blueberry pie cooling at one end of the counter. His mouth watered with the thought because it usually signaled that supper was ready. He laughed at himself. How odd it seemed that such trivial things, smells and such, were so clear to him, now.

His mind drifted to another sweet fragrance, the perfumed skin of Jessica. He thought about being with her, smelling the strong overpowering perfume she wore as they lay on a blanket, somewhere along the Neches River. He would be nibbling on her neck and hair in the warm afternoon sun, lying beside her after they'd made love. He remembered her smile that quickly turned sour whenever he told her he had to go home. And always she had the last say, pressing herself against him as if to dissolve his faint efforts to leave.

A banging noise caught his attention, interrupting his sensuous reunion with Jessica. Bramlette was trying to catch his eye, making hand gestures for Jason to take the plane to a higher altitude and change course back to Randolph.

Jason responded by moving the Stearman's nose up and watching Bramlette, periodically, for a signal to see when he'd reached the proper altitude. Bramlette finally waved his hand and pointed back towards the field, indicating it was time to turn around.

Jason nodded, easily executing the maneuver and setting a course for the base. The short distance for the return flight to Randolph gave him time to reflect on Jessica for a few more minutes before they would land. He decided at that moment that it would be prudent of him to write to her, if he ever intended to see her again.

He snickered to himself, realizing that his interests in her had been purely physical. He couldn't ever remember having much of a conversation with her. It seemed that they were always too immersed in passion to do much talking. When they hadn't been making love, he was usually reciting poetry and never really had paid attention to much of anything she had to say.

Jason made his final approach, turning into a brisk crosswind, cutting directly through his flight path. The light aircraft hung, almost suspended, above the end of the runway as he crabbed his way into position over the field.

The wind was gusting hard enough that he was having difficulty setting the plane down. To compensate for the additional lifting effects on the wing's surface, he cut his power back and pushed the nose down to force the aircraft onto the runway.

Bramlette went berserk, screaming, "Get your nose up! Give it more power, more power! Son of a bitch!" he yelled.

Jason only heard the order to pull up. The nose of the plane seemed to hang as if Jason were attempting to abort the landing. Before Bramlette could react, Jason gunned the throttle in panic, and stalled the plane, sending it up and over on its right side. The leading edge of the upper wing clipped the runway as the aircraft rotated over onto its back.

The forward momentum sent the Stearman into a somersault. The wires and framing disintegrated, tearing the fuselage loose from the wings and sending the cigar-shaped skeleton backward across the grassy field running parallel to the runway.

The two passengers clung helplessly to whatever they could hold onto as the plane rocketed over mounds of uneven dirt, tearing away its thin underbelly. A final deposit of sand offered just enough of a ramp to launch what was left of the fuselage into the air for one last flight before abruptly landing in a depression in the grassy field.

The force of the impact catapulted both men out of the cockpits, hurling them away from the mangled trainer as it continued on into a nearby mesquite grove.

The remaining fuel immediately ignited, causing an explosion and starting a grass fire around the wreckage.

A thick blanket of smoke billowed up from the ground, drifting over the crash site, with a black cloud rising directly overhead. Jason staggered to his feet. He was momentarily blinded from a stream of blood flowing into his eyes from several lacerations across his forehead. He made his way back to the twisted wreckage, stumbling through the debris, trying to find Captain Bramlette.

Bramlette had cleared the wreckage, but not without injury. Jason found him crumpled in a pile, unconscious, a few yards from the burning remains of the trainer. Because his left arm had been injured, it was difficult for him to pull the Captain away from the crash. Jason grabbed his parachute harness and dragged him along the ground and away from the incinerated Stearman. He had no idea if Bramlette was still alive.

Within minutes, emergency personnel from Randolph had arrived at the crash site with an assortment of ambulances and fire equipment. By the time help had come, Jason had passed out from a combination of smoke inhalation and the trauma to his arm. Bramlette remained unconscious throughout the entire ordeal. It was probably just as well, considering the circumstances.

Jason's eyes cracked open, still disoriented from the crash as they panned the darkened hospital room. He was trying to identify a vibrating hum, a roughly pitched propeller noise, that had been irritating him during the dream he'd been having.

'Too light for a Jenny,' he thought in the dream; 'maybe it's an old Newport or Stearman?'

His eyes finally opened, focusing on a heavy black metal fan oscillating back and forth and blowing a cool breeze across his face and chest. The wire cage over the blade was vibrating, banging metal against metal with an annoying tap as it made each sweep of the room.

The only noticeable light was filtering through a yellowed canvas shade pulled flush with the windowsill. The cord to the shade, with its cloth pull ring, flopped against the wall with each blast from the fan. The noise had added to his annoyance, making him think that the plane he was flying in his dream was having engine trouble. Then he remembered the crash and Bramlette lying out on the ground. He still wasn't sure his instructor had survived the smashup.

"How are you feeling, Lavoisier?"

Jason turned his head in the direction of the voice. "Who's there?"

"I'm Major Hanson, Flight Safety Officer."

"How's Captain Bramlette doing, sir?" Jason asked. "Is he dead?"

"No, he's all right...just banged up pretty good."

Jason breathed a loud sigh of relief as he relaxed back into his pillow. "With the way my luck's been going, I'm surprised I didn't kill him!"

"Oh, I'd say you're pretty lucky, considering that either one of you lived through that crash!" Hanson commented.

"Yes, sir," Jason replied, "I guess you're right."

"How's the arm?" Hanson asked.

"Still a little sore," said Jason. "But it's not hurt near as bad as my pride."

"I know this doesn't seem like the appropriate time to ask you this, but what happened up there?"

"I don't know, sir. A stall, maybe...I guess I might have hooked it in the wind; I really don't know." Jason answered candidly.

"A board of inquiry will want to know why all of this happened. Was Captain Bramlette handling the controls, or assisting you in the landing in any way?"

"No, sir."

"Was there a mechanical failure? A problem with the plane?" Hanson inquired.

"Not that I know of, sir."

Hanson shook his head as he stood up. "You've got yourself some serious problems if you were in command of that plane and the board finds you negligent, son."

"Yes, sir!" Jason acknowledged.

"Get some rest. When you feel a little better, we'll talk."

"I will, sir," Jason replied, turning his head away from the voice and closing his eyes as if to return to the dream he was having before the noise from the fan woke him up. At least the problems there weren't insurmountable.

"I'll give your folks a call if you'd like? No need to have them worrying unnecessarily over this."

"I'd prefer to call them myself, sir, if you don't mind. It would be easier on my mother."

"I understand," Hanson agreed. "Whatever you think!"

"They're probably going to lower the boom on me for this, aren't they, sir?" Jason questioned.

"I think that's probably about the size of it!" Hanson answered.

"Even if I weather the review board, they'll probably finish me off in my evaluations" Jason said. "Either way, I'm done for."

Hanson sounded sincere as he replied, "I'm sorry things turned out this way...for you and the army. Your record up to now indicated that you had the makings of a good pilot."

Jason moved his arm over his face to hide his anxiety.

Major Hanson, sensing Jason's devastation, left without saying anything else, deciding to leave him with some vestige of self-respect.

The Accident Review Board completed their investigation within the week. As expected, Cadet Jason Lavoisier was found negligent in the mishap. However, the board agreed that there had been some extenuating circumstances that may have contributed to the accident. Just the same, it was the finding of the board, after hearing testimony from Captain Bramlette, that he be dismissed from the Cadet program.

Jason packed his personal belongings after putting on the civilian clothes that he'd worn to Randolph. He turned in his military issue and quietly headed for the front gate, timing his departure to avoid seeing any of his fellow cadets. He walked the short distance to the transportation office to arrange a ride into San Antonio.

On the way over to the motor pool, he passed the Taj Mahal. He stood, staring up at the blue and gold dome of the tower, watching a formation of trainers leveling off over the field.

"I know I could have made it," he whispered to himself. "I'm as good as any of those guys! Someday...someday," he assured himself.

He turned away from the tower, trying not to think about what his father's reaction was going to be. It was more than he could handle now; but as sure as the sun would rise, he would have his day of glory.

CHAPTER 14

For nearly a month after the crash, Jason remained in seclusion, cutting himself off from any contact with his parents. Lora and James, after learning that he had been dismissed from the Air Corps, drove to San Antonio in hopes he might have left a forwarding address, or told one of his classmates where he was going. Their efforts were futile. Jason, for whatever reason, had vanished from the face of the earth.

James could see the emotional strain that Jason's disappearance was placing on Lora. It was unlike Jason to avoid his mother. He always had relied on her reassurance and encouragement whenever life had gone wrong for him, which was often. But this time it was different. Apparently the magnitude of the failure, at least in Jason's mind, seemed more than even she could compensate for.

James had exhausted every possible lead that might provide an answer to Jason's whereabouts, save one. Jessica, the paragon of sensuousness and cunning, had persisted in dogging his heels whenever he had shown his face at Tate City, so much so that he still dreaded making his rounds in the camp, anticipating being cornered by her with endless questions about his son. Jessica had remained relentless in her efforts to get any news of Jason she could from him. James had purposely kept Jason's separation from Randolph a secret, wanting her to have as little involvement with his son as possible.

Strangely enough, on his very next visit to the camp, six weeks after Jason's summary drumming out of the Corps, she suddenly became aloof, showing absolutely no interest in his presence and acting as if she didn't know him. James' intuition suddenly alerted him to the fact she knew more than she was letting on about where Jason was holed up. He decided, before going home that day, to confront her.

After making his rounds of the camp, he casually strolled over to the company store, under the pretext of buying a cigar, knowing that sooner or later Jessica would show up there. He hadn't waited long before she appeared on the front porch, cooing up to a young oil field worker who'd bought her a soda and a bag of candy from his paycheck. The young man was thrilled simply to be standing beside her, with his arm draped around her waist and his hand resting on her rump. There was hope in his eyes for something more.

Jessica made her usual show of unveiling as much of her cleavage as possible by complaining of the heat, much to the delight of her many admirers. James wasn't amused by any of it.

"Good afternoon, Miss Dunraven."

"Doctor Lavoisier," she answered, coolly, "how are yah?"

"I'm getting along as well as can be expected," he said.

"That's nice to know," she replied smugly.

James cleared a wad of chewing tobacco out from under his lip before he spoke again. "I don't suppose you know anything about where my boy is holed up? His mother and I are worried about him!"

"Why, Doctor Lavoisier, whatever gave you the notion that I would know anything about your son? I thought he was in San Antonio, flying his little airplanes." She laughed, smiling at the young man next to her, as she squeezed up closer to him.

"I see," James said. "Well, I'm sure he'll turn up, sooner or later."

Jessica looked him straight in the eye with a peculiar expression and then almost a smirk.

'She knows Gawd damn good and well where he is,' James thought. 'I'd lay odds that she could lead me to him, right now.'

Jessica smiled again as if she'd read his mind. She turned and walked down the steps with the young laborer still hanging onto her. She fidgeted with her dress with one hand and combed her hair with the other, pausing occasionally to wrestle the man's hand off her breasts. She took a quick peek back at James to see if he was watching, convinced that he'd swallowed her story.

Working on a hunch that Jessica had been seeing Jason all along, James decided to drive back over to Tate City late in the afternoon on the following Saturday. He parked his car in the refinery just after dark, slipping into the compound where he could watch Jessica's house from an inconspicuous vantagepoint.

Shortly before seven, a black sedan pulled up in front of the Dunraven place. The horn sounded a few short blasts before the driver of the car got out and walked up to the front porch.

It was Jason. James got a clear look at him as he escorted Jessica back to the car. It was obvious by the way she was dressed that she'd been expecting him. They stood next to the passenger side door for a few minutes, pawing at each other. James thought about the young laborer he'd seen her with just a few days earlier. He couldn't help but wonder how many other men she'd been 'in love' with that week.

Jason closed Jessica's door and stepped around to the driver's side. He pulled a silver flask from his hip pocket, slugging down a few hefty snorts, then quickly lit a cigarette before getting into the car. Another lengthy embrace by the couple, and the car sped away, heading along the river, then over the bridge towards Palestine, where the couple could dance and drink all night without being bothered or seen by anyone connected to Jacksonville's Gospel society.

James was hesitant to tell Lora what he'd seen until he was certain that Jason hadn't run off and gotten married to the 'black-haired harlot,' as he now referred to her. He decided that he'd have another meeting with Jessica as a showdown over what he'd seen.

James made an unscheduled visit to Tate City, three days before his normal day at the company clinic. He visited a few patients at their homes and then walked over to the store, assuming again that Jessica would be somewhere in the vicinity.

He was greeted by the usual group of domino players, cheerfully red-faced from an afternoon of imbibing their home-brewed whiskey, faintly concealed in pint bottles between their legs. The bottles were shared with the piety of a communion plate, each player downing a generous portion before his turn to bid or deal. To have declined most certainly would have been taken as unsportsmanlike conduct, or downright cheating, for that matter.

Jessica was roosting by herself on a bench swing at the end of the porch. She was reading a worn-out magazine, with her bare leg stretched across the seat so that no one else could sit down. Her eyes followed James as he moved towards her, tracking him over the top of the frayed paper. When he got close enough, she slipped her face down behind the pages. James stood next to the swing without announcing himself. He reached down, grabbed her ankle and pulled her leg off the bench with a jerk, then sat down next to her. He slowly wiped his face with his handkerchief as the girl continued to ignore him. Finally, he stuffed the pillowcase-sized hanky back into his pants and pushed his hat back on his head, before speaking. "You know, I got a bad feelin' about you, young lady," James remarked as he forced the magazine away from her face.

Jessica snorted and turned her head away.

"It's kinda' like a young mare I used tah own. The fella that sold me that horse kept tellin' me what a beauty she was. A real looker, he'd say. And it was, a real pretty animal. Had the makin's of a show horse.

"Well, that horse was about the meanest damn animal I ever saw. I finally had tah kill that mare because it was so damned sorry. I came to hate that horse so bad that I killed it myself, just to have the satisfaction of watchin' that miserable beast die, after it'd kicked and bit me more times than I care to mention," he finished.

"I don't care about your horse or anything else you've got, Doctor Lavoisier!" Jessica shot back.

"Well, you see, I'm tryin' tah make a point about something," James answered.

"I know what your point is, Doctor Lavoisier, and I don't care about hearin' it, neither."

"Maybe not," James replied, "but we're gonna have ourselves a little parley, you and me. I've got a few things to get settled with yah," he added, glancing across the porch at the domino players, to be sure none of them were listening.

"I don't have tah talk to you, Doctor Lavoisier. You got no right to bother me," she quipped, casting a fiery glare at him and then down at her bare feet.

"Well you see, I think you do, unless you wanta have a passel of trouble for yourself...bad trouble! I think you'd be smart to listen to me, 'cause I'm only gonna go through this once," James warned.

"Yeah, and what is it that's so important that you gotta say, Doctor Lavoisier?"

"I know you been seein' my boy, Jason. I know he's been comin' over here to get you, so the two of you can go off somewhere and mess around."

Jessica interrupted him, "I haven't seen your son! I don't know what in the world your talkin' about!"

"I think you do. I also know all about what you're plannin' on doin to him."

"Oh, you do, huh?"

"That's right, girly. There's nothing original about your little fantasy. The only problem is, if you're planning on improving your lifestyle, you better get yourself another beau, 'cause this one's stone-broke. And he ain't likely tah be gettin' any richer 'till he's gotten over the likes of you...if you catch my drift?"

"You know your son likes me, Doctor Lavoisier? He thinks I'm beautiful and exciting!"

"No, I don't really think so. I think he's just hornier than a damn rattlesnake!"

"I'm going to do whatever I want to do with him, or anyone else, and you've got nothing to say about it. I'll make him dance like a spider on a string if I want to! And there's not a thing you or anyone else can do to stop me."

James stood up, staring at the belligerent young woman and having a hard time deciding how to handle the situation.

"You know, Jessica, I think I've underestimated you. I did a little research on you, thinking you were just a misguided, ill-treated little girl, suffering the effects of a poor home life. But the truth is that it's more than that. I think the fact is that you're a demon, hiding behind a child's face, using everything and everyone to get just what you want!

"You do what you want to, young lady. But I promise you this...I'll fight you, tooth and nail, before I let you have my son," he finished, before walking away.

Jessica let out a loud, affected laugh, drawing the stares of the drunken domino players.

"See you later, Doctor Lavoisier. Have a nice trip home. And do tell Mrs. Lavoisier hello for me," she jeered, followed by an artificial laugh that had everyone staring at her.

Two small children, who had just gotten out of school, walked over to the swing and turned to sit down. They were sipping on their sodas from the store and smiling affectionately at Jessica. She stared at them, returning their smiles and threw her leg back across the swing seat, laughing as she spoke. "Get outa' here, you little twerps! Go sit somewhere else! Can't you see I'm busy?"

Her eyes followed James across the yard to his car. He stared back at her, exchanging a fierce look, as if they had just declared war.

It was nearly nine in the evening when the phone rang in the hallway at home. James could hear Lora answering the call. She was doing more listening than talking, a sure sign to James that it must be a relative.

"I'm so glad you called, honey!" she said. "Let me get Daddy to come to the phone; I know he wants to talk to you!"

James put his paper down and started for the hallway, almost running into Lora.

"It's Jason...he wants to talk to you," she told him, as if he hadn't heard the conversation.

"How are you, son? When you plannin' on coming home? Your mother and I sure would like to see yah."

For a few seconds James listened intently as Jason was making an explanation to him about something.

"Railroad, huh?" James responded, "over in Palestine? Well, that's not much of a drive from here. Why don't you come on home for a few days...I'd like to discuss some things with you."

Lora inched nervously towards the phone, as if she were going to spring on it. She was mouthing directions to James not to upset Jason. "Just ask him to come home, and we can talk about it then," she cautioned him.

James ignored her. "Like the Dunraven girl, that's what!" he said, suddenly getting louder.

"Oh, since when did this come about? Well...that's good tah know! So you won't be seeing her anymore?" James asked, repeating Jason's words so that Lora would get the message. She clasped her hands together and looked up, as if a prayer had been answered.

The intensity of James' voice softened as he continued the conversation: "That'd be mighty nice, son. It'd be good tah

315

have you home for a spell. We'll look forward to seeing you on Friday evening then," James repeated. "I know your mother will be excited about your comin' home."

Lora smiled, grinning like a child on Christmas morning.

As James hung up the phone, he was troubled by what Jason had said about Jessica. 'There's no way that jezebel would give up that easy! What the hell is she up to?' he wondered. 'Something is wrong...seriously wrong. Somehow I got a bad feelin' Jessica's involved in this,' he thought, as he strolled back to his room.

Friday had been a blistering hot day that had scorched the roses along the drive, leaving them limp and flaccid. Even the noisy blue jays had fled for the cooler pine forests outside town. The small red ants that usually marched in long weaving strings along the ground had slipped deep into their red earthen mounds, to escape the deadly scorcher.

James had gone to Catfish row earlier during the day with one of the yardmen to buy some fresh vegetables and a juicy melon or two for supper. Jason was partial to the sweet, deep red meat of the rattlesnake variety. James had plugged several of the huge melons with his knife, tasting one after the other until he'd found two that were perfect for his son's homecoming. He bought peaches and pears, even a few apples and a stalk of sugar cane. It made him feel like he was doing something to let his son know he cared.

Lora had spent most of the morning helping Nellie wash the sheets and prepare a sumptuous spread for supper. The aroma of fresh turnip greens cooking in a pressure cooker filled the air; fried chicken, breaded with a heavy coating of batter, sizzled on the stove, popping a flare of grease into the air. Cornbread cooled next to the cakes set in a row at one end of the counter, awaiting a thick icing to be plastered over each layer. And tomatoes and cantaloupes were sliced and arranged on a large platter, fanned out in the plate like a card player's hand.

Jason quietly slipped into the kitchen, waiting for the exact moment to catch his mother from behind, wrapping his arms around her and kissing her on the neck.

"Guess who, momma?"

Lora turned, wiping her hands on a dishtowel wrapped around her waist, before she answered: "You caught me lookin' a mess, honey, but I'm so glad you're home!"

"It sure is good to be here, momma."

"Go let daddy know you've gotten home, honey. He'll be so glad to see yah, too. It's so wonderful to have you back, darling. Momma sure has missed yah."

James, upon seeing Jason, stood and embraced him. The two spent a moment in silence, just holding each other. It was the easiest way for them to show their feelings.

The conversation during supper was confined to culinary remarks about the tastiness of the meal as Lora orchestrated the passing of second helpings to Jason. She offered him another helping of "good old peas, good old okra, and a few more slices of tomatoes," fresh from the garden that morning. She passed him a little more fried chicken, then warned him not to get too full or he wouldn't have room for dessert.

Jason stopped to savor the flavor of the food in his mouth in a theatrical way to show his approval for his mother's cooking. When Nellie came into the room he re-acclaimed his complete delight with the turnips: "Only place on earth where turnips taste this wonderful...you're some cook, Nellie!"

Nellie would smile predictably and quickly head back to the kitchen waving her hand and saying, "You been eatin' 'em since you was a youngin', they's jess plain old turnips."

"This is wonderful, momma! You can't get food like this around the railroad camps. Everything those Yankees eat is boiled or raw."

"How long you plannin' on working for the railroad, son?" James inquired. "Seems to me that a fella with a college degree isn't gonna have himself much of a future workin' alongside a bunch of white trash and coloreds," he added, studying Jason over the top of his wire-rimmed glasses.

"It's just too hard uh work for a white man to be doin'. The coloreds can work in that hot sun all day long and it doesn't bother them," Lora remarked.

"Oh, it bothers 'em, momma! They lay down just as tired as I do when quittin' time comes. Some of 'em jest get along a little easier 'cause they been doin' it all their lives. What's sad is that they can't do nothin' else. Most of 'em can't even read! And they all seem to know they aren't goin' anywhere."

James took a sip of his coffee and then asked again, "So what are your plans?"

"I don't know, dad. I guess, just have some time to think things through. I don't have any sense of direction right now," Jason admitted.

"You should pray about it, son," Lora quickly interjected. "You know God's got the answer."

"I'm sure you're right, momma," Jason responded, "but I just gotta work this through, by myself. I'm still down about getting the boot from the Air Corps."

Lora looked up from her plate, saying, "Why goodness sakes, of course you need some time to get over what they did to you, darlin'. Momma still worries about that lickin' you took on your little head. I wonder if daddy shouldn't take a look at it?"

"I'm fine, momma," Jason countered. "My head's fine."

"That reminds me," Lora announced, "you got some kind of a letter from the government...the army. I guess it's something to do with that flying school you were in," she added, apathetically forking a piece of pie as she spoke. "I hope they aren't trying to make us pay for that expensive aeroplane that got torn up?"

"I'd better take a look at it," Jason said. "Where'd you say it was, momma?"

"I'll get it," she offered, disappearing into the hallway. "You got another letter...from that Dunraven girl," she added casually as she came back.

The mood turned cold for what seemed an eternity before Jason spoke. "Wonder what she wants? I asked her not to bother me anymore," he said, as if to affirm the covenant he'd made with his father a few days earlier. He looked over at James and then back at his mother.

"My word," Lora said, "it was mailed from Frankston just yesterday. I wonder how she knew to mail it here?"

"I don't know, momma. I don't wanta even read it! Just throw it in the trash," he insisted, smiling over at James before taking the other letter from Lora.

"They try to give us any trouble over that plane you wrecked and I'll have to get Lyles Haggerty involved. He's a good lawyer," James declared, sorting through the last few bits of pie for a final assault.

"I can't imagine, dad. They did everything they could do, short of putting me against a wall and shooting me," Jason said, half-laughing.

"Just the same, we better be careful. Damn government gets your ticket and you'll never shake loose of 'em." James warned.

As Jason opened the letter his face stretched into a huge grin.

"My God, they want me to come back in!" He laughed excitedly.

"Oh, honey, are you sure?" Lora asked.

"I'm sure, momma! They want me to re-up for a new Bombardier Instructor School, up in Denver, Colorado...at Lowry Field. The letter says they're looking for prior cadets with flight experience to become instructors."

He was almost shouting as he walked around the table to show the letter to James. He snapped his fingers as he laid the letter down in front of his father.

"This is won-der-ful!" He chuckled. "I knew they weren't done with me, not by a long shot! No sir'ee!"

"I'm not sure how excited I wanta get about this, boy," James offered. They kick your ass out and then come back wantin' you to train someone else to fly their damn planes? Sounds like a bunch of crap to me."

"Nah, dad, don't you see? It's a chance for me to get back into the Air Corps. With the war coming, I'd be in a slot for a top assignment...bombers! I'd be at the top of the list for the first crews they'd send overseas. When war comes, they're gonna get me anyway. This is my chance to get what I want, what I've always wanted! It's the answer to my prayers."

"Praise His name," Lora whispered under her breath, still not certain that she liked the idea of Jason leaving home again, but still approving of him getting what he wanted.

"Well, if anyone can handle those big old planes, I'm sure you can," James acknowledged. "Lord knows, any fella as excited about flyin' as you are is bound to make a good airman. I'm real proud for you, son!"

Jason and James spent the rest of the evening talking about the war and what it would mean to the country. James recalled a few well-worn stories about the Great War. He began by describing, in resplendent detail, his first days at the front, talking enthusiastically about his experiences, as if it had been a most wonderful, fun-filled adventure. Jason had heard it all before, but still was intrigued by every detail. Then suddenly, as if snapped to his senses by some spirit set to the task of preventing such sacrilege and desecration of the truth, James began to realize what he was saying. He had gone too far! He had been ameliorating the events, as if they hadn't been tragic and gruesome enough, trying somehow to suggest that there was something heroic about his being an accomplice to the carnage and genocide that had taken place in France. He stopped midway through his story, looking in defeat down at his lap, as if praying for forgiveness. Jason was both surprised and concerned, thinking his father might be ill.

"Are you all right, dad?"

"No, son, I'm not. I've been sittin' here talkin' like an old fool. I'm handin' you a pile of bull that's contrary to everything in life I believe in.

"War's an evilness, a festering boil that takes benefit of the same part of the brain that God gives a woman to help forget the pain of childbirth, so she'll tolerate bearin' youngin's again and again. It's sort of a built-in spinal block, except it works on the memory.

"In reality, the devil uses it to make young men and old fools like me forget the stench of battle for nothing more than a pair of polished boots and a steel bayonet. There's nothin' pretty or honorable about any of it! Never has been and never will be!"

James cleared his throat and sipped on the glass of water on the nightstand next to his chair before he continued, "If it comes, I pray to God it gets done quick! They'll be a world of heartache for mothers mournin' over their dead children. It'll tear this country to pieces. But those same mothers u'll get out there and beat the drum and send their youngin's off to fight, every time, never expectin' tah have 'em come back to 'em in pieces in a box. It's the last remnants of primeval stupidity that men and women seem to suffer equally.

"And the sorry part about it is that the old bastards that start these ruckuses u'll never suffer so much as a scratch. And when this one's done, we'll all forget about it and they'll come at us again with another one. We never learn," he added, philosophically, patting his son on the shoulder as he walked past him to his bed. "We never learn!"

Jason smiled and excused himself for the evening, wondering about his father's change of mood. He could only attribute his sudden pacifism to a mellowing in his old age. No one had ever been more eager for a fight than his father.

'Old men seem to flatter themselves by always feeling like they have to warn everyone about the evils of life.' Jason thought, as he retrieved Jessica's letter from the hallway trash can on his way to his room.

The next day Jason responded to the offer from the Army, putting his affairs in order to report to Lowry Field by July, 1940.

But, for the rest of that day, a day that had affirmed his future, he was content with the simpler things of life. With a borrowed car and loan of a few dollars, he made his way to Tate City to lie quietly beside the cool banks of the Neches River with Jessica locked in his arms. And as he lay embracing the Great Deceiver, so slept the world, oblivious to the hell that awaited all mankind. While Lucifer danced with joy knowing how many young hearts would be his in the coming struggle, Jessica was content with her moment of triumph.

Part Two

Stephen D. Boyett

CHAPTER 15

Dale was James' youngest grandson and the only surviving heir to the Lavoisier name. At twenty-seven he'd seen much of the world and had experienced more than most men in a lifetime. He'd come to the old home to pay his last respects to the place where he'd grown up as a young boy. Shortly, the home would be demolished, and the spirit of the old house and the memories of those who'd lived there would be cast to the wind like so much litter.

He'd come to reflect on the events of his life and try to reconcile his past by being close to the magic of the old place for the few days it had left. Everything had started and finished here for him, with only his crusade to find his personal Grail in between. But, as in so many stories of the search for the Holy Grail, it had all come back to this one spot, as if his guardian angel had waited here patiently, knowing he would return to discover the answers to life's questions.

It was very strange, after so many years, for Dale to stand in James' room. It was obvious that his sacred domain had been cared for with great love and devotion. Everything had remained virtually unscathed by the passing of time in the outside world. The smallest of details had been carefully attended to, leaving everything as he always had insisted it be…his exacting way. Combs and hair brushes, talcum dusters and hair oils, even his colognes, were all arranged where he could find them if he ever happened that way again. But he wouldn't.

The smell of tobacco still permeated the air. It was a little less potent than Dale remembered, but, just the same, it gave the room the scent that inspired memories of the old man, his grandfather. It was strangely pleasing to smell the sweet fragrance of the polished cherry wood furniture, and the strong musty scent that lingered over his high-backed, stuffed rocking chair. Its arms were still saturated with a trace of his grandfather's hair oil and hand lotions, where the old man's body had touched the fabric over so many years.

It was as if every fragrance that belonged to James had been carefully captured and sealed into the spacious bedroom. It was not offensive like the stench of aging things but a more pleasant ambiance, evoking emotions of happiness and warmth. It created a sensation so powerful that the young man could almost step back in time, when life had seemed wonderful and secure.

Medical books, long outdated by modern technology, were still displayed in a bedside bookcase, with their topics embossed in brilliant gold letters stamped deeply into the black binders. A collection of classic literature, richly bound in red leather covers, were set next to the bed, for convenience sake, where James would read himself to sleep each night. The Harvard Classics, the Masonic Bible, poetry and various novels, all reflected his striving to improve his understanding of the world. The books were also reminders of his loneliness and reclusiveness. They were old friends who had never disappointed or disagreed, comforting the old man when it seemed the world had gone mad, racing away from all that he believed in and trusted.

A flimsy nightstand stood next to his bed, supporting the necessities of his final years. The stand was stained with a proliferation of watermarks, eaten into the finish from drinking glasses set there to hold his false teeth and wet his throat during the hot summer nights.

A small drawer in the nightstand still held the syringe and ampoule of powerful adrenaline wrapped in brown paper, kept nearby, in case he'd felt the first gripping pains of a heart attack. A small silver dinner bell lay just inside the drawer to signal Lora if a deathly malady had come knocking at his door...but it never had. A small- caliber pistol, another old comforter, lay in the same drawer, primed to handle the intruder who also failed to materialize.

The young man fingered through the contents of the nightstand drawer, finding a plug of Black Mule chewing tobacco, too lethal for even the elements of time to attack. The white paper liner of the drawer was dotted with cigarette burns that had smoldered, scorching deep into the woodwork. A magnifying glass that had served failing eyes lay in the very back, next to a letter opener given to James by the Masonic Lodge one Christmas.

The young man stood silently next to the bed, with its beautifully carved headboard ornately embellished with cherubs and spindles, as if the occupant had been sleeping upon an altar of sorts. A deep oval trench had been worn into the mattress, the spot where the old man had placed his weary body each night to position himself for sleep with the least amount of pain from his infirmities. The young man's hand moved over the depression in the mattress, as if James' soul still lay sleeping in the bed. He remembered it all, the times he'd come down during the night to escape a bad dream, or crying for relief from a childhood ailment, or just for the comfort of being next to the old man, knowing he loved him.

He'd picked the bed to recuperate in when he'd had his tonsils taken out and his foot stitched, thinking there would be something magically healing about it. After all, his grandfather was a doctor. He stood for a moment, reminiscing about how he had kissed his grandfather each evening for the years he had lived in the old house, pleased with himself that he never had missed saying good night.

The closet still smelled of cleaning fluid diffusing into the air from the double- breasted suits and wide colorful silk ties and shirts, covered in loose-fitting garment bags from Zodie's Laundry. Rows of black and brown narrow-toed shoes lined the closet floor, interrupted by an occasional pair of white oxfords or straw bucks. The shelves above the suits were lined with a variety of boxes with labels as fancy as an ambassador's sash at a state dinner. These boxes held James' favorite hats. The fedoras and wide-brim Stetsons, Panamas' and plain fishing hats were stacked to the very ceiling. Each was worn with a particular event in mind, be it business or pleasure. Whatever the occasion, James believed that to bare one's head in public was rude and unmanly. It was certainly unbecoming a Creole gentleman.

The visitor's eyes moved in the direction of the smooth walking stick hung on the door. He remembered James' versatility with the cane as he directed the workmen at the sheds, like a conductor at a symphony, pointing to his selection of fruits and vegetables at Catfish row, or probing the soil for vermin, and weeds missed by the gardeners. And he was most adept at pulling down a fully weighted limb of ripe peaches or plums in the back yard with the cane for his grandson to select his choice of the delicious fruits. He remembered it all.

Even the floor held a record of his grandfather's habits. Foot trails were worn into the carpet where the old man had followed his routine after he'd retired from his medical practice.

He followed the heavily worn path to the dresser, positioned next to an outside door. The oval mirror of the dresser was framed in a thick routered cherrywood molding, artfully carved around the beveled glass. So often he'd watched James dress in front of it, tying his wide silk ties into small imperfect knots. He recalled studying him as he sloshed small squirts of Fitch's hair tonic onto his thinning hair and then brushed the silky strands back with his wooden hairbrush, doing little to cover his balding head.

He would apply a puff of talcum powder and a slap of cologne to sting the face and bring out a healthy red glow in the cheeks, and then the ritual was complete. Then, ever so patiently, he would turn his eyes to the young face staring up from beside him. He'd bend down and pat the small boy's tiny face with a generous handful of the sweet bouquet of cologne, strong enough to take the child's breath away.

James would pick up his bankroll from the dresser, the magical green wad of thousand-dollar bills used to titillate the senses of the small town merchants. He never went to town without ten thousand dollars in his pocket. He entertained himself with the confusion of the clerks trying to find change for the large denomination bills for some insignificant purchase he'd made. The young boy would emulate his grandfather with a roll of one dollar bills the old man had given him, sticking it in his pocket with a rubber band wrapped around the money like James had done.

Dale's hand caressed the worn top of the dresser. 'Here, too,' he thought, 'the old man's soul would come to visit if it still paced these halls...if souls do that sort of thing before God calls them home.' His finger stopped at the jewelry drawer on the right-hand side, on top of the dresser. Pictures filled the drawer, some familiar, some ancient and yellowed from time, and a few pictures of people he didn't recognize. Those who were closest to James were arranged in tiny gold frames on one side of the dresser where he could always see them. Only relatives of lesser importance, or those who'd lost favor with him, were banished to the small bureau drawer.

His attentions turned towards the duplicate drawer on the other side. He pulled it open, eager to reveal the treasures that might lie inside, a pocket knife, a hog's tusk, and a few coins from places James and Lora had traveled over the years. But there was nothing of any real value to anyone, except to those who loved the old man.

Dale reached for the first large drawer in the dresser. Inside were neatly stacked sleeveless T-shirts, underwear, socks, garters and a horsehair whisk broom, all still as fresh as the day they'd been placed there. He closed the drawer and reached for the one next to it.

James' old forty-four-forty revolver, so much a part of his grandfather's life, lay inside along with its worn leather holster and a partially emptied box of shells. He felt a strange sense of awe as he surveyed the tarnished piece, reverently leaving it where it lay. As romantic and sentimental as it seemed, he couldn't help but sense that there was something mystical about the weapon. It was, after all, the only witness to the truth of what had transpired throughout most of James' adult life. It seemed to have been as much a part of his colorful character as his hats and cane, although neither of these were ever kept under his pillow at night.

More pictures filled a shoe box in the next drawer. He claimed one here and there to examine, turning each of them over to study the notations written on the back. A black metal lock box caught his attention as he cleared away the final pile of pictures heaped in one corner. His mind raced with the stories about his grandfather's hidden stash of money, a pile of thousand-dollar bills still banded together from the bank. He stopped himself, realizing how absurd it was to believe that his grandfather would ever have left his fortune in such a conspicuous place.

The facts were that even though James was eccentric, he was more of a pragmatist than that. He had taken great care to insure his holdings would never fall into the hands of anyone except those he'd intended to have them. He'd been clear on that, long before he'd passed away. There had been speculation by some members of the family that the money had been buried in the back yard, or sealed in the walls of the house. Even the granite fence posts in the back lot had fallen suspect. A few people even surmised that rats had made nests of the money and that James, upon discovering the loss, had kept it a secret, not wanting to diminish his importance with a few distant relatives who had hoped to be included in his will.

The truth was that James had been very careful to see that a generous amount of his assets had been given to Lora to support her for the balance of her life. The rest, wherever and however much there may have been, were a secret that he purposely had taken with him to his grave.

Dale pulled the box from the drawer and placed it in his lap as he slipped into a nearby chair. For a while he fumbled with the stubborn lock, trying to open the mechanism that had been sealed for so many years. He examined the surface of the container, sure that something of importance must be inside. He was finally able to pry open the lid, handling the contents as carefully as an archeologist who'd discovered some ancient artifact. And indeed it was as if he'd found a canopic vessel, a container holding the most sacred reflections of the old man's life, the essence of his heart. It almost seemed as if he'd prepared the box to be with him in death. It became obvious that it was, in fact, an attempt to preserve his most precious memories in life.

There were pictures: a portrait of Jason, David and Dale and a picture of the entire family with one person torn from the photograph. That one person was his mother. Other pictures had suffered the same defacing. Somehow his mother's expressions, whenever he'd managed to find a portrait of her intact, were chilling and evil, although she was always stunningly beautiful.

He smiled at a photograph of Jason, his father, lying on top of a stack of other pictures. He was decked out in his flying suit with his foot propped up on the wing of a Jenny. The picture was inscribed simply with: 'To Mom and Dad...Love Son.' The corners were dog-eared from the many quiet moments the old man had spent alone admiring the picture.

There was a picture of a small boy. It was an old picture, yellowed and faded from the elements of time. It too was inscribed on the back, 'Sweet Baby Boy'. A small curl of hair was taped below the inscription. He thought at first it was a photograph of James or Jason as an infant. But when he saw the date on the picture he realized it was the child his father had accidentally killed with the car. He remembered James taking him to the cemetery in Frankston one afternoon when he was small. He had watched the old man's eyes become swollen and pained as he answered his question about who Billy was with a simple, "My other little boy."

An envelope lay near the bottom of the stack. In it was a collection of newspaper advertisements seeking the whereabouts of one Jaques Lavoisier. There were at least two dozen newspaper ads from various coastal cities along the Gulf, from Galveston to New Orleans and Mobile. The most recent of the ads was dated before the beginning of WWI. There were none after that date.

There was a stone carver's invoice and a sketch for a headstone, for the same name as in the advertisement. It was inscribed only with the man's name and a date of birth. There was no date of death, just a notation in that space, 'Known only to God.' James had obviously ordered the stone after his return from France. It had been delivered to Lalleville, Louisiana, with instructions that it be placed beside the headstone of Benonia Lavoisier.

Dale let his head rest against the back of the chair and unconsciously began rocking himself as he had done when he was a child. When he realized what he was doing he stopped and smiled, suddenly aware that old habits die-hard.

'The mighty throne of Zeus,' he thought, closing his eyes to savor the moment. He laughed out loud as he was reminded of James in one of his less serious moods, playing the role of the Hoochie-Goochie Man for his brother and him. Each time he'd shout 'Hoochie-Goochie,' the boys would run around the room looking for toy soldiers that the old man had hidden under the furniture, or in a drawer. James would chuckle with delight as one of them would find a 'little man'. The game would usually end with Lora coming to the rescue of whichever child had come up short on the number of toys. The despondent loser would be escorted to Lora's room, all the while being reassured that a trip to the store would equal things out. James would return to reading his paper, having thoroughly enjoyed himself.

It always had been a special treat for Dale to sit in the old rocker when he was a child. It was the place where his grandfather held court and expounded upon topics of great wisdom or so it seemed at the time, and where the old man had spent most of his waking hours reading and telling old stories or giving advice to anyone who'd come seeking his counsel. Dale remembered how special he'd felt whenever he'd had an opportunity to sit in the chair, but only when his grandfather had walked down the hall to take a bath, or had gone to town to handle business. He would rock and swivel, making as many rotations as he could until he heard the old man coming up the hall again, clanging his Johnny pot as he walked, blowing a muffled tune as he struggled for a breath of air for his weakened lungs.

He pressed himself deep into the chair, as if to steal a moment for himself, again. He listened to the wood in the chair creak as the taut springs moaned, complaining that their long rest had been disturbed. But, even so, the chair seemed to remember him.

The room was comforting and wonderful. It was something that no one would understand unless they'd known his grandfather and had been through the hard times they'd faced together. He'd loved the old man with all his heart. He wanted to remember again...one last time and then everything would be put to rest. It would be finished, and then the course of his life would be free to continue to have its way, without interference from the past.

His hand held up another picture from the box. "That's dad," he whispered to himself. The black and white photo was of a young man dressed in a uniform, standing stiffly beside a flagpole and saluting. An inscription had been penciled on the back: 'Lowry Field, 1940, first graduating class, Cadet Jason Lavoisier, Army Air Corps".

It was July, 1940. A long winding train from Dallas lumbered into Union Station in Denver, jerking as it surged forward and then reversed a foot or two. A steamy exhaust billowed up from below the train, gathering under the wide awnings that sheltered rows of straight tracks on either side.

Jason, already attuned to what cadet life would be like, stepped off the train carrying only a small ditty bag. A young lieutenant searched the thick fog of steam that had retreated to chest high level. Each time the officer spotted a young man with the look of a cadet, he would inquire, asking, "Bombardier? Lowry Bombardier?" He'd scored correctly enough times that he had managed to gather a pride of candidates milling around in a group behind him.

Jason moved towards the lieutenant, introducing himself with military correctness, and then, after being duly noted, stepped towards the group of men talking excitedly behind the officer. One of the men, an oddly dressed figure, already peeled of his hair and wearing an outlandish sports coat and slacks, looked up, noticing Jason coming towards them.

"Lavoisier...you reckless bastard, Gawd damn!" he shouted. "They must be desperate for troops to let you back in!" The man laughed, rushing towards Jason. "Now I know they've got us pegged for some suicide mission!" he said loudly.

Jason smiled, moving towards the man and slapping him on the shoulder as he shook his hand.

"How are you, Carl?"

"Good, Jason," he answered. "Hey, fellas, I want you to meet Jason Lavoisier, the crazy son of a bitch that gave 'Ball-Buster-Bramlett' that wild ass-ride over at Randolph I was tellin' you about!"

Jason pulled on Carl's arm, trying to get him to shut up.

"Hell, Bramlette's still walking around somewhere mumbling to himself, battin' his eyes and tryin' to figure out what the hell landed on him!" the man blurted out, giving Jason a wink.

Jason squinted with embarrassment as his friend, Carl Overman, continued to harass him with the story.

"Old Bramlette thinks he's this hard-ass case, so he makes Jason, here, give him a short field landing. Boy, did he! Old Jason sees this creep needs a religious experience, so he plants the jerk in the concrete and walks away without a scratch. What a belly buster!" Overman proclaimed. "They're still tryin' to get Bramlette's head screwed back on straight."

There was nothing Jason could do to refute the story. He managed a faint grin and hoped Carl would find someone else he knew getting off the train.

"Hey, Overman!" someone in the group shouted, "at least he busted out for something besides bein' stupid." Overman laughed and gave the man an obscene hand gesture as the group filed out of the station to trucks waiting to transport the men to Lowry.

Unlike most recruits, all of the men had been washouts from a prior aviation cadet program. It was the first class of the newly formed Bombardier Instructor School. The course was to be a highly concentrated, sixteen-week program, designed to develop instructors to train thousands of bombardiers the country would need when war finally broke out. The army knew that time was short, deciding to use men already familiar with basic military discipline and trained in the principles of aviation. Precision bombing had taken a lethal step forward with the invention of the Sperry bombsight. It was hoped that the combination of the new bombsight and the prior training of the men would give the Air Corps a valuable headstart in the coming conflict.

Jason found the atmosphere to be less stringent than that at Randolph, with instructors concentrating more on applied physics than rousting a cadet for some minor infraction of military discipline. There was a sense of urgency that set aside much of the traditional training philosophies. The pace was almost frantic as, day after day, more aircraft touched down at Lowry for use in training the bombardier instructors. Lowry was undergoing an extensive restoration in preparation for the second class of men, a class that would be three times the size of Jason's ninety-six-man contingent.

The student's time was split between classroom lectures and flying, usually in the B-18-A bomber. Bombing target ranges had been built due south of Lowry, chalked into circular target images on the open plains. Because of the scarcity of bombing ordinance, bags of white powder were used, falling from the bomb bay with a vaporous trail blowing from under the belly of the aircraft as the load was jettisoned over the target. The substitute was messy, but provided a good measurement of the accuracy of the bombardier and his equipment.

The hurried pace was not without cost as the Bombardier School suffered the first of many fatalities on August 22, 1940. All nine members of the crew on a training flight perished over Watkins, Colorado. Investigators released army news reports to the local press explaining that the aircraft had crashed after being caught in a severe hail and electrical storm.

The classified version of the report strongly suggested that the aircraft had been sabotaged. Investigators were unable to find any proof that the plane had gone down as a result of weather. They had determined that the aircraft's wiring showed no indication of being fused or burned, the telltale sign of being hit by lightning. The only plausible conclusion was that the plane had suffered an internal explosion from something other than exploding fuel.

It was a personal tragedy for Jason because Carl Overman was one of the dead, along with two other men who had been with him at Randolph.

The fear of infiltrators on the flight line made everyone conscious of the frightening prospects of more sabotage. Jason was jarred into the realization that his perception of the honored profession, the gentleman aviator, was not quite as clean and glamorous as he had envisioned. With skulking murderers planting explosives on aircraft and blowing his friends into small unrecognizable pieces, his image of life suddenly took a twist for the worse.

Several days after the crash Jason was relaxing in the bombardier's lounge reading a juicy blood and guts murder novel when he was paged to the phone. He'd expected to hear the Operations orderly on the other end of the line calling to advise him that his mission for that night had been scrubbed.

His face dropped as the caller began to speak.

"Hello, Jason!"

"Jessica?" he asked. "Is that you?"

"I can't believe I found you! How have you been?" she asked. "It's been a long time."

"How'd you get my number? I wasn't aware that I'd given it to anyone except my folks."

"Well, your mother gave it to me, but I had to make up a little white lie so she'd tell it to me. I told her that I'd gotten a letter from the railroad, something important and I needed to forward it on to you. I knew you wouldn't mind."

Jason didn't answer. He was still caught off guard by the call.

"Now, why haven't you written me?" she chided, "You know how much I miss you. I thought you cared about me?"

"I do, Jessica," Jason replied cautiously, "but I told you it was gonna be a long time before I'd be back in Texas. We won't get a leave until school is over. Closest I'll be is Barksdale Field, in Louisiana, this weekend, but it's too far for you to come. Besides, it's just a forty-eight-hour layover."

"Don't you miss me, Jason? I mean, being together like we were when you were here? I think about you all the time, especially when I'm by myself at home at night and it gets so lonesome."

Jason could hear people talking in the background, so Jessica was obviously at the company store phone. "Sure I miss you, sweetheart; I'm just a little down right now. One of my friends was killed in a crash yesterday," he explained. "I'm not sure it's a good time for us to talk."

"I miss you so much," she went on, ignoring what he'd said. "I wish I could see you! Everyone thinks it's just wonderful what you're doing, being a bombardier and all. They all think you're such a hero."

Jason laughed. "I'm no hero, Jessica, but it's nice you're thinking about me! I think a lot about you sometimes and wish you were here with me. It's been real lonesome around this place. We don't see many girls on the field, except for a few that work over at headquarters, and they're a couple of homely old souls." He laughed again.

"Jason, would you write to me and tell me what you're doing? I miss you so much!"

He could hear someone hassling her for the phone. "I wish I could see you, Jessica. Maybe when I get a leave I'll come home for awhile. We'll see each other then. I promise I'll write you and tell you what's going on here. It was wonderful to hear from you...really wonderful!" he repeated.

"When are you going to be at Barksdale Field?" she asked. "Could you call me if you have time?"

"Sure, that'd be okay. I've got Saturday and Sunday off, down there, before we do our turnaround," he answered. "I'll call you Friday night, after we land. How's that? We'll talk for a long time and I'll tell you all about my training program."

"That would be wonderful, Jason. I really love you. I want you to know that."

"Look, Jessica, I've got to go, but I'll be thinking of you."

"Goodbye, darling...I love you," she responded again.

Jason stood in a trance, still pressing the phone against his ear, wondering if he really cared anything about Jessica, or was just yearning for the affections of any female at that particular moment. He thought about the evenings they had spent sitting along the banks of Mud Creek or picnicking at Love's Lookout, watching the sun set. "She'd really be an eyeful for these guys!" he chuckled to himself.

Just as another passionate memory was materializing, he heard someone calling his name. "Lavoisier, you're drooling all over the phone." the voice announced. "Let me make a call, will yah?"

The man took the phone out of Jason's hand, breaking the spell. Jason made a halfhearted attempt at a smile, not really paying attention to the man standing beside him.

"Gawd damn, Lavoisier, go get a cold shower, will yah? You look a little flush." The fellow crewman laughed, shaking his head in disbelief at the stupor Jason was still in as he meandered back to his chair. His thoughts were still fixed on the image of another passionate encounter with Jessica.

The remainder of the week was a grueling schedule of cross country flights, simulating bombing missions, flown to the east of Lowry over isolated Kansas farm communities that were blissfully unaware they were a stand-in for some future air raid over Europe. In the latter part of the week they headed south over the rolling hills and thick forests of Caddo Lake country in Louisiana, to simulate jungle targets.

Jason's crew arrived at Barksdale on Friday afternoon, a few hours later than expected due to adverse weather. He slithered out of the bomber sporting a heavy growth of beard, and dragged himself across the flight line to Operations with his shoulders pulled down by the weight of his parachute and looking like a man doing hard time on a chain gang.

He sat in the debriefing room, lighting a cigarette and letting it dangle unrestrained from his lip, taking a drag whenever he happened to remember it was there.

After a while he began fumbling through an assortment of post-mission reports in his kit. In a few minutes he walked over to the planning table, all the while dreading the endless stack of reports he needed to complete, a postmortem of sorts outlining the delivery of his Pillsbury bomb load.

The operations clerk, a double for Ichabod Crane, slid up next to him with an irritating smirk on his face, and in a half-whisper said, "Sir, are you Lieutenant Lavoisier?"

Jason answered in the affirmative without looking up from his papers.

"Sir, you have a civilian visitor waiting for you. The Officer of the Day has escorted your guest over to the Officer's Club."

Jason looked up from his reports, squinting through his bloodshot eyes, then drawing a long pull off his cigarette, as if using it to fuel his response.

The enlisted man moved away, thinking that he had let something slip that Jason was trying to keep to himself.

"I'm not expecting any visitors, private...you must be mistaken," Jason finally answered. "No one even knows I'm here."

"Sorry, sir," the clerk said, "I must have gotten the wrong name."

Jason handed in his reports and bent down to pick up his parachute and B-4 bag, noticing that the clerk was still eyeing him with an obnoxious smirk on his face. He left the building scratching his head and looking back at the door, wondering what was behind the man's strange behavior. After a quick shower he changed into his uniform and headed over to the Officer's Club, still confused about the clerk insisting that he had a visitor waiting for him. The Officer's Club was alive with the Friday afternoon cocktail crowd.

Jason was greeted by several of his classmates who'd made the same trek to Barksdale, as he sidestepped his way through the standing room only crowd huddled near the bar.

"Jason, over here, over here!" he could hear someone shouting.

All he could see was a hand waving above a mass of bobbing heads. He made his way slowly through the crowd, cautiously greeting each instructor and ranking officer he encountered as he weaved his way through the throng of people.

Dana Becker, a fellow bombardier was perched up on a bar stool, making a number of undecipherable semaphore signals, surrounded by a crowd of men poised like they were shooting craps.

"I think you better get over here and rescue her, Jason, before the wolves get to her!" he warned.

Jason hoisted himself onto his toes, trying to see over the top of the crowd before turning back towards Dana.

"Rescue who? I haven't got any idea who you're talking about."

"Come on, Jason...your fiancée," Becker countered.

"My what? Say, what's going on here? I don't have a..." he stopped short of what he was going to say, finally getting a look at his visitor, smiling up at him from the circle of panting young warriors.

"Jason...darling!" Jessica shouted, leaping up and leaving her admirers to watch disappointedly as she embraced the young airman.

Jason could hear a chorus of moans from the gathering of men.

"What are you doing here, Jessica? How in the world did you get on the field? Why didn't you tell me you were coming?"

"I just wanted to surprise you, darling," she cooed, doing a one-hundred-eighty degree turn, and smiling as a reward to her party of admirers.

Jason looked around the room, noticing the attention they were getting and decided to maintain a stiff upper lip as if nothing were wrong.

"I would have liked to have known what you were planning. You're lucky I'm even here; we nearly turned around because of weather," he said, still shocked at seeing her. "And what's this about being my fiancée?"

Jessica was impeccably done up in a very revealing, dark green silk dress, with her black hair combed to perfection and a string of pink pearls dangling from her neck. It was a mature, well-organized, fashionable look, unlike the image of the camp urchin he'd remembered seeing the first time he'd met her.

"I just had to see you, Jason. I couldn't stand it any more. I thought it would look better for you if they got the idea that we were engaged. You said that you were going to be off this weekend, and it seemed as good a time as any for us to be together! Aren't you glad to see me?" she asked, dropping her head, as if she was going to bawl.

Jason reacted in panic, noticing that several high ranking officers were still watching his reunion. "Hey, sure I'm glad to see you. How'd you get the money to come up here? I mean, it's pretty expensive for a train, and I know you haven't got a car."

"It didn't cost me anything. Daddy's supervisor let me ride over with him in his truck. He had to go to Shreveport to get some parts for the pump station. He was a real nice man to go out of his way for me like that."

"Say, I don't believe I've seen that dress before?" Jason questioned, scouting out the fleshy terrain with a slight grin on his face.

"Do you like it? Momma gave me the money for everything," she said quickly.

"Momma?" Jason shot back. "What momma? I didn't know your mother was alive. Where does she live?"

Jessica was all smiles, sensing that the crisis had passed. "Over in Beaumont. She's so nice to me! You know her and daddy have been divorced for years, but she still does such sweet things for me."

"Sure is a generous woman," he replied politely. Why do I feel like I'm the last to know what's going on here? he thought to himself.

"Isn't this just heaven? All these men in their beautiful uniforms, with all the wonderful music and pretty lights," she exclaimed.

"Yeah," Jason concurred, reluctantly. It had seemed, by now, that he'd been to every officer's club in the Western Hemisphere since his training had begun. He was sick of the clubs and their food and would have sold his soul for a plate of his mother's fried chicken or a bowl of pot liquor.

"Have you had supper?" he asked, hoping to entice her to go somewhere so they could get away from the gawking of the other men.

"No, I haven't. But I think I'd just like to sit here and look at you in your uniform for a few more minutes. You're so handsome; no, I think dashing is more like it," she added, smiling at him. "I heard them say that at the picture show."

"It's okay that I came up to spend the weekend with you, isn't it, Jason? I just had to see you! Besides, it might be our last chance to be together before the war starts."

"War? Oh, yeah," Jason suddenly remembered.

He chuckled, thinking how alluring she was. "I think the war can wait awhile. Let's get outa here and find a quiet spot to spend the weekend. I think America is safe enough for a few more days!" he concluded, accepting the situation and electing to make the most of it.

Jason booked a room at the Adler Grand Motor Hotel, in downtown Shreveport. To say the least, the word 'Grand' was, at best, a loose description of the old architectural relic. The interior had been flocked and glitzed from floor to ceiling, but the effects of age had prevailed as surely as an old woman romanticizing about beauty long past, needing a surgeon's knife to restore her fallen radiance, a miracle that was not to be. The hotel was in the final stages of financial collapse, owing to the element that had begun to infest the neighborhood, and considerable competition. But apparently some of its clientele still appreciated the decorative appointments enough to overlook the lack of adequate heat or working plumbing. Loyalty, and modest prices, still carried the day for the old lodging, attracting young cadets and low- ranking officers, themselves barely eking out a living but still needing a fanciful place to bring their lady friends for the weekend.

The rundown condition of the outside of the hotel usually didn't matter, once the couples had entered the front doors. The interior was a marvelous extravaganza of European decor, lavishly set in thick turn-of-the-century carpets and oriental rugs, sconces and moldings that could never be replaced. Mirrors and crystal chandeliers confronted the guests at every turn in the lobby, leaving a few guests a little uneasy as they suffered an endless reflection of themselves on every floor before they arrived at their rooms.

Jessica was awestruck with the stateliness of the hotel. Never in her wildest dreams had she experienced such sublimity. She stood looking at the hallway ornamentation, gawking at it like someone having their first look at the gilded corridors of the Vatican. She stopped the bellboy every few feet to inquire about a particular painting or antique furnishing, as if he were a tour guide, well versed in such things. Jason was anxious to get to the room without being seen by anyone he knew. He patiently tolerated the interruptions, hoping Jessica would tire of asking questions, or that they'd reach the room before she encountered any more objects of virtu. The bellboy seemed eager, as well, to have the ordeal over with, shaking his head and mumbling obscenities under his breath each time he was sidetracked by her questions. After all, in his business, time was money.

"Oh, look, look, Jason, isn't this just the most wonderful picture!" she gushed, pointing to a tacky, oversized oil painting that obviously had been salvaged from the trash to cover a gaping hole in the wall.

"Down the hall, take a left, down two rooms on your right," the bellboy finally snapped, dropping the room key in Jason's hand and walking off.

Jason retrieved the bags and continued to follow Jessica through the corridor. "I wish my daddy could see this stuff," she remarked. "He wouldn't believe his eyes. He wouldn't believe the pretty ladies struttin' up and down these halls either! He'd probably break out in a cold sweat just thinkin' about it!" she added, laughing.

She popped a handful of candy into her mouth, making it impossible for her to talk for a moment until she swallowed some of it. It was then that Jason noticed that her purse was overflowing with the junk she'd bought at the cigar stand while he'd been registering at the front desk.

"It's just like I dreamed it would be," she announced, looking at Jason with a childish expression radiating from her face.

Jason gleamed back at her with his 'Gable and Bogey' look. Unfortunately, with all his appearance of confidence, he had knowingly registered at the front desk without one dime in his pockets. He'd been fleeced by some fellow bombardier, losing the last dollar of his paycheck the evening before his flight at a poker game. He had signed the register with the confidence of an oil tycoon, smiling at the desk clerk as he ordered a bottle of chilled champagne to be sent to the room. He also knew he didn't have enough change to give the bellboy a tip, so it was just as well the man had walked off.

"This is so exciting! I wanta live like this my whole life, Jason," she announced.

Her mood turned serious as she panned the room, studying the rich decor, emblazoned with an excess of gilt and bright warm colors.

"I'm gonna be a wealthy lady and live in a place as big as this...with butlers and maids takin' care of me hand and foot! And I'm gonna have flowers, and fancy clothes, and wonderful food...and a swimmin' pool made out of black marble, with a nanny to wash my back!" she proclaimed.

"I don't suppose you'd settle for a bottle of lukewarm champagne and the basket of fried chicken I had sent up to the room?" Jason said, a little deflated by her grandiose vision.

For a moment she seemed angry at his statement, looking at him as if he'd pillaged her lifelong dream with his insensitivity about the chicken and warm champagne thing. But one look at his face and she knew that there was nothing premeditated about what he'd said...it was just Jason, being Jason.

"Oh, darling," she exclaimed, "...don't you just feel so wonderfully elegant here? Couldn't you just run away and live your entire life in a place like this?"

"Well, I probably could until my daddy took a stick to me, when he got the bill!" Jason laughed.

Jessica didn't find his remark funny. "Your daddy...it's always your daddy!"

Jason ignored her, picking through his wallet one last time to see if he'd overlooked any cash for a pack of cigarettes. Then he turned his back to her as he struggled to uncork the champagne bottle.

"Besides, I'm sure your daddy would understand," she continued, stripping off her last item of clothing just as Jason turned around with a glass of champagne in each hand.

Jason didn't say a word, standing frozen as he savored her naked form from head to toe. He realized his memory had failed him again, but it was a realization he had each time they had been together.

After quickly guzzling down the two drinks and performing a juggling act with the empty glasses, he untied his shoes and tie, and managed at the same time to step out of his trousers. The last button on his shirt was expended with a hard tug as he leaped under the covers still holding onto the two glasses. Jessica calmly removed the glasses from his hands and dropped them on the floor as Jason concentrated on other priorities.

Jessica was eager to dress and go downstairs to the ballroom. An orchestra was playing the latest swing tunes, and everyone had congregated out on the dance floor.

Jason would have been satisfied to stay in the room and sleep, but Jessica was having no part of it. He reluctantly joined her, and after a few slow dances and several more drinks, Jessica finally relented and allowed him to sit down for awhile.

He was content to remain at the table, sipping his drinks and satisfying his craving for a smoke from a pack of cigarettes that he'd finally been able to charge to the room. She, on the other hand, was up and dancing with anyone who asked. Jason begrudgingly observed the goings-on, fondling his glass of bourbon and kneading his cigarette between his fingers as the evening unfolded. He drank, smoked and snapped his fingers to the beat of the music, trying not to let his jealousy show.

On came the admirers like a horde of locusts prepared to ravage the unharvested field. And to each of them Jason would reluctantly nod a halfhearted approval, toasting the couple's good health until he was almost under the table.

For more than an hour he could catch only an occasional glimpse of her face, glowing after some flirtatious utterance by one of a dozen suitors, packed around her like the petals of a flower.

And then, as if a heavily weighted curtain had been pulled over him, the lights faded and his vision began to blur. Voices became indistinguishable from the 'bump, bump, bump' of the bass player's thudding strings and the drummer's staccato rhythm. Laughter and conversation blended into a roar before everything suddenly went cold and silent.

"You looked a little peaked last night. I hope your tummy isn't going to be upset?" the voice questioned. "There's nothing nastier than the smell of vomit, first thing in the morning."

"I'm not gonna be sick," he replied, somewhat uncertain of himself.

Jason's eyes opened on command although they felt like peach halves that had been sutured to his eyeballs, including a layer of fuzz. Jessica was sitting beside him in a chair. She was chewing a cud-size wad of gum and reading a newspaper, at the same time loudly sipping the last drops out of a Coca-Cola bottle.

"Turn it down, will yah?" he shouted before he caught himself. "Just...sip it...a little...slower...please!" he pleaded, swallowing hard and closing his eyes simultaneously.

His hangover engendered a flashback up to and including the point where he'd passed out at the party the night before.

"How come you're up?" he asked.

She answered nonchalantly, "It's nearly noon. I couldn't sleep any more."

Jason tried to focus in her general direction, asking, "How'd I get back to the room last night?"

"Oh, that's cute!" she remarked, sarcastically. "A real fine how-do-you-do. You were all over me last night, like a grizzly bear. You even tore my new dress!" she announced, clicking her gum and turning the page of the newspaper. "I guess that was a real waste of a passionate night!"

"I wouldn't know," he murmured. "Look, I'll buy you a new dress, if you're upset about it."

Her voice softened as she spoke: "It's okay...I've already fixed it. I just wanta go downstairs so we can enjoy the beautiful morning...maybe have lunch."

"Oh, Gawd," he moaned, rolling to one side, and searching for a less painful position for his aching head as he contemplated the word 'lunch'. Finally, he propped himself up on one arm after Jessica disappeared into the bathroom. It wasn't the first time he'd been accused of being a little out of control, but it was the first time he'd done it with most of his uniform still on, including his shoes. He was a little suspicious about just how wild he'd actually been, considering the fact his shirt, though wrinkled, was still tucked in to his belt. And, oddly enough, his buttons, zipper and tie were still in the proper places. The only thing he hadn't worn to bed, apparently, was his parachute.

It was just as well that he had to wait for room service to press his uniform; it allowed him time to recuperate and at the same time piece things together from the night before.

Part of the mystery was solved when one of the guests inadvertently mentioned that they'd remembered seeing Jessica dancing the last dance of the evening with someone other than Jason. He knew he'd passed out around one o'clock and from what he'd been told the party was over at three thirty. Jessica seemed uneasy, vehemently denying that she'd stayed at the party after he'd been carried to bed.

Whatever the case may have been, Jessica was careful to forego any further outside distractions, dedicating herself fully to Jason for the balance of their retreat at the Adler Grand. He was curious why she'd made such a point of telling him over and over again about their having intimate relations that night. But, after all, it didn't matter. He was sure it would be a long time before he would see her again.

Sunday afternoon Jason drove Jessica to the train station. Their conversation became a psychological fencing match, with her trying to maneuver him into a dialogue about marriage while Jason carefully avoided any hint of the subject. When she realized he was sidestepping the issue, she changed the subject, deciding there was too little time left to pursue it.

At the station they held hands, exchanging promises to write, and see each other again as soon as he got leave. However, somehow Jessica knew it was over, at least as far as he was concerned. She could tell from the expression on his face that she would never hear from him again. She waved halfheartedly from the window as the train began to pull away from the station, but she was secretly determined that she would endure whatever it took to have her way with him. She also knew that the weekend had given her everything she needed to insure her success.

CHAPTER 16

Dale opened a letter he'd found in a box in the bottom of James' dresser. He was surprised by its contents. It was a rather revealing communiqué from Jason to James, sent shortly after his marriage to Jessica. It was, more precisely, a note of apology to James expressing his profound sadness for disappointing both parents and for letting himself get into such an untenable situation with Jessica.

The letter was dated just three weeks after Jason had graduated from bombardier school in Denver. Dale opened the envelope, finding a picture of Jason and Jessica standing beside an elderly woman on the steps outside the Denver County Court Building, where the couple had been married just minutes earlier. The old woman was clearly an accessory to what had happened, although her full involvement would remain a mystery.

Dale had remembered his grandfather's anger whenever he talked about the marriage. It was, as he described it, a shotgun wedding carried out with the delicacy of an execution. It wasn't a matter of 'forever binding love', but more the implementation of a contract giving Jessica her ticket out of Tate City, and, worst of all, granting her the Lavoisier name.

He examined the picture. His father was elegantly dressed in his dark brown military tunic and polished Sam Brown belt, with his newly earned second lieutenant bars on his shoulders. He was a handsome young man in his uniform, smiling slightly from under an Errol Flynn mustache. He didn't seem too bothered by the graveness of the occasion, but then again, nothing ever seemed to ruffle Jason's feathers. The bride was standing beside him, wearing a hat and a drab, unflattering overcoat, too large and too long for her petite figure. Her doll-like face was looking up at Jason with a submissive smile. The older woman was Jessica's mother. She appeared serenely pleased with the union, or else she was smiling from relief at having the matter concluded. It was difficult for Dale to tell which. But knowing the story as he did, he was surprised that anyone was able to smile.

Dale's thoughts turned to what happened at Lowry Field just before his parents were married. It was a story that

346

James had explained in detail to him years earlier when he was a young man. He had listened with interest, even though the pain of hearing such unpleasant things about his parents was agonizing. With the information the old man had provided, and what he had experienced himself, he felt that he could make a fairly good assessment of what had transpired during those early years.

Jason was constantly on T.D.Y., usually for two or three days at a time. Day after day, the formations of bombers practiced precision daylight bombing over the remote Colorado plains and mountains to simulate targets that they would soon face in North Africa and Europe. He was relegated, because of his job description, to the confines of the cramped bombardier's compartment, chain-smoking his cigarettes and reading his dime store novels as he waited for his target to appear briefly below him. Once the explosives were dumped, the bomber would make a sharp bank and head directly back to Lowry for a twelve-hour layover, and then he would repeat the same schedule.

Jason took the long flights in stride, taking advantage of the time alone to read or daydream or fall asleep to the drone of the engines. It was the perfect life for him. He found his comradeship with the other students enjoyable, spending whatever free time he had at the officer's club or playing cards in someone's room, disposing of his army pay with a fervor.

As the class approached graduation day, many of the students had made plans to marry girls they'd been engaged to from home, or had met while in Denver. The wedding ceremonies were as much a part of graduation as the commencement services. They offered a pleasant relief from the khaki-colored environment and stench of aircraft fuel, temporarily swapped for white lace and perfume.

Marriage was the last thing on Jason's mind. He was content to remain a bachelor, enjoying the many conquests that availed themselves to a debonair young officer. His life revolved around maintaining his dapper image with the ladies. No longer was he cursed with the stigma of failure that had haunted him since Randolph, or even earlier at the University of Texas.

During the last week of training the pressure eased up, allowing the men to relax from the hectic flight schedules and academic workload. Jason had totally lost interest in Jessica after his short weekend fling with her in Shreveport. He was relieved to be rid of her and assumed that it was the last he would hear from anyone in east Texas, except his parents.

On graduation eve the First Cadet Bombardier Squadron was treated to a traditional 'Dining In'. Jason and the survivors of the original class of ninety-six had prepared a comic skit to entertain the officers hosting the evening affair.

After the short performance, the guest speaker garrulously lauded the coming of air power and aerial bombing and then mercifully finished with the customary toasts to the President and other dignitaries, in absentia. The cadet body finished the evening by singing a selection of melancholy tunes composed by cadets with bombardier and Air Corps themes.

When the evening festivities were concluded the cadet class retired to the officer's lounge for drinks and conversation, and a chance to visit one last time before their departure for their new assignments the next day.

Jason was busily exchanging his views on a formula to defeat the Axis powers when he was interrupted by a page from the reception desk.

"Cadet Lavoisier...Jason Lavoisier...a call at the front desk, a call at the front desk," the Page chanted, walking nonchalantly through the assembly of men.

Jason excused himself and made his way to the reception area.

"Lieutenant Lavoisier," he answered, speaking into the phone, looking back at his friends at the bar and still thinking about the topic they'd been discussing. "Hello?"

"Hello, Jason, how are you?"

"Jessica?" he responded.

"Hi, Jason," she answered.

"What a pleasant surprise," he replied, somewhat incredulous over the call. He was stunned at hearing her voice again, still remembering the last time she'd called him. "I'm surprised to hear from you. Where are you calling from?" He asked cautiously, panning the room to be sure she wasn't there, calling from an inside phone.

"I'm in Frankston, and I desperately need to talk to you, Jason," she said, urgently.

"What is it? What's the matter?"

"I really didn't wanta bother you, but I just didn't know what else to do!"

"What's wrong? Is someone hurt? Your dad...is he okay?"

Jessica answered quickly, offering, "No, he's fine."

"Look, I'm sorry about not writing, if that's the problem?" Jason apologized.

"No, Jason, that's not the problem. I wish it was something that simple...I'm pregnant!"

An eternity passed before Jason could speak. "You're what?"

"Pregnant, Jason, you know...pregnant!"

"You can't be serious, Jessica? This has got to be some kind of a..." he stopped himself from what he was about to say. "Look, I can't do anything about this; I'm being transferred in a few weeks to another field. You have to understand, I'm just not in a position to help you right now! All right?"

"No, it's not all right, Jason, and I don't understand. Neither does my daddy!"

"Daddy?" Jason echoed.

"He was so mad when he found out. I mean I've never seen him so furious. He wanted to call your commanding officer and talk to him right then, but I asked him to let us try and work it out," she explained.

Jason mumbled incoherently into the phone, "Why would he want to call my commander?"

"Anyway, I told him we'd talk about it. That's why I'm calling you," she offered.

"Jesus, I don't want him calling anyone! That'll ruin everything, including my career. Look...just stay calm and I'll do something to handle this. I'll call you back tomorrow, so just let me take care of it and don't talk to anyone, including my parents, or you'll screw everything up!"

"I'll do whatever you say, Jason," she said, her voice suddenly making a miraculous recovery. "I love you, Jason!"

Jason set the phone back on the receiver and wandered back to his friends, still in a daze from Jessica's startling announcement.

Stephen D. Boyett

"What's the problem, Jason? You look like death warmed over," one of his friends remarked.

"Yeah," someone else offered, "what you need is one of these aviation gas martinis they're handin' out. Just don't eat the little khaki-colored turds floatin' around in it...they ain't real olives," the cadet cackled, grinning as he turned and snapped his fingers loudly to catch the waiter's attention.

Jason smiled, recovering from his low ebb enough to join in the group's merriment. For the moment he tried to keep his graduation a priority over the revelation by Jessica that he was going to be a father.

The following afternoon, after a considerable amount of soul searching, he placed a call to James, asking for his counsel. James was livid when Jason told him what had happened.

"I knew it would come to this!" James insisted. "She was gonna find some way to get her hooks in yah, and, by Gawd, she did! She set you up, son, but you'll never be able to prove it!"

"Maybe so, dad. But now what? If I don't marry her, my career will be ruined...her father will see to that." Jason warned.

"Don't worry about that son of a bitch; I'll take care of him. But you'd better get a handle on this, 'cause you're gonna have to face your responsibilities for the child, assuming that she's really pregnant or that it's yours?"

Jason quickly answered, "I dunno, dad...I'm pretty certain she is...I think it's what she's wanted all along."

"I'd try and buy her off," James suggested, "if I thought it'd work. Problem is, you'd never get loose of her, once she got the first dime. You'd never get her to submit to an exam, either!"

Jason could tell that his father was frustrated. Neither of the men spoke for awhile, each pondering what should be done.

"I'll have to tell your mother what's happened. This u'll damn near kill her!" James warned.

"I promise you I'm gonna see things through, dad. I know I'm responsible for gettin' myself into this. Gawd help me for being so damn stupid!"

350

"Well," James said, trying to console him, "I'm not real sure you are totally responsible. But that's beside the point, now. Do what you gotta do, and you can sort things out after the child comes. If I didn't think she'd done a lot of talkin' over at the camp, I'd take care of this another way," he muttered.

"I don't want anybody hurt 'cause of this, dad. I think it's something that I need to handle myself! I really think you and mother should stay out of it!"

The two of them talked a while longer, discussing the fact that Lora and he wouldn't be going to Denver if Jason decided to go ahead and marry her. Jason felt that anything more than a private civil ceremony would be inappropriate under the circumstances, especially since there had been no love lost between Jessica and his parents.

Three weeks later, the decision for the two of them to marry was made and Jessica set out by train for Denver. Jason was surprised to find that Jessica's mother had accompanied her on the trip and was waiting with her at Union Station when he arrived. Jessica had downplayed her mother's presence by telling Jason that she, Mrs. McQuinn, had procured free employee railroad passes for the two of them to make the trip to Denver, an employment benefit that required her mother be present on the trip.

The truth hit Jason like a rock when Mrs. McQuinn ostensibly shuffled up to the marriage license clerk at the county courthouse and announced that she was there to sign the parent's consent form for her underage daughter to wed.

As it turned out, Jessica was only fifteen, a small fact that left Jason paralyzed with astonishment. Jessica had led him to believe that she was eighteen, so he was punch drunk from yet another surprise disclosure. It left him little doubt that he was totally out of control of the situation.

At this point there was little he could do but pay the license fee and sign the marriage application. He lit a cigarette, an act of defiance not unlike that of a man trying to forestall his execution, and then proceeded to the Justice of the Peace, who performed a short, sterile and impersonal ceremony. A fellow cadet and close friend of Jason's, Jim Myron, had come along to act as best man. He was also the person who snapped the infamous photo of the trio on the courthouse steps. He later likened the experience to trying to pose three people who had just been told they'd contracted a terminal disease.

A few days later, after depositing Mrs. McQuinn at the train depot, the newlyweds set out for their first duty assignment. As the luck of the draw would have it, Jason had been detailed to Grand Island, Nebraska, certainly not the most revered station of choice for anyone who knew their geography and climates. Jason had a rather insouciant attitude over the transfer, since most of his time would be spent in a classroom or the belly of a bomber. Most of the airfields were being built on the same master plan, which left Jason's environment fairly predictable wherever he was stationed. There was a tendency on his part, even then, to forget that he had acquired a wife in the process.

For Jessica, the field bore a strange resemblance to the place she had come to loath most in the world, Tate City. It seemed the perfect justice for all the conniving she'd done to get herself there. And arriving in the dead of winter only compounded her misery.

Six months before the war, Jason was rotated to a new assignment at Ellington Field, just outside of Houston, Texas. Jessica, plumply endowed with child, eagerly followed in his footsteps a few weeks later, after he'd managed to find what was loosely described as dependent housing. She'd gone to Houston hoping that her life would become more bearable than what she'd experienced in her first encounter as an army dependent. She knew that at least the weather would be warm, and was eager to trade it for the harsh winter snows of Nebraska.

Due to a housing shortage, several barracks, once designated for noncoms, had been reassigned as staff housing for junior grade officers. Jessica found the conditions deplorable, even by her standards, and insisted that Jason immediately find quarters for them away from the field.

With financial assistance from his parents he was able to locate a furnished garage apartment near Ellington that had met with Jessica's approval. Jessica found herself alone and unhappy much of the time that Jason was flying. Because of the distance to Houston and the rationing of gas, she was forced to spend most of her time either at the apartment or at the field. She opted to spend her evenings at the officer's club where she could at least find comfort with certain young and admiring officers who were eager to engage her in conversation.

Because of her young age she was shunned socially by most of the wives of the other officers. She did manage to find a few girls to befriend near the apartment, but those acquaintances were usually short-lived. She had little in common with girls who were just starting to discover boys and dating. Their parents were quick to end the relationship as soon as they discovered that Jessica was married and pregnant.

Her pregnancy seemed to be the only thing that was progressing as planned. By August of 1941, David Michael Lavoisier had arrived without benefit of the presence of his father. As usual, Jason was away on a mission, this time en route to the bombing ranges near Roswell, New Mexico. Jessica was beginning to realize that the quality of life she'd envisioned for the army was not going to be much different than what she'd grown accustomed to at Tate City. It was certainly less glamorous than she'd anticipated, but then the war had created a slight miscalculation on her part, as did the reality of taking care of a baby.

At the start of the war, Jason had begun a relentless quest to be assigned to combat duty in either of the theaters of operations. His pleadings fell on deaf ears, primarily because of his importance to the Air Corps as an instructor. He was keenly aware that his chances for promotion would be hampered without having had combat experience on his service record. Aircrews were being lost at an alarming rate over Europe. The staggering tally left the odds better than even that virtually none of the first crews shipped overseas would survive to complete their allotted number of missions. But that wasn't a major deterrent in Jason's mind; neither was having a wife and child.

The army training command was frantically pumping crews out of the schools as fast as the cadets could absorb the training. It was a fact that left Jason all the more eager to join in the scrap. He watched with envy as hundreds of his students were shipped overseas for combat. Jessica, on the other hand, was content to have Jason kept safely stateside, not wanting to become a war widow. Her sense of patriotism was easily overshadowed by her fear of ending up back at Tate City with little more than a gold star in her window to indicate that she, not Jason, had made the ultimate sacrifice.

In September of 1942, Jason was again transferred, this time to Boise, Idaho, and now he was frantic to find some way to escape his duties as an instructor. He was certain that now he would be successful in landing a transfer to combat. He discovered very quickly, though, that, barring death or a general court martial, there was no way he was ever going to be released as a ground school instructor. As a result of his frustrations, he began to fantasize about the war.

At first, it was nothing more than idle daydreaming whenever he had moments to himself. But suddenly, on his off-duty time, he began hanging out in bars and nightclubs in downtown Boise. He had decided to become a self-appointed undercover operative. He was determined to seek out enemy agents known to frequent local establishments on the outskirts of the field, so rumor would have it.

There was no doubt that a few enemy agents had infiltrated Boise. And it was almost certain that they were busy counting aircraft and observing much of the training that went on at the field each day. But it was doubtful that they were fiendishly practicing their trade in the numbers that Jason had gleaned from his collection of spy gazettes, mystery novels and even the Stars and Stripes. The death of Carl Overman at Lowry had been enough in itself to convince Jason that there was a spy hiding behind every tree and bush on the field. He'd been stunned by the loss of his close friend and angered by the way he'd died. It justified his slinking around, night after night, dressed in an idiotic-looking trench coat and packing his forty-five automatic inside his coat as he sought out the Nazi scourge.

He made the rounds to as many popular nightspots as he could in an evening, listening for anyone who might be discussing sensitive information. His reports, while meticulously kept, were never turned over to the authorities, either fearing one of them might be a collaborator, or perhaps because he had enough sense about what he was doing to know that his sanity would be suspect if anyone found out what he was up to. None of his investigative efforts was officially sanctioned; the reports were quickly brought to the attention of his commander by secret service, agents and other intelligence operatives who'd been observing him night after night. His name began to appear on reports directed to the commander frequently enough that he was finally ordered to report to headquarters to explain what he was doing.

Jason was summoned to report to Colonel T.A. 'Butch' Rudman, a hard-core, up from-the-ranks officer, and a seasoned veteran with a short fuse for incompetence and non-military demeanor. In the process of trying to guess what Colonel Rudman wanted, Jason theorized that he was being ordered to report for a secret mission, or at the very least a transfer to combat duty. He spiffied himself up for his audience, all the while thinking it odd that he would be required to appear before such a high- ranking officer. It just wasn't proper chain of command.

He entered Colonel Rudman's office precisely on time, mindful of his reputation for stringent discipline. Rudman was closing what was obviously the jacket of Jason's file as Jason executed the customary military etiquette.

Rudman looked up, still mulling over the information in the folder as he spoke in a gruff tone, saying, "Sit down, Lieutenant Lavoisier."

Jason took a seat, half-smiling, expecting to have been met with a little friendlier tone of voice. It was still on his mind that he was going to be asked to volunteer for some extraordinarily daring mission.

"You got some kind of a problem goin' on here you wanta tell me about, Lieutenant?" Rudman questioned.

"Sir?" Jason responded. "I'm not sure what you mean."

Rudman stood up and walked around his desk, taking a seat on the corner. "It seems that you've been observed on a number of occasions doing some kind of intelligence gathering, making notes, listening in on other people's conversations at several bars around town."

Jason cleared his throat, realizing the gravity of the situation.

Rudman continued: "My people have been watching you for some time. No one seems to know who you are working for or what you're up to. Now, we can't seem to link you to any agencies on or off this field, so what the hell's this all about, Lavoisier?" he demanded to know.

Jason forced a fist-sized knot down his throat as he answered, "Nothing sir!"

"Don't tell me nothing, by Gawd!" he shouted. "You better have a Gawd damn good reason for putting my people to this much trouble when we've got a war to fight!"

Jason scrambled for a story, quickly deciding that it was going to take more than a creative yarn to save his bacon from a general court martial. His instincts told him that the truth was going to get him skinned just as fast. The real story would sound too idiotic, because it was! Something in between...that was his only chance.

"I've been concerned that some of my students might be doing a lot of talking about the training we're doing, sir," he offered.

"I wasn't sure they'd gotten the message about keeping their mouths shut! I certainly didn't realize that your people were keeping an eye on them," Jason added, in an apologetic, yet uncertain tone. Rudman shook his head, holding his eyes on Jason as he said, "I don't know what your game is, Lavoisier, but I haven't got any more time for you. You're about a hair away from getting yourself arrested for espionage. You understand me?" he demanded.

"Yes, sir!" Jason answered.

"What's worse, you've got everyone in the place sticking their nose into my command because of this, and that's annoying as hell!"

"I'm sorry, sir! I never intended to cause—" Jason started to say just as Rudman interrupted him.

"Save the bull shit, Lieutenant. I'm not gonna put this little talk in your file. I don't have any problem with your loyalties...you're too damned obvious to be a spy. What I am going to do is ship your ass outa here before you cause me anymore trouble with this funny business of yours.

"Yes, sir!" Jason replied. He cringed at the thought of the endless places Colonel Rudman could send him as an instructor.

"You're so all-fired determined to see combat, I'm gonna give you a chance to see some real soldiers in action. You've requested a transfer to combat a half dozen times; well, I'm gonna see if I can't oblige you."

"Quite frankly, Lieutenant, there's always a few like you that get in at the beginning of every war, thinking all this is some kind of a game. Let's see how you fare in the real thing," he suggested, gritting his teeth as he looked up. "You're excused, soldier; now get your ass outa here before I say something I shouldn't!"

Jason's thoughts were volleying back and forth. It was like being thrown into the proverbial 'Briar Patch'. Amazingly enough, he'd walked out of Rudman's office with exactly what he'd come for. The ass chewing from his commander was inconsequential; fate finally had dealt him a lucky break.

'Now', he thought, 'I'll have my chance to show them, all of them, what I can do.'

His ecstasy was short-lived. Colonel Rudman countermanded his own orders within a week after their meeting. He had decided, for some undisclosed reason, to transfer Jason, instead, to the Army Air Force Bombardier School, San Angelo, Texas. It would be more of the same old grind and still no closer to combat. In fact, it was worse. He'd been exiled to the very edge of humanity itself. For the fourth time in less than two years, the family struck out by car, this time heading deep into the west Texas desert, carrying whatever possessions they owned lashed to the trunk and roof.

After two horrible and torturous days of traveling in the torrid temperatures, soaked in perspiration and suffering from a mild touch of heat exhaustion, the family finally arrived in San Angelo. Jessica took one look at the bleak military installation and burst into tears, crying hysterically, swinging and clawing at Jason as he tried to comfort her. To make matters worse, they had arrived in the hottest part of the summer. It had become impossible even to hold the baby without having a heat rash break out on his sensitive skin. And the wind, what little there was of it, felt like the exhaust from a furnace, sporadically blowing through the car along with a portion of sand and dust.

Jason drove straight to their new quarters, thinking Jessica and the baby would find some relief from the heat by getting into a tub of cool bath water. They found they'd been allocated one section of a four-unit, one-story frame billet set aside for married officers. The entire unit was whitewashed, and every building had black asphalt shingles and dark green wood trim. The field looked more like a prison camp than a military installation. It was the worst-looking facility that Jessica had yet experienced. But there was more to come.

She stepped through the front entrance of her new abode, pushing back a foot high pile of sand that had seeped through the door as she inched her way into the darkened apartment. A wave of hot air that had built up inside during the afternoon, nearly pushed her back out the front door. She caught a glimpse of a dark fuzzy blur scurrying across the floor in front of her and exiting through a hole in the nearby wall. A small avalanche of sand, built up on either side of the exit, slipped into the hole after being disturbed by the escaping creature.

Jessica's whimpering prompted David to begin screaming at the top of his lungs, miserable with the heat and covered in a profuse rash. Jason bounced gingerly up the wooden steps, carrying a double arm full of luggage. He assumed that Jessica would need a little time to become accustomed to their new assignment. It had been that way each time they'd moved. He tried to be in a jovial mood as he flipped on the light switch, as he declared his customary approval, announcing loudly, "Say...this is wonderful!"

No sooner had he finished than both of them became mesmerized by the movement on the floor as hundreds of scorpions and assorted spiders darted for the shadows of the room. Each of the multi-legged varmints had left their telltale tracks in the thin layer of sand that coated the floor.

This time, even he couldn't deal with the wildlife that had overrun the living area. Boise had been bone-chilling cold, Grand Island even colder, and Ellington Field had been plagued with roaches and dampness. But this was more than a broom and fly swatter could cure.

At this point he mercifully sought a room at the V.O.Q. for himself and his family for the night. Jessica was finally able to slip into a tub with David, to give both of them some relief from the heat. Meanwhile, Jason made his way over to the club to get the three of them supper.

They spent the evening in their underwear, lying on the top of bed covers with the lights out and the window to the room wide open as they tried to sleep in the hot night air. The windows didn't have screens, leaving sand and leggy visitors free to come and go during the night. It was a trade-off, pure and simple, where survival dictated the necessity of coexisting with the beasties of the desert.

It went without saying that Jessica hated San Angelo. She complained incessantly about the sand that found its way into every nook and cranny of the small apartment. There were bugs that stung and bit, snakes that slithered onto the sidewalks and streets in the evenings when the temperature dropped. And there were dust storms that blew with such force they sandblasted and pitted every inch of glass in the windows and choked anyone caught outside without a mask or handkerchief. But, worst of all, there was the damnable heat that never relented until the sun had totally vacated the desert sky. When it did, the nights turned to a frigid chill that always caught the inhabitants off guard.

Jessica had learned to tolerate her circumstances, but she made no bones about hating where she was. The sand and dust impregnated everything in the house, as did the stench of kerosene blown across the field from the engines of the bombers. The noxious fumes from the engine exhausts sparked her ire, reminding her of the pungent smell of crude oil and methane gas lingering over the oil fields of Tate City. The noise made by the huge R-2400 radial engines became commonplace; like the hum of a fan near a sleeping man's head, disturbing the listener only at that moment when the sound was interrupted.

She had endured the relocation, continuing her plebeian lifestyle, however reluctantly, but always waiting for that day when something better would come along. However gruesome life seemed at the moment, she was always reminded that it was better than what she'd grown up with as a child. That thought in itself made life a little more bearable, but not much.

The transfer to San Angelo had in no way dampened Jason's yearning for combat. He continued his campaign of requesting reassignment, barraging his commander's desk at every opportunity with written requests to be forwarded through channels. When he wasn't dogging his commander's heels for a transfer, he was lobbying at the officer's club with anyone who'd listen. He was most persistent with in-transit officers on their way to assignments overseas, or with friends at other fields, pleading for them to find him a slot in some forward area near the fighting. He reasoned that if he could make it that far he'd eventually finagle his way onto a combat crew. He was afraid, at this point, that he might miss the war altogether.

Shortly before Christmas, 1944, Jason received welcome news. His wish had finally been granted. He was to be transferred to the 502nd Bomber Group, a combat composite operating in the Pacific Theater. This time the orders had definitely been cut and placed in his hands. Everything had been approved, including travel orders to San Francisco and onto his final destination in the Pacific. There was no doubt that this time it was the real thing, and Jason was ecstatic.

For Jessica, life had become dull and uneventful except for the fact that she was two months pregnant with their second child. Her world revolved around an obsessive battle to maintain her disappearing girlish figure. When she wasn't complaining about her unwanted pregnancy, she was preoccupied with having her hair done, or finding maternity clothes suitable for evening wear so that she could attend bingo or cocktail hour at the club and not look too pregnant. The last thought on her mind was Jason being transferred again.

Jason was a little reluctant to tell her that he was being shipped overseas, knowing that she would be upset. For some reason she'd become convinced that it would never happen. It wasn't until he'd decided to tell her at supper that night that he realized why she'd been so adamant about his never being transferred to the front.

"I called my folks today," Jason announced, shortly after they'd been seated in the Club dining room.

"Oh," Jessica answered, "what about?"

"Just about your coming over there to have the baby."

"That's ridiculous, Jason! Besides, why would I go all the way to Jacksonville for that? Your mother and father hate me."

"That's really not true, honey. I think it would give them a chance to get to know you a little better."

Jessica laughed. "You'd be here all alone. Why would you want to do that?" She hesitated for a moment, realizing that there was more to his story than what he was telling her. And then she knew. "What is it, Jason?" she asked. Where are we being transferred to now?"

"We're not," Jason responded. "I've been ordered overseas!"

"That's not possible!" Jessica snapped. "Colonel Rudman promised me that he wouldn't..." she caught herself, quickly trying to cover up what she'd just said.

Jason was dumbfounded. "When did you talk to Rudman?" he asked.

Jessica remained silent, staring down at the floor.

"You went to my commanding officer? That's why he changed my orders for a transfer before? What right did you have to interfere with my career? For Gawd sakes!"

"I had every right! You have a responsibility to your family to take care of us, not go gallivanting all over the world just to prove what a man you are!"

Jason's eyes swept the dining room, noticing a few concerned looks from some of the people having dinner.

"The orders are cut, Jessica! And not even you can get them changed this time. I thought, since you'd complained so much about having David under such primitive, medieval conditions at Ellington, that I'd arrange for you to have this baby in a civilian hospital at home."

"It's your home, not mine!" she asserted.

"My folks would be there to take care of David and help you with the baby," he said. "There's no other choice, unless you want to go back to Tate City. I'm shipping out next week!"

He watched Jessica's jaw muscles flinch as she rolled her eyes back.

"You'll never make me go back to Tate City, ever!" she huffed, loudly.

By the time Jason had left for San Francisco the following week, Jessica and David were on their way by train to Jacksonville. Their parting moments had been as endearing as anyone else's during the war. It was a wonder things had turned out so agreeably between them, considering Jessica's reaction to the idea of staying with his parents. But that had quickly changed, the more she thought about leaving San Angelo. It seemed to be the lesser of two evils.

Jessica had resigned herself graciously to accepting her banishment to Jacksonville. She actually had begun looking forward to living in the grand style that the Lavoisier's home would provide for her. Life under James' and Lora's constant vigil would be difficult, knowing, as she did, how they felt about her, but she would survive.

Her arrival in Jacksonville was met with an unexpected outpouring of warmth. Lora was beside herself. She would finally have the chance to dote over David, something she'd been deprived of, except for a brief visit she and James had made after he was first born. James wasn't going to lose any sleep worrying over whether Jessica was happy or overly content living with them. His attentions and concerns were directed more towards the well being of the grandchild she was carrying. He allowed her little personal freedom, taking it upon himself to confer with her physician and make his own evaluations about her diet and well being. By the time she finally went into labor her relationship with Lora and James had been strained to the breaking point.

Although she had given up most of her independence in order to live with Jason's parents, she had reserved one privilege for herself. It was to be a personal victory of sorts, something that she had planned on since arriving in Jacksonville. She had diligently set aside the money for the hospital expenses and for the delivery of the baby. Each month she had deposited money into a savings account at Jacksonville Building and Loan, from an allotment deducted by the army from Jason's pay. It was an opportunity to spare herself the final humiliation by not having to accept a handout for her maternity expenses from James.

While the atmosphere in the old mansion was strained at times, Jessica and David were provided with a generous quality of life. Lora had seen to it that the upstairs had been totally redecorated to Jessica's taste. Jessica's propensity for garishness was a test of Lora's humility and patience. But she endured, quietly attributing the gaudiness of the wallpapers and furniture to Jessica's improvised childhood.

Lora had employed Nellie's eldest daughter, Sophie, as a second housekeeper to care for David and keep the upstairs. Her motivation was to allow Jessica the freedom to devote her full attentions to the little boy. Unfortunately, that soon became a point of contention when Jessica used the opportunity instead to spend less time with the child and more time away from the house. It became obvious that David was unaccustomed to the pampering he was receiving from Lora and James. The more the Lavoisiers tried to compensate for Jessica's inattention to the little boy, the more it provoked a problem.

Finally in July Jessica went into labor. Her stay at Nan Travis Memorial Hospital provided everyone with a welcomed break from the tension that had overshadowed the family for so many months.

On the day she was to be discharged from the hospital, Jessica was wheeled to the cashier's window by an orderly to pay her hospital charges. A nurse walked behind her, cuddling the newest addition to the family, Dale Carlton Lavoisier.

Mrs. Bradley, the hospital cashier, smiled, oohing and ahhing at the baby as Jessica scanned the statement and then confidently handed her a check drawn on her account at the Building and Loan. It was normal procedure for the cashier to verify with the bank that there were sufficient funds to cover patients' expenses; as Jessica patiently waited, Mrs. Bradley telephoned the Building and Loan for the normal approval of the check.

"We could just as well send the bill to Doctor Lavoisier's home, if you'd prefer?" Mrs. Bradley offered. "There's no need for you to have to go through all of this!" She assumed it would be easier for Jessica than having to wait for someone at the bank to pull her account records.

The very suggestion of James being involved in any way sent Jessica into a rage as she responded, "I'll take care of my own bill, thank you!"

Mrs. Bradley, who was taken back by Jessica's terse reaction, turned away for a moment to listen to the clerk on the phone who'd been checking on Jessica's savings account.

"I see," Mrs. Bradley answered. "You're absolutely sure?" she asked. She looked over at Jessica as she spoke, trying to keep her voice to a discreet whisper.

Jessica could see that something was wrong, so she asked, "Is there some kind of a problem?"

"Yes, I'm afraid there is," Mrs. Bradley replied. "Your account is insufficient to cover this check."

"There must be a mistake," Jessica shot back. I have my passbook right here in my purse. You can see that there's more than enough money to cover everything."

"I'm afraid there isn't," she answered, embarrassed over what was happening. "Mrs. Tillerman, at the bank, says your husband withdrew everything in the account two days ago. I'm very sorry!" she apologized.

Mrs. Bradley tried to think of a logical reason for something else that may have happened, feeling almost unpatriotic at having to tell her that Jason had cleaned out the account, but her excuses fell on deaf ears. Jessica lowered her head and covered her face with her hands as she began to sob. Mrs. Bradley handed the bogus check to the nurse who was holding the baby and then marked the file to have the bill forwarded to James for payment.

Lora and Nellie arrived at the hospital a half-hour later to take Jessica and Dale home. Nellie held the baby, bundled in her arms, while Jessica sat staring out the window, mumbling inaudibly to herself.

For the next several weeks the tension in the house heightened as Jessica did her best to avoid any contact with Lora and James, seeing them only at supper. The rest of the time she kept to herself in the upstairs apartment when she wasn't out walking with David and Dale. James immediately fired off a letter to Jason, demanding an explanation for his actions. Jason was quick and candid with his response, explaining that he'd incurred a substantial gambling debt with some unsavory characters in Honolulu who'd threatened to kill him unless he made good on the markers they were holding. He admitted that he knew Jessica was saving the money for her hospital bill and that he'd planned on paying it back just as soon as he could. Unfortunately, his survival had dictated that he use whatever resources he had in order to preserve his life. The next paragraph went on to ask his dad for a loan until he could get a few more paychecks under his belt.

James knew that Jason's flimsy excuses weren't going to cool Jessica's fury. It was in perfect character for his son to pull just such a stunt. He hadn't changed at all since college. He also knew it was pointless to refuse him the loan since Lora would eagerly send the money if he didn't. It would be consolation enough for her that he was still sitting the war out in a safe, rear-echelon assignment.

Besides the money he'd sent to Jason, James deposited a hefty amount of cash into Jessica's depleted bank account. He considered it an act of kindness that he hoped would promote a feeling of good will between them, but his generosity didn't work. She accepted the peace offering like Caesar extracting a tribute from a conquered nation. It was as if she considered the money payment for punitive damages, a sort of complicity on James' and Lora's part for Jason's actions.

James never heard another word about the money he'd sent Jason and could only assume that he had received it in good order. It didn't matter. James had little doubt that the money would be used for gambling. Not a dime of it was ever deposited back into Jessica's account.

Jessica received a letter and a package a month later from Jason telling her that he was finally being transferred from Hickam Field, Hawaii, and assigned to a B-29 crew. His destination had been censored. In the letter Jason made a weak attempt at an apology for the ill-timed withdrawal of the money.

A black lacquered box had accompanied the letter. In it was a strand of large pearls that he said he'd bought from a marine corporal. The marine supposedly had told him that he'd taken the pearls off a dead Jap during the invasion of Peleliu.

The Japanese soldier, so they story went, had placed a note in the box expressing his enduring love for his wife and thanking her for giving birth to his new son. Shortly afterwards, the marine had caught the Jap in a cave and killed him. Strangely enough, the note failed to show up with the box.

'I'm sorry,' Jason wrote, 'but I was so taken by the story about the Jap writing home to his wife, that I just had to have the pearls for you! I didn't have time to raise the money, so I wrote a check to this guy just before he shipped out. I was going to keep the pearls a secret for Christmas, but you had the baby before I had a chance to cover the check.'

The truth was that Jason had purchased the pearls in a hockshop near Hickham to mitigate the fallout from his ill-timed stunt with the money. He knew he was in disfavor with everyone and assumed the gift would be adequate reparation for his misdeed. Fortunately for Jason, Jessica had never gotten a look at the letter he'd sent earlier to his father. Lora, upon examining the pearls, extolled their beauty as if she were something of an expert. She was obviously pleased that 'Sonny' had vindicated himself with such a sensitive gift to his wife.

James, on the other hand, privately likened the theatrical story to a wheelbarrow load of something removed from a corral, which infuriated Lora. James kept his mouth shut, hoping to placate Jessica's hostilities in any way possible. At least for awhile, her excitement over the gift provided everyone in the house with some relief from her quarrelsome personality.

Jessica's cheerful and forgiving behavior was as short-lived as a kid with a new toy. She returned to her old self, continuing to show her resentment for James and Lora by instigating a confrontation with either of them whenever they happened across her path.

James wrestled with an unrelenting desire to pack her up and move her across town, to a rental house, but he'd decided against it, for fear of losing contact with his grandchildren. They were one of the few pleasures in life that he had left.

Jessica was fully aware of James' deep affections for the children, and she schemed continuously to keep them away from him. Whenever she would hear James calling David, or heard him coming up the stairs to see the boys, she would quickly place them in bed or sit with Dale in the rocking chair in the dark, as if she were nursing him to sleep. James would turn around and leave, not wanting to be impolite.

Her mastery of deceit was unparalleled, as was her lack of conscience about depriving James and Lora, not to mention the children, of the opportunity of sharing each other's company. She'd threatened, on more than one occasion, to pick up the boys and leave, knowing full well the panic it created with James and Lora each time she made the threatening declarations.

Boredom headed the list of Jessica's complaints about Jacksonville and life in general around the house on South Jackson. She had made a ritual of going shopping once, or sometimes twice a day, to 'get some fresh air'. She often disappeared from early morning until late afternoon. She was ambivalent about nursing Dale, cooperating only when she was in the mood, otherwise leaving him for Lora and Nellie to feed.

Several months after Dale was born, James happened to be walking across the street from the clinic to handle some business at the bank. Just before noon he'd stopped to take a fix on the mammoth Victorian clock mounted on a pole in front of the building. He stood a few feet away, listening to it toll its Big Ben chime as he reset his watch. Just as he was glancing down from the clock he noticed Jessica walking out of Buell's Dry Good Store with a strange man. She paused a few feet from the store, glanced nervously up and down the street and then stepped quickly into the man's waiting car. In her eagerness to leave she'd missed seeing James standing immediately across the street. The black coupe sped away, heading out of town in the direction of the Old Tyler Highway.

James immediately became suspicious. He knew every one of her relatives, and none of them even slightly resembled the man accompanying her. It was rare at that juncture of the war even to find a young man around town, much less one that wasn't in uniform.

James decided to follow the car out of town. The coupe drove slowly, weaving on and off the road, as if the driver had been drinking. When the car reached Love's Lookout, it turned off the blacktop road, heading down into the woods towards the main picnic area.

James waited on the highway, keeping the coupe in sight as it continued. He was certain they were heading towards the abandoned Forest Service fire tower, a few hundred yards past the stone picnic tables. He watched from the overlook as the car parked just below the old metal structure. After he was sure they were there to stay, he shut off his engine and coasted down the hill stopping far enough away that they wouldn't hear him. He cut himself a plug of tobacco and waited. Fifteen minutes had passed before he decided it was time to take a closer look at what was going on.

Before getting out of the car, he slipped his pistol into his belt from the holster strapped to the steering column. The road was still damp from an early morning rain, making the footing soft and quiet as he approached the parked car. He could hear Jessica and the man laughing and talking when he'd gotten within ten feet of the car. At that point the conversation lapsed into to a loud chorus of moans and groans.

James positioned himself where he could peek through the back window. He wasn't the least bit surprised to see Jessica and the man, going at it, locked in a wild gyrating heap of flesh, hell bent for leather on the front seat.

The pistol slipped easily from James' belt as he leaned against the car and pushed the weapon through the open window. He positioned the barrel against the man's head with a hard tap.

"What the hell, Gawd damn it!" the man screamed, kneading his scalp as he rolled off Jessica and onto the floor of the car. "You son of a bitch, what'a you think you're doing?" he demanded, going silent as soon as he saw the pistol.

"Get your ass out'a the car, both of yah!"

"What for? Who the hell are you? What'a you gonna do with that damn pistol?" the man asked.

"Better do what he says," Jessica warned; "he's got a fondness for hurtin' people."

"I'm gonna shoot your nuts off right where you lay if you don't get out'a that damn car, and I mean now!" James ordered. He reached over, grabbed a handful of the man's hair, and dragged his naked body onto the road. Before the man could say anything else, James slammed him face down into the gravel. Jessica sat up in the seat and covered herself with her abandoned dress as she cursed James under her breath. By the time she'd gotten her clothes on, her companion was on his knees in front of James with his hands locked together. He looked as if he were praying before being baptized, with James clutching a fistful of his hair and preparing to anoint him with his forty-four-forty. Sweat, mixed with blood, rolled off the man's face as he looked up, concentrating on the rifling in the barrel. A few seconds later his face turned towards his captor, pleading for his life with his eyes as wide open as humanly possible.

James delivered a kick to the man's groin, sending him sprawling backwards on the ground. It was all the man could do to tuck himself into a fetal position, twisting in the dirt before stopping to vomit. When he'd finished, he sat up, still trying to find enough air to refill his lungs. He held his hand out, trying to keep James at arm's length until he could muster enough air to talk. The other hand clutched his ailing testicles.

James placed the pistol between the man's eyes and cocked the hammer with a quick snap. "That's my boy's wife you been messin' with, fella; my boy who's riskin' his life fightin' for this country while a pissant like you is layin' out in the woods with the likes of her. I oughta finish yah off right now!" James suggested.

"Oh Lord, Gawd, Mister...I had no idea she was married. She ain't even got a ring on."

"Bull shit!" James retorted. "You just thought she was a little free merchandise that you'd hustle up for yourself in town, there."

"I swear to Gawd. She told me her husband was dead! You gotta believe me! I wouldn't have done nothin' if I'd known she was a soldier's wife, honest. It was her idea all along."

Jessica stepped out of the coupe, buttoning the last two buttons on her dress and then bent down trying to straighten the seams of her hose and shuffle into a pair of high heel shoes at the same time.

She ignored James and her companion of late, as she leaned over looking into the side mirror, combing her hair and touching up her lipstick.

When she finished dressing she retrieved the man's clothes from the car and started to hand them to him. "You oughta put these on," she said. "You look a little silly sittin' there naked when everyone else is dressed."

James jerked the clothes out of her hands and waved her away. She turned around and stepped back a few feet, ignoring the man's pleas for her to intercede.

"Gawd damn, lady, aren't you gonna stop him? He's gonna shoot me!" he whimpered, reaching out for Jessica as she strolled by, still combing her hair.

"I really don't care if he shoots you or not, honey. We all got our little problems," she said, slapping his arm away as she lit out for the main highway.

"What'cha gonna do with my clothes, Mister?" he hollered. "I gotta have somethin' to wear back to town."

"You aren't gonna be goin' back to town!" James countered.

"Oh, shit...Mister, don't kill me!" he cried.

James stepped back alongside the car until he reached the trunk. He was still holding the gun on the man as he squatted down and pulled his pocketknife out of his pants.

"Oh, Jesus, fella, you ain't gonna cut my tires, are yah?" he hollered, watching James pull up the ice-pick blade on his knife. "I can't replace them tires!"

James looked the man straight in the eye and launched an enormous wad of chewing tobacco in his direction. It landed just short of the man's legs like a brown rope. Without saying a word, he slammed the ice pick into the car's gas tank several times as the naked captive watched in horror. Thin streams of fuel began to trickle onto the ground.

"Now what'd yah want's tah go and do that for?" the man complained. "I done told yah I didn't know she was married!"

"Yeah," James said, "I know that. That's the only reason I haven't blown your brains out. The way I figure it, you got about enough gas to make it to a station, if your tank's full. Now, if I was you, I'd git while the gittin's good! And if I catch you sniffin' around her again, I'm gonna slit you wide open!"

The man was shivering, even though the temperature was past ninety degrees. "I don't suppose you'd reconsider givin' me my britches?" he pleaded one more time.

"You must not of heard me very well, Bub? Now I said, git!" James shouted, firing a shot into the ground next to him. "And if yah have tah do a little walkin' this afternoon in your birthday suit, maybe someone else's wife u'll get all excited about seein' your naked ass. Who knows, they might even take you in. On the other hand, maybe somebody u'll jess shoot yah 'cause they think you're a damn pervert," he added calmly.

The black coupe tore out, fishtailing down the gravel road, the naked driver looking back over his shoulder at James and Jessica. A trail of fuel followed behind the car as it turned onto the Tyler Highway and headed away from Jacksonville.

Jessica had meandered about thirty yards down the road by the time James pulled up beside her.

"Do I have to walk back to the house, or do I get a ride?" she asked.

James didn't answer, but instead tossed the man's waded-up clothes at her and pulled forward another twenty yards. Jessica fell in line behind the car, pilfering the man's wallet of its cash. She discarded the clothes on the side of the road before catching up to James again. She knew he wouldn't make her walk home.

Neither one of them spoke on the trip back to Jacksonville. But, as soon as they turned onto South Jackson, Jessica began sniveling and blubbering about how sorry she was for what had happened. She was quick to attribute her falling from grace as a result of being lonely for Jason.

"Save it for someone else. It isn't gonna work with me," James said, refusing to even look at her. "You ought'a be horsewhipped for actin' like a Gawd damn bitch in heat."

Jessica turned off the tears. Her character was suddenly all business, having remarkably regained her composure.

"I suppose you're gonna tell Jason about this? You've been looking for something to use on me ever since we first met."

"I'll tell you exactly how its gonna be, sister. I'm not gonna say anything to anyone, 'cause you and I are gonna make a little deal, a sorta 'come to Jesus meeting', just between you, me and the Lord," James said.

"Oh," Jessica responded, "and what might that be?"

"First off, you're gonna start by living the life of a nun until my son gets himself home. And if I catch you tomcattin' one more time, you're gonna find yourself wishin' you'd never been born.

"Secondly, if you step out of line one more time, I'll have those youngin's taken away from you by the courts. What you

371

did today is all I need to get your ass run out of town, and there won't be anybody liftin' a hand to help you!" James warned. "People around these parts don't go for whores, especially one who's got youngin's, and a husband off fightin' for his country."

"Oh really? It'd be your word against mine," Jessica challenged. "You'd never be able to prove a thing!"

"Well, it wouldn't be hard, missy. Yah see, we'd just give that fella a call that spent his afternoon walking the Tyler Highway, as naked as a jaybird, and see what he has to say about it. Truth is, I doubt that he made it more than a mile 'fore that car of his ran outa gas. There'd be plenty of folks tah testify they'd seen him. I don't suppose he'd be on the best of terms with yah, after what he'd been through."

Jessica didn't say another word. Instead she opened her purse and unwrapped an entire pack of chewing gum, stuffing all five pieces into her mouth.

"Oh, yes," James continued," there's one thing more."

"I'd appreciate your being a little more respectful of my wife, and I want you to start payin' attention to those children of yours. You step outa line again and I'll tack your promiscuous ass to the wall!"

She almost leaped out of the car after James pulled around to the back of the house and stopped at the kitchen door. She scowled back at him, wondering if he'd keep what he knew a secret. There was no doubt in her mind that he'd use it on her the next time she pushed him too far. James, better than anyone else, understood her thinking. He refused to be manipulated like other men. He seemed to have an immunity to her charm and calculating personality. It was that discernment, from then on, that left her uneasy whenever she was in his presence.

Life went on as usual, except for Jessica's miraculous change in attitude. Lora was convinced that Jessica had been confronted with something in the order of divine initiative, although Jessica certainly would never admit to it. Nonetheless, Lora knew. After all, why else would she have had such an instant change of personality?

Lora's motherly reaction to her was proof enough, in Jessica's thinking, that James had kept the covenant, so

Jessica didn't push her luck. She knew that the sooner she got out from under James' thumb, the better chance she would have of surviving the consequences, if and when Jason found out about the incident at the Lookout.

Even though the war effort had forced most people to tighten their belts, James continued to prosper. While his medical practice had fallen on hard times, with so many people gone off to the service or having moved away to work in the war industries, the government more than offset his losses by purchasing everything he could ship to their supply depots from the packing sheds. Not only was the packing business extremely lucrative, but it also provided him a generous subsidy of gas and other benefits.

Most people in the South who had money to deposit, still had a deep mistrust of banks, as a result of their collapse during the depression era. The government's efforts to restore confidence in financial institutions by regulating their operations and insuring deposits was seen as little more than 'Yankee government meddling'.

That reasoning, as strange as it may have seemed, led most people in the South to do their business in cash, and James found that little idiosyncrasy to play in his favor, as he was usually paid in cash for his services or produce.

Much of what he collected was socked away in secret niches around the house. Some of the funds were deposited in bank accounts under Jason's or Lora's name, and one particularly large account was opened under his nurse's name. In addition to the deposits in Jacksonville, a lock box was kept in Frankston with several thousand dollars under his brother's name. His purpose was simply to avoid the scrutiny of the IRS in his business. He transacted just enough of his dealings through his personal account at the bank to keep from calling attention to what he was doing. The balance of his business was done in cash. Eventually his cash holdings became so large that he was forced to deposit money in other banks in nearby communities. When that became a problem, he began buying cemetery lots, knowing that it would be easy to resell them if the need arose. But still, most of his cash was hidden in his room or sealed in metal cans and mason jars and buried in the back yard or sealed in the fence behind the house.

It was customary for him to come home from the office and stash his take for the day in an old red thermos jug that sat in the corner of his closet. He and Lora referred to this as 'jug money'. Then whenever there was too much 'jug money', he would fill a paper sack full, and either bury it or open another account as far away as Alexandria, Louisiana.

He'd come home from work one afternoon and, as was customary, he'd gone to the closet to deposit his take for the day in the thermos. Shock waves reverberated down the halls of the house when he discovered the thermos had disappeared. He went wild, tearing through the closet, pulling everything out onto the floor. Lora, thinking he was being accosted by a burglar, rushed into the bedroom, gun in hand. She'd expected to find him locked in a death struggle. Instead, she found him sitting in his rocking chair, cutting himself a plug of tobacco. It was obvious that something was wrong. He shook his head several times before explaining. Nellie and Jessica arrived on the scene a few minutes later.

"Which one of you took the thermos jug out of my closet?" he demanded, staring at each of them. He took an extra long look at Jessica, who had been the last to wander into the room. She looked disappointed he wasn't dead.

"You mean dat old rusted thing, in dah back of yow closet?" Nellie answered. "Why I done throwed that nasty thing out 'dis mornin', Doctor!"

"You did what?" James shot back, lurching forward in his chair.

"I done figured it waran't no good anymore...dah bottom was plum gone off it," she explained nervously. "Dah trash man hauled it off dis mornin' tah dah dump."

James looked down at his johnny pot, shooting a black streamer into the white ceramic container. "You got any idea what you've done, woman? Gawd almighty, damn!" he proclaimed. "Well, do yah?" he asked.

"Naw, sir, I sho' doesn't," she answered.

"All of yah, get yourselves a pair of gloves on and get a flashlight. We got work to do!" he announced. "Nellie," James instructed, "you tell your daughter she's gonna need to stay here with the boys until we get home. And tell her we're gonna be awhile!"

374

The four of them arrived at the Jacksonville City Dump just as the last flicker of daylight had faded behind the pine trees encircling the garbage heap. Smoke from fires, set by caretakers, drifted lazily over the mountains of debris. Bloated animal carcasses lay with their legs stretched straight out, their bellies distended with gas. James confronted one of the custodians, demanding that he show them where the trash for the day had been deposited. Fortunately for James, the day's haul hadn't been covered in dirt by the tractors. James waded, seemingly unaffected, into the waist deep mix of sewage and trash, probing through the wet rot with his cane.

Rats, giant opossum-sized creatures, raced frantically out from under the cans and boxes, with high-pitched squeals as their habitats were disturbed. Lora and Nellie followed James' lead and marched into the putrid medley of rubbish right behind him. Jessica was less eager, tiptoeing only about ten feet into the grizzly muck before she bent over, coughing and emptying her stomach with a loud bellowing noise, like a cow in pain from bitterweed. Lora came over and mercifully wiped her mouth with a piece of tissue. When she'd finished, she gave her a clean hanky to hold over her face to filter out some of the gagging stench.

As soon as she'd recovered, Jessica stood holding her hands out, as if she were a child experiencing mud for the first time. Her expression was sour as she wiped her hands on her slacks even though she'd been careful not to touch anything.

"I can't believe I'm standing in this nasty crap, tearing my legs to pieces so that you can find an old rusty thermos bottle!" she complained.

Her eyes concentrated on the shadowy terrain, keeping guard against any creepy crawleys that might be slithering in her direction.

After forty-five minutes of this, James stabbed his arm into a darkened lump of offal and suddenly produced the thermos. He held it up into the reflection of the fire, echoing a joyful howl of success across the smoldering mounds of refuse. He stood like a devilish haint, silhouetted in the soft orange glow of the trash fires burning in a circle around him. As if driven to madness by the whole affair, he began dancing a jig over the spot where he'd located the prized container.

After a few minutes he stopped, grinning with a crazed look on his face as he twisted off the metal cap to the thermos. He pulled a fist full of bills from inside the container, stuffing most of it into his pockets. Several thousand dollars slipped from his hands and landed at his feet as he shook the thermos, trying to remove the last few dollars.

Jessica recovered instantly from her nausea as she stood staring at the money lying all over the ground. It was more money than she'd ever seen in her life. James noticed her curiosity and quickly gathered the cash back up, pushing it into the already bulging pockets of his suit pants.

"Why would he have all that money in an old thermos?" Jessica questioned Lora on the way back to the car.

"You'd do well to forget you ever saw anything here tonight, honey," Lora warned. "He wouldn't take kindly to anyone talking about our personal family business. Someone around these parts would just as likely kill all of us if they got wind of this. Besides, it just looked like a lot of money...there wasn't but a few hundred dollars in there."

Jessica was just about to argue the point, first with Lora, who quickly turned her back, and next with Nellie who obviously could tell what she was going to ask her. She shook her head before Jessica could utter a word, and disappeared through the open door of the car.

Just as Jessica started to walk over to the window to ask Lora another question about what she'd seen, James stepped up to her. "You keep this to yourself, young lady," he ordered, tossing the empty thermos over onto one of the trash piles. "Let's get outa this filthy place before one of us gets snake-bit."

The vision of all that money lying on the ground next to James' feet was more than Jessica could easily forget. 'There must have been thousands of dollars in that can,' she thought. 'Why in the world did Lora say it was just a few hundred dollars? And if that's all it was, then why was everyone acting so funny about it?'

None of it made any sense to her. She lay awake most of that night thinking about the money she'd seen and fantasizing about what she'd do with it. She wondered where he kept it. Maybe he had another thermos bottle or a can in his closet or under his bed? But mostly, she wondered how much money he had managed to hoard over the years. The more she thought, the more she hated him for having it. But even more than that, she despised him for choosing to live such a paltry and subdued lifestyle. It seemed such a waste. So much money just lying in a closet in his room, and there wasn't the slightest possibility that she'd ever get her hands on one thin dime of it, not if he had his way.

James had made a fatal mistake in ever letting Jessica see the money that night at the dump. From that moment on she would never quit thinking about how she would take it away from him, and he knew it. Unfortunately for her, being married to Jason posed a particular problem in her normal process of scheming to get what she wanted. She couldn't very well steal the money, being family and all. And, on the other hand, she knew James wasn't about to hand it to her. So now began the great siege. And for the tragedies that it would bring upon both of them, it had certainly begun in the most appropriate setting...the Jacksonville dump.

CHAPTER 17

Dale looked at the glossy photo of himself as a toddler in the arms of Osamu, a young Japanese Imperial Marine. The man in the picture, once a committed believer in Bushido, seemed to be at peace with life. His smiling face was in stark contrast to the usual battle-hardened stare of most Japanese soldiers.

Osamu had been captured during the invasion of Guam with a number of his comrades who had elected to spare themselves the ritualistic death demanded by their faith, the code of honor that only a few had challenged. He had parted company with his more fanatical fellows-in-arms who had elected to accept neither suicide nor surrender, fighting on in the jungles after the fall of Guam to the Americans. Most were killed within the first few months of occupation by the U.S. Marines.

Osamu had made a decision to live in peace, accepting his shame for being captured, in exchange for someday being allowed to return to his family. It was difficult to believe that an Imperial Marine, the Emperor's finest, could ever accept serving his enemy, but he found it a manageable exchange in the place of suicide.

The photograph took Dale's thoughts back to that time when he had been a child of two, living on Guam, and what life had been like there. It was the first time he'd been away from his grandfather, the beginning of the coming and going cycle that would become so commonplace in his relationship with the old man.

Jessica had finally been given the opportunity to make good her escape from Jacksonville. Her salvation came with the ending of the war and the transferring of families to the repatriated pacific islands. It would be the last time that Jessica would ever darken the door of the house on South Jackson.

James and Lora agonized over their grandchildren moving to such a distant place. They decided to grant themselves a reprieve by driving Jessica and the boys to San Diego, instead of letting them take a train.   At least it would give them another week with the children.

They made the arduous trek across the deserts of West Texas, New Mexico and Arizona in record time, finally arriving without incident in San Diego two days before their scheduled departure for Hawaii. From Pearl Harbor, Jessica and the boys would continue on to the Marianas where Jason awaited them on Guam.

James had arranged for a suite of hotel rooms in San Diego for the family when they arrived. On the last day of their stay they decided to make a quick excursion across the border to Tijuana, before Jessica and the children were scheduled to report to the ship.

Once they'd crossed the border, they stopped for lunch at a quaint cantina located on a back street, some distance from the main thoroughfare.

After lunch they decided to return to San Diego to let the boys take a nap at the hotel before going on to the ship. They left the Tijuana restaurant and walked the short distance to where James had parked. When they turned up into the alley where he'd left the car, they found themselves face to face with a Mexican policeman ransacking their luggage. He was taking clothing, cosmetics and anything else that would fit in his pants and shirt pockets. He'd obviously broken out one of the front window wings to gain access into the Packard.

James reacted by grabbing the back of the man's shirt and giving him an undiplomatic tug that launched the policeman out of the car and onto his rear end. The policeman responded in turn by jumping up and going for his pistol.

James was alert enough to realize that the man was going to shoot him. He managed to land a well-placed punch to the policeman's chest that separated him from his pistol and planted him back on the street for a second time.

The policeman pulled a whistle from his pocket and began blowing an alert to other federal police working the same vicinity.

Before James had the sense to realize what the man was doing, two other policemen were on him, beating him with their nightsticks and kicking him.

Lora retreated from the melee, pushing Jessica and the children into the door of a nearby shop to keep the police from

379

turning on any of them. By this time James was down on the ground with his face bloodied from several blows he'd taken on the head. The two assisting officers held James' arms while the first man, the one he'd pulled from the car, slapped him several times. After giving him a short lecture in Spanish, the policeman relieved him of his wallet, and then ended the confrontation by bouncing his nightstick off James' head.

Lora was hysterical, but Jessica seemed delighted to see James beaten to a pulp. She stood there with a spiteful smirk on her face, hypnotized by the drubbing that he'd taken.

James was finally carted off to the Tijuana jail in a pickup truck, which the 'Federalies' commandeered from a passerby. Lora knew the Mexicans would be expecting a ransom, the customary fine as they always put it, for disturbing the peace.

Because of her concern for James' injuries, Lora paid the amercement levied by the local Mexican Jurist without debating the amount. After she'd paid his fine, she loaded James, now conscious, into the car and headed back across the border.

James' face had been split open above his right eye, the side of his head had a finger-length contusion that was still bleeding. His cheeks and chin were swollen, making him look as if he was suffering some dreaded disease. The worst of his injuries appeared to be his nose, broken from a punch he'd taken from one of the assailants. He also suspected that two of his ribs had been fractured. He was suffering from the effects of a concussion, as he held his tie against the side of his head to control the bleeding. Lora tried in vain to convince him to go to a hospital, once they'd crossed the border, but James would have no part of it. Instead, when he got to the room he gathered what he needed from his medical bag to treat himself with Lora's help.

A few hours later, he had managed to suture the cut over his eye, and Lora had been able to close the wound on the side of his head by following his instructions as he watched with a mirror. His ribs were wrapped, just in case they'd been broken, giving him a little relief from the pain. There wasn't much he could do with his nose, other than try and tape it back to its original position.

Lora had taken Jessica and the children to the pier while James slept. Not being able to see them off upset him more than the beating.

By late evening the next day, James and Lora had checked out of the hotel and were on their way out of San Diego. It took Lora a while to realize that James wasn't driving towards Texas. Instead, she discovered that he was heading back towards Tijuana. She threatened him with everything she could think of to try and coerce him into turning around.

"Please don't do this!" she pleaded. "We don't need any more trouble with those people over there. They'll kill you if they see you again!"

James had hardly spoken since he'd gotten into the fight. It hadn't occurred to her that he was brooding over what the Mexicans had done to him.

It was dark by the time James pulled over at a diner, a few hundred yards on the American side of the border. He handed her the car keys and instructed her to wait there until midnight. If he didn't show by then she was to go on to Jacksonville without him. She knew there was no way she could stop him. No one could.

He hired a cab to drive him over to Tijuana. He was primarily interested in finding the one who started it all, the one who'd slapped him and taken his wallet, but at this point any of them would do. For what seemed hours he drove up and down the narrow brick streets, parking outside the adobe cantinas and whorehouses as he searched for his assailants. The streets were flooded with American sailors from San Diego congregating around prostitutes who seemed to outnumber the sailors.

Tijuana was no different than the rest of the Mexican border cities. The smells were overwhelming. And every doorway seemed to hold the villainous shadow of someone waiting with larcenous thoughts, looking to relieve the gringo of his money, or carve him up, if they were inspired to do so. During the day the people were like tree roaches, disappearing into the cracks and crevices of the walls at the first sign of sunlight, doing whatever it was that kept them occupied until the next night, when they reappeared on the streets to crawl among the filth and ply their trade.

By 9:45 that evening, James and his driver, Jesus, had spotted their man. He'd recognized the fancy gold toecaps on his boots. He had remembered them matching the gold caps on the man's front teeth.

'Gomez,' James thought, recalling the man's name from the jail, when he finally came to. Gomez was standing in the door across the street, dressed in the same sweat-stained khaki shirt and pants that James remembered so vividly from the ride over to the holding cell. But it was James' watch, dangling out of Gomez's pocket, that sealed the Mexican's fate.

He was standing in a door near a streetlight, hassling a young prostitute whom he suspicioned was holding out on paying him his percentage of the night's take. Gomez had his hands up her dress, frisking her for cash and whatever else he wanted. Before long he followed up by jerking her head back and punching her in the stomach.

James could see the gold crowns on his teeth. Gomez stood there momentarily, watching the young girl fold over onto the sidewalk, and then turned and walked into the cantina next door.

James already had negotiated an arrangement with Jesus to become an accomplice in his mission—for a fee, of course. They'd rehearsed a short simple plan that would draw Officer Gomez out of the cantina. The cabby had only to mention to Gomez that he had an American woman passed out in the backseat of his car, and James figured he'd leave the cantina and his friends to harvest the spoils.

His hunch was correct. Here came Gomez, following Jesus out of the cantina, directly towards the car. The cabby stopped, looking up and down the street to make sure that no one was watching. Gomez wasn't impressed with the driver's caution. He pushed him to one side as he boldly stepped up to the cab.

James had locked the door and left just enough of the window rolled down that Gomez was forced to remove his hat before sticking his head through the window to take a look at the woman in the back seat.

What he found was the barrel of James pistol landing across the side of his head with such force that Gomez bit completely through the hand rolled cigarette pinched between his teeth. James cranked the window tight against Gomez's

The Saints of Mercy Bayou

neck and arm and ordered Jesus to move down the block with the Mexican's body still hanging limply outside the window. James opened the window and pulled him inside with Jesus' help.

Once James had the situation under control, Jesus started the car and tore down the street, heading towards the border.

"Senor," Jesus advised, "it would perhaps be best to cross the border somewhere besides the usual checkpoint. Especially, Senor, if you would like a quiet place to kill the policeman?"

"Anywhere will do!" James responded. "Just step on it; I wanna get this business done with!"

"Si, Senor!" The driver smiled, knowing it was going to be a lucrative trip for him, since the American had promised a reward if he succeeded in getting Gomez.

James unstrapped the policeman's holster and tossed it out the window as they skidded back and forth over the dirt road leading to the U.S. side. He'd also gotten his watch back in one piece. By the time the driver announced that they were safely back in the States, Gomez had come around. His head was bouncing against the window in sync to the tires colliding with the potholes on the dirt road.

His eyes were the only things that moved for the first few seconds that he was awake. He looked as though he thought he was having a bad dream. The patchwork of bandages, stitches and swelling made James appear almost ghoulish in the shadows. James slid the barrel of his pistol into the man's mouth and cocked the hammer. Gomez rolled his eyes back and clinched the barrel with his teeth and lips.

"You know who I am, you little bastard?" James demanded to know.

The Mexican shook his head with a short side-to-side movement, carefully avoiding doing anything that might disturb the stability of the trigger.

"You don't, huh? Well, take a real good look, cause I'm the last son of a bitch your gonna lay eyes on till you land in hell!" Gomez inhaled a deep breath, indicating he was aware of the seriousness of his situation. In the next few minutes he realized who his abductor was.

When they reached the outskirts of San Diego, James ordered Jesus to pull over in a vacant field. He grabbed his prisoner by the collar and led him to a small dry arroyo. Jesus didn't have the stomach to witness a murder, and after all he hadn't been paid for that part of the deal.

Gomez had gotten down on his knees, facing away from James, preparing to be shot in the back of the head. He tapped him on the shoulder, motioning for him to stand up and face him, a move that somehow reassured Gomez that he wasn't going to be harmed. Wrong idea! James unloaded an upper cut that broke off both of Gomez's front teeth. Gomez was surprised to find his gold crowns lying in his hands when he reached up to clear the debris from his mouth. James slugged him again, this time sending Gomez backward into a pile of sand. He still wasn't sure if he had broken his ribs earlier that day. He was in severe pain, his side feeling like it was torn open.

Gomez was on his hands and knees, pleading for his life with a mix of whimpers, supplications and a few prayers thrown in for good measure. He seemed to be having a little trouble remembering the prayer part.

James turned as if he were going to walk away, and then planted a hard kick to Gomez's head. The Mexican gave a loud grunt, landing face down in the sand. He was out cold. James removed the man's shirt and one boot and then emptied his wallet. James relieved him of the two gold tooth caps he still had clenched in his fist.

Jesus was surprised when James appeared back at the car without having heard any shots fired. He had one of Gomez's boots in his hand, full of large rocks collected in the arroyo.

"This policeman was a very bad man! Senor did right to cut his throat," Jesus said, staring at James for some sign that he had indeed dispatched his victim. Jesus carefully surveyed James' clothes for some sign of the gruesome murder. He was puzzled by the one boot full of rocks.

James ignored the comment and ordered Jesus to help him carry Gomez back up to the car. James revived him just enough to slip him a couple of strong sedatives and painkillers from a prescription he'd gotten for himself. He forced Gomez to wash them down with a shot of whiskey and then poured the rest of the bottle all over the Mexican's pants.

By this time, Jesus had become confused with the whole scenario. When James ordered him to take them downtown, all the cabby could think was that the gringo had gone crazy. He'd beaten the man senseless; now he was taking him on a goodwill tour of downtown San Diego. Gomez wasn't complaining; in fact, he wasn't feeling a thing. It was all he could do to sit upright.

Jesus nearly came unraveled when James asked him to find a large store, preferably a jewelry or department store.

"Senor, everything in San Diego closed hours ago. There is nothing open!" he advised him.

"Pull over...here," James commanded.

They stopped in front of a large apparel store that was closed.

Jesus helped James drag Gomez onto the sidewalk and sit him up next to one of the windows of the store.

"A little exercise in foreign relations, you son of a bitch!" James advised, calmly retrieving Gomez's rock-filled boot from the car. He launched it through the department store window, instantly setting off the burglar alarm.

James and Jesus then pulled away, leaving Gomez happily listening to the alarm and waiting for the authorities to arrive. The charge of attempted burglary, vandalism, illegal entry into the U.S., public drunkenness and a few other charges would provide more retribution than James could have possibly delivered with a single shot to the head. He was satisfied that Gomez would spend enough time in prison that no one would be bothered by him again.

Jesus delivered James back to the diner where Lora was waiting. She knew he had resolved the situation to his satisfaction, the details of which she was content not to know anything about. The trip home was quiet except for a few brief conversations about the children and their well being.

Jessica and the boys arrived in Hawaii nearly a week and half after they'd left San Diego. The voyage had been exhausting. They had inched their way through the Pacific in a worn-out vessel that had, of late, been relegated to transporting invasion troops to the same islands.

They had weathered two ferocious tropical storms at sea that kept the ship constantly pitching and rolling, creating an epidemic of seasickness among the passengers for most of the voyage.

Jessica and the other wives were graciously received at Hickham Field while they waited for transportation on to Guam. The officer's wives club hosted several get-togethers to give the wives a chance to renew old acquaintances from previous duty stations. It also gave them a chance to become acclimated to the tropics. However, very little information was available to the wives about the living conditions on Guam. Everyone had assumed it would be similar to Hawaii. Guam had been all but forgotten until the beginning of the war. Its strategic importance as a refueling base for long-range bombers was quickly realized. The thirty-mile-long island was ideal for just such a mission. It didn't necessarily follow that its living accommodations had received the same priority from the U.S. High Command. But no one had bothered to tell the wives that little tidbit before they shoved off on the last leg of their journey.

Jessica and the other dependents finally landed at Guam, arriving at Apra Harbor near the town of Agana.

They found an island cloaked in dense jungle, a deep verdure-colored blanket of foliage that was fully encircled by creamy sand beaches and crystal clear waters that blended into shades of light green on the outer reefs, and finally a dark blue as the ocean floor dropped off. There was more to the jungle than its tropical beauty. Beneath the intertwining vegetation were shrouded the horrors that had befallen the friendly and loving people of Guam from their Japanese invaders. The Japanese had used the jungles to cover up their crimes. Much of the population had been executed in an orgy of killing during the years that the Imperial Marines of General Takeshi Takashina had controlled the tiny island. The Japanese had been determined to establish a pecking order for the peoples of its captured provinces, ranking the pacific islanders among their least revered subjects and treating them accordingly.

The U.S. military installations appeared like festering sores on the smooth silky terrain. They were like garbage dumps hidden by the beauty of the land until a turn in the road revealed their sudden ugliness. Seabees had hurriedly erected a city of corrugated metal Quonset huts to shelter the troops from the sun and monsoon rains. There had been little time to worry about aesthetics, as the Seabees raced to keep pace with the invasion fleets heading towards Japan, and war's end.

Jessica moved down the ramp of the transport, gripping one child with her hand and supporting the other on her hip as she navigated the gangplank in her three-inch high heels. Sailors working the dock whistled and whooped at the lacy spectacle, as a sporadic gust of wind revealed more flesh than Jessica had intended. The ovations continued, much to her delight, until she finally reached the warehouse where several naval personnel offered to help her with the children while she stood in line.

It wasn't until she'd had her travel orders processed and been released to continue on to Oreta that she realized that Jason wasn't there to meet her. She made a quick survey of the crowd, worried that he might not have received her letter about the arrival date. She wasn't particularly worried about having a place to stay, considering the abundance of enlisted men and officers milling around her, like buzzards circling fresh meat. She realized that she was probably the first American woman most of the men had seen since they'd left home. Just as she was rewarding them with a flirtatious smile, she heard Jason shouting for her from somewhere behind the tightening wall of admirers.

"Jessica, I'm over here!" Jason screamed. He was met with a playful round of boos and moans from the crowd. He shoved his way through the onlookers until he was finally able to pull Jessica and the children into his arms. The same group of sailors suddenly cheered and whistled, congratulating him on claiming his voluptuous prize.

"Let's get outa here, honey," Jason said, giving the other men a victorious grin. "Gosh, it's good to see yah; you look wonderful," Jason whispered, kissing her and the boys in unison. "You won't believe it! I won one of the only cars on the island last week in a crap game. It's a real heap, but it's all ours!"

Jessica smiled, more interested in the half-naked stevedores standing near the gangplank than Jason's mention of his good fortune.

"How was the trip?" Jason asked, almost shouting over the throng of people moving towards the warehouse exit.

"It was horrid!" she answered. "David has been sick all the way from Pearl. The kids haven't had anything but powdered milk and oatmeal in a week. It gave both of them the GI's; Gawd, you'd think the navy would have known small children would be on the ship. It'll be nice to get some fresh milk down them!"

Jason looked at her with a surprised stare. "Jesse, hon, we don't get fresh milk out here. Everything is powdered, so it'll keep. The Gawd damn Japs killed most of the cows, all those that didn't run off into the jungle. Anyway, the kids will love goat's milk. It's not too bad, once you get used to it."

"Oh Gawd, Jason!" she complained.

"Hey, no sweat, hon," he said quickly. "I'll have some of the fellas ice a few gallons down at Hickham and fly it over on the next hop."

Jessica straightened her dress and checked her stocking seams before pushing her shoulder-length hair back away from her face. "I'd really just like to go home and take a nice cool bath. This heat is unbearable and I'm absolutely exhausted from lugging these damn kids around!"

Jason let loose with a nervous combination laugh and moan. "Well, we don't exactly have our own bathroom with a tub. It's more, of a...communal type thing. We have to share a latrine with our hut mates, Jessie and Sally Burman, and their four kids. But they're really great folks, you'll like 'em, especially Sally! And say, the shower's great."

Jessica looked at Jason as if she knew she hadn't heard the worst of it yet. "Fabulous!" she acknowledged sarcastically. "They sound just wonderful."

"Guess what the good news is?" Jason quickly offered, trying to diffuse the situation. "I got you a house boy, to help with the kids. He's a Jap prisoner, a real tough little monkey, but he's a hard worker and real clean, too!"

Jessica studied Jason's face for some indication that he was kidding about the houseboy.

"And where does he sleep?" she asked, in a condescending tone.

"Oh, he doesn't stay with us," Jason laughed. "They lock him up every night in a stockade with the rest of his pals. Keeps them from stealin' food for their buddies, still holdin' out in the jungle."

"I see. And who watches him while he's in the house?" she asked.

"Oh," Jason snorted, "he's harmless...wouldn't hurt a flea."

Jessica rolled her eyes back and patted her neckline with a hanky, all the while mumbling under her breath, "I have my choice of having my throat cut by him or being trampled to death in the bathroom by the brats next door. I can hardly wait!"

Jason wiped the sweat from his sunburned forehead before picking David up, then said, "I think we need to saddle up and get going before we get caught in the rain, don't you? These old roads aren't too good around here!"

"Maybe we could go over to the club pool and cool off a little," she suggested. She realized that he was ignoring her. "They do have a pool, don't they?"

"Oh, the officer's beach is swell. It's a lot better than a pool. It's a hell of a lot easier to take care of too." He laughed. "We even got the navy to put in shark nets last month, so it'd be safe."

Jessica squinted a faint smile, adjusting Dale on her hip.

"Guess what else? I'm Club Officer. You know what that means, don't you?"

Jessica shook her head reluctantly, afraid to ask, "No, not really," She said finally.

"We'll have all the fresh food and powdered milk we want, and plenty of liquor, too. And say, you'll love the gang at the club. They're a great bunch of fellas. We're gonna have some wonderful times, you'll see."

A black sedan, with all the windows knocked out, except the front windshield, sat baking in the sun next to the warehouse. The fenders were partially eaten away from rust, and the headliner and seats looked as if they had contracted one of the many varieties of jungle dermatitis. The more sparsely used parts of the cushions were covered with a black mildew and spots of rust that had bled through from the wire supports underneath. The tips of the bumpers had been bent up, resembling a set of chrome horns on some threatening variety of Asian buffalo. The stuffing was hanging out from under the deteriorating seat covers, with springs curling up from wounds here and there, forcing passengers to make careful decisions about where they sat.

Jason stopped in front of the car, sweeping his hand from front to back like a salesman showing off the latest Rolls Royce.

"Can you believe it? Only Gawd damn car on the whole island. What luck, eh?" Jason declared.

Jessica gave an ugly sneer before holding out her hand as if she were afraid of catching something. She tried in vain to find a clean spot to bless it with her finger, but gave up after a few seconds of searching.

Jason opened the door, politely helping her into the front seat. Jessica immediately began sniffing the dank air, suspicious of the stench that had hit her between the eyes as soon as she sat down. After inspecting Dale's diapers she looked over at Jason for some explanation.

"Oh," Jason said, reassuringly, "you'll have to get used to the smells. Everything around here rots 'cause it's so wet all the time. Soon as we get moving, the sea air will make everything smell better."

Jason drove along a shell-covered road that ran parallel to the beach. "I thought I'd take you on the scenic route...let you see some of the native color."

"Is this place always so damn hot?" she complained, ignoring him.

They passed a row of ominous-looking Japanese naval guns, aimed towards the sea from concrete revetments. The emplacements were strewn with palm leaves and tree trunks, along with other debris. A thin layer of ivy and moss had taken root on the walls, signaling that the jungle had begun to reclaim the small plot of ground. Most of those who knew what it was hoped the jungle would quickly have its way with the unwanted reminder of those terrible years.

"That's where the Japs held off the Third Marine Division. They really gave our boys hell!"

Jessica looked out to sea and then asked Jason, "Why are they still keepin' all those Japanese prisoners here? Lord knows what they're really thinkin' about us?"

Jason lit a cigarette and blew, forming a short-lived rolling donut into the air with the smoke before he answered in a typical unconcerned tone. "The ones that are walking around have given their word...they're not the ones to be worried about. We've got a few holdouts that the Marines are still tryin' to dig outa caves up in the hills."

Jason continued along the beach and then turned inland towards Oreta. They passed long rows of grass huts set on small plots of ground where the jungle had been burned back. Naked Guamanian children seemed to be everywhere, playing in front of the stilted hooches. They mingled with chickens and pigs running loose in the small yards. Several children were splashing and swimming in an enormous bomb crater that had filled with rain water, making a convenient bathtub and reservoir. Occasionally a Guamanian man or woman could be seen sitting on the front steps of the rickety houses, caring for a child or plucking a freshly killed chicken for supper.

The car's heavy jeep tires began to vibrate and hum as they made contact with the metal Marston mats used to cover the roads and keep the vehicles from sinking up to their axles. Jason gave a snappy salute to the guard as they passed through the front gate of the field. A short distance later he pulled up and stopped in front of a neat row of rusted, half-moon-shaped buildings.

"Well, here we are, honey! What'a yah think?"

Jessica glanced over at the buildings and then turned to Jason. "Here we are what? What is this?" she questioned, confused.

"We're home," he said, a little taken back by her disapproving tone. "It's real nice and roomy, even if it doesn't look so good from the outside."

"Good Gawd," she groaned, "It's horrible!" She turned away, plopping her forehead against her arm and laying it across the open window of the car. Just as she started her predictable whimpering, her arm made contact with the scalding hot metal window frame, burning her exposed skin. She let out a deafening scream that quickly had both of the children following suit. Jason leaped to the rescue, consoling her with one arm as he held Dale with the other. Somehow, in the midst of all of the hysterics, he had managed to coerce everyone into the arched bungalow. He gave Jessica one of his 'It'll be all right' pats on the back as she nursed her blistered arm, whimpering in harmony with the two boys.

Jason ran his hand up the wall, finally flipping on the main power switch, turning on the lights and several overhead fans, simultaneously. Much to her delight, she was suddenly faced with a room full of furniture.

"It's rattan," Jason offered. "The Guamies make it for us. They soak the wood for weeks, then hit it a lick with a blowtorch. Makes the stuff soft so they can form it around nails to make the arms of the chairs and sofas. The fellas at the parachute shop made the cushions from a couple of old mattresses. Hey," he said with a smile, "how about this material? Pretty neat, huh?"

"Oh, its wonderful, Jason!" Jessica proclaimed. She was thrilled beyond his wildest expectations. The tears instantly vanished.

The rest of the hut had been decorated in a postwar Japanese motif bought a few pieces at a time and transported to the island in the belly of a B-29. Jessica examined the carvings on the teakwood coffee table, along with a small set of sake cups and black lacquered rice bowls. A small dark teakwood Buddha smiled from across the room, with its delicate ivory teeth emitting a soft fluorescent sheen that seemed to catch the interest of anyone who looked at it.

Jason suggested that she make a wish and rub the idol's stomach. "The Japs think it's a god." He chuckled. "Your wish is supposed to come true, as long as your heart is pure and in tune with Buddha."

Jessica ran her finger over the polished wooden stomach, making short circular motions. "I don't know what kind of idiot would ever believe that hooey," she scoffed. "The damn thing gives me the willies."

A knock at the door interrupted their conversation about the idol. An unusually small Japanese man stepped sedately into the room, bowing as Jason introduced him. "This is Osamu, our house boy. He speaks pretty good English when you can get him to talk. He'll be here to help you with the boys and keep the house."

Jessica conjured up a nervous smile as she studied the gaunt man still bowing a reserved greeting, a few feet away.

Jason was quick to explain, "It's kinda' against his grain to serve a woman, but they do whatever we want. He may look a little puny, but he's a good worker."

Jessica looked over at Jason for reassurance that it was safe having an enemy soldier in their home. Osamu stood up straight, suddenly grinning from ear to ear as he listened to the baby crying on the couch next to Jessica. He seemed mesmerized by the white-skinned child. He stepped over to the couch, picking up the baby and holding it in his arms. Osamu's head cocked to one side as a faint smile erupted across his face and he wiped back several tears.

Jason watched with curiosity as Osamu walked outside with the cooing baby, apparently thrilled to have the child's tiny wet hands exploring his smiling face.

Jason shook his head in disbelief. "That's the first time I've seen him crack a smile since he's worked for me. I think he's got a son back in Japan he's never seen. Feel kinda sorry for the old boy." Jason acknowledged. "You'd never guess he was a noncom in the Imperial Marines."

Jessica quickly settled into her new life on Guam, enjoying the company of other wives she'd known as far back as her first visit to Lowry Field. The arrival of dependents to the base gave a new dimension to life for the men as well. Jason was gone much of the time the family was stationed on Guam, flying missions to Japan or Wake Island; sometimes going back the opposite direction, through the Marshalls to Hawaii. Jessica had, on very rare occasions, spent an afternoon at home rather than her usual schedule of sitting on the beach until dark and then going to the officer's club for dinner, with or without Jason.

The weather had become particularly bad, even by tropical standards. Rain had fallen in a light sprinkle most of the morning, indicating that something far worse than the usual four o'clock monsoon was in store. But no one quite knew what to expect. By three in the afternoon the storm had come ashore, quenching the last vestiges of sunlight with sheets of fiercely driven rain. The huge droplets hammered the metal structure with a deafening roar, bleeding through the seams of the metal skin. So much rain was falling that every vent and flue of the structure became an artery for the flowing water, momentarily backing up toilets and sinks.

Jessica had been indulging herself since lunch with a half-dozen gin and tonics, unaware of what was brewing a few miles offshore. While trying to anesthetize her boredom, she had become knee-buckling drunk. She'd gone to the boys' darkened bedroom to make sure that the runoff outside hadn't breached the sandbag walls around the hut, and flooded the closets where her high-heels were stored. Both children were napping comfortably, taking advantage of the cooler than usual temperature. Osamu was working in the kitchen, preparing supper, as he did each night for the children and himself, since Jessica was rarely home until long after midnight. He'd noticed the increased rain, but thought that it would surely pass after a few minutes.

Jessica had stood in the boys' room just long enough for her eyes to adjust to the dark. And then, as if blown backwards by some indescribable force, she stumbled into the hall with her hands over her mouth and her eyes glaring into the darkened room. Almost before she could bring herself upright, she turned, half- running and half crawling, towards her own bedroom. In an instant she emerged from the room carrying Jason's loaded forty-five automatic.

A blast rocked the hut, sending Osamu diving to the floor until he realized that the shots weren't aimed at him.

There was no question that what he'd heard was a gun, a very close gun, fired from the back of the hut. He raced to the boys' bedroom, finding Jessica holding the pistol, still smoking from the discharge a few moments earlier. Her face was twisted with a grimacing look as if she'd just thwarted a burglar in the act and was waiting for the next one to show himself. A huge rat was kicking and flipping itself wildly around the floor, half its head blown away.

Osamu panicked when he realized what she'd done. "Missy, no shoot...no shoot...no, no, no! Kill with stick!" he said, making a motion of swatting at the dying, Dachshund-sized rat with a make-believe broom. He was astounded that Jessica, in her drunken stupor, had fired off a round only a few feet from Dale's bed.

Osamu walked slowly over, picking up the frightened child and held him in his arms, comforting him as he sat down next to his brother, who also appeared to be very shaken. He wiped David's eyes with his finger as he tried to soothe both of them, talking softly in Japanese.

Jessica put the automatic down on the dresser and turned to leave, stopping momentarily to look at the huddled heap on the bed. She stood in the door like an enraged demon, glaring at Osamu, examining the small man as if he alone were the reason for all that she disliked about Guam, the military, and anything else that might have fit the bill of fare at that particular moment.

She weaved back and forth for a time, licking her lips and batting her eyelids, trying to focus.

"Get your hands off those brats of mine, you filthy Jap! And get outa my house before I call the Provost Marshal and have you arrested!" she slurred. "You got no right to tell me what I can and can't shoot at. That Gawd damn rat needed killin' and it wasn't for you to say how he was gonna get it, either, so get outa here before you get some of the same!"

Osamu had picked up enough of what she'd said to know he would be better off leaving. He lay Dale back in his crib and gave David a final caress across his small forehead, stalling until Jessica had left the room. When she had gone, he reached for the pistol, ejected the round in the chamber and removed the clip, which he dropped into in his pocket. He put the pistol back down on the table and walked out into the downpour, back to his own living quarters where the other prisoners were billeted.

The storm had been upgraded to a full-blown typhoon later that afternoon, and Jason had been grounded on Wake Island to weather out the storms. Jessica had decided around six o'clock to head over to the officer's club, unaware that a typhoon was bearing down on the island. Unfortunately, Jason had tried to place a call to Jessica to warn her about the storm, but all communications to the base had been cut off.

Dale and David had gone back to sleep for the night by the time she left the house. Normally, Osamu would have stayed with the children while she was gone. However, since Jessica had ordered him out of the house, there was little she could do but take her chances that the boys would sleep through the night.

By eleven o'clock that evening Jessica and a male companion she'd picked up at the club had passed out drunk, locked in each other's arms in the man's bed, as air-raid sirens blared a warning of the typhoon bearing down on the island. Winds had reached one-hundred to one-hundred-twenty miles per hour, sending anything that wasn't tied down flying into the wind like shrapnel. When Jessica was finally aroused from her drunken stupor, she could do little except dress and make her way to a nearby bomb shelter with her bed-mate, along with others lucky enough to be near the bunker.

The winds had become so intense that trees were being uprooted and flung through the air. Quonset huts had a remarkable resistance to high winds because of their odd shape, but the winds were driving trees and other airborne objects through the metal skin of the shelters, ripping them wide open.

By the time the full force of the storm had hit Guam, the base was coming apart, piece by piece. Osamu, realizing that Jessica had had too much to drink, and concerned for the family's well-being, had slipped out of his underground shelter and somehow gotten to the Lavoisier's; once there, he found the side of the building facing the incoming storm partially collapsed with a tree lodged through it. He worked his way inside, grabbed the two boys, and sprinted to the nearest bomb shelter.

Osamu had been badly cut from flying glass and spent the next week in the dispensary. Jessica made no effort to visit the man or thank him for saving her children, fearful that Jason somehow would get wind of her late-night rendezvous with her admirer on the other side of the base. Because of Osamu's courage, neither of the children was injured in the storm. It wasn't until months later that Jason realized the true reason why Jessica had insisted that Osamu be dismissed as their houseboy. She'd used the excuse that she was afraid of him. Because of it, the soldier would sit out the remainder of his imprisonment on Guam in confinement in a minimum security area, unable to have the same privileges as those offered to his comrades working on the base. By the time Jason found out what had really happened, the family had been transferred back to the States and Osamu finally sent home to Japan. It was too late for him to apologize to the man, or at best relieve him of his humiliation at being discharged from their service, shamed in front of his fellow soldiers.

None the worse for their primitive life on Guam, the family returned to stateside, first to Mather Field in Sacramento, California for a year of duty and then on to Barksdale Air Force Base outside of Shreveport, Louisiana, for another year.

James and Lora were delighted at having Jason and the family stationed only ninety miles from Jacksonville. Jason and the boys often would spend the weekends with Lora and James while Jessica would stay home or drive to Beaumont to visit her father.

Jessica had become even more overt in her coquettish inclinations. She was openly teasing married and unmarried officers alike; entertaining herself at club functions by raising a furor among the wives. She played a game of psychological tug-o'-war with some officer's wife, over her husband, especially if Jessica had taken a dislike to her for something the woman had said, or just for the way she looked. She would appear at the festivities dressed to kill, thoroughly enjoying the lustful stares of the men. She delighted in the uneasiness of the wives, pathetically tucking and twitching at their evening wear, desperately trying to improve on their matronly figures, unable to compete with the shapely, black-haired beauty who had drawn the attentions of their husbands.

Jason would watch from a distance like a recently beaten dog, boiling inside and cowering with humiliation. When she finally decided to indulge him with her presence, her conversation would dwell on the reactions she'd gotten from the wives and the obvious weakness in their marriages, as evidenced by their husbands' lascivious reaction to her. She gloated over her successes, laughing at having made the men make fools of themselves, enjoying the pain she'd inflicted on the demoralized and embarrassed wives. "Good Gawd, if the poor old thing would give him what he wanted at home, he wouldn't be out chasing everything with a skirt," as if there hadn't been any premeditation on her part. She was always the innocent victim when a pass was made by some admirer, supposedly not understanding why an incident had occurred, yet always pleased that it had. There was no shame, no remorse, and never any consideration as to the consequences of her actions for her or Jason, or her victims.

But there were indeed consequences. Behind every great military command staff, stood the network of officers wives, trusting their husbands to deal with the less important matters of war, and the strategy of running the base. The wives were quick to admonish the staff for rewarding any officer whose wife failed to step into line and follow accepted social behavior by openly violating the sovereignty of someone else's marriage.

Jason had been newly promoted to major, and transferred to headquarters to rub elbows with the top brass in a cushy new squadron slot. No sooner had he moved into his new office than he found himself being ordered to Ramey Air Force Base, in the Caribbean, on the island of Puerto Rico. There was little doubt in his mind that he had just received a reprimand for the unsavory conduct of his wife by Barksdale's female inner circle.

Jessica was little concerned with the bruise she'd administered to Jason's career, happily accepting the reassignment as a vacation opportunity. But her reputation had begun to follow them like a shadowy specter, passing from ear to ear with the speed of sound as soon as she would arrive at a new installation.

Before leaving for Puerto Rico, the family spent Christmas with James and Lora, all except Jessica who had elected to stay at the base, with the excuse of packing for the transfer. Jason accepted her alibi, turning his attentions to the children's excitement over Christmas. Their fantasies of a fat little man in a red suit being pulled around from house to house by smiling reindeer and delivering free gifts began to seem like less of a fantasy than what was going on in Jason's life. He desperately needed the time away from her to try and understand what was happening to him, and the recklessness with which she was dismantling his life.

CHAPTER 18

Dale swiveled around, forcing a groan from the threadbare old rocking chair. He glanced through a small pane of glass in the French door, staring into the dark dining room as a picture formed in his mind. It was a picture he'd seen a thousand times before, of the family sitting around the long dining table that once had provided some of the most tranquil moments of his life. He could see Nellie serving up dishes of steaming foods, caught up in the excitement of the holiday, singing to herself as she delivered pies and freshly baked cakes to the buffet table next to the congregation of diners.

'Those were wonderful days,' he thought. 'Every meal was a spiritual experience, a coronation of life where the dining room became the ultimate destination for each member of the family by day's end, sharing their problems and gathering the sustenance of life, be it manna from heaven or Lora's roasted chicken.'

James always seemed his happiest sitting at the head of the table in his regal, thronelike chair, dressed for dinner in a white shirt and tie, pleated pants and house slippers. Lora was never still, always passing food and never eating, just extolling the nutritional quality of each dish. Jason, the prodigal son, was content to be home, like a child returned from summer camp, not a father but just another one of the boys. Dale could remember looking at David, and trying to follow his lead in picking the correct utensil from the array of silver and crystal set out on the white linen tablecloth. He always noticed the empty place where his mother should be sitting, but she was never there, though Lora always set a place for her to show the boys that their mother was welcome.

The meal was consumed in silence, something from Lora's way of life as a child, saving the conversations until the end, with the delivery of dessert. Those wonderfully artful pies and cakes, or puddings and homemade eclairs were a tantalizing reward for finishing an already delightful meal. Then the stories would begin.

The children were excused to cuddle next to the flaming white ceramic gas heater, just inside James' room, where they could listen to the stories in warmth, playing with their toys as the adults talked. James would conclude his tale telling by standing and then retiring to his rocker, followed into the bedroom by Jason, for a final hour of menfolk conversation before going to bed. Lora would go her own way, refusing to listen to the third or fourth version of a tale she'd already endured over the years.

Dale remembered one evening gathering in his grandfather's room and his father telling him and David that the family was being transferred to Puerto Rico. Although it was the first that anyone had heard of the transfer, it meant little if anything to either of the boys. Life already had been a continuous shuffling from one place to another, so even at this early stage of their lives the boys were veteran travelers. Besides, home was Jacksonville, with their grandparents. It always had been considered that way. Moving amounted to nothing more than getting a series of painful shots, attending a new school and settling into a new house for the duration, on a base that would probably look just like all the others.

Maybe it was that he was older when they made this move, or maybe it was what occurred there that made this place become so vividly etched in Dale's mind.

Dale turned and sat back down in the rocking chair, remembering San Juan the day they'd arrived. Standing on the deck of the rust bucket of a ship with his brother, as they watched the water in the harbor turn from a deep, sedate blue to a polluted pastel green color. It was laced on the surface with oil slicks from the tugs and tenders, as they pushed the ship against the wharf.

He could hear his mother screaming for the two of them to come to her as the crowd of people began to funnel down the gangplank. He could recall the horrible smells of rotting foods and diesel fuel that hung over the wharf, causing him to run to his mother's side as if he'd never again get a breath of fresh air.

Many of the passengers who had weathered the gyrating movements of the ship's pitching and dipping for five days from New York, were suffering fevers from the immunizations given to them before they embarked on the journey. By the time the ship docked in San Juan, the crew had become incensed at having to clean up vomit and plugged toilets, change messed sheets, and pull children off the rails of the heaving ship. The captain contemplated confining most of the crew to quarters until the passengers had left, fearing reprisals against his cargo of women and children.

Jason wasn't there to meet them. He wouldn't be coming. He'd not only been exiled to Ramey as his punishment for his wife's indiscreet tackiness, but he'd had the additional bad luck, as far as Jessica was concerned, of catching up with his new squadron just as they were being sent on an extended TDY to England. Jason managed a rather weak protest over his stroke of misfortune, and then left merrily for Britain like a man going out for a night of drinking and poker.

So there the family sat, on a new base, husbandless, fatherless and friendless. No one who cherished their military career or valued their marriage would have come around, once they got wind of Jessica's seamy reputation.

Ramey was a kind of Elba Island for many of the wives, putting them just close enough to the continental U.S. to remind them constantly of home. But it was far enough away that there was little they could do but sit out their tour of duty, pining away for life in the States.

Jessica moved towards the waiting yellow school buses, dragging Dale and David along beside her as she spotted an airman flipping through a clipboard of documents, trying desperately to sort out Navy personnel from Air Force families.

She adjusted her dress, unlocking both boys from the death grip they had on her belt, and pushing them out of her way as she approached the airman. She cut into the front of the long line of people who had been waiting to board the bus.

"Excuse me, Sergeant...could you tell me which bus I should take to Ramey?" Jessica asked, knowing full well that the slick-sleeved airman was no Sergeant. She smiled, patting her exposed cleavage daintily with a hanky to remove small beads of sweat that gave her breasts a wet shiny reflection in the tropical glare.

"Yes, ma'am," the airman responded, gawking at her chest. "Just put 'em on that bus over there...the children," he said, trying his hardest to recover from his embarrassment at the irretrievable statement.

"Thank you," Jessica answered with an entertained smile, grabbing both boys and stepping quickly onto the bus ahead of the complaining line of women who had been waiting in the hot sun for hours. The interior was stifling from the steamy atmosphere created by the passengers' breath and the heat from the afternoon sun. People hung out of the opened windows, gasping for air, blocking any hopes of a cooling breeze. Children cried with discomfort as the acrid sting of sweat irritated their tender flesh. Once they'd gotten under way, the bus swerved down the narrow highway, heading into the interior of the island, dodging sugar cane carts. The driver ignored his panting passengers as his small overhead fan blew cool air over his uniform, turning the dark wet stains under his arms into whitish patches of dried salt.

Jessica closed her eyes, bouncing on the seat in perfect, uncomplaining rhythm to the movement of the bus as it navigated the cratered surface of the old highway. Puerto Ricans moved along the road, slowing the movement of the traffic in the towns, their vintage trucks creatively repaired with a fender, a door, an engine cowl from different makes of cars, all bent and twisted to somehow fit.

As the bus twisted and turned along the narrow streets, packs of children emerged from alleys, leaping onto the rear bumpers, pressing their faces through the windows, and smiling with decayed grins as they demanded a reward for their daring stunts. Obese Puerto Rican policemen, dressed in tailored brown uniforms and riding boots attacked the children with black whips that cracked in the air until the leather stingers, weighted with metal tips, hooked into the young flesh, flinging the thin-bodied beggars onto the cobblestone streets. Dale remembered how queer it was that the children were laughing as the whips cut them away from the bus, watching them crash into the stone street, and run off as if nothing had happened.

The town disappeared behind the heavy jungle foliage as they climbed into the mountains, the daylight suddenly disappearing as monstrous trees began to curl over the road. As the bus rifled its way down the dark tunnel, stone-sized droplets of rain thumped its metal skin like hail splattering against the front windshield. Warm water splashed into the open windows, soaking the occupants who feared asphyxiation more than the torrential downpour.

As they crested the mountains, the rain turned to a thin fog that hung like a cloud over the jungle. The driver, chewing his gum to the beat of the noisy and ineffective windshield wiper, moaned a tune that he had remembered from some local night spot as he missiled the bus over the slick, narrow mountain pass.

Jessica watched the countryside drag by, lifting her skirt up to her waist and fanning her legs with a small fan she'd bought in San Juan. She bounced her legs open and closed in time to the movement of her fan as she continued to stare out the window, caught up in a dream and listening to the driver repeat his monotone song for a second half-hour. Suddenly she realized that the driver had stopped his obnoxious howling. She looked up towards his seat with a half-interested curiosity, catching the airman looking down from the angled mirror at her gyrating thighs as he adjusted it for a better look. Jessica took short notice of his interest, making a face at him and continuing to fan herself as she returned to watching the countryside and drifting back into her daydream.

The children on the bus had reached a mutinous frenzy, climbing over the seats, pulling and fighting with each other as mothers pleaded and halfheartedly threatened. Jessica resolved the insurrection of her offspring with one swift thunderous slap to the two small heads. The stinging blows were quickly followed by a body slam to the seat for both boys, bringing them instantly under control. For a brief moment, a dead silence moved over the bus as everyone turned towards the popping sounds of Jessica's hand making contact. After a few incredulous glares from observing mothers, the action returned to its previous tempo, all except for Dale and David.

As with most military installation, every effort had been made to make the personnel's stay as comfortable and pleasurable as possible, exchanging the drab standard military issue architecture for a touch of native flare in the design of the base housing.

Despite Jason's unofficial wrist slapping by the Air Force as a result of Jessica's egregious social behavior, he had still managed to wrangle an unusually beautiful home, located within the confines of the base. The yard was splattered with shade from tall, svelte, segmented palm trees. Large bunches of dark green, unripened coconut pods, pressed together like a string of verdant balloons, hung just below the broad palm wings. Some of the trees leaned at an obtuse angle as if bowing in servility to some mystical island god.

The center of social activity for the officer ranks and their ladies was their club, built along the sheer edge of Devil's Cliff, overlooking Goat Island, a lumpy barren stone extrusion, nosing up from the ocean.

A constant cooling sea breeze, squeezed from ocean waves crashing hundreds of feet below, climbed the sheer precipice that dropped to the ocean floor from the club's outer perimeter. An evening of dining and dancing on the outdoor terrace of the club was an enjoyable break from the blistering daytime temperatures under the tropical sun.

During the day, the swimming pool at the club would become the center for social gatherings for the officers and their families. Jessica quickly reconnoitered the club social arena, establishing herself as a regular among those who basted themselves daily in the intense sun as they sat around the pool's edge.

Jessica would routinely arrive at the water's edge at ten a.m., dressed in the most fashionable swimwear and rubber bathing cap. She took a single lap across the pool and then spent the remainder of the day provocatively oiling herself with tanning lotion, until she was slicker than a piece of boiled okra fresh from the kettle. She would strike an inveigling pose, planting her arms back behind her as she sat pressing herself towards the sun, an exercise that enhanced her already generous figure.

At five in the afternoon the informal festivities would be interrupted as retreat sounded from overhead loudspeakers, blaring the national anthem from a well-worn record of military tunes, as all were required to stand facing the approximate direction of the ceremonial lowering of the colors near the front gate. The instant the music stopped, the grounds would clear, as everyone rushed to the nursery to retrieve children and then to their homes to greet husbands who had just gotten off work.

For those lonely hearts who had met at the club pool during the day and discretely agreed to have a friendly, innocent evening together, the club was the only accepted place to rendezvous. Since the rules of social behavior forbade one officer to visit the quarters of another while he was gone, it was usually understood that whatever went on at the club was purposely being done under the scrutiny of everyone, a kind of public chaperoning. It was accepted socially as long as each participant was careful to stay at arm's length.

Jessica, on the other hand, loathed self-discipline, electing instead to flaunt her disdain for the system by foregoing any phony pretenses. She assumed that everyone else had to be secretly carrying on the same as she was; as she so often rationalized, she simply had the courage to dispense with the formality of having to pretend she was only interested in casual conversation or a few twirls around the dance floor. In her mind, there was little point served in diluting the 'goings on' of a perfectly good evening by playing some childish game. After all, as she loved to mumble under her breath, "What am I supposed to do, check into a convent while he's away?"

Jessica would stake herself out like a decoy at the pool, sometimes with her children, but usually without in order to present a younger more detached image to the field of men. She always put on an air of innocence, acting as if she were unaware of the alluring picture she was presenting, pretending to be surprised when a man would happen onto her beach towel to talk, like a bug landing unsuspectingly on flypaper. It was a ritual that usually involved a juvenile conversation about money, cars, travel and an exchange of adolescent, sexual innuendoes. At some particular point in the conversation, Jessica either would put on the captured, submissive act or go ice cold, to the suitor's surprise.

If Jessica found the man desirable, then she would consent to 'do the club with him.' She would delight in showing up in something threateningly revealing, giving the old crows, as she referred to the officers' wives as a group, a quick supremo glance before walking off with a smile to dine and dance on the terrace in her escort's arms until the early hours. There would have been little difficulty in finding a volunteer from that particular group of women to deliver the fatal coup-de-grâce to Jessica if lechery had been punishable by a firing squad. However, the best the group could hope for was that she would be found out, caught in the act, so that the vigilance committee, the officer's wives, could pass judgment that would be a fate worse than anything the military could impose, as Jason already had found out at Barksdale.

However, as hard as they tried, no one ever succeeded in catching Jessica with one of her gentlemen admirers beyond the confines of the club, much less in some compromising position. They were as sure of her debauchery as they were that the sun would rise, but much less able to prove it. And there were some who would have gone for her jugular without proof, had it not conflicted with the business of the Air Force.

So Jessica continued her libertine lifestyle, ignoring the damage she was inflicting again on Jason's career, unconcerned with her own image, boring full speed ahead to satisfy her insatiable appetites. She whiled away the hours, spurned by everyone except her spontaneous lovers, biding her time until Jason returned. She soon began to look forward to being transferred to another base, with a new set of faces, and a fresh start at the same game; never mind what had instigated the transfer. So she spent her 'wanting to be alone days' sunbathing quietly on her private perch, an open-air, second-story patio at one end of the house. She was fully aware that only forty yards away a three-story barracks overlooked her private pavilion. When the mood struck her she would shed her swimsuit and move out away from the low privacy wall, to give the gallery of enlisted men a better view of the hills and valleys of Puerto Rico. Nonchalantly, she would go about her business, to the occasional whistles and catcalls from the windows, enjoying every second of the attention.

During Jason's absence from Ramey, Jessica frequently enjoyed the company of enlisted men. Since this was strictly prohibited, it was much more difficult for Jessica to arrange an evening with one of them than an officer. However, most of the airmen had been stationed on the island long enough that they would have gleefully climbed the one-hundred-foot walls of Devil's Cliff to have the opportunity of an intimate evening with an English-speaking woman, especially one as attractive as Jessica.

During an officer's wives club style show, Jessica had occasion to meet a young airman from Photography who had been assigned by the base newspaper to do a series of pictures for a local interest story. She saw the photo essay as an important career opportunity, since she was one of the models in the show. When it was brought to her attention that the story would be circulated worldwide, she became even more ruthless in her efforts to dominate as many of the posed photographs as she could. She approached the photo opportunity by laying on the charm and flirting with the photographer to the point the other participants quickly realized her intentions and retreated.

The young airman was an unusually handsome man, a tall, dark-haired, swarthy Italian, well endowed with his native accent and European mannerisms. Between Jessica's stalking the attractive young man and his suave, hand-sucking European hustle on her, there was enough hot vibes radiating from the pair to wilt a flower. It was an uninhibited circus, her maneuvering to stay in front of his camera lens, and him with his Italian blood boiling over as he dreamed of splitting the sheets with the dark-haired beauty.

As the young airman, Fraddie Delanoe, artistically snapped off his shots, slinging the black film clips in and out of the box camera, Jessica smiled and giggled with loud, contrived laughter. She slipped into one pose after another, telegraphing a promise of reward for his preferential treatment with a certain look on her face. Small groups of women from the club stood gawking at the exhibition, shaking their heads in disbelief as Jessica ignored them to pursue her dream of becoming a cover girl.

Fraddie had snapped enough exposures to fill the Sunday edition of the New York Times, leaving an observer reminded of watching an old western movie where the six-shooter seemed to have an inexhaustible supply of ammo.

When Jessica had finished her debut into the modeling world, they moved onto the terrace of the club to discuss further photo techniques. It was mutually agreed that another meeting would be necessary to select the best pictures for the upcoming publication, and of course provide Jessica with an excuse to see more of the dapper young man.

See more of him, she did. In fact, she saw so much of him that he was able to make a complete anatomical study of Jessica with and without film, for the sake of art, of course. Unfortunately, another airman had happened onto several prints while they were being processed at the photo lab, innocently selecting a few for his walls, unaware of the model's identity.

While making an inspection of the airmen's barracks an observant officer had spotted Jessica's exposed likeness, discreetly taking custody of all copies of the pictures, and turned them over to his commanding officer, along with the name of the photographer. Airman Delanoe was strongly advised to find another subject for his photoplay, which he willingly did, slipping into obscurity rather than attend remedial training at Leavenworth Prison.

Jessica was totally unaware of the discovery of the pictures, thinking instead that she'd been jilted by her lover. After a barrage of attempted phone calls and notes to the man, Jessica realized the hopelessness of her efforts. Her ego had been sorely bruised and demanded revenge, which she pursued with a fury. She relentlessly shadowed the poor devil until he was forced to disappear completely. Her last resort was his commanding officer. When the commander consented to talk to her she presented him with a lengthy fabrication about the airman trying to take advantage of her during an innocent photo session. She was unaware that the officer had a portfolio of the confiscated work in his desk, and most of her correspondence to Airman Delanoe. Jessica appeared satisfied that Fraddie's desertion was a result of his transfer and nothing to do with her. When she'd left the office, the officer pulled the manila envelope from his desk, retrieving the glossy photos to compare his thoughts about his visitor with the pictures. "Nice legs," he remarked, slipping the photographs back into the envelope. He pressed the intercom key, "Sergeant Walker?"

"Yes sir," a voice answered.

"Get hold of that airman Delanoe. Make sure he keeps his ass put until we can get him shipped outa here next week. That Lavoisier bitch is gonna have his balls if she figures out he's still on base."

"Yes, sir," the Sergeant answered with a snicker.

"Find out when her husband's squadron is due in from Bentwater, England; I want'a see him as soon as he sets foot on this base."

CHAPTER 19

Jessica revved the car engine, rolling a few feet forward as the car in front cleared the security checkpoint. The guard gave her identification card a quick glance as he checked her name against his roster. He handed the I.D. card back to her, shining his flashlight through the back window on the two sleeping children. "Okay, ma'am, just follow the car ahead of you," he grunted.

Jessica drove on, following the chain of red lights weaving in front of her. Another airman, armed with a carbine, motioned for her to pull her car into line with the others, parked in neat rows, outside the enormous silver and black hanger. A mix of orange and red road markers were the only source of light, giving the people that were filing into the building, an eerie, zombie-like appearance.

Jessica took her place in line, tugging unsympathetically on her two children as they continued to submit to the overwhelming desire for sleep. She pulled them to waiting chairs set in orderly rows across the floor of the massive hanger. Most of the women sat sipping on scalding coffee, talking to other women as their children squirmed and shifted in their metal chairs, looking for a comfortable spot to continue their sleep.

A loud electric screech ripped through the tranquil mood of the crowd, shocking the children awake and jolting the semiconscious adults into an attentive posture. The officer at the microphone stood looking over at the amplifier of the P.A. system as if he had expected the system to malfunction.

"Good morning," he said, as another burst of feedback escaped from the bullhorns encircling the listeners. "In a few minutes the squadron will be landing. As you know, it's been a long TDY, and many of you have had to endure a lengthy separation from your husbands. General Sullivan, Commander of Ramey Air Force, has asked me to thank you for your patience and support for coming out this morning to welcome the squadron home from their mission to England. The tower has notified us that they have radio contact with the first aircraft and that their ETA is twenty minutes."

The room came alive with cheers and excitement as hundreds of women began to apply makeup and unleash waves of combs and brushes to attack the uncooperative heads of children.

After a quick lecture on keeping control of the children and staying behind the barricades, while the crews unloaded, the families were dismissed and allowed to move to the flight line to await the arrival of the squadron.

A flickering metallic reflection sparked a bright explosion of light from the opposite end of the runway as the first aircraft angled into the sunlight and touched down. Applause broke loose from the crowd as sounds of reversing engines reached the anxious gathering. A lumbering B-29 Stratofortress rolled towards the reception area, the deafening noise of its engines drowning every sound except that of its squealing brakes. The Air Force Band began to strike up a medley of patriotic marches.

Jessica took her place in the crowd of onlookers as the more impatient women moved to the front and tried to identify the heads that bobbed inside the cockpits of the mammoth aircraft. As the engines stopped, an arm poked out of the pilot's window and gave the thumbs up sign, prompting another round of applause from the crowd. The belly hatches of the bomber's fuselage popped open, and ladders slipped with a jarring clank to the ground, quickly followed by men in loosely fitting jump suits and discarded parachutes dropping down onto the concrete apron.

Women leaped over the barricades, out-maneuvering the guards with moves that would have caught the eye of a professional football scout. Even when the identity of their husbands was mistaken, airmen would joyfully embrace the charging wife, taking advantage of the mood to have a little fun. The crowd would roar its approval, as the embarrassed woman would return to the starting line after being given a generous kiss by the flyer.

The B-29s moved into a single line formation, pivoting until each faced the direction of the crowd. The roar from the engines made a deafening drone as they burned off the last residues of fuel before the yellow striped propellers would stop. The crowd, ignoring the security guards, moved down the line of bombers, searching for their loved ones. Huddles of husbands and wives with children clinging to the fathers' legs or nestled in the flyers' arms held emotional reunions up and down what now looked like the fairway at a carnival. Jessica spotted Jason as he dropped to the ground from the ladder. He paused, looking at her with a funny boyish smile and then dropped his bag to grasp her tightly in his arms. They stood for a moment, ignoring the rest of the world, talking, whispering, embracing. Then Jason felt the tug from the two boys, finally reaching out and pulling David to his side and lifting Dale into his arms.

It was an exciting day for the children, who were now wide awake, climbing through the forward cabins of the giant bombers with their fathers, getting short lectures on knobs and switches. The highlight of the tour was the trip through the tunnel that connected the forward compartments from the rear areas with a trolley car mechanism. The children moved through the tunnel on the small-wheeled cart, preferring to stay and entertain themselves in the 'tube' rather than continue the tour.

When Jason and Jessica arrived home they were met at the front door by Carmel, a young Puerto Rican girl whom Jessica had hired as a maid and sitter for the boys. Jason set his flight bag in the living room and slipped upstairs with Jessica for a moment together. They boys had trapped the small maid in the kitchen to examine each and every one of nearly a hundred lead soldiers that Jason had brought them from London. Carmel nodded and made a few remarks in Spanish, not understanding a single word the two boys were saying as they showed her their prizes.

Jason and Jessica had a passionate reunion, finding themselves hot and sweaty as they separated and lay facing the ceiling fan as small prisms of light projected through the wooden, louvered slats in the windows. Ribbons of light striped their naked bodies, as if they were wearing skintight prison garments. Jason held Jessica in his arms as both of them lay quietly, acting more as if they had just experienced a new lover than a reunion of husband and wife.

"I'm really glad to be home, Jessica. It was too long for us to be separated. A lot of the fellas are going to resign because of the problems they're having with their wives."

"What kind of problems?" Jessica asked quickly.

"Ah, like Charlie Kincade's wife. She's gone back to the States for detox; tried to do herself in with booze and pills 'cause Charlie's been gone so much. It'll give him a chance to get home a little early and try to straighten things out.

"Oh, that's too bad…so what was it like in England?" she said, half-interested in his statement. "Was it as beautiful as they say?"

"It was fabulous, Jessica! The countryside is lush with flowers and the darkest green grass you've ever seen. The English really know how to live. They have the most elegant homes, most of them older than our country," Jason went on, with his eyes fixed on the window as he tried to dream his way back.

Jessica pulled herself closer to Jason, pressing her head against his bare chest before she asked him, "What do English girls look like? Are they as pretty as I am?"

Jason didn't answer for a few seconds, then said "Pretty fast gals. I mean, they think different than we do. A lot of fellas got married to English girls over there. A lot of them are really attractive, especially when you see a pretty one and listen to her speak the Queen's English. A couple of the boys are even gettin' divorces from their wives to go back over there and get married."

"Why would they ever want to do that, marry some foreigner?"

Jason looked over at her. "The Air Force can take the blame for most of that. I mean, they should have brought some of those fellas home sooner!"

"You missed me, didn't you, Jason?" she quizzed him, licking her upper lip.

"You know I did," Jason replied. "I never have wanted anyone else. It's just nice to be home," he said, crushing his cigarette out in the ashtray next to the bed and turning his attentions to Jessica's beckoning pull.

Jason was taken back by Jessica's beauty, as if he had forgotten her stunning, almost supernatural loveliness. It was a loveliness that was strikingly pleasing to look at, but somehow seemed more at home in the dark, like the black widow with its exotic beauty luring its prey to a greater fate than just an intimate encounter.

Jason slipped into a deep sleep as Jessica dressed and went downstairs. She began to unpack his flight bags, removing his clothes for Carmel to wash. She was distracted by several gifts that he'd brought for her and the children, trying on a necklace or ring, or admiring the delicate bone china and silver he'd carried home in a separate box. In one crate she found two gold anniversary clocks and a china music box with a tiny petite porcelain ballerina that danced out of sync to the tune that played from the box. Jessica smiled as she watched the dancer spin effortlessly in a circle to a now faster tempo as she wound the automaton with its brass key. While she listened to the music her hands moved through Jason's luggage, pulling out clothing and packages. Then they discovered a heavy flat object lying at the bottom of his bag. She pulled the rectangular-shaped package out and unwrapped it, coming face to face with the picture of a woman that she'd never seen before. It was a relatively recent photograph with an inscription to Jason written across the lower portion of the picture.

Jessica analyzed the black and white photo as if she were studying an animal, deciding where to place the killing shot. Her temper raged as she read the note. It was a poetic verse that announced the woman's admiration for Jason and an appreciation for his kindness towards her family while he was a guest in her home. The inscription could have been interpreted a thousand ways, or simply taken at face value as an expression of sincere appreciation for Jason's thoughtfulness for something he'd done for her.

No matter the reason, almost anyone, except Jessica, would have given her husband the benefit of the doubt over the circumstantial evidence until the matter had been discussed. Jessica, on the other hand, seethed with a desire to collar the woman, standing her up for a blow with an accusative statement and then delivering a finishing verbal shot that would have weakened the knees of a Marine drill sergeant.

She sat braced at the kitchen table, drafting her charges into a letter, as if a tribunal would deliver the document to the English woman. Jessica smiled to herself as she applied her skillful manipulation of the scanty facts into a repugnant attack on the woman's character. When she'd finished with her scarlet note, she sealed it, searching through Jason's personal effects until she located the woman's address and then slipped away to send the stinging letter secretly on its way.

Jason was unaware of the letter Jessica had sent to his English admirer for nearly two months, accidentally coming across the woman's confused response to Jessica's scalding indictment, stashed in a niche in Jessica's closet. The woman had addressed her letter to Jason, pleading her dismay and embarrassment at Jessica's unprovoked attack on her and her family. Jason was outraged. He walked down the stairs, hustled the boys outside and then stormed into the kitchen where Jessica was throwing supper together.

He flipped the letter onto the kitchen table, staring at her until she turned around, noticing his clenched jaw.

"Good God, what's the matter with you?" she asked.

"You're the matter with me…you and your vile temper!"

Jessica glanced at the letter lying on the table, suddenly realizing that Jason had found the evidence of her ill-conceived deed.

"Why did you send that letter? Why in God's name would you do somethin' like that?" he demanded.

"Why shouldn't I? I'm not going to stand around while you carry on with her behind my back!"

"Do what?" Jason responded.

"I saw your little memento, her with the cutesy little smile on her face!"

"You wrote that horrible letter because of a picture? A picture that had nothing to do with anything? And then you hid her letter to me, so that I wasn't able to apologize for your filthy attack on her and her family? Why would you do something like that?"

"Why? I could tell from that picture that you had something going on with her…that she was trying to keep the spark alive until your next little visit. I'm nobody's fool!" Jessica shouted, taking a swipe at the letter and sending it flying.

Jason wiped his face with both hands in frustration. "I'm gonna tell you something about that picture, and then I'm going over to the club and get as drunk as I can, to drown my embarrassment over what you've done."

"What I've done?" Jessica snapped.

"That's right," he said. "Dave Benson, Art Howard and I were on our way to London for a weekend. We watched an airman from our base, drunk on his ass, plow into a car, head-on. The three of us pulled the airman's body out of the wreck; then we pulled the body of the driver out of the other car that was burning."

Jessica interrupted, "That's real touching, Jason. So, what's the point?"

"The point is that the man that our guy hit had his son in the car with him. The little boy was badly burned by the time we finally were able to get him out of the wreck. The three of us spent a lot of time raising money and doing blood drives to try and help the little fella make it. Well, he didn't pull through."

"What's that have to do with you getting involved with her?"

"I wasn't involved with her, Jessica. The three of us were invited to stay with the family after the boy died, some sort of appreciation for what we'd tried to do. When we got word that we were being sent home she gave each of us a picture, her picture, as a memento to remember Mark, the little boy, because she didn't have any pictures of him. The picture had nothing to do with anything, except to say thanks to us. She lost her husband, her only child, and you managed to do a super job of finishing off her self-respect," Jason continued, standing up and shaking his head. "What the hell ever happened to you to make you so goddamn cold and ruthless with people? What is it, Jessica?"

Jason turned around and started up the stairs to his bedroom, with Jessica staring at him, having only heard his final remarks. "I'm not buying that bull shit, Jason. I'll tell you what happened to me; I married a damn wimp, a spineless coward! You know how I can tell, because I've had better men than you right here in this house, in your bed. And if you don't believe me, just ask your kids. Ask them about Uncle Fraddie and some of the others. I don't have to sit around waiting for you!" she shrieked. "I can have any man I want, any time I want him. I certainly don't need a cowering worm like you!" she yelled, before Jason slammed the bedroom door.

Fraddie's name hadn't gone unheard by Jason. After a week of investigative snooping, Jason was able to confirm Jessica's true confessions to be anything but idle boasting. Airman Fraddie Delanoe had indeed been real, as Jason soon found out, while standing in Fraddie's ex-commander's office.

The Colonel surprised Jason, acting as though he had been expecting him to come. "I guess you're here about the pictures. Well, I've got 'em all," he said, opening his desk and pulling out the envelope. "Look, Major, nothin' personal, but this is delicate stuff that could get both our names in front of the General. I got a shot at a promotion coming up, and I don't need your family problems gettin' between me and my career. My part of the problem has been resolved; Airman Delanoe is gone.

"All you've got to do is handle this thing with your wife with a little discretion, and everybody will be happy," the Colonel added, almost pleading.

Jason was dumbfounded by the pictures. He'd come for information about his wife's affair with Airman Delanoe and instead had a blockbuster dropped into his lap. He saluted the senior officer and stuck the well-worn envelope under his arm, acting as if he'd known all about the photographs.

"Look, son, I don't know what your problem at home is all about, but I think if I were you I'd spend a little time with that good-lookin' wife of yours. Take some time off, go over to San Juan or catch a hop over to Havana for a few days…the change 'ull do wonders for yah, for both of yah! See if you can put this thing behind you!"

Jason left the office, stunned and humiliated. He drove to an isolated beach that he knew about near the base, a gunnery range known as Crash Boat Landing. He made his way down a suspended metal staircase that dropped to the ocean, thirty yards below. The waves had cut a small cove into the cliff, cutting the beach off from the rest of the shoreline, and leaving a fifty-yard patch of white sand, dotted with empty shell casings and spent bullets.

For awhile, Jason perched himself on a boulder several yards out from shore, squatting down with a cigarette trapped in his lips, his mind somewhere on the horizon. He dreamed of another time, trying to call upon a pleasant memory that would take the pain away, but all of his good memories had left him when he needed them most.

The crashing of waves brought him back, alerting him to the rising tide that would soon make it impossible to reach shore, a trip that would be much easier to deal with than what he'd experienced in his life thus far with Jessica. He waded back to the small strip of beach that hadn't been consumed by the waves, digging a hole with his bare foot. He opened the package, realizing his worst fears. He looked briefly at the first shots and then, without going further, set fire to the package with his lighter, laying it in the small hole he'd dug in the sand. He watched as the fire sent a black puff of smoke into the wind, then sizzled as a blanket of foam from the ocean washed over the incinerator, putting out the fire before it had done its work.

Jason watched the waves carry the pictures out to sea, spreading the unburned prints out on the water as if on display. "Even the satisfaction of doing this is taken away from me. God, what have I gotten myself into?

He climbed the metal ladder, looking down as the tide swallowed the last stretch of sand below him. The steel ladder swayed in the wind, moving the stairs against the side of the cliff and moaning as the cables stretched from the movement of the breeze and Jason's weight.

Two months later, in July of 1952, James and Lora made a trip to Puerto Rico to visit Jason and his family. They arrived in San Juan by ocean liner from Miami, taking two rooms at the Caribbean Hilton. James had elected to stay in San Juan, at the resort, to give Jason and his family a break from the monotony of the base and give him a chance to discuss some business with his son, in private.

The reunion was noticeably subdued as Jessica stood by while James and Lora heartily embraced the children and Jason, then offered her a reserved greeting. The family visited for several hours, and then Lora suggested that she take the boys swimming while James and Jason had a chance to visit. Jessica had deserted the group a few minutes earlier to visit the dress shops in the hotel's lobby.

James poured two shots of whiskey into a glass of ice and handed one to Jason. He sat down, twirling the ice cubes in his drink, lost in a private moment as Jason studied him, aware that he had something on his mind.

"I can't stand all these damn ninny drinks these Puerto Ricans like to concoct down here! I'll stick to my whiskey," James said with a laugh, breaking out of his trance.

Jason chuckled nervously in response, taking a swallow from his glass.

James stopped fiddling with his drink, then looked up at Jason. "Boys looked a little quiet; you and Jessica having some problems?"

Jason hesitated for an instant. 'Yeah, things aren't exactly what you'd call great.

"She giving the boys a hard time?"

Jason snorted, "Hell, she's giving all of us a hard time. The kids are gettin' the worst end of most of it, though, I guess cause they're the first ones she can tie into when she's pissed off about something. She's been actin' this way ever since I got back from England."

"I suspect it's been going on longer than that, hasn't it, son?"

Jason looked surprised. "I've been gone so much, Dad, I guess I don't know what she's been doing. David's got somethin' seriously wrong with his stomach and Dale's teachers are saying he's got a learning problem."

"What about you?" James asked. "How are you faring with all of this?"

"Other than being humiliated constantly by her cavorting with every man on the base, I guess I'll survive," Jason answered, lowering his head in defeat.

James reflected silently on the incident at Love's Lookout before replying. "Look, son, I'm not trying to pry. You're a grown man. You need to get a grip on this problem and get that bullshit taken care of, once and for all. I don't wanta see you or the boys going through hell because of her. You've always known how I felt about Jessica, so we won't belabor that point. I don't look kindly on what she's done to my grandsons either!"

"I know, Dad, and I'm going to have to do something about it! It's just that I haven't had time to take care of the problem. It's easy to let the situation slide when I'm gone all the time. I know you're worried about the boys, but I'll take care of them; I promise."

James slugged down his drink and poured himself another one before continuing. "That's not the only thing I came down here to talk to you about. I've got some problems of my own that I need your help with, but, by God, this other thing with her better get taken care of, and I mean it."

James reached for his medical bag that was sitting next to the table. He reached inside and pulled out two large stacks of bills held together with rubber bands, laying them on the table in front of him.

"Jesus, Dad, why the hell are you traveling with that much cash? How'd you get through customs with all that?"

"Being a doctor still has its privileges," he said, downing another shot of his drink. "I'm gonna need for you to hang onto this for awhile, until I ask for it back."

Jason picked up a packet of cash, thumbing through the bills, trying to mentally count as he responded, "Sure Dad, but why'd you bring it down here?"

"All of a sudden I'm finding myself a little top-heavy with cash from a few real estate deals. I've gotten a little concerned about rumors that the government's got treasury agents snooping around banks all over east Texas. Rumor has it that they want to see if they can catch a few tax evaders as an example to everyone else, a little Yankee extortion to fill Washington's coffers."

"I don't see any problem; we can put it in my lock box at the base," Jason said.

"Not unless you've got one hell of a big safe deposit box," James responded, hoisting first one and then a second shoebox-sized stack of bills onto the table next to the two smaller packets.

"Good God," Jason gasped. "If I didn't know better, I'd think you'd knocked off a bank!"

"Not quite, but if the treasury people find out about this I could be in just about as much trouble. You've got to make damn sure that Jessica is kept out of this. There's two-hundred-and-four-thousand dollars here, the four-thousand is yours."

"Where the hell am I going to put this much money without raising a few eyebrows?" Jason asked, still trying to fully grasp the reality of what was sitting in front of him.

I've arranged for you to have a safe deposit box here in San Juan. We'll go down to the bank later and put this in the vault. You can sign the authorization card and make me the beneficiary, in case anything happens. If anything was to come of me and your mother, use the money as you see fit for you and the boys. Just do me a favor and make sure that no one else gets their hands on it! If anyone gets wind of this, you may have to take a quick trip to Havana and deposit it there."

The visit was short, with Jason having to return to Ramey the following Monday for a two-day flight. Before they left, Jason had arranged to give James and Lora some time alone with the boys. James felt a deep sense of compassion for what he knew the two boys were going through. His years as a physician had made it all too easy to diagnose the abuse that was taking place at Jessica's hands. Unfortunately, there was little James could do about it.

Dale was responsive, acting almost starved for the outpouring of affection from James and Lora, while David was withdrawn, preferring instead to sleep or be alone, playing with the toys that James and Lora had brought for him from the States. Jessica made no excuses for the strange behavior, except to say, over and over again, that it was from living in the hot climate.

With James and Lora gone, Jason and the boys returned to their usual routine at home, going about their daily existence just as they had before the visit. Jessica, on the other hand, had become increasingly temperamental, suspicious that James and Lora had been plotting against her with Jason. In the weeks that followed, she unleashed a wave of stinging, unprovoked attacks against Jason, always in front of Dale and David. One of her tirades had been so vulgar and loud that the air police had been called by neighbors, concerned that something might happen to the two boys. The incident with the air police was enough to calm the storm of discontentment for a few days, long enough for the neighborhood to return to normal.

Jason had received an invitation to attend a formal affair at the officer's club, a promotion party being given for a senior officer from his squadron. The invitation was, of course, extended to both Jason and Jessica as a matter of protocol; however, there were those who would have liked to have made an exception. The very mention of a party, and Jessica would begin a strange metamorphosis.

She would feel an odd sense of urgency as she plotted and prepared her tactics with exact precision, deciding what she would wear, her mood for the evening, and which females she would target for her meticulous emotional defacing during the evening's social exchange, a contest, as she saw it. An evening like this was as serious to her as an athlete pursuing a medal.

The evening was unusually calm with the wives of the other officers duly warned of Jessica's 'MO', like a herd of gazelles moving ahead of a stalking lioness on the Serengeti. All was uneventful from the receiving line to the orchestra's last melody of the evening. Jessica had had her usual overdose of champagne, becoming light-headed enough to loosen what little inhibitions she still possessed. Her frustrations for the failed evening landed squarely on Jason, and she cut into him with insults that increased in volume as her drinking continued and the other guests steered clear of her. By the time they had left the club and had begun to drive home, Jessica had launched herself into a rage, swinging her verbal knife to castrate the last vestige of Jason's manhood and devour his self-respect.

The next day was Sunday, and Jessica had sobered up but she continued her siege of Jason's ego, chipping away with a relentless abuse of his character. Jason finally had had enough of the battering and he moved into the dining room. She could hear him rummaging through the front closet before he finally sat down at the dining room table.

Jessica interrupted her assault as she studied Jason's movements, trying to see what he was doing through the opening into the dining room. Suddenly she froze in panic as she watched Jason remove a pistol from the gun case he'd taken from the front hall closet. He jerked back the action with a loud metal-on-metal clatter, and then inserted the clip. Before she could move out of sight he held up the pistol, raising it up level to his eye, sighting it at an imaginary target on the wall, then squeezed the trigger. 'Click'.

Jason gave her a quick look and then quietly began to remove springs and screws from the weapon, creating a puzzle of parts that now lay heaped on the table, prompting Jessica to return to her insults, confident that no harm would come to her. Within seconds she was back to full power, and leaving him cringing as he worked to reassemble the gun. She moved towards the table, carrying her taunting remarks with her, delighted with his frustration as she stood with her hands on her hips, rocking her head from side to side as she became louder and louder.

Jason peered up at her as he inserted the last piece to the puzzle, blindly reaching into the gun box for an ammo clip and slamming it into the butt of the automatic. As he felt the clip lock into place he charged the action with a single effortless flip, holding the pistol in Jessica's direction as he looked down at the mechanism. Without thinking about the direction the muzzle was pointing, he pulled the trigger. The pistol discharged with a deafening roar, slamming Jason's arm back from the recoil and filling the room with a soft haze and tiny sparks of burning powder. The projectile traveled past Jessica's head, hit the plaster wall and left a cratering hole that opened to the sunlight outside.

Jessica reached for her face, feeling the spot on her forehead where the bullet had tickled her skin as it passed on its way to the wall. Fragments of white chalky dust drifted down, landing on the table where Jason sat, still holding the smoking weapon.

Jason looked at the hole in the wall, taking a quick glance at Jessica to assure himself that she was still alive, and then looked back down at the smoking pistol. His left hand moved over to the weapon as if to relieve the other hand, clicking on the safety as he laid the firearm down on the table. He stood up slowly, shaking his head at her with his mouth partially open, then swallowing as he backed away from the table.

"I swear to God I didn't mean to fire that shot, Jessica! I had no idea that there was anything in there! I swear to you it…just went off!"

Jessica was still stunned from the loud report of the blast that had been amplified by the walls of the room. She covered her ears with both hands, looking at the thin beam of light cutting across the room from the hole in the wall. As she followed the beam from the wall to the table, Jason could see her eyes light up as they landed on his.

"I'm not sure whether you're surprised how it happened, or surprised how you missed, you bastard! I can't believe you did this, you gutless imp!" she screamed, walking towards the foot of the stairs.

"Don't worry, Jason, I don't really think you did it on purpose. You haven't got the balls to kill me. You're too much of a coward to kill anyone, and you only pretend to be a man," she snipped, then walked up the stairs, shaking her head, trying to clear the ringing from her ears.

Jason pulled the clip out of the gun, staring at it. He wondered if he'd done it on purpose. The clip was empty. A single brass shell ejected from the pistol lay on the floor, taken from a full box of ammunition that lay open in the bottom of the gun case. He wondered if he'd purposely slipped the single shell into the clip, wanting to kill her.

Perhaps she'd done it, he thought. Maybe she'd hoped he'd accidentally shoot himself. It was just one more strike against him, almost as if she were expecting him to try it, knowing that he'd fail, knowing that she'd have one more thing to humiliate him with.

CHAPTER 20

The details of the family's transfer to Forbes Air Force Base from Ramey seemed as clear to Dale as if they had arrived that morning. Now, sitting in James' room, his recollection of their first arrival at the base in Topeka, Kansas stirred his memory only for a brief moment. It was his remembrance of the last visit he'd made to Forbes, years after everything had happened and after his family had come apart, that held him spellbound in James' rocking chair.

He'd gone back, to walk himself through ten years of memories, to visit his boyhood home, as people often do; but the visit was more typical of a jury being taken to observe the scene of a crime than a happy reunion with one's past.

Dale remembered his visit, how queer it was that it had been so easy for him to find his way around the huge site that the base once had occupied. Street signs still rested squarely on metal posts as if expecting whoever had taken the buildings to return them and place them back on the stumps of concrete showing from behind stands of weeds.

He drove down the streets, stopping frequently as something would catch his eye, a landmark that would evoke an image of a structure where a part of his life had passed. He could see the ghost of the buildings, hear the sounds of the people who had filled the streets, and hear the noises and taste the smells as if he were an intruder in a colossal dream.

But his dream finally faded, leaving him standing in front of an open field filled with rubble and piles of debris. He drove on further into the base.

He could still hear the officers responding in his vision to orders echoing across the flight line as columns of airmen moved into position to pass in review. The families would sit in the hot morning sun, patriotically enduring the heat and winds to do their duty, filing onto the bleachers to sit and watch the parades that they'd seen a hundred times before. He'd remembered watching as some officer would out-distance his men because the guidon wasn't paying attention; and of course there was always someone out of step, skipping endlessly in the moving column, trying to find their rhythm, only to upset the pace of those marching behind.

Dale's mirage of his khaki-uniformed legions faded again as he stirred from his dream, sitting in his car looking out over an empty expanse of weed-infested concrete and asphalt, void of any life except a rabbit gone berserk, trying to find its burrow.

'So many people,' he'd remembered thinking, 'it was like something had devoured a city and everyone who had lived there.'

Dale sat deathly still in the rocking chair, thinking about the deafening roar of jets firing their engines across the flight line, leaving the smell of spent fuel drifting across the base, watching the heat from the hot Kansas sun lifting the waves of fumes into the atmosphere. Even the vision of B-47s landing with their bright orange drag chutes trailing behind was as clear as it had been when he was a boy. His vision suddenly materialized into little more than a dust devil in a distant Kansas wheat field, breaking his concentration on the past as he decided it was time to move on.

He remembered that his last stop on the base that day, oddly enough, had been the base hospital, or what had been the base hospital. It was the only brick building on the base, an extravagant structure built just before the winds of austerity had fallen upon the Air Force for the umpteenth time.

It had been one of the more unpleasant places he'd visited that day. It was where human remains of crash victims were brought, fathers of Dale's classmates, killed when their planes had crashed near the base.

Dale thought about the times he'd seen the officers from the base crash team come to his classroom to get one of his fellow students for a ride home because that student's father had been killed. There was always that moment when the children would hold their breath, wondering who would be selected. They tried to understand why it had happened to that particular person, and thinking that now that family would have to leave, to go wherever it was that families went after the father had died; a sort of banishment to some unknown world.

But that wasn't all that this place reminded him of; he'd had his first look at death here, a boy forced to face the reality of death by his father, thinking in some distorted way that it was for his son's benefit to see what death was like.

Jason had brought David and Dale to the hospital because he had to identify one of the airmen in his squadron, killed in an auto-train accident. Jason had decided that it would be good for the boys to experience the reality of death, since they both would be driving in the future, a little incentive to be careful.

Dale remembered being paraded past the wire stretcher that held the man's remains while an airman sat in the corner of the sterile-looking tile room, filling out paperwork to process the man's remains out of the Air Force.

The pungent smell of alcohol hung in the air as Dale shuffled past the corpse, looking down at the stilled figure and wondering how everyone could act so calm, talking and smoking, none of them shocked, as he was, at seeing the man asleep under the examination lights.

Dale stopped at the end of the basket to look at the man's face, waiting to see if he would breathe, wondering how it had felt to die.

"Come on, Dale, quit lookin' at him," he heard David whisper, pulling him out of the room.

Even after all the years had passed, he couldn't understand his father's reasoning for doing such a thing, not to boys that young. His dad seemed to have been pleased with himself as he noticed the profound effect the experience had had on both boys. Dale and David were in a state of shock as they left the morgue.

Dale remembered leaving Forbes and driving across the highway to Capehart, a housing reservation for Air Force personnel working at the base. The elements of time had taken their toll on the housing project, leaving few of the homes inhabitable. Like the base, Dale had little trouble finding his way around the old neighborhood.

"Trees...I don't remember there being trees out here," he said to himself. It brought home the reality of how long it had been since he'd left, but it seemed like yesterday. He drove slowly past the playgrounds and derelict homes devoid of windows and curtains, a random door hanging on by a single screw in the hinge as the wind patiently worked to loosen the house's final grip on the door.

His mind fought off his first impression of the deserted community, an impression that a disaster had taken place here, but he knew better. He remembered the people who had lived here as he drove by a house or favorite gathering spot.

'That was Candy's home, and Hal Hammond lived over there,' he thought, 'and Floyd lived up on the hill; his dad was a bird Colonel.'

His car rolled to a stop, and his eyes glanced over at one of the houses as if some force were beckoning to him. A cold eerie feeling that something was calling to him, something that had been expecting him to return, made his heart race as he stepped out of the car.

'We really are creatures of habit,' he thought, knowing now that he'd taken the path to his old house. This was the place where the hard realities of life had exploded in front of him, much the same as his shock at having his first look at death, across the highway at the hospital.

He struggled to make himself step into the house, moving through the darkened hallway, stepping past the debris that littered the floor. He stopped, looking back at the kitchen, hearing his mother and father talking, and then fighting, about something she'd done.

The rooms were smaller than he'd remembered. He stood in the living room trying to place the living room furniture in his mind, but for some reason he couldn't remember there being any furniture in there. And then it occurred to him that Jessica had taken all of the furnishings with her when she'd left.

He opened the door to his bedroom, stepping inside, moving from habit to the farthest corner from the door. His eyes closed as he struggled to control his thoughts, trying not to see the figure standing at the door, swearing at him, waving her hands and then charging him as he slid down in the corner, trying to conceal his body, and fend off the blows from her fists. He realized that he had slipped into the same position, sliding down against the wall, squatting in his old defensive pose, gasping for breath with perspiration soaking his shirt as he remembered one of many attacks. It was so long ago, but somehow the rage, the hate, was still there.

She'd come like a wild animal whenever she needed to vent her anger about something. Standing in the door at any hour of the day or night with a wild look on her face, she would scream some obscenity and then the beating would start.

She was like a bear, clawing and slapping, intensifying her attack the more he struggled, until he finally learned to lie still as she beat on him. He knew that if he didn't cry out she'd tire of listening to herself and then she would leave, mumbling her justification for the attack as she'd walk back to her own room.

Her room was at the end of the hall. It was the room where she'd kept company with the demon. Dale always had thought so anyway, when he was a boy.

He'd never wanted to go into that room after the night he and David had opened her bedroom door and unleashed her fury. That night she appeared at his door, standing like a monster in his darkened room, outlined by the lights from the hallway. She surged towards him, beating him this time until he passed out, lying on the floor until morning when, David came into the room and helped him up.

He remembered getting up, regaining his composure, having had enough of past memories, and leaving the house, thinking something was watching him from her bedroom, the only room he hadn't visited on his tour, the room where she'd kept the demon.

Dale wiped his face as he sat in James' chair, forcing himself to go on thinking about what had happened in Topeka.

Capehart hadn't been the only place they'd lived when they came to Topeka, but it was where Jason and Jessica's marriage finally had ended and, along with it, the start of an infinite number of tragedies for everyone. He leaned back in the chair, thinking about when they first arrived in Topeka.

Dale could remember the Kansas countryside, flat fields of wheat moving in waves, changing colors as if the nap of a golden rug was being rubbed by the fingers of some invisible giant. Thick hedgerows or dark green billowing trees lined the fields, breaking the winds back and separating the deep contrasting green of barley or Alfalfa crops growing on the opposite side. From the air, the fields were an artful composite of patterns as beautiful as a quilter's design. Here and there great silos towered over the land, marking the location of the farmer's home like an enormous surveyor's stake.

Jason had rented a new tract home located midway between the base and downtown Topeka. It was a small three-bedroom home built in a project where the designer's imagination had been limited to one floor plan. Because of the GI Bill and the huge number of people moving into Topeka looking for housing, Jason considered himself lucky to have found a place to rent at all.

Jason had been assigned to a combat-intelligence squadron ordered to photograph Chinese and Soviet military installations and troop movements. The flights required frequent intrusions into the hostile air space of both powers, to snap pictures and record response times, once the bombers were detected on enemy radar. One flight from Forbes already had found its evasion of Soviet fighters deathly inadequate, requiring extensive diplomatic maneuvering to retrieve the bodies of the RB-47 crew.

Jessica willingly accepted her husband's absenteeism, looking at it as an opportunity to test the water, especially since their relationship was still on shaky ground.

At this point, she had decided that her indiscretions could best be concealed if she were to operate within the civilian sector of Topeka, staying clear of the gossip at the base. This was not to say that an occasional dalliance with an airman or lonely officer wouldn't be entertained if the opportunity availed itself.

She had determined that the wealth and power that was so important to her would, after all, be found in the civilian society. Unfortunately, Jessica's concept of a wealthy man was a low budget fantasy, someone who owned a house and didn't have to negotiate with the finance company on a month-to-month basis in order to keep from having their car repossessed. She had not yet evolved to the point of dreaming of diamonds and furs bought for her by a tailor-dressed lover spangled with a gold watch and smoking a fat Havana cigar—at least not yet.

Jessica was determined to become a part of Topeka society. She had no qualms about letting anyone who might have the slightest social influence in the community into her bedroom. Dale and David had watched what had seemed an endless trail of strangers traipsing through the house when their father was gone.

At one point she latched onto David and Dale's school principal, an attractive, recently divorced gentleman whom she'd met at a PTA gathering. He was not particularly well off financially, but seemed to know everyone in Topeka. His hypnotic blue eyes and jet-black hair accentuated his fair complexion, slightly shadowed by the hint of a heavy beard that added a rugged hue to his manly charm. He was an extremely attractive man, but much too pompous for her taste. Nevertheless, he served the purpose for what she wanted.

Jessica would have been satisfied to linger awhile longer with her stunning companion if the affair had not come to the attention of the school board after a complaint from a student's mother, an officer's wife from Forbes who was familiar with Jessica's unsavory reputation.

She abruptly broke it off with the principal just as Jason was returning from a short T.D.Y. in Germany. She was prepared to explain away anything Jason might hear about her escapade as jealous gossip because of her association with the principal while she was innocently involved in PTA work at the school.

Jason returned home from his mission, dreading the revelations about Jessica's activities that always surfaced shortly after he walked through the front door, usually from her own lips. He called her from Operations, informing her that he was home and needed a ride. Jason was standing outside of the Operations office, looking like a derelict who'd just been released from the drunk tank. A cigarette hung from his lips and a two-day growth of beard covered his face as he leaned up against the building in his wrinkled, sad-sack flight suit, wearing a pair of dark aviator sunglasses and a blue uniform cap.

"Hi, Jessica," he said, giving her a quick ceremonious peck on the cheek. "How are you boys doing?" Jason asked, receiving his usual eager embrace from each of the boys.

Jessica looked over at him. "So how was it this time? Your flight jacket is covered in stains; did you get sick?"

"No…just spilled coffee. We got into some really rough weather over the Atlantic. It was knocking the hell out of us…thought that damn plane was coming apart. Colonel Potter got us lost for about an hour, so I'm just glad to finally have my feet on the ground."

"So how long are you home for this time?" Jessica asked, blurting out what she'd been thinking all the way over to the base. "I don't suppose they've said anything yet about your next trip?"

Jason lit a cigarette, leaning towards the driver's side window to return a salute from the air policeman who was peering into the car as they passed the front gate. It gave him a minute to compose his thoughts, to control his temper.

"As a matter of fact, they have. I was going to wait until we got home to tell you that I have orders for another trip in thirty days. We're supposed to go on leave starting tomorrow. I thought we'd all go to Jacksonville to see the folks," Jason added, looking out the window to keep from seeing her reaction. She was as hostile as he had imagined she would be, with or without the news of the impending TDY.

"Why in God's name are they doing this, Jason? How can anyone's marriage survive with the husbands being gone this much? I don't understand why they aren't more considerate of the families."

"I don't like it any more than you do" Jason answered, vexed at the insinuation that he was enthusiastic about another separation from the boys.

Jessica pursed her lips. "I don't suppose you can tell me where you're going and how long you'll be gone this time?"

"I'm not supposed to, but I will…North Africa…Rebal. The orders say, for a year, but that's not firm."

"This is insane, Jason. How can anyone put up with that…or have any kind of a life?" she challenged, raising her voice.

"Yeah, I know…it's tough on everyone. Some of the fellas have put in for transfers to get off flying status because of it. There'll be some families splitting up over this one."

Jessica perked up. "Then why don't you transfer to another squadron? Why are we always forced to go along with everything the Air Force wants us to do? Why can't you just resign?" Jessica muttered.

"Because there's a chance that I'll make the promotion list this time. I'm bound to make Lieutenant Colonel as soon as I get back from this trip. When I get back, I can get off flying status and get my own squadron. There's no way I'm going to resign. This is my life…it's all I've ever wanted to do and I'm not giving it up!"

Jessica sat gritting her teeth for a moment. "Then there's something I want for myself. I want the boys to stay with your parents while you're gone, or at least for awhile, for part of the time while you're away."

Jason looked back at David and Dale. "For God sake, Jessica, don't you think we could discuss this later? The boys don't need to hear us arguing about this!"

"I want the chance to have some peace and quiet…a chance to live a little without being tied down to housework every day, and two kids. Let your mother and dad take care of them, be the martyrs…that's what they've always wanted, anyway!"

"All right, Jessica, maybe everyone would be better off if they did stay with my folks for awhile. You boys wouldn't mind staying with your grandparents, would you?"

Dale and David sat quietly looking at each other, wanting desperately to please their father, a little taken with the idea of getting away from their mother for a while. It wouldn't have mattered if they had objected to the idea. Once Jessica made her wish known, it was a closed case; they would go to Jacksonville, like it or not.

Jason understood the boys were witnessing much of her freewheeling lifestyle while he was away. It had occurred to him that it was in the boys' best interests to live with his parents, to have some stability in their lives. It was the only alternative to his being gone.

It was too much to expect Jessica to make the trip to Texas for the vacation. Jason waited in Topeka for a week for the boys to get out of school before leaving for Jacksonville, bidding Jessica farewell as she stood at the front door, hardly able to control her elation at being alone.

They arrived in Jacksonville about ten o'clock the next morning, turning off South Jackson Street onto the narrow dirt drive that curved around behind the house. The huge pecan trees shaded parts of the yard like a giant circus tent, allowing only a random patch of sunlight to shower the carpet of thick St. Augustine grass. White sheets and pillowcases fluttered on the clothesline; a woman stood behind the wall of clothes, hidden except for a wash basket and her thin pale legs.

A cloud of red iron ore dust rolled over the car as it stopped next to the back porch. Two blacks working in the back lot stopped for a moment to study the car's occupants and then returned to their hoeing.

As soon as the doors of the car opened, the clothesline drooped down low enough to reveal Lora's smiling face. At the same instant that Lora started for the car, Nellie walked onto the back deck with another load of wash.

The housekeeper smiled, wiping her hands on her apron after setting the basket of wet clothes on the steps. "Oh, precious Lord, bless their hearts! Mrs. Lavoisier is gonna be so glad her babies are home!" she exclaimed.

"Oh, my little darlings! I'm just so pleased you're here! Daddy will be so excited," Lora gushed. "What a delightful surprise!" She rushed quickly to embrace Jason and the boys.

"Hi, Momma, it's so good to be home! How've you been? Where's Dad?" Jason asked, looking down towards the garage to see if James' car was there.

Lora answered Jason while she was cuddling the boys: "He's down on the Neches River, honey. Some colored got himself bit by a cottonmouth while he was working down on the river. Daddy's down there with some men tryin' to get the poor old soul out of the water. He should be home directly," Lora motioned everyone into the house. "Would you look at my little darlin's; haven't they grown?"

"I see you still got the best cook south of the Red River workin' for you," Jason praised. "I can't figure out how a woman can cook food that delicious and keep such a girlish figure?"

Nellie smiled, answering with a slight giggle, "Oh, go on now…I's gots works tah do, and ya'll be gettin' hungry 'fore I get done cookin' 'dis pot liquor!"

Lora glanced out the window as a car flew around the drive, heading towards the garage. "There's Daddy now. He'll be just tickled to see you boys. The two of yah go outside and say hello to Granddad."

Jason could hear David and Dale laughing as they walked back to the house with James.

"I wish you'd look what I found in our yard, two big old yea-hoos…don't believe I know who they are," James said, with his arms locked around David and Dale's neck. "They sorta look like my grandsons, but I'm just not sure," James added with a huge grin.

"Oh, granddad, you know who we are! I'm Dale and this is David," Dale said, looking at his dad for confirmation of what he was saying, in case James was really not sure.

James laughed, giving the boys a squeeze and then turned them loose. James walked over to Jason, embracing him with a bear hug, while pats on the back were exchanged by both men.

"How ya doin,' son? All three of yah are lookin' good!" James said.

"You're looking like your doin' all right, Dad," Jason responded.

"Oh, I'm gettin' along real fine, son. It's awful good to see you and the boys. I'm glad you decided to come home for awhile. Let's have a little supper and then we'll talk."

"How's the man that got snake bit?" Dale asked.

"He's real sick, son. I don't know if he's gonna make it or not. Damned old snake bit him six or seven times 'fore anyone could get him out from under the brush pile. Man had no business workin' down in that mess. It never fails...they'll get down there, knowin' the water's full of snakes, and get bit every time."

"Why was he down there, granddad?" Dale asked.

"Poor old thing was tryin' ta make a livin', boy, settin' a trot line, using a seine, maybe after catfish or turtles...hard to say. Poor folks don't have a lot of choice in what kind of work they gotta do. Let's get washed up," James finished, still feeling concerned for the old man.

After dinner Lora walked up the stairs to the boys' room where Nellie had prepared their beds, pulling back the top sheet and fluffing a large feather pillow for each of them. A ceiling fan hovered slowly above the beds, sending waves of cool air down to the sheets. Lora spent a few minutes talking with the children and then left the room to draw a cool bath for them in the tub at the end of the hall. When it was full she organized the order of bathing, giving each of the boys a kiss before disappearing down the curved stairway to James' room.

Jason was there, reclining in an overstuffed chair and smoking a cigarette as James rocked slowly back and forth in his rocker, dressed in his suit pants and a sleeveless T-shirt. Both men sat quietly, lost in their own thoughts, Jason searching the rings of smoke that he launched into the air and James reading his Dallas Morning News, as if he were unaware of his son's presence.

Lora came into the room without speaking, taking a chair in a corner. She sat down, and leaned her head back to relax.

James put his paper down in his lap and removed his wire-rimmed glasses, then wiped his eyes with a handkerchief before speaking.

"What's happening with you and Jessica? You gettin' along any better?"

"No, it's not any better. We've pretty well been the course. She's more deceitful and conniving than I've ever seen her. My career's in jeopardy constantly from her gallivanting around with everyone on base, and now she's got herself tied up with a couple of civilians downtown."

James cut himself a plug of tobacco with his pocketknife. "The boys know anything about all her whorin' around?"

Jason looked down at the carpet, taking a long draw from his cigarette. "I'm sure they know she's been doin' something. She's been so damn mean to both of them, I don't think they mind her being gone all the time. It's when she comes home, drunk, on a tear, that all hell seems to break loose."

"She still beating up on them?" James asked, knowing that Jason had a hard time admitting he knew she was doing it.

"I suppose she is...I never catch her at it. Neither of the boys ever say anything about what she's done, but I guess you can see it in their eyes," Jason said, ashamed of himself for his inaction.

Lora sat up straight in the chair before speaking: "I want those children to stay here. Neither one of them is going back up there with her."

"Yes, I'm going to drive over to Rusk tomorrow, see what Judge Harmond can do about this," James said.

"She's agreed to leave them here for the summer, and I wouldn't want to make her mad at this point, so let's wait and see what happens when school gets ready to start," Jason said, trying to mediate the situation before James started any legal proceedings.

"That woman's got a mean streak in her worse than those damn snakes down on the Neches. Bad mean! I know you still love her, son, but I have a terrible feeling that she's gonna do somethin' to one of yah!"

"I know she thinks I'm blind. Everyone on base knows about her. Someone saw her with one of her boyfriends, some school teacher, the other day at a night club, all wrapped up in the guy, crawling all over him," Jason sputtered. His frustration was obvious to his parents.

"The boys will be all right, here. We can't replace what they've lost in all of this, but we can give them a good home. Your mother and I love both of them very much. Maybe…just maybe, that will heal some of the damage," James assured him.

"I wanted to spend a few weeks here at home with them. I've spent so little time with either one of the boys. Maybe we could drive up to Love's Lookout tomorrow, do a little crappie fishing over on Mud Creek. I'd like to take them over to the packing shed, spend some time seeing some of the folks around town," Jason said. "It would be good for them to know there are decent people in this world."

Dale remembered his father departing for North Africa when his leave was over. He'd left early in the morning, having said his farewells the night before to all of them. He didn't wake anyone before he left; he didn't want to disturb them so early in the morning. All of them knew he was unhappy with the circumstances that had brought them to Jacksonville, the failure of his marriage, and not being able to do anything about it. It was easier for him to handle his departure this way, not seeing the looks on the boys' faces at that moment when his parting had become a reality, or the looks of his parents as they grieved silently for their son's unhappy life.

James and Lora committed themselves, heart and soul, to creating a warm environment for the boys at a time in their lives when most couples were thinking about retirement. Both boys were approaching the teenage years, Dale ten, almost eleven, and David twelve, which made the old couples' effort that much more courageous.

Dale reflected back on his grandparents' sacrifices, realizing that they had answered the call with a vitality that not only benefited the boys, but gave the two of them a new perspective on living, an awakening of intuitions normally put to rest at this end of life.

The once-tranquil residence became a beehive of activity as carpenters worked to construct a barn for two ponies James had bought for the boys. Watermelon benches were built for the evenings under the great pecan trees when the family would enjoy the sweet red meat of an iced melon after a scorcher of a day. Long strands of rope hung from the overhead branches of the trees, supporting old tires suspended in the cool shade, carrying the young adventurers into their fantasies, swinging them above the imagined deadly jaws of giant alligators or hungry piranha. A tree on the back lot hosted a raw interpretation of a house, a scantily constructed sanctuary erected by the young builders to give themselves an escape from the adult world. It was a miracle that it survived the storms that twisted and pulled on the tree, yanking away branches, but never doing anything to the hideout.

In the evenings, after supper, Lora would read to the boys from one of Agatha Christie's works or some other shoot-em-up, or play a game of pick-up-sticks on the floor of her bedroom. Sometimes they'd sit quietly in the parlor, playing the victrola, listening to classical music as Dale and David lay on the floor absorbed in a comic book.

After supper James would retire to his room to read in his rocker, chewing on a plug of tobacco, ignoring the fluttering pages of his newspaper as his fan oscillated across the room.

A fierce storm had blown in from the Gulf, dropping the temperature in the house to an uncomfortable chill. The boys had huddled in James' room to warm themselves in front of his gas heater, watching the lightning flash above the pecan trees like so many strobe lights. The power had been interrupted so often that James had given up trying to finish reading his newspaper, seizing the opportunity because of the eerie setting to tell the boys the story of 'Old George'.

The heater whispered a constant hiss as gas burned with an orange and blue flame, transforming the white clay briquettes into an array of translucent reds. Gusts of icy air would slip into the room, pushing the flames to one side for an instant before relenting, allowing the fire to right itself. A suspicious youngster would glance cautiously in the direction of the cool draft of air, and shift a little closer to his grandfather to settle his nerves. James recognized the mood, as seasoned storytellers often do, knowing it was a good night for a story.

"You boys know this old house used to be a funeral home." James started, watching both boys' eyes respond as he planted the seeds of his tale. "Yes, sir, it was a night just like this when old George Murphy was brought in…right down there where the kitchen is, that's where the fella put him."

Both boys turned their heads in unison to look through the dining room into the darkened kitchen.

"Yes, sir, it was pourin' rain outside…a downpour like we hadn't seen in these parts for years…kinda like the storm we're havin' now. Water had come might near up to the front door of the funeral home." James hesitated, cutting himself a plug of black mule, and letting the suspense build.   "Old George was quite a drinker, comin' downtown after gettin' off work over at Stephen's Mill, and buyin' himself a jug of whiskey down on catfish row from a bootlegger. It was almost midnight.

"Well, old George was drunker than a hoot owl, stumblin' down South Jackson, soaked to the gills, holdin' a newspaper over his head so's the rain wouldn't get into his whiskey. He was right outside, right next to that old pecan tree, when, all of a sudden, just as he was takin' a slug of whiskey, he stepped out into the street, still holdin' that paper over his face. I'll be danged if a truck didn't hit him, sendin' him flyin' across the yard, right up on the sidewalk of the funeral home. The old boy that was drivin' that truck never saw George before he laid into him."

James shook his head as if he'd been there. "Well, that old boy panicked when he saw what he'd done, sure that George Murphy was dead. When he realized that he was standin' in front of a funeral home, it occurred to him that he might be able to drag old George inside without anyone seeing him, since it was so late."

James launched another streamer into the white ceramic pot, wiping his mouth and stealing a glance at his young listeners.

"The truck driver figured that he'd take George around to the back of the home, knowing that the morticians lived upstairs, where your momma and daddy's room is. He found the door to the kitchen unlocked, so he carried George inside and laid him on the table in the embalming room, then lit out, tryin' to get away before anyone saw him."

Dale and David stared at each door, expecting to see George standing there with each flash of lightning.

"Well, that wasn't the worst of it. One of the old boys that worked there had come in early, before anyone else was up, seein' George laid out on the table and thinkin' he was there to be embalmed.   That fella had stripped old George's clothes off and started to open him up, to pump him full of embalmer's fluid, when George sat up, screaming at the top of his lungs, delirious from the knock on his head he'd gotten from bein' hit by the truck.

You can imagine the look on that mortician's face when George leaped off that table, plumb nekked, runnin' around that room, still half-drunk, screamin' and actin' crazy wild. That old boy didn't know what to do, thinkin' he'd come face to face with a zombie…you know, a dead man who doesn't know he's dead cause he's had too much to drink." James chuckled, careful not to break the mood. "That mortician was in shock, scramblin' for anything he could find to bring old George down. That fella picked up a meat cleaver, leapin' on old George, and givin' him a whack across his neck, cuttin' his old head clean off!

The mortician didn't want anyone to know what he'd done so he buried old George right here in the house. But he had to bury his head separated from his body 'cause he couldn't find a spot big enough for all of him. Now I can't swear I seen him, but the story I heard was that old George was seen walkin' around in this house, lookin' for his head. When the funeral home moved out, well, old George got left behind by the fella that did the killin'. I reckon if a fella was to listen real close, he could hear old George walkin' around at night," James added, knowing full well that the old house creaked and moaned enough to convince anyone that George was on the prowl. He ended his story and bid the boys good night, giving each of them a kiss on the cheek and sent them on their way.

Dale and David moved through the hall listening for any noises that might warn them of George's whereabouts. They could see a thin ribbon of light coming from under Lora's door, and both of them were relieved that she was still awake. They went in.

"What are my little darlings doing up so late? Don't you boys want to go on upstairs and go to bed? It's so late, all this nice rain makes it such good sleeping weather," she added, returning to her novel.

Dale was the first to speak up. "I think I'd like to stay down here for awhile, if you don't mind, grandma. That storm's kinda givin' me the willies," Dale said, keeping an eye on the door to Lora's room.

"Yeah, me, too!" David said, moving over to a chair next to her bed. "I'll just wait until Dale's ready to go," he announced, not wanting to admit that he was scared like his brother.

After an hour of waiting for the boys to wear down, Lora finally insisted that they go to bed. She turned out her light, sending both boys scurrying to find a lighted room. Dale stared down the darkened hallway, making a razu up the old staircase, with David following only inches behind. The thundering stampede woke James from his sleep as Dale and David bolted for the lighted bedroom at the top of the stairs.

Sometime between midnight and one in the morning Lora woke up, aware that someone was sharing her bed. She turned on the switch to her floor lamp, finding not one, but both boys buried beneath the covers.

"What on earth are you two boys doing in my bed? Do you know what time it is? Gracious sakes alive!" Lora demanded, noticing that both of the young men's eyes were fixed on her heavily cold-creamed face and sleeping cap.

"No, ma'am," Dale answered, trying to decide whether or not his grandmother belonged in the bad dream he'd been having upstairs as he checked out her mask.

"I have the funniest feeling that your grandfather has had something to do with this! I think he's been doin' a little story tellin'," Lora said, looking over at both boys as she finally understood what was going on. Lora closed her eyes and turned off the lamp, "I suppose it was that ridiculous story about Old George, and it's just a bunch of hooey; there isn't any such person," she said. "Now let's get some sleep!"

Both boys slipped back beneath the covers anyway, not taking any chances on her being wrong about the matter. They fell asleep, certain that George would respect the sanctity of their grandmother's room. After all...ghosts were only supposed to do their creeping and crawling when there were no grownups around. Safe at last!

CHAPTER 21

"Behold, I send an Angel before thee, to keep thee in the way, and to bring thee into the place which I have prepared." Exodus 23:20, always had come to mind whenever Dale recalled those years of sanctuary he'd had with the old couple in Jacksonville, especially his grandfather.

They'd made such a committed effort, taking it upon themselves to provide a home, to reverse the insanity that had gone on in Topeka. Like most children, Dale had failed to appreciate the value of what they'd done for him until years later, or perhaps not until now, this very instant. He smiled as he reflected back on those times. The old home, the couple's efforts to make him feel a sense of worth, of belonging, of knowing that being alive, was important. They'd taken such care to restore their fragile hearts, to mend the wounds of Jessica's vicious abuse. When Dale was young, it was as if James and Lora had been placed on this earth to provide sanctuary for him; but then that's always a child's perspective, that he is the sole voyager on the journey through life.

The rescue had come too late for David. He withdrew from the outstretched hands, eating, sleeping, existing in their home, but never accepting the generous affection offered by his grandparents. He had struggled to understand why he'd been abandoned by his parents, wondering if there was any complicity on his part for the separation. He'd been warned never to reveal what he knew, and he hadn't. She'd said if his father found out what he'd seen, the separation would be his fault. What he'd seen, what they'd both seen, was the demon in an orgy of passion in their parents' bedroom. But their father wasn't the man in the bed.

It had been the night that she'd beaten Dale unconscious, because he'd accidentally intruded into the room behind David. He never understood what it was that he saw, what had prompted the attack. But David knew. He was old enough to know what she was doing, and now he would spend his time in an endless nightmare trying to understand his fear of his father finding out, knowing when he did that the divorce would be his fault—his mother had said so. Although Jessica physically abused David less than Dale because he was older, what she did was every bit as damaging, if not more so.

Dale, unlike his brother, eagerly accepted his grandparents' affections. He was starved for any form of attention, deliriously happy that someone cared. James often had Dale accompany him to town while he made his rounds at the hospital or visited a patient at home. James was always excited to have an opportunity to show off his grandson. He would take Dale to the bank, proudly introducing him to the clerks and bank officers. Dale could see the power and influence his grandfather had as he watched the tellers and department heads making every effort to accommodate the old man.

James was greeted constantly on the street by patients or business acquaintances with a, 'Hello, Doctor Lavoisier', or 'Hello, Doc'. It was one such greeting where a friend paid his respects to James, and then said good morning to Dale with a 'Hello, little Doc' that left Dale beside himself, thrilled that anyone might place him in the same category of respect as his grandfather.

One day, in Afton's hardware store, James spent a half-hour casually lecturing his young protege on the finer points of hardware linguistics. It was a lesson in Americana, an accumulation of standards and measurements as old as Texas history itself. It gave Dale a revealing look at the man he most admired in his life, an understanding why his grandfather was so well respected by the people who knew him. He'd risen from the ranks of poverty to become a success—not a byproduct of some highbrow society, but a simple man who'd pulled himself up to a better position in life by sweat and toil—never forgetting where he'd come from, still proud to look back at his Creole roots.

When they'd finished their business at the hardware store, they walked down the street to Willy Springer's barbershop. James was received with the same respect and admiration that he'd been given at the bank and on the street. It was more than southern hospitality; he was their doctor, and in a way he'd succeeded for all of them.

"When's that granddad of yours gonna take yah fishing, young fella?" Willy Springer asked, popping his last customer's hair off the striped barber's bib and holding his hand out for Dale to slide into the chair. Willy held Dale's head straight with one hand as he managed the clippers with the other. "You know how to catch them whoppers, them old black bass, don't cha, boy?"

Dale smiled nervously as he watched the other customers waiting for his response. He tried to get help from his grandfather for the answer, but James sat buried in his paper. Dale finally responded, "No, sir!"

"Well, yah gotta slip up on 'em like an old fox, real quiet 'til you're right on top of where they're layin', usually by a big old stump. Then yah stand yourself up in the boat, pull out yer tally whacker, and wet your bait real good, hollering 'I'm a friend of Willy Springer's? Then yah gotta put that line in the water real...slow, 'cause them old bass are smart! Now the Gar and the catfish, he'll jump on anything, but the black bass...he's a special kind fish! He's real temperamental."

"Willy Springer...I'm a friend of Willy Springer," Dale repeated with a smile.

"That's right! If yah do it thata way, those big old black bass u'll leap plumb out the water tryin' to get on your hook. See, it's 'cause, when I was a young feller, like you, I got into a mess of 'em, catchin' so many I used up all my stringers! But, I was always real careful to turn them little ones loose, tah have a chance tah grow up, tah become big daddy bass. Well, the word got around that 'Willy Springer was an all right feller!' That's why, today, wherever you wet a line the way I told yah, there's always a big old Black Bass just itchin' to do old Willy a favor, like lettin' himself get caught by those who know the magic words."

Dale quickly turned his head towards James to check the accuracy of Mr. Springer's advice. James held a straight face as the men along the wall laughed and elbowed each other. Dale accepted James' nod to mean it was good advice, never mind what the others might think.

The morning trip always ended at catfish row, where James would select the melons and peaches for their supper. The Packard would thread its way through the narrow lanes created by old pickup trucks and trailers sitting side by side, with bushel baskets of fruits and vegetables piled on their tailgates or sitting on homemade stands.

James would drive slowly through the crowded street, stopping only when he'd spotted a particularly attractive selection of melons or peaches, maybe okra or snap beans and sometimes ears of corn, but corn was usually better if it had come from up North, from Opossum Kingdom, rather than local fields.

Dale would watch, as James would have the farmer plug the melon with his knife, handing him the triangular wedge of red meat to taste like a man sampling a fine wine. He'd savor the meat in his mouth for a moment and then discuss the effects the weather had had on the man's crop. He'd jaw with the farmer, looking over his other offerings, before making his knowledgeable selection. He would begin to dicker and haggle with the farmer on his price, only after he'd skillfully tantalized the man with his interest in six or seven bushel baskets of produce, a full day's sale for any farmer on the row. James would lecture the man about which of his crops had sat in the fields too long or had been picked too early. The farmer would quickly lower the price, surprised at the accuracy of James' statements about how he'd grown his crop or when he'd harvested it.

When James had satisfied himself that he'd gotten the rock-bottom price for the selection of produce, he'd hand the man his original asking price. "It's more than I oughta pay, but if a feeler was to deliver all this to my house, I figure I could live with the price he was asking'."

It never made much sense to Dale why James would have debated the price with the man to begin with, getting him down to half the price, only to end up paying just what he'd asked at the start. He learned that it was not only a source of entertainment for James, but it was the way things were done, a way of preserving the farmer's self-respect. James could justify paying the top price by having the produce delivered to the house, and everyone was satisfied with the deal.

One such venture to catfish row had resulted in the purchase of several stalks of Cuban bananas that James had hung in the lower shed to ripen.

Dale and David both had retreated from the unbearable heat in the house to the shade of the pecan trees in the back yard.

Dale had discovered the green stalks of bananas suspended from the rafters in the barn. The discovery came at a perfect time with both boys wanting something to eat.

Dale untied the smaller stalk and placed it between the two of them, on burlap sacks. David commented, "I'll bet we could eat this whole stalk of bananas! They gotta be good for yah, bein' fruit an all." Dale giggled, holding one of the dwarfed morsels between his fingers, peeled of its bright green skin, sticking it into his mouth like a cigar.

Lora discovered the 'banana caper' when she opened the shed door, finding both boys laid out on the floor with their heads supported on gunnysacks. She'd been attracted to the shed by a constant moaning that she had heard coming through the door.

Neither of the boys said anything to their grandmother, rolling their eyes pathetically towards her, never breaking the tempo of their moaning, as both of them continued rubbing their swollen bellies.

Lora was satisfied that they hadn't gotten into rat poison or bug spray when David released a deep, long belch that attracted her attention to the pile of peels just on the other side of a bag of pecans.

James was summoned home, alerted that there was some emergency at the house. He pulled into the drive, leaping from the car at a dead run as Nellie directed him to the back shed.

When he got to the open shed doors, he made a quick assessment of the situation, doing a double-take at the two figures sprawled out on the floor with their bellies exposed from under their opened shirts and unzipped pants. James immediately noticed the pile of discarded banana skins heaped on the opposite side of the floor by the young 'banana poachers'.

James stood with his hands on his hips, shaking his head and muttering, "Gawd...ah...Mighty! Don't you two boys know what eatin' all those green bananas will do to yah?"

Both children were taken to the master bathroom on the main floor where James retrieved a bottle of clear mineral oil from the medicine cabinet. "Both of you are going to be as constipated as a Christmas goose if you don't swallow every drop of this stuff. Now, bottoms up!" James said, laughing to himself as he watched the small 'fruit bandits' suffering to swallow the tasteless oil.

He was satisfied that the boys had served penance enough for their escapade. To make sure they finished the greasy elixir, he pulled an enema bag from the cabinet, theatrically stretching out the hose to its full length and slowly screwing on a plastic applicator that looked to be a foot long. He hung the contraption on the knob of the cabinet and turned to Lora, smiling where the boys couldn't see him, struggling to keep a serious tone, "I'll have to hit 'em a lick with 'the bag' if they don't drink all their medicine."

Lora was speechless, staring first at the giant cups of mineral oil that both boys were holding, and then at the hose hanging threateningly on the knob of the cabinet. Dale looked over at David, confused about what the device could possibly have to do with a Christmas goose, bananas, or the cup of clear liquid he was holding with some uncertainty.

David had picked right up on the threat from his Grandfather, gulping the cup of clear syrup, gagging and heaving as it worked its way down. Dale followed suit, motivated by the reaction of his brother, knowing there must be something terrible about the rubber contraption if David was willing to polish off the tasteless vile remedy because of it.

James started out the door, sticking his head back in the bathroom, and giving instructions to Lora: "Keep 'em in the bathroom for awhile, hon; things ought to start happening pretty quick when that stuff hits bottom." James howled as he headed off to his room.

These were the lighter moments, but there were some that were more somber. There were times Dale could remember when just being in his grandfather's room had such a warm, soothing effect on him. He thought about the evening he discovered the small red velvet sack in the dresser drawer, while he was helping to put James' freshly laundered shirts away. It had been carefully concealed beneath an old shirt that James had never worn, a shirt that seemed to have been kept strictly for the purpose of hiding this particular treasure.

When he'd shown the small pouch to his grandfather, James stared at it as if he'd seen a ghost. The old man held the bag cradled in his shaking hands, his head bent down, studying the worn cloth as if he were looking at a long-forgotten friend. His fingers stroked the material with soft, unconscious movements as his head straightened and he looked off in the distance, having traveled somewhere far beyond the room, journeying to wherever it was that his memory had called him.

Dale watched, knowing that his grandfather had forgotten about him. He could see the old man's face move with slight twitches and spasms, as if he were in pain or distressed with his thoughts. His face relaxed, calmed by what he'd seen. Now, it seemed that he was at peace with his memory, almost smiling, as his fingers stilled against the material. James inhaled a deep breath, casting a last look back at the place he'd visited in his mind and then glanced down at Dale.

"What is it, granddad? What's in that old bag?" Dale asked.

James closed his hands over the small purse, answering, "Just memories, son...just memories."

"Memories about what, Granddad?"

James held the bag by the cord, staring at it, then spoke in a low voice: "Just memories of people I've known, some places I've been! Nothing important."

He leaned over, placing the sack back in the drawer, and buried it beneath the shirt that had covered it for so long.

"You know, when a fella makes his journey through life, he leaves a little of himself behind wherever he goes...the products of his heart, of his energies. At the same time, he picks up memories, some good, some not so good; things that let him look back to see where he's been. After awhile, he gets where he doesn't collect so many thoughts.

"I guess the true quality of a man's walk through life can be measured, somehow, by the satisfaction he gets from those memories, from those things that his mind has sorted out as important to him," James continued. "It's the only thing in this life we really get to keep. It's even stranger that we keep it bottled up in our minds, just about the way it happened. I guess I'd like to believe we get to take a few of the good memories with us when we leave this old world."

James could see that his young listener wasn't fully understanding him. He pushed the drawer shut and smiled at Dale. "It doesn't matter," he said.

"You know, it doesn't seem like that long ago that I went off to fight the Great War. Now France, that's a place to see! Course, I'm sure it's changed a lot since I was there. But, land sakes, it was somethin', seein' all those famous places, and knowin' our family came from there."

Dale's interest perked up. "We came from France?"

"Why, sure," James answered. "You're as pure a Frenchman as a fella could be, 'cept for your momma's side."

James thought for a moment before continuing. "You know, the countryside in France is one of the prettiest places I think I've ever been! The farms are small, but beautiful. The Germans tried to destroy most of it; did a pretty good job of it, too, but I figure that's all been rebuilt by now." His head lifted so that he was staring at the wall above Dale's head. "The roads are covered with so much shade from all the trees, that it's...like...walking...through...a dark...tunnel." James hesitated, looking back to the dream he just left, then went on: "It gets so cold in there, even in the summer, a fella would wanta be wearin' his jacket before he took himself a stroll down that road."

James knew what was happening, what was coming back to him. He struggled to keep the thoughts from materializing, thoughts that had been silenced for so long, thoughts that began to materialize so vividly. "There was the prettiest little farm up on the frontier. Just outside of Pont-a-Mousson. Beautiful fields of uncut green grass with a river flowing through the property. And you could always hear church bells ringing off in the distance."

James paused, finding himself consumed with the memory; a memory of the interfering priest who had led him away from the one thing he had wanted most in his life. "Priest!" James mumbled.

Dale looked at him, answering his grandfather's questions, "You say somethin', grandad?

"Nothing, son. I was just thinking about someone!"

Dale, eager to hear more, said, "Tell me more about France, granddad! Tell me about the beautiful farms!"

"They were a sight to behold, no doubt about it! Pretty as a picture post card. Probably what made 'em seem so beautiful was that so much of France had been destroyed by the war. Terrible destruction! But not this place. It was a queer little island of farms, stuck smack dab in the middle of all the hell that was going on around it!"

"Did anybody live there? Were there people on the farms?" Dale wanted to know.

"Oh yes...like there was no war going on! Lots of folks lived there! Why, on one of the farms I was tellin' you about, the most beautiful lady I'd ever seen had a place that looked like something from a dream. She was a pretty French girl! She was really a sight to see."

"Prettier than Grandma?" Dale asked.

"Well your Grandmother's a pretty lady, all right, but this French girl was a real looker!" James stopped, looking over at the drawer that held the velvet sack; "She was as pretty and delicate as a bisque ballerina."

"I think I left my heart there," James mumbled to himself, still looking off in the distance.

"Wha'd you say, Granddad?"

"I hope you'll get to see France someday, son! Maybe you'll have a chance to visit Pont-a-Mousson."

James talked awhile longer about his visits to the town, but more about the farm and the beautiful young French girl who had lived there. Not once did he mention anything about the war. Then he stopped, tired of the painful reflection, abruptly announcing that it was bedtime.

"Whatever happened to the beautiful French lady, granddad?" Dale asked, infatuated with the description of the fairy tale setting.

Again, James' eyes drifted towards the dresser before he responded: "She died right after the war...after I'd gone home," James said. "I never saw her again. It was such a long time ago."

James turned out the light, lying in his bed, forgetting that Dale would want to kiss him good night.

Dale walked to the side of his grandfather's bed, leaning over and kissing the old man as he always had done, then saying, "I'm sorry the beautiful lady died, granddad."

"Me, too, son...me too." James responded, and gave a deep, labored sigh as he closed his eyes.

As Dale started to pull the door shut to James' room, he heard the old man say in a soft voice, "I love you, Dale."

Almost eight months to the day that Jason had left, the family was reunited in Topeka, as Jason's squadron of B-47s returned to Forbes from North Africa. The boys had returned a week before Jason. James and Lora had a difficult time allowing the children to leave, knowing that they would be exposed again to Jessica's cruelty; but because of the boys' eagerness to be reunited with their father, James decided to back off and let well enough alone.

Jason was greeted with a promotion to Lieutenant Colonel, as he had predicted. For a while, his new position of authority gave Jessica a fresh surge of interest in the Forbes social circuit. For no other reason than Jason's appointment as a squadron commander, Jessica was kept busy attending a full calendar of insignificant social functions sponsored by the other officers' wives. They were designed as little 'getting to know you' parties, but few of the attendees had any problem knowing who Jessica was. Obligations of protocol were reasons enough for most of the wives to bury the hatchet long enough to perform their social responsibilities, but there was no noticeable change in attitude once their obligations had been met. Jessica made the rounds of obligatory coffees and teas, unscathed by the icy reception she'd receive wherever she went.

Shortly after taking over as Squadron Commander, Jason's attendance was requested by the base Commander at a public relations extravaganza. It was being thrown at the officer's club for the high collars from Topeka. Included were jurists, city officials, the police chief, attorneys who'd worked with the Judge Advocate's office, and Chamber of Commerce representatives, all on the guest list of prominent influentials invited to the get-together. Even a few state legislators were invited on the list of distinguished guests.

Jessica made her grand entrance at the gala, radiantly outfitted in a filmy cocoon body dress, sparkling with semi-precious jewelry and a strand of pearls dangling over the exposed cleavage of her décolleté creation. Her entrance into the 'soiree de gala' was, as always, Jessica's finest moment, executed with the same cool-handed precision as a seasoned battle commander launching an offensive. She smiled her way through the receiving line, clinging to Jason's arm for appearance's sake, tolerating the procedural formalities until she'd passed the uniformed dignitaries. As soon as they had been introduced to everyone she knew, Jason would be called upon to join the staff officers from Headquarters to mix with the guests. She had attended enough of these gatherings over the years to know that she would be on her own until the party had ended...exactly what she wanted.

Jason had tactfully sloughed Jessica off into the hands of the city attorney, a prehistoric fossil named Willard Bybee. Bybee looked old enough to have been delivered in the first wagon load of settlers to stake out Topeka. He was a well-weathered, Paleolithic specimen with a bushy head of hair dyed a bright glowing red. He had the obnoxious habit of spitting as he talked, compounded by a threatening saliva residue at the corners of his mouth that kept his listeners captivated as they tried to predict when the white bubbly foam would be launched in their direction.

Despite Bybee's crusty appearance, he was probably the single most influential individual in the room. His age made little difference to Jessica, as she honed in on the fact that everyone seemed to be making a point of paying their respects to him. She had attached herself to a star, a wilted star, but nonetheless he was providing her the opportunity to be introduced to many of Topeka's notable citizenry.

"Hello, Willard," a voice boomed from behind her.

"How-do, L.C.," Bybee answered, slipping a stogie between his lips. "Meet Jenny Lavosonae," Bybee said, nonchalantly introducing Jessica as he concentrated on chewing the tip off his cigar.

"Hello, I'm L.C. Spinner," the man said, offering Bybee a light from his lighter.

"Hello...it's nice to meet you," Jessica responded, eager to correct the error made with her name.

"L.C.'s one of the attorneys that works with the Judge Advocate General's Office here at Forbes. Damn good counselor," Bybee remarked, still trying to get his cigar lit.

Jessica made a quick survey of L.C., hawkishly eyeing him as he held up his lighter, patiently trying to spark Bybee's unlit cigar. He was a heavy-set man with wavy, prematurely gray hair and stunning blue eyes. He was impeccably dressed in a well-tailored black pinstripe suit and white shirt with an appropriately matched tie.

"Are you Air Force, Mrs. Lavosonae?" L.C. asked, finally dropping his arm after getting Bybee's cigar stoked up.

"It's Lavoisier," Jessica corrected, nervously.

"I'm sorry...what?" L.C. asked, confused.

"Lavoisier...my name is Jessica Lavoisier," she said, not wanting to embarrass Willard Bybee.

"Where the hell did Jenny go?" Bybee asked, staring down his cigar as he let loose a billowing cloud of smoke. "So Gawd-damn many folks running around this shindig, you can't tell who's who!"

"Well, it's still nice to meet you, Jessica," L.C. announced, aware that Willard Bybee was stewed, having had an early start at the open bar. "Did I understand you to say you were Air Force?"

"Yes, Colonel Lavoisier is my husband. He's just been given his own squadron."

"I see. Maybe that's why I haven't had the opportunity to meet him yet," L.C. said, giving Jessica the once-over.

"So how are you involved with Forbes, Mister Spinner?" Jessica inquired, fully enjoying L.C.'s overt head to toe survey.

"I occasionally handle a court martial, whenever they need a civilian attorney for one of the men. I had a hand in helping write the Uniform Code of Military Justice, so I get a few calls to assist, once in awhile, because of that."

"How interesting!" she acknowledged.

"Oh, I'm not out here very often. Most of my time is spent with my private practice, or over at the capitol, doing work for various Senate and House committees, or the State Attorney General's Office."

"It sounds marvelous!" Jessica exclaimed. "It's certainly got to be more exciting than living this dull existence here at Forbes. It appears that you have a very interesting law practice, Mister Spinner! Are you a native Topekan?" Jessica asked.

"Yes, I've lived here most of my life. After the war I went to college and law school at Kansas University, married a local girl, so I consider myself a native," L.C. remarked.

"Do you have children?"

"We have a little girl...Debby. She's three. How about you, Jessica?"

"No, unfortunately, we don't have any children." Jessica smiled.

"And what part of the country are you from?"

"Dallas. My Daddy was an oilman. I'm just a simple southern girl," she lied, clearing her throat and taking an evasive look off in the distance to change the subject. "Working with the legislature probably gives you an opportunity to meet quite a few important people around Topeka?" Jessica asked. "It sounds so interesting!"

"It is...sometimes! Maybe you'd like to come down to the Senate for a tour one afternoon. Meet a few of the lawmakers. Of course, your husband is welcome to come, too, if he'd like," L.C. said, careful not to make his interest too obvious. Jessica let loose a cold, condescending laugh. "I don't think Jason would be interested. His idea of a fun-filled afternoon is to slide under the hood of his car with a wrench."

"Well, anyway," L.C. continued, "I'd like to call you, have you come by sometime. Maybe we could have lunch, then take a tour of the Senate Chambers. My office is next door to the State Office Building, so we could eat in the Senate cafeteria. The food's horrible, but you'd get to meet a lot of people."

"I'd like that," she said. "I think it would be very educational. I've always been interested in politics. I would imagine that your wife enjoys being involved in the social fanfare, being able to rub elbows with such important people?"

"Jean? No! She's too much of a homebody. She's never cared anything about all the hoopla that goes on over at the Capitol. She really finds it quite boring, as a matter of fact," L.C. added, pulling his wallet out and handing Jessica his business card.

"Well, L.C., I've enjoyed talking to you. I hope we'll meet again!" Jessica said, giving him an eager smile.

L.C. paused for an instant, locking in on Jessica's eyes before he said, "I'm in trial the next two weeks. I'll try to give you a call, as soon as I'm free. Maybe we can arrange something."

"Maybe so," Jessica agreed, shrugging her shoulders, then handing him her phone number, "...maybe so!"

The inhabitants of Kansas learn early in life to recognize the changes in inauspicious clouds that ebb their way over the sky like a black sea, as the light dims to an eerie incandescence and winds cease to move the gentlest of leaves on the trees. And then, with the voice of a thousand demons, comes the horrific roar, the train of Satan, the tornado dropping from concealment in the sky. In an instant the unsuspecting are torn asunder as they break and run, too late, always too late. A lifetime of dreams and hopes are destroyed, and then the tornado is gone without remorse.

Never once did L.C. heed the signs of what was before him.

Stephen D. Boyett

CHAPTER 22

A week later, after both of L.C.'s cases were dismissed from the court docket, L.C. and Jessica were enjoying lunch at the Senate cafeteria. Jessica felt a certain measure of satisfaction, having gotten her foot in the door at such a prestigious place.

L.C. was savoring his own feelings of success, enjoying the muted accolades from his colleagues, silent applause for his choice of a little something on the side, and his boldness in showing her off.

"So tell me about L.C. Spinner," Jessica inquired, "and how he got to be such an important attorney for the State of Kansas. It's always so exciting to me to find out how some people have made it to the top. I'm so used to living around losers! It's like a breath of fresh air when I have a chance to meet someone who's done something with themselves...actually being successful. I'm sick to death of all these so-called men who hide themselves behind a uniform to keep from having to face the real world."

"That's very flattering, Jessica, but I think you're overly impressed with what I do. You have to remember that this isn't Washington!" L.C. laughed.

"Oh, I think I have good reason to be impressed with you," Jessica said, smugly.

"Really...and why's that?"

"Well, for instance, I know you graduated cum laude from Kansas University, you're licensed to practice before the Supreme Court, you were decorated in WWII with an Air Medal and D.F.C., and..." Jessica laughed, "...you played minor league baseball before college!"

L.C. was surprised, wondering who was pursuing whom. "Sounds like you've been doing a little pretrial discovery for our luncheon date. I'm afraid you have me at a disadvantage, as I know nothing about you except that you're married, and that you're an extremely beautiful woman."

Jessica exhaled a breathy response. "I'm afraid you'll find that I'm a very ordinary person, just trying to find happiness in life. Unfortunately, I was swept off my feet by a man who offered me the world to marry him. I was a young girl, star-struck by a man in uniform who appeared to have everything going for him."

"And what happened?" L.C. asked. "I'd think a man would have to be crazy not to keep <u>you</u> happy."

"I don't know...maybe it was because I was so young and naive. I tried to put off getting married, but he wouldn't wait...wouldn't stand for it. He felt that the war would start before we could have any time together. I guess now I feel like I was taken advantage of. Being such a child, I didn't know about life, and that I was getting myself involved with such a weak individual!"

L.C. was touched by her obvious suffering. He reached for her hand to comfort her as she continued. "And now, now that I can see him for what he is...I wish to God I hadn't been so gullible, so weak when he demanded that we get married. It just makes me feel like I've wasted my life," Jessica complained, even managing a few tears.

L.C. was moved by her performance. When they'd finished their lunch, he escorted her through the underground tunnel to the Capitol building, stopping several times to introduce her to his acquaintances as they walked the short distance to the Senate galleries.

"Hello, L.C.!" a figure shouted from a crowd of people in the tunnel. A well-dressed man stepped up to L.C., ignoring Jessica as he spoke: "Davidson is looking for you. He's steaming over that change in Milborne's tax bill. He's in a sweat about having some kind of trouble getting it out of committee. Some stupid son of a bitch in the House..." The man caught himself, staring at Jessica.

"Oh, Tom, meet Jessica Lavoisier, a client of mine," L.C. said. "She's taking a little tour of the State House with me. Jessica, this is Tom Crawford. He's one of our senior senators from western Kansas, over in Washington County," he explained, pulling Jessica into handshaking distance of the senator.

The man smiled, giving L.C. an approving smirk and Jessica a quick, patronizing, plastic grin, then shook her outstretched hand. "Davidson's got a meeting set for four o'clock. Why don't you drop by my office as soon as you're done with your tour?" he said. "The shit's gonna hit the fan when the Governor finds out we've got a problem with <u>this</u> thing."

"Sure, Tom, I'll drop by later. We're going up to the Governor's office in a few minutes. I'll talk to him if he's in," L.C. said.

"See you later," the senator replied, obviously a little perturbed by L.C.'s lackadaisical attitude over his crisis.

"We can do this another time, L.C., if you need to be somewhere else," Jessica offered.

"No. That fickle son of a bitch has always got a problem. Makes me nervous as hell, just being around him! You can always tell when he's up for reelection. Any other time, you couldn't get that guy to budge without a kick in the ass."

L.C. escorted Jessica up to the second floor of the capitol building, past an opening in the stone-quarried floor, an atrium that opened from the first level to the suspended glass ceiling, hanging just under the dome. Jessica looked over the enormous spindled railing down to the first level. She stopped, admiring the huge murals by John Stewart Curry. Their voices echoed down the massive hallways as they moved past statues of Amelia Earhart and Dwight Eisenhower, both honored Kansans.

The Senate chamber was empty except for a page distributing a flyer to each of the wooden desks in the paneled room. L.C. gave Jessica a quick blow-by-blow of who sat where and what was going on in the way of business in the present session. He stopped at one of the desks, picking up a copy of the committee report that Tom Crawford had discussed with him in the tunnel.

They left the Senate chambers and walked down a corridor that led away from the gallery. An aged elevator shaft, fenced with a Victorian wrought-iron grille, filled one side of the hallway, a stairwell angling around behind it. A narrow walkway led to a light-colored wood and glass door, barely visible at the end of the hallway. A hollow thumping sound came from behind it, the sound of an ailing mechanical device or someone unfamiliar with the machine they were using, or perhaps both. A woman momentarily peered up from her work as they entered, patiently trying to adjust a document in an ancient typewriter.

"Afternoon, Claire...is he in?" L.C. asked, keeping his eyes on the report he'd picked up earlier, instead of the woman behind the desk.

Jessica was confused about where they were, thinking at first that L.C. had changed his mind about introducing her to the Governor. "Go on in, L.C., he's just on the phone. He should be done in a minute," the woman said, concentrating on the paper in the typewriter.

Jessica thought the exchange was a little odd, still confused where they were. They obviously had come in the back way to someone's office.

L.C. walked past the woman's desk through a small paneled door into a large plush office, crowded with rusted western and agricultural memorabilia. A man was mumbling into a phone, sitting behind a heavy wood desk. The Kansas State Seal hung on the wall opposite. The man faced away from Jessica and L.C., his body hidden by a high-backed leather chair.

"Tell Byner that I'm expecting his support this afternoon, and he damn well better be there when they call for the vote," the man was saying. Jessica could easily hear the conversation. "We need that piece of revenue legislation wrapped up, so he better be there if he knows what's good for him!"

L.C. cleared this throat, alerting the man to their presence. The individual swiveled around in his chair, just enough to identify L.C., but not noticing Jessica, then returned to his conversation.

"Wait just a minute," the man said, with his back still to L.C. "Let me ask him. L.C., Burke wants to know if you're sure about this committee report on H.B. 2366 this afternoon. Byner doesn't want to support us; he's afraid it will never get out of committee! He's doing his usual low crawl under the woodwork."

"Bull shit! I already got word that the votes are there!" L.C. laughed.

Jessica stared at L.C. and then at the man at the desk, trying to understand what was going on.

"You heard him, didn't you, David? All right, I'll see you after the vote this afternoon," the man said. "Tell Byner he needs to get a little backbone," he finished tersely, hanging up the phone and swinging around, then stared at Jessica with a startled look on his face. His eyes darted immediately over to L.C. for an explanation.

"Oh, Governor, I'd like for you to meet Jessica Lavoisier. She's with me today...on a tour," L.C. announced, seeing that the Governor was shaken at finding that his conversation had been shared with a perfect stranger. "Jessica, this is Governor Gray!"

The Governor straightened his tie and reached for the coat lying in a crumpled heap on the credenza behind his desk. "Well, it's a real pleasure to meet you, Jessica! Have you been here long?" he asked, leaving both L.C. and Jessica at a loss to know how to respond. "I mean, in Kansas," he corrected, still nervous after having possibly said something that would come back to haunt him.

"It's very nice to meet you, Governor. No, I've only been in Kansas for a short time…my husband is stationed at Forbes."

"Oh, I see," he said, relieved to find that at least she wasn't a constituent. "Well, I hope L.C. is giving you a first-class tour of our Capitol. We like to believe that we have one of the most magnificent capitol buildings in the country."

"It's very beautiful," she replied, "really wonderful!"

"It always amazes me how L.C. manages to get such beautiful clients. It makes me very envious of him. I almost wish I was back practicing law," he added, shaking Jessica's hand as he patted L.C. on the shoulder with the other, and gave him a quick pinch on the neck.

Jessica handled the compliment with a little smile, locking her fingers together after the Governor had released her hand.

"I assume, from your name, that you're French?" he asked, rattling off a few rough lines in his own version of the language.

"I'm afraid my husband is the only one who speaks French in our home. But it sounds like you handle the language very well, Governor!"

"Well, thank you, Jessica. I spent a little time in France during the war," he said, delighted. "Now, let's see, you said your husband is out at Forbes?"

"Yes. He's a squadron commander," Jessica said, trying to hide her concern about revealing anything that might get back to Jason.

"I know General Dorick, but I don't think I've met your husband. Maybe we'll meet sometime when I'm out that way."

"It's very nice of you to let us visit. I know how busy you must be. I just can't tell you how thrilling this is for me! Thank you so much!"

"It's my pleasure, young lady, my pleasure. Okay, well, how about a picture?" the Governor said, turning his chair and motioning Jessica to have a seat.

"Picture?" Jessica asked. "I don't—"

Before Jessica could finish, the Governor had leaned over his desk and was talking into his intercom: "Claire, bring the camera in...we need to take a picture of our pretty visitor."

L.C. had a slight smirk on his face as the Governor positioned himself behind Jessica, standing to one side of his seated guest.

"Get over here, L.C., I think you ought to be in this with us," he suggested, with a smile that only L.C. could see. "A little celebration shot for our coup today, eh?" he laughed.

"Sure," L.C. chuckled, grinning down at Jessica as he stepped behind the Governor's chair.

Jessica stayed a few more minutes, and then left the office through the main entrance instead of the back 'get away' door, as it was called, waiting in the reception area for L.C. to finish talking to the Governor.

They had only walked a few feet down the hall before Jessica stopped, turning to L.C. "What in the world was this business of taking the pictures all about?" she asked, glaring at him.

"They always take a complimentary picture of visitors meeting the Governor," L.C. responded. "I think he was knocked out with you!"

"Who was this Byner he was talking about?" Jessica asked. "Don't ask," L.C. replied. "Two years ago, that pathetic son of a bitch got himself involved in a landmark Supreme Court Case, here in Topeka...Brown versus the Topeka Board of Education. Funny thing was...he didn't have a thing to do with litigating either side of the case; just jumped on it for all it was worth politically. He had his name smeared in every newspaper in the State."

"So?" Jessica questioned.

"Kansas had always been an advocate for equal rights. Hell, even in the civil war, Kansas was one of the strongest abolitionist states in the Union. I don't think anyone ever disagreed with the decision of the Supreme Court. But Byner gave us a black eye, keeping the thing in the papers, out front where the people of Kansas would have to bleed over the humiliation of the case, for something that was going on all over the country. The case could just as well have been brought by someone in the South, where you'd expect there to be segregation problems, but it happened in Kansas.

"Anyway, Byner's been on the Governor's shit list ever since that little stunt. The jackass committed political suicide in his own district. Now he's up for reelection, and he hasn't got a prayer!"

"Well, Senator Byner sounds like a man with a career problem. But I think Governor Gray is a charming man," Jessica said. "I wish I had a chance to know him better."

"It's funny you should say that," L.C. responded. "We were just talking about a little smoker we're having tomorrow night over at the Kansan Hotel. I thought you might like to join us; the Governor and his wife will be there, along with some of the senators and their spouses. It should be a good party, a nice chance for you to meet some of the more influential people in our Legislature."

Jessica's eyes lit up. "It sounds delightful, but I'm not sure how Jason would react to my going out without him. I mean, I don't know how I could get away from the house. Maybe he'll be flying tomorrow night," Jessica went on, anguished by the idea of missing such a social opportunity.

"Why don't you see what you can do, and I'll just go ahead and plan on you being there tomorrow night. If you'd like, we could meet at the club for a few drinks before the party. It would give me a chance to introduce you to my partner, Sam Laughlin. He's a little hard to take at first, but I think you'll get along okay," L.C. added, holding Jessica's hand, rather than give her a handshake.

The next morning, as soon as Jason had left for Forbes, Jessica drove into town, trying to complete a tight schedule of appointments in preparation for the evening's social invitation. She knew that the family's finances were on the stretch. They usually lived from paycheck to paycheck, trying to stave off the creditors each month with a juggling act that would have been the envy of the most proficient con-artist. However, Jessica's quest to find the perfect ensemble was in no way dampened by the size of her bank account. She began with a furious assault on the women's specialty stores in Topeka, looking for the most exquisite evening clothes. Price was the least of her concerns as she papered the city with a storm of hot checks.

By the time Jason arrived home, Jessica had thrown a facsimile of a meal on the table for the boys and was joyfully enroute to her rendezvous with L.C.

Jason stood next to the bed, a stupefied expression on his face, angrily gripping the stack of sales receipts he had found mixed in with the clothes scattered about the room. Jason slid down onto the bed, mentally adding the tickets, realizing that Jessica was involved in more than just a spending foray on this particular evening.

At two-thirty in the morning, Jessica walked through the front door of the living room, radiantly attired, in her new clothes, hanging onto the doorsill, passionately embracing anything that might keep her upright. A few feet into the living room she knocked over a table lamp, sending it crashing onto the wooden floor.

Jason had taken up his vigil on the couch across from the front door, watching her fumble like a blind person, stumbling across the room to an overstuffed chair in the corner.

"Jason, sweetie! You look a little peeved," Jessica slurred, twisting her mouth into several grotesque contortions. Her hand moved over her eyes, trying to shield her sensitive eyes to the overhead light fixture. "Don't worry about the clothes...I'm taking them all back tomorrow. Or is it today? Anyway, I had a wonderful time! L.C. is just so perfect! He knows everyone!"

"I think you owe me an explanation, Jessica. Where've you been?" Jason asked in a weak, barely audible voice, more out of his obligation as a man than from really wanting to know for himself.

"Well, let's see, I was asked to be a hostess at a little party, for some senators and judges. I even got paid for going," she said, pulling a wad of cash from her bra, leaving a single bill hanging limply pinched between dress and cleavage.

"You think I'm some kind of fool? I don't know what you got that money for, but I can only imagine," he said, his rage building.

"You're such a jackass, Jason," she chortled. "I'm going to bed. I don't care what you think. You're a nobody! A tiny little nobody and I want'a go to sleep. She staggered towards the bedroom, tripping and stumbling as she tried to navigate the hall. She stopped and looked back. "You're not even important enough for me to worry about anymore, Jason. I've met the most important people, and you weren't on the list. So put that in your hat and mail it home to your rich father!"

The next morning Jessica was awakened by the sound of the front door slamming as Jason left for Forbes. She pulled herself out of bed, fighting the torturous hangover from the night before. She dressed, then headed back downtown to return the clothes she'd purchased the previous day. After she'd finished returning the parcels of clothing to the stores, she lit out for home, to attempt to bandage up another gaping wound in her marriage. She waited until after lunch to call Jason, hoping that a full stomach had put him in a less argumentative mood.

She reached him immediately after lunch, opening her conversation with, "I know you don't believe me, Jason, but I really was invited to help Mister Spinner host a party his office was putting on for the Senate. The lady in their office who usually helps with these wing-dings was ill. He's asked me to help again the next time they put one of these on because they thought I did a fantastic job. I just thought it would help you have an inside track to know some of the people in the legislature. I really thought it was important to your career, and they did need the help! I've taken all the clothes back, so we won't have to pay for them. I don't know what got into me," she continued. "I guess I just saw it as an opportunity to help the family get ahead, in my own stupid way." She looked at her watch, and rolled her eyes back, as if to speed up the process of her obligatory apology so she could be off to her next rendezvous with L.C.

Jason hesitated to answer, then said, "I'm having a real hard time swallowing this whole thing. It's hard for me to believe that you couldn't have called or left a note at my office."

"But I did, Jason. I called at noon. I talked to some airman who said he didn't work there, but promised he'd leave you the message."

"No one in his right mind would believe such preposterous excuses, Jessica. It's just more than I can tolerate," he responded. "I'm not going to listen to any more of this…I've had it."

Jessica sobbed theatrically "I'm really sorry you don't believe me, Jason. I was just trying to help. I wanted to be a part of your life, to be included, but I can see that was a mistake! I'd better let you get back to work. I'll see you when you get home," she whimpered, knowing that Jason would never jeopardize his position in the Air Force by filing for a divorce. "I'm sorry that you always think something is going on every time I leave the house," she snipped as she hung up the phone.

Within five minutes after her conversation with Jason, Jessica was on the phone with L.C. "I'm just so glad I was able to reach you, L.C.," she said. "I'm just out of my mind trying to live with that pathetic little man. He's such a coward. He won't fight for anything. I thought he cared enough for our marriage that he would stand up for himself. He's just so spineless, just pathetic! I can't go on living with someone who doesn't want to be a man." She reprised with the same melodramatic sympathy act she'd just given Jason.

"You're just upset. Look, I'm going over to the club. Why don't you meet me over there? It'd be good for you to get out of the house for awhile," L.C. offered. "Anyone asks, tell them you had an errand to run."

"I need to be with you so badly, L.C. I'll be at the club as soon as I can get dressed and do something with these damn kids. They're just driving me up the wall!"

"Kids? Whose kids?"

Jessica realized what she'd said. "Neighbor kids! I've had them over here all morning, taking care of them for a friend down the street."

"Oh, I knew you said you didn't have any children. Anyway, I'll see you at the club whenever you can get there."

Jessica's clandestine meeting with L.C. at the club eventually adjourned to a local motel. L.C. had become drunk enough that Jessica was easily able to maneuver him to where she had the home court advantage, slipping into bed with the well-inebriated lawyer. The encounter was brief. Within minutes, L.C. was sprawled out naked, making a thunderous snore.

Jessica slipped out of the bed, still undressed, and began pilfering L.C.'s wallet. When she'd finished helping herself to his cash, she dressed and then sat down at the small desk in the room to write him a note. She composed a masterfully written love scribble, exalting his performance. She knew she held the only clear memory of the brief encounter that had transpired in the motel bed.

L.C. neither missed his cash nor had a conscious recollection of his performance the previous night, assuming that his resources in both cases had been adequately spent. Jessica and L.C. began to frequent the same motel several times a week, dispensing with the formality of having to have dinner and cocktails before having their passionate romps.

Jessica usually tried to arrange her meetings with L.C. to coincide with Jason's out-of-town trips or mandatory evening functions at the base. It was becoming increasingly difficult for her to keep her schedule with L.C. secret from Jason. Little hints of her infidelity, such as matchbook covers or candy wrappers with the hotel name on them, began to attract Jason's attention. He'd tried to follow her several times, but was foiled each time by a change in Jessica's plans that diverted her away from the motel at the last minute.

Early one morning, Jessica had stopped by Jason's office to tell him she was going shopping and would be home late that evening. The truth was, she had accepted an offer from L.C. to accompany him to Kansas City for the day to attend the trial of one of his clients.

Jessica walked into Jason's office unannounced, sitting behind his desk and rummaging through his paperwork with a halfhearted interest, while she waited for the staff meeting he was attending in another room to adjourn. She picked through the papers on his desk, scanning his mail and interoffice memos, placing them back into their original position after she'd finished reading through them.

One of Jason's many squadron responsibilities was to prepare newsy articles for a monthly Air Force publication, The Air Schooner, distributed throughout the world and selectively shared on occasion with the civilian press. He was enthralled with the power of his tiny newspaper. The temptation to use it to elevate his own opinions on various topics was frequently more than he could handle. The Air Force had carefully structured a 'fail safe' system for the approval of all articles written by such aspiring journalists, to protect the integrity of the Air Force from controversy. More than once Jason had seen his journalistic efforts purged, without comment, by higher command, like so much sewage.

Jessica's prying nature, compounded by her eagerness to be on her way with L.C., kept her hands busily opening files and drawers within her immediate reach. She found a folder in Jason's middle drawer stamped confidential in bold red letters. Inside, under a cover sheet were several reports stapled together, with the upper- most report defaced by a handwritten message scrawled in red ink.

The note had been addressed to Jason, in response to his request for approval of an article that he had submitted to headquarters. The note read:

> Under no circumstances are you to publish this article. The repercussions from such an ideological fantasy, coming from the military and getting into the hands of the civilian press, would create an absolute furor from the civilian sector, not to mention the Joint Chiefs. It's absolutely contrary to our constitutional authority. You're to destroy all copies of this article and refrain from authoring any further creative compositions on this or any other controversial topics. I hope I make myself clear! You are neither qualified nor authorized to speak for the Department of the Air Force concerning its philosophy or public policy! Get rid of this stuff, now!'
>
> signed: Colonel J. J. Marshal

She began to read the article, in which Jason had suggested that the military become "Big Brother" to oversee a misguided American society led astray by infectious socialism and communism. It was one thing for the more conservative element of the military to think such a thing in private; but for them to officially admit that society needed a good housecleaning under the supervision of the armed forces would have sent shock waves all the way to the President. Jessica was by no means an expert on militarism, or politics for that matter, but she knew a well-brewed scandal when she saw it. She lifted a copy of the article from the folder and slipped it into her purse. A few minutes later Jason walked into the room, frazzled from his meeting and caught off guard when he found his wife sitting at his desk.

"Hello, Jason!" Jessica said. "I just came by to see if you'd take me to dinner at the club tonight. I think we need to discuss a few things, and I don't particularly feel like cooking at home."

"It's not like you've been doing a lot of cooking lately, Jessica, but I'll be more than glad to take you out to dinner if it will resolve any of this cat-and-mouse game we've got going on. Why don't you go home and take care of the boys until dinner and I'll pick you up in a few hours," Jason added, suspicious of her motives.

Jessica canceled her scheduled rendezvous with L.C., throwing a meal together for the boys and outfitting herself for dinner at the club. The evening degenerated into the same old arguments, resolving little except to confirm to Jason that Jessica was hell-bent to liberate herself, and determined to continue her unconscionable behavior. She made no effort to deny her meetings with L.C., but only protested Jason's infringement on her privacy. "You have no right to follow me around town, doing your little cloak and dagger act, trying to catch me doing something that's none of your concern!" she huffed.

"None of my concern?" Jason responded. "Jesus, I'm your husband. I ought'a kill that no good son of a bitch!"

"What a joke, Jason. You haven't got the guts to kill anyone, much less fight for anything else in this world. Your father's the only one with enough grit to do that, and you certainly didn't inherit any of his backbone. What I do with my time is my business!" she snapped, glaring at him across the table.

The next day Jessica was reunited with L.C. at the motel, and she produced a copy of the document filched from Jason's desk, giving it to L.C. to read.

L.C. shook his head in disbelief, mumbling under his breath as he continued to read Jason's article, "Stupid jackass! My Gawd, heads would roll if anyone ever got a look at this thing!"

"I'd rather figure out some way to make his father cough up some of that cash he's got hoarded in his room," Jessica said, staring out the motel window, massaging L.C.'s neck while he continued to read over the document. "That old man's got more money than he knows what to do with." she added.

"You never told me your husband came from a wealthy family!"

Jessica shook her head. "It hasn't done me any good. I've never seen a penny of the old man's money. He hates the ground I walk on. Jason's the only one who'll ever see any of it, if he lives long enough."

L.C. was amused, laughing as he quizzed her more about James. "How'd he make it?"

"Growing tomatoes, peaches and selling real estate, if you can believe that! He's a physician, but I think the bigger part of his income has come from deals he's made selling oil property around J-ville. That old man's got the touch. He's as crooked as the Mississippi River."

"How so?" L.C. asked, more attentive than before.

"I just know that he's always done everything he could to keep from paying any income taxes," Jessica replied. "He keeps his money stashed in cans and jars all over the house and yard."

"You ever seen any of it? I mean, how do you know he's not just talkin'? Tax evasion is pretty heavy duty stuff," L.C. told her.

"He never talked about it," she retorted. "In fact, he'd have probably killed anyone who ever discussed it. I know he's got it, 'cause I saw a wad of money one night when the old nigger that works for him threw a load of it in the garbage."

L.C. chuckled again. "Maybe he needs a good tax attorney, if he has enough to be throwing money away like that. It'd be nice to have a client that could pay his bills."

Jessica laughed condescendingly. "What in the world would he need a tax attorney for? Like I said, he never pays any taxes!"

"Maybe you ought to think about turning him in to the IRS, unless he gives you a little of what he's got stashed away," L.C. suggested. He only partially believed Jessica's story about the old man and his concealed horde of money lying around the house.

"God, I don't know, L.C.; he's not like anyone you've ever met! He's a really tough old coot."

"Really," L.C. snorted in a less-than-impressed tone. He thought James couldn't possibly be as tough as the elements that slithered into his office, who were looking to have him or his partner keep them out of jail, having been accused of everything from tax evasion to murder.

"I don't know if I wanta be on his bad side, L.C.," Jessica said, dropping her hands from his shoulders and turning towards the window, as if she were watching to see if James was standing outside. "They'd have to pay me an awful lot of money to get me involved in a rift with him."

"Look, the worst thing that would happen is that you'd get a reward for turning him into the IRS. I mean, come on, what's an old man gonna do, anyway?" L.C. asked, a gleam of criminality in his eyes. He was anything but serious about the suggestion, doing most of the talking to impress Jessica that there was a tough, manly side to his usual intellectual personality. After all, who said an Ivy Leaguer couldn't hold his own against an old man from Texas?

"It's probably the only way I'd ever get my hands on any of that money," she said, "the way Jason and I are going. I wanta think about it for awhile, L.C. The man really scares the hell out of me." Jessica turned away from the window and started putting on her clothes, as if she needed to escape from the room, from the heresy just discussed.

L.C., was amused by Jessica's fear of the old man. She dropped the idea of blackmailing James, at least temporarily until she was certain of her future with L.C.

L.C.'s wife, Jean, had been his childhood sweetheart. She had persevered through the college and law school years, working to support the family while L.C. attended school. She was a woman of almost angelic personality. Other than the few months she'd had off for the birth of their daughter Debby, Jean had worked for the same company since marrying L.C.

Jean's existence with L.C. appeared to be anything but auspicious, living in an extremely modest home, tucked away in the same GI Bill housing project that they'd lived in since he had come home from the War. Until now, he had lived a typical middle-class lifestyle, committed to his career, belonging to all the appropriate organizations aspiring young lawyers can be expected to join. He was always mindful of his image as a family man with others in the community, and vehemently guarded his reputation from anything that might tarnish it. His social commitments had over the years, been tastefully met alone, respecting Jean's request to be allowed to stay out of the social mainstream and concentrate on raising their daughter. Except for a few short-lived escapades while he was under the influence, L.C. never had ventured far from his devotion to Jean.

Although L.C. was considered one of the brightest legal minds in the field of income tax and finance, he had little success in retaining much of his own personal income. He typically piddled away most of what he made on poor investments and business expenses, leaving little for his family except what they needed to live on.

He had been a compassionate and caring husband before Jessica slipped her hooks into him. She was hell-bent on creating a new image of success for L.C., and herself. A new car, new clothes and expensive outings to posh Topeka night spots were a top priority in her plan of attack, so that they both would be noticed by socie'te.

It took little prodding for L.C. to realize that his career could use an overhaul, a spiffing up, a little harmless dressing with his beautiful companion latched to his arm.

Jessica, on the other hand, had other motives for her clinging association with L.C.

When the opportunity availed itself, they would sneak away on overnight junkets, bar association conventions and mini-vacations to Cancun, Mexico and Ocho Rios, Jamaica. All the while, Jean and Debby sat home, convinced that L.C. was faithfully pursuing his profession for their sake, a devoted husband and father. His lack of talent for money management soon created a bleak dawning of financial worry for L.C. He idolized his dark-haired mistress, spending himself into a financial labyrinth that was beginning to take its toll.

Jason hadn't been eradicated from the picture altogether. He had his suspicions of her extramarital activities, but still preferred to look only superficially at Jessica's outings, for fear of rocking his soon-to-be-capsized career.

Out of the mire of tangled reasoning and distorted rationalizations by her husband and her lover, Jessica strutted forward, committed to nothing but herself. She schemed and maneuvered, feasting joyfully on the resources of both men, immersing L.C. in the same financial woes that she'd placed on Jason. At home, her violent temper was frequently unleashed on her children. David and Dale both had experienced her unprovoked beatings and abusive language. The catalyst was usually something totally unrelated to the children, a fight with L.C., a comment from Jason, a mood from drinking.

Late one evening Jason returned home from a flight to find Jessica standing over Dale, holding him by his hair and driving her fist into the boy's face. The child lay silently, accepting his terror without a sound, knowing that crying only increased the frequency and severity of the blows.

David had developed his own set of problems, in the midst of all the turmoil between Jason and Jessica. A young doctor on call at St. Joseph Hospital happened to notice the number of similarities in David's symptoms from previous emergency visits. When he realized how many times the boy had been in the emergency room, and the consistency in the time of the evening when he was there, he became suspicious. No one had been able to diagnose the problem. On an intuitive hunch, the young doctor arranged to have David examined by a psychiatrist from the Menninger Clinic. He kept David overnight, with the excuse that he wanted to run tests on him. By mid-afternoon, the doctor had his hunch confirmed. When Jason arrived at the hospital to take David home, the young doctor ushered him into his office where the psychiatrist was waiting with his report.

"Colonel Lavoisier, I'm Doctor Preston. I was on call last night when David was brought in."

"Yes I remember," Jason answered. "Did you find out anything? This stomach problem of his has really been giving us fits!" Jason said with a smile. We've absolutely agonized over what could be wrong with him."

"What's wrong with David is not his stomach!" the doctor said bluntly.

Jason gave the two doctors a look that said, 'I've been through this before.' "Well, let's hear what you think it is…I've heard everything from gall stones to puberty," he laughed.

Both doctors sat straight-faced, neither of them responding to Jason's sense of humor. "This is Doctor Blair, a psychiatrist from the Menninger Clinic."

Jason perked up. "I can assure you my son hasn't got anything wrong with his mind. That's certainly a different approach, though!"

"I'd like for you to listen to what Doctor Blair has to say. I think he can help David.

"I'm listening." Jason said, with a disingenuous smirk.

Doctor Blair opened his file, "Colonel, I'm going to ask you some personal questions that may be uncomfortable for you, but we can't help your son unless we understand more about what's going on at home."

"Sure," Jason said nervously. "I don't have anything to hide...I mean, there's no reason why I shouldn't answer your questions."

Doctor Blair looked at Jason over the rim of his glasses and then returned to his file. "Are you and Mrs. Lavoisier having problems at home? Marital problems?"

"Not any more than anyone else," Jason answered, laughing slightly, then nervously cleared his throat.

"Is your wife seeing anyone else?" the doctor asked.

"No!" Jason said quickly. "We have our ups and downs, but nothing major."

Doctor Blair became a little agitated, "All right, Colonel, let me put it another way. Are you aware that your wife is having men over to the house while you're gone?"

Jason looked up at Blair, gritting his teeth before he said, "Who told you that?"

"Your son told us, Colonel," Blair answered.

"My son? Well, you know how kids are...they're always imagining things," Jason said, trying to disguise the fact that Blair had hit a raw nerve.

"We don't think he's imagining anything, Colonel. And, quite frankly, I don't think you're being entirely honest with us either," Blair said, closing the file and pulling off his glasses. "I believe that your son's concern for your relationship with his mother has manifested itself into this stomach problem he's having. The short of it is, Colonel, your boy's scared."

"Scared of what?" Jason questioned. "I mean he's not the one, she's..." Jason stopped himself. "You're right, Doctor...I'm not being honest with you. Jason bowed his head, closed his hands into fists and placed them against either side of his face as if to punish himself for, again, failing to deal with the circumstances.

"Look, Colonel, we're not interested in blaming anyone. The best thing for your son at this point is to find the source of his problem."

"I'm sorry," Jason apologized; "of course I'll answer your questions! I'll do whatever's best for my boys, whatever'll help them...both of them."

"Let's go back to my questions about you and your wife. Are you aware that she's been having other men over to the house while you've been gone?" Blair asked again.

"I've been suspicious of it," Jason answered. "I've never been able to prove it, or catch her in the act."

"You know your sons have caught her in your bed with someone! She apparently threatened David, told him that if you found out...if you did anything about it, it was all going to be his fault."

Jason looked up. "What?"

"Yes," Blair explained. "She told him he'd be responsible if the family was forced to split up over what he saw. Quite frankly, Colonel, what it looks like to us is that your son thinks that you and his mother are having problems because you've discovered his little secret."

Jason closed his eyes and gave a long exasperated sigh. "What about my other son? Is he going to have the same kind of problem with all of this? I guess you know that she's been beating the living hell out of him. David's gotten to where he'll take off whenever she tries to start something, the beating, screaming, slapping, and all."

"They're both going to need professional help, Colonel; but it's possible that we can clear this thing up before it gets any worse. Sometimes these things can be straightened out without much problem. Sometimes it takes years, depending on how much damage has been done. What we've got to determine now is how deep-seated this problem really is."

"All right, Doctor. Where do we go from here?" Jason asked, finally determined to do something. "I've always put my career ahead of my sons, but that's over now. Just tell me what you want me to do."

As Jason began to disclose the myriad of bizarre events that had occurred during his marriage to Jessica, both doctors sat speechless. After two hours of talking, Doctor Blair interrupted Jason.

"From what I've heard so far, Colonel Lavoisier, this situation is far more complex than I'd imagined. We'd want to talk to your wife...if you think she'd cooperate with us. I think you and your wife are going to need a lot of help, if you're going to have any hope of salvaging your marriage," Blair added, looking at his colleague for confirmation.

"You know, Doctor, there's no doubt in my mind that you've got my son's best interest in mind, and that you're very sincere about wanting to help Jessica and me! The reality of this thing is that my wife and I are beyond reconciling our problems. You know this as well as I do. There's no way she'd ever cooperate in any of this." Jason wept for brief moment. Neither doctor said anything.

"I've been a pitiful failure at much of what I've tried to do with myself over the years, including my marriage. I might as well tell you that, at this point in my life, I'd consider a divorce from her as a positive accomplishment, especially if it would help my children. What I can do, if there's any way in this world to do it, is to take my sons out of her realm of influence, have them live with my parents. At least, they'd be where she couldn't get her hands on either of them."

"Well, that's really the bottom line in this whole thing, Jason. One way or the other, the environment that your children are living in has got to be changed. As I see it, there are three alternatives. One would be for you and your wife to seek psychiatric counseling, preferably from the same center where the boys are being treated, but you've obviously canceled out that option.

"The second alternative would be to send them to your parents' home. I normally wouldn't be in favor of this, except that I understand that the boys have a very positive relationship with your parents and that your father is a physician. It's probably the only alternative that makes any sense at this point.

"A third alternative, an option I would find most unpleasant, would be to have Social Services become involved," Blair continued, looking at his colleague.

Preston looked up at Jason. "The physical abuse by your wife, and your failure to intervene, would be grounds to legally have the boys removed from your custody. Doctor Blair and I both agree: while we have a responsibility to report all of this, we also feel that it would be in both your sons' best interest to try and handle this thing without getting Social Services involved."

"I assure you, it'll be taken care of," Jason said, emphatically. Blair stood up, tucking the file under his arm before he spoke: "For everyone's sake, I hope so! I'm going to hold my decision on this matter until you get back with me about your plans to send both boys to their grandparent's home.

Jason spent the next two days pondering how best to approach Jessica about giving up her control of the children to his parents. He knew she would resist any change that would appear to make her look like an unfit mother. He also knew that she would fight any effort to allow James and Lora to have custody of the boys. He decided that his only solution was to offer Jessica a bribe, a large lump sum of cash to convince her to abrogate her legal rights to the children. Since he was virtually penniless, James would have to be called upon to bankroll the deal, as always. For Jason to have to approach his father for the money to buy his children from the clutches of his raving wife was almost more difficult for him than having to confront Jessica with the proposition.

Jason finally called his father, giving him the blow-by-blow evaluation and ultimatum by Doctors Preston and Blair, knowing that their opinion would weigh heavily with James' decision.

"That's the situation, Dad," Jason finally said in a defeated tone, as he talked to James on the phone. "I've got to get this handled or they're going to take the boys away from me and place them in the custody of the State."

"Nobody's going to take <u>my</u> grandsons, I'll promise you that!" James vowed.

"I'd be free of Jessica and could send the boys whatever they needed in the way of money to live on while they stayed with you and mother. I'm afraid, if we try to fight her, she'd get one of those legal weasels she's commiserating with to step in and help her."

"How soon do we need to move on this, son?"

"Right away," Jason replied. "I just can't take a chance on her doing something to one of them again. Both of the boys have been through hell with her. I really wish I knew what to say to them, to tell them both that it's all gonna be okay."

"I'm gonna wire you the money tomorrow, Jason, but I want you to know that I don't like the idea of paying her off. I'm gonna tell you right up front: if this doesn't work, if she doesn't take the deal, it'll be handled my way."

"I know she'll go for it, Dad, and we'll be rid of her, once and for all," Jason concluded.

James wasn't as sure. "Craig Fisher, my attorney, will dictate an agreement to a local attorney up there, and I want you to make sure she signs it!"

"If she hesitates," he ordered, "back off and don't press it with her. I'll take it from there. The only condition I have for all of this is that you go through with the divorce. No second thoughts, no cold feet: just get away from her before it's too late for you and the boys."

Jason followed James' instructions, setting aside a time to meet with Jessica when the boys were out of the house. He had a check and the agreement in his coat when he confronted her with the deal.

Jason began cautiously, "I think you need to know that David was seen by a psychiatrist from Menninger Clinic when he was in the hospital."

"Now why would David be seeing a psychiatrist? Something to do with me, I suppose," Jessica remarked, batting her eyes.

"When the doctor talked to David, it seems that it came out about you having your boyfriends over...in our bedroom. David told him about the man that he caught you in bed with...L.C., I presume. David told the doctor that you beat Dale because they walked into the room."

"Not really...I beat him because I'd told the man I didn't have any children. I couldn't care less if they catch me in bed; I told both of them to stay in their rooms. They didn't do what I said."

"You expected them to sit in their rooms, in the dark, while you did your thing in our bed with your boyfriend? You're sick, Jessica!" Jason snapped. "The authorities know all about you and your tough stuff with the kids," Jason went on, starting to explain what Doctor Blair had said when Jessica interrupted him.

"Beating up the kids? How about living with a wimp? How about living with a child instead of a man? Did you tell them that? They don't know the half of it, and you don't either! You want something to get upset about? Try this on...I'm pregnant! One month pregnant! Now what do you want to talk about, Jason, darling? And you're sure as hell not the father! Do you think this is the first time I've gotten pregnant from another man? I guess you would, you naive little boy!" she snarled.

Jason was stunned, shocked senseless by Jessica's statement. He stared at her for a moment, forcing himself to continue, as if she hadn't made her startling announcement.

"The psychiatrist said that if David and Dale aren't taken somewhere else to live that he'll have no other alternative but to inform the authorities about what's going on." Jason said, reaching into his pocket to retrieve the check and agreement from James.

"I don't suppose you told them about the abuse I've had to endure with you and your lousy job. Well, your self-righteous mother and that beast of a father of yours can have their little brats, under one condition!"

"What's that?" Jason asked, surprised that she had willingly offered up the children. He knew there would have to be a glitch in the agreement.

"Oh, nothing except that I want you to agree to say that you're the father of this baby."

"Do what?" Jason blurted out.

"You heard me! I know that there's been, how do they say, a little alienation of affection on my part for the last year, darling," Jessica continued, "but I think that would be a little difficult for you to prove, under the circumstances. Oh, yes, and one more thing...I want an immediate, uncontested divorce from you and this sorry excuse of a life."

Jason pushed the envelope back into the inside pocket of his coat. "Why would you want me to admit to being the father? You know who the real father is...or have you slept with so many men that you're not sure?"

"I'm sure," she said, hesitating for a second. "It's just a little insurance, in case he gets cold feet about getting a divorce from his wife. If that happens, you get to pay child support. If he comes through, you get what you want, and I get what I want!"

"I see...another one of your little cold, calculated maneuvers." Jason declared.

"That's right, Jason. It's the only way you're going to get what you want from me. After all, I've got to look out for myself. So, go call your father and tell him he's getting his lovely little darlings and

I'm getting my divorce.   Just don't think for a minute that you've gotten the upper hand in this!"

That evening when the boys returned home, Jason took them aside in the back bedroom and told them what had happened. He told them what Doctor Blair had said about the problems they were having. He told them that he knew what their mother had been doing when he was away from home. He carefully confronted David with his guilt over the encounter with Jessica when he'd caught her in the bed with the stranger. Finally, he told them that their mother and he had decided to get a divorce.

Both boys sat speechless, listening to Jason explain, none of it making any sense to either of them. He realized that, even with the amount of abuse that both of them had taken from Jessica, neither of the boys understood the necessity for their parents separating.

David covered his face with his hands as he lay across the bed. Dale sat stone-faced, watching his father leave the room. He walked over to the wall switch and turned off the light, sliding down against the wall in the corner of the room, listening to David's muffled crying.

The next afternoon, while Jason was at work, a moving van arrived in front of the house and began loading the furniture. Dale and David sat on the curb in a dreary slump, watching the movers carry out Jessica's confiscation of all of their family's personal effects. She had been gone since the previous day, showing up with the movers to make sure that nothing was missed. When the van was loaded, Jessica walked out to where David and Dale were sitting.

"I just want you boys to know that this is your father's doing. I love you both, but I just can't live with him anymore. I've tried everything to be a good mother and wife, but it takes two to make a marriage work. Your father's never made an effort to make me happy. I've got to do what's right for me, to make a life for myself, where I can have what I want. You'll never know how hard I tried to make things be the way they should, for all of us! I've agreed to let you go to your grandparents' house, only because I think it will help you appreciate what you had here, how well off you really were."

Both boys looked up at her, saying nothing as she continued. "I'd love to have you visit me, but the place I'm moving to is so small I'm afraid it wouldn't be very comfortable. Well, anyway, I'll talk to you before you leave for your grandparents," she finished, smiling as if she were saying goodbye to a casual neighbor.

Both boys watched as the moving truck followed Jessica's car, disappearing behind a row of trees. Neither one of them spoke, standing up and walking back into the emptied house to their room, to wait for their father to come home.

Two weeks later David and Dale were in Jacksonville, with James and Lora. Jason had given up his base quarters and moved into an apartment just outside the entrance to Forbes. Jessica was comfortably settled into a rental house that L.C. had leased for her so that they could be together whenever he could manage to slip away from Jean. But, when L.C. found out about Jessica's pregnancy, he made himself scarce, fearing that Jessica might implicate him in a paternity suit, or at the very least create a scandal for him that surely would find its way to the halls of the Kansas Capitol.

His hesitancy to divorce Jean added to Jessica's smoldering rage. Days passed with little more than a phone call from her lover, and it wasn't what she had expected. She'd committed herself to their new togetherness, but where was L.C.?

CHAPTER 23

Jessica anguished over her apparent abandonment. She was consumed by paranoia, believing that Jason must somehow had been involved with L.C.'s decision to stay away from her. A threat, blackmail, she wasn't sure. She finally concluded that it was Jason's presence in Topeka that was causing L.C. to keep his distance.

'I've got to get him out of here,' she thought. 'We'll see if keeping his career is as important to him as slithering around trying to destroy my life!'

Jessica knew who the people were in Topeka with the right pull, even though many of them had not yet had the unenviable pleasure of her acquaintance.

"Hello, I'm trying to locate John Ragsdale, and I was told that he could be reached at this number?" Jessica said, trying to disguise her voice.

"Hold on, ma'am," a man answered. "Rags, it's for you on line three!" he screamed.

There was a brief pause before another man answered, "This is John Ragsdale...what can I do for you?"

"Mister Ragsdale, I understand—" Jessica started to say before she was interrupted.

"I'm sorry, I can't hear what you're saying. You'll have to speak up, ma'am," Ragsdale complained.

Jessica started over again, "I understand that you write a column for the Journal?"

"That's right, can I help you?"

"I have something that I think would be of interest to you. I'd like for you to write an article on it; I think you'll find it most informative."

"Well, I'll have to see what it is before I commit to anything. Who am I talking to?" he asked.

"That's not important. Just wait a day or two and you'll receive the document in the mail," Jessica whispered, then hung up the phone.

John Ragsdale had been an outspoken critic of the military establishment for more years than Jessica had been married to Jason.

But he wasn't prone to publishing his exposés without substantiating his sources, especially when it was one that had the aroma of a vendetta. Credibility was hard-earned in the newspaper business, and Ragsdale had learned long before that the underlying motivation for his getting the exclusive on a story was as important to verify as the story itself.

After he'd read the article written by Jason, his instincts led him to contact the Base Commander's office for some background on the document. After an informative conversation with the Base Commander, General D.O. Dorlick, Ragsdale was convinced that there was nothing official about the article, and agreed to return the document to the commander's attention. Dorlick was enraged by Jason's essay, prompting a chain of phone calls to subordinates that filtered down the ladder of command, landing on Jason like a wrecking ball.

Before retreat sounded that afternoon, Jason was standing at brace in Dorlick's office.

"Sit down, Colonel Lavoisier!" the General ordered.

Jason sat down, hat in hand, totally in the dark about the reason for his appearance before the General.

"You know, Colonel, I've never liked having to convene a court martial to send a man from my command over to Leavenworth, especially an officer!"

Jason gasped, almost collapsing back into the soft chair.

"I put a mechanic from this base there for five years after we caught him sabotaging aircraft engines, because he was mad about getting passed over for promotion. I even had a fella shot on Saipan, during the war, for raping a nurse. I never liked what they did, but in a way, I understood what motivated them to do it.

"In your case I'm having a difficult time understanding why a career man, a Lieutenant Colonel with everything going for him, would go out of his way to commit such a blatant act of insubordination!"

"Sir?" Jason questioned, "I don't understand."

"Well, understand this," Dorlick said, holding up the document returned by Ragsdale. "Look familiar?"

"General Dorlick, I assure you that I haven't got the slightest idea of what this is all about. If you're referring to this…the article I submitted for publication in the Sky Schooner, I received that back through channels and destroyed every single one of my copies, as I was ordered."

"Apparently you disposed of every single copy except…one," he said, throwing Ragsdale's copy onto the desk in front of Jason. "Fortunately, the columnist had some integrity about who he smeared. Now, I want to know who the woman was that sent this to the Journal."

"Sir," Jason said, "I've just recently gone through a divorce, and, as much as I hate to admit it, I think my ex-wife may have been responsible. She was alone in my office, just before we were divorced. It's entirely possible that she took a copy of it to use against me."

"You know, Colonel, if it wasn't for the fact that you're so close to retirement, I'd push for a general court-martial and watch them lock the damn doors on you. Personally, I don't give a damn about your personal life. What I care about is my career, which you and your ex-wife have just about finished off. I've got no way of really knowing if that goddamn reporter is on the level about not publishing this piece of trash! All I know is that he's got me by the short hairs for as long as he wants a piece of me. The only thing I'm certain about is that I've seen all of you I want to, you and your problem wife that I've heard so much about!"

"Sir, I don't know what to say. I wasn't aware that she'd taken anything out of the office!" Jason said, strangling on his tie, as the anxiety began to build.

"Don't bother to explain, Colonel. I'd be thrilled to see you resign, but I'll settle to have you transferred. Apparently, your C.O. has had several phone calls from your ex, complaining about insufficient checks you've written to her, for one thing or another. She's also given him some rather startling reports about you slapping your children around. You seem to have a problem keeping your dirty linen to yourself, Colonel. The service has no place for an officer who can't keep his family problems under wraps…and doesn't follow orders, to boot."

"General, you're really not getting the truth about all of this!" Jason tried to explain.

"You're going to be off this base in a week, one way or the other. If you elect to take the transfer, I promise you...you won't see a stateside installation until the day you're mustered out. That's all I have to say, Colonel, and you can thank your sweet ass that I didn't throw the book at you!"

Jason sat quietly listening as General Dorlick finished his chewing out. When it was over, Jason saluted and left headquarters, astonished at finding his career once again on the brink of disaster, a la San Angelo.

He left the base and drove towards town, stopping at a local dive to ponder his dilemma in the company of several stiff drinks. He couldn't figure out why Jessica had seen fit to set the dogs on him, weeks after the verbal battles from the divorce had died down. When he'd bolstered his courage with enough drinks, he called her house, deciding that it was time for a showdown.

It wasn't until ten o'clock that evening that someone finally answered the phone. It was L.C.

"I'd like to talk to Jessica. This is Jason! I've been trying to reach her all day," Jason muttered, vexed at hearing L.C. answer the phone.

"Jessica," L.C. screamed, "it's Jason! I think he's pissed off about me being here," Jason heard L.C. say, as he made an ineffective effort to cover the phone with his hand.

"What's he want?" Jessica's voice thundered from another room. "Why the hell didn't you tell him I wasn't here?" she said, fumbling with the phone. "Hello, Jason, what a pleasant surprise to hear from you."

"Let's cut the small talk, Jessica. I know about the article you clipped from my desk and sent downtown. It didn't work. The paper sent it back to the Base Commander."

Jessica reacted in disgust, challenging his statement, "I don't know what you're talking about! I haven't sent anything to anyone."

"You didn't get me court martialed; I thought you'd wanta know that. I'm being transferred overseas. It really doesn't matter, though. I'd just as soon be as far away from you as I can get," he snapped as Jessica tried to interrupt.

"You're making things up, Jason. Just more of the same, trying to blame everyone else for your problems!"

Jason laughed, feeling the numbing effects of the half-dozen drinks he'd had. "I don't think so, Jessica. The General asked me to let you know you're going to be subject to an investigation by the FBI if that article raises its ugly little head again. Ask your lawyer friend to tell you what they do to people who steal military documents."

"You're drunk, Jason!" she yelled.

"Yep, I sure as hell am. It's the only way I could bring myself to talk to you."

"I'm not concerned about you or your general! Fortunately, I don't have to associate with you and that low-class trash out there anymore! I really don't have any more time for you or your threats, Jason," Jessica snipped, holding the phone away from her ear.

"Believe me, Jessica…you won't be hearing from me again. But I think it's appropriate to tell you that my experience with you has certainly been an adventure! You're the most sordid, cold-blooded, slithering animal I think I've ever met. I'm just thankful that my children are finally out from under your grip! I just pray to God that they never find out about their mother's reputation!" Jason continued hoping he'd had the last word.

"What do you mean by that? I have an impeccable reputation!" Jessica screamed. "You're the one that's the social outcast, not me!"

"You know, Jessica, you've always had your way. You've wrecked my career, my self-respect, and finally my family, everything that was important to me! But you're not any different from the rest of us. You're gonna pay. No one can live such an insane existence, ripping and clawing the heart out of everyone, not without paying a price sometime in their life. At least with the boys living with my folks, they'll learn about caring for someone else, about what personal integrity means!"

"Oh? I don't see where your parents are any trendsetters with integrity. Your father is nothing but a low-class thug…lording it over everyone, and taking whatever he wants. He's not any better than the rest of us! We'll see what kind of pillar of righteousness that old bastard really is," she said, pausing. "Then let's see who the kids end up with. Just don't push me, Jason; I can do a lot more than I've already done, and don't think I can't." she growled.

"No one's pushing, Jessica. Believe me, everyone is trying to stay out of your way. Just don't hurt the boys. Leave them alone. My parents' home is the last vestige of sanity in their lives. Just don't destroy that, like you've done with everything else. See if you can't make yourself care for someone else, just once," he finished, hearing the phone disconnect.

Jessica sat in the living room, tapping out a cadence on an end table next to her chair, making a small figurine rattle as it vibrated its way to the edge.

"Everything's my fault, never his, never anyone's but mine. All I've ever tried to do is make a better life for myself," she mumbled. "They sit there on their thrones, watching everything I do, deciding if I'm moral or immoral. Who the hell do they think they are, telling <u>me</u> how to live?"

Jessica slammed her fist into the table, finally sending the figurine crashing to the floor.

"And that old man, that son of a bitch, sits there, counting his money, hiding it from the Feds. And he dares to say <u>I'm</u> the one with no integrity? They want me to leave them alone, to be quiet. Well, I'll be quiet…just as quiet as they'd like…as long as they're willing to pay for it. Let's see what the Great Doctor Lavoisier is willing to fork over in exchange for his self-respect, in that dumpy little town of his," Jessica murmured, shouting for L.C.

"For God sake, Jessica, I'm trying to listen to the game. What do you want, darling?" he answered from the bedroom.

"What did you tell me about getting Jason's father to pay some money to keep me from turning him into the IRS? You said you knew how to do it, without him being able to get me for blackmail," Jessica said, with L.C. still ignoring her. She stood up and walked to the back bedroom, crawling onto the bed, next to him.

"I've got to go, Jessica," he complained. "Jean's left Debby with someone, a friend, and I've got to pick her up. I'm already late! Jean's gonna know I've been with someone, and you're getting my clothes all wrinkled."

"Jean already knows that you've been with someone! She just doesn't want to admit it. She could never treat you the way I do. She's too timid, too reserved for a man like you. You know you like the things I do to you, L.C., admit it."

L.C. grunted, trying to ignore her persuasive moves, pulling a deep draw from his cigar with his arm tucked behind his head as Jessica teased at him, trying to lure him away from his ball game.

Finally he sat up in bed, and placed his cigar in the ashtray. "I guess it won't hurt for me to be a little late picking Debby up; I think they've gotten used to it."

Jessica repeated her question with a whine as he pulled at her clothes: "What about Jason's father? How do I get the money out of him?"

L.C. was more interested in what he was doing with Jessica than answering her question. He panted out a response as he continued to struggle to undo her clothes. "Come by the office tomorrow, and we'll work on it then," he said, burying his face in her neck.

Jessica glared off in the distance, detached from her lover's efforts, thinking only about her revenge on the Lavoisiers—all of them.

The receptionist looked at her with a nervous smile and then glanced at the door to L.C.'s office.

"Martha, would you let L.C. know I'm here, whenever you have a chance? He's expecting me for lunch," Jessica said, smiling at the tense secretary.

"Aren't you early, Jessica? You might want to come back a little later. I think he's going to be awhile," she said, glancing nervously at his door for a second time.

Jessica could hear voices coming from L.C.'s office, voices that turned to crying as the door to his office opened. A woman slowly emerged, and stopped at Martha's desk. "You've destroyed all of our lives. I don't understand why you'd want to hurt us like this. He doesn't know what he's doing; neither do you," she whimpered at the rattled secretary, before turning towards the entrance to the office. "I'll have my attorney send over the divorce papers as soon as he can prepare them," she announced, looking back at L. C. "He had a daughter, a family; I just don't understand," she said, softly closing the door behind her.

Jessica turned with a jerk, looking first at L.C., stoking up his cigar and then at Martha who was sitting with her hands over her face.

Martha jumped up and disappeared down the hall. Jessica watched her leave and then followed L.C. into his office.

"What in the hell was <u>that</u> all about?" Jessica demanded to know.

L.C. shifted his jaw back and forth, his eyes fixed on the hallway door. "That was my wife."

"Are you having an affair with your secretary?" Jessica asked, not quite sure if she should be outraged or not.

"Hell, no! I'm not having an affair with her! I'm having an affair with you! Jean was mad at Martha because that's where she thinks I've been every night! Martha is upset because she knew that I'd fire her if she said anything about us. Look, let's get out of here. I need a drink!"

Jessica and L.C. sat at a table in a darkened corner of the club, discussing their plan to extort part of James' hidden booty.

"I just want to know how to do it so that he doesn't turn this thing around and get the police down on me. I need your help." Jessica pleaded. "I know he's got the money, and we can get it all if you'll help me."

"All you've got to do is send him a letter demanding that he pay you what he owes you, some trumped-up debt or something. It's a smoke screen to make it look like you're legit about him owing you money. You just slip a little something in there about telling the IRS about the money he's got rat-holed if he doesn't cooperate," L.C. suggested. "If he tips off the Feds that you're trying to nail him, you can squeeze out of it by saying he owed it to you!"

"Lord, L.C., I can feel that money in my hands. I just hope that old bastard doesn't come after me," Jessica said.

"Look, he's an old man. You're remembering someone from fifteen years ago. He's not gonna mess with you, not when you've got an attorney working with you. He comes around here and I'll have him roughed up! Now quit worrying and send him the letter. Hell, in two weeks you'll have fifty thousand dollars in those pretty hands."

"I hope it's that easy," Jessica said, fidgeting as she looked nervously around the room. "I'll rest a lot easier when I've got the money in my pocket! My Gawd, it'll be wonderful!"

Within three days Jessica's extortion letter had arrived at James' office. When James was handed the letter he stepped into his private office, closing the door as he slipped the wire earpiece of his glasses around his ear. When he had finished reading, he calmly removed his glasses and inserted them, with the letter, back into his coat pocket.

"Angela," James said in a soft-spoken voice, "would you please call my brother Bill? You've got his number in your book. Tell him that I'm planning on coming over to do a little fishing with him. Have him call me tonight at home."

"Yes, Doctor Lavoisier," she answered. What about your appointments?"

"Oh, yes! See if Doctor Brandon will handle our patients, starting next Friday, 'til I get back. Reschedule anyone he can't see until week after next," James ordered, pulling on his suit coat as he left the office.

That evening Bill called James at home. "James, Bill here. How are you?"

"Doin' just fine, Bill," James responded, "thanks for calling!"

"Understand you wanta do a little fishin'. The water's muddier than hell, but I reckon we can find a spot somewhere where the crappie are bitin'," Bill said, excited at the prospect of having James spend a few days with him.

James listened, then finally spoke up. "I'm not comin' over to go fishin' this time, Bill!"

"Oh?" Bill said.

"Got some business to tend to. I'm gonna need an alibi. I gotta head up North. A lawyer fella in Kansas has got himself in bed with my son's whorewife, and they're tryin' ta clean me out."

"Is that a fact?" Bill declared.

"I'll need to have you take my car over to Keso's, so's it'll be seen. You gotta make sure you get plenty of folks takin' notice. I'll bring along some clothes so you can find a fella about my size to dress himself up in my stuff."

"I know'd that woman your Jason married was a real looker, but sure never pictured her as no swindler, though." Bill remarked. "Maybe that lawyer feller put her up to it?"

"He hasn't seen enough of her to care about anything but gettin' in her drawers. Nah, this thing stinks of Jessica, not some smart-ass

Yankee lawyer. She's the one behind this and she's tryin' to clean me out, like she did my boy."

"What'a ya reckon you're gonna have to do, James?" Bill asked.

"Dunno! I may have to kill both of 'em to bring this thing to a stop! I don't see any other way to keep her from bleedin' Lora and me dry."

"Might be the best way to handle it!" Bill said, "but sure don't like the idea of havin' ta kill anybody."

"If I get in trouble up there, I'll try and get a note to yah, tellin' you what to do. Whatever happens, make sure that Jessica doesn't get the boys away from Lora. Take the boys as deep into Gator's Trot as you can; keep 'em at Keso's if anything happens to me."

"Won't nobody from outside get in there," Bill said. "Especially a bunch of Gawd damn Yankees."

"I don't think I'm gonna get caught. I'll be at your house Friday mornin'. We'll need to get an early start. I'll see you Friday," James said. "Keep this to yourself. The fewer folks that know about it, the better off I'll be."

James arrived in Pollock about ten the following Friday morning, pulling a boat and trailer behind his blue '51 Packard. He visited with Bill's family, and then the two men headed into town. James drove slowly down main street, honking and waving at anyone who might know him or Bill, trying to be as conspicuous as possible.

"You reckon that Kansas fella's a fighter, James? Some of them folks up there would jest uh soon see a southern man shot as look him in the eye, with all this trouble we're having with the coloreds. You're sure gonna need ta be careful." Bill said, catching his breath after taking a swallow of whiskey.

"I'll be all right," James said. "It isn't the Yankees that I'm concerned with. And that white trash bitch isn't gonna have anyone pining over her carcass, if I know what she's been up to. Most folks up there u'll probably consider it a favor to have her done away with. Anyway, I'm not countin' on getting myself caught!"

Bill doubled back, once they were out of sight of Pollock, heading towards Alexandria where James could catch a train north to Topeka. Then he turned back towards the swamps after letting James out at the train station. He hired a stand-in along the way, making sure that he stopped regularly so that the two of them would be seen together.

When James got to Topeka, he registered under the name of Earl Walters, at the Kansan Hotel. The next morning, he dressed and went downstairs to have breakfast and meet Mister Chiles Crawford in the Brown Cow coffee shop. Crawford was a disreputable sleezebag private detective who officed in a deteriorating twenties vintage gas station on Topeka Boulevard, an appropriate habitat for such an iniquitous-looking character.

Crawford arrived thirty minutes late, sporting three or four days growth of beard and wearing a suit that had lost its luster several years earlier. His suit smelled of whiskey and body odor. Stains from meals that he had gorged himself on for the past few days spotted his sweat-stained shirt. A stump of a cigar hung between his fingers. His uncut nails were packed with black grime and filth, leaving the impression that Mr. Chiles Crawford was keeping the history of his life stored under the tips of his fingers, to advertise his scurrilous character.

James studied the unpleasant figure sitting across the table with the interest one would have watching a roach feed on an abandoned plate of food.

"You Walters?" Crawford asked James.

"Yeah," James answered. "You got something for me?"

"I got what you want…it's just that it's gonna be a little more expensive than we agreed upon earlier. I had expenses," Crawford added, grinning at James, his tongue pushed through a hole where a front tooth had rotted out."

James looked at him, gritting his teeth as he reached into his coat. Crawford smiled, assuming James was reaching for his wallet. The smile quickly dissolved when he heard the all-too-familiar clicking of a hammer being cocked.

Crawford plugged his cigar back into his mouth. "All right, no need for that; I'll give you what you want. She's seein' more men than Spinner. I counted three others since you called. Could've been more. One's a judge…other two are lawyers. I got their names for yah. Looks to me like she's got a little enterprise goin', the way them fellers are sneakin' in and out of the back door of her house all night long. A couple more drove by and stopped, but they didn't get out of their cars."

James accepted Crawford's information, including the list of visitors to Jessica's residence.

"Pleasure doin' business with ya, Mister Walters," Crawford announced, accepting an envelope containing a cash payment for his services from James.

"Don't flatter yourself by thinking I owe you anything else for this, Crawford. And don't try to follow me for any more money. I catch ya snoopin' around and things will get real serious for yah, if you catch my drift!"

"No problem, Mister Walters," Crawford said, understanding James' insinuation perfectly well. "Pleasure," Crawford said as he stood up and left the restaurant.

That afternoon, around five-thirty, James made his way to L.C.'s office. He had purposely made a late appointment with L.C., hoping that his secretary would have gone home for the day. He'd told L.C. that he needed to see him on an urgent tax problem, introducing himself again as Earl Walters.

James was surprised to find Martha still at the office when he walked into the reception area. "Good afternoon, young lady. I'm here to see Mister Spinner. I'm Earl Walters...I believe he's expecting me," James said, checking the office to see if anyone else was there.

"Oh yes, Mister Walters, Mister Spinner told me you'd be coming this afternoon. We were planning on working late anyway, so it worked out fine for Mister Spinner," she said.

"I see," James responded, caught off guard. "I understand Mister Spinner has a partner? Is he working late this evening, too? I'd like to meet him if he's here," James inquired, trying not to raise any suspicion as he tried to find out who was in the office.

"I'm sorry, Mister Walters, he's out of town for the week. He's vacationing in Miami. That's where I'd like to be right now," she said, smiling at him. "Maybe you can meet him next time you come in?" she added.

"Florida is a pretty place this time of year," James answered, trying to be friendly with the secretary as his mind raced, also trying to figure how to get her out of the office. "I've spent a number of summers fishing off the Keys. Beautiful country," James exclaimed, trying to make small talk as he continued to try and case the office.

L.C. stepped into the reception area to ask Martha a question and noticed James standing there. "You must be Mister Walters. I hope I haven't kept you waiting too long," L.C. announced, holding out his hand.

"I'm sorry, Mister Spinner," Martha apologized. "I was just going to tell you Mister Walters was here for his appointment!"

"That's quite all right. I was just enjoying a pleasant conversation with the pretty young lady," James said, returning Martha's smile.

"Well, come into my office," L.C. said, motioning towards his office door. "Let's see if we can take care of this pressing problem of yours."

James followed L.C. into his office, looking back over his shoulder at Martha. "Looks like you're doing pretty well, Mister Spinner. I guess you lawyers make a pretty good living handling the tax problems that all us ordinary folks get ourselves into?"

L.C. smiled, letting out a nervous chuckle as he sidestepped the question. Just as L.C. started to ask James about the reason for his being there, James bent over, clutching his chest and gasping for breath. L.C. shot up from his desk.

"What is it, Mister Walters? What's wrong? Are you sick, are you having a heart attack?" he questioned anxiously. "Martha!" he screamed. "Get in here, quick!"

Martha flew into the room, dropping down beside L.C. as they both waited for some indication from James about what was wrong with him.

"I better call an ambulance!" Martha suggested, standing back up.

James leaned back in the chair. "I feel like an old fool. I'm sorry," he said. "This happens every time I forget to take my medicine!"

"Have you got it with you?" she asked. "I'll get you a glass of water!"

"I was supposed to have my prescription filled yesterday, but I forgot to go by the drug store."

"Have you got your prescription with you, Mister Walters? I can run downstairs and have it filled. There's a drugstore down the block. I still think we should call an ambulance." she repeated.

"If you could get the pharmacist to give you one pill," James panted, "I'd be fine! It's just angina. I'm really embarrassed about this. It's bad enough, getting sick in your office, without asking you to get my medicine for me," James continued, handing Martha a note he'd written in the reception area with the word 'digitalis' scribbled on it.

"It's no bother, Mister Walters! I'll run across the street and get this for you. It'll just take a few minutes."

"I apologize," James said again. "It'll go away as soon as I get that digitalis into my system."

James watched as Martha left the office, knowing that it was going to be impossible for her to convince the pharmacist to give her the strong drug without a doctor's approval. L.C. left his office, returning a moment later with a glass of water in his hand, only to find James sitting up, fully recovered from his attack.

"You're looking better, Mister Walters. You had us a little worried!" L.C. said, with a short laugh, relieved that the crisis apparently had passed.

"You're not half as worried as you ought to be, Spinner!" James coolly replied.

"Come again?"

"I think we better finish our business, Mister Spinner, before anyone else has to be included in our problem," James ordered. He shifted himself up to the edge of the couch, clutching his cane with both hands, as if he were preparing to shinny up the thin pole.

"I don't think I understand, Mister Walters. Do you and I have some sort of problem? I wasn't aware that we'd ever met before. If you'd like to tell me what this is all about, perhaps we can get whatever it is that you want taken care of, so that I can get back to work." L.C. said, understandably upset about the theatrics that had taken place.

"You know, Spinner, where I come from, people don't take kindly to a fella that tries to swindle a man out of his money, or destroy another man's marriage, or run off with his wife. In my book that man's a cuckolding son of a bitch!" James stated, pulling his knife from his pants pocket, pointing it at L.C. and then cutting himself a chunk of tobacco from a plug he was holding in his hand as he supported his cane.

"What the hell is this all about? I think you've got the wrong attorney, mister. Maybe you should be talking to my partner. I don't know anything about your wife or your money," L.C. huffed, moving towards his desk and pulling a cigar from a glass humidor on the edge of his credenza.

"I've got the right man, all right. You're just a little foggy about your personal habits, Spinner!"

"I think this conversation is over, Mister Walters, or whatever your name is. I'm going to have to ask you to leave!" L.C. ordered.

"I heard you're considered to be a pretty important man, Spinner! A man that's done real well by himself, making it to the top, and all! Problem is…sometimes you get a little ahead of yourself, steppin' on the wrong toes; toes of people that don't take kindly to havin' someone interfere with their life and their families' lives." James said folding his knife, and slipping it back into his pocket.

"I don't know what you're talking about. You get yourself up and get out of here before I throw you out, old man," L.C. demanded, standing up and starting to walk towards James.

James' hand dropped smoothly from his cane and slipped into his coat as if he were reaching for a handkerchief. Before L.C. had cleared the corner of his desk he could see that the man on the couch was tracking him with a revolver that gave off the sound of the clicking of castanets, as James pulled the hammer back.

"That'll be close enough, Spinner. You know I killed a fella with a pistol during the war in France. That son of a bitch died real hard. I can still remember the look on that fella's face, watchin' his own brains drip down the wall. I got absolutely nothin' to lose by killin' yah."

"Now look," L.C. said, swallowing hard. "I think there's been a misunderstanding here! I haven't done anything to anyone, and I'm sure we can straighten this whole thing out!"

James walked over to the desk, motioning for L.C. to sit back down in his swivel chair. James then reached up and pulled two heavy law books from the bookshelf, stacking them directly in front of L.C. "Put your head on those books!" James demanded. "Do it now, or I'll kill ya where you sit."

"This is crazy, Walters! I swear I don't know why you're doing this!" L.C. pleaded as he reluctantly laid his head down.

It's James Lavoisier, not Walters, Mister L.C. Spinner." Spinner rolled his eyes up at James. "I want you to call that whore you've been layin' up with and tell her to get over here."

"Who?" L.C. panted. "I don't know who you're talking about!"

"Jessica," James said.

"Jessica?" L.C. repeated. "She's—" he started to say.

"You heard me. Get that whore on the phone, now! I ain't gonna ask yah again!"

"I'll try," L.C. said raising his head up to dial.

"Keep your head on those books. I don't want this bullet gettin' lost if I decide to shoot ya," James said in a cool, matter-of-fact tone.

"For God sake, don't kill me, Doctor Lavoisier…there must be some way we can work this thing out!"

"You got a tape recorder, counselor?" James demanded.

"Sure," L.C. came back. "In my desk."

"Lay it up here, on the desk, and hook it up to your phone. Turn it on when I tell you to. Now start dialing and get that bitch on the line. When she answers, I want you to go over your little extortion plot with her and make sure you don't tip her off that I'm listening."

"All right…just don't get careless with that pistol, please!"

James knew that Martha would be coming back anytime, still thinking he was suffering from what she thought was a heart attack.

L.C. listened earnestly for Jessica to answer the phone, praying that she was home.

"Oh, Jessica, Jesus, I'm glad you're home. I need to talk to you about Doctor Lavoisier," L.C. said, shaking as he adjusted the tape recorder that he had turned on while the phone was ringing.

"What do we need to talk about him for? I already sent him the letter, L.C.; you know that," Jessica said. "Did you hear something from him?"

"No, but I think you need to reconsider your idea of blackmailing him, the more I think about it!"

"What are you talking about, L.C.? I thought we'd already been over all this. We made a decision! I said I already sent him the letter," Jessica repeated, sounding confused about his change of direction. "Why the hell are you getting cold feet now, after we've already committed ourselves?"

"Look, I know what's best. You need to let this thing drop before someone gets hurt! I just don't think it's right to do this. You need to just drop it!" L.C. suggested, trying to make himself seem as uninvolved as possible.

"Well, you sure as hell thought we should do it when you put the letter together," Jessica retorted, sparking a nervous squirm from L.C. as he looked up at James and then the pistol in his hand.

L.C. wiped his face, then continued "Look, it was your idea to threaten to turn him in to the IRS unless he paid you the fifty-thousand. I sure as hell wasn't going to get any of the money! Now, I think it's wrong and I say we drop this whole damn stupid idea, now! There could be some long-term problems if you persist with this. So I want you to drop it!" L.C. demanded, his head still set uncomfortably on the stack of books.

Jessica didn't answer, pausing for a moment, then finally saying, "I don't like the way you're making this look like it's all my idea. I'll do whatever you say, L.C., just don't be mad at me! I thought it would be easy to get him to pay us. Are you sure we shouldn't wait to see what he's gonna do?"

"What I want you to do is swear to me you'll forget the whole thing! I know what I'm doing, Jessica. It's for your own good," L.C. went on, his voice quivering as he tried to coach her into agreeing.

"Gads, L.C., first you're hot, then you're cold. I don't understand what's got you so rattled. Did he call you or something? Hell, he'd never do anything; he's just talk! He's just like Jason. He'll pay it and that u'll be that," Jessica lectured as L.C. stared down the barrel of James' Colt.

"It's settled, Jessica. I don't want to hear any more about it! I've got to go…I'll talk to you later," he announced, hanging up the phone.

James stood silent for a second before he spoke. "You know, it worries me that you might not understand that I mean business," he declared, suddenly bouncing the barrel of his pistol off the back of L.C.'s head and sending him sliding to the opposite end of the desk. "I got a good mind to cut your nuts off, you overgrown ninny. Get back up in that chair!" James ordered.

"God damn it!" L.C. moaned as he struggled back into his chair, holding the back of his head.

James lifted the small tape reel out of the recorder and dropped it into his pocket. "I figure out of all this conversation there's probably enough to get you a little jail time, or at least have you disbarred. But you know, Spinner, I'm just a tired old man, lookin' to be left alone. If I ever so much as hear your name from anyone again, I'm gonna send this stuff to the folks that go after trash like you. And if they don't take care of you, then I'll be back to get you myself! As for Jessica, her time u'll come."

L.C. flinched as James waved his pistol past him to stuff it back in his coat. James walked towards the door and then turned back, standing at the corner of the desk. "I almost forgot. Here's a little gift for you...a list of folks your girl friend's been layin' up with on the side whenever you and her are apart. You might tell her that I'm givin' her some free medical advice; if she's plannin' on havin' that bastard child of yours, she ought ta lay off whorin' for awhile, at least until after it's born! I'd stay away from her, Spinner. She's a whole lot tougher than you are! She's likely to get you killed." James spat, sending a slug of tobacco onto the carpet.

"You know," James said, "we got a sayin' down South that, 'A dog can whip a coon, a coon can whip ah possum and ah possum can whip a dog.' If I was you counselor, I'd find out which one you're screwin' with before you try playin' these games!"

James walked out the front door of the office and into the elevator, tipping his hat at Martha as she raced down the hall to the office, still thinking there was an emergency. She stopped, confused as the brass elevator doors closed; then she swung around, glancing through the open doors of the office where she could see L.C. sitting at his desk, holding his hand over his bruised head. He was reading the penciled list of Jessica's suitors that had been graciously left on his desk, by James, alias Earl Walters.

CHAPTER 24

Dale's finger moved along the smooth, cold edge of the hog's tusk that he had retrieved from the shoebox lying in his lap. His eyes followed the graceful curve of the tooth, remembering when he had found it in the swamp and presented it to the old man as a gift.

He reflected on that time in his life, a time when it seemed he had crossed into another world. He remembered his apprehension as he stood, mentally disarmed, without any sense of what he was to face in his new environment, surrounded by so many unfamiliar sounds and creatures. It was a time when he would rely on James to teach him to survive, like a child looking to his father to show him how to walk.

It never occurred to him why they had made the trip to the swamp, not until he was older; it never really mattered until then. There, he had come to know the old man as he'd never known him before. He saw a side to his grandfather as different as the forbidding black waters that lay before him. The language, the culture of the swamp people, even the noises after dark in the mysterious Atchafalaya were unlike anything he'd known in the outside world.

Despite all its cruelty and venomous inhabitants, the order of things made perfect sense to the young man, after he'd been introduced into the strange prehistoric world. Unlike the civilized life he'd just left, revenge, hatred and jealousy were not a part of the scheme of things in the marvelous slough. Everything had its purpose. Every effort was accomplished purely for the sake of the preservation of life, nothing more, nothing less.

It was an experience that would remain with the young man for the rest of his days. He knew it had been the essence of life for James, the rare drop of difference that somehow had given his grandfather a glimpse into the reality, the truth, of the outside world. There was something there, something different that he yearned to understand about this stunningly beautiful and strange place. Again, he thought back to the time in his life when events had brought him there. He remembered only that it had been a great adventure.

He realized now that James and Lora had protected David and him from the dark facts behind their slipping silently, into the depths of the swamp. He began to recall the events that would bring him back to this room, to sit and ponder his life and confront himself with the truth of what had happened.

He eased back into the rocker as his mind wandered back to the days just before they'd begun the trek into that New World.

James had enjoyed a period of serenity and happiness since he'd returned home from his business in Topeka. He was somewhat surprised that Jessica had given up so easily, but assumed that she had seen fit to take L.C.'s advice. His concerns were redirected to his medical practice and the enjoyment of raising his grandchildren.

Life returned to its old routine as summer gave way to the cooling winds of winter that swept through east Texas. The wet winter frosts turned the twisted skeleton forests of hardwood, circling Jacksonville, into a glistening white crystalline barrier. Like a cloud suspended in time, rolling over the countryside and clinging to the naked trees, snagging themselves on the bony limbs to cloak each tree in a transparent robe of glass. The St. Augustine grass stayed a dark blue green, protected in the wrapping of ice that coated each blade.

The old house took on the familiar smell of winter from the fumes of the open gas heaters that roared their fierce warming breaths into each room. Quilts were piled onto the beds in stacks so thick that the sheer weight became uncomfortable for the young boys as they hid deep within the warm caverns.

Every morning the hibernating boys were called back to life by the aroma of pastries and hot chocolate, sizzling bacon and steaming eggs. A small silver bell signaled the morning feast.

Winter's long dreary overcast days and damp windy nights slowed the usually active pace in the old house. The morose weather was broken only for those brief moments when the sun penetrated the thick layers of clouds, burning away the listless gray mood of the family.

An occasional letter from Jason would spark a bright light into the monotonous gloom, encouraging everyone to turn their attentions away from their confinement.

Their reading of the letter was a family ritual. Lora would pick up the letter at the post office, keeping it first in her purse until she went home, then placing it in her apron while she worked in the kitchen. She would stop periodically to touch the envelope and think about her son.

After dinner, she would announce that she had the letter. The family would adjourn to James' room where Lora would relinquish control of the envelope, handing it to James to share with the family. As James would begin to read aloud, the room would fall silent, except for a whispered commentary from Lora: "Oh, poor darling", or "Bless his heart!"

As James read, he would occasionally stop, passing the letter to the boys so that they could study a short personal paragraph written to them by their father. They would look at the lines and then return the letter to James to continue.

When the reading was finished, Lora would fold the letter and place it back into her pocket, then walk to her room to be alone with her son's words. It was as if she were able to communicate with Jason through some special form of telepathy that was not for the others to know.

On those nights when a letter had been read, Dale often would find himself wide-awake, thinking of his father and family. He could see the lamplight from Lora's room as she lay awake, examining her son's letter, reflecting back on those times when she hovered over him, cared for him and loved him, never thinking he would be anywhere but home.

Jason's exact whereabouts was classified by the Air Force because of the sensitive nature of his assignment to a reconnaissance squadron. Anything that could have suggested his whereabouts, was thoroughly censored, clipped, or marked out with black lines. But letters were invaluable in reassuring the family that Jason was at least alive and well. They understood that it was in Jason's best interest that his squadron's location be kept a secret. However, there was always a feeling of helplessness, not knowing where he was in the world. The secrecy always left James and Lora with a feeling that their son was in imminent danger, and rightfully so.

Dale bound himself closely to his grandparents. He and James became almost inseparable companions, spending their spare hours together, talking or fishing, or just being in each other's company. The companionship began a miraculous, but slow, healing of the scars of Jessica's abuse.

David, on the other hand, had turned strangely away from his grandparents' overtures of affection, uninterested in substituting James' and Lora's attentions for those of his parents. He spent his time brooding, ignoring everyone and hoping to somehow re-establish life with his parents, dreaming of their reunification.

Lora was keenly aware of David's fantasy, knowing that he was pursuing a dream that would never be. She committed herself to try to remove the ominous cloud of despair from the boys' minds over what had happened because of their parents' divorce. As the winter days warmed, Lora decided that the boys might enjoy going with her into the country, to the small farming community of Galatin where she was teaching school. Her students were girls from local farms in and around the small settlement.

The town consisted of little more than a new red brick post office with its freshly erected white flagpole, contrastingly straight in relation to the bleached gray, framed buildings leaning hither and yon on either side. The feed store and next-door grocery were the hub of activity in the single row of buildings lining the highway. Twenty yards from the post office, the blacktop road abruptly turned into a red dirt gravel road.

Lora's student visit was scheduled for Sally Bolton's house, two miles down the unpaved road on a twenty-acre river bottom farm. Lora had planned to spend the afternoon with the girl, helping her with her required homemaking project of making a new dress. David and Dale occupied themselves on the front porch of the Bolton home, observing the rudiments of country life. An experience that quickly turned boring for the energetic and adventurous young men.

David and Dale were both in their teens and were shyly aware of Sally Bolton, or any girl for that matter. The Boltons had a twelve-year-old son and two other daughters besides Sally. All three of them were sitting on the front porch with David and Dale, watching their every move, while Lora was inside with Sally and her mother.

"Y'all boys from J'Ville?" Sammy Bolton questioned. "Ever been on a farm before? I bet y'all never been ridin' before."

The girls giggled, covering their mouths and huddling together with every utterance from their brother.

"Oh, yeah...we do a lot of riding," Dale responded instantly. "We been riding all our lives," he said, elbowing David. "You got a horse to ride around here?"

"Got Butterscotch! He's old, but got plenty uh spunk. Y'all boys wanta go fer a ride?" The Bolton boy asked.

"Why not? Sure! This isn't any fun just sittin' here. We could ride around and check out your place, take a look at your cattle and stuff," Dale boasted, winking at David.

"Let me get him saddled, and we can go for a ride down to the lake. Y'all boys can come on down and help me saddle him up...less ya wanta stay here and keep lookin' at my sisters?"

Dale and David leaped to their feet instantly, their faces flushed from the statement. The girls stared at the two boys, continuing to giggle as Dale and David followed Sammy Bolton to the barn. Dale looked back over his shoulder at the girls and then hurried to catch up with the Bolton boy.

"What kinda cow is that standing over there?" Dale asked. "Sure is a big sucker!"

"Cow? Don't you see them balls hangin' down under that fella? Shit, cow! That ain't no cow. Don't you know nothin'?" He laughed, throwing a well-worn saddle up on the rail next to a barebacked animal standing in the corral.

"This your horse?" David asked. "He's nice lookin'," he continued, trying to appear a little more informed than his brother.

"Y'all boys 'er dumber than a stump. That there's a bull," he said, pointing back at the 'cow', that Dale had mentioned, "and this here is a mule, M...U...L...E," he scolded, spelling loud enough that Dale and David knew the girls could hear their brother.

"Hey, he was turned wrong, otherwise I could've seen he was a bull," Dale assured him. "We have a lot of bulls in Kansas. They just aren't that color, that's all," Dale said, watching the boy sling a stack of burlap bags, his substitute for a blanket, onto the mule's back, sending an explosion of dust in all directions.

"Why don't y'all boys get on up on Butterscotch...I'll take ya over to Honey Lake. We can git away from all these damn horny girls," Sammy added, loud enough that his sisters heard the remark.

"Sammy Don, I'm gonna tell mama about your nasty mouth!" one of the girls screamed, launching herself inside the house.

"Git up, Butterscotch, git up!" Sammy screamed. "They sure did think you boys was pretty! Next thing you'd know, Becky 'ud wanna be kissin' on one of yah!" Sammy yelled with a hyena laugh.

When they reached Honey Lake, Sammy slid off the mule and immediately began peeling off his trousers and shirt. Dale and David were horrified to see that he wasn't wearing any underwear as he shed his well-worn britches.

"Sammy," Dale spoke up, "how come you're not wearin' any undershorts? Doesn't that chap your butt?" he asked laughing.

"Shit, naw! Undershorts are for sissies. I don't wear 'em less I'm goin' tah the doctor. Only seen him once ta get a boil lanced off my ass!" he shouted back, making a break for the water.

Sammy landed like a pink sheet suspended on the surface of the brown water for an instant before sinking totally out of sight. Dale and David stood at the edge of the water watching Sammy splash and swim in the glassy lake, diving under just far enough that his cheeks reflected in the sun like two submerged pink buoys.

"Jesus, aren't you cold, Sammy? You gotta be freezin' your nuts off swimmin' in the middle of winter," Dale chuckled.

"Kid's crazy!" David whispered to Dale. "He's gonna drown."

"Naw, it ain't cold. The water gets heated on the other side of the lake from the power plant. It's really great. Y'all boys come on in, less your chicken to get nekked! Ain't nobody around to see ya, so come on," Sammy taunted.

Dale and David looked at each other, then started undressing. Within a minute, the boys had shed their clothes, joining their alabaster companion in the dark soupy puddle.

Sammy was accustomed to swimming in the warm shallows of the lake, and lying on a sandbar twenty yards from shore to sun himself. Dale and David swam out to the small island, rolling over on their backs next to Sammy, and floating motionless in the water, resembling, at first glance, a row of undersized beached pilot whales.

"Sammy, this is all right!" David remarked.

"Yeah, great spot, Sammy. This is something!" Dale agreed.

"I knew you'd like it. I come here a lot when I wanta get away from my sisters. It's sorta my secret hideaway," Sammy declared, suddenly craning his neck towards shore.

"What's the matter?" Dale questioned.

"Don't look now, but my sisters are standin' up there in the bushes. Gawddamit," he added, "I wish mama would whip their butts! Always followin' me everwhere I go!"

"I thought you said they didn't know about this place!" Dale shouted, horrified that girls were seeing him naked.

Dale and David moved into deeper water, immersing themselves as far into the murky depths as they could, poised to make their way back to shore for their clothes. Before the two boys could commit to a decision, a bare-skinned herd of young ladies descended into the water, flowing into the lake in a single wave of giggling flesh, sending a small tidal wave towards the sandy island.

Dale sat staring at the girls, as if he'd found himself privy to some once-in-a-lifetime phenomenon, his eyes fixed on the two Bolton girls and a friend standing in waist-high water, wading casually in his direction. Sammy was in hysterics watching his sisters and their friend moving towards the sandbar with David and Dale in a panic, retreating to the clothes they'd left next to Sammy's mule.

"Them city boys sure are modest, Theresa," Sammy remarked to his sister, as he lay back on the sandbar, continuing to enjoy the sun.

"God, they're all naked, David!" Dale said, hyperventilating from the swim. "Look at Sammy, just layin' there with his giblets hangin' out! I've never seen so many naked girls in my life!"

"You've never seen any naked girls, and if Grandma catches us here with all these buck-nekked people were gonna git a lickin', for sure!" David warned.

Just as David and Dale had retrieved their clothes and had moved towards a thicket to dress, they could hear several more girls coming towards the lake. The two boys crouched down, peering over the top of the scrub brush a few yards from the water's edge.

Sally Bolton had apparently decided to go for a swim with a girlfriend, alerting David and Dale to the fact their grandmother had finished her business and would be wanting to leave.

"Are they gettin' naked too, David?" Dale stretched himself up, trying to get a look at the new arrivals.

"I don't know. My best guess is that they are. Some secret place this kid's got! I've never seen so many people tryin' to get in the same swimmin' hole, and all of them jumpin' out of their clothes. We better get going back to the car; we can put our clothes on when we get there," David ordered.

Dale and David struggled to walk across the freshly plowed field between Honey Lake and the Bolton house. Lora was sitting on the front porch with Mrs. Ella Bolton, who was facing her, sitting in a swing. Lora had just raised her coffee cup, daintily holding it up to her lips, when she caught a glimpse of what appeared to be two naked figures slinking across the open ground immediately in front of her. She continued her conversation, at the same time keeping her eyes fixed on the two disrobed forms. Her eyes darted towards the car as she watched the door on the opposite side open and then saw the two glowing white bodies slip into the back seat.

"Excuse me, Mrs. Bolton, I think I've left my handkerchief in the car. I'll be right back," she said, smiling a faint apology. She walked calmly to the car.

A cold duel of staring eyes ensued as Lora peered through the open window of the car, with both boys silently going about the business of trying to don their trousers, all the while looking up at her. Still wet from the dip at Honey Lake, they twisted and struggled to pull their clothes on, trying to keep a low profile as Lora turned back towards Mrs. Bolton.

"I need to be going," Lora said to Mrs. Bolton, walking back to the porch, hooking her arm in the strap of her handbag and charging for the car before Mrs. Bolton could get up. "Thank you for the coffee and tell Sally I'll see her in class next week," she finished, revving up the engine and slamming the car in reverse with a cloud of dust enveloping the car.

Mrs. Bolton had hardly enough time to stand before the car reappeared on the opposite side of the dust cloud, swerving across the dirt road and disappearing over the hill.

James was standing in the back yard, talking to one of the yard men when Lora goosed the car into the garage, slamming on the brakes and leaping out at a run. As she marched by James, puffing her infuriation, she blurted a summary of what had happened. James followed her, trying to decipher what she was saying.

"I've never been so absolutely humiliated, never in my entire life. Strutting naked as jaybirds, soaking wet, right up in front of my student's mother. I'm just humiliated beyond…oh! They ought to have their bottoms blistered," she snapped, slamming the screen door leading into the kitchen.

"For Gawd sake, Lora," James roared, breaking into a laugh, "if you'd tell me what this is all about, I'd have a better chance of understanding what you're so upset about! You boys wanta give me an idea about why she's got her feathers all ruffled?"

Dale looked over at David before answering. "I guess she's mad 'cause we went swimmin' in the lake while she was doin' her work. We had tah head out from where we were swimmin' 'fore we could get dressed, 'cause we thought she was fixin' ta leave us."

James looked first at David and then at Dale and burst out laughing, "I guess a fella's got a right ta take a dip if he's got a mind to. Good swimmin' holes are hard to come by. I'm sure Mrs. Bolton's seen nekked youngin's before! Damned if I can understand her moods sometimes," he added, then turned and walked back to finish his business with the yard man, snickering and shaking his head.

Dale and David gave each other a reassuring look, relieved that the crisis apparently was over. Suddenly, James turned around, looking at both boys as they were starting for the house.

"Those country kids take to swimmin' like ducks take to water, ya know," James said. "Some of 'em would rather get buck nekked and barefoot than eat. A fella's gotta be careful, standin' around with his tally whacker hangin' out, though!" He laughed. "A good swimmin' hole is like a good restaurant;

once the word gets out, you're likely ta have a whole passel of folks droppin' in on yah before yah know it. Sure can catch a fella off guard, just when he thinks he's got the place to himself," he went on, smiling knowingly as he returned to his conversation with the yardman.

The boys' eyes met in shock at how frighteningly accurate his remarks had been. Why it was almost as if he was being coy about saying all that he knew. Perhaps Lora had seen more than she was letting on, and told James what they'd done. James and Lora hadn't spoken except for the brief conversation they'd had as Lora marched towards the house. But adults had a way of communicating with each other, some magical skill of talking with their eyes—every youngster knew that!

What they didn't understand was that James was being an authority on the obvious, having spent countless hours at his own favorite swimming hole when he was a youth. He became a veteran at the protocol for 'skinny dipping' and knew the goings-on better than most. Why else would they have left the swimming hole without getting dressed? Girls, that's what.

Life rebounded to its usual routine. Lora quickly forgave whatever it was that had created the stir, one of the few occasions the boys ever saw the gentle woman upset about anything.

A mortuary like stillness struck the house each evening as the restless energies of young men were quelled for the sake of the older inhabitants. James and Lora had tired hours before the boys, slipping off to sleep as Dale and David occupied themselves reading and talking.

Sooner or later the story would turn to Old George, still a permanent resident of the house. David had gone all out one evening, not only recalling the story but testifying to a personal sighting of Old George. It was a revelation that sent chills up and down Dale's spine. Never had anyone in the family ever said they'd seen the ghost, not even James.

Dale was awakened that night by a storm raging outside. He looked up, catching a glimpse of a figure sweeping past the foot of their beds and disappearing into the darkened hallway.

He was shocked, but not immobilized. Actually, he was quite pleased finally to see the haint. There was something strange about what he'd seen. It wasn't the grotesqueness of the spirit, or any threatening movements, but rather the cigarette hanging between the spook's fingers. 'Now that was odd,' Dale thought. 'Why not,' he figured; 'if they can walk, I guess they can smoke.'

With the arrival of morning, Dale leaped from his bed, waking David up to give him a blow by blow of what had happened. David listened, irritated at being disturbed.

"There's no such thing as ghosts! I made all that up about seein' George," he stated.

"I'm tellin' you I saw that sucker. He was standin' right there...right by our beds.

"Smoking a cigarette?" David interjected.

"Yeah, that's right!" Dale answered.

"Well, I'm tellin' you," David lectured, "there's no such thing as ghosts! There sure isn't any such thing as one that smokes!"

What Dale had actually seen was Lora, slipping into the room to close the windows because of the storm. She was bedecked in her usual night attire of cold cream stuccoed to her face, and a long robe. She was drawing from a cigarette, and trying to be as quiet as possible.

Lora's sister, Katherine, made an unexpected visit from her home in Fresno, California. Her visit happened to coincide with another massive tropical depression that was sweeping across east Texas.

David and Dale observed the customary niceties of hugging and kissing the overweight relative and then sat quietly minding their manners.

Dale listened to the thunderous storm outside, a storm that surely would inspire 'George' to make his rounds through the house on such a night.

Dale lay in his bed, patiently reading, listening for signs of the elusive ghost, waiting for each of the family members and houseguest to retire.

Aunt Katherine appeared at the head of the stairs, looking into the boy's bedroom and wishing them a comfortable night's sleep, then walked into her room.

Dale listened to the straining compression of the bedsprings in the guestroom as Aunt Katherine's heavy body flattened the coils against the wooden slats.

Finally, he heard the click of the bed lamp switched off, signaling that Aunt Katherine had gone to sleep. He waited another half-hour, careful not to be caught off guard by a preemptive arrival of the ghost.

When he was certain everyone was asleep he reached for a cigar box that held the tools for his clandestine operation. The box contained a large tin of talcum powder, a spool of black thread and several cigarettes borrowed from his grandmother's purse. He moved down the hallway to the entrance to each room to shake talcum powder on the floor directly under the doorsill. He returned to each door to string a web of thread, crisscrossing from one side to the other. He selected one of the rooms to lay the cigarettes out on a nightstand, assuming that George might be tempted by a little nicotine bait.

When he'd finished, he made his way back to bed listening for signs that his ghost had become entangled in one of the traps. Several hours passed, leaving Dale drifting in and out of a shallow sleep.

At four in the morning Dale was awakened by a succession of sounds, something trying to untangle itself from the web he'd strung in the hall. His breathing increased as he listened to the creature struggle to free itself from the trap.

"I got him, by Gawd, I got him!" Dale whispered. "David, you're not gonna believe this! I got George!"

As soon as Dale realized he couldn't wake David, he slipped out of bed and moved down the hall, with flashlight in hand, squinting into the pitch-black alcove. He aimed the beam in the direction of the door, moving quickly to the white talcum powder on the floor.

Footprints...he was thrilled. The powder had been disturbed and there were several clear prints still visible in the film on the wooden floor. The snare that he'd strung across the door was torn, ripped by the force of the monster trying to free itself.

Dale was pleased with the evidence. He slipped back into bed, deciding that he would sleep until he could call everyone upstairs to see the evidence of his night's work.

Dale was startled by Nellie moving around the room, whistling an old spiritual tune, pushing the dust mop across the floor, stopping to pull the drapes back and opening the windows.

Dale smiled at her until he realized the threat she posed to his ghostly evidence.

"Nellie, you didn't wipe up the white powder on the floor in the hallway?" Dale asked, sprinting down the hall.

"Lord sakes, I doesn't know what dat stuff was. It was on everything. I gotta ask Mrs. Lavoisier 'bout dat mess," Nellie mumbled. "Y'all white folks is white enough without havin' tah always be coverin' yourselves wit powder. Makes you look sickly!

"You better quit worryin' 'bout that mess on the floor and git yourself down stairs tah breakfast. You knows how Doctor Lavoisier feels 'bout you boys bein' late to dah table. I done cleaned up de mess, and dat's dat!"

"Ah, Jesus!" Dale hollered.

"Don't be usin' the Lord's name in a spiteful way, child, especially when he give us a fine day like dis," she admonished, smiling.

"I had that sucker right in my hands!" he said. "Now you've gone and ruined everything! I'll never be able to prove I saw Old George!" He declared as he dressed and bounded down the stairs.

"Got enough bad in 'dis old world without goin' out lookin' tah try and hawg-tie dat old devil! I jess' doesn't know bout dese chillen," she added, with a laugh. Dale stopped just outside the door to the dining room to listen to Aunt Katherine complaining about something that had upset her during the night.

"I just never saw anything like it, Lora! My word, I was covered from head to foot with string, and basted in some kind of powder. It was like a nightmare! I had to fight my way out of that horrible mess just to get back to my room! I've just never been so scared in all my life!" she complained, downing a massive shovel full of grits.

James looked over the top of his morning paper, making a patronizing grunting sound that he always made when he thought someone was packing the room full of bull, "Uh-uh-uh."

"Oh, sweet Katherine," Lora said, "I can't, for the life of me, understand what it could have been!"

509

"Huh," James grunted, keeping his face concealed behind his newspaper.

Dale stepped into the dining room. David glanced up at him with a suspicious look.

As soon as Lora and Katherine left the room, James lowered his newspaper. "Crazy old biddy," he announced. "She hasn't got the sense God gave a pissant! Sounds to me like she was doin' a little nippin' on the jug last night, probably wanderin' around drunk upstairs and got lost. Dale and David both gave a faint grin in response, continuing to keep their faces turned towards their plates. Both boys listened as James muttered a final declaration before disappearing towards his room: "Powder, black string...hell, she's hallucinating...got the damn DT's! She's lucky Old George didn't get her," James casually remarked, grinning to himself, knowing he'd laid the trap to rekindle the yarn with the two boys, and knowing full well their attempt to capture the elusive ghost had failed.

CHAPTER 25

The year was now 1958. Excitement electrified the family at the news that Jason was coming home on leave. Lora was in a tizzy, blowing through the house to make sure everything was in readiness for Jason's homecoming. Nellie moved thoughtfully, working to tidy and freshen up the already sterile residence. James prepared himself by clearing his calendar of appointments for the first few days that Jason would be home.

Two days later a city cab pulled into the drive, rolling through the lugustrum tunnel growing next to the house, then pulled around to the back steps and stopped next to the porch where David and Dale were sitting.

Jason emerged from the worn-out vehicle, with a flight bag in one hand and a burning cigarette locked between the fingers of the other. He handed the driver his fare and turned towards the porch, capturing a final draw of smoke from the cigarette, then flicked it into the air behind him.

"Hi, boys! How you fellas doin'?" he asked, holding out his arms as Dale and David raced towards him. "It's good to see you guys again! I really missed you," he said, locking both boys in his arms. "It's been a long time!"

"Boy! It's great to see you, dad! We didn't know when to expect you home," David explained.

David gave Dale a shove, nudging him towards the house as a messenger to announce Jason's arrival to the rest of the family.

"Oh, land sakes alive, my baby's home!" Lora gasped, wiping her hands on a dishtowel as she stepped from behind the screen door to the kitchen.

"It's wonderful to have you home, honey," she greeted him, "just wonderful! Daddy will be so excited to see you! The boys have just been beside themselves ever since we got the wire you'd be coming home!" Jason cuddled her in his arms, giving her a peck on the cheek as they separated. He gave her a long look, a smile of relief, the look of a voyager contented to be in a safe harbor after a perilous journey. He bowed his head, as if to acknowledge that he'd had his fill of adventure. He turned to the boys with a smile. "I missed you, all of you…"

James stepped onto the porch, holding open the screen door checking to see what was going on in the backyard. "Hey son, bless my soul, it's good to have ya home! We've been real anxious about when you'd be gettin' here," he added. Jason embraced his father, then smiled at the small gathering, pulling the boys back into his arms. David and Dale carried his bags as the group headed into the house.

Nellie stood at the sink, holding her greeting in reserve until Jason had entered her domain. As he walked into the room, everyone went silent as Jason slipped over to the sink, clutching her in a bear hug from behind.

"I sure does hope you came home hungry, Jason! Your momma says you'd probably need fattenin' up with some good old collard greens and blackeyes after dat old army food!" She laughed, pretending to be embarrassed by the show of affection, but all the while expecting it.

"It's just wonderful being home, with all of you," Jason said. "It's been an awful long time…too long!"

"Well, come on in and let's get the dust off of yah. The boys can take your things to your room. I'm just so happy to have you home, honey. You just don't know!" Lora exclaimed, gripping Jason's arm, her head resting on his shoulder.

Jason sat in James' room for nearly an hour until Nellie announced that supper was ready to be served. Everyone migrated into the massive dining room, standing behind his chair until Dale had assisted Lora into her seat.

After a short blessing by James, Nellie began to serve the platters of meats and vegetables. The noise of silver and crystal clanging and rubbing against the china plates drowned out what little conversation came from the diners. The traditional silence was observed until Nellie brought in the dishes of hot cobbler, steaming as vanilla ice cream was dished onto the warm peaches and crust.

As the meal wound down, James and Jason began talking, discussing what Jason had been doing in his new assignment. Lora and the boys listened intently as he told where he'd been, giving them a rough outline of his secret duty.

"The Communists, Chinese and Russian, even the Koreans, have been shipping a tremendous amount of war contraband into the Sea of Japan through the Formosa Straits and into the Gulf of Tonkin, stockpiling it in Indochina. We've been watching them move the stuff across the Chinese border for some time.

"Why should we care where they're sending it?" James asked. "Just as long as they don't go after any of our allies."

"That's just the point, dad! The Communists are really active in Asia. They've started guerrilla actions everywhere they can find a sympathetic ear. It's not the same thing as declaring a war, and it's a whole lot cheaper for them than fighting a conventional action. Anyway, they've got us flying photo recon' along the Russian coast, down to the South China Sea to keep an eye on the tonnage their moving. It's a whole new situation we're dealing with this time. You can't even be sure who your friends are. We're not even supposed to be over there, officially. It's scary, dad! We don't even put our insignias on our aircraft. No one's sure what'll happen if they catch us with our cameras rolling," Jason continued.

"Dammit, son, that doesn't sound very safe for our boys! I hope the Air Force is doing something about this, something to protect our flyers."

"Our people are having to play a diplomatic chess game. If we don't tell our allies what we've got, they're furious. If we do, the Soviets have it within hours".

James cupped his hands together, looking down at the table, "What's the point of all of this then?"

"I guess it's the same game that was played in Korea. If we complain too much, the sensitive nature of our work will be compromised back home by Communist sympathizers who would love to see us jerked out of there in a flash. We either stay and take our lumps or go home and rely on British and French intelligence."

"I'd feel better if they would make you leave," James stated.

"So would I!" Lora interjected.

"We carry a United Nations duty card and hope like hell the guy on the ground believes us, if we're captured. It's pretty dangerous," Jason said, noticing the concern on everyone's face, "but so far we've been able to fly above anything the enemy can throw at us."

513

"I don't like the sounds of it, son," James complained, noticing that Lora was becoming upset by the conversation, glancing at the two boys.

"Maybe we should talk about this later, Dad," Jason said, noticing his mother's concern about what the boys were hearing. "We've got plenty of time to chat before my leave is over."

Later, Jason sat in James' bedroom, talking long past the time that Lora and the boys had retired for the evening. He sat in James' old rocker, closing his eyes as he listened to his father, opening them whenever he answered a question. He savored each special moment, the feeling of being secure in his father's room as they visited late into the night.

"What'a yah hear from Jessica, son? Is she leaving you pretty much alone these days?" James asked.

"Oh, I guess so, dad. You knew that she had that attorney, that Spinner fella that knocked her up, get a court order attaching part of my pay. They claimed it was for child support for Jessica's little girl and the boys, even though David and Dale are living here. She's been like a plague in my life! This overseas duty seems to have been my only salvation from her."

"The woman's a demon, son!" James answered sharply.

"I'm really thankful for you and mother taking the boys in like you did. I don't know what we would have done without you," Jason said, pressing his head back into the back of the chair and closing his eyes again.

"They're good boys! They've been through a lot these past couple of years. Your mother and I are just glad to be able to offer them a little stability in their lives. Neither of us could stand them being raised in that environment, in Topeka. The woman's a Jezebel if I've ever seen one. She's contemptible!" James snarled.

"You know, dad, I used to listen to her tell me how she enjoyed making someone dance on the end of a string like a spider. I always thought it was funny. That is, until I began to realize that it was me doin' the dancing. She got a strange sense of power watching people suffer because of her manipulating their lives. Never any remorse, sorrow, or even regret for destroying someone. She always acted like she was paying the world back for something," Jason added softly, looking down at the ash on his cigarette, pondering the wasted years he'd spent with her.

"What's done is done, son. Let the past lay where it will. What you need to do is carry on with your life, doing the things that make you happy. Stay clear of her; she's more of a demon than we would like to believe. I'll deal with her if she tries to get the boys back, I'll promise you that!"

Jason stood up, grinding out his cigarette in the ashtray next to the chair. "I guess I'll get some sleep. It's really good to be home with you and mother! I had a feeling for awhile that I'd never see this place again. Funny, how being away from the people you love, makes you start having all sorts of funny thoughts. Anyway…it's great being back."

"Good night, son. We're glad you're home!" James replied. "I'm really glad to be home!" Jason said, turning back to his dad. "I never realized how precious this place is to me!"

Lora was an avid fisherman, fishing off an old pier that she'd leased at the lake. Jason enjoyed going with her to talk and sit on the wooden pier, feeling the cool east Texas breeze against his face and the warm sun beating down on him from a bluebird sky. Jason cooled his legs, pulling his pants up to his knees and letting his feet dangle in the murky water of the lake.

"It's really lovely out here, mother! It's nice to be somewhere where it's cool and the wind is a little chilly. Clark Field is so stifling hot most of the time. When it rains, the heat turns the air into steam."

"Oh, honey," Lora stated, "I wish you could stay here and not have to go back. I worry so about you."

"I know, momma. It seems so long ago when I was here and living with you and dad. Those were wonderful times in my life. I've really missed the boys while I've been gone! I'm sorry I haven't been much of a father to them," Jason apologized, looking forlornly up at his mother.

"The Good Lord knows what's best. They're doing fine. Both of them have done well in school. I think a few more years and we'll have the damage healed over!"

"I hope so, mother!" Jason replied.

"They're such loving children, warm and affectionate as they can be. It's a shame that Jessica will never appreciate the joy of having them share their lives with her. And they think a lot of you, son. They're both extremely proud of their father," she emphasized, "real proud."

"I'm glad to know that, momma. I've often thought about what they would think of me after all of this was over. I haven't had much opportunity to get to know either of them very well. David seems a little aloof from everyone, but maybe it's because I'm not used to him. I've worried about him for so long. And Dale...I guess he and dad are the greatest of buddies?"

"Oh, yes," Lora answered, with a smile. "They're inseparable. Dale's the spitting image of his grandfather down to his walk. It's been such a pleasure for your daddy to have Dale be so close. They're just so much alike!

"That's wonderful, mother, really wonderful!" Jason exclaimed.

"This job I have is pretty dangerous. If anything were to happen to me...I'd want...well, I'd want the boys to know that they were important to me. I'd never want them to think that I'd just abandoned them here. What I'm trying to say is that I'm really concerned for 'em. I don't have much to give 'em, now, not even my time, but I've set a little something aside for them in a trust."

"You shouldn't trouble yourself about that, Jason. Your father has made provisions to see that both of them are well cared for."

"I know, mother, but it's something I want to do. At least, I feel like I'm providing a little something for them. I just don't want Jessica to get her hands on anything that belongs to them."

"Hush up now about all this morbid talk. The Lord's not gonna let anything happen to my boy!" Lora responded.

"Well, just don't forget about what I've said, just the same; in case push comes to shove, I want the boys to have what I've set aside for them. Don't let Jessica get after you and dad," Jason cautioned, suddenly giving his pole a jerk and launching a fish into the air. "She'll try to grab every penny she can from the boys or from you."

"I wouldn't spend any time worrying about that happening, son. Your father is more than capable of handling Jessica." She looked over at him with a caring smile on her face.

A curtain of depression lingered over the family for several days, as it always did with each farewell, after Jason finished his leave and left to return overseas. The boys moped around the house, listless and upset. Lora was as concerned with the children's downtrodden mood as she was at Jason's leaving. She made a vigorous effort to break the spell that was affecting the usually happy atmosphere.

Several weeks after Jason had left, he wrote to his mother, advising her, much to everyone's delight and relief, that he'd been transferred out of the dangerous intelligence assignment. While still on flying status, his new duty was primarily concerned with reconnaissance interpretation and evaluation duty, at a desk. His flying would be limited to the minimum required to remain on flight status for his flight pay.

It was an answer to everyone's prayers, a relief during the months that would follow when the family would find itself thrown into an unexpected crisis.

CHAPTER 26

Several months had passed since Jason had returned to duty. The boys received an occasional telephone call from Jessica, who could barely bring herself to inquire about their well being before trying to pry the whereabouts of their father from them. When they informed her that they didn't know where he was, she would become incensed, certain that James had instructed them to withhold the information to keep her from finding Jason.

Jason was, as usual, behind with his alimony and child support payments, and Jessica was frantically trying to track him down. His security status was working to his benefit, the Air Force refusing to give her any information.

Jessica's lack of success in connecting with Jason for her back alimony and child support sent her into a relentless pursuit to locate him. She resorted to threatening James with L.C., still unaware of L.C.'s previous encounter with James at his office. The lawyer had failed to mention that he was terrified of James, wanting nothing to do with instigating another visit from the doctor.

The truth was that neither James nor Lora had any idea where their son was stationed. He had managed only an infrequent letter to his parents and sons, and those had been forwarded, censored from Travis Air Force Base in California. He was constantly being transferred to new duty stations in his less dangerous assignment, not having a permanent mailing address.

It appeared that Jessica would persist until the Air Force finally gave in to her dauntless badgering. Then suddenly, the calls to the Department of the Air Force in Washington, letters to various political figures to intervene, and visits by her to the Forbes Air Force Base Personnel Office all suddenly, and without explanation, ceased.

James was making his rounds at Nan Travis Hospital, preparing to leave for his office at the clinic when he was paged at the nurses' station to answer an emergency phone call from the receptionist at his office.

"Doctor Lavoisier, this is Edna. I don't know what to do! There are two men here who say they're federal marshals, and a man from the Internal Revenue Service from Dallas. They're going through our files and boxing up all of our records. They won't let me back into the office. They even took my appointment book."

James paused for a moment. "Did they have a warrant?"

"Yes, Doctor Lavoisier!" Edna answered.

"Call my attorney. Tell him what they're doing and have him meet me at the office! Whatever you do, keep quiet!"

James made his way quickly across town, racing into his office still wearing his white lab coat from the hospital.

"What the hell do you people think you're doing? These files are confidential. What's this all about?" James demanded to know, as he stormed through the door.

"Doctor Lavoisier, we have a search warrant issued by Judge Arthur Myers of the Federal Court in Dallas, District V, ordering us to seize all of your records. Your nurse was duly served with the appropriate warrant," the marshal stated, continuing to place the files into a cardboard box on the floor.

"Who's behind this? Who are you people with? What office?" James demanded to know, throwing his lab coat on a chair next to the desk.

"I'm special agent Mac Covey, Federal Marshal's office out of Dallas," the man answered. "You'll have to leave, Doctor. This office is closed for investigation and collection of evidence," the young marshal announced rudely, hoisting a box onto a two-wheel dolly.

James looked at the marshal, then turned towards his office. "You don't mind if I get my coat, do you?"

"That'll be all right," the marshal said.

James stepped out of sight into his office and then returned, standing in the door. "You boys can put those boxes down until my attorney gets here," James ordered, pulling the hammer back on the pistol that he'd taken out of his desk.

All three men moved back several steps. "Look, Doctor...it'd go a lot easier on yah if you'd put that piece away. You're just makin' it harder on yourself. Someone could get hurt!" one of the agents pleaded. "Put it down!"

"Not a chance," James responded. "This is a medical office, mister. You may be government agents, but I'm a physician and you aren't going to close this office. I've got patients to treat…patients with serious medical problems. Nobody's gonna move anything until my attorney gets here and says it's okay!" James announced.

"Look, Doc, we got a legally executed warrant. Your fixin' ta get yourself into somethin' you can't get out of!" the revenue agent warned, nervously wiping his forehead with his sleeve.

James sat down at the desk, still leveling his pistol at the threesome. "You people come waltzing in here, telling me I've got to close my doors so you can ransack my office. Hell, for all I know you're a bunch of thieves going through my cabinets for drugs. I ought'a blow you away and take my chances on anyone proving it wasn't a case of mistaken identity," he threatened, gritting his teeth.

"Come on, Doctor, this ain't gonna get you anywhere!" the marshal pleaded. "Put the gun down and we'll forget all about it!" the agent continued.

"Put it down, James," a voice came from the door. It was Craig Fisher, James' attorney. He walked into the office, ignoring the threat from James' pistol, as he approached the three men.

"You got an arrest warrant?" Fisher asked. "I'm Doctor Lavoisier's attorney."

"Just a search warrant," the agent answered.

"Can he go?" Fisher questioned. "I think he's just a little upset about seein' you boys take his office apart!"

The agent looked over at James, relieved to see the old man slip the pistol into the belt of his pants. "I guess so…he didn't hurt anybody!"

"Go on home, Doc," Fisher commanded. "I'll call you after I sort through all this with these gentlemen."

James left the treasury agent, marshals, and his attorney discussing the legality of their search while he headed for the bank. Once there, his worst fears were confirmed, finding that his accounts had been frozen and his lock box sealed.

A hearing was convened within a month after the incident at the office. James agonized over the effects the lock on his account and the restraining order were having on his business. The growers had begun to take their business elsewhere because of his inability to pay for their produce. His undisclosed funds would have provided the federal investigators with crucial evidence, aiding their attempts to prosecute him for income tax evasion. James was forced to watch as his packing shed operations began to falter, forced to sit idle during the prime months of the harvest season.

To make matters worse, the government had prepared a surprisingly thorough case, a case aided by someone who knew James very well. He had little doubt about the source of their information. He tried desperately to stay one step ahead of the investigators, knowing that Jessica would continue to provide them with everything she knew about his business.

James had retained a prominent law firm in Dallas, on the advice of Craig Fisher, to defend him against what appeared to be the inevitable closing of his medical practice and packing sheds, and the possibility of heavy fines or a prison term. The IRS had thwarted every effort by the defense attorneys to keep the practice open. They knew that the pressures they were exerting would force James to resort sooner or later to spending his concealed funds, thus incriminating himself even further.

The case was critical to the IRS, because of its relevance to the prosecution of other similar cases. His trial was targeted for an all-out effort by the government after they had examined the evidence gathered over the months of investigation. The conclusion, drawn by the investigation team, was that the case was solid enough to establish legal precedence for future prosecutions. At the very least, they had James. Ideally, they hoped they would have the tools to go after a host of tax evaders.

Pretrial motions were heard in federal court in Dallas. James and Lora attended the hearing, leaving the boys with Nellie at home in Jacksonville. James listened as the attorneys debated and negotiated the legalese and procedural mumbo-jumbo, establishing the rules for his trial that had, as yet, not been placed on the docket.

The government called its first witness, a doctor from Nacogdoches, Texas. The witness, Doctor Cletus Burls, a general practitioner like James, had been called to testify as to what a practice the size of James' would normally produce in the way of income. His testimony was designed to show that a medical practice half the size of James' would have produced as much or more revenue than James was admitting to. After a heated cross-examination, Doctor Burls conceded that his figures were pure conjecture, and agreed that a physician's income might vary substantially, despite the number of patients in his practice. James' attorney brought it to the attention of the judge that Doctor Burls himself was under investigation by the IRS and had felt obligated to cooperate in the case as a very friendly witness.

The hearing continued, as locals from the Jacksonville area were paraded reluctantly into the courtroom, one by one, to testify as to what they had paid for James' medical services. In each case, the prosecutor showed that there was no record of the cash payment made by the patient for James' services; but neither was there a record that James ever had charged them for his services. In several cases the witnesses testified to James' benevolence, much to the shock of the prosecutors.

Next, the government began to call witnesses to testify concerning the details of real estate transactions made over the years by James. Again, the prosecutors contended that a difference existed between the profits James had actually realized and what he had reported as income to the IRS. The exact amount of each sale was unsubstantiated because most if not all of the deals had been in cash.

James' attorney was again easily able to discredit the witnesses because the buyers themselves had attempted to deceive the IRS by paying cash in order to conceal their future gains on the same properties. Each of the witnesses had readily admitted to the deception.

After the fourth day of testimony, the government was beginning to realize that their case was anything, but wrapped up. They were still confident of a conviction, but not with the sweeping victory they had predicted.

The prosecution had taken a statement from Jessica, getting details on safe deposit boxes and other dealings between Jason and James over the years that she and Jason were married. The prosecution had been trying to arrange to have Jessica appear as a key witness, but L.C. had become involved, vehemently opposing her participation, using his influence to keep her from being subpoenaed.

L.C. was doing it more to save his own life than to aid and abet Jessica. The prosecutors finally got her to agree to appear as a witness.

L.C.'s experience as a trial lawyer had taught him that the momentum of a trial could change very quickly under the right circumstances. If he could keep Jessica away from the trial long enough, it was possible that the prosecutors would become frustrated, deciding to change their strategy and offer James a plea bargain without Jessica having to appear. It would also prevent a confrontation between Jessica and James. In L.C.'s mind that, God forbid, might make James somehow believe that he had some hand in the matter.

Jessica was still unaware of the tape recording made in L.C.'s office during James' visit to Topeka. It had been confiscated by federal agents during the seizure of James' office records. James had advised his attorney Brett Hamil about the tape and had planned on using it in the hearing to discredit Jessica's testimony. Oddly, either by coincidence or through L.C.'s ability to get to the right people, the tape mysteriously disappeared after James' attorney had executed a request to have the evidence subpoenaed.

As it happened, Jessica did finally appear shortly after it was announced that the tape couldn't be found. She went into the courtroom as if she'd left her royal entourage just outside the door, dressed in a stunning black suit, and holding the gallery spellbound as she took her seat. The Judge snapped out of his trance, barking an order for the hearing to continue. Heads in the gallery and at the defense and prosecutors' tables turned reluctantly back towards the bench.

Mister Gerri, the federal prosecutor, called Jessica to the stand, almost drooling with excitement, stumbling over himself with politeness as she took her place. There she sat, an omen from a dark dream come to life, smiling as she locked her eyes on James. Her lips were blood red as if she'd already savaged her prey, coolly letting him know that she not only intended to deliver his death blow, but was going to savor each moment.

After the customary inquiries for the record, Gerri began his questioning of Jessica. At first she told of finding herself captive in the Lavoisier home during the war, after she and Jason were married and he finally had been sent overseas.

"At the time, I thought they—well, at least Doctor Lavoisier—had asked me to stay with them because they wanted me to have the best medical care when my second child came," Jessica said. "I'd had a hard time with my first baby."

"And what did you realize later, Miz Dunraven?" the prosecutor asked.

"I suddenly saw that I was a prisoner in their home. They refused to allow me to go anywhere, to be with friends, or do the things other young people would do, under the same circumstances. They guarded me and my child, night and day," Jessica confessed, suddenly becoming teary-eyed.

"Objection, your Honor," Brett Hamil, blurted out. "This testimony has no relevance to this case, other than to discredit the character of my client with hearsay and innuendo."

"This is leading us somewhere, isn't it, Mister Gerri?" the Judge asked.

"Yes, your Honor, if the court will be patient," Gerri replied.

"Very well, objection overruled. Proceed!"

"Go on, Jessica," the prosecutor ordered.

"Several times while I was living there, Doctor Lavoisier made remarks suggesting that he wanted to keep the children, to have me turn over legal custody of them to him. When I had Dale, my second child, I tried to pay my hospital bill, only to find that Doctor Lavoisier had conspired with my husband to force me to give up my children by taking all of my money out of my bank account. When I went to pay my bill, I was told the account, an account I had carefully kept my hospital money in, was overdrawn."

"Your Honor," the defense pleaded, "I protest this blatant attempt to paint my client as a child stealer, a kidnapper. This is ridiculous!"

"You got a point to this, Mister Prosecutor, or are you sending us on a wild goose chase here?" the Judge questioned.

"Your Honor, I think the testimony Miz Dunraven is about to give has a great deal of bearing on our case. If you'll be patient with me for just a few more minutes."

The old Judge nodded and leaned back in his chair with his eyes closed.

"Then what happened, Jessica?" Gerri asked.

"When I couldn't pay the bill, because I didn't have any money, Doctor Lavoisier offered to pay it out of his pocket. He even made a deposit into my bank account to try and get me to give him the boys.

He followed me around town, everywhere I went, accusing me of doing the most horrible things. He was trying to make me look like a bad mother to my children and some sort of vixen as he called me, to everyone in town."

"He did this because he wanted you to give up custody of your children?" Gerri reiterated.

"Yes! A few weeks later, he asked me down to his room and offered to give me a lot of money to help me start a career in the movies if I'd leave the children in his custody until his son came home," she said, whimpering.

"How much money did he offer you, Jessica?"

"Seventy-five-thousand dollars," she said. "He said he'd pay me in cash. While I was standing there, he pulled out a roll of bills, thousand-dollar bills, and began counting them in front of me. I'd never seen so much money!" she exclaimed.

"Was that the only time you'd seen him with a large amount of cash?" Gerri asked.

"No! Later, before I left for Guam, the maid had accidentally thrown away an old thermos jug that Doctor Lavoisier had in the closet. Everyone in the house was forced to go out to the city dump that night and dig through the garbage looking for that old jug."

Gerri looked at the Judge, "Did he find his thermos, Jessica? And if he did, what was in it?"

"Yes, he found it. It had nearly fifty-thousand dollars stuck down inside of it. I was told that he had money hidden all over the house and the backyard. When I asked Lora, his wife, why he was hiding money everywhere, she told me I'd be killed if I talked about it to anyone." "Objection", Hamil interjected. "Overruled," the judge replied. Gerri cleared his throat before continuing: "Now later, I believe you stated in the interrogatory that you'd seen an even larger amount of cash."

"I never actually saw it, but Jason had mentioned to me that his father had made him get a lock box in San Juan, Puerto Rico, when we lived there. He said he had so much of his father's money in the box it almost wouldn't fit. His father had apparently brought the cash with him when he came to visit us."

"Objection, hearsay!" Hamil complained.

"Sustained."

"Were there other times when you saw or heard about him having large amounts of cash around the house?" Gerri again inquired.

"It became sort of a family joke. Everyone in the family knew he kept cash so that he wouldn't have to pay for anything with a check. Why, all of us knew that he'd had a fence built in the backyard just to be able to hide cash in the fence post. I never was positive it was true, but I had heard that he owned cemetery lots all over the state. They were deeded in different names that he liked to use. I guess he thought they'd be easy to get rid of."

"What other things did he invest in?"

"Jason was upset for years because his father had given Bill Lavoisier, his brother, a two-hundred-and-thirty-acre peanut farm near Pollock, Louisiana. I was told that he'd bought that with cash, but no one would ever talk about it. Mostly, it was common knowledge that Doctor Lavoisier owned property...oil, gas and other real estate all over Texas and Louisiana, but that no one would ever know where it was or whose name it was in. He also bought his sister an office building in Ruston, Louisiana. She's in real estate."

"Did, uh, Doctor Lavoisier ever discuss what his earnings were with you?" the prosecutor asked.

Jessica sat with a stupid look on her face and then, as if she were insulted by the remark, answered Gerri's question. "The man hated my guts. He wanted to kill me. Hell, no, he didn't tell me what he made! He went out of his way to make sure I didn't get my hands on one thin dime of his money. Any money I did find out about, he threatened to shoot me if I ever told anyone about it," she added, causing a few laughs from the gallery.

"No more questions, your Honor," Gerri said abruptly.

"Mister Hamil, your witness," the Judge stated.

Brett Hamil approached the witness stand, wiping his face with a handkerchief before turning to look at Jessica. "You look to me like a woman who pretty much knows what's going on in her life. What I mean by that is...I guess, when you were married to Jason, you knew how much money he brought home, what he bought, what he owned?" he inquired.

"Jason didn't make spit for an income, and he sure as hell didn't own anything. He owed everybody in town and then some! It wasn't any problem keeping track of his net worth. He didn't have one, except for a deck of cards and set of dice for a crap game!" Jessica laughed, again causing the gallery of onlookers to erupt.

After a few loud bangs of his gavel, the Judge was able to quiet the room before the defense continued.

"So, what you're saying is that Jason pretty much let you know whatever he was doing with his business? He wasn't a secretive type husband?"

"Jason," she said, half-laughing, "he couldn't keep a secret if his life depended on it. He told me everything."

"And you and Doctor Lavoisier…it sounds as if you didn't get along very well with each other? Wasn't it true that you've hardly spoken to him since you left his house after the war?" Hamil quizzed her.

"I never wanted to see him again! He spent his time maligning me with everyone, trying to make me look like trash! I hated him!" she snapped, looking at James coldly. "He was nothing but a selfish old man, doing anything it took to make a dollar."

"Nothing but a selfish old man, that is what you said, isn't it, Miz Dunraven?" Hamil challenged.

"That's right…that's exactly what I thought of him!" Jessica reaffirmed. "He was cruel and hateful," she added, turning her eyes away from James.

"This man…this man takes you into his home during the war to have your child, and pays the bills, and he's cruel and hateful? This man," the attorney went on, "takes your children into his house after you were threatened with having them taken away from you for abusing them, and he's cruel and hateful? This man—"

The prosecutor suddenly interrupted, jumping to his feet, "I object to this line of questioning…defense is just badgering the witness!"

"Objection overruled…let's get on with it, counselor; it's getting late!" the Judge commanded.

"The truth is, that you've hated Doctor Lavoisier for years because he wouldn't be blackmailed into buying his own grandchildren from you? You're the one maligning that <u>old man</u>, as you called him. Doing everything in your power to squeeze him for cash!"

"That's not true!" Jessica screamed.

"It is true. You're either a liar or an accomplice in the same thing Doctor Lavoisier is being accused of. You say you knew your husband's business, what he owned, what he made? He couldn't keep a secret, were your exact words. What about the large sums of money kept in your account when you were married to Jason? You knew that was money his father had given the two of you so that you could have a better life for you and his grandchildren. You certainly knew it wasn't Jason's. We can produce the checks with your signature on them. And yet you never reported it as income, did you?"

"I never asked him for any of his money!" she shouted. "And I've already started proceedings to regain custody of my children. He's the one that's abusing my children, not me!" she screamed. "I'm their mother, and I want them back. I have the right!"

"I see...pangs of conscience," Hamil muttered to himself. "And you also know," he went on, "that the very home that the government is attempting to take away from Doctor Lavoisier and his wife was in fact deeded to you and your husband before your divorce. You apparently tried to gain title to the property and obtained a restraining order during the divorce proceedings to keep Jason from giving the house back to his parents. When you realized that you wouldn't be able to take it away from Doctor Lavoisier, you agreed to relinquish your ownership, knowing full well that you were going to turn in Doctor Lavoisier to the IRS. Cruel and hateful, indeed...speak for yourself, young woman! No more questions, your Honor," the attorney concluded, walking back to his chair, shaking his head in disgust.

"Mister Gerri, do you have any further questions of the witness?"

"No, your Honor," Gerri said, startled by the revelation about the ownership of the house at 625 South Jackson.

James had agreed to testify in his own behalf. After he had been questioned by his attorney, he was faced by the formidable young Mister Gerri, who opened his questioning with a contemptuously abusive assault, prompting the defense counsel to protest bitterly. All the while, James sat quietly enduring the verbal lashing.

The Judge was a Southern-bred man, an oddity for the Federal Bench in Texas. While fully aware of the prosecutor's privilege skillfully to harangue the witness, the Judge preferred a more chivalrous climate in his courtroom than what Mr. Gerri had been accustomed to on the East Coast.

James was startled when the silver-haired magistrate, who had appeared either asleep or hard of hearing during most of the proceeding, interrupted the government attorney in the midst of his cross-examination. "You know, young fella, I've listened to you cross-examine Doctor Lavoisier for the past twenty minutes. At first I thought you might not be feeling well, maybe got up on the wrong side of the bed this morning, or maybe you're just a little nervous about the trial. But I'll be danged if I can figure out what's got you so riled."

"What?" Gerri reacted.

"Now I realize that you probably went to a fine Eastern law school and all, but I make the rules in this courtroom. Now, Mr. Gerri, in case you've forgotten the premise of this court, it's to give Doctor Lavoisier a fair and just hearing. I will decide if we need a trial here, and how I'm gonna run that trial. We are not here to provide you with a platform to ridicule and express your indifference towards the folks who live down here in the South. Now you straighten up your act, or you and I will just have to have a little set-to in my chambers."

"Your Honor," Gerri said, caught off guard by the Judge's remarks, "I assure the court, I meant no disrespect towards Doctor Lavoisier or the citizens of this state. I'm merely following accepted courtroom procedure," he added, with a smug grin to the other members of his team.

"It may very well be accepted courtroom procedure where you come from, counselor, but you keep it up and I'm warnin' ya, I'll send your tail packin' and someone else u'll be finishing this case for you! I hope I've made myself clear," the Judge directed, vexed at the attorney's arrogance.

"Understood, your Honor!" the young man promptly replied, turning back to James with his face tomato red.

"My apologies, Doctor Lavoisier...gentlemen! I think we can continue now, if the prosecutor will go ahead," the Judge ordered.

"Doctor Lavoisier," Gerri continued, "our investigation shows that, during the last three years, substantial incomes were derived from your produce operations, medical practice and real estate transactions. Each of these businesses, however, seemed to have been carried out almost exclusively on a cash basis, with little or no record keeping. How do you explain the fact that hardly any of the payments for goods and services that you received were made by check or other traceable documentation?" he questioned.

"Well, I guess I never thought about it much, except that most folks around these parts have enough trouble readin' and writin', much less tryin' to keep up a checkbook. They'd have a hard time understanding a bank statement, even if they were of a mind to trust the banks with their money...which most of 'em aren't. If a fella wants to pay me in cash...that's his business," James replied.

"Isn't it odd," Gerri asked, "that your bank deposits from these cash transactions don't seem to be consistent with what one would expect from such a diversity of business?"

"You tell me, young fella. You're the one sittin' on all my records," James responded coolly, causing the gallery to break into laughter. "If you're askin' me if I made more than I'm telling, the answer is no. You ought to know by now what I spent and what I deposited."

"As a matter of fact, Doctor, we can't begin to account for all of your income, and I believe you know that. It appears that most of your cash-paying patients and business associates either won't cooperate or are untraceable. We are prepared to show that your income is inconsistent with your lifestyle, that you have a net worth substantially greater than what you now admit to. Put quite simply, Doctor, I believe that I can prove that you've filed fraudulent tax returns, evading your obligations for tax liabilities far beyond those you've reported. I also believe, and I will prove, that you've perjured yourself in an attempt to conceal your crimes." Gerri stated, turning towards the Judge.

"Your Honor, I'd like to petition the court at this time to issue an order allowing our agents to search the properties of the defendant, in order to perform an audit, as well as look for records that may be in the defendant's possession. The audit would be done for the purpose of placing a valuation on Doctor Lavoisier's estate. The government feels that such an audit is critical, not only in establishing proof of his under-payment of taxes, but would also prevent any further disposal of assets by the defendant similar to what was done with the deed to his residence in Jacksonville."

"Your Honor," Hamil interrupted, "the transfer of title to the Lavoisier's home was done over ten years ago. I think it's absurd for prosecution to insinuate that Doctor Lavoisier knew at that time that they would levy these charges against him, and that he made any conscious effort to conceal his interest in the property."

"I'm going to order a thirty-day continuance in this hearing in order to review the prosecution's request for a search and audit of the defendant's estate and also to handle some other matters pending before the court," the Judge suddenly stated.

"Your Honor," Gerri interrupted, "thirty days will give the defendant time to further conceal or convert his assets. We beg your Honor's reconsideration in granting an immediate order, allowing us to investigate his assets and issue a restraining order preventing him from dispersing those assets! At the very least, we'd ask that a bond be considered in the amount of five-hundred-thousand dollars."

"Mister Gerri," the Judge replied in a terse voice, "you have his bank accounts, his medical practice and his produce business under tight wraps. It seems to me, that your time would be better spent in trying to locate all of those unconfirmed properties that your star witness alleges dot the state of Texas and Louisiana, rather than worrying about the man's furniture and dishes. I doubt seriously that if Doctor Lavoisier has all of those thermos jugs full of money sitting around the house that he would have waited for you to drop by for coffee before he put them somewhere else. Motion will still be considered in thirty days," the judge answered, slamming down his gavel.

The young prosecutor leaped from his chair, almost outrunning the judge as he walked to his office. The judge stopped at the door to his chambers, wondering if Mister Gerri intended to run over him. Once inside, Mister Gerri and the defense attorney took a seat in front of the judge's desk. The defense attorney accepted a cup of coffee, calmly stirring his brew as the prosecutor continued to plead for the judge to reconsider his decision on the audit and search.

After nearly thirty minutes the door opened. Brett Hamil walked from the judge's office, noticeably upset with the meeting that had just taken place.

"There's more to it than the judge wanting thirty days to handle some other business of the court; that's not the worst of it," the attorney advised James and Lora. "Apparently Mister Gerri slipped up and told him that Jessica has already been successful in getting a court order issued to have the boys returned to her custody. She's planning on having you served with the order within the next week. The judge was trying to be considerate by postponing the hearing and the trial until the matter with the boys has been resolved. He thought you might want some time to be with the boys and get things settled. I guess she really rubbed him the wrong way," the defense attorney told them both. "He thinks Gerri is nothing but a smart-ass henchman for the government."

"Jesus," James said, "how can she do this to the boys at a time like this? Anyway, I appreciate you telling us what she's up to!"

"I wouldn't count on the full thirty-day continuance. The way that attorney is acting, anything could happen. He'll probably get the thirty-day recess shortened. I'm sorry you have to face this thing with your grandchildren, along with the trial. It's a lot to have happen at one time," Hamil finished.

"Let's go home, Lora," James said, watching her as she began to sob. ""We've got business to take care of!"

As James stopped the car near the back porch and cut off the engine, Lora turned, looking at him with an uncharacteristic sadness. "I almost can't muster the strength to go on, James. I'm tired of fighting...fighting for every crumb of life. And when we think we've made it, everything we've worked for and loved is torn out of our arms. It's just more than I can stand!" she sobbed.

"We've got to go on, Lora. We can't afford to lay down now. We'll lose everything we've worked so hard to build for ourselves. We just can't quit in the middle of this!" James said, putting his hand on hers, the first time in years that there had been any sign of affection from either of them.

"How do we handle this, James? The government is going to come in here, and do their audit and probably take everything we own. And that vile woman is coming after my grandchildren...I just can't stand it! What do we do?" she cried.

"We'll fight, that's what we'll do. Let them do their audit; they won't find enough to fill a bushel basket. And let Jessica come after the boys, I'm taking them to Keso's. I've been planning it for some time, ever since this thing started. We'll load everything we can get on a truck and head over to the swamp. Bill will take a lot of the stuff at his farm. I've worked this thing out so that we can make it look like I took the boys on a fishing trip. We'll go deep into the swamp, all the way to Choctaw Lake. They'd never be able to find us in there...not and get out alive!"

"How can we possibly take all of our things? And what about the boys? They don't know anything about living in bayou country," Lora said, overwhelmed with the idea of such a trip. "What if something were to happen to one of them?"

"The boys will do fine. I'll be with them. It might give them a chance to grow up some. God knows they're gonna need it, with that demon on their heels. I'll keep them there until the attorneys can get enough on her to reverse the court order."

"I'm so worried about them," Lora said, "they've never been around anything like that!"

"As far as the things we own, we just take the most valuable items. They're going to get a lot of what we have, but the more we put on the truck, the more we'll end up with. Besides, I have a feeling they're more interested in getting their hands on my records and seeing if they can find the money. There's no way in hell I'm leavin' those for them tah go through. If we don't fight, we'll lose the boys forever," James said, determined in his mind what he had to do.

Lora knew the look that James had on his face. He'd never give up—never! He would leave the face of the earth, descending into a place that most of the world never knew existed.

Five days later a new Chevrolet stake bed truck was parked in the back yard. It was loaded with a mound of household items and covered with a chocolate-colored tarp. A fishing boat and motor were hitched to the truck to make their trip look like a legitimate vacation, in case they were being watched. The boys were convinced that they were setting out for a great adventure.

It was several hours before dawn as Lora followed the truck out of town, driving James' blue Packard. Both boys slept on the seat next to James as he shifted the gears of the truck, heading slowly towards

Pollock, Louisiana, stealing into the curtain of darkness that still blanketed Jacksonville.

By mid-day they began to see signs of the lush Louisiana bayou country. Blacktop highways turned into gravel roads that sent volleys of rocks clanging against the fenders as they slipped deeper and deeper into the submerged world before them.

Each step of the way, as James slipped along the green tunneled paths that led deeper into the swamp, they were confronted by bayou people, unfriendly at first until they realized that James and Lora were natives of the area, and spoke its colorful French dialect. That brought friendly and affectionate responses from everyone they came in contact with. It was as if a feudal land baron had returned to tour the distant outlying holdings of his estate. The people they met would guard the secret of their presence in the swamp with their lives.

Not only was it a jubilant occasion to welcome home a local son, but especially one of such notable success. James' prominence was well recognized among the impoverished citizens of the swamp, many of them distant relatives to the Lavoisier clan. His entourage proceeded farther and farther into the heart of the wetland.

The gravel road abruptly ended at the edge of the water, as if the road gang had been swallowed up by the swamp. A short, lightly built black man waited at the water's edge, greeting James in French and tipping his hat to Lora. He began to unload the car and truck, re-packing everything onto a barge, tied to a pier at the water's edge. When he'd finished, he helped Lora and the boys board a small, flat-bottomed boat moored to the back of the barge. They appeared as the image of royalty escaping from a recent coup de' etat, fleeing for their lives...and so they were. James followed the small band into the boat, wearing his usual slacks, white shirt, and paisley tie with a straw fedora to shade his eyes from the blistering sun.

The group sat quietly watching the shore as the gaunt man maneuvered his cumbersome rig between the giant cypress stumps, sliding over the dark green hyacinths that blanketed the waters. The shade from the towering cypress trees offered a cooling relief from the sting of the afternoon sun. Soft-shell turtles flopped like falling depth charges into the water along the bank and from limbs poking up from the murky water along the boat's path as they motored away from the landing.

Dale was spellbound, watching a lumbering gray cottonmouth, suspended from a bush above the water, gulping down something that was fighting to keep its legs from the snake's mouth while the rest of its body was being digested.

James kept a stern look on his face when one of the boys pointed towards a huge black bird floating like a kite above the open spaces between the trees.

"What's that?" Dale asked, pointing straight up towards the bird. "Is that a hawk?"

"Turkey buzzard," James replied, laughing as he turned back towards the boys, relieved to be back in the swamp. He was at peace now, more peace than he'd known in years. Lora could see the change come over him as James began to relax, no longer fearing the government might be following him. They would never find him in this place.

After a two-hour ride through the submerged cypress forest, the boat's engine dropped to a faint metallic idle, and the boat drifted towards a peninsula hidden from the direct view of the waterway. A man waited at shore to help the boatman unload the cargo of household goods, boxes of files, records, and a commissary of food and supplies.

Dale stood staring at the six-foot-high chicken wire fence that surrounded the encampment, sitting twenty yards from the water's edge. Two other men walked down to the boat, greeting James in a language that seemed strange to Dale; it wasn't the French he'd heard his grandfather speak before.

They talked to James for a moment, then climbed onto the barge to start unloading building materials already on the boat before the family had arrived at the swamp that day.

The camp had been erected a few days earlier with as many of the comforts of home as James could arrange on such short notice. Two large military wall tents, faded from previous use, stood inside the compound with the walls rolled up and tied with cord. Two rows of cots with white mosquito bars suspended above them were already in one of the tents. A wooden picnic table had been set up in the other. The back wall was lined with a row of crudely constructed bookshelves waiting to hold the cases of canned foods that James had carried with him from Jacksonville. A white enamel refrigerator sat just outside the kitchen tent, waiting to be plugged into a gasoline generator that James had brought on the barge. Several fifty-five-gallon drums of water and gasoline were positioned on sawhorses close to the river side. Fresh water would be delivered weekly by the boatmen.

James could tell from the look on Lora's face that she was less than pleased with the quality of life that had been provided for her grandchildren.

"I just don't feel right about this, James," she said under her breath. "They've never lived like this. What if something was to happen to one of them? I'd never forgive myself."

"They'll be fine. I can take care of them! Quit worrying," James advised, cutting a chunk of black mule as he started his inspection of the camp.

Both boys followed James into the compound, stopping at the gate as he turned around and pointed to the fenced door panels with his cane.

"You gotta keep that gate closed, 'less you want hogs rooting around in here. Gators u'll come in here at night, too, when they smell the cookin'. Best get in the habit right now of closin' the gate," James instructed, continuing with his tour of the camp.

"I'll whip up some supper for us," Lora said, moving into the kitchen tent, followed by one of the men carrying a box of groceries.

"I don't want you boys to drink any water except what's in these barrels. And nobody's to take a crap around the camp without burying it; that's the first thing that'll get one of us sick, you understand?" James asked, ignoring the boys' inquisitive expressions as he scratched a line along the ground outside one of the tents with his cane.

"Yes, sir," both boys answered.

"You boys get a shovel and cut a trench around the outside of these tents. We're likely to get rain tonight and I don't want to get water inside where we're sleepin'."

James left the boys to carry out his orders as he finished directing the men where to place the cases of food and supplies in the tents.

Lora was busy at two portable white gas stoves that stood near the edge of the kitchen tent.

Within a half-hour Lora had finished cooking the meal, filling the three workmen's plates with a heaping mound of food. All three of the men thanked her and then left the tent to sit outside the compound.

Dale thought it odd that the men were eating on the ground outside the fence while the four of them sat at the long picnic table having their supper.

"How come they don't come in here and eat with us, granddad?" Dale asked, looking over at James. "We got lots of room at the table."

"'Cause they got their place and you got yours, boy. It's the way things are," James answered.

"It's not that we're any better folks," Lora tried to explain; "it's just that they'd feel mighty uncomfortable sittin' with us, just the same as we would with them. Since they've been hired to do a job for your granddad, they figure it's best to keep a respectful distance."

"Is it because granddad is their boss?" Dale interjected. "And because he's Creole?"

"That's part of it. It's also 'cause he's an important man in their eyes, bein' a doctor and all. They respect him for what he's done."

James looked over the edge of his coffee cup. "You boys be careful not to be disrespectful of these folks. They're proud people. In time, you'll understand the order of things here, in the swamp. They can be your best friends if they're on your side. You make 'em mad and they can give yah hell! They'll be expectin' you boys to behave like guests in their home. Mind that you remember that while you're here." He stood up and placed his dishes in a bucket.

When they had finished eating, James walked with the boys down to the edge of the water to wash the dishes. He sat on a canvas stool a few feet from the water, and primed a Coleman lantern that he'd brought along, touching a match to the new mantles suspended behind the glass. The brilliant white glow illuminated the shoreline. James set the lantern several feet away from his stool to avoid the swarms of mosquitoes that instantly honed in on it. Dale and David washed the dishes and then, at James' instruction, peeled off their clothes and slipped into the dark waters of the bayou for a bath. Dale and David quickly learned the value of using Ivory Soap, easily spotted in the muddy waters at night because it floated, almost sparkling in the light from the lantern.

When they returned to camp, Lora was dressed in her nightgown, her face fully coated in cold cream and her hair wired with dozens of hair rollers. She kissed the boys goodnight and slipped under the white mosquito netting hanging over her cot. She seemed unaffected by the drastic change in her living conditions. But then, she too had been from the swamps, never really forgetting the early years as a child when life always had been the way it was that night. It made things seem a little more acceptable for the boys, watching their grandmother adjust so easily to what seemed to them, a strange and uncertain experience.

In the morning both boys were awakened by the heat of the sun beating down on the canvas tent. Dale opened his eyes to find Lora standing over him. She bent down and kissed him on his forehead.

"Grandma's going to leave now. I'll be back in three or four weeks to check on you. You mind your grandfather and do what he says." She kissed David and Dale, then walked to the gate where James was waiting for her.

"I'm not going to let anything happen to the boys, I promise you," James stated again. "You head on over to Bill's. He'll finish loading the other things that he's got at his house. Give him this list of what I need for him to pick up in Pollock. You head on home after you've seen him…we'll be all right," he reassured her, looking down at the ground as if to avoid her questioning eyes.

Lora acknowledged his instructions with a reluctant nod, waved to the boys, and then stepped into the waiting boat. She was on her way to Bill Lavoisier's home to instruct him to transport the last cases of incriminating files and other evidence secretly into James' hands, and to re-supply the hideout.

Dale rolled over in his cot, pulling back the white netting to get a better view of his grandmother in the boat disappearing into the Cypress swamp. He'd miss her, the touch of gentleness that was always so much a part of life whenever she was around.

He thought about the prisoners and mental patients working on the road gangs they'd passed on the highway, on their way deep into the swamp. He realized it was a better prison than any man could ever build. His heart pounded as it occurred to him that he was locked into this place, hidden away from everything he'd ever known except his grandfather and brother. His mind raced with panic. Only his trust in his grandfather made it seem all right. 'It must be,' he thought. 'He'd never let anything happen to us.'

But the more he thought about it, even at thirteen years old, the more he realized how appropriate this place really was for him. He would learn that survival outweighed all else, including pride and arrogance. There was no place for self-pity, lest one become a meal while caught up in such sorrowful contemplation.

CHAPTER 27

The day had been uncomfortably hot again, even after the sun had disappeared, turning the swamp pitch black. The routine that night was the same as it had been the first night, except that the meal consisted of little more than cold Vienna sausages and crackers. James laid the bland selection on the table in front of the two boys and slipped into his bed, leaving David and Dale sitting alone in the faint yellow light from a kerosene lantern.

Dale could see that his grandfather had been drinking. He could tell that James had been upset about something all day. He had watched him pacing in the compound earlier in the afternoon. By nine-thirty, the partially full bottle of whiskey dropped from under the mosquito netting of James' cot and rolled a few feet across the palleted floor of the tent.

Dale moved towards his grandfather, listening to the old man moaning something in his drunken stupor, a verse, something from the Bible. "If I ascend up into heaven thou art there; if I make my bed in hell, behold thou art there." He picked up the bottle and set it upright next to the cot, gently tucking in the netting near James' feet. He watched the old man's sleeping face for a brief moment, and then returned to the picnic table to finish eating the tasteless meat and soggy crackers.

At four that morning, Dale was awakened by a burning sensation in his arm. When he was finally able to focus his eyes, he realized that his arm had been pushed against the mosquito bar during the night. He'd provided a feast for enough of the huge mosquitoes that his arm looked like he'd contracted measles. A heat rash had broken out under his neck where he'd perspired in the sweltering night air. A dozen varieties of spiders and other critters clung to the inside of his netting, invited into his sleeping chamber through an opening where his feet had unhooked the tuck from his mattress. Fortunately, none of these species had elected to sting or bite their host during the night.

Dale sat up in his cot, miserable from his intermittent sleep. It was light enough that he could see around the perimeter of the camp. Besides the unbearable heat and infestation of ravenous bugs, the swamp had come alive with an ungodly noise, screaming from the murky shallows of the swamp to the tops of the towering canopies hovering over the canvas habitat.

He'd had enough of the heat, and decided to slip over to the water jug to quench his thirst. Less than six steps from his cot, he felt the struggle of a moist animal skin slithering under the pressure of his naked foot. Dale leaped straight up and bounded back to bed, leaving the fist-sized tree frog flattened in the mud.

His thirst disappeared as he began to hear a low snorting growl coming from just the other side of the fence. Whatever it was had begun to dismember the wire barricade, shaking it with a tremendous force. Dale could feel his heart beating, as if someone were punching him in the chest. Every muscle in his body strained as he listened to the monster tearing at the wire, ripping at the posts and wooden slats of the fence.

'It has to be a bear,' he thought, and his tongue made a nervous circle around his lips. He was sure it was a bear; nothing else was big enough to take the fence down. The prowler was pulling the wire off the wooden frame. Dale began to breathe in cadence to his heartbeat, trying to conceal his presence by holding his hand over his mouth. The creature had, by now worked its way inside the main perimeter of the camp.

For a moment the place was still, returning the night to the more peaceful overture coming from the swamp, the very sounds that had earlier kept Dale awake. He lay as still as he could, listening, waiting, wondering where the monster was lurking. He couldn't understand why James and David were still asleep.

A piercing squeal tore through the tent, bringing with it the sounds of crashing cans and supplies in the pantry. A wall of one of the tents collapsed as the monster made its charge towards Dale.

Just as Dale was cocking himself to leap for the safety of the wire fence, deciding to take his chances in the swamp, James appeared out of the darkness.

For an instant, the crazed animal stopped its charge, studying the shadow of the human looming in the dark in front of it. And then it charged, going after the man standing only a few feet away. Just when the two forms were about to collide, James caught the intruder with a walloping blow from an axe handle he was holding next to his leg.

The animal screamed in terror, retreating a few feet from his adversary before charging again. James delivered a second round of blows, knocking the beast on its side.

"Git, pig!…git, git!" James screamed. "Damn razorback bitch, git outa here!"

He chased the hog around the compound, landing one blow after another to the animal's head and carcass. Dale was frozen with fear as he watched the duel taking place in front of him.

"By God, I'll knock you back to hell, you try to rip me with those damn tusks, you rotten bitch!" James yelled, moving towards the razorback. Each time James would adjust his stance to get a better angle to strike the hog, the animal would shift positions, blowing a warning snort and making an upward thrust with its curled tusks. It was a stare-down as James backed the pig into the corner of the wire fence, cutting off the razorback's retreat. The animal dug in for the charge, springing forward and then stopping just short of its target.

"You piece of swamp shit, I'll beat the livin' crap out of you, you wanta fight!" James threatened.

Dale was amazed at his grandfather's agility and courage, sparring with the tusks of the giant pig with nothing more than a club. He watched as James ended the contest with a lightning fast blow to the hog's head, knocking the charging tusker flat on the ground. The blow hadn't killed the razorback, but it had broken its spirit to fight. The animal slipped away from James, running through the hole in the fence and back into the swamp.

"You all right, boy?" James asked.

"Yes, sir!" Dale responded.

"Why didn't you let me know we had a razorback in the camp, boy? You could have gotten yourself ripped wide open by that hog!"

"I didn't know what it was. I've never seen anything like it!" Dale exclaimed, shaken.

"We're gonna have tah double the wire on the fence," James said, walking back to his bed. You boys have been dumping the garbage too damn close to the camp. You better move back two or three hundred yards; otherwise, we'll have a slew of em rootin' around here."

"Yes, sir," Dale replied, falling back onto his cot, trying to catch his breath.

David suddenly sat up, with one eye still closed as he panned the camp trying to see what was going on. He looked at James and then at Dale, finally flopping back into his cot as he returned to a deep sleep.

"Man-eatin' pigs, mosquitoes that suck your blood, snakes…what kind of place is this?" Dale wondered as he tried to go back to sleep.

In the morning, feeling a little guilty about the sparse meal he'd served the night before, James prepared a spread of biscuits, grits, pancakes and an assortment of canned fruit cocktail for the boys' breakfast.

After the tasteless meal from the night before, the boys woke up famished. When they had finished eating, James sent them down to the bayou to wash the breakfast dishes and do the laundry. When their chores were finished, James called them over to the tent where he kept a black footlocker next to his bed. He opened the trunk, producing a quart bottle of a clear liquid. He poured each of the boys a serving of the thick fluid, handing it to them to drink in a tin cup.

"Worm and Malaria prevention…get it all down," James ordered. "It may taste like hell, but it's good for you!"

Dale took a small sip, gagging and grimacing. "This is the same stuff you gave us when we ate the bananas! That tastes horrible! Gawd!"

"Mineral oil," James chortled, "now get it down…we got work to do."

David had the same reaction as Dale, holding his breath as he painfully gulped the ooze, letting a few droplets of the oily liquid drip onto his shirt.

"Gawd dang, that still tastes like motor oil!" David complained.

"I think I'm gonna puke," Dale moaned, trying desperately to cancel out the overwhelming urge to throw up.

James returned the bottle to the footlocker and left the tent, with both boys still trying to deal with their nausea.

Shortly after drinking the viscous cocktail, the two boys were hard at work in the hot morning sun, moving brush away from the outside of the camp perimeter. James wanted to try and do away with the large population of bugs crawling into the compound. He had decided to strip the under-brush and ground cover away from outside, so that he could spray the area with bug poison.

David dropped his shovel, looking as if he'd slipped into a trance, and acting as if something earthshaking suddenly had taken hold of him. It had! He moaned, and then turned, sprinting as fast as he could for the woods.

"Hey!" Dale screamed, "Where are you going? We gotta get this done! I'm not gonna do all this by myself!"

David ignored his brother, disappearing into the forest. Dale kept working, shaking his head at his brother's desertion. Just as he was muttering another complaint, the same revelation came over him, sending Dale dashing for the privacy of the tree line in the same direction David had taken.

James caught a glimpse of the last member of his labor gang racing into the woods. "Darn kids…never will get them to understand what hard work's all about! All they wanta do is play." James shook his head and returned to the medical journal he was reading.

Half an hour later Dale walked back into camp, holding up his unbuttoned pants with one hand. "Granddad, I gotta have some toilet paper, I'm sick. I got the runs from that stuff you gave me."

James laughed when he realized why the boys had vanished into the woods. "Havin' a time with that snakebite juice I gave you, huh?" he joked, entertained by what was going on.

"I'm really sick," Dale answered, wiping the sweat from his face as he waited for James to issue him a roll of T.P. from the supply tent.

"You boys better get used to taking that stuff. You're gonna have it everyday," James said, looking back down at his paper, still entertained as he thought about what must have been going on in the woods.

"I'd rather have worms," Dale whined; "it can't be any worse than this!"

Chuckling to himself as he tried to answer with a straight face, James said, "You'll live!"

By afternoon the boys had recovered from the slick potion and were sitting along the banks of the bayou, fishing. Dale's attention was drawn away from the water and his cane fishing pole as he watched a line of army ants moving across the ground in a single column, carrying bits of leaves and pieces of freshly killed insects. A small tumblebug was pushing a piece of animal dung the size of a marble with its hind legs. Dale was amazed at the bug's strength, considering its load had to be at least a hundred times heavier than it was.

Dragonflies roosted daintily on the water, sometimes coming to rest on the fishing poles and then launching themselves into the air to down a mosquito or a fat deer fly. A woodpecker caught Dale's attention as it tapped noisily at a cypress tree a few yards away from where the boys were sitting. Occasionally a gar would break the surface of the water, lured out of his basking in the sun to enjoy an irresistible tidbit that had landed on the water nearby.

Both boys were barefoot, wearing cutoff jeans and no shirt, with a hunting knife hanging from their belts. David was busily whittling a piece of soft cypress with his knife as Dale continued to watch the ground, amazed at the menagerie of wildlife moving around him. The more he focused on the ground, the more he realized that an intricate world had existed beneath him, and he'd never seen it.

By three in the afternoon the sun had become so intense that both boys headed back to camp to nap under the shade of the open canvas tent. More mosquitoes than usual had gathered in the inside of the roof of the tent, forcing the boys to sleep under the mosquito bars.

An armadillo waddled up next to the wire, near the tent, digging a hole in the soft earth under the fence as Dale lay in his cot with his eyes fixed on the tenacious scavenger. As soon as the animal had cleared a tunnel under the wire, it entered the enclosure, scouted a few feet from the hole and then turned and made its way back outside. It was as if the animal had come to prove that the fence meant nothing, that if the creatures of the swamp wanted him they would have their way.

Around five o'clock in the afternoon, the sky had changed to a thick black ceiling of clouds. The winds began to whip through the compound, jerking at the tie-down ropes and sending the light mosquito bars sailing into the prevailing breeze. Lightning flashed across the blackened sky as thunder boomed loudly in the distance. James got up from his nap and stood at the edge of the tent, studying the storm. He had seen something in the color and movement of the weather that bothered him, something different from the predictable afternoon showers they had had the past few days.

He ordered the boys to follow him down to the water's edge where the boat had been pulled up on shore. He fastened one end of a rope to a cleat on the bow of the boat, then stretched the rope out, walking up the bank to a tree, forty-five feet away. He wrapped the other end of the rope around the tree. When he had finished it, he had David and Dale, help him pull the motor off the boat and carry it back to camp.

A few minutes after they got back to camp, the rain started to fall. It sprinkled in a light drizzle at first, turning to a solid sheet of water as the storm moved in over the island. The roof sagged from the weight of the rain collecting on top of the tent. The small trenches dug along the outside of the tent were overflowing, allowing waves of water to flow under the walls.

By noon the next day, the bayou had risen to the front gate of the compound. James was concerned that the camp soon would be lost in the flood. James had left the tent, slipping out of sight into the wall of rain. Only a slight glimmer of daylight remained, making it difficult for Dale and David to see where James had gone. They were worried that he might drown in the storm. They waited, neither of them sure of what they would do if James didn't return.

James walked back into the tent a few minutes later, directing David and Dale to follow him to the front gate. The three of them trudged back into the blowing gale, standing at the wire gate as James ordered the boys to help him pull on a rope that he had tied to one of the gateposts. The boat, submerged nearly to the gunnels, moved slowly into sight, still afloat because of the air chambers built under the seats. The weight of the water that was in the boat made it difficult to haul in the small aluminum craft as they worked it into the shallows.

Once the boat had been retrieved, James handed the boys buckets to bail it out, as waves of rain continued to sweep the bayou. When they had emptied enough water out of the boat, they dragged it up into the tent, rolling it on its side to finish draining off the remaining water.

David was ordered to stand watch at the edge of the tent, as James and Dale hurriedly reattached the motor back onto the boat. James set two boxes of documents in the boat he thought were somehow important, and handed Dale and David life preservers to wear, in case the boat was capsized during the getaway.

The ground around the camp began to vanish as waves of water lapped against the slats of the fence. A cottonmouth slithered into one corner of the kitchen, looking for a dry roost and was quickly dispatched by James with a boat oar. A short time later, a red squirrel crawled out of the water, lying just under the edge of the tent, exhausted but still keeping a wary eye on his hosts as he joined the vigil.

By early evening the storm had slowed to a light mist. The squirrel had long since taken to the water, preferring the sanctuary of a tree rather than the small sinking island. By midnight, the sky had cleared and fog hung over the bayou as the moon cast a fluorescent glow above the calm waters. The swamp population rejoiced with a deafening choral.

By morning the water had receded to its original level, leaving little indication of how high it had risen the night before. Dale and David woke up to the smell of breakfast cooking on the stoves. James had tidied the tent, even shoving the boat to the outside and rolling up the walls to dry their supplies. Except for the unusually high humidity, the morning was the same as any other, so much the same that immediately after breakfast James ordered the boys to the black footlocker for their morning dose of snakebite juice.

Dale stood grasping his cup of mineral oil with his eyes closed as he reluctantly downed the slick awfulness. David had tried to escape, swearing that he was heading for the latrine. James called him back to the tent, giving him his serving of elixir, unconvinced by his grandson's halfhearted alibi.

James knew the camp would have to be moved to higher ground. In the next few days, while they were fishing from the boat in different areas of the swamp, James kept his eyes open for another campsite. When he was sure about the elevation of an area he thought desirable, he plotted out a new site, a more permanent and comfortable facility than the first camp had been, and certainly one that would stay dry.

On a Saturday morning after the storm, James and the boys made the two- hour trek back to the landing where the truck had been parked. They drove to Alexandria and rented a motel room. James left the boys in the air-conditioned room while he went on a shopping spree to outfit the new campsite.

When he returned, he was pulling a small house trailer behind the truck. He had arranged ahead of time with one of the men in the swamp to tow the trailer on a pontoon barge over to the new campsite. He'd brought a more powerful generator and several canvas halves to connect the two tents and trailer together. He'd also purchased a water pump and several sections of pipe to bring water into the camp for bathing and washing dishes. The truck was full of lumber and boxes of equipment to make the camp more comfortable.

As soon as they had moved to the new location, the small trailer was unloaded, and winched into place on a pier and beam foundation. After the trailer was in position, James went about wiring the tents and newly fenced perimeter with lights powered by the bigger generator. He had two workmen build a shower and an outside sink for washing dishes, in the kitchen tent. He also installed a small propane water heater to provide hot water for the shower. They would sleep and eat in the air- conditioned trailer and store their food and supplies in the tents. James had even purchased a small freezer to keep vegetables and fruits stored, to insure that they avoided getting scurvy. Wooden pallets were laid throughout the camp to keep them from having to walk through the mire and standing water that never seemed to drain off despite the intense heat during the day.

James had built smudge pots to burn inside the compound, sending blankets of thick acrid smoke over the campers in the evening when the mosquitoes seemed to congregate in ever-larger numbers. Dale even noticed that his skin had turned a pale yellow from the bug repellent, giving him a jaundice appearance. Mildew and fungus grew on everything, coating the equipment and walls of the tent with a brownish green film. The bed sheets had lost their original crispness, turning to a dingy brown color from the river water that was used to wash the camp laundry. Their bedding had begun to rot from the dampness. The monsoon weather left the boys with little to occupy their time but lie in their cots and watch the downpour drench the already saturated terrain.

Dale was watching a scorpion trying to find its way across the water-filled moat cut around the outside of the tent, when he was distracted by a shadow moving through the rain. Whatever it was, it was moving towards the front gate of the camp.

Dale could see a man standing in the downpour, rain draining like icicles from his hat to the ground as he waved at him from the front gate. He leaped to his feet, running as fast as he could to the trailer to tell James about the visitor. James got up, pulling his pistol from under his pillow and tucking it into his belt. He put on his hat and grabbed his umbrella, walking quickly out into the downpour with Dale following behind him.

The man greeted James with a polite, unhurried salutation in French, acting as if it was a warm sunny afternoon and he was just out for a casual stroll. Dale watched as James shook the man's hand, returning his greeting in French and introducing himself as they stood in the torrent of rain. James offered their guest shelter under the tent, as soon as he was convinced that the man was there on friendly business.

"My apologies, Doctor. My boy has gotten himself gored by a hog," the man said, with a heavy French accent. "His leg is split open and he is bleeding badly. I wouldn't bother you, but I worry that he might die if I don't stop the bleeding."

James questioned him in French, asking him where his son was being kept. The man answered that he was in his boat under a tarp at the water's edge. Dale could only pick up part of the conversation as the two men switched from a broken English back to French and then back to English.

"David, Dale!" James shouted, "come with me. We've got to get this man's son out of his boat. He's gotten himself chewed up by a razorback."

The four of them hauled the boy up to the trailer, laying him gently on James' bed. James moved a lamp over to the bed, handing it to David to hold while he examined the boy's leg. James unwrapped several layers of old newspaper that the boy's father had used to bandage the wound. When he had removed the final layer of newspaper he discovered a thick pad of Spanish moss stuck to the gaping, foot long wound in the boy's leg.

"Gawd damn it! Why'd you put this crap on his leg? The whole leg is filthy, absolutely covered with this stuff!" James realized that he had embarrassed the man, so he softened his tone. "Well, at least you got the bleeding slowed down. You probably kept him from bleeding to death!"

James talked to the boy's father, trying to be a little more tactful as he picked pieces of moss out of the open wound with a pair of forceps.

"What's your name?" Dale asked, smiling at the boy. "I'm Dale Lavoisier. This is my granddad...and that's my older brother, David. My granddad's a good doctor...he'll have you back on your feet in no time."

The boy lay still, staring up at Dale without any response to what he'd said.

"He can't understand you, son. He's a deaf mute," James said, lifting up the boy's leg to slide a folded sheet under it. "I'm going to have to clean this leg up or he'll lose it. Dale," James continued, "I'll need you to help me. David, take the boy's father outside and get him a cup of coffee or a soda. There's too damn many folks walking around in here."

James worked on the boy's leg for several hours, cleaning and suturing his ripped calf. The boy was a year or two older than Dale, but not much bigger. He seemed to be comforted by Dale's presence in the trailer as James sewed the jagged wound back together.

When James had finished dressing the wound, the father, a poor river-man and part-time trapper, tried in earnest to arrange to pay for James' services. James diplomatically declined the man's offer to pay, requesting instead that the father do some work for him at a later date. The boy's father was pleased to be able to maintain his dignity by paying his bill the way James had requested.

James was aware that money was always a scarce commodity for the river people. He also knew that their pride was easily bruised. It would have been an affront to the man for James to forgive the charges. James immediately made friends with the father because of his handling of the delicate question of the payment.

The boy's father had signed what Dale had said to his son, generating a smile from the boy's face. The boy's name was Leon

Covair. He held out his hand to Dale, then to David, and finally to James, moaning his version of a greeting as they shook hands.

When James realized that the family lived only a quarter of a mile from camp, he arranged to call on his patient later that week. James knew that if he didn't continue to treat the sutured leg, and remove the drain that he'd inserted in the wound, the boys father would return to his own form of treatment, placing more Spanish moss or mud packs on the leg, or purposely infecting the cut with maggots. The maggots would eat away the dead tissue, an old cure that worked remarkably well. But the leg would probably turn gangrenous without cleaning and have to be amputated, if the boy didn't die first.

James could see that Dale was excited about making friends with Leon and was unconcerned about the boy's handicap. James seized the opportunity to make a house call, pleased to have someone for Dale, and David, if he was interested, to occupy their time.

Leon had been born and raised in the swamp. He'd only made two trips out of the bayou country during his life. One had been to deliver his mother to Alexandria to a hospital, where she died hours after being admitted with a concussion received in a fall. His other visit to the outside world had been to ride with his father when he'd taken his older brother to Baton Rouge to enlist in the army.

Leon had a vivacious character. It was hard to find him without a smile on his face. And even though his formal education had been neglected, the love and dedication of his family had helped turn him into a happy and outgoing young man. He was as curious about life as any teenage boy, and he hungered to understand his small world at Keso's Marsh, as well as the world that he'd seen on his excursions to Alexandria. Dale and David quickly came to admire him, realizing that there was much they could learn from the enthusiastic backwoods boy. It was obvious to them that he was extremely intelligent. He had mastered sign language from a pamphlet given to him at the hospital by a nurse when his mother had died. He also was an accomplished artist, masterfully recreating his world in drawings kept in a notebook tucked under his arm.

But his greatest talent was his knowledge of the swamp and his enthusiasm for sharing his wealth of information with the two 'city boys'. Neither Dale nor David understood sign language, but they quickly overcame that obstacle by creating an alternative form of communication.

Dale had discovered that Leon could feel sound vibrations. Once they had Leon's attention, by yelling or beating on something, they would converse with a crude combination of hand and facial gestures that symbolized, as best they could, what they were trying to get across to their deaf companion.

When Leon had something to say, or wanted their attention, he simply let out a loud mooing sound. Leon thought it was funny, how Dale and David always overemphasized what they were trying to say. Most of the time he'd watch them struggle through a long series of gestures, totally entertained by their efforts, but all the while knowing exactly what they had been trying to say.

Leon was a self-proclaimed archeologist, often taking the boys miles from the camp to visit an old Indian potters' village. The three of them would spend hours, collecting bits of pottery from off the ground, or picking pieces from the piles of dirt at the old village where the Indians had practiced their trade centuries earlier.

Leon tried to tell a story about a seven-foot Indian that a team of archeologists from Southern Methodist University had dug up near the sight. He'd made up his own version of an 'Old George' tale, trying to sign to Dale and David, as best he could, about seeing the chief's ghost all the time, just about where their camp had been built. Leon had so much of a problem keeping a straight face that the story never had much impact on Dale or David, despite the fact they only understood parts of what he was trying to tell them.

But the story of Old George terrified Leon. Dale had done too good a job of communicating the story to him. From then on, Leon avoided coming around their camp after dark, even though both boys had assured him that George lived in Jacksonville.

Leon had become their best friend and, as it was, their only buddy. As great a friend as he was, he sometimes made a pest of himself, arriving in the camp shortly after sunrise and waiting patiently outside the trailer for the boys to get up for breakfast. He'd occupy his time by peeling through a selection of old Saturday Evening Posts and comic books that were stacked near the picnic table. He would walk in and out of the trailer, continually, to see if they were awake. James would finally run him outside and lock the door.

When Dale and David had finished their morning chores, the three of them would strike out to a fishing hole or a favorite swimming spot. More often than not, they'd do both, swimming out deep into the gator grass and lily pads until they could find a likely fishing spot. They'd stand in the water up to their chest, stripped of their clothes and cast for bass. Leon had taught them that it was a good fishing hole if they felt cold currents of water against their legs. While highly improbable, the possibility of having one's vitals snipped off by a passing gar or a gator was a fear that was constantly on both boys' minds. But neither of them was about to admit to any such phobia.

Doodlebug calling, another of Leon's endless talents, became one of the favorite pastimes. The trick was to get the doodlebug to start kicking sand at the bottom of his funnel-shaped trap.

Leon, with his well-developed moan, was able to fool two or three bugs at a time into kicking sand. The vibration from his voice would signal the doodlebug that a meal had fallen into its trap. Once the doodlebug started kicking, a small bb-sized shot of cotton hooked to a thread was dropped into the hole where the doodlebug would hook on to it, thinking he'd trapped some kind of fuzzy snack. Doodlebug calling could occupy half a day before the threesome would move on to another adventure.

They'd been in the swamp for two months when Brett Hamil successfully appealed to the judge for another continuance in James' trial after a heated confrontation. James had been told by phone that the judge's patience was wearing thin. The judge had been advised by Gerri that he had reason to believe that James had skipped town. Hamil had been put on notice that he was being held personally responsible for James being present at the trial when it began, two months hence. Mister Gerri had threatened to file a grievance against Judge Leonard because of the way he had conducted the pretrial hearing. The prosecutor demanded a bench warrant be issued immediately for James' arrest, but got a search warrant for an audit of James' property instead.

James had made up his mind, despite Hamil's promise to Judge Leonard, that he was going to continue to hide out at Keso's Marsh up to the day before the trial. He was determined to keep Gerri from looking at the records he had with him in the camp, and to continue ducking the process servers trying to deliver Jessica's custody order. He had, in fact, decided to leave the boys in the swamp even after the trial had started. He'd decided to have his brother Bill care for the boys until the trial was over.

The maneuvering by everyone concerned with the trial had created a legal nightmare. The prosecutors hadn't found anything of substance at the Lavoisier home during their search, and Gerri had turned his frustration on Lora, demanding that she reveal James' whereabouts. Marshals from New Orleans had made two attempts to search the swamp for James, to no avail. Lora was being followed everywhere she went by federal marshals hoping to be led to James and the boys. Jessica's attorney was threatening to have kidnapping charges brought against James and Lora. She'd even gone as far as having her attorney write to Bill Lavoisier and threaten him for aiding and abetting James in his plot. The situation had begun to wear on everyone.

Lora had reached her breaking point. She was physically exhausted trying to teach summer school and operate the house with nothing but her measly salary to live on. She constantly worried about James and the boys. Jason hadn't written home in months, adding another concern to her growing list of worries. Most of all, she longed to see the boys, knowing full well that it was out of the question for her to visit them, since she was under constant surveillance.

Hamil had his own set of problems, wondering if James was going to appear in court on the appointed trial date. Or else, as the Judge had warned, Hamil was going to do time in jail for contempt by his client. Gerri had lost valuable time in pursuit of his test case. Other indictments were to be postponed, creating problems for him with his superiors. Judge Leonard had hung himself out on a limb with his unorthodox procedure in the courtroom. He knew he might be called to task for handling the trial the way he had.

James stood to face the greatest disaster. It wasn't so much the loss of his livelihood and his wealth, or even the possibility of prison that he feared as much as losing his grandsons. They had become his world, his reason for life itself. His battle with Jessica was a personal crusade. But now, with the trial and Jessica's overt attempt to regain custody of the boys, James saw a sign of what was to come. He knew that it would take all of his resources to defeat her sinister maneuvering to drag her sons back to Topeka. If he failed, his life, as he had wanted it, would be ended, giving her the victory and the revenge she had sought for years against Lora and himself.

James lay in the swamp, keeping to himself in the trailer, struggling to deal with his fear of losing Dale and David. He was tired of fighting. In a way, he regretted not having killed Jessica when he had the chance. But even that desire had left him. Nothing seemed to matter anymore except keeping the boys next to him as long as he could.

CHAPTER 28

James had been away from camp for two days. He'd driven over to Winnfield to visit an old classmate from Tulane University, and then on to Ruston to take care of business. Dale and David had stayed in camp, preferring the meager comforts of home rather than enduring the long tedious trek by boat back to the landing.

The evening had turned to a black sinister shroud, leaving the boys without the soft moonlight that usually accompanied nightfall in the swamp. An electrical storm burst in jagged streaks across the sky, threatening to rain all during the evening. Rain would have been a welcome relief from the stifling heat that hovered just under the forest canopy. It almost suffocated the boys in its muggy stillness as they sat reading in the tent. David had lit the smudge pots to thin out the swarming mosquitoes that were drawn by the light hanging from the center of the shelter.

Dale was consumed by a feeling of loneliness, even though David was sitting only a few feet away. The past seemed to well up within him as the storm continued to threaten outside. He knew better than to let the morose mood take hold of him. The haunting fears and memories of the past were much too painful and too intense for him to deal with in this bleak place.

He looked over at David, hoping that he would sense that he wanted to talk. Nothing happened. David continued to read, oblivious to Dale's mood.

"You ever think about mother and dad and the way things were before they got divorced?" Dale finally asked.

David finished the line he was reading in his book and then turned towards Dale, studying him for a moment with an irritated look, "Sometimes...why?"

"I always wonder what it would have been like if they hadn't split up. I guess we'd still be in Topeka!" he said staring at David while waiting for some instantaneous response.

"I wish they were back together," David announced after a long pause. "I guess if Dad had'na had to go overseas again, things might have worked out okay and we wouldn't be here. Mother would have told L.C. to get out, so that she could be with Dad again," he added, staring off into the dark.

Dale was surprised, "I don't think she would have done that, David. I don't think she loved Dad...or us, either!"

David stood up, knocking the bench over that he'd been sitting on. He rushed Dale, grabbing him by the shirt and pulling him forward. "I don't ever wanta hear you say that again...ever! They're gonna get back together again someday! Dad's just gotta get done with his job overseas, that's all!"

"Turn loose," Dale demanded, jerking his shirt out of David's fist.

"They just had a misunderstanding, and they'll work it out...it's nothing. They just had a fight!" David railed, pushing Dale backwards as he turned him loose.

"They didn't have a fight, David; they got divorced. It isn't the same as when she used to run off and leave us all the time. She isn't coming back this time...and I'm glad!" Dale screamed. "I hated her guts. I'd rather live with Grandma and Granddad!"

David jerked around, burning a stare at him, "Yeah...this is just like heaven livin' here, isn't it? Hangin' around here with that old man in this slop is great! You don't even know why we're here, do you?"

"What are you talking about?" Dale responded.

"You think this is some kind of a holiday. You're stupid, that's all. You're just stupid. He's makin' us stay here so that mother can't find us!" David shouted. He's trying to get back at her 'cause he knows she wants us to come home, so that she can get the family back together."

"That's a lie. Granddad and Grandma care about us! They just don't like the way she's treated us. They're trying to do what's best for us. They wouldn't do anything to hurt you and me...either one of them."

"They're trying to keep me here because they think I might get mother and dad back together. They're trying to keep them from getting remarried because they hate her. She told me exactly why they were keeping us hidden in the swamp!" David suddenly announced.

Dale was shocked, watching David's face to see if he'd meant something else. "When did you talk to mother?"

David looked confused, wiping his face with his hand as he took a final glimpse at Dale and then turned his back and walked out of the tent.

Dale followed him as far as the entrance to the tent, screaming at him as David disappeared into the dark, "What are you talking about? You haven't talked to her. You're makin' it up! She's never said anything to you about any of this. You never called her...you couldn't have! She never said she wanted to get the family back together, either...she doesn't care about us...any of us!"

Dale turned around, making his way back over to the table, bothered by what David had said. He knew something was wrong. He'd never seen David act so strange. He was scared, more than he'd been in a long time, as he realized that something had happened to David. David, the one who'd always been the pillar of strength when James and Lora weren't around, now seemed out of control.

'He meant something else,' Dale thought. 'He knows he hasn't talked to her. He's just confused.' His mind raced with scenes of Jessica standing over David, slapping him across the face, his nose bleeding from a blow from her hand. He wondered how David could feel any different than he did, after what he'd been through with her.

He turned out the light and lay down on one of the cots, remembering back to a time at the house on South Jackson. He thought to himself how peaceful it always had been in the backyard of his grandparents' home, or better still was his grandmother's room, lying across the foot of her bed near the fireplace. None of these black thoughts ever crossed his mind there. He drifted off into a comforted sleep.

In the morning Dale woke up to find Leon sitting at the picnic table in the tent, as usual. Dale looked at him and then rolled over, covering his head with a pillow. "How come you like lookin' at those books so much, Leon?" he asked, rolling back over and throwing a pillow at Leon's back.

Leon smiled, making a loud moan, not realizing that Dale had said anything.

"Yeah, good morning to you, too," Dale chirped, making a half-hearted 'hello' sign with his hand.

Leon moaned again, throwing the pillow back at him as he charged the cot, dumping his young friend out on the dirt.

"Jesus, Leon. What're you doin'?" Dale laughed. "You got buckshot for brains, you dope," Dale went on, slowly enough that Leon could get the drift that he was being cut down with a sarcastic remark.

Leon made a succession of circle motions around his head, letting loose with one of his hideous laughing sounds as he jokingly signed that Dale was crazy.

"You throw me out of bed, and I'm crazy? Let's go get something to eat."

While Dale and Leon were having breakfast, David came into the tent, acting as if nothing had happened the night before. It was the way he always reacted. He'd blow up about something but that would be the last time he'd ever say anything about it; it was over.

Dale was the first to hear the boat heading towards shore from the swamp. All three of them raced down to the water as James threw a line out for the boys to drag the boat up on shore.

"Mornin', boys!"

"Hey, Granddad," Dale yelled, smiling back at James.

David felt like he ought to say something, but only smiled.

Leon moaned a short hello after James signed to him.

"Anything been goin' on since I left? Looks like you fellas handled things okay," James remarked as he started for the front gate of the compound.

"Everything's fine," David answered. "Thought we might have a storm last night, but it passed over."

James smiled, stopping and looking over at Leon. "I'm glad you're here, Leon, I've got something for you." He motioned for Leon to come over to him. James reached into his coat, wadded up across his arm, and pulled out a letter. He handed it to Leon to read and then continued to walk towards camp.

"What was that, Granddad?" Dale asked.

"I got Leon into school up at Ruston, if his daddy u'll let him go. They got a program up there for boys with Leon's problem. It'd be just the thing for him," James continued, taking a look back over his shoulder at Leon.

Leon struggled with the contents of the letter for a few minutes, suddenly realizing what it said. Then he let loose with the most God-awful noise any of them had ever heard. Before James had made it into the trailer Leon had him locked in a bear hug, and then began dancing around the three of them like a wild man, singing at the top of his voice.

James smiled, patting Leon on the back and at the same time telling him to take the letter home to his father. Leon showed the letter to Dale and David. When the boys had finished reading, they handed it back to Leon, smiling their congratulations to him. He smiled back, stuffing the letter back into the envelope as he took off at a sprint for home.

Dale followed James into the trailer, sitting down on the bed while James unpacked his travel bag. Dale looked up with a questioning look on his face. "You think his daddy will let him go?"

"I really don't know, son. Folks down here can be cantankerous as all get-out about givin' their youngin's any kind of education. His daddy may think he's protecting Leon by keepin' him home as long as he's alive and able to support him."

Dale was concerned about why Leon's father would do something like that. He didn't understand, if Leon was as smart as everyone knew he was, why his father wouldn't want him in school.

"It's not the school that he's worried about, Dale. His pappy is probably worried that old Leon might be treated poorly by someone. Pride's more important to these backwoods folks than a fella havin' a chance to go out in the world and earn his way. I'm just hopin' his daddy will think highly enough of that invitation from the Dean of the school that he'll give Leon a chance."

"I hope so, too, Granddad," Dale agreed. "Leon sure would be happy about goin' to school."

James cut himself a generous chunk of tobacco, then slipped it into his cheek, talking at the same time. "The worst of it is…when Leon's pappy dies, Leon u'll most likely be sent to the Louisiana State Asylum, over at Ruston to be taken care of. That'd be a mighty poor setting for a boy that smart!"

Dale dropped his head, consumed by the prospect of his friend ending up with such a dismal finish.

James noticed that Dale was upset with what he'd said. "I'll talk to his daddy as soon as he has a chance to give the letter a little thought. Let's don't get down and out about it until we know what his daddy is gonna do," James added, resting his hand on Dale's shoulder. He loves that boy a lot; I'm sure he wants to do the right thing by him."

The boys had taken to the woods, a few days later, looking for a new swimming hole. Leon had discovered a clear pool of water between two sandbars washed up from the bayou. The boys could see turtle tracks where a female had left the water to lay her eggs in the warm sand.

Leon knelt down with David and Dale hanging over his shoulders as he began gently to uncover the buried stash of turtle eggs. Leon picked the soft-shelled turtle eggs out of the wet pocket of sand, one at a time, laying them in a handkerchief. He pointed to the wet hole and then went about trying to explain that the female was keeping the eggs warm by urinating on them. Dale and David finally got the drift of what he was trying to explain.

Dale suddenly caught the sound of a boat moving down the channel, a few hundred yards from where they were standing. He crouched down, moving closer to the water to get a close look. He realized that it was Uncle Bill, skimming over the water in a flat bottom boat, rented back at the landing.

He raced back to the sandbar to put on his shoes and then took off through the woods for camp. David followed, leaving Leon to gather up the eggs, confused about what had caused the sudden desertion of his friends.

Bill already had arrived in camp by the time David and Dale got there. They knew he'd be in the trailer with James. Dale pulled open the door and started to walk in when James ordered, "You boys wait outside for a few minutes until Uncle Bill and I are through talking! We'll be out in just a minute!"

Dale thought it was queer for James to react that way. He'd never excluded them from a conversation, no matter who he was talking to. They waited outside, eager to visit with their uncle and hear the latest news of what was going on in the outside world.

James finally opened the door, waving for Dale and David to come in. "You boys sit down...I've got something to tell you." The look on James' face gave David a clue that something was terribly wrong.

Dale smiled at Bill, flopping down on the bed and giving him a hearty, "Hi, Uncle Bill!"

Bill didn't answer, just hung his head with a slight nod and looked down at the floor.

James was sitting on a stool with his elbows resting on his knees and his shoulders slumped forward. Then he looked up, and Dale could see James' chin quivering as he began to speak. "Your daddy's plane crashed last night...while he was flying a mission up in Alaska."

James paused, giving the boys a moment to deal with what he'd said before he continued. "They found the plane this morning. The Air Force has got people up there checking out the area for survivors."

James cleared his throat and wiped his eyes with his handkerchief. "I don't feel good about tellin' you this, 'cause your daddy's a fighter. He's been through tough spots before. But the Air Force is sayin' that they think there's a possibility that he was killed when he bailed out of the plane."

He could see the heartbreak in the boys' faces. David turned away from James and stared out the window, to keep from letting anyone see the tears in his eyes. James walked over to his dresser and pulled out several handkerchiefs handing one to Dale and then David. "We'll be headin' home at the first light of mornin'. I know your grandmother would want us to be with her at a time like this. Pack up the things tonight that you'll be wanting to take home with you," James said. "We'll have an early supper so we can all turn in, right after we've eaten."

David glanced down at the floor, trying not to look at James or Bill as he walked out of the trailer.

Dale waited a moment, wanting his grandfather to say something else, to tell him that there was a chance that his father was still alive. James studied Dale's eyes, knowing what the boy wanted to hear, but he shook his head slowly and turned away, looking out the window as Bill sat quietly watching the two of them.

The sun was setting when Dale made his way down to the water to be alone. He sat down on an old fallen pine tree. A cottonmouth had twisted himself into a tight curl farther down the log, trying to save some of the heat it had absorbed during the day. Dale ignored the snake as it eventually unwound itself and slithered into the water.

Dale ignored the loveliness that at any other time would have held him spellbound. Instead, he wanted to reminisce about his father. His eyes were fixed on the moon as he thought about the few times he could remember their being together. His emotions tore at him, filling him first with love and a desire to be close to his dad, as he'd never been before. A moment later he seethed with anger and pain, remembering the long separations from his father when he'd gone overseas, leaving him to fend for himself against his mother. He thought about the divorce and how confused he'd been. He remembered how secure he'd felt in his father's arms when he was small; things were simpler then. He knew he'd never have the chance to get to know him, to be with him the way he'd always dreamed. He loved the image of the man he'd created in his mind, even if he'd never really come to know him.

A bullfrog pushed its face up from the water, bellowing in response to Dale's muffled weeping. After a few minutes, Dale noticed his grandfather standing a few feet away. He was looking across the water at the silhouette of the tree line, starkly contrasted against the evening sky.

James stood leaning on his cane, laboring to catch his breath. He stared straight ahead, as if he hadn't noticed Dale sitting a few feet away on the log. It surprised Dale when he finally began to speak. "It's hard for a fella when he loses his daddy so early in life. When I lost my daddy, I was about your same age. All I could think about was all the things I wished I'd uh been able to say to him before he went away. It's sure not an easy thing to understand the 'whys' and 'how comes' of a man dyin'," James added, softly.

Dale watched him, wiping his face, trying to keep James from seeing his tears, even though the old man still hadn't looked at him. "You know," James continued…"your daddy spent his life doin' the things he loved. That's important for you to understand! Lotta folks come to the end of their days still searchin' for somethin' out of life. No, sir! I'd say your daddy was a pretty happy fella, bein' in the Air Force and all. He probably spent more time doin' what he wanted than he should have."

Dale's head dropped back down, resting on his knees as he turned his eyes away from James to look back across the water.

James paused, struggling to take a breath. He moved over to the log and sat down next to Dale. "When I was in France during the War, I remember comin' across an old wooden sign hangin' off a tree, up at the front. I'll never forget sittin' there lookin' at that thing, thinkin' about what it said."

Dale looked up, watching his grandfather as he went on with his story.

"The Frenchies had been gettin' the livin' crap kicked out of 'em up at Verdun. There were damn near as many casualties bein' carted back to Paris on that road as there were men bein' sent up to the lines. It was pitiful how many young fellas were dyin' up there. Well, it'd gotten so bad that some poor soul finally gave that road a name, nailin' a sign to a tree along the road that read "La Voie Sacree! The Sacred Way!""

Dale was confused why his grandfather had picked this time to start telling him war stories. James never spoke unless he had something important to say. Nothing was ever wasted with him, in conversation or otherwise. Dale listened, hoping it was something that would soothe the pain of his father's loss. "The Sacred Way?" he repeated.

"Yeah! I thought about that sign for years after the war. It finally occurred to me that maybe that old boy wasn't so much tryin' to honor the dead as he was the living. The more I thought about it, the more I realized something about what that fella was tryin' to say."

"What was that?" Dale asked.

"Well, I think he had his mind on those fellas going up to the front to fight more than those poor souls bein' hauled back to Paris; their worries were over. But a fella facing the uncertainty of life at the front…well, he didn't know from day to day what might come of him. The fear was almost worse than actually gettin' hit," James added, looking deep into Dale's eyes.

"I don't understand what you mean, Granddad."

"What I'm sayin', boy, is…don't feel sorry for your daddy. If he's dead, his troubles are over. He's at peace with himself. You've got to make your way on through life…doin' what's gotta be done to find your own happiness. The path you follow, that highway, is for the living," James said.

Dale studied the old man's face. "I think I understand what you're sayin', Granddad!"

"I hope you do, son. All of us have left a little of our hearts along the way for those we've lost. I guess that's the true tribute that we pay those people we loved. Just don't let yourself lose sight of your own right to a life because you hurt right now. You'll always have your daddy's memory. And I'll always be with you, no matter what happens," James assured him, embracing the young boy. "Your daddy's death, if he is dead, tears the life out of me, too, son...but we've got to go on!"

Hours before sunrise, Dale and David were helping to load the last of the boxes of clothes and documents into the barge tied at the water's edge. A man from the boat listened as James gave final instructions for taking the camp down after he and the boys were gone. What wasn't salvaged would quickly succumb to the elements.

Dale took a last look at the campsite. It would be a hard place to miss, but there had been some good times. He thought about Leon, wanting to tell him goodbye. He knew deep down that he'd never see him again. He wanted to wish him well in his new challenge as a student at Ruston.

Just as James was closing the gate for the last time, Dale heard Leon trumpeting a loud moan, signaling his approach from the swamp. His father had come with him to say their farewells. Leon locked David in a bear hug and then latched onto Dale, patting him on the back as they embraced. He stepped back, wiping the tears from his eyes as he put his arms around James, moaning a soft "thank you" for his help in getting him into school.

Leon's father stepped forward, thanking James in French for his kindness to his son, and offering his hand to him. "I owe you a great debt, Doctor Lavoisier! Your kindness will never be forgotten!"

James responded in French, while he pulled an envelope from his pocket and handed it to Leon. It was an envelope full of cash.

"Money for school. You study hard, boy!" James ordered, watching Leon's father translate his precise statement to Leon in sign.

Leon returned a wide grin and then quickly looked down at the ground. He'd been holding a coffee can in his hands. With a short nervous smile, he handed the can to Dale, a gift to his best friend. Inside were the soft-shell turtle eggs they'd found the day before.

Dale nodded a 'thank you'. It seemed such a contradiction for things to be so unhappy just as Leon had been given his new lease on life. Dale felt almost as if he were cheating Leon out of his happiness with the mood that hung over their departure. A chill surged up his spine as it occurred to him that he was returning to the other world, a world with an overabundance of pain and hate. And Leon, for a brief time, could live in peace behind these forested walls...if only for a little while longer.

'Maybe Leon's father is more aware of the rights and wrongs of life than anyone realized,' Dale thought. 'Maybe it's Leon who should feel sorry for us. We're the ones going in harm's way, leaving this simple, peaceful sanctuary.'

Dale never looked back as the boat motored away from Avalon, the name he'd given the camp...King Arthur's mythical place of rest, the Isle of Souls, Land of the Blessed. Leon bellowed a farewell that was drowned out by the noise from the boat's motor as the travelers made their way towards home.

CHAPTER 29

It was late evening when James drove the truck around to the back of the house on South Jackson. Nellie opened the back door and watched forlornly as the small column trailed their way into the house. She patted each of the boys as they headed for their room upstairs, each of them silent with their own thoughts.

James stopped, looking the short black woman in the eyes. What he saw told him what he had feared most. She wiped her eyes, as if trying to remove the telltale look. It was too hard for her to smooth the lines of grief that had been carved deeply into her face since hearing the news.

"Miz Lavoisier is in her room," Nellie said softly. "She's been in dare most of dah day. She didn't hardly touch her supper."

"I'll talk to her," James whispered.

He moved slowly towards Lora's room, stopping at the door to remove his hat. Lora was sitting in her rocker, near the large window that faced the street. She was still wearing her dress, with a small quilt over her legs and an open Bible lying in her lap.

She continued to stare up at the ceiling as James walked into the room. He took a seat in a chair a few feet away, staring into the flames of the heater near her rocking chair. The soft glow of a reading lamp next to her bed did little to illuminate the dark room.

James sat quietly, waiting for Lora to say something.

"It never occurred to me how God must have felt when his son died," Lora finally said, still staring at the ceiling. "It's odd how all these years I've always said I was a believer, and yet I never really understood what God's grief must have been like in those final hours. How painful it must have been."

James sat back in his chair, listening to the wail of a pulp train passing behind the house. He waited for Lora to confirm what he already knew.

She wiped her eyes with a handkerchief before she spoke again, still staring at the ceiling. "An Air Force officer was here earlier this afternoon to tell us that they found Jason's body. Apparently he was the only one to get out of the airplane before the crash. They just couldn't get to him in time because of a bad storm.

Lora's hand began to shake as she reached to wipe her eyes again. "They'll be bringing him home to Jacksonville tomorrow afternoon," she added.

James stood up and went over to her. He touched her face gently before kissing her on the forehead. He looked at her for a moment before asking, "Would you like for me to give you something to help you rest?"

She looked up at him, "No...I'd just like to be alone."

He nodded and then turned and opened the door to the hall, stopping as she spoke again: "I wish I'd been with him!" she said. "It wasn't right for him to be all alone out there." She cried softly.

James looked back, and then closed the door quietly behind him as he left the room.

On the day of the funeral James was up hours before Lora and the boys. He sat at the kitchen table sipping a cup of coffee, still stunned by Jason's death. He stared into the backyard, listening to the blue jays screaming in the giant pecan trees. All the loveliness that he had created there, everywhere, had gone.

His memories of Jason at the house on South Jackson were too few. He wanted to find a fond memory of his son, a recollection of the two of them together. It was an image as hard to recall as his first footsteps. He blamed himself for having been too busy, hot on the heels of success, eagerly pursuing his dreams of wealth, as Jason had gone his own way in life.

He dressed and left the house, driving to Frankston to be alone with his pain. There seemed an urgency in his mind somehow to recall some aspect of happiness with Jason before the funeral service put a ceremonial end to his son's life.

On the way, James stopped at the cemetery where he found that the preparations had already been completed. He stood at the headstone, staring at the gray marble monument. The stone was blank except for the inscription for Billy etched deeply into the face on one side.

James leaned over, pulling at a weed that had invaded the carpet of thick grass over the grave. The morning sun struggled to burn through a thick ground fog that blanketed the cemetery. A light breeze pressed the moisture from the fog against his clothes, leaving them damp as he perched himself on the edge of the stone monument.

The calmness of the early morning was broken by the old man's sobbing as his head dropped into his hand, his other hand caressing the smooth face of the headstone. He stopped, wiping his eyes with his handkerchief: "I'm sorry I wasn't with you, son! God knows I loved you…even if I didn't know how to tell you!" he murmured.

James stood up, wiping his eyes a final time as he turned away from the grave. "This place has become a stone abacus for the heartbreaks of my life!" he thought, walking back towards his car. Gazing across the gray broken horizon of headstones in front of him, his eyes suddenly fixed on the shadow of a person standing fifty yards away, staring at him from behind the trunk of a Mimosa tree.

For a split second, his mind recalled the uniformed apparition that had appeared to him during the carnage of the Argonne. But, just as at the crater, the person's face remained hidden from view as he stared across the open cemetery. A feeling of peace and contentment surged through James as it had when he lay in the bottom of the shell hole those many years earlier.

His mind raced, trying frantically to explain what was happening. 'It's a caretaker,' he thought, 'or an early morning visitor to a grave.' As hard as he tried to explain the reasons for what he was seeing, he continued to sense the warmth radiating from the image standing directly in front of him. It was as if he was being assured that all was well with Jason…that he was in the loving care of this fleeting eidolon.

James broke from his trance and started towards the figure next to the tree. He only had taken a few steps when he realized that whatever had been standing there was gone. James let out an agonizing cry. "Come back!" he pleaded. "Please! I just want to talk to you! Come back!" he shouted.

And then, as had happened, years earlier, he suddenly felt at peace about Jason, knowing now that he was safely across the river in the care of his mother and father. He could hear her softly whispering, "And ye now therefore have sorrow: but I will see you again and your heart shall repair, and your joy no man taketh from you." He was sure now that Jason was safely home.

He continued on to Frankston, with the sun finally ascending fully above the forested horizon behind him. He stopped at the old home where they'd lived while he'd begun his medical practice. He meandered through the yard, arousing a sleeping dog nestled comfortably against a corner wall of the front porch. A vivid image of Jason shot through his mind, a picture of a young boy swinging joyously from the old Model T tire suspended from a limb of the pecan tree. He was dancing endlessly above the worn ground during the hot summer, cooling himself in the shade of the enormous umbrella of leaves.

The tree, like the man now standing below its branches, had grown old, the deep scars from the bindings of an earlier time still visible to passersby. Its usefulness, its beauty, the great magnificence that had once cast a sea of shade as great as a cloud now belonged to the past.

James could see the small boy, clean and neatly dressed, playing like any other child, always offering an energetic smile whenever James came home from work. It still bothered him that Jason always looked so freshly pressed and groomed, when 'a boy needs to be a little gritty!' he thought. "It's God's way of makin' us remember where we come from. He always had a smile to match his clothes, so I guess that was good!" he whispered, nodding to himself.

He stood for a few short moments and then left the yard. He drove down to the town square, a little hamlet built like a box around a tiny cubicle of thick grass. The old buildings were disguised with new names and different purposes, but their old identities lingered on their sides and fronts, stained deep into the wood laths of these once-proud edifices. Milborne's Dry Good and Waltman's Five and Dime; James was pleased that the new owners had been unconcerned enough to leave the old advertisements, though his heart sank as his eyes wandered through the windows. The buildings had been gutted, turned into little more than storage barns to house junk cars and bales of bleached hay from seasons past.

James peered through the opened wall of Pfizer's Drug, staring at the chrome stump of the soda fountain stools and noticing the patches in the floor where colorful tiles once formed a dazzling mosaic. He remembered Jason twirling himself endlessly on a stool, sipping a phosphate as he waited for him to take care of his business with the pharmacist.

He looked across the street to the open park where the bandstand still stood like a magnificent gingerbread hub to the city. Old men would spend their days reminiscing along its perimeter, sitting on park benches next to the grass, their walking canes held perpendicular to form a man-made picket fence.

He recalled the grand occasions when he and Jason would don their brightly colored band uniforms, he with his French horn and Jason with his trumpet, to join the local symphony, as it were, to play the patriotic tunes of the time, from the pavilion. 'Those were good times!' he whispered to himself.

On his way back to Jacksonville he made one last stop. The old cotton gin, still standing next to the highway, had caught his attention as he turned towards home. Thick stalks of bull nettle and other weeds had grown so high that the gin seemed to have sunk ten feet into the ground. Cattails, stiffly braced against the morning breeze, their yellow stalks angling towards the sky, stood guard on the stagnant pool next to the old gin.

James squatted down at the water's edge, remembering the mob of youngsters that had cooled themselves in droves during summer vacation, in their own sacred Ganges. A homemade pier nosed into the water, half-submerged, twisted from its original form. The pier had been the flight deck to launch young divers into the center of the pond from its eight-foot platform.

James remembered going to the pond to fetch Jason home for supper, and how Jason would smile when he saw him. A certain ritual always followed with Jason clamoring onto the pier to show his dad a thunderous belly flop that he'd perfected. He'd leap into the air, cupping himself face down and landing with a painful thud on the waters. An ungraceful geyser would streak in all directions, soaking everyone, including James.

He stood for another brief look, feeling better about Jason's life, at least the part that he'd had something to do with. He picked up a flat piece of iron ore and tossed it into the center of the pond, towards the spot where Jason would land in a cannonball trick. He watched the fading energy of the widening ripples, wondering if Jason wasn't better off having his life end at the pinnacle of its momentum instead of becoming stagnant as his had done. He turned away, avoiding his own question.

At noon, the mourners came, bearing gifts of food and sympathy, crawling out from under the past. They'd come for the occasion, urged forward from curiosity, or love, some having touched the young officer's life and some there to give comfort to the family, out of dedication; some came only to eat and stare.

With the last volley of rifle fire echoing above the funeral tent and the bittersweet sounds of taps wrenching the last tears from the gathering, the ceremony ended.

James knew that Jason's funeral was far more significant than just an end to his son's life. For Lora, it was as if a great pillar had been left, to bear nothing, to stand as the columns of an ancient Acropolis, strangely left without purpose after the grand design had been dismantled.

For David, his father's death was an end to a dream, the termination of an everlasting flicker of hope that reconciliation would come to his parents, that he would have the family he yearned so desperately to be a part of. Now the renaissance would never come, and David gave up his dream.

Dale watched as his family dissolved before his eyes, each slipping away to deal with their own mortal wounds. James held him for a brief moment in a loving embrace, looking into his eyes as if to examine the severity of his grief. When the old man had finished staring at him, he leaned down and whispered, "Walk proud and straight on your path, boy! Remember it's a road for the living...not the dead!"

He watched the old man, once towering and proud, now slumped and withered from all that had happened to him. He watched as James looked towards the road where Jessica was waiting to take the two boys back to Topeka.

Everything was an opportunity for Jessica. She'd used the funeral finally to do what no one else was able to accomplish, to give the killing blow to the old man by taking away the last inkling of purpose in his life.

The words that James spoke as he saw Jessica standing at the open door of her car, a few feet from the dispersing funeral, would always be poignantly clear in Dale's memory. "Now cometh the Beast," he remembered James whispering. "How much she hath glorified herself, and lived deliriously, so much torment and sorrow give her!" the old man said, finishing the Bible verse with a sigh.

He gave Dale a final kiss and then walked away as the sheriff escorted both boys to their mother's waiting car.

The trial for income tax evasion had ended, stripping James of everything the government could sell for back taxes, including his medical practice. Only the old home and what was left of his hidden stash of money remained.

Despite all that had happened, a tiny glimmer of hope escaped with the old man, an ember of love hidden deep within his heart for his grandsons. The old man would judiciously preserve his resources for a final battle that he knew would come before his death. Of all the possibilities that life had brought, this single purpose that burned deep within him now would keep him alive until he had finished his appointed task.

CHAPTER 30

Dale's deep concentration was interrupted by the sudden opening of the glass- paneled door from the dining room. Lora stepped slowly into James' room, carrying a tray full of coffee and sweet cakes from the kitchen.

"You've been in here so long, Darlin', I thought you might be getting a little hungry. I just don't know why you wanta spend so much time going through all this old stuff. Lord knows, I hate to see you opening up old wounds. I should have had Nellie throw it all out after your grandfather died."

Dale took her hand after she set the tray down next to him. "I'm glad you didn't throw it away, Grandma…it's important to me!"

Lora leaned down and kissed him on the cheek. "I know it is, honey…you keep whatever you want. They'll be here Saturday to haul off everything we're not taking with us in the move. Seems like most everything has gotten so worn out and raggedy," she added, running her hand lovingly across James' dresser and letting herself slip into a brief moment of reflection.

Dale could see a tear slip down her cheek as she straightened the hairbrushes on the dresser and then turned away from him.

"I'm gonna miss this old place," Dale said. "I remember an awful lot of good times in this house."

"Oh, yes," she quickly responded, "there were some grand, grand times here! Your Grandfather always took such pride in taking care of this place…keeping everything so beautiful."

"He loved it here," Dale agreed, sighing deeply.

"It's a shame to let them tear it down. I know it would make your grandfather unhappy to find out that I'd sold it, but I'm just too old and tired to take care of it anymore. It was a wonderful place for your father and you boys to grow up, so it served its purpose very well," she finished, moving her hand softly across his face before she walked out of the room.

Dale ignored the tray of refreshments. Instead, he leaned back in the old chair and let his thoughts return to events after his father's death.

Life with Jessica in Topeka, for David and Dale, was predictably the same as it always had been. L.C. and Jessica were cohabitating in a small tract house that he'd bought on the outskirts of town. It was a peace offering to Jessica, to assure her of his matrimonial intentions sometime in the future.

As had always been the case with Jessica, once the thrill and excitement of L.C.'s love offering had worn off, she'd returned to her usual self-serving binge, energetically seeking out new plateaus of self-gratification from him or any of her other suitors who might happen by.

It was difficult for the boys to understand their status in the house. They were treated as neither guests nor family. The child that Jessica had had with L.C. received just slightly more attention than either of the two boys. L.C. was affectionate towards the girl, but had always had his suspicions about being her father. While Jessica had been pleading her child support case before the courts, L.C. was carefully documenting his file—he had seen the gleam in the viper's eye.

L.C.'s law practice had dried up to little more than the handling of random referral cases from sympathetic colleagues, or preparing an occasional income tax return for a pittance of what his time was actually worth. He had long since lost his position as a legislative counsel because of his heavy drinking. Even the military had lost interest in retaining him after he started showing up drunk at court-martials, or failed to show up at all. His partner had secretly bought L.C.'s interest in the law practice, agreeing to let him continue to use space in the office in order to keep Jessica or anyone else from knowing how serious his financial situation had become.

The second month that David and Dale were in Topeka, L.C. arrived home, swacked to the gills, managing to stay in the center of the narrow street by bouncing his T-bird off the other cars parked along the road. The turn into the drive at the house was even less graceful. The car came to a halt in the front yard, only inches from the front door.

David and Dale listened as L.C. fell into the house, landing face down in the hall. The two boys looked at each other as he appeared on all fours at the top of the stairs. They stepped aside like a parting of the Red Sea, allowing the overweight sloth to collapse onto the living room carpet.

Jessica blew out of the bedroom, planting her feet inches from the lump of sprawled flesh. "You revolting slob! I hope you broke your gawd damn neck," Jessica screamed, giving the heap a hard poke with the toe of her shoe.

Dale and David struggled to pull L.C. to the couch, arranging his arms and legs as if he were a corpse prepared for a funeral, or a Christmas turkey cinched up for basting.

"Probably should have let him take a dive down the stairs," David whispered, as he walked away. "Put him out of his misery!"

A half-hour after he'd been planted on the couch, L.C. stood up and began staggering towards the kitchen.

His feet never quite caught up with the lead his chin had given him as he fell face-first into the dining table. Food and drink catapulted into the air, spraying the walls as the table collapsed from the weight of his body.

Dale shook his head, looking down the hall for his mother to appear. "Jeez, he really did it good this time! Look at that table. He flattened that sucker like a steamroller. That's one that won't ever get put back together."

Dale turned just in time to see Jessica, poised with her feet spread and her teeth bared. "You drunk son of a bitch! You can just lie there, you fat pig! I'm not cleaning this crap up!" she shouted, turning and disappearing into the back bedroom.

L.C. had hoisted himself up on one elbow, bleeding from several small cuts he'd gotten from broken glass. Dale grabbed one arm and David took the other, dragging him back to the couch.

"Smooth move, pumpkin," David declared, using the sarcastic nickname that they had coined for L.C. "Now we get to clean up after you!"

"At least we can eat while we work," Dale commented angrily.

After they'd taken care of L.C. and the disaster site, the boys walked outside onto the small redwood deck at the back of the house.

"I hate this, David," Dale said. "Why did Dad have to leave us in this mess? He could have done something to make sure we wouldn't have had to come here if something happened to him! Why couldn't we have stayed where we were, in Jacksonville?"

"I don't know, Dale," David answered, "that's just the way things worked out."

"She doesn't care about us; all she wants is to get her hands on the little bit of money Dad left us!" Dale complained.

"Maybe she does care," David replied. "Maybe she just doesn't know how to show it."

"She doesn't give a damn about anything or anyone," Dale said. "You wait and see; she's gonna keep treating us like dog meat 'til she's got every dime that Dad left us."

"Look…give her a chance," David insisted. "We've only been here a couple of months."

Dale looked his brother in the eyes. "Sure, but do me a favor, and take a good look at that poor jerk on the couch if you wanta see what she can do to someone. Think about the first time you saw that guy in there. He sure as hell didn't look like that, did he?"

"The guy's a lush," David scoffed, turning away.

"She's killing him, little by little, so she can get what she wants, just like she's gonna do with us," Dale warned, leaving David alone on the deck to ponder what he'd said.

L.C. had become a pathetically predictable character, embalming himself with anything he could swallow to reach his desired anesthetized state, loading himself up with vitamin B to try to offset the horrible hangover he knew he would have every morning.

Jessica was little bothered by the stigma of L.C.'s degenerating condition. She was anything but dissuaded from attending her usual round of social galas, despite the hum of rumors that encircled her wherever she went.

For awhile, L.C. was a passive alcoholic, drinking himself into a self-destructive stupor to arm himself against her endless insults and deliberate confrontations. But as her flirtations became more open with other men, he began to react against Jessica's suitors. He would stand on the edge of the dance floor at social events, shouting insults at anyone who tried to have a conversation or a dance with her. On more than one occasion, L.C. had been ushered out of the festivities because of his behavior, with Jessica trailing behind, dragging her mink on the floor and huffing profanities at him, as they were thrown out.

Stephen D. Boyett

The High Mass of social affairs in Topeka was the party thrown by the Kansas bar Association for the returning senators and representatives and their wives as they prepared for the legislature to convene.

By some fluke, L.C. had received an invitation to the black tie event, which of course meant Jessica would attend as his lady, however loosely the term could be thrown about.

Jessica had slithered into a blue satin sheath dress, tight enough to reveal the label on her underwear, if she'd been wearing any. L.C. was on his best behavior, struggling to keep off the booze until they had made it through the reception line, which included his longtime friend, the Governor of Kansas. Many of L.C.'s friends were horrified, not only by his failing physical stature, but also by the collapse of his brilliantly promising career—promising, until he'd met Jessica.

Jessica paid little attention to those who disliked her. She'd become accustomed to such behavior over the years. She preferred, in fact, always to be with new people. During the course of the evening, she had managed to gather her usual crowd of admirers from the eligible, as well as ineligible men at the party. L.C.'s good behavior had gone flat, sending him to the first available opening at the bar. By mid-evening he had positioned himself, with a full bottle of scotch, at the edge of the dance floor.

As he watched Jessica dancing with an endless stream of fanciers, pulling herself tightly into their arms, pushing her face into their necks and massaging their shoulders, his passive character boiled into a rage. He sprang to his feet, pushed himself away from the table, knocked over several chairs, and dropped the full bottle of scotch as he stormed the dance floor.

With "String of Pearls" playing from the orchestra in the background, L.C. indignantly roared at the top of his lungs, "Get your Gawd damn hands off her! That's my meat!"

At the same moment, he reached for Jessica's arm, pulling her towards him. He reached into her strapless gown, presenting the horrified dignitaries with the sight of one of her breasts as he held her in a headlock.

"You jackass, get your hands off me!" Jessica shouted, wiggling free and calmly slipping her breast back into her gown, as if she'd just

578

finished nursing a child.   Then she returned to her stunned dance partner, who had retreated to the outer perimeter of the dance floor.

L.C. turned and left the party. He managed to navigate his way home, defeatedly marching up the stairs to the kitchen, where he grunted and belched as he devoured what was left of a turkey stashed in the fridge. He waited for Jessica while he ate, and complained to himself about her misbehavior.

An hour and a half later, Jessica was delivered home by one of her suitors from the party. L.C. pulled open the kitchen window and began screaming obscenities at the couple sitting in the car below. Bedroom lights on both sides of the narrow street began to flash on, as alarmed neighbors peered from their windows.

Jessica marched into the house, slamming the front door. She leaped into the kitchen, wide-eyed and ready for battle.

"Bastard!" She screamed.

"Slut!" L.C. responded, without looking up from his meal.

Jessica's eyes darted around the room, stopping at the electric can opener. She lurched towards the wall, grabbed the opener and hurled it at him. Fortunately for L.C., it was still plugged into the outlet.

"Hell, you can't hurt me...I'm magic," he slurred, grinning with a fang of turkey hanging from his upper lip.

"Like hell you are, you Gawd damn blimp!" she screamed, leaping at him with both hands and slapping at him as fast as she could move her arms.

L.C. gave her a quick push, sending her backward into the previously flattened kitchen table. At a point when most women would have retreated to console themselves and lick their wounds, Jessica bounced to her feet and launched an aerial bombardment with anything she could find. She picked up a quart-sized wine carafe and smashed it across his face, sending him sideways into the refrigerator and onto the floor.

Blood ran down L.C.'s face from the generous gash sliced along his jaw line and mingled with the cheap red wine that had splattered all over the front of his dress shirt.

Jessica stood over the downed man, raising another bottle, bent on delivering the coup de grâce when David and Dale walked into the room.

"Gawd, Mother, what are you doin'?"

She calmly let the bottle drop to the floor. She looked down at L.C. for another moment. Then, pulling a piece of meat off the turkey carcass and sticking it into her mouth, she walked to her bedroom and closed the door.

Dale pressed a dishtowel against the side of L.C.'s face as a compress, trying to slow the bleeding. David and Dale struggled for several minutes to get him to his feet. They tried to take him to a hospital, but he refused to go, demanding to be left alone. The boys finally gave up, leaving him on the couch where he fell asleep.

As the boys grew older they spent as much time away from home as possible to avoid the ugly goings-on between the 'Spider' and the 'Pumpkin', as the boys often referred to Jessica and L.C.

One afternoon, David and Dale left school early. Instead of going straight to work as they usually did, they stopped by the house to get some papers that Dale needed for his job. As David pulled the car into the drive, they found themselves face to face with two boys they recognized from school, who were coming out of the front door. David rolled the window down as the two walked past the car.

"Whata you guys doin' here?" he asked.

One of them, a short muscularly built fellow, laughed as he walked by, pulling at the fly buttons of his jeans. He grinned at David, laughing as he spoke: "Better hurry, buddy, before her old man gets home. I got her warmed up for you."

David's eyes shot towards the second floor of the house, just in time to see Jessica turning away from the kitchen window. Dale sat motionless, staring at his brother as he pressed his head against the steering wheel. Neither of them spoke as David finally started the car and pulled out of the drive. Nothing was said that evening when both boys finally returned to the house.

Hours before sunup, Dale woke to find David standing over his bed. The room was glowing from the moonlight, reflecting through the bedroom window. He could see that David was fully dressed. He was holding a piece of luggage.

"I'm leaving," David said. "If it makes any difference to yah, I think you've been right about her all along!" he added, shaking Dale's hand mechanically.

Dale cleared his throat: "Where you going?"

"I don't know. I've just got to get away from all this!" David answered. "They'll take me in the service since I'm eighteen."

"What about school?"

"That's the least of my worries right now," David replied.

"I don't want you to leave, David. What am I gonna do when you're gone?"

"I wish I could take you with me, Dale, but it'll be tough enough for one of us to make it out there. Stick it out as long as you can stand it; then get as far away from this God-forsaken place as you can."

Dale nodded his head with a slow, understanding. "I will, David!"

"Don't ever look back," David said. "Just keep going…get as far away from her and this place as you can possibly get."

"You'll let me know where you are, won't you?" Dale pleaded.

David stood still, staring at Dale without answering.

Dale watched as his brother disappeared into the dark of the hall. He lay on his side in bed as he listened to the roar of David's car starting in front of the house, the sound growing fainter as he drove away.

He never heard from David again. He found out from one of David's girlfriends that he had joined the Army shortly after that night. Dale would always search for his brother's face among the thousands of troops he saw after he had joined the Air Force several years later and was stationed in Vietnam.

Dale's own parting from his mother came a year later. He'd gone to the house during a tornado alert to pick up a portable radio to keep with him at the store where he was working. A storm had shut off the power all over the neighborhood. When Dale walked up the stairs of the house, he could hear someone talking.

"Gawd, you're so damn pathetic," he heard a woman's voice saying. "No one's gonna help you, not anyone! No one cares anything about you. Even your own daughter can't stand the sight of you," the voice said. "Why don't you just die and save us all a big problem."

Dale was startled to find Jessica sitting alone on the couch, staring out through the glass doors on the back deck. When his eyes finally adjusted to the dark room, he realized that L.C. was stretched out on the floor, staring up at the ceiling. Papers from L.C.'s lock box were scattered across the coffee table where Jessica had left them after carefully examining their contents.

Dale could hear L.C. wheezing on the floor as he struggled for a breath of air. Jessica remained silent, acting as if Dale wasn't there. He thought at first that L.C. might have been drinking again.

"I gave that no good son of a bitch the best years of my life," Jessica finally said. "And there he lays, dyin' on me without leaving me one red cent!"

"What?" Dale answered.

"There's not even enough here to bury the worthless bastard," Jessica prattled on, staring at L.C. like a hyena waiting for its prey to expire.

"What are you talking about?" Dale demanded, striking a match over L.C.'s stilled form on the floor.

The light glittered back from L.C.'s eyes. The man panted with short breaths as his hand tugged weakly at the leg of Dale's pants. Dale was horrified as he looked down at the man's face.

"He's having a heart attack; Jesus, he's dying and you're just sitting there! What are you trying to do?" he screamed as he ran to the phone. "How long's he been like this?"

Jessica never moved or said a word. She glanced at L.C. from time to time to see if he were still alive and then back to the window. Dale tried frantically to comfort L.C. until the ambulance arrived.

When Jessica heard the siren of the ambulance, she calmly stood up, finished the remains of a drink she had fixed herself earlier and then walked slowly out of the room.

.

Two hours after riding with L.C. to the hospital in the ambulance, Dale returned to the house. The power was back on in the neighborhood as he walked inside.

He climbed the stairs to his room. After a few minutes, he realized that Jessica was standing at the door.

"Well?" she blurted out.

"Oh, that's great, Mother! I know he'd be glad to hear you were so choked up with concern!" Dale said coolly. "He's dead, so now you've got whatever it is that you've wanted!"

Jessica lowered her head, struggling to produce a paper-thin whimper. She quickly turned around to hide her lack of tears.

"Save it, will yah! There's no one left to impress with your theatrics." Dale turned back towards his dresser and began folding his clothes in a neat stack on the bed.

"You smart-aleck bastard!" she screamed. "How dare you talk to me like that—I'm your mother!"

"I wish to God you weren't!" he retorted.

Jessica suddenly sprang at him, catching him across the face with her hand. Dale moved back a few steps, parrying off a second blow, then caught her arm and shoved her back towards the door. He pointed his finger at her, "If you wanta live, keep your distance or I'll kill ya!"

"That man never meant anything to you, did he? You can't even conjure up an ounce of grief, or pity, or real tears for him, after what you've done. He's just another insignificant lush, dumped on the road of your pathetic life!" Dale shouted.

"Oh, is that right?" she snapped. "You haven't had to live with him."

Something that James had once said came to him just as Jessica began screaming her indignation. It was a passage from Dante. He remembered James saying, 'I did not weep, so much of stone had I become within. They wept."

Dale turned away from her, ignoring her raving.

"Get out of my house!" she screamed. "Get out of here this instant!"

"I intend to, Mother. I'd just like to know one thing. What it is about you that makes you wanta destroy anyone that ever tried to love you?"

"I don't have to listen to this. This is my_house!" she yelled. "He owed me this much. Why should I have to put up with him? He was nothing but a drunk, a failure. He wasn't even a man. I can have any man I want…ask anyone. They'll tell you how beautiful I am."

"What are you…a whore who sells herself for whatever she can coerce out of some poor jerk, if he's foolish enough to believe you love him? You think people are weak and spineless because they wanta believe in you…like Dad and L.C.? They were nothing because they wanted to share their lives and dreams with you?

You're the one who's wrong! You're no better than a thief. They trusted you with their hopes and dreams, and all you did was find a way to use their weaknesses to destroy everything, including their self-respect; no, even worse, like a grave robber, you stole their souls.

"I've heard enough of this. It may surprise you to know that your sister is his child, not your father's. I've had my share of being used, too! So now, what do you think about your dead heroes?" she announced. "Maybe they aren't so wonderful after all?"

"Oh yes," he answered, "I loved my father despite his failings because I know he cared. And I liked L.C., because I knew what he was really like when he wasn't trying to run away from you. But that's the difference...you don't care about anyone but yourself! As far as my sister, everyone knew she was L.C.'s daughter. You always thought we were all blind to what you were doing," Dale added, taking a suitcase out of the closet.

"I had a right to have a good life. They owed it to me. I could have had anyone I wanted...men who would have bought me the world!" she proclaimed.

"I know that's what you've always thought, Mother. I know you believe it enough to steal this house from L.C.'s daughter, and to steal whatever else he may have left behind. I also know she'd be a lot better off letting you have it. She and her mother couldn't begin to stoop to your level to fight you for what little he had."

"What do you know about fighting for anything?" she screamed.

"You're right, mother...I'm not a fighter, not like you; not for what you believe in.

"How dare you talk to me like this, you ungrateful brat!" she raved.

Dale walked to the door, suitcase in hand, looking back at Jessica over his shoulder. "You know, mother, I know now, more than ever, that you're just evil enough to get whatever it is that you want out of life. But I'm just as sure that somewhere, somehow, you'll be held accountable for what you've done. I pity you...and everyone's miserable soul that you've ever dragged down with you," he ended, turning away.

Dale left the house. Following his brother's advice, he never looked back, fearing something of the fate forewarned to Lot if he turned to look upon the wickedness of Sodom.

CHAPTER 31

The green landscape of Vietnam seemed familiar to Dale, even though his only encounter with the country had been limited to a quick flip through a National Geographic magazine. There was survival school in the Philippines, but that was different.

The jungle conjured up vivid memories of his days at Keso's Landing, and Avalon, his self-proclaimed bayou sanctuary.

The raw smell and texture of the air was vaguely reminiscent of the bayou. Even the people and their creatures moving over the landscape had a familiarity to them. But there were too many people, too much movement. It was not the slow comfortable pace he remembered at Choctaw Lake. It was as if someone had stirred a bed of red ants, sending them scurrying for another hole in the dank earth to hide them from the scorching sun.

Vietnam was Dale's first duty assignment after completing tech school at Sheppard Air Force Base, at Wichita Falls, Texas. He'd been trained as a Load Master, assigned to a C-130 squadron, based out of Da Nang, shuttling 'grunts and grub', wherever and whenever duty called.

It was a pleasant enough duty compared to most, giving Dale and his fellow crewmembers a chance for a little relief from the sweltering heat once they were airborne. It beat humping it like the miserable grunts. At least there was a shower and clean sheets waiting at the end of the day.

Most of Dale's time was spent in preparing the C-130 for operations. The loadmaster was kept busy rigging pallets, or reconfiguring seats for troops or litters for wounded, checking weight and balance, and a million other details before the engines were turned over for the mission.

Once airborne, there was little to do but sit and wait for the final approach to the drop zone. The pallets of equipment were, at the pilot's command, gently nudged towards the door of the plane with the help of a roller conveyor system. Then, as if the plane's patience was spent, the pallets were slammed aft by the force of pilot chutes no longer willing to let the loads leave at their own lethargic speed. The cargo was virtually ripped from the aircraft. Great lines of silk cord unwound from the giant G-12 chutes, folded carefully on top of the cargo, straightening into stiff slender green stalks, connecting the load to a formless bulk of silk canopies at the other end.

Dale would have a brief moment to enjoy the bird's eye view of the countryside, watching from his windy perch at the back door of the aircraft as the huge chutes filled to form a bouquet of green silk flowers, nestled around the descending load. Watching...watching as the load drifted towards the DZ, he would count the chutes and triangulate the movement of the pallets toward their targets. Then the doors would be closed as the emptied aircraft would return home. Now he could relax, unlock the uncomfortable straps of the parachute and find a private place to huddle with his thoughts for the trip back to base. Now he had time to think about something other than the war. Usually, he thought first of his grandparents and home, and how much he missed them. He worried about his grandfather's failing health.

Time had healed some of the wounds inflicted by his mother. But, even as a young man, he still had scars from his ordeal with her. Most noticeable was his introverted personality. He was an attractive young man, yet he found it extremely difficult to associate with others. He was self-conscious and withdrawn, avoiding friendship, always fearing that he was inadequate, that there was something that made him unfit to be with others. He found it easier to be by himself, to rely on no one, like many men in time of war. It made the death of a fellow soldier easier to handle. But that wasn't the reason for Dale's aloofness. He carried a burden of responsibility for David, always yearning to somehow make up for what had happened with the family, the disappointment that David had felt over their parents' divorce. He loved David and hated the thought of never seeing him again. That was a part of his life that he never would be able to resolve.

In a sense, Jessica had cursed them, one and all. Each of them had borne the burden of her sins, bowing their heads so that no one could see their shame. The old couple in Jacksonville had been his salvation, by making them that special place where heads could again be raised with pride.

Here they were taught love and understanding. Still, there were scars. David had tried to run away from all that had happened to him, while Dale found solace with his grandparents in Jacksonville.

Any difficulty Dale had experienced over the years, dealing with the memory of L.C.'s tragic death, was of little consequence compared to the magnitude of death and misery going on in Southeast Asia. It overwhelmed any festering grief he might have held for his late stepfather. It was an experience that was difficult to prepare for, whatever the background of the newly arrived American soldier might have been. There was no room for sadness for a single tragedy.

The night of L.C.'s death had been the last time Dale had seen or spoken to Jessica. In the years after his self-imposed exile, he had time to reflect on the bitter past. Those awful childhood dreams of the demon slipping into his room, laughing as she mauled him or his brother before turning and disappearing back into the hall. The realness of those dreams had left him wondering sometimes if they were dreams at all.

He had remained close to his grandparents during his college years, seeing them often when he was in school. After graduation he remained devoted to James and Lora, visiting them as often as he could before he'd decided to enlist in the Air Force and had been shipped overseas. James was disappointed to see Dale enlist, having preferred that he take a commission. His grandparents were all the family he had.

He was faithful in writing home to the old couple, his letters filled at first with the bravado of an unseasoned warrior. But soon, too soon, the tone changed, softening with the sentiments of a man experienced in the world, burdened and compassionate for the people and comrades who shared his violent world. If the loss of one's youth makes one a man, then a man he'd become. Vietnam was quick to have that kind of effect on newcomers—those that survived long enough.

He'd searched for David when time allowed. Several times when he'd had a day off, he'd caught a hop to some distant base, or crossed into Thailand on a long weekend leave to see if he could locate him there. The military wasn't much help, either unwilling or unable to do a thorough job of checking their records. Dale eventually concluded that David had entered the service under an assumed name, to keep from being found. He had vanished, and that was probably what he wanted. Dale finally gave up the search for his brother, hoping that after the war they might be reunited. It would never happen. Unbeknownst to Dale, David would perish during the Tet Offensive, and his true identity would never be known to the government or his family.

On the morning of June 23, 1968, Dale's crew had been ordered to make an emergency airdrop to resupply the 28th Vietnamese Ranger Battalion, operating in the upper quadrant near the Cambodian border. The troops of the 28th had been engaged in a firefight with NVA regulars for several days and were running short of supplies. The Special Forces Advisors had been ordered to defend their positions and had dug in along the Cambodian border, despite heavy casualties among their remaining Vietnamese Troops.

At first light, the camouflaged C-130 was on final approach over the drop zone. Dale and three other loadmasters had lowered the tail gate and were handling a few final details as they waited for orders to jettison the load.

Dale caught a glimpse of two other C-130's that had joined them from Bien Hoa, positioning themselves for the drop on either side of their lead aircraft.

The sun shone through the portholes of the cargo bay, like golden rays of light shimmering on the opposite wall as the plane leveled off. The pilot maneuvered just above the top of the jungle, trying to avoid ground fire. A gale force wind whipped through the open compartment, pounding the men as they worked to unlock the last restraining devices holding the pallets in place on the rollers. The men ignored the deafening drone from the engine, attuned only to the change in pitch that would warn them that the pilot was adjusting the air speed in preparation to release the load from the plane.

Ben Robiack, one of the loadmasters, gave the group a 'thumbs up' as he watched the parachutes drift over the target area, eagerly pounced on by a swarm of Vietnamese Rangers in the fire base perimeter.

"The little bastards are jumpin' on those groceries like flies on shit!" Robiack roared. "Come to mamma," he chortled, waving his arms at the shrinking soldiers on the ground, as the pilot gunned the engines and nosed the aircraft up to gain altitude. "All right!" he added, walking back to give each of the other loadmasters a hand slap.

"Cut the shit, Robiack!" one of the other loadmasters screamed, bending over to look out of the window. He motioned for everyone to quiet down as he spoke into his headset. "That's affirmative, Captain, we got smoke comin' from number one and two starboards!"

The loadmaster paused for a moment before suddenly speaking nervously into his mike again. "Captain, we got a problem. Fire's comin' off both engines! She's cookin' real hot, sir!"

Again there was a moment of pause and then the load master answered with a sharp, "Yes, sir! Captain says get 'em buckled...looks like we're jumpin' if he can't choke that fire," he announced, cinching the straps of his parachute as tight as he could get them. He ignored the other men as he checked out the window.

Dale checked his harness, and helmet, then he felt for his pistol, pulling it off and quickly re-buckling it inside his flight suit so that it wouldn't be stripped off when he went through the jungle canopy. He pulled his APO jacket off and let it drop to the floor of the plane.

Everyone had moved towards the opened back end, keeping their eyes locked on Sergeant Piper as he continued to wait for orders to come over the headset from up front.

"Where the hell are we? "Robiack shouted. "What's our Gawd damn position?"

"Everyone, keep eye contact if we jump; don't get separated!" Dale yelled.

"Stay together...everyone just stay together," Sergeant Rodriguez shouted, trying not to sound alarmed. Dale noticed Rodriguez was fingering a small gold cross around his neck.

"Captain's gonna try to find a spot to put her down," Piper said, still listening on his headset. "The other ships are gittin' a fix on us!"

Unexpectedly, just as Sergeant Piper started to say something else, the C-130 made a sharp bank, rolling wildly to one side. The walls of the cargo bay collapsed into a ball of fire, engulfing Piper and everyone forward of the other three loadmasters. Then a huge explosion and sudden swaying of the plane hurled the remaining three men from the open back end of the aircraft, throwing them free of the burning plane.

Dale managed to open his chute even though he'd hit his head on the way out, losing his helmet. He was dazed from the blast, or the impact from the blow to his head. He had the presence of mind to check the horizon for the others, at the same time trying to see what had happened to the aircraft as he hung freely in the harness, floating towards the jungle floor.

He noticed a single chute off to the east, drifting on top of the trees below him. It was too early for anyone to have landed in the jungle. Either Rodriguez or Robiack had gone down with a malfunctioning parachute. He knew that Piper was finished. The C-130 had disintegrated into smoking fragments, falling like a pyrotechnic display, sprinkled over the jungle behind him.

His right boot had been blown away, and his face and hands were covered in blood.

Dale knew that the rest of the crew hadn't had time to follow the standard escape procedures, so he hoped that they had been blown free. It would have been their only chance to survive the explosion.

He landed on the floor of the jungle with a hard jolt. The fall through the trees had been the worst part of his descent. At one point, he'd been turned upside down when part of his chute had hooked on a tree limb, driving his face into another limb, breaking his nose and bruising the side of his head.

He lay, knocked out on the floor of the jungle, sleeping, at first, like an animal nestled in the elephant grass. The sweet fragrance of decaying vegetation drifted into his nostrils. The jungle teemed with life, moving over Dale's body as if a magnificent morsel had been delivered to the creatures of the earth. They probed and touched, trying to determine if he were ripe to eat, or how to divvy him up.

He dreamed and slept, unconscious from the blow to his head and the excruciating pain from a broken leg, driven up through his calf.

Visions of his days in the swamp played in his mind as the sun intensified. By mid-day it had turned to a searing blaze, burning his exposed flesh. The curiosity of the insects had turned to a ravenous frenzy, stinging and biting the stilled form, no longer content to wait for him to expire.

By mid-day his dreaming ended, and he awoke, shocked back to life by the pain from his leg and the stinging from the insect bites. He'd felt a sharp poking as he'd slept the last few seconds, a painful stabbing to his side and back.

When he was finally able to open his eyes he was startled to see a scrawny naked man, hunkered down in front of him. The man's mouth and teeth were stained red from a wad of betel nut he'd been chewing. He was wearing a dirty loincloth that covered his crotch.

Dale quickly realized the source of the pain in his side and back as he watched the wormy form poke him with a bayonet attached to a Chicom Ak47.

The creature was screaming at Dale, jabbing him, as he demanded that he get up. Before Dale had a chance to respond, the man jerked his parachute harness off, reached into his flight suit, and took his pistol. The man ignored his screams of pain. As Dale lay on his back, on the verge of blacking out, he could see several other Vietcong standing over him. They began trussing him to a tiger pole, ignoring his wounds as they bound him to the rail like a side of beef.

It was obvious to Dale what was going on. The Vietcong were racing to get him out of the area before the evacuation choppers came in. They knew that the minute the rescue aircraft had a fix on him the area would be crawling with helicopters.

The VC hoisted him into the air, tied and gagged and set off with their prize. Some time later, he was shocked to see another group of VC coming up behind them. They were carrying two other bodies attached to poles. As they came closer, he realized that it was Robiack and Rodriguez.

Half of Rodriguez's head was missing. The VC were obviously body snatching. Robiack was covered in blood, but appeared still to be alive.

A few minutes later, the three of them were shoved into a large spider hole in the ground, to wait out the rest of the daylight hours. The VC would move them north after dark, or so Dale thought.

The VC had little concern for Robiack's or Dale's wounds, leaving them unattended in the dark hole with Rodriguez's body. It was too dark for Dale to see if Robiack was conscious or even alive. He couldn't hear him breathing. He managed to work his hands down his side to try to examine his broken leg. He was shocked to find that it had swollen to the size of a ripe watermelon. Fortunately, the swelling had caused the pain to subside slightly.

Dale fell back, exhausted from his efforts. The stench from Johnny's body was becoming overpowering in the warm, cave, making it difficult to breathe. He tucked his face up under his arm, trying to filter the air. He wanted desperately to sleep, to conserve his energy, but he couldn't.

He lay on his side, remembering that, just the day before, he'd written his grandparents to tell them how beautiful he'd found the country. He'd been very positive about making it back to the real world, to home, sure that he was going to be okay.

The prospect of being left in the cave was terrifying. Oddly, he feared that his captors might be killed before they could retrieve them.

Dale's concerns turned to his grandparents. He knew that the military would be sending notification to Lora and James that he was missing. He also knew that James was seriously ill. He worried what the news of his missing in action would do to his grandfather.

The evening of their first night of captivity, the VC returned to the hole and retrieved Ben Robiack and Dale. They left Rodriguez behind, but Dale was sure it wasn't because of the condition of his body. They probably would come back for him, if and when it was to their advantage to bargain with his remains.

In the weeks that followed, Dale and Ben were kept continuously on the move. Dale had expected that the two of them would be taken north to Hanoi, but they continued to move them in the same vicinity where they had been captured. Most of the time they were kept underground in massive earthen complexes that the VC had built to hide their troops from aerial observation. A few times, they were taken to villages to be shown off to the locals for propaganda purposes.

Ben Robiack had recovered enough to be able to get up and move around. Dale's mobility was another matter. He was still limited by his injured leg that had never been properly set. The leg, in fact, had turned a sickening black tinge and was causing Dale to suffer continuous fever from the infection. Gangrene was his constant fear. For some strange reason it hadn't appeared, at least not yet.

Robiack had tried to help him set the leg, but the bone was badly shattered. They worried about doing internal damage that would be worse than the break itself. Because of the infection and severe pain, Dale remained delirious much of the first week, slipping in and out of consciousness for days at a time.

Despite the injuries already suffered by the men, the Viet Cong regularly administered beatings to both of them. Fang, the name they had given the VC officer who had captured them, took pride in beating his two prisoners whenever a visiting dignitary passed through the camp, which was quite often. Fang had an irritating smirk, accentuated by a lone black incisor that appeared whenever he opened his mouth. Fang would have preferred officers for his object lessons, but he managed with what he had.

Ben Robiack had been kept bound in a squatting position for so long that, by the third week, he'd begun to suffer paralysis on his right side. The torture had been used on him so frequently that he still imagined the excruciating pain shooting through his body from his bindings, even when he was untied. Dale was an easier target. Fang could simply deliver a few well-placed blows to his injured leg with a bamboo club that he carried with him like a riding crop.

During one of the punishment sessions, Fang had discovered that Dale was fluent in French. It suddenly reduced the number of beatings that Dale received. Since Fang could speak Vietnamese and French, but not English, he delighted in having Dale give prepared confessions at each of the villages where they would make short stopovers. Fang then became a little more interested in Dale's condition because of his special talent.

In addition to their physical deterioration from torture, both men were growing weaker by the day; they were slowly being starved to death. Their condition was worsened by the constant forced marches through the jungle, Robiack walking and Dale being carried.

The Viet Cong, as a common practice, had let the Americans know that prisoners were being kept in the area, in hopes of preventing B-52 strikes on their bases. At the same time, their strategy forced the constant changing of their location to prevent a rescue attempt by the Americans.

James began to show signs of strain over the disappearance of his grandson. He'd cherished the thought of their being reunited after Dale returned home. But now that possibility seemed remote. His hopes sank deeper when a news story was released about the wreckage of the downed C-130 and the report of bodies being found at the crash site. The news triggered a heart attack that nearly killed the old doctor.

A combination of events had brought the downing of Dale's plane to the attention of Jessica. The military had released Dale's hometown as Topeka, Kansas, so the newspaper in Topeka picked up the story off the UPI wire service, and Jessica read the article in the paper.

Sometime later, the Air Force unwittingly notified Jessica as next of kin from Dale's military records, even though he'd carefully selected James and Lora as his heirs.

Jessica had received an official telegram acknowledging her son's status as an MIA. This, she thought, was license to slip back into Dale's life, to gather a final reward for her motherhood.

She wasted little time in capitalizing on the situation. Coldly and deliberately, she notified James of her intention to contest Lora and him as the beneficiary for Dale's service benefits. In the same letter, she declared that no decisions concerning Dale or the disposition of his remains would henceforth be made without her consent.

The Topeka newspapers were duped into publishing a local interest story on a mother's grief for the loss of her son. Jessica played the part to the hilt, taking every opportunity to publicly express her profound grief, all the while happily basking in the limelight.

Dale's military benefits were of little concern to James. What concerned him most was Jessica's renewed interest. Worse yet, he was disturbed by her interest in the inheritance that James so carefully had preserved for his grandson. The prospect of Dale's death made it even clearer to James what Jessica was after. She knew better than anyone that James was seriously ill and that time was short. It wasn't hard for her to figure that James would have bequeathed everything he owned to Dale, including his secret hordes of money and titles to properties that had escaped the government's auction hammer.

She assumed that James hadn't made any contingency plans, in the event of Dale's death, and she was right. He'd never thought in his wildest dreams that he would be burying another member of his family before his own end came.

The legendary stash of money had grown to phenomenal proportions, in Jessica's mind. Visions of thermos jugs of cash, or stacks of neatly banded thousand-dollar-bills, concealed in the walls of the house gave her a constant source of sugar plum fantasies in which she tiptoed through crinkled heaps of cash, that fell from the ceiling to lie beneath her feet, like a carpet.

She'd even arrived at the morbid decision to have Jason's and Billy's bodies exhumed, once James and Lora had passed away and she'd gained control of his estate. She believed that James had hidden money in the caskets. It was simply a matter of having herself appointed by the courts as trustee of her son's estate. After all, she was his mother.

But James wasn't so easily convinced of Dale's death, nor was he willing so quickly to relinquish his grandson's future to the demon.

And come she did, as quietly as the dark shadow of a storm. In 1969, James suffered a massive heart attack. He lay near death in Tom Davidson Memorial Hospital. With his mind still clear of purpose, he sent Jessica a letter, an invitation for a final parley under the pretext of settling their long-standing dispute for the sake of his grandson's memory. It was an appointment known only to Jessica and him.

Jessica appeared in his room a few days later. She stood near his bed and stared at the emaciated form that barely broke the flatness of the sheets. Curiosity had brought her to her most hated enemy—curiosity and the prospect of money. She'd been hesitant at first, fearing that it was a trick; but, after carefully checking James' condition with the hospital, she decided to accept the invitation.

She seemed surprised that this frail old man had been such a formidable adversary. Now she was furious that she had allowed herself to think that this sickly old skeleton could be such an imposing enemy. But what did it matter, as she looked down on his scrawny defeated form? She'd won.

She moved closer to his face, to watch him struggle with each breath beneath the oxygen tent. She was surprised when his eyes partially opened, glaring at her as if he'd known the precise moment she would appear before him.

His lips moved, but there was nothing but silence. He motioned for her to come closer.

"It's yours...you can have all of it!" he whispered. "All I ask in return is that you leave my grandson alone. You've put him through hell!"

Jessica stared at him without expression, looking nervously around the room, as if she wasn't sure they were alone.

"There's enough to make you very rich and comfortable for the rest of your life," he struggled to say, closing his eyes.

"What are you doing this for?" she questioned.

"Because, if he's alive...I want him free from your influence...from your tampering with his life," he said, forcing himself to his elbow. "You're a godless monster. I wish I'd killed you when I had the chance!"

His voice began to break with rage and fatigue, then he fell back into the bedding.

Jessica let out a horrible laugh.

"It's all here, everything you need to know to get to the money," James groaned, handing her an envelope, his hand struggling to deliver it to her. "They'll be a man...waiting for you at Keso's. He'll take you to the island."

She stood up, opening the envelope to examine the contents next to a soft night light on the wall. After a short time she smiled to herself and turned to leave, ignoring her dying benefactor until she reached the door.

"I always knew I'd have your money someday...I just didn't think it'd be this easy. You've saved me a lot of trouble."

James fell back into the pillow, still watching the shadow at the door. "Go on, git out!" he ordered.

"You're really not stupid enough to believe that you could get rid of me this easy? I intend to have it all...everything you own. I've hated you for so long. You're nothing but a pathetic old bastard; you're just as sorry and no-count as that weakling son of yours.

"This gives me more pleasure than you know," she carried on, "being able to see you die. And I can't begin to tell you the thrill it gives me watching you agonize over your grandson's death. At least, there was some purpose to his miserable life." She laughed. "And you'll never lay your eyes on him again!"

James lay back, turning his eyes away from her, "Get thee gone, Satan. Get thee behind me!" he whispered to himself. He'd obeyed his mind, but not his heart. He yearned to tear the life from her, but he knew he had no strength left. A few moments later she was gone.

James looked towards the window of his room, with the curtains drawn back. He watched the thick gray clouds, puffed as full as wool waiting for the spinner's wheel. His eyes followed the droplets of rain that hung from the glass until their weight sent them careening down the length of the window. He could hear the howling wind, confirming what he already knew. He studied the movement of the heavily laden clouds, watching them as they raced away from the gulf, sagging and pregnant with moisture from an ocean storm. He'd seen the signs before. He'd known all along what was coming, the great swirling destruction from the sea. In a short while, his task would be completed. "The dogs shall eat Jezebel, in the portion of Jezreel, and there shall be none to bury her, thus saith the Lord God," he muttered to himself.

His eyes filled with tears as he thought of Dale. How dear the boy had been to him. He waited, as he'd waited every night for his grandson's goodnight kiss when he was a young boy. And then, as gently as it always had come, he felt the warmth of a loving caress. He held tightly onto the outstretched hand, reaching to him from the dark, as he closed his eyes and accepted the peaceful end to his life.

Jessica wasted little time in making her way to the appointed rendezvous at Keso's landing, as James had predicted. She was accompanied by one Edwardo Puccini, a Las Vegas hoodlum whom she'd taken up with some months earlier. He had noticed Jessica at one of the local casinos that she frequented whenever she could manage to gather the cash for a trip.

Lately Jessica had been living with the illusion that she was the mirror image of Jane Russell. She began imitating the actress's dress and style, copying every detail of Jane Russell's screen character. Her interest in Las Vegas and the particular hotel she had chosen also played an important part in her fantasy. She had read in a movie magazine that Howard Hughes owned the hotel where she was staying. She'd also read the story of Jane Russell's discovery by Hughes.

She reasoned that eventually she would meet Mr. Hughes, and obviously, he would make her a star. Unfortunately, Edwardo was as close as she had come to her dream.

Edwardo, despite his tough underworld mentality, found himself instantly captivated by Jessica. She not only refused to become one of his hotel harlots, but also maneuvered him into joyfully springing for her expenses each and every time she descended on Vegas.

That was not to say that Jessica had repented of her lustful ways; quite the contrary. She was shrewd enough to reason that since Edwardo held the key to the treasury, her favors were best invested with him.

Shortly after their association had begun, Edwardo had a rather startling personality transformation, something similar to that of a freshly castrated bull. Unlike his previously aggressive and ruthless self, he now seemed a submissive character, always trailing behind Jessica as she swept through the casino in search of Mr. Hughes.

Edwardo had faithfully accompanied Jessica to Jacksonville and then on into the swamp. He chauffeured Jessica in his bright orange Caddy convertible as she navigated from the map given to her by James. Edwardo, was of course, motivated by the promise of sharing in her bounty at the end of the trail. However, Edwardo had become increasingly uncomfortable with the adventure as Jessica's pursuit took them farther from Las Vegas. The extent of his outdoors experience had been in the bushes of Central Park where, in his youth, he would lie in wait to roll some unsuspecting passerby. Now he was terror-stricken by the dark ominous jungle that seemed to envelop the car on both sides of the road as they proceeded farther into the swamp.

Jessica urged him on, skillfully working him into a frenzy over the thought of finding James' horde of money. Before long, even that failed to overcome the stark realization of what he was getting himself into.

When she didn't get a rise out of Edwardo, Jessica began to browbeat him, bombarding him with an endless array of insults until they finally arrived at Keso's Landing that afternoon.

They stepped from the car, Edwardo in his white muslin slacks and gold imported Italian sports shirt, with his two-hundred-dollar shoes oozing into the black muck beneath him. Jessica was just as inappropriately attired, wearing a tight -fitting pantsuit, French spiked heels, and enough jewelry to dazzle an army of gypsy dancers. Her attempts to apply makeup ended when she discovered that it had melted from the heat.

They stood, staring at the short stretch of dirt road that had disappeared into the turbulent waters of the lake.

Jessica nervously examined her watch, looking up to survey the thick cypress stand surrounding the two of them. Edwardo had taken refuge back in the car, sipping a warm beer, and cursing a single mosquito that circled endlessly above him, attracted by his pungent odor. As he lay back in the front seat, sleepy from the effects of the beer and the heat, he was startled by something just on the other side of the door. He sat up, and saw an old man staring at him.

"You son of a bitch, what'a you think you're doin', sneakin' up here without sayin' nothin'? I ought to kick your ass!" Edwardo screamed.

The man ignored him, turning his back and walking towards Jessica.

"I'm to guide you to the Choctaw Lake...to the "island", the man announced with a heavy accent. He tipped his hat with a faint effort.

Jessica studied the man for a moment. His eyes were hidden beneath the wide-brimmed straw hat, and his shoulders slumped forward from age. She reached into her purse, pulled out a handful of bills, and handed them to the harmless-looking character.

"We'll need something to dig with; I'll pay you if you've got a shovel you can sell me?" she asked.

"Yes 'um, I have one in the boat," he replied, accepting another bill from her purse.

The man turned without saying anything else and began following a footpath leading along the shore into the cypress stand. Jessica followed, screaming back to Edwardo, who was watching with considerable reservation about following them farther into the swamp.

"You chicken shit, get up here!" she yelled.

With that, Edwardo leaped from the car like a child afraid of being left in the dark. He raced down the trail until he caught up with them, giving himself a few deep breaths to regain his composure before getting into step with the other two. "I don't like this guy. You mess with me, old man, and I'll slit your God damn throat!" he threatened, pulling a knife from his pocket and brandishing it in the air in front of the guide.

Jessica laughed. "You're such a jackass, Edwardo. Leave him alone."

Again, the old man ignored the threat from Edwardo, continuing to lead them deeper into the swamp. After a twenty-minute hike, their path ended in front of a wooden, flat-bottom boat, pulled up in a thick clump of swamp grass. A layer of brown foam covered the water around the boat, crusted against the waterlogged sides of the slender vessel.

Edwardo watched the old man push the boat out of the anchorage of grass that gripped it so tightly. He backed away from the muck lapping against the shoreline, preferring to keep himself dry and unscathed from the black ooze that sucked the old man down to his knees.

Jessica showed her exasperation with Edwardo with a loud huff, as she jerked off her high heels and stepped into the mud and onto the boat. Edwardo waited for a moment and then followed suit, removing his shoes and socks, then rolling up his pants and daintily tiptoeing after her. The old man effortlessly launched himself into the rectangular-shaped boat, still gripping the wad of money in one hand that Jessica had paid him for his services.

He cranked the small Evinrude motor, crudely attached to a two-by-four nailed to the boat's rails. On the second crank, the engine turned over, belching a gray cloud of smoke over the water as the boat lurched forward.

Jessica and Edwardo turned towards the front, concerned more with their final destination than the curious fellow steering the oddly shaped craft.

The old man maneuvered through the thick hedge of brush beneath the cypress trees. Twisting and turning, he worked his way in and out of the shallows for nearly a half-hour before finally slipping under a barrier of low-lying tree limbs and then out into a wide-open channel.

He glanced up, studying the clouds and the winds as they sat in the middle of the opening. He hesitated for a moment before goosing the throttle and following the open water south towards Choctaw Lake and James' Island.

Jessica concentrated on the water, lost in her dreams of wealth, as Edwardo nervously watched the wake splashing over the bow of the boat, filling the floor with water up to his ankles.

The swamp man ignored his passengers, instead taking every opportunity to watch the horizon, looking south, mentally judging the speed of the clouds. His eyes scanned the shoreline, aware that the watermark on the trees was far above the bellowed trunks of the cypress where it had been a day earlier. The hyacinths had long since disappeared from the surface, and he could see from the cloudiness of the water that great currents were swirling through the channel, pushing the silt up from the depths.

An hour passed as the group motored slowly through the rough waters towards their destination. The old man then turned the dugout sharply to the west, veering into a heavy forest of submerged oaks, bumping logs and stumps dangerously concealed just beneath the muddied waters.

Another hour passed as he followed an invisible trail, moving by instinct, darting through narrow crevices in the wall of timbers until he came to an opening no larger than a small country road, cut cleanly through the trees.

Again, he continued on, moving slowly along the waterway, skirting past animals swimming in the water, suddenly evicted from their perches by the swelling of the swamp.

Edwardo was spellbound, as he watched a small deer, struggling to free itself from the grip of a huge gator, which was taking advantage of the migration of its prey into its private domain. He laughed, secure in the safety of his wooden platform. Neither he nor Jessica had noticed anything strange about the level of the lake.

Jessica turned with a jerk as the old man cut the power on the boat, sliding the last few yards to a small tongue of land immediately in front of them.

"Is this it?" she asked excitedly.

"Yes, ma'am," the man responded, forcing the bow of the boat up on the shore with a final burst from the motor.

"Least I can get out of this God damn leaky rowboat," Edwardo complained, doing the splits as he tried to step from the boat onto the shore. "Noisy son of a bitch! I can't hear myself think," he added, relieved finally to be on solid ground.

Jessica stepped from the boat and quickly strapped on her high heels. She reached into the boat to retrieve the shovel, ignoring the old man who continued to sit quietly next to the motor.

While Edwardo slipped his socks and shoes on, Jessica flew past him, pushing the shovel into his arms as she walked up the bank trying to get a fix on the place once called— Avalon.

"There it is!" she screamed, racing towards the front gates of the camp. "Get up here!" she commanded Edwardo.

Edwardo broke into a sudden burst of speed, slipping and falling headfirst onto the ground. He jumped to his feet, wiping his hands on his pants, and hurried to where Jessica was waiting impatiently for him.

The fence had fared poorly over the years, torn and twisted from the weather and scavengers from the swamp. The gates were still standing but void of any of the wire that once ran around the perimeter of the camp. The wooded pallet floors of the tents were barely visible in the patches of weeds that had overgrown the compound.

Jessica raced through the remains of the camp looking for the marker on the map. She found the steps that once led to the trailer. She pushed over the stones, and fell to her knees as she attacked the rubble. Even a small copperhead, comfortably nestled in the crack of the stones got little more attention than a whack from the shovel as Jessica and Edwardo feverishly cleared the site.

Like imps dancing on the floor of the forest, Jessica and Edwardo screamed with delight as they retrieved container after container, chock-full of cash from the freshly dug pit.

Only the noise of the boat's motor being started interrupted Jessica's merriment. She raced to the bank where they had first landed, still clutching a fist full of money in each hand. The old man had backed the boat nearly twenty yards from shore as she and Edwardo looked on.

Jessica ordered the old man to return to shore, surprised to see him indignantly throwing the money she'd paid him into the water. She listened to the strange man in the boat suddenly come alive with expression, standing up as he shouted back at them: "My dear friend has been delivered into the hands of God, and you have been delivered to hell."

Jessica could not hear him mumble his final remark: "My debt to you, my friend, for my son Leon is paid. Now...we both will rest in peace! Adieu, my good friend...your revenge is at hand."

With that, he started the boat and slowly moved away from the island, never looking back as Edwardo begged and pleaded on his knees for him to come back for them.

Jessica walked slowly back to the pit, pulling the final container from the hole and laying it in front of her. She sat down on a stone, her eyes fixed on the open canisters of money, thinking not of the great fortune she had acquired with James' blessing, but now understanding what he'd done. She let the money fall to the ground in front of her, ignoring the whimpering of her companion.

She looked skyward as the first drops of rain began to plummet through the thick canopy overhead. The clouds, now darkened as if night had come, rolled over the swamp. Before long the ocean storm would crawl across the swamp, cleansing the land as God once had used the great flood to purge the evilness of man from his sight. And when the flooding waters had consumed the land beneath their feet, the creatures of the swamp would feast upon their remains.

Here she contemplated her destiny, knowing that her enemy had been victorious. The old man, her lifelong adversary, had skillfully executed the serving of his revenge, even unto death.

'He knew,' she thought, 'even while he closed his eyes to die...he knew I wouldn't be far behind, following him in anything but a peaceful death.'

She hated his victory more than she feared the end of her life, which she knew was but a short time away. He had held on, to the last moment, to the very thing she always had wanted: the temptation of money and wealth, using it to lure her to her end.

A small fire, built from the pile of money pulled from the canisters, burned and smoked as the storm closed in, a storm as great as any that had come that way in twenty years.

And when the storm had passed, the swamp was again calm and flourishing with life, its creatures content with their good fortune.

CHAPTER 32

Dale felt an emptiness as he thumbed through the memories that the old man had lovingly preserved in a shoebox, in his drawer. He could sense the despair that his grandfather must have felt as he sat in his rocking chair and began to unfold the clippings. They had been written when the journalists of the day found it out of vogue to offer hope to loved ones at home about anything concerning the Vietnam War. It was as if his capture by the enemy had been a victory for America and the world, or so it seemed from the press's point of view.

'It was so long ago, and yet it seems like yesterday,' Dale thought, as he glanced through the articles and carefully bundled letters that James had collected until his death.

The worst part of it was having missed being with his grandfather in his final hours. He felt much like an amnesia victim, robbed of precious moments of his life. When all is made right, the amnesia patient is rewarded with the return of his lost moments. Dale's loss, however, would never be satisfied. The time had passed, with James believing him to be dead, never knowing that Dale lay alive on the floor of a hooch, dreaming of going home someday to be with him. "If only he'd known," Dale muttered, "perhaps it would have made a difference!"

Dale remembered anticipating the end of the war when peace talks had begun in Paris in May of '68. It had given the world a glimmer of hope that the horror of the war would soon end. It was a time to breathe a sigh of relief.

"Surely," he remembered thinking, "the North Vietnamese want peace as badly as we do."

Unfortunately, that was not to be the case. The North Vietnamese were determined to increase the pressure during the negotiations to give them leverage in Paris. They had no interest in decreasing hostilities during the peace conference, preferring to let their opponent bleed from his wounds while he was dealing not only with them, but a desperate political situation at home. By the end of '68, the war had taken a turn for the worse for America and for Dale.

Dale had swallowed the rumors of peace along with everyone else. He had failed to understand the proverbial problem that always had confronted western minds in dealing with the Asians, their persistent waiting game, believing that an impatient man has reason for his haste, racing ahead of himself and truth.

Dale found out the hard way just how patient the powers in the North could be.

Perhaps it had been his overwhelming desire to go home, the feeling that it was almost over, to have this madness ended made him begin to feel invincible. He remembered his shock at being captured in the first place.

The worst was still to come, the struggle to survive after his capture. But he had been more fortunate than most. When his ordeal was over, he finally made it home. But it wasn't only to his rescuers that he was grateful; there was something else that had happened, something unforgettable and wonderful.

His thoughts, returned to those hideous final days; slowly, methodically, he began to recall the details of the strange but marvelous events.

The VC were terrified of B-52 raids. So devastating were the attacks that American and South Vietnamese troops, sweeping the fire zone after a raid, would be in danger of drowning in the quagmire of mud created by the churned and displaced earth.

During the latter part of 1969, Dale and Ben Robiack found themselves in the Mekong Delta, after two months of forced marches through thick jungles, zigzagging through Cambodia and back into South Vietnam with their captors.

It had been a harrowing experience for both men, carried part of the way stuffed into bamboo cocoons. At other times they were gagged and bound by their hands and feet in the bottom of a boat as the VC slipped silently past patrols on the Mekong River at night.

Little concern was shown for the comfort of the prisoners, who were at times dragged bodily through the jungle on a traverse pole. Dale still suffered from his injured leg, and Ben Robiack had become so emaciated, weighing little more than 92 pounds, that he resembled a skeleton. He was often carried on the back of a much smaller Vietnamese man or woman. The twosome appeared as some odd creature, scurrying along the jungle floor with Ben's naked torso clenched to his host. His legs dangled like withered limbs of a tree, as they bounced along the trail in line with the other troops. His motor skills were gone, collapsed from the constant amoebic dysentery and the paralysis from being tortured. Even Colonel Fang's threats at gunpoint eventually failed to rouse enough fear in Ben to make him cooperate.

Their final destination was a small village in Vinh Long Province. They arrived there with their captors, apparently in preparation for another all-out push modeled on the Tet offensive of January, 1968. Dale's and Ben's importance had become secondary as the Viet Cong prepared for the forthcoming assault.

In the midst of the movement by his VC captors over the two months, an infection in Dale's leg had recurred. Fang's prize had become a liability, interfering with his efforts to meet his timetables for the assault. Both prisoners were pathetic figures. Had it not been for orders from Viet Cong headquarters concerning the two airmen, Fang would have long since dispatched the two of them in a ditch along the trail and gone on about his business.

In a token effort to treat the infection in Dale's leg, a Viet Cong surgeon opened the wound to drain it; but through a combination of carelessness and poor hygiene he only succeeded in further infecting the leg. In a matter of days, Dale contracted pneumonia.

Neither antibiotics nor clean dressings were applied after the operation by the surgeon, who suddenly vanished from the camp for the next two days. Dale always held a suspicion that Fang had arranged for the surgeon's disappearance, in hopes of having an alibi for ridding himself of at least one of his prisoners.

As the days passed, the condition of the leg grew worse. Ben tried to give some comfort to Dale by giving him a drink of water when it was available. He washed Dale's body to try and relieve the fever whenever he could muster the energy to drag himself across the floor to his comrade's side.

When Dale was awake, Ben would try to feed him with the small amount of food he had been able to collect. Robiack had devised a mortar and pestle contraption to grind some of the rice he'd saved into a gruel so that Dale could swallow the unsavory concoction without having to chew.

Much of the time that Dale was conscious he would dictate letters to his grandmother and grandfather. Ben would pretend to jot down the sometimes incoherent mumblings, knowing that there was no way of sending the letters, even if he actually had transcribed them. He also was aware that the VC would use anything they could find to brainwash either of them, especially personal information about their homes and families.

As his fever intensified, Dale began to have nightmares. He would hallucinate, seeing the feared black demon from his childhood standing in the cell. The stark terror of that image would bring on a seizure that left him in convulsions, shivering in a pool of sweat for hours at a time.

Ben would sit next to Dale, trying to comfort him as best he could. During the lengthy hallucinations Dale remained silent, a habit from his days as a child when he had learned that to cry out only increased the wrath of the demon. When the fever broke, it would leave Dale exhausted. He might eat a few handfuls of rice and gulp down as much water as Ben would give him. The two men would talk, exchanging assurances that they both would be going home soon; but both of them knew that Dale could never survive under the present circumstances, and Robiack wouldn't be far behind him.

Ben Robiack had become Dale's only chance to remain alive. Ben was a tough, streetwise young man who had joined the Air Force to avoid jail in Rochester, New York, on a plea bargain worked out with a judge at Juvenile Hall. He hadn't done anything too severe, but the war had given the judicial system an alternative to sending first offenders into the prison population. Now, however, it looked as if he too had received a death sentence.

Ben was mesmerized by Dale and his heritage. He was totally enthralled with the stories that Dale told of his family. It was a world he was totally unfamiliar with, but he made a point of insisting that Dale invite him to his home as soon as they returned to the 'real world'. He seemed to take special pride in having someone to rely on him, for once in his life.

His own childhood had been difficult enough, never knowing his father and being raised by an older sister after his mother had died of alcoholism. Up until his capture by the VC, his life in the military had actually been an improvement over his previous existence.

On the morning of November 13, 1969, Dale lay awake on his cot, too weak to resist a giant rat that was attacking his leg, attracted to the stench of rotting flesh. He cried out for Ben, trying to arouse him from a deep sleep.

At the exact moment that Ben awoke to Dale's plea for help, the door to the cell opened. A Viet Cong officer strutted into the hooch, smiling at the rat gnawing on Dale's leg. He studied Dale for a brief moment and then turned to face Ben. The rat ignored the gathering to continue its feast.

Both prisoners sensed imminent danger, knowing that something was desperately wrong with his being there, the smile on his face. They both had lived too long with the threat of death not to understand what the man was going to do.

Ben pressed himself against the wall, crying as he pulled his knees into his chest, tucking himself into a tight ball on the floor. Dale turned his eyes towards his companion, unable to do anything to help.

The VC unholstered his pistol and calmly pulled back the hammer. He fired a single shot into Ben's head. Ben's lifeless body rolled over on the floor, still tucked in a fetal position.

The rat was disturbed by the shot. It leaped from the bed and ran through the open cell door. Dale stared towards the ceiling as he waited for his turn to die. He was surprised to hear the officer leaving the hooch, the cell door left wide open, as if to taunt the American, knowing there was no chance of his escaping.

For most of the morning Dale could hear the VC loading equipment into trucks, recovering their stashes of arms and hurriedly leaving the camp. He waited, thinking that the officer would return to finish him off before abandoning the village. But the soldier never came back to complete the execution. Dale could only assume that the officer thought the rat would finish his work, and saw no reason to waste a bullet.

By late afternoon the camp was deserted. Dale hadn't been able to muster the strength to crawl to the door of his cell. He had an insatiable thirst, and a stifling heat had made the cell like an oven. He became delirious, fading in and out of consciousness.

The heat dissipated only slightly at dusk. His mind floated, disassociated from his body, no longer feeling anything except the pain throbbing from the open wound on his leg. His breathing became shallow as he lay still, acutely aware of any sounds coming from within the camp.

He thought of his grandmother and her wonderful kitchen. He closed his eyes, and saw the dining room table. A cut glass pitcher full of the deliciously cool bronze tea sitting in the middle of it, small chips of ice clinging to its sides, and a frosty coating on the outside of the glass.

His dad and James were there, each sitting at opposite ends of the table. Lora was sitting across to one side, handing plates of food to each of them. It seemed odd that even his mother was sitting at her place, the place that Lora always had set for her, out of respect, even though she was never there before. Jessica sat with her face turned away from everyone else, enduring the gathering, as if serving out some divine penitence.

David was sitting quietly across from Lora and his mother, dressed in his uniform, a peaceful look on his face. He was smiling at everyone, content, at last, to have the family back together.

When Dale awoke, he was in excruciating pain. His throat hurt from the dryness. A current of sharp penetrating aches surged through his side, and he knew it wouldn't be long before he was dead. He lay in the dark of the night, listening to his own breathing drowning out the noise coming from the jungle, outside the village. The rats had returned, but for some reason preferred to work on Robiack rather than his leg.

A sound from inside the room caught his attention, breaking his concentration as he waited for death to arrive. He listened, hearing the faint clear resonance of a waltz playing somewhere in the room. Over and over, the brief tune played; and the sound, although strangely inappropriate, was soothing to him. After a while, the tune stopped. Dale's eyes moved from side to side trying to find the source of the music.

He convinced himself that he had been hallucinating, but again he heard the music, this time closer to his bunk. He strained to roll his head to one side, alarmed by the appearance of a figure moving in the dark towards him.

He watched the man move out of the shadows and lean over him. He would never forget feeling the cool wet cloth pressed gently against his eyes. His head was raised by the stranger's strong hands. He felt a cup pressed against his lips and cool water trickling into his mouth. The figure never spoke to him as he lay blinded by the wet towel over his eyes. He remembered feeling the strange sensation that his visitor was making every effort to comfort him.

Dale remembered feeling his leg being bandaged. And then, the most wonderful of his memories, he could feel his head being stroked. He remembered this touch. It was identical to the way his grandfather had stroked his forehead when he was little. That special soothing touch that did more than any medicine ever could do to relieve the pain and let him know that all was well. It was as if he were lying in his grandfather's bed, receiving a miraculous healing that took place just because of where he was.

Dale suddenly felt the concussion from a horrific blast. The explosion lifted his body upwards and then dropped him down for an instant before the next detonation came.

He felt the weight of his protector pressing against him, taking the force of each charge. He remembered wanting to wrap his arms around his ghostly defender, screaming with a final burst of energy as clouds of dust and burnt powder folded over them. He gasped for air, his lungs choking with smoke and soot from the black fog. The concussion from a nearby explosion ripped at the membrane of his nose and mouth, filling the openings with blood. Then he was knocked unconscious, leaving him tucked beneath the stranger, still pressing him tightly against his chest.

When it was over, he was helpless to do anything but lie where he was, and pray that his savior had survived the attack.

Tears hovered beneath his eyelids, for lack of enough fluid in his body for them finally to be spilled from his eyes. He remembered his hand moving along the edge of the bunk, reaching out to communicate his gratitude for saving his life from the bombing.

A warm grip clasped his hand, pulling it against the protector's face. It was a sensitive moment that brought a feeling of warmth and reassurance, a feeling that all would be well.

Dale's guardian held his head up and began to give him sips of water and food. Dale remembered the offering, feeling that he was receiving a final communion before his death. Now, he could hear a faint whispering coming from the being. He listened, struggling to hear what he thought he was saying to him. He remembered the voice whispering, "I'll always be with you."

Dale tried to speak, but there was nothing. He was unable to make a sound to show his gratitude. Only the welling up of tears showed his anguish. The voice in the room grew silent.

Dale's hand again searched for his benefactor, but there was no response. He could hear the soft thudding of rain starting to fall on the leaves of the Elephant plants near the cell, slamming against the broad leaves, sounding like the surface of a poorly tuned kettle drum.

Droplets of rain cascaded through the open roof, washing his face and body, cleansing the film of dust and chemicals from his eyes; finally he could see.

Darkness had consumed the entire camp, except for small pockets of light glowing in soft auroras of yellow and white from phosphorous fires started by the bombing. Immediately in front of him, on the other side of a small wall was the silhouette of a man, standing with his back to him.

Dale listened as the familiar waltz he'd heard earlier rang out from the direction of the shadowy figure. He watched, paralyzed with exhaustion but still yearning to know the identity of his guardian spirit. The man stood deathly still, glancing over his shoulder at Dale, and then faced the dark night, slumped in repose.

In the midst of the tinkling chime of the waltz and the accompanying beat of the rain, Dale could hear the man's voice, praying softly to himself. Then the praying stopped.

Dale watched as the figure moved out of the shadows and walked to the side of his bunk. Still, the man's face was hidden. The figure leaned over, whispering into Dale's ear a second time:

"You've been the greatest pleasure of my life, and my being here this moment with you is the reward of all that I desire. If you can find solace with my presence, then there is justification for my soul, at last.

Have courage for what lies beyond this moment in life. I will be your devoted sentinel for eternity, always loving you, moving beside you, until we are reunited in the perfect world. I will always be with you...forever."

There was something about the apparition that made him feel they had known each other at some time in his life. And the melodious, beautiful chime, where had he heard it before? His mind raced to identify the tune so familiar and yet so evasive. Dale struggled to focus on the vision, fighting to stay conscious until he was sure that it had not been a dream or hallucination. He closed his eyes, succumbing to fatigue and the pain of his open wound. As he slipped into a deep sleep he felt the soft touch again of a hand across his forehead.

A thick milky fog lingered over the jungle in the early morning light, cooling the stagnant air and coating the foliage with a delicate mist.

Dale was awakened by the touch of a hand pushing against his shoulder. He opened his eyes, expecting to see his gentle guardian, returned to reveal his identity.

"We'll get you dusted out, buddy, soon as we can call in an Evac!" the voice proclaimed.

"Look at this guy," another voice said, coming from somewhere else in the room, "he looks like he's been through hell! He's a Goddamn skeleton!"

"I don't understand how he lived through the bombing. Look at this place...there ain't nothin' left of it," someone else said, stepping forward to treat Dale's leg. "The fifty-twos blew the living shit outa everything within a quarter-mile of this place! The damn concussion alone should have wasted him."

Dale ignored the men around him, nervously scanning the room for his visitor from the night before. A soldier pressed a canteen against his lips, noticing Dale's concern as his eyes moved past the people standing around the bed.

"Did you find someone else here, besides me?" Dale whispered. "Another prisoner, someone else? Please...I've got to know!"

The soldier leaned over to answer Dale's question. "Sorry, pal...you're the only one that made it. The other guy bought the farm. I promise you we'll make sure he gets home."

Dale lay back in the stretcher as they started to carry him out of the room. He still wasn't sure that his experience with the ghostly purveyor had been a dream; but, on the other hand, he wasn't entirely certain that it hadn't been. He watched as the rescuers hemmed Ben Robiack's body into a black plastic bag, stretching him unceremoniously out on the ground next to him on the DZ as they waited for the choppers to come in. His mind and emotions were cold to the corpse lying next to him. For the moment, he was still mesmerized, by what he thought had happened before the arrival of his rescuers.

Dale was airlifted to Cam Ranh Bay for surgery and recuperation before being sent to Japan for additional surgery on his leg. Once his physical wounds had healed, he was transferred to a psychiatric facility at Wiesbaden, West Germany, for the standard evaluation and debriefing given to all repatriated POW's.

There was a lingering confusion in his mind, about everything that had happened to him. Dale's efforts to deal with the imprisonment, the torture, and the incident during the bombing led to a severe depression. Much of his problem was assumed to be a result of suffering at the hands of his captors.

But it was the revelation that his grandfather had died while he was captive that suddenly caused him to become more deeply withdrawn. He began to suffer the recurring nightmares of his childhood.

The psychiatrists approached Dale's condition as a 'textbook consequence of his confinement and physical abuse at the hands of the Viet Cong'. When Dale failed to respond to treatment, the doctors assumed that his condition had been obviously exacerbated by his having witnessed Ben Robiack's violent death.

A veteran army psychiatrist, Colonel Scott Holland, experienced with cases of POWs, was assigned to Dale; and, after several months of working closely with him, he reached what he felt was an acceptable diagnosis for Dale's condition.

Dale remembered Dr. Holland's explanation of this diagnosis during one of their final sessions before he was to be discharged from the base hospital.

"You know, they always got a new label for the same old stuff. The new generic term for cases like yours, they say, is Delayed Stress Syndrome.

At this point, about the best I can do is tell you what I think is causing your depression and nightmares. They always manage to tag new names onto the old infirmities, but never seem to figure out a cure for anything by the time the next war rolls around."

He stood up, walking over to the window with his back to Dale, obviously ill at ease with his scant explanation that he was about to make.

"What I think happened to you started long before you ever went to Nam. Your capture, and the things that happened while you were being held, was nothing more than a catalyst that kicked up an old problem.

There's no doubt that what you experienced in Nam made this other problem surface...but I don't think that's all of it! I think something else happened to make you believe you saw someone out there...the someone that we've talked about over and over again, your grandfather. He was a very authoritative, strong individual, as I understand?

And he was usually the one who came to the rescue when things went wrong?" Holland questioned.

"I'd say that's right," Dale replied.

"Each time you experienced difficulty in your life, your grandfather...not your father, or mother, was the one who came to your rescue. He was everything your mother and father couldn't be, or wouldn't be," Holland continued. "That man represented survival to you long before you were in the situation with the Viet Cong. When your life was threatened in Nam—and we both know that was no dream—you called out to the only power you knew would never fail you. You created, in your mind, the angel that visited you during that bombing," Holland asserted.

Dale's head dropped to his hands. He sat shaking his head in confusion, as he answered Holland's accusation.

"No," he answered. "I mean, I don't think so! Everything is so damn mixed up. Most of the time I couldn't see. All I could do was listen to what I thought he was saying."

Holland, squatted down next to him. "You never saw this ghost, this creature that appeared after the VC had left...did you?"

"No, I don't think I ever saw him. At least, I never saw his face," Dale replied.

"You never saw his face because he wasn't there. You wanted him to come to you because you were scared. He'd always come when you were being hurt by your mother. He was even in your dreams, fighting the demon that haunted you when you were little," Holland went on.

Dale nodded his head slowly. "I don't know. I don't understand why I feel so damn depressed about something that never happened."

Holland sat on the edge of his desk, clasping his hands and staring at Dale. "You feel depressed because you want to believe your grandfather is alive...that he was with you out there in some spiritual form. But you've got to face the truth. Your grandfather died while you were a POW. He didn't go anywhere but to his grave."

Dale looked over at the psychiatrist. "But I didn't know that he'd died when I saw him...I mean, the guy, the thing...out there."

"It doesn't matter whether you knew it or not. You were uncertain enough about what happened that, when you were told he'd died, it destroyed this belief that you had some sort of guardian angel following you around. It took away the security that had been a part of your scheme of survival all your life." Holland knew that what he was saying was painful for Dale. "There was no ghost, no angel, no ghostly Florence Nightingale. You were alone with the corpse of your buddy, stretched out on the floor next to you for three days. That's all. There was nothing more to it!

You suffered a short term mental breakdown when the situation seemed hopeless. Of course you would have an illusion of some spirit coming to your rescue. Children do it all the time. Let's call it an acquired defense mechanism," Holland added.

"If you could somehow put your feelings aside and see a new perspective on your grandfather, then look at him as a fellow human, not as a Godsend, placed on this earth to protect you. He was a man who cared very much for you...and you for him, so deal with his death...accept it and let it go at that."

Dale nodded with uncertainty. "I guess I never realized that I relied on him that much. I just know I cared a lot about him. I always will."

"Don't be too hard on yourself for this happening; it's perfectly understandable. Give yourself a chance to see things as they really are. Take some time to find out about your grandfather. It was probably very difficult for him to live up to everyone's expectations."

"I'm sure it was," Dale agreed.

Holland smiled. "You were fortunate to have someone who cared for you that much; but I think as soon as you realize that your grandfather was just another human being, everything will work out for you. Give yourself some time to adjust. Your mother, with her sociopathic tendencies, purposely crushed your father's authority within the home.

There's a reason your mind has responded as it has. It's like having a fever. It's your body's way of trying to tell you something is wrong, while it sorts things out. Go somewhere. Spend some time alone. Take this thing apart in your own mind. Try and see your mother and grandfather for what they really were. Get it out of your head that your mother was some fiendish demon caught up in a battle with your grandfather for right and wrong," Holland suggested, looking compassionately at Dale.

Dale, wrung his hands, and nervously slipped his fingers through his hair, and said, "that voice that came to me...it knew things about me that no one else would have known. Everything that happened was as if he was standing right there, trying to tell me that he was there to help me!"

Holland lit another cigarette before responding, "Of course your visitor knew everything about you. It knew your innermost desires and longings. It knew your pains and memories. It knew everything that there was to know about you, because it all originated in your own mind. Your mind knew the life-threatening circumstances you were facing. In one last desperate grappling for survival, your mind projected the image of your grandfather coming to help you. It was nothing more than coincidence that he was dead. It would have happened if he'd still been alive," Holland stated.

"Then, what you're telling me," Dale interjected, "was that I imagined all of this! That my mind took me on some damn trip to get me away from the reality of what was happening to me?" he laughed nervously, shaking his head.

"Precisely!" Holland answered.

"You ever had a dream, Doctor, where you ate and drank and stared at someone for three days while they stood guard over you? Or survived a saturation raid by B-52s, with this dream stretched out on top of you to keep the Gawd damn shrapnel from taking your head off? I'm havin' a real tough time with the explanation you're givin' me, Doc. I just gotta believe there's more to it than that."

Holland looked exasperated, trying to ignore Dale's obvious failure to appreciate his professional diagnosis. He snuffed out his cigarette, walked over to his desk, and began writing a note on a prescription pad. When he'd finished, he turned to Dale and said, "There's not any point in continuing our discussion about this until you've had some time to think over what I've said. I'm recommending that you be given a short leave. Anyway...it'll give you a chance to get away from this place for a few days."

Dale stood still for a moment, staring out the window at the manicured lawn.

It suddenly came to him where he wanted to go as he gazed down on the massive shade trees hovering over the street that ran along the hospital grounds. The French border was only a short distance away. For the first time since his nightmare had begun, he felt a wonderful anticipation about something in his life.

He felt an urge to go to the small village in France that he'd remembered hearing about as a child. It seemed such a magical place when he was little. It was always special to hear James talk about Pont-a-Mousson. He could remember seeing James' eyes glitter, enthralled with his memories. How rare it was, he reflected, to see the stone-hard man ever surrender to a sensitive moment. But there was never any doubt about his passion for that marvelous spot and for the trace of his life that had passed there when he was a young man.

It seemed appropriate to go to Pont-a-Mousson. If understanding his grandfather would bring peace to his own mind, then surely it would allow his grandfather finally to be freed from his earthly bondage, however real or imagined it may have been. At the very least, it would give him a chance to be alone with his thoughts.

Dale knew that he could not expect to find anyone, who would have known his grandfather, in the village after so many years. But, at the very least he might have the opportunity to experience a part of his grandfather's life that no one else in the family had known about. The Great War had been the best and worst of times for his grandfather, as much as he could tell from the stories he'd heard as a child. It had been the part of James' life, besides his youth in the swamp, that had had the most effect on his life. No one knew better than Dale how special the village was to James. And, although James had never admitted it, Dale knew he always yearned to return to experience its loveliness one last time. But the ugliness of his memories of the war always overwhelmed his eagerness to make the journey.

Having never quite understood what had been so special about the village, Dale was curious enough to decide to spend his leave there, in obedience to Doctor Holland's orders.

Within two days, he was crossing the frontier into France.

CHAPTER 33

The thick foliation of the French countryside concealed the lost chastity of the frontier, torn and twisted beneath two separate German invasions. To the unsuspecting visitor it seemed peaceful enough. Dale knew the history of what had happened. Somehow, the landscape seemed undisturbed, its blemishes from the two wars wiped clean by nature's powerful healing forces.

His entire life, he'd been consumed by an unceasing curiosity about his grandfather's love for this place he was about to visit. He'd often dreamed as a child that he would visit the tiny village, lazily occupying the banks of the Moselle. He imagined standing on the banks of the sweeping river with his grandfather, seeing the old man exuberantly happy again.

In a small way, he still remembered his dream, saddened now that he would have the experience without being able to look into his grandfather's eyes for some sign of his joy, a smile, or a happy comment. 'If he were only alive,' Dale thought. 'The things I'd do for him...the places we'd go.' He made himself stop. He remembered the psychiatrist's warning about his spending too much time thinking about James.

From St. Mihiel to Flirey and finally Pont-a-Mousson, the train lumbered up next to the old Gothic stone station with a belch of steam blanketing the worn tracks.

Dale made his way to a small room above a local tavern in the center of the village. After having dinner downstairs in the pub, he returned to his room, tired from his long journey.

At the first light of morning, Dale was awakened by the tolling of church bells ringing across the village commons. He dressed and walked to the church, hoping to find the parish priest. He knew the church would hold the records of births and deaths of most of the people who had lived nearby. He hoped the archives would provide him with the records of one Marie Gresoire and her place of burial, assuming that she had been buried in Pont-a-Mousson. They would also give him information about her family and her farm.

Dale found the priest talking with a parishioner in the narthex of the medieval basilica. The priest was a young man, in his mid-twenties. His greeting was somewhat reserved until Dale began to explain why he had come to the village.

The men spoke in French, talking for a few minutes until the priest was finally at ease with his visitor. He invited Dale to join him in his study where they talked for most of the morning, each sharing what he knew of the history of the small settlement and a superficial chronology of their own lives.

The priest had lived in the village for three years. He was passionately interested in the ancient history of the community, as well as the more current goings-on of the last sixty years. One of his first privileges, upon arriving at the church as a priest, was to be taken to the exquisite cartulary of the ancient cloister. This is where he was allowed to wander through the archives with the zeal of an historian, given access to endless genealogical records dating back to the beginning of French civilization. He had devoted a portion of each day in the library, enthralled with this marvelous opportunity. If anyone should have an interminable amount of information concerning his flock, he would.

Dale related the story of his grandfather to the priest, what little he knew of the events that had brought James to Pont-a-Mousson during the First World War. He shared the story of his childhood with James and his devotion to the man. Finally, he revealed that he had come to the village in an attempt better to understand the man he had admired so much in his life.

As he spoke, Dale realized that the priest, for some odd reason had an intense look of concern on his face all the while they were talking. He finished his story, telling his listener of his encounter with the strange vision he'd had while he was in Vietnam and the therapy he'd been given at Wiesbaden.

The priest continued to listen, bowing his head and fumbling with his rosary, and then returned his attentions to Dale, shaking his head as if he were deeply disturbed by something Dale had said.

"I'm sorry, Father," Dale suddenly interrupted himself. "I know that my story of the vision I had while I was being held prisoner, sounds a little far-fetched. It's just that all of this has come from so far back in my past. The vision seems to have been the culmination of a great many things in my life.

I've always felt that my grandfather would have wanted me to see the village, and it just seemed an opportune time to experience something he loved very much."

The priest stopped him, holding up his hand and shaking his head. "It's not anything that you've said or done," the priest responded. "Quite the contrary...it's something else."

"I...don't understand what you mean." Dale questioned.

"Your being here, and the miraculous vision you speak of can be nothing less than divine providence. And I must tell you that I find myself confronted with a great injustice that has burdened my heart."

"I'm not following you, Father"

"I'm afraid that I know much more of your grandfather than I've let on. Your coming here at this time leads me to believe that it's God's divine will that I tell you what I know. I think the hearts of those involved would want it that way. I think it would bring peace to their souls. I pray to the Almighty that they'll forgive me for violating their sacred trust."

Dale sat speechless, shaking his head slowly in confusion.

The priest stood, walking over to a small, pot-bellied stove in one corner of his study. He kept his back to Dale for a short moment before turning, his face distorted as if in pain. "One of my first official acts upon arriving at the church was to give final absolution to the curé...Father Alliot. He'd ministered to the people of the village for many years. He'd been a faithful servant to God for most of his life, trying to do what he felt was desired of him by our Lord.

At the moment of his death, he revealed something to me, in trust, that had weighed so heavily on his heart for years. He had born an error in judgment so painful, so horribly painful to him at times, that he had questioned his usefulness in serving Christ.

I tell you this now because you are in search of the truth...a truth that must be settled for all our souls, including your own. I think I've always known that this thing that was done would never be laid away so easily. And now I must believe that it is divine initiative that brought you to us!"

"I'm really confused by all of this," Dale said.

"The woman that you're looking for...Marie Gresoire...is alive!" the priest suddenly confessed. "She was never killed, as you and your grandfather had thought."

Dale was incredulous, even dumbfounded by the priest's disclosure. "But my grandfather said she had died...immediately after the War had ended."

"In a way, she had...because of what Father Alliot had done. Your grandfather was in love with Marie. And she with him. As sad as it was, your grandfather accepted Marie's death, believing all that Father Alliot had written him. Your grandfather was truly devoted to the memory of Marie, over the years believing that she had been killed near her farm. He'd even been faithful in sending flowers to her grave each year until, we assumed, he had passed away. It was a bitter reminder to Father Alliot each year of what he'd done when the flowers arrived and were used on the altar so that they were not wasted."

"Why would this priest do such a thing?" Dale said angrily. "Why would he have perpetrated such a heartless lie for all these years?"

"I know it's difficult to understand why such a thing could be done by a man of God. In his zeal to protect Marie and remain a faithful proprietor of his responsibilities to the church, he did what he felt must be done. As time passed, he came to realize that his deceit was no better than the sin he was attempting to prevent. As it always is...truth would have served him much better."

Dale looked away from the priest, trying to absorb what he'd been told. "Was the woman a part of this?"

"Not a willing part," the priest answered. "She was doing as she was instructed in obedience to God, or so she thought. She was alone in a land that was torn from war, and the church was all she had. Marie has always been a faithful Catholic. She knew that her involvement with your grandfather would never be condoned by the church, despite the fact that she was deeply in love with James, but certainly, this was not the way to handle it. We all know that now!

When Father Alliot found out that your grandfather was going home to divorce your grandmother, he seized the opportunity to make up a story about Marie's death, in an attempt to stop him from following through with his plans. As much as Marie loved James, she wanted to do what was right in the eyes of God. She has paid a dear price for her subjugation by Father Alliot."

"As did my grandfather!" Dale interrupted.

"I know," the priest continued. "I also know that they both continued to love each other. I know your grandfather's heart was broken over losing Marie. And she...closed her life to all others...never marrying anyone. I think Father Alliot realized that he had merely forfeited one sin for a multitude of others."

"I never had any idea that he had had an affair with someone. I guess I could have figured it out, from the way he acted whenever he mentioned her, or this village. Perhaps it's just as well that he believed she died. It would have been just one more tragic circumstance in his life if he'd known that she was still alive. And I think your priest would have had to fear for his own life if my grandfather had known what he'd done!"

"Your grandfather was a very generous and compassionate man. It's ironic that gifts of money your grandfather sent the church in memory of her eventually did find their way to Marie. She'd lived such a meager existence on her farm, being helped by the church in those hard years. She had no idea that Father Alliot was giving her money that James had sent. That too had weighed heavily upon Father Alliot, each time money would arrive from America."

"This isn't really what I had expected to hear. I don't know how much this helps me find peace about his life. I came here hoping to find something else, an answer to why I had the vision."

"But there was good in his life here!" the priest said forcefully. "From what I've learned of your grandfather, he was a warm, caring man. He was someone of great courage, who could, I believe now, have lived among our people very happily. I only hope you can forgive our dishonesty with him."

"I don't have any hard feelings towards the people here. I was just looking for something else...something that might give me peace of mind about his life," Dale reflected.

"You should know he was a very charitable man. Over the years he provided money for many of our people who were in need. I think that's why Father Alliot finally became so distraught over what he'd done...his misjudgment of the man. Although none of us ever saw him again, his generosity was overwhelming. Even after World War II, his benevolence helped rebuild our village from the destruction of that war. He is remembered by many of us because he cared.

When he was here, after the war, he was very much at peace with himself. The idea of Marie's death hurled him into despair with life. And, you should know that Marie was very faithful to her memory of him. I wish you would come with me to visit her. It would be a blessing for her to see you and talk to you. She's old and in poor health. I know it would give her a great deal of comfort just to see you! Would you go with me to her home, to visit with her?"

"I'd like that, Father," Dale answered; "I'd like that very much!"

It was mid-afternoon when the two men left the church. A brisk wind had moved across the road as they walked to Marie's farm on the outskirts of town.

Dale knew when he saw the tunnel of trees leaning over the road, curved as the arms of so many ballerinas, that he had arrived at her home. The leaves had fallen from the trees, plucked by the cool winds of fall, lining the road with a golden carpet, smooth and glistening in the soft rays of the afternoon sunlight.

Halos of clouds billowed in the distance, rolling in great white velvet swirls beneath graying skies. Dale could see the Moselle River in the distance, swollen and muddy from water collected from the German frontier. The river moved slowly against the banks, as if to show its satisfaction, as a cat might rub against its master.

They stood at the door of the old farmhouse, Dale and the priest; then, after a few soft knocks, the door inched open. An old woman glanced at the priest with a smile, starting to return his greeting before her eyes fixed on the young man next to him.

Before the priest could introduce Dale, the woman's hand flew to her mouth as she gasped in shock. She stepped back away from the door, tears suddenly filling her eyes. Her face turned away from Dale. She moved back from the door, nearly falling into an old rocker near the fireplace.

The priest knelt next to her, holding her trembling hand. Dale walked closer, offering his hand in greeting, leaning next to her.

"Bonsoir, Mademoiselle Gresoire! I'm Dale Lavo—" he started to say.

"I know who you are, young man," she stammered.

"I'm sorry if we startled you!" Dale apologized.

She said nothing, motioning him to move closer. With his face close enough for her to touch, she placed her hand along his cheek and temple. Then her hands clasped his, embracing them as she wept.

For a short time, she sat staring at him. The priest had moved away from the pair, standing with his back to them as he faced the warm coals of her evening fire. He knew that their joy did not involve him.

"You look so much like him. Is he still alive?" she asked.

"No, he died a short time ago," Dale answered in a soft whisper.

She reached for a white linen handkerchief in her pocket, blotting the surge of tears welling up in her eyes. Marie leaned over and kissed Dale's hand with a soft, loving caress. When she'd finished, she motioned for Dale to pull up a chair from the table and place it next to hers.

"You must have loved him very much." Dale said calmly.

She looked at him and then nodded slowly, still wiping her eyes.

"I came here because he'd told me so much about you and your home when I was a small child. It's as beautiful as I imagined."

"James loved it here. He was so happy whenever he could come to the farm," Marie sobbed. "Was he happy with his life?"

"Yes...I think so!"

"And you," she said, "I think you must have been very close to him?"

"Yes, I was," Dale smiled. "He was a wonderful grandfather!"

Her hand again pressed against her mouth in an attempt to veil her shock at seeing Dale. She cast her eyes towards the fire to inspire some long-lost dream of her togetherness with James. She glanced back at Dale, seeing the same youth who had vanished so many years earlier, taking her heart with him. Her eyes closed tightly, giving her time for a last reflection. "You must forgive me; I've been alone for so long!"

"Please," Dale asked, "tell me about him, the way he was then. I'd like to know about my grandfather when he came here, during the war and afterwards."

Marie smiled for the first time since the visitors had come to the house. She leaned back in her rocker, glancing up at the ceiling. The priest turned to look over his shoulder, obviously pleased at her change for the better.

"The Americans were so young. That was what most of us remember so vividly about them," Marie said, "that and their innocence. By the time they had come to help, all of our young men were gone, slaughtered! They had all perished at Verdun, or with the English at the Somme. The young Americans thought the war would end just because they had paraded through the streets of Paris. But they were magnificent!

James was not like the rest. He had a sincere love for France and our people. His heart struggled to understand the reason for the war and the destruction of our country by the armies that marched back and forth, spoiling everything as they went.

When I first met James, he had tired of life. I think he would have welcomed death at that time. I know he never feared dying, as many men did; he had seen so much death at the front.

The village and my farm were like a seed that had survived a great fire. We were his hope that France could be rebuilt, pulled from the crumbled fortresses that lay in ruin after the last shots were fired.

I think, most of all, he loved the simple life of a farmer. He would push his hands deep into the soil whenever he had the chance to stand along the river and in the freshly turned fields. Those were his happiest moments.

What he saw waiting for him in America after the war were obligations, not dreams. But life is a little of both. Somehow, he felt that he would find a way to do the honorable thing with his family and still have his dreams. He was completely torn over what to do. His great gallantry would never let him leave your grandmother or father. I knew that, from the moment I first met him! And I would never have forced him to give up his honor. He had fought too hard to survive the war for that. And, I think he still loved her.

I knew it was better to have had his love, if only for a moment, rather than have him stay, wondering always about those he'd left in America.

I'm ashamed of what I did to him. God forgive me," she said somberly, crossing herself out of habit. "But even now, as I look at you, I know it was the right thing to do. No one can ever take that away, the love I have for him, or the moments we shared together. These things have lasted me a lifetime, as your memories will for you! It's odd, though, that you've come so far in search of his past."

"Why do you find that odd?" Dale asked.

Her eyes fixed on his with a curious understanding as she answered, "Because he also searched desperately to know his father. He admired him much the same way as you admired James. But that, too, seemed to have been resolved here in France, during the war, from something that happened that brought him peace. He left France a very different man than when he first came to us. Happier in some respects, older for his years. Scarred by much of what he'd seen."

"I never knew anything about his father," Dale said. "He never discussed him with any of us. I didn't know anything about what my grandfather was like during the war or afterwards with the occupation forces. My grandmother would never discuss those times with us."

"And your father...is he alive?" she asked.

"No. He died several years ago, before my grandfather passed away."

"I'm so sorry," she said. "My father died only a few years before I met your grandfather. We've all lost our share of those so very dear to us."

She moved slowly from her chair and retrieved an old framed picture from above her mantle. She dusted the glass before handing it to Dale. He studied the faded photograph, realizing that it was a picture of James in his uniform.

"It was made in Paris. He was a handsome soldier!" she said, smiling first at Dale and then the priest.

Dale nodded, carefully laying the frame down on a table near her chair. He continued to stare at it as Marie carried on with her conversation. "I'm an old woman and my life is almost over. The little bit of wisdom and intuition that I have acquired over the years leaves me with the feeling that you are searching for something, something about James that is stirring deep within you."

"I suppose that's true," Dale acknowledged. "The encounter left me wondering if I had known him as well as I thought I did. I guess I'm searching for the spiritual part of his life to reconcile this with the man I knew and loved. That's part of why I came to Pont-a-Mousson."

She shook her head slowly in disagreement to what he'd said. "No...you <u>knew him</u>. It's your mind that tells you to doubt your feelings about him. <u>But trust your heart</u>! There is where the truth lies!" She paused for a moment, then continued, "James believed that a person left a part of their soul with those they had grown to love whenever they parted. It was a permanent gift, that would spark the fires of the heart, inspiring wonderful memories, while each remained apart from the other. Your devotion to him is justified," she added, as is mine!

I've cherished his memory for so many years, and I see him now as if we were both still young. It's as if he'll always be with me, just as he was then," she ended, putting her delicate hand gently over her heart.

Dale was entranced as he listened to Marie. "I think he would have been very happy here, if life had turned out that way for him. And I'm sure that if he were here, this moment, he would say how deeply in love with you he was!

When I first heard about what had happened between you and my grandfather, I was angry. But, I think now that what you did took a great deal of love <u>and</u> courage. I thank you for caring enough for him to have made that decision. I also believe," Dale continued, smiling, "that he has certainly left a part of his soul in your care. Thank you for sharing your life with him!"

She looked up at him, her eyes suddenly flooded with tears again. "Thank you, young man, for bringing a little joy to an old woman. It means more to me than you'll ever know!"

They stayed a little while longer before Dale and the priest decided it was time to return to the village. They stood outside the small cottage, after bidding Marie a sad farewell, making promises to return that Dale knew would never be kept.

It gave Dale a few minutes to enjoy a last look at the old farm and think about Marie, and this small island of happiness that had been surrounded by such violent unrest in years past. He knew the old woman would probably not be alive if he ever returned to France, but he was very happy that he had come to Pont-a-Mousson.

As they turned to walk back through the tunnel of trees and the path back to the village, Dale could hear faint sounds of music drifting from inside the cottage. The uneven resonance of the music was obviously coming from the vintage gramophone Dale had seen in Marie's front room.

He was startled by the tune coming from the house. Although it was barely audible, he knew the music. Marie was alone with her dream, and more at peace than many who had made the walk along the sacred way of life.

Now, back in his grandfather's house, Dale leaned forward in the old rocking chair, emotionally spent from his reminiscence. The hours of reflection had resolved little in his mind. He was no surer of his life and what had happened to him than he was before he decided to plunge himself into his painful review of the past. But, at the moment, he felt more at peace with himself than he had for many years.

It had occurred to him, as he contemplated the events of his life, that he was nothing more than a product of his own environment, much the same as James and his mother and father had been.

But, the contemporary hypothesis did little to explain his experience with the ghostly vision in Vietnam. He was still bothered by the vividness of his encounter.

Perhaps it was due to the extreme trauma he faced in those three days, as the psychiatrist had suggested. It had been an opportunity for his mind to purge his anger and hostilities over a life of disappointment with those that he loved. 'Even James,' he thought, 'had disappointed me by not being alive when I finally came home!' There was so much to try to understand, so much that would never make sense.

But still his grandfather's touch was far greater than the capabilities of any dream. It was an ethereal act that had truly comforted and saved his life. There was never a dream that could accomplish that.

His eyes swept the room as he caught a final hint of the familiar fragrance of the old bedchamber. He wished that there were some way to take all of it with him, to have it to hold and touch for the rest of his life. But, this, too, would have to be committed to memory.

Life certainly had been no harder on him than it had been on his grandfather. And he'd been fortunate to have had such a wonderful guardian. Still, it was reassuring to think that just possibly there was some truth to his feeling that it had been James standing beside him and nursing him back to life while he had suffered the final days of imprisonment.

Despite what the psychiatrist had said, he always would feel a sense of obligation to James, if not for that time in Vietnam, then certainly for all the other times he had interceded to protect him. But, mostly he felt gratitude that his grandfather had loved him enough to be there when he needed him most.

And, as far as having been bequeathed a part of his grandfather's soul to comfort and protect him since they had parted, that would be something to accept like one's belief in God...purely a matter of faith.

He stood up, and placed the open box of pictures on top of the dresser. It was time to leave the memories behind. He satisfied himself that he had dissected the circumstances of his life as carefully as he knew how, even though many of his questions remained unanswered. And, they would remain that way forever. Perhaps that wasn't all bad.

As he started to walk away from the dresser, his eye caught sight of the small crimson bag that held his grandfather's watch.

He'd forgotten how tantalizing the small treasure had been to him when first he'd seen it as a child, and been allowed to hold it. He still remembered the reverence that James had held for the piece, watching the old man's mood become wistful at the mere sight of it.

Now, as he thought back to Marie and his visit to France, the watch held even more significance. It had been the very proof that the deceitful priest had used to tear his grandfather's heart from him. It was the essence of that point in time when James' chance to dream had ended.

Dale opened the bag, unfolding the gold chain from the sheath until the watch finally emerged. He remembered the story of the deep notches on the side of the watch. The slices from the American fencing master's bayonet as he tore at the German, in no-mans land, with the lethal upward stroke that had dispatched the watch from the soldier's blouse.

He knew now that James hadn't preserved the watch for so many years just to remember a fallen comrade. Nor had he kept it o n l y to remember the sad message that had been brought with it from France, telling him of the death of his lover. There was more to it!

Dale knew, of all the truths he'd failed to understand...this one was no mystery. It was the single possession in James' life that he had cherished most; reminding him of the ardent love he'd experienced in another time. But, even more than that, it was an indelible source of the inspiration he'd found so hard to hold onto in life. It was a symbol of his caring, for all those who, had indeed, been given a small piece of his soul.

Dale now believed that James had been reunited with those he loved. And in the end, the watch was the one undeniable truth to Dale that James was finally at peace and had been beside him in his darkest hours.

As the back plate of the watch opened, an orchestrina began to play, sounding a tune, seeming to have been saved within the watch just for this special moment. The tune, so familiar, was the same tune played within the cottage where Marie lived, the exact tune...whispered from the shadows of his cell when he'd envisioned that James stood beside him in those perilous   times. The words echoed in his mind as he listened, thinking of the old man and his promise: "I'll always be with you!"

ABOUT THE AUTHOR

Stephen Boyett was educated in the South, and is deeply influenced by the Southern environment that was so much a part of his childhood. His family heritage reaches back to the founding of the country, and gives strong inspiration to the creation of the fictional characters in his story.

"My greatest challenge as a writer was to bring the spirit of these characters to life, to immerse the reader knee deep in their world, to love them, and at times, hate them for what they were, but never forget them."

www.ingramcontent.com/pod-product-compliance
Lightning Source LLC
Chambersburg PA
CBHW052339020726
47503CB00001B/35